Outremer III

'In the beginning'

D N Carter

Clink Street

London | New York

Published by Clink Street Publishing 2019

First edition.

ISBNs: 978-1-912562-46-6 hardback
978-1-912562-47-3 paperback
978-1-912562-48-0 ebook

Dedicated to
Pamela Smith
1937 – 2016

Authors' Foreword

Welcome to the third volume of Outremer. As with books one and two, I have had cause to refer again to factual research for both religious and historical accuracy, as well as many documents, abstracts and books on a wide range of subjects. I have therefore likewise inserted bibliographic references, all of which are listed at the rear of this volume.

The story becomes a lot more fluid and faster with historical and religious information being revealed in an easy to follow and understand format as Alisha and Paul's lives settle into a new routine of normality...but the world around them is changing rapidly. Whilst Paul strives to learn as much as he can about the mysteries in Egypt, new people enter their lives that have direct, immediate and profound affects upon them and the direction they will follow. As confusion grows about their own beliefs, so does whom they can trust. As mysteries from the past call out to them, they have to make decisions that not only affect their lives, but the lives of countless thousands, the repercussions of which echo out across time to the present.

The genuine historical facts as revealed within Outremer are all there to verify and confirm if the reader wishes to validate their authenticity.

Acknowledgements

I have already covered my acknowledgements and made my thanks known previously but I would like to express my gratitude to those few friends who have gone out on a limb and well beyond what was asked or expected of them over the past year. They know who they are but without them, book three would not have been completed.

Characters

Brother Baldwin (Upside)

Abi Shadana

Queen Sibylla

Master Douglas

Ailia Plantavalu

Luke

Pauls mother

Master Elek Aldin (Aldin Angelus)

Count Henry

Master Jakelin de Mailly

Husam al Din Lu'lu

Queen Tamar

Contents

"In The Beginning."

PART IX

Chapter 49
Cairo. The Path is Followed Again

Alexandria, Egypt, late April 1180

Paul lay awake looking at Alisha. He could see her smiling at him in the dim light of the bedroom. After their bout of training with Tenno and subsequent late night with their guests, both felt tired but could not sleep. They both looked towards the door as they heard Theodoric and Sister Lucy laugh out loud briefly then snigger in the opposite room.

"At their age...," Paul whispered, joking, and put his arm around Alisha.

1 - 9

"I think it is wonderful they still feel so much love for each other. I hope we are the same when we get to their age," Alisha whispered then moved her hand to unbutton her night shirt.

"Are you hot?" Paul asked quietly.

"I am...but, but I am wanting you...I wish to show you my love," Alisha replied and smiled as she placed her hand near to his groin. Paul instinctively pulled away a little as her hand reached his groin gently rubbing her hand against him. "Do you not want me?" she asked softly and moved her hand away.

"Ali, it has been some while. Are you sure, I mean, can we?" Paul blurted out and pulled her close. His eyes immediately looked upon her cleavage as her night shirt pulled apart slightly.

"More than anything. I knew today as we trained that I was again ready...and I wanted you right there and then," she replied and leaned into him and kissed him, her hand moving back down to his groin. She broke the kiss and looked at him. "Did not take much for you to respond did it?" she laughed quietly as Paul became aroused.

"Ali, what if you fall with child again?"

"I have been taking that silphium...and if I fall, then so be it, but I need to feel you...be a part of me as one."

"But I have not bathed properly."

"Nor have I...," she laughed as Paul rolled her onto her back and lay beside her looking down at her intently.

Quickly Paul sat up and pulled his night shirt over his head and flung it across the room, which made Alisha laugh. She started to unbutton her top until it hung loose completely open revealing her milky white stomach and breasts in stark contrast to the dark blue night shirt. Paul gently grabbed the waist band of her bed chausses, untied the fastening at the front and then pulled them down. She raised her legs so he could remove them completely and he threw them across the room, which made Alisha laugh again. She covered her mouth trying to quieten herself. Gently Paul moved himself between her knees and pushed them apart as he lowered himself between her thighs. Alisha raised her legs and wrapped them around his waist pulling him closer. He held himself up upon his elbows as he looked down at her as she lowered her legs so her feet were pressed against his upper thighs and pulled him even closer.

"I do not think this will last long," Paul whispered and laughed.

"Then we shall have to repeat it and practise more," Alisha smiled back and put her arms up and pulled him nearer. As Paul lowered himself further, he looked at her firm breasts and gently started to kiss between them and began to kiss toward her nipple. Alisha put her hands on his face and raised his head so he looked at her again. "My dear, if you kiss me there, be warned, you may get some of what Arri gets," she laughed. Paul started to laugh as Alisha then moved her hips upwards toward him, instantly meeting Paul. "Just go gently this first time for I do not know how it will feel... but I am so unbelievably ready and wanting you," she said softly.

Paul kissed her on the lips, her gentle response sending a surge of feeling through him as he tasted the sweetness of her kiss. He lowered his hand and delicately felt between Alisha's thighs. He was already beginning to sweat from holding himself up on just his left arm. Alisha used her legs to pull him closer and he felt the soft wet warmth of her meet him.

"My beautiful Ali, you are most certainly ready...wetter than I have ever felt you," Paul remarked.

"Probably wet myself then," she joked back and laughed.

"That, my woman, is why I love you...for I truly feel as one with you,"

Paul replied and very gently guided himself slowly toward her. He shuddered with joy as his senses exploded as Alisha opened up for him completely and he slowly penetrated her, her warmth slowly enveloping him as if for the first time. It felt more intense than when he had first made love to her. He suddenly felt overwhelmed with emotion and as if he would cry. He closed his eyes and stopped moving as Alisha tried to pull him closer and deeper inside her. He froze almost, shocked at the massive amount of emotion that was welling up inside of him.

"Paul…what is it, what is wrong?" Alisha asked softly wondering why he had stopped and closed his eyes. He opened them slowly and looked down at her as he took his weight upon both arms. He went to speak but words failed him. A single tear fell from his face and splashed upon her cheek. She gently wiped it then cupped his face with her hands. "Oh my dear dear man what is it?" she asked as Paul held his position and looked at her.

"Does it hurt or feel different after having Arri?" he finally asked.

"More sensitive...in a nice way, but no, Abi did a good job after the birth," she answered and smiled. She moved her hand lower and started to gently feel herself and move her hips slightly. When Paul pushed down, he felt her hand as she pleasured herself faster. She started to moan and gyrate her hips. Paul could feel the surge in his loins build rapidly in intensity and tried to slow down his movements but Alisha wrapped her legs around him even tighter and pulled him inside her deeper. The muscles in his arms flexed and his face contorted as he tried to control himself, but Alisha laughed softly and pleasured herself harder as she felt Paul's body shudder. She gasped as her senses became overwhelmed as her entire body suddenly and without warning climaxed. She wrapped her arms around Paul rapidly and pulled him very close and held him tightly as the orgasm flooded every sense of her being in a way she had never experienced before. She moaned and had to bite her bottom lip, but even then, as she felt Paul start to come inside her, his head beside hers as he fought to remain quiet, she bit into his shoulder. Her feet felt as if they were curling inwards. Paul shuddered involuntarily and he pushed his arms beneath her and hugged her tightly, as he let his body completely give into hers. Alisha kept thrusting her hips against him and jerked in spasms for several long minutes until her body started to come down and relax. She slowly ran her hands over his shoulders, now covered in sweat, but she did not care as he lay between her not moving or speaking a word.

The love making had been short but more intense than they had ever experienced before and it had taken them both by surprise. Paul softly kissed Alisha on her neck beside her ear, then her cheek and then upon her lips. He stopped as he heard Theodoric laugh out loud and moaned at the same time as Sister Lucy could be heard telling him to shush and quieten down. Alisha and Paul both laughed quietly. Alisha relaxed her legs down as Paul just lay between her, stroking her hair as he looked at her, her eyes wide and glistening. Softly he kissed her upon the lips again then rested his head beside hers, rolled himself sideways pulling her over with him so she lay on top of him. He pulled up the sheet over her back and as she rested her head upon his chest still joined as one she closed her eyes. She could hear his heart beating and with every minor movement from Paul, she jolted as the intense sensation still ran through her body. Wrapped in each other's arms, they fell asleep.

Megalithic Hypogeum of Hal Saflieni, Malta, May 1180

Philip, dressed in a simple cream coloured robe, a short cloak and sandals, looked around the empty open space, the ancient Holm Oak tree still standing where it had always stood. Much of the area had been cleared away since his last visit many years previous with the other trees appearing to have been cut back. He threw his cloak over his shoulder as the midday sun beat fiercely down, but a cool breeze blew in from the seashore. The soil seemed to reflect almost white in the sunshine as he strained to look for the entrance. The sea sparkled in the distance a brilliant turquoise colour. He closed his eyes and took a deep breath.

"It has been a while," Kratos said, causing Philip to jump in fright. "Sorry, I did not mean to startle you," he said softly as he moved to stand in front of him. He wore his simple white mantle, which only added to his air of authority.

"Kratos…it has indeed…," Philip replied and sighed and looked upon his old friend.

Both looked at each other in silence for several moments as Kratos rested his hands upon his staff and smiled.

"What brings you here?" Kratos asked.

"Why ask when you already know I am sure?" Philip replied smiling.

"I know Abi is here…and I know that it was you who saved Paul and Taqi back in La Rochelle."

"Well, my friend, I kept my side of the bargain and kept away all these years as you asked me too…until," Kratos started to say and stood up straight. "Until I was certain that you were all in immediate danger and harm's way…then I had to intervene."

"I received a letter from Paul. He informed me of your visit to Alexandria, that Theo is there and I am a grandfather."

"Well, I always told you that one day you would be, did I not?"

"That is what concerns me…for you said many other things. He said Abi was badly injured, 'tis but one reason why I am here."

"Then come inside, meet Abi again for I know she will be pleased to see you. We have much to catch up on," Kratos said and proffered with his outstretched hand for Philip to approach the small, almost hidden entrance to the buried temple complex. "As you can see, I have almost hidden the site entirely. Your arrival is well timed for we are soon to leave this place for good."

Philip paused for a few minutes and looked around as he approached the stone cut steps that led down into the complex. His mind returned to an earlier time when he had visited with his wife. Happy memories, he thought, as he recalled in his mind her beautiful face as she laughed and danced around him as if in front of him again. He took a deep breath, then stepped down into the temple entrance.

Philip stepped into the main room of the complex running his fingers along the smooth walls carved directly out of the solid rock. He recognised the various designs painted in red-ochre on the ceiling with their familiar honeycomb pattern that transformed into a collection of floral spirals, most of which appeared enclosed in pentagons. Black and red ochre images of a 'fat lady' holding an axe were still visible in various sizes just as he recalled them. It had been many years since he had last entered this room but he could remember it all as if it was only yesterday. Theodoric had been present with him on that occasion. Two long poles illuminated the inside in a bluish white light.

"I see you still have them working," Philip commented, pointing at the lights.

"Yes…but the power grows weaker yearly. Soon they will cease to function anymore," Kratos explained as he followed Philip.

"So you know Theo lives?"

"Yes. But then I have known that all along. Are you angered with him?"

"Angered…no. I was when I first read Paul's letter, but then I read all about what he has done since meeting them in France. I will probably hit him hard if I get the chance to see him again."

"You shall have that chance…but not yet. You cannot visit them until you have finished other business as you probably already know," Kratos said softly and stood still looking at him.

"You have aged much since last I saw you. How so?" Philip asked, puzzled.

"Oh you know…life," he laughed in reply. "But, like Abi, I have aged more these past fifteen years than…oh, let me see, the past three hundred," he said and laughed again.

"Why. I do not understand it. I thought you were born to last until the next return of the Dark Sun," Philip asked, puzzled.

"Oh that I am and shall, but the many injuries I have sustained these last few years alone I am afraid have done more damage than was expected or that I am capable of sustaining. But I am recovering…as is Abi," he explained and looked across toward a stone archway just as Abi slowly stepped into view, her hands placed across her stomach. She wore a simple one piece white dress, her hair hanging loose except for a band of braided hair tied across her forehead and behind her head. Her hair shimmered a pearlescent light blue and purple in the light. She smiled and stepped down and approached Philip. "I think perhaps you two should speak."

"Abi…," Philip said then shook his head, lost for words.

Abi stepped closer, put her arms around him and hugged him, both with their eyes shut, for several long minutes before Abi took a step back and looked at Philip intently. She gently ran her finger down the creases beside his right eye and smiled.

"You have aged well. These character lines suit you," she said softly and smiled.

"Character lines. Always the diplomat," Philip replied and laughed and held her hands as he looked at her.

"You have come at the right time for we leave here within days. Kratos said you would come," she explained softly.

"Did he now? And you...you sound and appear different," Philip said still holding her hands but looking at Kratos.

"What, more feminine?" she asked and smiled broadly. "It is the dress I am sure."

"Abi," Kratos said and raised his eyebrows. "She is with child."

"What...but I thought that was impossible...I...I...who?" Philip asked awkwardly then laughed.

"Oh you know him. A good man and it would appear of our line," Abi replied.

Philip looked at Kratos, confused.

"Tenno," Kratos informed him and nodded.

"Tenno...!" Philip exclaimed, surprised.

Abi simply nodded yes and smiled.

"How...no, do not answer that. Tell me later," Philip laughed. "I have missed you all so much, more than I realised until now."

"And we you," Kratos said and ushered Philip along to sit. "I knew you would come again and now you have, perhaps you will help us seal this place?"

"Of course I shall help. What of the other sites here?"

"Oh they have been sealed for many years past already," Kratos answered.

"Where will you go from here?" Philip asked.

"We shall take our vessel and hide it away in Atl, then go to the Emerald Isle and wait for you to join us, in good time of course," Kratos explained.

"But what of Tenno and his child. Does he know?"

"No he does not. But he shall," Abi explained and sat down upon a rock cut bench.

"And before you leave us again, you must take the plans drawn up for the new temple structure to house the nine and the gateway," Kratos said as he offered Philip to sit beside Abi.

"And where shall that be if moved from La Rochelle?"

"Where I am afraid you must travel next...if you are willing of course?" Kratos replied with a wry smile. "Not far across the border of England into Alba. You have been before so you know it already."

"By any chance...Temple Parish...near Balantrodach?" Philip replied as Kratos nodded yes. "And what will happen with your child?" he asked turning to look back at Abi.

"We shall see. But after a year, maybe two, he shall leave with Kratos to a safe place whilst I finish my work," Abi replied.

"Where exactly? And why did Tenno not return home? So many questions…where will you go that is safe?" Philip asked and held Abi's hand.

"Philip, our days of living amongst you draw near to a close. We stand out as a little too obvious would you not agree?" Kratos asked.

"Not that much, you do not."

"I am surprised Paul did not inform you why Tenno stayed. I shall explain later over a meal…but where are your belongings for you travel light?" Abi asked.

"No he did not explain. He detailed their journey to Alexandria and what that evil minded Turansha tried to do. That affected me badly…for that man will stop at nothing, I fear. I should have killed him when I had the chance," Philip replied and shook his head. "And as for my dear friend Firgany…truly a great loss."

"We know…but I have since spoken with him. He watches over Alisha still," Kratos said and winked. "Philip, when you have hidden that which must be hidden again, near Balantrodach, only then can I resume the installation on the island in the New World."

"Kratos…I have always felt and known that the day would come when I would be tasked to do so. 'Tis why I have spent so many years preparing everything…the stories, my writings and my cathedral designs," Philip answered and sighed.

"And you have done more than was expected. But the time will also come when you must pass on that mantle to another…And who, will be your decision alone," Kratos said with a reverence of tone that made Philip look at him. "You tried to find a better way to carry the messages from the past to the future…but please accept that it shall now fall to Paul to find that way so please listen to him when he tells you there is a better way to guarantee the message and codes from antiquity can be carried across time without the use of force or religion…for that is his gift to the world."

"And what is that?"

"He does not even know himself yet, but he shall…should he get to Cairo as he has been advised."

"And in the future, people will remember as promised?"

"That, my dear friend, I can indeed promise. Even if they lose the very codes, there will be those souls reborn whom, despite the veil, will remember and tell them within new stories…new technologies and new legends will be born from the higher imaginings of those enlightened ones…but having physical proofs, as that is what the majority in this world seem to need and see, they will greatly help to re-educate man…help him remember who he really is," Kratos explained solemnly.

"And this island in the New World…what shall it be called and how can you be so sure what is hidden shall remain so?" Philip asked as Abi looked at him, the tiredness in her eyes growing.

"Why, Philip, there is but only one name we could call it…Oak Island of course," Kratos replied with a large smile and raised his eyebrows. "And once sealed, it will only again be accessed when the very world itself enters the ring of light and changes its position…only then will its sealed vaults empty. And only then will it confirm what will then be found within the recovered Chambers of Creation from the four corners of this world… for only then will the vibrations that govern this realm of existence be correctly matched!"

"Oak Island…how appropriate," Philip smiled.

"Indeed. Before you leave, you must take with you the Crimson Stone to place in Scotia," Kratos said and began to walk toward the remnants of a small fire in the centre of the room. "You have much to do and not a lot of time to do it in. Now you must tell me how your plans for the Temple Church in London are progressing."

Port of La Rochelle, France, Melissae Inn, spring 1191

"Crimson Stone...and Abi pregnant!" Sarah remarked utterly bemused.

"Tenno...the dirty sea dog," the Genoese sailor laughed.

"Lucky sea dog," Simon commented, his eyes wide as he stared off in thought.

"Atl...New World...New Scotia, Oak Island...can you explain more?" Gabirol asked.

"Check the map I gave you. You will see New Scotia already marked upon it. 'Tis where Tenno went and passed through as he claimed. And there are Templars there right now as we sit here this day," the old man explained. "And Atl, well that is a land of great antiquity now buried and hidden beneath snow and ice, apart from a small inner sanctum. A paradise on earth almost."

"Then if this is so, why are we not told?" the Templar asked.

"Only the most trustworthy have been selected so far to venture there...to prepare the way. It may be many more years, perhaps even hundreds, before all will know

of its existence...to reveal it now would confirm this world is not flat and open up a whole new exodus to the New World...before its time," the old man explained.

"But you tell us now. Why?" Gabirol asked, looking confused.

"Because you in this room...'tis to you that a new responsibility will be passed on to, if you so choose to accept what I offer when this tale concludes."

"Me...but I have never been chosen to do anything, certainly not of any worth," the Genoese sailor interjected loudly and laughed.

"No...but there comes a time in everyone's life when an opportunity presents itself to be called to a higher calling...one of which, of course, you are more than free to reject," the old man explained, looking at him directly.

"I think I know who you are now," the Templar said quietly and raised his sealed envelope and waved it before placing in back upon the table. The old man raised his eyebrows. "But I shall not say until you have finished this story," he smiled and winked.

The old man part nodded his head in acknowledgment.

"Why does Philip need to go to Scotia, Alba whatever it is called?" Peter asked.

"And Crimson Stone...what is that all about?" Sarah interrupted, asking again.

"Let me answer Sarah first then, if you will? For the Crimson Stone is one of the reasons why crimson became a holy sacred and now royal colour," the old man started to reply and discreetly pushed the crimson coloured wristband up his arm to hide it from view. The Templar however saw him and smiled again. "It will be, as explained previously, at least another eight hundred years before the full knowledge relating to the Crimson Thread will again be fully revealed...as Theodoric detailed, and that the Crimson Thread would have to be hidden and protected. You may recall it was the Prior de Sion who made the active decision to form a military arm to protect that line...the Knights Templar!" the old man said and paused. "Do you recall how I explained how Abi told Paul to know and accept that the Crimson Thread of an ancient bloodline that far outreaches any of the royal bloodlines now being sowed within royal families runs through his veins? How he had the right to wield this sword?" the old man said and placed his hands upon the sword. "How Paul carried the wishes and ambitions of all his ancestors to establish a line of leaders who would heal, protect and educate their peoples? To lead by example doing service to others, not service to self?"

"I do," Simon interrupted enthusiastically.

"So do we," Sarah said immediately and looked at Simon scornfully.

"Then know that the use of crimson as a symbolic colour originated from stones found near Stonehenge in Britain. For there, a river runs through the land and

through ancient stone monuments, many now buried and still hidden, that have stones with a unique property. When the stones are taken from the river and left to dry in the sun, they turn a bright crimson colour. Truly a magical thing to see. So they were regarded as special, holy almost, especially as they were used for healing."

4 - 19

"How can stones heal?" Ayleth asked, puzzled.

"By their very properties," the old man answered and took his hands off the sword and sat back. "The evil Turansha knew all of this and the significance of the Crimson Thread."

"Yes, you previously explained that," Gabirol mentioned.

"Oh good...I thought I had," the old man smiled and continued. "And as Kratos explained, Philip had sought a better way of carrying the codes across time, but it would fall to Paul to find a way," the old man said and paused for several long minutes. "And is why Kratos wished for Philip to travel back to Balantrodach and bury one of the Crimson Stones with letters etched upon it deeply...letters that would lead any who discovered its location to Oak Island and its very entrance..."

"Why Balan what's it called?" Simon asked.

"Balantrodach...'tis the name of the area in which the main Temple Parish is situated, and in the year AD 1128, 'twas one of the founding Knights Templar, Hugues de Payens, who visited Alba and was granted a meeting with King David I of Scotia. The king subsequently granted Hugues and the Knights Templar the Chapelrie and Manor of Balantrodach. There is a wonderfully built Templar church there..." The old man trailed off for a few more minutes.

"The Crimson Stone...'tis buried there yes?" the Hospitaller said and leaned forward.

"Alas and sadly no...for it remains here in La Rochelle," the old man replied.

"What...where?" Simon asked excitedly, which made the old man laugh.

"Philip was tasked by Kratos to remove bodies laid in La Rochelle, in Cougnes, to Balantrodach, where they were to lay until a greater more sacred chapel could be constructed not too far away...where they would remain interred until the vibrations of the world again match when it passes through the ring of light...a task which he succeeded in doing...but the Crimson Stone he did not place...hide," the old man sighed.

"I do not understand all this talk of ring of light and vibrations," Ayleth remarked, puzzled, and bit her bottom lip.

"Then let me explain very briefly...you see all sounds make vibrations, and even light travels in waves as the ancient knowledge tells us...'tis but another reason why the Grand Master of the Prior de Sion and others are known as Navigators, for they understand and can symbolically ride those waves...and as our planet traverses the great heavens, time is measured by the distances between the sun and the centre of many stars...the stars we see that make up the Milky Way...that is proper time, time as used by the gods, or our understanding of God. Every great year, which is roughly twenty-five thousand years, our entire system of planets and sun passes through a ring of light that vibrates differently. It raises our conscious levels as well as physical bodies...that ring of light is over 2,160 years in our time wide... as in that is how long it takes our world to pass through it."

"When does this start?" Gabirol asked, looking serious.

"Not until the Age of Aquarius... AD 2003 give or take a few years."

"And stones vibrate...is that connected then?" Gabirol asked.

"Yes they do. 'Tis why the architects of sacred stone monuments chose their stones carefully. 'Tis why Stonehenge has specially selected stones taken from Wales...for their unique resonating and vibrational properties. Sound vibrates to form various patterns. This can be demonstrated if you place salt or sand upon a shield and vibrate the sides or especially so upon a large drum. The patterns they make are all geometric and perfect...'tis a practice the higher initiates of the Templars have observed and documented. Many of those sound forms Philip knew all too well and had drawn them down...images he included within the designs of several of his plans, including one he compiled alongside Kratos that is to be encoded within a new sacred chapel."

"And where exactly is that to be built?" Peter asked. "I would love to be involved in that," he added.

"Then perhaps you shall for its foundations have already begun...but it shall take many more years before the chapel above is begun...and it is in a place called Rosslyn...," the old man answered.

"Rosslyn...sounds identical to Roussillon where Theodoric's family came from and where you claim Mary really came ashore," Gabirol noted.

"Linguistically identical even...and for that very reason." The old man smiled.

"Can I ask why was Kratos sealing his home?" Ayleth asked.

"'Twas not really his home, Ayleth," the old man answered. "But the time had come when he had to seal off the entire complex, including the many others on the island and neighbouring island too. To make sure that it remained intact along with the many ancient ancestor remains...remains that will one day be recovered

and seen for what they really are. When it is discovered again, its construction will remain a mystery for many years until mankind's awareness and knowledge has increased enough to recognise what it is they are really looking at. They will argue over its purpose, its age and who built it. It has been sealed so that only the first thirty rooms located over three levels can be accessed. But eventually, nearer the time of the passing of the dark sun and ring of light, deeper passages and rooms will then be found. Of course as is the nature of man, they shall at first claim it was but a simple rock cut tomb, just as they will claim the pyramids at Giza are just simple tombs of Pharaohs..."

"So when was it built?" Peter asked.

"Kratos said it was finished during the period as the earth passed through the zodiacal sign of Taurus, the Bull...so many thousands of years BC. Huh, the very last thing Kratos did alongside Philip as they sealed the entrance was to leave a sleeping woman figurine...Kratos laughed at how that would cause so much intrigue later when it is recovered," the old man laughed.

"Why?" Simon asked.

"Man in the future will find items from the past but sadly place upon them their own perceptions as they see things then, not as they necessarily were...he also laughed at how future man will wonder how they illuminated the temple, just like the Giza pyramids, for no trace of soot nor burning torches is present. You have all seen how much a roof can darken from burning torches..."

"So what did the little woman figurine mean?" Ayleth asked.

"It was Kratos's way of saying that Mother Earth sleeps but will awaken. It represents a rite of initiation, incubation to be more precise as to sleep within the Goddess's womb is to die and to come to life anew. Just like all the other sacred initiation rites where the candidate enters a sealed cave or room and where more often than not, this type of initiation was known as 'temple sleep' whereby if he or she falls asleep, any dreams were thought to be influenced by deities, and might provide insight about the past, the present, or the future."

"Like Paul's dreams," the wealthy tailor commented.

"Yes," the old man replied and paused before continuing. "Upon Malta, there are many many more temples and stone circles that lay buried. In time they will be uncovered just as those many thousands all across our world will be and prove that they are all linked. What are missing though are the original temple structures that once stood above the underground chambers. Great structures long since dismantled but which many more temples across the world were copied from."

"So the other passages below it...where do they lead?" the Templar asked.

"My friend, as I have explained before, there are indeed great passages and pathways that cross our world. In Malta, there are many that stay hidden, and shall remain so, of great halls. There was a time when what we would truly call giants did inhabit and use them. Not just giants symbolically but real physical giants at a staggering height of some twenty-four feet tall...," the old man explained and nodded it was true.

"Twenty-four feet...!" Simon almost yelled out.

"Yes, as unbelievable as that may sound. And in time, their remains will be recovered and their existence proved. They will also learn of the different doorways to other realms as some have stumbled across by accident in our times...gateways."

"Gateways again. Did you not say that the place in Alba was a gateway or did I hear that wrong?" Gabirol asked.

"No you are correct. I did mention a gateway. 'Tis part of the land itself between Ballantrudich and a town known as Stirling."

"Other realms I do not understand," Simon remarked.

"Again, no surprise there then," Sarah said folding her arms.

"So is the Hypogeum a cemetery or a temple or initiation cave or what?" the farrier asked.

"A mixture of all. But the spirals painted in red ochre, just like the spirals found all over the world, represent both a physical event that occurs within our sphere of existence, but also as experienced within visions during hallucinations. Attar was able to mix a herbal remedy that would induce hallucinations that would help open doorways into other dimensions, out of which deities, the ancestors, are said to come into this realm. But those practices are now oft deemed evil and of being in league with the Devil."

"This Crimson Stone you mention with an inscription upon. What is the inscription and where is it now?" the Templar asked.

"The stone...'tis in this very building. But first let me explain that the Crimson Stones were collected from a river that runs near to Stonehenge itself. Understand that Stonehenge is not only a very precise astronomical observatory for all manner of calculations, but is also a generator of energy and accumulator of memories, for it records events across time as well as harmonises sound. And it is the sound qualities that have an immediate and direct impact upon us all now. Strike the stones and they hum and make sounds, some similar to a bell being struck. There was a time when they could be struck to make a musical sound and communicate over vast distances, but the system has been broken...you can still see the marks where the stones used to be hit to make the sounds," the old man explained and paused as he watched Gabirol

write as fast as he could. "Do you know that in Wales, many churches use the same bluestones used at Stonehenge as bells?" He looked at them all in turn as they all shook their heads no. "You have all heard of Geoffrey of Monmouth...well in the myth of Merlin bringing the stones to Stonehenge, he states that the stones have medicinal properties that can be accessed by washing the stones and then pouring the water into baths. The water absorbed the healing virtues of the stones. This is exactly the same as the rocks taken from the river that turn crimson. Many springs and wells in Wales are believed to have healing properties and you will find innumerable numbers of them issuing out of the mountains with deliberately manmade enhanced springheads, enhanced in the sense that the water source has been cleared out and enlarged, and a little wall was usually built thus creating a pool where the water emerges. This indicates that such springs were viewed as special and that the ancient people who so viewed them wished to obtain water at their source, as it came out of the ground, Mother Earth, rather than further down the mountain where it becomes a rivulet and so less pure. As mentioned, the stones, mainly the so-called bluestones at Stonehenge are known to ring like a bell or gong, or resound like a drum, when struck with a small hammer stone, instead of the dull clunking sound rock-on-rock usually makes. In Wales such stones are known as 'Maenclochog' for 'Ringing stones' but their sounds are now muted..." The old man sighed.

"Can we see the Crimson Stone then if it is here...please?" Ayleth asked.

"Of course," the old man replied and reached down into his saddle bag beside his chair. After a few moments he lifted onto the table a smooth stone of roughly a foot long and four inches wide at its thickest. It was flattened and appeared more pinkish than crimson as the old man slowly peeled away the soft leather covering wrapper completely. "You will notice the carved letters...and before you ask, Simon, yes I shall reveal what they stand for."

Simon stood up and leaned across the table to read the letters carved into the Crimson Stone.

Fig. 51: Crimson Stone Engraving.

O·U·O·S·V·A·V·V
D ·   M·

"That is impossible to decipher," the Hospitaller remarked.

"There is no such thing as impossible," the old man smiled.

Alexandria, Egypt, June 27th 1180

Attar stood beside Paul as he looked over some diagrams Theodoric had laid out across the table in Paul's study room. Theodoric stood with his hands upon his hips pleased with himself as Attar rolled up his baggy sleeves on his dark green robe. Outside the morning air was still cool as the sun broke over the top of the outer wall.

"And you say you drew these yourself from the actual site?" Attar asked and looked up at Theodoric.

"Aye I did that, along with your father," Theodoric answered, looking at Paul.

"But these are all sealed and their locations hidden," Attar remarked, puzzled.

"Aye...I know. 'Twas not easy getting inside and even harder getting out," Theodoric replied with a proud smile.

"I bet," Attar said and looked closer at the images. "And you swear this was copied at a site within the Thebian Valley?"

"Yes. And if our understanding of the language is correct, it is the underground temple no less of Thutmose the Third. I knew the image was important so I copied it...," Theodoric answered and held out his hand toward the drawing.

"'Tis well executed, my friend," Attar said, admiring the drawing even closer.

Fig. 52: Thutmose – The Underworld Realm.

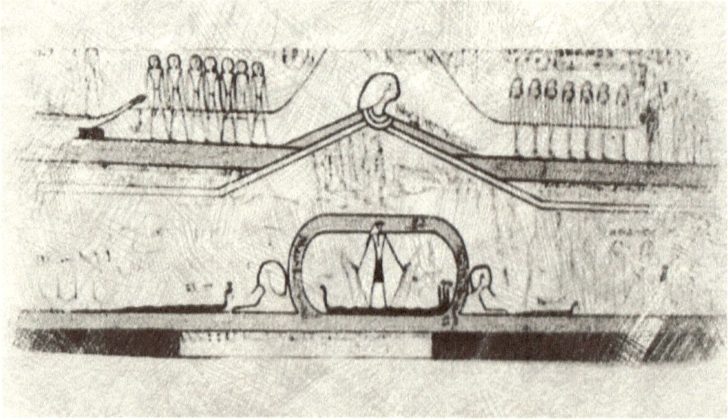

"And this gives clues to what is beneath the Giza pyramids?" Paul asked.

"It does and your father and I used it to gain access to the many tunnels beneath," Theodoric replied.

A light rap on the door drew all of their attention to it. The door opened slightly as Percival slowly peered in.

"Sorry to disturb you but Alisha says you have a visitor," he started to explain and fully entered the room. "'Tis Turansha's secretary and an escort."

"Why...what has happened? Are we in some kind of trouble?" Paul asked, concerned.

"No...Turansha demands your most urgent attendance at his palace... and not to delay," Percival replied.

ഇ൬

Paul quickly followed Turansha's secretary along the wide marbled floor corridor towards a large ornate door bordered by two columns. Percival followed closely watching the four Mamluk guards carefully. No one else had been allowed to come upstairs and the sense of urgency and concern was written all across the secretary's face. At the door, they all stopped.

"Please, wait here a moment," the secretary said before quietly entering the room, shutting the door behind him.

Paul and Percival looked at each other, puzzled.

"They let me keep my arms," Percival whispered, placing his left hand over the pommel of his primary sword.

"Alisha was not too pleased we left before eating the breakfast she had prepared," Paul whispered back just as the door opened again.

The secretary beckoned them both in. Percival looked at Paul, puzzled, wondering why he too had been called to see Turansha.

Inside the room, large white see through screens hung from poles. Paul immediately saw Turansha sat in a large wooden lattice chair with cushions set to prop him up comfortably. It was positioned just outside the main room on the balcony allowing him to look out across the Mediterranean Sea just a short distance away. The secretary motioned for Paul and Percival to sit on a stone bench to the side of Turansha. Paul acknowledged Turansha with a slight nod as he feigned a pained smile back, hardly moving. His eyes were sunken and he looked exhausted. Paul tried to hide the look of concern upon his face, which made Turansha laugh briefly, then cough, his chest sounding coarse and full of fluid.

"My good friend...and of course Percival," Turansha finally blurted out, his voice dry and whispered. "Thank you for coming so quickly...my time is done in this world..."

"What do you mean?" Paul asked and looked up at the secretary stood behind Turansha. He shook his head sadly. "Please, I do not understand. What is wrong?"

"I am dying...I am not sure how or why...but there is nothing anyone can do. My lungs fill with fluid," Turansha explained and coughed, gasping for air. "I believe...I believe I have been assassinated, somewhat slowly," he said and coughed again, screwing his face up in pain as he held his chest. "Paul...I am of the mind that it was...Conrad."

"Conrad?" Paul exclaimed, shocked.

"Yes...Conrad. For he is the only person from whom I have accepted any drink from when first his embassy met my caravan for the exchange of Saint Armand...all of my food and drink is carefully prepared, and I know I can trust my cook..."

"The bastard!" Percival said aloud shaking his head with disapproval. Both Turansha and Paul looked at him. "Sorry. I speak out of place."

"No, you speak as it is," Turansha replied and smiled at Percival's obvious embarrassment. "Paul...'twas a great pleasure and honour knowing your father, and you also, but now, now my time is done and Allah wills it that I must depart this world. But before I go, I had to warn you about Conrad...If you think Reynald is bad, he will but pale by comparison to what Conrad will do."

"Tell us what we must do?" Percival interrupted.

"Percival, I cannot tell you what to do. But I can ask that you keep careful watch upon that man...and Percival, I charge you with guarding this man's back always," Turansha said painfully as Percival looked at Paul and frowned, a little confused. "Paul has great knights, warriors of great strength and courage who protect him and Alisha...and of course young Arri...but Paul," Turansha said as he coughed again and tried to sit up higher. "Paul, you will need this man in the years ahead," he explained and looked across at Percival. "And you must let Percival accompany you to Cairo, for to Cairo you must go, and soon. I have already sent word ahead. By day, if you accept my commission, you will labour working with a good friend of mine, whom you have already met, designing ships…great and mighty ships, and by night and your days of rest, you will continue that which your father started. I failed in securing the continuation of his work as I had promised him, but I may redeem that promise in you if you will," he said and grabbed Paul's hand tightly and looked into his eyes intently.

Paul could see the intensity in his reddening eyes. Turansha's face was yellowish and pale, his colour seeming to drain even more as he looked at him.

"I do not know what to say…I shall certainly be cautious with Conrad and watch him closely…but Cairo. And designing ships…'tis a great dream of mine, but I could not if those very same vessels were to be used against my own kind in warfare," Paul replied.

"No…the ships you will work upon are not ships of war…they are to be ships of exploration, that I promise you," Turansha explained and coughed again very heavy. It took him several minutes to regain his composure. "And whilst you are in Cairo…let Attar guide you in the ways of the Giza complex. Do not repeat the mistakes of your father and Theodoric…and Percival, remind him of this conversation if he ever does."

"How will I know?" Percival asked quickly.

"Promise me!" Turansha coughed deeply as he forced the words out, his eyes widening. He clenched Paul's hand even tighter as his face turned red. "Promise me," he blurted out again in pain and coughed, black looking blood beginning to seep from the corner of his mouth. His secretary rushed to kneel in front of him and beside Paul, but he raised his left hand and shook his head indicating he says nothing. He focused upon Percival as he held his breath. He opened his eyes wider and raised his eyebrows at him, his pained expression almost begging for his response.

"I…I promise," Percival replied awkwardly and looked at Paul, bemused.

Paul felt the tension in Turansha's grip immediately weaken fast, then go completely limp just as Turansha looked at him. He smiled, the black looking blood dribbling down his chin onto his white robe. The frown left his face and his eyes seemed to widen briefly as he smiled. He blinked once more as he looked at Paul as if by way of a final gesture of thanks. He then sank slightly into the cushions as the pupils in his eyes widened. His fixed open eyes just stared forwards. Suddenly a woman sat just out of sight stood up quickly a few feet away and rushed off in tears. Paul and Percival had not even noticed her presence.

"He is gone," the secretary said quietly and lowered his head in respect.

Percival looked at Paul, bemused and concerned. Paul looked down at his own hand still holding Turansha's. 'How and why would Conrad poison him?' Paul thought and looked at Turansha. 'If his secretary tells Turansha's brother Saladin that it was Conrad who poisoned him, what manner of hell will he unleash upon Christians in reprisals?' he thought, alarmed. Just as he thought that, the secretary stood up slowly, walked over to a set of white drawers where the female had been sat unnoticed. Within moments he withdrew a leather wallet and handed it to Paul. Paul released his grip on Turansha's hand and stood up fully. As he lowered his arm, Turansha's body made a noise as his bowels opened, the smell instantly filling their noses. The secretary gently arranged a sheet across the lower half of Turansha, placed his fingers over his eyes and closed his eyes before looking at Paul.

"That, I shall clear and sort out before the others enter to bid him farewell," he explained sadly. "But in that wallet is a letter of recommendation I drafted on his behalf. He has signed and sealed it. It also absolves you all of any party to his death. So there can be no blame! For all our sakes he has not mentioned being poisoned by Conrad. Pray you keep his wishes and that it remains so for he wants no more bloodshed in his name."

6 - 2

Paul looked at the wallet then back at Turansha.

Main port, Cairo, July 1180

Alisha held Arri close despite his being strapped around her chest tightly. Tenno stood beside her holding the aft deck balustrade looking at the approaching dockside as the boat they were travelling upon drew up closer. In the distance Alisha was able to make out the faint outlines of the three main pyramids on the horizon visible above the city's other buildings and minarets. The port was busy and bustling with all manner of ships and vessels.

"Do not be too harsh upon him," Tenno said and looked down at her.

"I am trying not to be…but I love our home in Alexandria. I do not wish for this place but as his wife I shall follow and go where he goes," Alisha replied and squinted in the afternoon sun. "But look at him and Theo... they are like two excited boys," she commented and looked down where Paul and Theodoric were laughing as they moved boxes toward the main deck gangplank opening.

"Those pyramids may fascinate Paul and his father before, but they do not fill me with the same excitement. They do nothing but cause me concern," she explained looking up towards the distant pyramids.

"He is here to build ships," Tenno stated bluntly.

"Yes...you believe that too?" Alisha asked pointedly.

Tenno looked down at her again and raised a single eyebrow.

Alisha shook her head, saddened, kissed Arri on the forehead and looked out at the port side as they slowly edged ever closer, ropes being thrown to secure the boat. Tenno could see she was not happy but there was nothing he could do to alleviate her concerns or her feelings.

੨ଓ

Two hours later, Theodoric stood with his hands upon his hips looking up at the three storeyed house before him. Sister Lucy linked her arm into his as Paul ushered Alisha beside them. Percival and Tenno steadied the two horses of the large old open cart, its elderly owner sat on the driver's seat smiling a toothless grin. The house fronted onto a wide pathway. It was set back from the main thoroughfare road, the hustle and bustle of which could be heard in the distance. Alisha looked up at the house. Its walls were immaculately plastered a pale stone colour but with a hint of pink. A large double wooden door was protected by a metalwork grate. All the left hand side of the building, which only went two storeys high, was covered in an intricate and very ornate wood lattice frontage, the top sections having areas highlighted in white relief. Further to the left her eye caught sight of a swing gate that entered into a courtyard and stabling for several horses and two carts. On the three storeyed section, beautifully carved wooden balconies stood out from the walls on each level. Mainly built from smooth stone, the building quietly impressed Alisha, who could not help it, much as she did not like to admit it.

"When Thomas and his lot get here, they will find more than enough room in the outer buildings set back near to the river," Theodoric said aloud and smiled.

"There is more?" Alisha asked.

"Of course. If you thought the house in Alexandria was big…just wait until you see what is beyond those doors," he replied and put his arm around Sister Lucy.

"How long will it take for Thomas to get here?" Tenno asked.

"Only two days," Theodoric answered just as the front door opened and the metal gate pushed aside.

A dark haired young female dressed in a long bright blue dress stepped into the street and walked towards Theodoric smiling. In her hands she carried several large metal keys.

"All is ready for you, master," she politely said to Theodoric and bowed, offering up the keys for him to take.

"No…'tis their home, not mine," he replied and nodded toward Alisha and Paul.

"So sorry. So sorry," she quickly repeated and turned to face Alisha and Paul immediately offering up the keys. "I am Nyla…and I have prepared the baths and put food out ready for you," she smiled.

Her hair was jet black, but her skin almost white. Her eyes were a dark brown but filled with youth and happy looking. Percival raised his eyebrows quickly and smiled at her. She was elegant and spoke softly. A slight breeze made the large leaves of a palm tree sway and rustle set just a few feet from the front door. She again offered the keys up for Paul to take. He looked at Alisha, smiled and indicated she take them. Gently she took the heavy keys and nodded at the young woman.

"There is much history here, Paul…much indeed," Theodoric said aloud and nodded toward the main doors.

Alisha looked at the friendly smiling face of the woman again then back up at the building before her. She clasped Paul's hand and led him toward the doors.

Port of La Rochelle, France, Melissae Inn, spring 1191

"The house sounds to me like a small palace," Sarah commented.

"It was a grand house indeed. Bigger than the one in Alexandria even…and built in the area once known as Heliopolis," the old man explained. "Once inside, Theo took Paul to what was once Philip's study as Alisha and Sister Lucy looked around

the huge house...very pleasantly surprised. Percival...well he spent an awkward hour trying to make conversation with Nyla," the old man chuckled.

"And the house was Philip's?" Gabirol asked.

"And Theodoric's too."

"Does he tell Alisha and Paul it is part his also?" Peter asked.

"No...no he did not," the old man smiled.

"Why not?" Ayleth asked instantly.

"Because a home can only have one master at a time. As I told you before, Philip, Firgany and Theodoric had invested in several properties during their travels. They had left them all in capable hands who administered them and rented them out accordingly by trusted agents. Theodoric knew it would best serve them all well if they all believed the house to be just Philip's, and by rights Pauls accordingly," the old man explained.

"And built upon ancient Heliopolis, yes?" Gabirol asked.

"Yes indeed. 'Tis why it was purchased in the first place," the old man replied.

"This Heliopolis...I have read much from old sources on the area. Can you tell us more for it greatly interests me for I know it is connected with the ancient firebird, the Phoenix," Gabirol asked.

"You are certainly well read, my friend," the old man remarked. "Let me tell you that the house was situated in an area of Cairo that had a cosmopolitan population that included Jews, Muslims and Christians alike. Very much like Alexandria. But what most of them fail to realise is just how sacred the ground is beneath their feet... or what still lies beneath them!"

"Such as?" Simon asked bluntly.

"And who is the girl again?" the Genoese sailor asked.

"Her name was Nyla as said. She was the daughter of the agent Philip had commissioned to manage his estate in Cairo many years previous. When word came from Theodoric they would be returning within the month, it was she who helped move out the previous occupier, clean the home completely and have it ready for their arrival. Percival certainly took a shine to her. Paul had likewise written to his father explaining they would be moving to Cairo whilst he worked with Husam designing boats."

"So Paul found his career path thanks to Turansha," the wealthy tailor remarked.

"For then, yes," the old man answered.

"For then! That can only mean his career changed," Gabirol noted.

The old man simply nodded in agreement.

"'Tis by understanding our history that we will guarantee our future," he said quietly,

paused as he took a sip of rose water and continued. "For thousands of years Egypt was home to a series of important Jewish communities. These groups are a vital part of the pluralistic society that characterises Egyptian life. One of the most significant Jewish communities is that of Fustat, a city founded in the seventh century BC on the east bank of the Nile. Cairo was founded north of Fustat in AD 969 and became the political and cultural capital of the Muslim province of Egypt and has been ever since. Today, Fustat comprises an area of Cairo known in Arabic as Masr al-Átiqa, or 'Old Cairo'. Some of Judaism's most distinguished figures spent time in Fustat. Among them is the philosopher, rabbi and physician Moses Maimonides, who has written both his major philosophical works, 'The Guide for the Perplexed', and his fourteen-volume anthology of Jewish law, the 'Mishneh Torah', there. Located in the heart of Fustat, the Ben Ezra Synagogue is a centre of prayer, study and celebration for Egyptian Jews from at least the last century. The panel of the ark door on that synagogue dates back to the last century too with its dominant carved decoration at the centre of the door that also reflects the direct influence of Islamic, specifically Mamluk and Ottoman design while the Hebrew inscription on the panel, 'Open to me the gates of righteousness' is based on verses from Psalm 118. The ark door has a fascinating story to tell, as the face of the Holy Ark, which holds the Torah scrolls and marks the direction of prayer, it was the threshold to the most sacred place in the synagogue. At the same time, the door faced outward toward the broader community. Its absorption of Islamic vocabulary reflects the synagogue's place in the larger Mediterranean world. I tell you these facts to add weight to the fact that in Cairo as well as Alexandria, all creeds could, and they did demonstrate, how they could all live together," the old man explained.

"If Paul was to work upon designing ships...what was Alisha to do?" Ayleth asked.

"Keep a home, look after Arri and make new friends. Exactly the same as she did in Alexandria," the old man answered.

"And Thomas and his men?" she asked with a raised eyebrow.

"And what about Paul's horse, Adrastos?" the farrier interjected loudly.

"Thomas brought his men overland...with Adrastos," the old man replied and smiled at the farrier. "And Alisha employed the agent's daughter Nyla to help Sister Lucy around the home, especially in regard to Thomas and his men...and she in turn introduced Alisha to a lot of women who were involved in the very profitable textiles business. She would in time turn her designs into clothes much sought after."

"A woman of her own means then?" the wealthy tailor stated.

"Yes indeed. She would make more than enough of an income by her trade and new found interest. You see, the social interaction with textiles and their production formed, literally and physically, the fabric of life for most women in Cairo. The

Fatimid dynasty that ruled Egypt from AD 969 to 1171 famously intensified and perfected the production of textiles and the tiraz style in particular. Alisha took that style and made her designs based upon it far more practical. Cairo is perhaps the most important centre for the export of this precious commodity across the Mediterranean and beyond and I would not be surprised if you were to find one of her garments in Paris or London. The textile business in Cairo had a life-changing impact on most men and women, as women became not just consumers of textiles, but also producers, traders and investors. As ladies-in-waiting in charge of the wardrobe of the royal household, they acquired both prestige and visibility. Women belonging to the upper echelon of society could display publicly their status and authority through what they wore but also through the fabrics they gave as gifts just as Turansha had offered Alisha when she had first arrived in Alexandria as a gift if you recall?"

"I recall all right. Wish I could have access to such textiles," Sarah joked and laughed, looking at Stephan.

"In furnishing their houses with silks or wools women from all walks of life could assert their styles and aspirations. In death, lavish shrouds or simple wraps served as the ultimate mark of respect to accompany women in their final journey and Alisha introduced vibrant and colourful styles that quickly became popular. Cairo was at the centre of a rich, cosmopolitan cultural society and it was there that Alisha discovered her talents for both design and a business woman.

"I went to Cairo once when I was very young...with my father," the wealthy tailor said glumly. "All I can recall is that it was a warren of streets just bustling with life. There are mosques at every corner, Coptic churches, huge gates and bazaars selling everything from silks to perfumes, to slaves and camels. My father did take me to what he said was the oldest university in the world, but it looked just like any other mosque to me." He shrugged his shoulders.

"You mean the Al-Azhar mosque which does indeed house the oldest university in the world...from AD 970 roughly?" the old man said as the wealthy tailor shook his head, unsure. "During the earliest Crusades, a man named al-Mustafa, who lived in Alexandria, helped the Crusaders by rescuing Jerusalem from the Ortokids, which ultimately led to its conquest by the Franks in AD 1099. He later tried to undo the fact that he had helped the Crusaders advancing into Palestine himself, but he was defeated at the battle of Ascalon, and retired to Egypt. Many of the Palestinian possessions of the Fatimids then successively fell into the hands of the Crusaders. In AD 1118 Egypt was invaded by Baldwin the First of Jerusalem, who burned the gates and the mosques of Farama, and advanced to Tinnis, but then illness forced him to retreat. In August AD 1121 al-Afdal Shahanshah

was assassinated in a street of Cairo, it is said, with the connivance of the Caliph, who immediately plundered his house, where fabulous treasures were amassed. The vizier's offices were given to al-Mamn. His external policy was no more successful than that of his predecessor, as he lost Tyre to the Crusaders, and a fleet equipped by him was defeated by the Venetians. In AD 1153 Ascalon was lost, the last place in Syria which the Fatimids held, and its loss was attributed to dissension between the parties of which the garrison consisted. In April AD 1154 the Caliph al-Zafir was murdered by his vizier Abbas, because the Caliph had suggested to his favourite, the vizier's son, to murder his father and this was followed by a massacre of the brothers of Zafir, followed by the raising of his infant son Abul-Qasim Isa to the throne. In December of AD 1162, the vizier Shawar took control of Cairo. However, after only nine months he was forced to flee to Damascus, where he was favourably received by the prince Nureddin, or Nur al-Din as I have called him previously, who sent him to Cairo with a force of Kurds under Asad al-din Shirkuh, at the same time Egypt was invaded by the Franks, who raided and did cause much carnage on the coast. Shawar recaptured Cairo but a dispute arose with his Syrian allies for the possession of Egypt. Shawar, being unable to cope with the Syrians, demanded help from the Frankish king of Jerusalem, Amalric the First, who hastened to his aid with a large force, which when united with Shawar's forces, besieged Shirkuh in Bilbeis for three months. At the end of this time, owing to the successes of Nur al-Din in Syria, the Franks granted Shirkuh a free passage with his troops back to Syria, on condition of Egypt being evacuated in October AD 1164."

"What, did I hear you correct that a Muslim commander helped Franks take Jerusalem...and then they in turn helped Muslims take Egypt! Why are we not told of these facts?" Peter asked.

"There is more, my friend. For just two years later Shirkuh persuaded Nur al-Din to put him at the head of another expedition to Egypt, which left Syria in January AD 1167 and again a Frankish army hastened to Shawar's aid. At the battle of Babain April 11th AD 1167 the allies were defeated by the forces commanded by Shirkuh and his nephew Saladin, who was made prefect of Alexandria, which surrendered to Shirkuh without a struggle. In AD 1168 Amalric invaded again, but Shirkuh's return caused the Crusaders to withdraw. Shirkuh was appointed vizier but died of indigestion on March the 23rd AD 1169, and the Caliph appointed Saladin as the successor. The new vizier, Saladin, professed to hold office as a deputy of Nur al-Din, whose name was mentioned in public worship after that of the Caliph. Nur al-Din loyally aided his deputy in dealing with Crusader invasions of Egypt, and he ordered Saladin to substitute the name of the Abbasid caliph for the Fatimid

in public worship. The last Fatimid caliph died soon after in September, AD 1171," the old man explained in detail. [81]

"I think you already explained that previously," Gabirol stated and looked up.

"Thank you for pointing that out. I do try not to repeat myself unless it is necessary." The old man smiled as he replied. "And so it was into this at times crazy world of constantly shifting alliances, truces and engagements that Paul found himself commissioned to work upon new ship designs. Of course he would receive tutelage by the best ships draughtsmen Husam had at his disposal."

Husam's residency, banks of the Nile, Cairo, Egypt, July 4th 1180

"And you are sure Alisha is okay with this?" Theodoric asked Paul as they approached the impressive columned entrance to Husam's home and also his operational headquarters in Cairo.

"I have the letters from Turansha, plus he did invite me personally as I reminded Alisha. She worries too much I fear," Paul replied as two Mamluk guards blocked their way. Paul looked behind at Tenno, who was following close behind them. "At least she and Sister Lucy can sort the house out without us getting in the way."

"Until Thomas and his men arrive today," Tenno stated as he studied the two Mamluk guards.

"If we are not here too long, then perhaps we can visit the pyramids on our way back afterwards. There is so much to show you," Theodoric remarked.

"I promised Alisha I would not go exploring just yet," Paul replied as he caught sight of Husam walking towards the gated entrance accompanied by Gokbori and Saladin's deputy, Karaksh.

Two other Mamluk guards appeared from behind the walls and proceeded to open one of the large metalled gates and swung it outwards. The two guards stood near to Paul moved aside as Husam greeted Paul with a large grin.

"Assalamu Allakham," Husam said and bowed his head slightly at Paul.

"Wa Allakham Assalam," Paul replied and grabbed Husam's forearms.

"We are so honoured you have taken up our offer. We aim to make your stay here in Cairo as enjoyable and productive as possible," Husam said and shook Paul's arm.

"'Tis good to see you again. This is a long way from Abrahams Oak, yes?" Gokbori said and stepped closer, part bowing his head. Paul bowed his head in acknowledgement. "Husam tells me you are to design us new ships...I look forward to seeing what you plan. I am as you know a lover of ships and the water," he explained, smiled and looked across towards a jetty set parallel to the main building.

"That it is...and I do not think I ever thanked you properly," Paul replied and broke his grip with Husam. "Alexandria did not afford me that chance either as Alisha was with me then, but I offer it now."

"No thanks are...how you say, necessary. I simply did what was right. And your wife...she is indeed a rare beauty. I hope I will be acquainted with her again soon. But if you really wish to thank me, then between you, put a ship there for my next return," Gokbori said and pointed to the empty jetty and dry dock beside it.

"But I am not trained yet," Paul replied and looked at Husam.

"Not yet, but you will be and you have the mind and eye for it I am told... reliably," Gokbori said and looked at Husam as Karaksh stepped forward.

"I shall make sure you both have all you require to accomplish your task," he said in a low voice, almost a whisper.

Tenno looked at Theodoric quizzically.

"Task?" Theodoric said aloud as if to question the point.

"Task indeed," Gokbori laughed.

"If you help design and build ships here, does that not put you at odds with your fellow Christians?" Tenno asked bluntly as Theodoric put his hand across his face and shook his head. "'Tis a valid question no?"

"'Tis valid indeed," Gokbori replied. "But this is not about choosing sides, 'tis about working together for that is the only way our peoples will ever prosper. Together."

"And you have our assurances of protection. You are safe in Cairo no matter what happens elsewhere," Karaksh said and paused. "We know that you are no enemy of ours during these testing times...with Reynald."

"We are far from perfect neither, but we try," Gokbori said and gestured for Paul, Theodoric and Tenno to walk through the gates.

"And it would appear the path is followed again," Theodoric said to himself, smiling as he placed his hands behind his back.

Tenno looked at him, suspicious of his remark, and frowned.

Chapter 50
A Queen, Camelot & a Land of Dolmens

Cairo, Egypt, July 4th 1180

Paul sat himself down at the main dining table as Theodoric settled himself into the chair opposite him. Tenno sat at the head of the table having beaten Theodoric to it. It had become a new daily game between them. Sister Lucy brought over two plates of hot food as Alisha served out another.

"Is that all for dinner?" Sister Lucy asked aloud as she placed a plate in front of Paul and Tenno in turn.

"Erm…yes. Percival dines with Thomas and his men tonight, and I believe Ishmael is sourcing some materials with Nyla still," Paul answered.

"You mean they are all in the town again?" Alisha laughed as she picked up two more plates of food and approached the table. "So tell me…how was your first visit to work?"

"It was…interesting. Both Theo and Tenno were allowed to accompany me," Paul replied as Alisha placed a meal in front of Theodoric, the other beside him and promptly sat down next to Paul closely. "Arri sleeps well. I think he missed you today," she said and rubbed his arm gently before looking across the room at the small baby crib in the corner.

Sister Lucy started to sit down when Attar knocked on the rear entrance door. His face was just visible above the closed half of the lower stable type door as he pushed himself past the long strings of hanging beads. He feigned an apologetic grimace when he realised they were all about to eat.

2 - 19

"Please, enter," Paul said and stood up. "You are just in time if you have not eaten."

Sister Lucy opened the latch and swung the half door open and beckoned Attar to enter.

"Sorry for I do not wish to intrude. I shall come back tomorrow," Attar said politely and bowed, his hands held together.

"No please...you know you are more than welcome to stay. Besides, I have questions to ask about the pyramids," Paul said and offered Attar to sit beside Theodoric.

"Paul...I told you. No exploring in dangerous tunnels. You have other responsibilities now," Alisha interrupted and nodded toward Arri asleep in his crib.

Tenno looked at Theodoric and raised an eyebrow as if to question what Alisha had said. He shrugged his shoulders at him.

"Ali...I came to enquire how he found his new work. I shall not speak of pyramids or matters relating to them," Attar replied courteously.

"Sorry, I speak out of turn for I do not wish to sound rude or impolite. I just worry that this one here," Alisha explained as she nudged Paul's arm, "is influenced by the many tales his father and Theo have filled his head with regarding them. I just want him safe and to myself for a while."

"That is understandable. But they are not just tales for they speak truth in what they did and saw," Attar replied, still standing, his hands clasped as if in prayer.

"I do not question that...I just meant...," Alisha said and felt slightly awkward. "I shall be quiet for I fear I am saying too much the wrong way."

"A woman saying too much! Never!" Theodoric joked.

Sister Lucy shot him a look of disapproval and shook her head.

"She is right to have concerns," Attar replied and bowed again at Alisha.

"Please dine with us...perhaps you can educate the old fool better," Sister Lucy said loudly and walked over to the main cooking stove and began to dish out two more plates of food, glancing back at Theodoric frowning and indicating toward Alisha.

"Ali, I promise I shall do nothing stupid. I have all that I need right here," Paul said reassuringly and held Alisha's hand as she looked at Attar.

"I shall say no more!" Theodoric said and raised his hands as Tenno shook his head very slightly.

"Paul...I simply cannot bear to think of losing you, especially down some dangerous long lost tunnel, and for what?" Alisha asked quietly and looked at him intently.

"For what? Perhaps Attar is better qualified to answer that than I," Paul replied.

"Wrong reply," Sister Lucy said loudly as she approached carrying her own meal and a plate for Attar. She placed hers next to Theodoric heavily with a thud then placed Attar's at the other end of the table. "Eat before it gets cold and then Attar can enlighten Paul why it is foolhardy and dangerous to go to such places as I know some will actively encourage him," she said and looked at Theodoric with an exaggerated scowl.

ꕥ

After finishing their meals in relative silence, Paul stood up and offered to help Sister Lucy and Alisha clean up, but both turned on him immediately demanding he get out of the dining room and retire to the other large room to relax whilst they cleared up. Tenno and Attar stood to leave with Paul but when Theodoric stood up and started to follow, Sister Lucy grabbed the back of his shirt.

"No not you. You can help us," she bellowed to him and indicated with her thumb to follow her. He feigned a pained protest but then smiled as he walked over to a large cleaning board with her. "The scouring ash and grass is over there. I need your strength to clean the grease away, my darling," she mocked as she then pointed him toward the end of the main cooking hearth.

Alisha gently pushed Paul towards the main room adjoining the dining hall as Attar followed. She looked back at Tenno and tilted her head that he should follow Paul.

Within minutes Paul was opposite Attar, both sitting in large single chairs made from wicker and wood lattice but cushioned. Tenno eased himself down in another chair beside Paul.

"'Tis not often I get to sit upon a chair," Attar remarked as he sank back into it.

"Nor I...could make me lazy," Tenno stated as he felt the soft cushions attached to the wide arms of the chairs.

The large open room had several chairs centred around a dark wooden low table that looked more like a travel trunk with its metal covered corners, but the centre of it was beautifully carved in ornate detail and lattice work. Nyla had placed several vases around the room with scented flowers that filled the air with a pleasant fragrance. Two large embroidered tapestries hung on opposite walls, with the northern wall mainly taken over by a large set of wooden shuttered windows. The south wall led into a small enclosed courtyard with a shallow fish pond surmounted by a small wall with stone bench areas to sit on. Alisha had already asked to have the water covered in netting to stop Arri from ever falling in. A whole collection of different swords, daggers, shields and many statuettes adorned the wall furthest from the dining hall. Paul laughed as he remembered how Alisha had raised everything in the room above the height of what Arri could possibly reach. He wondered from where all the various items and ornaments had come and what stories his father could tell him about them. Tomorrow Paul would attend Husam's residency alone, though Tenno insisted that either he or Thomas would escort him both there and home afterwards. Paul moved in his chair as he felt something press against his thigh. He reached down and pulled out Clip clop, Arri's little comfort horse. As he raised it Tenno immediately stood up and reached to take it from him.

"There it is. Do you know how long Ali and I looked for him," he said and took Clip clop from him and walked back toward the dining area.

Attar smiled as Tenno walked away, Clip clop raised triumphantly in his hand.

"He is a very good man," Attar said quietly.

"I know," Paul whispered back. "Why am I whispering?" he asked and laughed.

"Alisha…she worries for you…no?"

"My Ali…yes she does," Paul answered as he turned and leaned sideways to look through the kitchen and dining hall divider hatch in time to see Tenno return Clip clop. She laughed and snatched him from Tenno. "But it is nice to know she cares so much."

"That she does. But Paul, and I may speak out of turn when I say this, you must not stop or deny your own spirit of adventure and growth. If you do, no matter how noble the sacrifice is and no matter how much you convince yourself otherwise, you will come to resent her. Slowly but surely bit by little bit. You must find a compromise balance whereby she will allow you to grow," Attar explained quietly.

Slowly Paul turned back to face Attar. Part of him did not want to hear his words, but part of him felt excited as if he had been given a way to still engage his thirst for knowledge and exploration.

"But how do I approach her and explain that it is not danger I seek…just knowledge?"

"You will find a way...and she will likewise find a way to develop herself in directions she has not even considered yet."

"I pray you are right for I love that woman more than life itself," Paul remarked and sighed.

"Paul...you cannot hide from what you desire and know you will end up doing. I am not advocating you lie, but I am saying you should visit the pyramids and explore them if that is what you desire for I know it is an itch you must scratch."

"Huh...easier said than done. And I thought you of all people would have come up with some greater or deeper and meaningful way of conveying that message than just an itch you must scratch!" Paul laughed.

"Why over complicate a fact with words that only dress up what needs to be said?" Attar asked back and nodded.

"What words?" Alisha suddenly asked as she appeared through the doors from the courtyard carrying a tray with a jug and tall blue glasses. She smiled beautifully as she looked at Paul and placed the tray on the low table. Upon the tray was a small oil lamp with the flame flickering away. "I shall light the lanthorn before Arri awakes for his last feed...now tell me, what words?" she asked again and sat down beside Paul and clasped his hand upon his knee.

"'Tis rude to ask upon a private conversation," Paul replied, joking, and smiled at her as she raised her eyebrows high. "We were just talking about how to address certain things in life and how to best explain them...especially to those we love the most!"

"Truly?" Alisha said and looked at Attar, suspicion written all across her face as she frowned further in an exaggerated fashion.

"Truly. We were just going to talk about pyramids," Attar replied as Paul's eyes widened in alarm and he shook his head very slightly to indicate no. "How they are connected to giants and people similar to Abi."

"Really...that I must hear. Please hold that conversation until we are all done and settled for the eve. That I must hear," Alisha repeated as she stood up, kissed Paul on the head and walked away back to the dining hall area. She flicked her hair over her shoulders as she left.

"Oh dear...she will quiz you hard this eve now," Paul smiled.

"No matter. It will be a delight to discuss it and I know Theodoric will certainly speak upon the matter...I had to say something believable!" Attar said quietly as he grinned.

ꙮ

The evening air was cool as it blew gently through the hanging net curtains drawn across the doorway into the small courtyard. The room glowed with a comforting warm yellow from the three lanthorns set upon wall mounted brackets when Theodoric coughed and cleared his throat.

"I can tell you that Abi's mother came from an area that is part of the Tori province in Georgia, a land full of myths and legends about giants who were all nine feet tall on average. Blonde and blue eyed no less. Her father came from Sardinia, another place with identical myths, and as you know, the line is passed down through the mother...," he explained as Alisha looked at him intently.

Tenno sat perfectly still as he listened.

"So where was she born exactly?" Tenno asked bluntly.

"Sardinia...but sadly her parents both died when she was just three years old. That is why she went to live with Kratos," Theodoric answered. "But her true homeland, where her ancestors came from, is an area dotted by a series of forts guarding the strategic crossroad of routes leading to the western, eastern, and southern provinces of Georgia. Georgia's flag is identical to that of England's...as in a red cross upon a white background... but they also have many identical legends related to St George and dragons as well as being a country covered in ancient stone structures just like England. They also have many wells and springs of healing waters. Many old stories speak of 'the valley of the giants'. Much of the ancient history of the Caucasus region remains a mystery, because of the remote locations, but as your father and I discovered, megalithic structures are found all over the region and many sites have similarities with other, better-known megalithic structures such as the ones at Stonehenge, in Malta, or Baalbek. On the slopes of the Trialeti mountain range, at an altitude of over five thousand feet, we saw cyclopean castles and menhirs dating back to the second and first millennium BC and they extended for many miles. Near the village of Tejisi we helped design and build a church where we used a sixteen foot tall menhir set into it," Theodoric explained and paused as his mind wandered back to that time as Sister Lucy rubbed his back.

Paul looked at him and was amazed at just how far his father had travelled and how much he simply did not know about him still.

"Please, Theo...tell us all you know," Paul asked.

"Please do," Alisha said and held Paul's hand.

"Then let me start by explaining that English, the language as you understand it, was not from the country you now call England. No…for it originated in the lands of the north, before its people were driven out. Many went to Britain whilst others went to Georgia. In time, people will learn of this simple truth again," Theodoric said and sighed before continuing. "But the nation of Georgia was not unified as a kingdom until the Bagrationi dynasty of King Bagrat the Third in the ninth to tenth century, arising from a number of earlier states of the ancient kingdoms of Colchis and Iberia. 'Tis the Colchis aspect you should pay attention to for it is connected to the town in Britain with its hidden sacred past. A great mystery hidden in plain sight no less."

"How so?" Tenno asked.

"Because Colchis in Britain became known as Camulodinum, the Roman capital of the country. It was shortened to Camulod…Sound familiar?"

"Camelot!" Paul commented.

"Exactly and even more so when you apply the Latin principle whereby you can use or interchange the D and T and we have Camulot. Plus, in the surrounding landscape, over a hundred and thirty lines of energy converge on a place named Beacon Hill. Lines that stretch out across France, through Italy and start from here in Cairo no less. Plus there are three major tumulus mounds also set that mirror the three belt stars of Orion north of Camulod, which many already now call Colchester."

"Just like the three Giza pyramids do," Paul interjected. Alisha looked at him and frowned.

"Yes, you are correct, Paul. The same," Theodoric remarked and smiled.

"Then why is this not known, more widespread?" Alisha asked.

"To hide the fact. Hence why many legends and stories give details of Camelot with many confusing and conflicting accounts to deliberately conceal the truth. To protect the knowledge until mankind wakes up from his amnesia. Your fathers certainly knew this fact well," Theodoric answered.

"Do not forget the Georgian flag also has a white Unicorn set upon a black background…," Attar said quietly.

"Yes…and God willing if all goes to plan, the day will come when Britain will adopt the symbol of the rose as its national flower as well as the unicorn upon its banners…," Theodoric said and shook his head.

"I recall my father did once mention King David...the Fourth. He is known as the Builder is he not?" Paul asked.

"See. You paid more attention to your father than you thought," Theodoric laughed. "But yes, he was known as the Builder. In AD 1118–1119, having considerable amounts of free, unsettled land...a result of the withdrawal of nomads...and desperately needing manpower for his new army, King David invited some forty thousand Kipchak warriors from North Caucasus to settle in Georgia with their families. In AD 1120 the ruler of Alania recognised himself as King David's vassal and sent thousands of Alans to Georgia, where they settled in Kartli. The Georgian Royal army also welcomed mercenaries from Germany, Italy and Scandinavia where all those westerners were defined as Franks just as here. In AD 1121, the Seljuq Sultan Mahmud declared Jihad on Georgia and sent a powerful army under one of his famous generals Ilghazi to fight the Georgians. Although significantly outnumbered, the Georgians managed to defeat the invaders at the Battle of Didgori, and in AD 1122 they took over Tbilisi, making it Georgia's capital. Three years later the Georgians conquered Shirvan. As a result, the mostly Christian-populated Ghishi-Kabala area in western Shirvan was annexed by Georgia while the rest of an already Islamicised Shirvan became Georgia's client-state. In the same year a large portion of Armenia was liberated by David's troops and fell into Georgian hands as well so in AD 1124 David also became the King of Armenians, incorporating Northern Armenia into the lands of the Georgian Crown. In AD 1125 King David died, leaving Georgia with the status of a strong regional power. In Georgia, King David is called Agmashenebeli, which in English means 'the builder'."

"So, if the ancestors who made Georgia are connected to the English, how was their history lost?" Paul asked, bemused.

"I shall come to that. But there is far more to Georgia than most people suspect...even by those who live there now," Theodoric answered. "You see, near Lake Paravani, in the region of Akhalkalaki, there is a megalithic fortress at an altitude of over nine thousand feet. Your father and I had some serious trouble walking up that one I can tell you," Theodoric laughed. "But there is another site, called Gochnaris Lodovani, 'the great rocks of Gochnari', near the town of Manglisi in the Algeti river valley as well as another megalithic fortress located at an altitude of over nine thousand feet in the Eastern Georgian province of Kakheti, near the village of

Patara Abuli. They are all constructed using huge basalt blocks, some of them thirteen feet long. The gates are far too big for our average size, and the walls are up to thirty feet tall. There are over three thousand dolmen stones in the Western Caucasus, and more are constantly being found. These dolmens are still of an unknown origin. The dolmens of Abkhazia mainly consist of four upright stones and a capstone, some of them weighting as much as fifty tons we estimated."

"So who built them?" Alisha asked, intrigued.

"That is what Philip and I tried to confirm," Theodoric replied. "Just as now, people living there today cannot provide any information about the civilisation that lived there before them other than vague folk legends that claim gods or giants of the distant past made them. But it is as if the builders of the megalithic structures across the world just vanished from the face of the earth…though they left their legacy hidden for us to one day recover…"

"From where?" Alisha asked instantly.

"The codes that lead us start and end with the great pyramids…," Theodoric replied and looked at Alisha and raised his eyebrows.

"I don't want you going in those tunnels still," she said, looking back at Paul.

"Tell them about Tamar," Sister Lucy suddenly interjected, looking serious.

"Who?" Paul asked.

"Tamar. She is a young woman both of your fathers knew. She is also related to you both believe it or not," Theodoric started to explain and looked at Sister Lucy as if for guidance.

"Please, you must tell us more then…for we both know so little of our families' pasts," Paul asked and held Alisha's hand tighter.

"Well I can tell you she was made Queen Regent of Georgia, Queen of Queens in 1178 just two years past…a fact that would not have occurred but for your fathers," Theodoric said and looked down briefly.

"And you also," Sister Lucy interjected sternly.

"Perhaps! She was born in the year of our Lord AD 1160. Huh, there was once talk that she would be betrothed to Stewart…or you," Theodoric explained looking up at Paul. Alisha immediately held Paul's hand with both of hers, looking slightly alarmed. Theodoric laughed. "Fear not, Ali, that time has long since gone."

"Good...I am glad to hear so," she replied.

"Tamar is of the Royal House of Bagrationi, her father was George the Third and her mother was Burdukhan. She was a fine woman...," Theodoric said and smiled as Sister Lucy playfully thumped him. "Tamar is a Christian woman but knows much indeed. Your father told her one sentence when she was just a small child and yet she can still recount it perfectly."

"What is that then?" Tenno asked.

"'We have to stay true to our convictions, no matter how high the price'... that is it. Nowadays Tamar has a dream whereby she aims to merge both the Georgian and Roman Empires. She has already practically succeeded in this despite her youth. She is also known as Tamara, her Latin name. Tamar uses the name Tamar Johanna Georgia in her term as Pope, she is already known to some initiates as Pope Joan."

"What...Pope Joan! How so?" Paul asked, utterly intrigued.

"Tamar's youth coincided with a major upheaval in Georgia. In AD 1177, her father, George the Third, was confronted by a rebellious faction of nobles. The rebels intended to dethrone George in favour of the king's fraternal nephew, Demna, who was considered by many to be a legitimate royal heir of his murdered father, David the Fifth. Demna's cause was little but a pretext for the nobles, led by the pretender's father-in-law, the amirspasalar 'constable' Ivane Orbeli, to weaken the crown. George the Third was able to crush the revolt and embarked on a campaign to crack down on the defiant aristocratic clans. Ivane Orbeli was put to death and the surviving members of his family were driven out of Georgia. Prince Demna, castrated and blinded on his uncle's order, did not survive the mutilation and soon died in prison. Once the rebellion was suppressed and the pretender eliminated, George went ahead to co-opt Tamar into government with him and crowned her as co-ruler in AD 1178. By doing so, the king attempted to pre-empt any dispute after his death and legitimise his line on the throne of Georgia. At the same time, he raised men from the gentry and unranked classes to keep the dynastic aristocracy away from the centre of power. Tamar is good at diplomacy and politics and she overshadows her father in the government. Her father lets her do all the hard work and she is now the most powerful person in the kingdom. She set up new laws for more equality and less corruption in the kingdom. The kingdom is flourishing and is growing into a mighty nation. Tamar despite her young age has already reunited the Orthodox and Catholic Churches who split up in the Great Schism of AD 1054. She has also built many churches to convert many people and spread Christianity. If I told you that I know she will become a pope, would you believe me?" Theodoric asked and looked at Sister Lucy who hit him again.

"A pope?" Paul remarked.

"Yes...'tis written in her charts and is why some higher initiates already call her Pope Joan as I just said."

1 - 3

"That I should like to see," Paul replied, looking incredulous.

"Paul, there has already been one female pope, though much of the facts have been obfuscated and erased from history...well, as much as could be."

"What does this woman have to do with us here, now and in Cairo?" Alisha asked.

"She has in her possession a manuscript...one that she has vowed to have copied and placed back in the Vatican or wherever the popes of the future will reside. 'Tis an authentic manuscript that could turn the whole philosophy of the Christian Church upside down, for it details that Mary Magdalene was indeed the thirteenth apostle and that she was Jesus's fiancé and later wife. The manuscript describes her as Jesus's most trusted and closest disciple. It also describes her as the actual founder of Christianity. Tamar demanded from the Church an explanation for this act of secretion but the Church responded that if these secrets were to be revealed, then the whole of society as we know it will collapse. It is why she allows women to be ordained and hold offices in the clergy. Although women may be elected as Pope, none have been elected openly so far. She will do much to change how women are perceived within the Church...and there will come a day when the Church finally admits that Mary Magdalene was in fact, actually the first pope...not Peter!"

"Is this all true?" Paul asked quizzically.

"Yes...every word. 'Tis why despite her age she is already called a king. Granted in Georgia they have no masculine and feminine differentiation as such, but she is called Mepe, which means king...or sovereign. She is much like you," Theodoric said looking up at Alisha.

"Then Paul shall never meet her," she quickly replied and pulled Paul closer.

"But how does this have anything to do with Abi?" Tenno asked as he sat up straighter.

"I shall explain," Theodoric replied and cleared his throat again. "According to written documents and family legend...and as the Georgian chronicler Sumbat Davitis-Dze writes, the ancestors of the dynasty trace their descent to the Biblical King David and came from Palestine around AD 530. Yes, the same David who killed the giant Goliath with a stone from his sling! Paul...Remember before that I told you that even King David was tall himself? The bronze helmet they tried to put upon his young head before the fight did not fit...remember?" Theodoric asked as Paul then nodded yes. "Good. Then know that native Georgians call themselves Kartvelebi, and their land Sakartvelo, which means 'a place for Kartvelians'. According to the ancient Georgian Chronicles, the ancestor of the Kartvelian people was Kartlos, the great grandson of the biblical Japheth...Noah's son Kartlos was son of Togarmah, son of Gomer, the eldest son of Japeth. Kartlos should have been 'a brave, gigantic man, the legendary giant'. Well Mount Kazbek is a major mountain of the Caucasus region not far from where Abi's ancestors came from. It is associated in Georgian folklore with Amirani, the Georgian version of Prometheus, the Titan from Greek mythology, who was chained on the mountain in punishment for having stolen fire from the gods and having given it to mortals. The legend is traced to between three thousand and two thousand years BC. The location of his imprisonment later became the site of an Orthodox hermitage located in a cave called 'Betlemi', almost identical in both written and spoken words as Bethlehem, at around twelve thousand feet level. According to legends, this cave housed many sacred relics, including the biblical Abraham's tent and the manger of the infant Jesus. In the Monastery Shemokmedi in the western Georgian province of Guria you can find a painting of a six fingered angel, and it is said that giants often had six fingers. The site even pre-dates the monastery's early Christian origins and there is also a 'Stone of Giant'. According to a legend a giant used to terrify the village until Saint George was called to help. He killed the giant, as he had killed the dragon, and the grateful people erected the church for Saint George. See how similar the tales are to those of Britain?"

"And?" Tenno asked bluntly as if impatient to learn more.

"And...and in Greek mythology Aeëtes was a King of Colchis, an ancient Georgian kingdom. Aeëtes was a son of the Titan Sun God Helios and

Perseis, a daughter of the Titan Oceanus. His daughter Medea, sometimes known as the witch of Colchis, helped Jason of Argonaut fame secure the Golden Fleece. Medea then fled with Jason. Her son Medeus became the eponymous founder of the Persians. Now according to the gospels of Luke and Matthew, David was an ancestor of Jesus Christ through both Joseph and Mary. He is depicted as an acclaimed warrior, musician, and poet…and he is also known for having red hair, based on the description of his physical appearance as 'admoni', 'red-haired', in 1 Samuel 16–17. He had a fine appearance and handsome features and his life is conventionally dated to 1040–970 BC. Jesus Christ of the Bible will be proved to have been a genuine historical person just as King David was…and that he was tall, blonde and had blue eyes just as the letter from Pontius Pilate to Tiberius Caesar stated."

"Why what did it state?" Alisha asked.

"It said…if I can recall it all, but you can verify the facts as it is all written down…'His golden coloured hair and beard gave to his appearance a celestial aspect.' Or from the Archko Volume in The Vatican where its states 'He is the picture of his mother. His hair is a little more golden than hers. He is tall, and his shoulders are a little drooped. His eyes are large and a soft blue.' According to Genesis and Ruth, David is the fourth son of the patriarch Jacob of Israel and ancestor of the tribes of Israel, which were named after his descendants. He was the grandson of Abraham. Father Abraham made according to the scriptures a covenant with God, who promised land and descendants as numerous as the stars. Abraham's father, Terah, was born in Nippur into a priestly-royal family, but moved later to the ancient city of Ur and then to Haran, which was an ancient city in Upper Mesopotamia and now a village in Sanliurfa. Nippur was one of the most ancient of all the Babylonian cities of which we have any knowledge, the special seat of the worship of the Sumerian god Enlil. The Sumerian scriptures say that when Enlil saw that the humans created by his brother Enki were demi-gods, giants, he decided to kill them by sending a flood. Christians believe that Jesus was a descendant of Abraham through Isaac. Isaac who was saved by an angel when God tested Abraham's faith by telling him to sacrifice his son on an altar…at the very place where the dome of the rock now stands in Jerusalem. Abraham was a descendant of Noah's son Shem. Noah of the Great Flood had three sons, Shem, Ham and Japheth. We all know the biblical story about Noah and the Ark yes?" Theodoric explained and asked then looked at Tenno.

"Yes I too know full well the story," Tenno replied.

"Good…Well to remind ourselves again…God saw that man had become wicked and decided to send a great flood to cleanse the earth. But God told Noah to build a large ark. When Noah, his family and all the animals were on board, God sent the Flood, which rises until all the mountains are covered and all life on earth is destroyed. According to the Bible the Ark came to rest on one of the tops of the mountains of Ararat. Noah and his family were safe and could start to repopulate the earth."

"Forgive me, but I fail to see how this has anything to do with Abi or giants," Tenno interrupted as Attar smiled at his look.

"In short," Theodoric started to reply then thought on his choice or words and laughed briefly. "Okay, not short, but in simple terms, there is a clear link between the ruling family of Georgia and Noah of the Great Flood. As the scriptures state… 'There were giants in the earth in those days, when the sons of God came in unto the daughters of men, and they bare children to them'. Some biblical literalists say that the ones that God wanted to cleanse from the earth with the Great Flood were the children that his sons had with humans…the giants! So let us say that the giants were wiped from the earth by the Great Flood but obviously a few of them survived. Some say that one of the women aboard the Ark was already pregnant with a giant. It could even have been Noah's wife, as some speculate! The giant's blood-line survived through the Great Flood, and was brought to what was supposed to be a giant-free earth! A Jewish legend tells that the giant King Og begged and prayed to Noah to come aboard the Ark, and that Noah made an agreement with him that he could sit on the back of a giant unicorn that was tied to the outside of the Ark since there was not enough room inside for it. Recall that the flag of Georgia has a unicorn upon it? Og was the king of the Amorites, described in Genesis 10:16 as descendants of Canaan, son of Ham, son of Noah. They are described as a powerful people of great stature like 'the height of the cedars', who had occupied the land east and west of the Jordan. King Og is being described as the last 'of the remnant of the Rephaim', the giants.

"It is a sad but real truth that many in the years ahead will disbelieve our holy books and label them as purely the ignorant ramblings of a people in time who simply did not understand the past and the reality of our world," Attar said quietly.

"True…but likewise, that attitude will go full circle as man learns even more and again recognises the hidden truths carried within all holy books," Theodoric commented.

"But there is no physical evidence to support most of what the holy books claim," Paul remarked.

"Oh yes there is, my young man…and plenty of it. Just travel beneath the pyramids and you will see," Theodoric replied instantly with a large smile upon his face.

"Oh no you won't," Alisha snapped and scowled mockingly at Paul but meaning it none the less.

"Many doubt that the story from the Bible about Noah and the Flood has anything to do with reality, and say that no physical evidence of the Ark has been found. Well, the biblical version is but a copy and borrowing of an even earlier telling of the story, but it is a story that really happened and now carries over into our times. All the mathematical and esoteric codes are likewise all carried over within them. All across the known world, including China and even your own home lands," Theodoric said looking at Tenno, "all have great flood stories and legends as recounted for millennia before our peoples made contact. Your fathers and I found seashell fossils on mountain tops all over the high places we have visited. How could they possibly get deposited there?"

"My father says because the lands changed…what were valleys became mountains and what were mountains sank beneath the seas…," Paul remarked.

"Yes…all of those things happened. We found on more than one trip great stone harbours…but thousands of feet above sea level. On Mount Ararat we discovered a piece of ancient wood but also a strange metal trestle over 450 feet long by 75 feet wide buried on the side of the mountain. It still lays beneath the earth now. The measurements correspond to the dimensions of the Ark given to Noah in the Bible. But as we also learnt… there were many arks, not just the one," Theodoric explained and paused as he took a sip of some water from a glass upon the low table. "Have you heard of Gog and Magog?"

"Yes," Paul answered as Alisha and Tenno shook their heads no.

"Well Magog is the second of the seven sons of Japheth, one of Noah's three sons, as mentioned in Genesis. The land given to Magog after the Flood was the region north and east of the Caucasus, and his descendants were referred to by the Greeks as Scythians. Gomer was Japeth's eldest son, and it has been debated what land he and his ancestors populated. According to the fifth century BC Greek historian Herodotus, Gomerians or Cimmerians inhabited the region north of the Caucasus and the Black Sea during the eighth and seventh centuries BC. Stone stelae found in the region and the northern Caucasus have been connected with the Cimmerians, and they are in a style clearly different from both the later Scythians. Military intelligence reports to the Assyrian king Sargon in the eighth century BC described the Cimmerians as occupying territory south of the Black Sea, while the first century Romano-Jewish historian Josephus placed Gomer and the Gomerites in ancient Galatia…an area in the highlands of central Anatolia. Some believe that Galatia was named after the immigrant Gauls, the Celts from Thrace, who settled there and became its ruling caste in the third century BC…and remember the Greek myth about the hundred Thracian giants who waged war on the gods? The Scythians were a race of superb horsemen and archers. The Kurgans were quite literally the original Caucasians, having originated from the area around the Caucasus from which the term has derived almost a thousand years before the Scythians, even if the Scythians can be said to be Kurgans, for they were tall, blonde-haired and blue-eyed, expert horsemen and chariot riders. They buried their dead in large burial mounds, the term kurgan means 'burial mound'. Now Meshech was another son of Japeth. He is named with his brother Tubal as principalities of Gog, prince of Magog. Yes, Magog is in the Book of Ezekiel as a place and not an individual. Son of man, direct your face towards Gog, of the land of Magog, the prince, leader of Meshech and Tubal."

"So who was Gog?" Alisha asked, even more puzzled.

"It is hard to find any reference to Gog in the ancient writings besides the Book of Ezekiel where it is purely referenced as a symbol of the evil darkness of the north, a king that should come from the east and make war with Israel. Ezekiel also mentioned that Gog is the ally of Gomer, Japeth's eldest son. Aurelius Ambrosius, better known as Saint Ambrose AD 340–397, was a bishop of Milan and he claimed that Gog was a name for the Goths. The Goths were according to some scholars an East Germanic tribe of Scandinavian (Denmark, Norway, Sweden) origin but the ancient Greeks considered the Goths to be Scythians as detailed by Herodotus. Gog and Magog became identified by some ancient scholars with the Khazars, whose empire dominated Central Asia in the ninth and tenth centuries. So did also a Georgian tradition, which called them 'wild men with hideous faces and the manners of wild beasts, eaters of blood'. King Joseph of Khazaria claimed to be a descendant of Magog's nephew Togarmah. The ancient Khazar Empire was a major but now almost forgotten power in Eastern Europe, which in AD 740 converted to Judaism. It is said that Kazaria was divided between Ak-Khazars, 'White Khazars', and Kara-Khazars, 'Black Khazars'. The Arab writer Istakhri claimed that the White Khazars were strikingly handsome with reddish hair, white skin and blue eyes while the Black Khazars were swarthy verging on deep black as if they were some kind of Indian. We know that some identify two of Magog's sons as Suenno, progenitor of the Swedes, and Gog is also known as Gethar or Gogus, as the ancestor of the Goths. We have even been told that Meshech, another of Japeth's sons, first ruled in Britain. The Georgian people have traditions that they, and other Caucasus people, as well as Armenians, share descent from Meshech. And according to the tradition, the giants Gog and Magog are guardians of the City of London. The story is that the Roman Emperor Diocletian had thirty-three wicked daughters. He found thirty-three husbands for them to curb their wicked ways but they chafed at this and under the leadership of the eldest sister, Alba, they murdered them. For this crime, they were set adrift at sea. They were later washed ashore on a windswept island, which after Alba was called Albion, the oldest name for Britain. Here they coupled with demons and gave birth to a race of giants, among whose descendants were Gog and Magog. Another version of the story has it that these two giants were the last two survivors of the sons of the infamous daughters, who were captured and kept chained to the gates of a palace on the site of Guildhall to act as guardians."

"Yes my father has told me that part several times. 'Tis but another of the reasons he sees fit to travel to London often," Paul said and looked down as he thought about his father. Alisha sensed the sadness in Paul and rubbed his shoulder gently. He looked up at her and smiled.

"I shall not bore you much longer," Theodoric said and shuffled in his chair.

"I am far from bored. Are you?" Paul answered and looked at Alisha. She shook her head no.

"Okay to keep this short…if I can? The ruling family of Georgia seems to be related to persons of the Bible, from Noah to Jesus. But is there any truth to the Christian Bible or is it just folklore and religious rhetoric as some believe? Well, there exist many other historical documents going all the way back to the time of Jesus and even before. Egyptian history and culture generally match the biblical accounts. When it comes to the Greek myths and ancient scriptures it is quite astonishing to learn they also correspond with the biblical scriptures in many cases and that the ancient Greeks believed their myths to be true is a well documented fact. A major work of Greek mythology was The Iliad by Homer. The Sumerians were one of the earliest societies to emerge in the world, in Mesopotamia. They developed a writing system known as cuneiform, written on wet clay with a sharpened stick, or stylus. Over thousands of years Sumerian scribes recorded daily events, trade, astronomy and literature on clay tablets. And when they all speak of giants, we should take them seriously. We found many skeletons in the Caucasus region, some unbelievably huge...many over nine feet tall. Now the 'Narts' were a tribe of heroes. They were huge, tall people as retold in the Nart sagas, a series of tales originating from the North Caucasus. They form the basic mythology of the tribes in the area, including Abazin, Abkhaz, Circassian, Ossetian, Karachay-Balkar and Chechen-Ingush folklore. The Narts themselves were a race of giants and some motifs in the sagas are shared by Greek mythology...such as the story of Prometheus chained to Mount Kazbek and the myth of Jason and the Golden Fleece in which Colchis is generally accepted to have been part of modern-day Georgia. Some believe that many aspects of the legends about King Arthur are derived from the Nart sagas, like the one where Arthur kills a giant living on a mountain. In the Georgian myths you can also read about the 'Devi', giants, usually believed to be evil beings. The devis lived in the underworld or remote mountains, where they hoarded treasures and kept captives. The myths usually depicted a family of devis, with nine brothers being the average number. Bakbak-Devi was most often the strongest and most powerful of the devis." [82]

"Sounds very much like devils," Alisha remarked.

"It does indeed. The bible says that God created apes and humans, not apes that turned into humans...Genesis tells us that God created Adam, the first human, from the dust of the ground and then he created Eve from one of Adam's ribs so that Adam should not be alone. And that we are of course the descendants of Adam and Eve. Remember how I explained before the meanings behind 'rib' and that it meant spirit? That they were created the way we look today. But we also remember that Genesis tells us that the sons of God, or more correctly 'Gods' in plural, found the females of man pleasing and had children with them. Some believe the sons of God were and are the same as the 'fallen angels', the 'watchers' who according to the scriptures had come down from heaven to earth. That they gave rise to a race of hybrids known as the Nephilim...giants so tall that the Hebrews were like grasshoppers in comparison. Most traditional Christian scholars believe them to have been powerful demons."

"So Abi is of the Gods," Tenno stated more than asked.

"That is just it. We are all the children of the Gods. Some are just taller than others and some still have the blood running through their veins that the ancient tools will work with," Theodoric replied.

"And our souls can migrate from a small body to a larger, depending upon what path one chooses to experience," Attar said and nodded.

"Look, the Sumerians developed one of the earliest civilisations on earth, from the fourth millennium BC in the area known as Mesopotamia. Their creation myth is almost identical to the Christian Bible version. Their gods created the world with sky, water, animals and humans. In the Bible we are made from dust, in the Sumerian texts they are formed from clay. In both the Bible and the Sumerian texts we are created in the image of the gods...not just a single god. Also the sons of the Sumerian gods begot children with the humans, and their offspring were giants, like Gilgamesh. Some of the ancient Sumerian clay tablets depicting the creation of the human race show the struggle their gods seem to have had trying to make us as it seems to have been an intricate process. Some texts say that this creation process was in fact a medical experiment, done by beings from the stars and we were created so they could use man as their servants, or slaves if you like. Tablets reveal texts and images that talk of these people from the stars named as the Annunaki. But the ancient Sumerians also had stories of a great flood. Their supreme god Enlil wanted mankind to vanish because they had become too many and powerful, but the god Enki, who had been responsible for creating the humans, warned the hero Ziusudra (Atrahasis/Utnapishtim) and gave him instructions on building an ark. So according to the Christian Bible, the Sumerian tablets and similar flood stories all over the world, the human race more or less was wiped out in a worldwide flood. Only a few survived and started repopulating the earth. Afterwards, very tall, white skinned, blonde and blue-eyed gods came back and helped educate mankind again. But as soon as they departed, the highly advanced civilisations deteriorated fast and completely vanished leaving only monuments in stone memories."

"So what is so special about Colchis other than it was renamed Camulod as you explained earlier?" Paul asked.

"According to the Greek historian Herodotus, Egyptians occupied the area of Colchis at the eastern end of the Black Sea. He states that these Egyptians knew more about Egyptian history than the Egyptians themselves. Apollonius of Rhodes, who lived some years later, stated that the Egyptians of Colchis preserved as heirlooms a number of wooden tablets showing seas and highways with considerable accuracy. The kingdom of Colchis, which existed from the sixth to the first centuries BC, was regarded as the first Georgian state. Some believe that secret tablets have revealed that Colchis was built on the remains of the legendary Atlantis. Well, the only source we have of Atlantis is the Greek writer Plato, who in about 360 BC mentioned in his writings a story from his ancestor Solon. While visiting the priests of Sais in Egypt, the Athenian statesman, lawmaker and poet Solon learned the story of a magnificent ancient civilisation that disappeared nine thousand years earlier, that great earthquakes and floods had destroyed Atlantis with its survivors fleeing to Egypt. Some of the mountain villages in Colchis should have been relatively untouched by the cataclysmic disaster, and that is why the ancient Greek historians talk about Egyptians in what today is Georgia for they were the proto-Egyptians! There is an ancient link between Georgia and Egypt, and there is definitely a link to Greece. The Greek historians had an intriguing knowledge about the country they called Colchis, and ancient Greek legends told of a fabulously wealthy land where Jason and the Argonauts stole the Golden Fleece from King Aeetes with the help of his daughter Medea. The Golden Fleece was the fleece of the gold-haired, winged ram. Well, the ancient Greeks referred to Colchis as 'polychrysos', meaning 'rich in gold' and it is a fact that gold has been mined in Georgia. It was said that gold was carried down by the mountain torrents, and that in ancient times was obtained by means of perforated troughs and fleecy skins! Golden Fleece...but not on a living ram! Did I forget to mention that Jason and his brave men had to fight off a gang of giants before they reached Colchis, with Heracles, Hercules, killing most of them? Also the giants of the earliest Greek legends were nothing like the stupid trolls of the Nordic myths for they were represented in human form and equipped with armour and spears. The ancient Greeks believed that their legends were true…that the gods, giants and heroes had lived. So many of the Georgian legends are so similar to the Greeks' that there must be a link, there must be something true to the basis of the legends! And it is quite strange that so many of their legends include Colchis and the Caucasus mountains. Why would Prometheus, the Titan from Greek mythology, be chained to a mountain in Georgia? Would it not be more natural that the gods chained him to Mount Olympus? Not only is it the tallest mountain in Greece but it was here the ancient gods lived! Also where the gods were attacked by twenty-four giants, quite successfully until the god Heracles immobilised the leader of the giants by tossing him over his broad shoulders, and rushing him over the Thracian border. Yes, the giant was sent back to where he came from but history does not really give clear information on where Thracia was situated but it was somewhere to the north or northeast. In one ancient Greek source, the very earth is divided into Asia, Libya, Europa and Thracia. Another giant from Thracia was Maximinus Thrax and we know that he was real. His name is translated to 'The Giant from Thracia' and he was a Roman Emperor from year AD 173 to 238. According to Historia Augusta, he was of such a size, so Cordus reports, that men said he was eight foot, six inches in height. We have busts and coins showing Maximinus with his prominent brow, nose and jaw." [83]

"And Abi is connected to all of this?" Tenno asked, looking confused.

"Tenno, I am sorry. Alas once I start to talk, I find it hard to stop…but yes. For Abi's ancestors were of a direct descent from what we would call those very same tall, blonde haired, blue eyed giants from antiquity."

"Why could you not just say that at the start?" Tenno quipped and sat back.

"Because I wished for Paul to learn about Colchis and the history behind it, for much that was secret and begun in the Colchis of Georgia was taken to the new Colchis of Britain," Theodoric replied just as Percival appeared at the rear entrance, followed in by Thomas. Quickly Percival and Thomas walked across the small courtyard and entered the far side door which led to their own private quarters without saying a word. "An early night for them two I am guessing."

"So this queen you mentioned…Tamar, she is important then?" Paul asked looking back at Theodoric.

"Yes and much so. I speak of her now so that hopefully you too will remember and make a special note of her," Theodoric replied, which made Alisha look at Paul, puzzled, almost suspicious.

"Ali, do you know that in the region I speak of, the word Ari means a 'bee'?" Theodoric remarked, seeing her expression.

Ishmael suddenly appeared at the main entrance doorway leading in from the dining area. He bowed his head slightly and looked toward Paul.

"Sorry to disturb you all…but Nyla has arrived and asks to enter with a friend. She has brought many textiles and silks for you," Ishmael explained and looked at Alisha directly.

Alisha stood up fast and quickly rushed across the room excited. As she past Ishmael she kissed the side of his face and hurried off through the dining area and toward the front door.

"I think Ali has found a new best friend," Theodoric joked.

"I shall join them…and you can all talk man things," Sister Lucy said as she stood up.

Paul pointed to her chair with his hand and gestured for Ishmael to join them.

"If you are sure?" Ishmael said.

"Of course. Please join us," Paul replied as Attar sat himself up further.

"Now that Alisha has gone, perhaps we can talk on matters of more interest to you," Attar said as Ishmael sat down.

1 - 23

"I do not wish to conceal anything from Ali," Paul commented.

"Then do not. Tell her all that we speak of but if you wish to learn, and more importantly understand, the wisdom of our forefathers, then you must learn of the secrets of the pyramids. To understand that we, as a people, are all one," Attar said softly.

"See…I am not the only one who says it," Theodoric said and nodded.

"We are all one. If you learn and understand the mathematical codes, the true reality of this world will be opened to you. You will truly see the beauty of our existence in a way you never believed possible. You will understand the saying 'from one many, from many one', and how we are all responsible in equal measure to save ourselves…from ourselves," Attar explained as Theodoric nodded his head in agreement.

"He speaks correctly for, as your father would confirm, we all must learn again the simple truth…that we are all one regardless of race, colour or creed…we are all One Spiritually! Our world is broken, and it is breaking more, as many prophecies claim…but self fulfilling prophecies of a negative and destructive kind must be stopped," Theodoric explained and sat forwards on his chair.

"The pyramids at Giza all hold truths. 'Tis why we must visit them and learn from them even though it scares Alisha," Attar said.

"What, even the small third pyramid?" Paul asked.

"Yes…that one teaches us the truth about light…that light is simply the by-product of matter, regardless of how fast matter moves, light always leaves matter at a constant. That is one of the truths recalled within the legends about the EYE in the centre of a pyramid that it is trying to tell us. The other is how to truthfully view our reality…but also truths about a free and limitless energy form," Theodoric explained, excitement registering across his face.

"Paul, many come to these lands seeking answers to the greatest mysteries. They do so as they instinctively remember that the answers are to be found here…a memory almost and that includes some of the greatest minds from Europe. A primordial tradition transmitted from generation to generation within closed communities of initiates which still exist, such as the secret Islamic communities like the Druze, the Ismailis and the Nusairis, who have been responsible for transmitting ancient wisdom to Europe through their influence on the Knights Templar," Attar explained.

"Sorry…you say that Ismailis have transmitted wisdom to the Templars?" Paul interrupted.

"Yes…and because the Templars recovered certain items, they were able to confirm facts from antiquity that proved what the secret initiates taught was in fact based upon truths. 'Tis why they work so closely together now. They have a common goal…one which unfortunately the likes of Reynald are not privy to," Attar explained.

"Then why not make him so and perhaps then he would not be so hostile," Paul remarked.

"No…we tried that years ago. His answer was to go out and try and slaughter as many Muslims as he could. He does not wish to share any knowledge…," Theodoric answered, his tone turning serious.

"The Knights Templar derived several of their doctrines and practices from the Ismaili Ashashin, who in turn inherited them from ancient Gnostics. The Druze and Nusairi sects were for many years the custodians of the most complete system of secret knowledge. The doctrines of the Nusairis are identical to those of the Cathars," Attar explained further. "That is one aspect the likes of Reynald could not accept…that the key to spiritual enlightenment among the Orient's arcane secret groups all point to the Muslim lands of North Africa and the mysterious East. Here in Cairo we have the Muslim 'House of Wisdom' where one of the greatest Frankish kings ever learnt secrets from when he was taught there. You have heard of him I am sure. He was Charles, King of the Franks…better known to you as Charlemagne. His legacy subsequently led to the creation of many cathedrals across Europe for the Templars and he founded a lodge for the Rosicrucian Order in Toulouse. Even the name Rosicrucian, a follower of the path of the Rose Cross, is to all purposes identical to the Moorish Sufi phrase 'Path of the Rose'," Attar said quietly as he studied Paul's reaction carefully.

"My father has explained about Charlemagne already…and his sword being made similar to mine," Paul replied and placed his left hand over his sword handle.

"Yes…and I note you carry that sword always," Attar remarked, looking at the sword.

"I carry mine also always," Tenno said.

"I know. These points are not missed," Attar replied and rubbed his chin as he thought for a moment. "You, Tenno, I know are aware that a true master can put away his weapons, but sadly, and I hate to agree with this fact…sadly you must continue to carry them in the face of so much hatred and violence that still resides in the world," he explained and sighed before continuing. "Knowledge is but only part of a whole body of ancient wisdom as was known to Noah and Abraham, to Zoroaster, to the Chaldean, Egyptian and Greek masters, and to Muslim mystics."

"Like you?" Paul asked.

"Paul, I still have much to learn, but I have been blessed so far for I have been fortunate enough to learn that the teachings contained within all the holy books have two aspects to them…one exoteric and the other esoteric. That may seem contradictory but in reality complementary. I am sure Theodoric has explained this before," Attar remarked as Paul nodded yes. "Even when this distinction is not openly acknowledged, or even denied, there none the less exists a state of an outer and inner, like a bone and the inner marrow, the visible and invisible, the wide and narrow road and the mind and flesh. All has an equal and opposite. Black and white, light and dark…but you know this already," he said, raising his eyebrows.

"Your God and your Devil," Tenno stated and shook his head disapprovingly.

"Yes, I suppose so. But why do you say that with almost contempt in your voice?" Attar asked.

"Oh that is just the way he is normally," Theodoric joked.

"Why," Tenno said and looked at Theodoric hard before looking back at Attar, "I just find so much about both of your religions that contradicts itself and confuses. Tell me, why if this Jesus was indeed married and had children…why does this fact upset so many Christians? For so many dismiss it because there is apparently no obvious 'evidence'. The irony there is self evident, no?" Tenno asked.

Theodoric sat back in his chair and roared with laughter. Tenno frowned at him and raised a single eyebrow, which made Theodoric laugh even more. Paul chuckled seeing him laugh so much. Attar smiled and tried to remain composed but even he was impressed with the irony of Tenno's statement. Ishmael forced a smile not quite sure why Theodoric was laughing so much.

"Oh my Lord…I know people who would claim you were a devil worshipping demon in disguise," Theodoric laughed, holding his stomach.

"Devil…," Tenno said and looked harder at Theodoric. "So far on my travels in Christian lands I have as yet to be insulted by any so called devil worshippers…for not believing in their Devil…but I have been insulted more than once by Christians for questioning their God!"

Theodoric laughed even more at Tenno's comments. Paul laughed but stopped when Tenno looked at him puzzled. Alisha looked around the doorway of the dining hall holding some silk strips in her hand. Paul raised his hand all was okay as Theodoric continued to laugh. She smiled then disappeared from view again as Paul struggled not to laugh at Theodoric's comments. It was good to see him laugh so heartily he thought. He was always good company.

"Let me explain then that if we look closely at the life of Isa…your Jesus, in the New Testament and the so called apocryphal Gospels, where it is easy to read that he himself made a clear distinction between the inner, hidden or esoteric teachings and outer, external or exoteric ones. Jesus publicly gave exoteric teachings to the masses, while privately instructing his trusted disciples in the inner, esoteric meanings. After the manner of the apostles, the early Christians preached openly to the public the Gospel message, while preserving the esoteric doctrines for those who became initiated disciples. The distinction between outer doctrines and their higher inner meaning was also known to Moses, whom you know was an initiate of Egyptian wisdom, and the Israelite prophets. The exoteric form of the Mosaic revelation contained laws and commandments purely suited to the people and conditions of that period, Taurus no less as it traversed into Aries, the Ram, whilst the esoteric doctrines, explaining the meanings behind the external forms and rituals, were preserved by the real priests and prophets. By the time of Jesus, the esoteric spiritual side of the Hebrew religion had been corrupted and almost lost. People were enslaved to the 'letter of the law' and consequently kept in the bondage of ignorance by false teachers, not realising that 'the letter killeth, but the spirit giveth life'. Thus the Essenes, being the true Israelite priests and the mystic precursors of the early Christians, concerned themselves with rediscovering the inner meaning of the Mosaic Law. That is why within the first four centuries after Christ, his teachings underwent the same corruption and loss as those proclaimed by Moses. Christianity emerged as a powerful institution dominated by a clerical hierarchy largely ignorant of the original esoteric truths. The Gospels, like the books of the Old Testament, underwent editing and revision to comply with the exoteric Christian creed. The many Christian Gnostic texts, which spoke of esoteric doctrines, were denounced and confined to the flames," Attar explained as Theodoric composed himself.

"Yes...yes I agree absolutely with you, Attar...," he said and sat himself up properly and wiped his eyes, Tenno still looking at him, frowning deeply.

"At that time in the West the Church of Rome emerged triumphant, whilst in the East arose a new prophet and Messenger of God. In the ancient land of Arabia, in fulfilment of age old prophecies, Muhammad himself began to proclaim complete surrender to the One God of all mankind. His message became known as Islam, the last of the great revealed religions. And after the manner of Moses and Jesus, the prophet Muhammad distinguished between the exoteric and esoteric dimensions of religion too. Being the last of all the celestial faiths, Islam contained the essential divine truths of all the earlier revelations. This is something, Paul, your father understood as Theodoric I am sure will also confirm," Attar said and looked at Theodoric to confirm.

"Aye, that he does know and understands," Theodoric replied, having stopped laughing now but still smiling broadly.

"That explains his extensive collection of Islamic books and manuscripts," Paul remarked.

"I am not sure how much you know or understand about Islam but I can tell you that as a youth, Muhammad spent time in the desert conducting caravans from Mecca to Syria. Here, according to some, he first encountered seekers looking for the 'original religion of Abraham'. He would later travel each year to Mount Hira near Mecca to meditate and pray. It was during one of these visits that he entered a level of higher consciousness when the Archangel Gabriel revealed to him the first chapter of the Holy Qur'an, the sacred book of Islam and the direct Word of Allah. Muhammad confided his experience only to a small group of close associates but soon, an inner circle or secret school of disciples began to form around him, and in time they publicly proclaimed the exoteric message of surrender to Allah. But understand that Muhammad, just like Isa…Jesus…never claimed or intended to found a new religion. In fact, he always said he was just continuing the primordial tradition that was working long before him. Like Moses and Jesus, Muhammad came in a long line of prophets who from time to time delivered to their people, under divine inspiration, the same revelation of God's nature and of man's relationship to Him, as had been given to Adam. Muhammad came to reinstate this eternal pristine message that had been obscured by ignorance, idolatry, and used to enslave rather than liberate humanity. From this perspective the Holy Qur'an teaches the primordial unity of all religions and the common origin of each. If you remember nothing else of this meeting, please remember that fact alone for it affirms that there is not a nation or people to whom a prophet has not been sent. The central message of Islam is the declaration of faith, shahada, as in 'There is no god but God and Muhammad is the Messenger of God'. From the esoteric perspective this is also understood as 'there is no reality except Reality'. The exoteric practice is summed up in the 'Five Pillars of Islam'. These are Faith, Prayer, Fasting, Almsgiving and Pilgrimage."

"It sounds like you are trying to convert us to Islam," Tenno stated bluntly in his usual manner.

"No, that I cannot do…but would it be so bad if I was?" Attar replied and smiled.

"It makes no difference to me," Tenno answered.

"I shall continue then…The Holy Qur'an has both an exoteric, as in the zahir, the outer or apparent meaning and an esoteric, as in batin, the inner or secret meaning. Within Islamic esotericism, as in the original Mosaic and Christian revelations, knowledge is made accessible depending on the integrity and ability of its recipients, with the consequence of requiring the withholding of information from the uninitiated. This is why there has always been a gradual unveiling or communication of spiritual truths to mankind. What Muslim esotericists call the 'wisdom of gradualness' of 'hikmat at-tadrij'. For spiritual knowledge, states a highly regarded Islamic esoteric text, is like food and light."

"How do you mean?" Ishmael asked.

"Just as a small child needs to be fed gradually, stage by stage, until it reaches adolescence, so that it may not eat something harmful to its constitution, and just as light is appropriate only to persons with open, healthy and strong eyes, so that a person whose eyes have been shut, or had just emerged from darkness, will be severely dazzled by daylight, in the same way, those who get hold of this higher esoteric knowledge should communicate it only to those who are in need of it and can accept and understand it. Now know that many Christian mystics have travelled to Arabia seeking a genuine spiritual Master Teacher. In fact, many mystics surrounded Muhammad during his life. These Companions, as they are known, he privately instructed in the doctrines of Islamic esotericism. Two of these Companions, the Prophet Muhammad's close friend Abu Bakr and his son-in-law Ali, later inspired their own Orders. Although Muhammad, as the last of the prophets, was the repository of a complete treasure of precepts, Muslim tradition asserts he publicly declared only some of them, leaving the rest undeclared. This was due to their inapplicability at the time, but also because of the expediency of disseminating them in that particular period of our history. It is said even Prophet Muhammad himself mentioned certain secret moments of revelation, saying, 'If the Muslims knew of them, they would stone me.' He therefore entrusted the undeclared precepts to the Companions and through them to the worthy of succeeding generations so that they would progressively reveal them at appropriate junctures according to their wisdom, whether by inferring the particular from the absolute, or the concrete from the abstract," Attar explained.

Ishmael nodded he understood but he was still not sure of Attar's explanation.

"Who knows…perhaps there will come a day when we all do join as one faith…though I prefer to say join as one understanding of the truth," Theodoric remarked.

"Not in our lifetimes," Attar commented before continuing. "After the death of the Prophet Muhammad in AD 632, the Companions, particularly Abu Bakr, Ali and Salman al-Farisi, continued to preserve the esoteric tradition within the exoteric faith of Islam. Abu Bakr became the first Caliph, leader of the Muslim community. However, in time, just as Muhammad had warned before his death, the thirst for power and political intrigue soon caused strife and division among Muslims. The mighty Islamic empire became divided as positions of authority were usurped by individuals bereft of spiritual understanding. Those who seized power and wealth did so in the name of the prophet and the exoteric creed of Islam. The outer creed represented by the law, which is Sharia, the accumulated customs of the Prophet, which is the hadith, and a literal reading of the Qur'an, emerged as 'orthodox' Islam. Again, exotericism appeared to vanquish esotericism. Many Muslim initiates, custodians of esoteric wisdom, went into hiding or exile. Yet a number of Muslim spiritual teachers, considered by the people to be saints, did not conceal the fact they had been initiated by members of a school or brotherhood, the tariqah founded by one of the Companions."

"I think I am beginning to understand what both my father and Firgany were trying to explain and inform me all about now," Paul mused as he looked down in thought.

"Men ahead of their time," Theodoric said quietly.

"That they were…," Attar remarked.

"But now you…you are an initiate, yes…a Sufi?" Paul asked as he looked up at Attar.

"That you could also say is true. But my cause…our cause is the truth of truth. It is the exoteric, the esoteric of the exoteric and the exoteric of the esoteric. It is the secret of the secret; it is the secret of that which remains wrapped in secret," Attar remarked and winked.

"Well that will certainly only serve to confuse," Theodoric remarked and grinned as Tenno and Ishmael both looked puzzled before Attar continued.

"At the end of the eighth century and the beginning of the ninth century, many Muslims who followed the spiritual path openly declared their connection with Islamic esotericism. They divulged truths based on spiritual experience that, because of their outward appearance, brought on them the condemnation of orthodox Islamic jurists and theologians."

"Nothing new there then and is the same as Christians, yes?" Tenno commented.

Attar nodded his head yes then continued again.

"Some were imprisoned, flogged, and even killed. Historically, the practitioners of esotericism were associated with the descendants of the family of Prophet Muhammad himself. Ali, who was Muhammad's son-in-law, was universally regarded as the fountainhead of esoteric knowledge. The relationship between the Prophet Muhammad and Ali was symbolic of the exoteric form and the esoteric core of divine religion. This is similar to the Christian Gnostic idea of the relationship between Jesus, representing the exoteric, and the beloved disciple John to whom the esoteric doctrine was divulged."

"You know of the John connection?" Paul asked, surprised.

"Of course. I would not be a very good Sufi if I did not know now would I?" Attar replied smiling. "Sadly, just like Christianity, from Islamic esoteric tradition emerged distinct Muslim groups such as the Fatimids, Ismailis and the Nusairi, the Alawis. Certain mystical brotherhoods and Orders formed within Muslim communities and became known as Sufis, the mystics or esotericists. It is commonly thought the word Sufi comes from the Arabic word suf, meaning 'wool' from the rough woollen clothing worn by early ascetics to demonstrate their detachment from the world," he explained and pulled out his own green woollen top slightly. "All Sufi, like all genuine mystics, aim for a glimpse of the eternal whilst trapped by this physical world. To that end, the Sufis have laid out the 'path', the 'tariqah', that will lead to gnosis, marifah or mystic knowledge of the Lord. The 'path' of ascension to divine union with God passes through stages known commonly as 'stations' or 'states'…the last stage being that of fana, or passing away in God, which is the ultimate desire of a successful mystic. The Sufi at this point ceases to be aware of his physical identity even though he continues to exist as an individual. But I caution all who would follow this path that although the majority of Sufi Orders meticulously observe the Islamic law, Sharia, they believe it to be only the outer clothing or external shell protecting the core, the esoteric truth. The Holy Qur'an calls those who know the essence of things 'the possessors of the kernels'. The Sufis liken esoteric wisdom to a 'kernel' hidden within a shell. Exoteric Islam, experienced as a traditional way of life, creates the environment, the culture, the community, and necessary psychological orientation, from which certain individuals are called to initiation into esotericism. The authentic Gnostic and mystic is always a minority when compared with the great mass of humanity who are fully satisfied with exoteric religion."

"Paul, in case you think Attar is indeed trying to convert you, let me tell you that the Sufi schools and brotherhoods are renowned for propagating Islam throughout the world. Their piety, deep spirituality and tolerance enabled Sufis to attract a large following. The brotherhoods have rendered an incalculable, monumental service to Islam in three different ways. They have prevented Islam from becoming a cold and formal doctrine by keeping it alive as an intimate, compassionate faith...they were mainly responsible for spreading the faith in east Asia and sub-Saharan Africa and they were among the foremost leaders in Islam's military and political battles against the encroaching power of the Christian West. By the tenth century, descendants of the Prophet Muhammad through his daughter Fatimah, and her husband Ali, established the Fatimid Empire over a large part of North Africa. Many Muslims see this as a fulfilment of a prediction attributed to the Prophet that a time would come in which 'the Sun, of Islam, would rise in the West'. Prior to accepting Islam, North Africa had been home to a number of Gnostic communities. Some have claimed that the Fatimids are the philosophical descendants of Bardesane, the renowned Gnostic Christian Master Teacher. This fact has not escaped Saladin himself has it, Attar?" Theodoric asked.

"Not much escapes Saladin, my friend," Attar replied as Tenno sat up intrigued.

"Please, tell us more," Tenno asked.

"If you wish," Attar replied. "The Fatimids are responsible for ushering in a new 'golden age' for Islam. They have established this city of Cairo calling it 'The Victorious City of the Exalter of the Divine Religion' as the new capital of a new and growing empire. Public devotions of the Fatimids differ very little from orthodox Muslims', but the esoteric teachings are restricted to those of the community best able to receive them. A proper understanding of their books requires a special education and years of training. Here in Cairo the Fatimids have now established the Grand House of Wisdom, the Darul Hikmet, for the training of missionaries, dais, skilled in the propagation of Islamic esoteric philosophy. Students come from all over the Orient to the House of Wisdom for instruction and initiation. Twice a week, every Monday and Wednesday, the Grand Prior convenes meetings, which are frequented by adepts dressed in white. These gatherings are named 'philosophical conferences' or Majalis-al-Hikmet. The Fatimid Caliph is also the Grand Master of the House of Wisdom. One of the earlier students who attended was Hasan Sabbah who upon his return to his native Persia, formed the so called Ashashin, with his headquarters at the mountain monastery-fortress of Alamut."

"So Taqi is indeed embraced within a great order," Paul said to himself but clearly heard by all in the room. "Sorry, I did not mean to interrupt... please continue."

"From here, Fatimid rulers despatch missionaries, dais, throughout the known world. Under cover they have even infiltrated Christian Europe. Accomplished in the esoteric doctrine, the dais can use any outer form, be it artistic, scientific, religious or secular, to impart universal and perennial truths. Even poetry, for which we Sufis are renowned, can be used to transfer spiritual insights from one culture or religion to another. Our use of allegory and ciphers amounts to a secret language, the universal language of initiates...and mainly based upon mathematics," Attar smiled as he explained. "It is accepted that Sufis have even dealt with some of the greatest Celts. That is why there is a well known ninth century Celtic cross bearing the Islamic Arabic inscription 'Bismillah ir-Rahman ir-Rahim' meaning 'In the name of Allah, the Compassionate, the Merciful' as Theodoric I am sure will confirm."

"Aye that I can as I have stood beside it myself," Theodoric replied.

"I would love to visit this House of Wisdom," Paul said as he looked up, hearing Alisha and Sister Lucy laugh out loud in the dining room.

"Then perhaps we can arrange that," Attar said quietly as he looked at Paul intently as if searching out his every thought. "Saladin himself tries to live by the principles he has himself been taught of tolerance, prosperity, love of knowledge and peace over war...and he has helped greatly in maintaining the renowned al-Azhar University, today the most venerable orthodox institution in the Muslim world. It is where the great Mansur al-Hallaj spent some time. He was a Persian mystic, revolutionary writer and teacher of Sufism, who wrote exclusively in Arabic. He is of course most famous for his poetry, accusation of heresy and for his execution at the orders of the Abbasid Caliph Al-Muqtadir after a long, drawn-out investigation."

"I am sure I heard Firgany speak of this man…in regard to the Templars and Ashashin but I cannot recall exactly what…but why was he executed if he was a man of peace?" Paul commented.

"That does not surprise me, Firgany speaking of him," Attar said and paused for a moment. "He was executed for heresy and claiming to be God, though that was not what he claimed at all. You see, he said 'I saw my Lord with the eye of the heart' and 'I asked, "who are you?" He replied, "You"'. That statement drew much attention and condemnation. He was also a prominent figure in Alevism and Bektashism, famous for his saying of 'I am the Truth', 'Anal Haq', which is confused by orthodox Muslims for a claim to divinity. Sufi Muslims link this quote to the Qur'an verse 50:16 where it says 'And We have already created man and know what his soul whispers to him, and we are closer to him than his jugular vein'. I am sure these sayings sound familiar to you…almost identical to some Christian sayings, yes?" Attar asked.

Tenno shrugged his shoulders as Paul shook his head yes.

"Similar yes," Paul replied quietly.

1 - 5

"Al-Hallaj was born around 858 in your calendar in the Fars province of Persia to a cotton-carder. Hallaj actually means cotton-carder in Arabic. His grandfather was a Zoroastrian and his father lived a simple life, and this form of lifestyle greatly interested the young Al-Hallaj. As a youngster he memorised the Qur'an and would often retreat from worldly pursuits to join other mystics in study. Al-Hallaj was originally a Hanbali Sufi Muslim and later turned to be a Qarmatian Batiniyya. He later married and made a pilgrimage to Makkah, or Mecca as you call it, where he stayed for one year, facing the mosque, in fasting and total silence. After his stay at the city, he travelled extensively and wrote and taught along the way. He travelled as far as India and Central Asia gaining many followers, many of whom accompanied him on his second and third trips to Makkah. After this period of travel, he settled down in the Abbasid capital of Baghdad. During his early lifetime he was a disciple of Junayd Baghdadi and Amr al-Makki, but was later rejected by them both. Sahl al-Tustari was also one of Al-Hallaj's early teachers. But as you can probably guess, amongst other Sufis, Al-Hallaj was an anomaly. Many Sufi masters felt that it was inappropriate to share mysticism with the masses, yet Al-Hallaj openly did so in his writings and through his teachings and consequently he made enemies. This was exacerbated by occasions when he would fall into trances which he attributed to being in the presence of God. During one of these trances, he would utter الحق أنا Anā l-Ḥaqq, 'I am The Truth', which was taken to mean that he was claiming to be God, since al-Ḥaqq, 'the Truth', is one of the Ninety Nine Names of Allah. In another controversial statement, al-Hallaj claimed 'There is nothing wrapped in my turban but God' and similarly he would point to his cloak and say, الله إلا جبتي في ما Mā fī jubbatī illā l-Lāh 'There is nothing in my cloak but God'. This type of mystical utterance is known as shath and it was statements like these that led to a long trial, and his subsequent imprisonment for eleven years in a Baghdad prison. He was publicly executed on March 26th, AD 922."

"Why do you tell us of this man?" Tenno asked bluntly.

"Why…because it was during the spectacular rise of the Fatimids here, together with the influence of their underground networks, which provoked the largely orthodox Abbasid rulers in Mesopotamia to launch a campaign against 'heresy' as they saw it here. With the backing of the strictly orthodox scholars and the legalists of the more exoteric religion, Mansur al-Hallaj was condemned to death. He had penetrated the outer shell that is exoteric Islam, to reveal the inner core. He realised illumination, fana, or what the Sufis know as 'death to one's self' and 'passing away in the Divine Beloved', exclaiming 'I am He whom I love, and He whom I love is. We are two spirits dwelling in one body. When thou seest me thou seest Him, And when thou seest Him, thou seest us both.' Viewed in mainstream Islamic law, such a declaration is indeed shocking and forbidden. However, understood esoterically it is nothing less than the sentiment of an illumined mystic. Hallaj further offended the legalists with such statements as 'To claim to know Him is ignorance, to persist in serving Him is disrespectful, to forbid yourself to struggle with him is folly, to allow yourself to be misled by his peace is stupid, to discourse on his attributes is to lose the way.' So as you can see, he was bound to upset the larger community of the exoteric faithful...and I would caution you that Christians are just as guilty within their exoteric behaviour and condemnations."

"So what happened to Hallaj...I mean how was he executed?" Paul asked, intrigued.

"As said, he was publicly executed in Baghdad in AD 922 of your calendar which attracted large and sympathetic crowds but he was nevertheless scourged, gibbeted and finally decapitated. As he was near to death, he prayed for mercy...mercy for his executioners. Years after his murder he was openly hailed by Sufis, dissident Muslims, and even some orthodox writers, as a martyr of exoteric incomprehension. But his legacy is great and far reaching. For many years Hallaj had travelled widely and I can tell you that the rumours that he presided over a secret network of missionaries and wandering Sufis was true. Three decades after Mansour al-Hallaj stood upon the gallows in Baghdad, a secret society emerged in the Iraqi city of Basra. Like the Fatimids, the group, known as the Brethren of Purity, or Ikwan as-Safa, dedicated themselves to the pursuit of science as well as political action. They published a veritable encyclopaedia of existing knowledge. Their works covered such subjects as philosophy, theology, astrology, metaphysics, cosmology and the natural sciences, including botany and zoology. The brotherhood recognised truth wherever found, accepting the wisdom in other religions. A seeker of truth must 'shun no science, scorn no book, nor cling fanatically to a single creed'. They attempted to compile a common doctrine of Islamic esotericism beginning with self-knowledge and the emancipation of the soul from materialism leading to a return to God. The first letter of the brotherhood restated the Sufi axiom of 'He who knows himself, knows his Lord'. Condemned as 'heretical' and burnt by the authorities, their writings enjoyed a wide influence, even reaching Europe." [84]

"I know...for I have seen their writings...in my father's study and in Niccolas's crypt library...where he taught me much also about Sufi mysticism, but he called the Brethren of Purity the Brethren of Sincerity," Paul remarked and shook his head slightly. His mind flashed back to a small stone carving set upon the far wall of his father's study with the very words 'He who knows himself, knows his Lord'. Was there no end to the surprises he kept learning about his father? he pondered momentarily.

"You okay, Paul?" Theodoric asked after a few minutes sat in silence.

"Yes...just my mind wondering back to past events, that is all. Please Attar...will you continue?" Paul replied and looked across at Attar.

"My pleasure...and yes, the Brethren of Purity is but another name for the Brethren of Sincerity," Attar said and smiled before continuing. "Knowledge is power, yes...you have heard this statement before?" Paul nodded yes. "Good. Traditional esotericism is at one and the same time doctrine and practice. It implies for the whole of the being, body, soul and spirit a fundamentally different way of existence. Running through all cultures are the threads of an 'underground' primordial tradition. In our current 'Dark Age' of banality and materialism this great spiritual tradition is well concealed, and for good reason lest it is destroyed forever. That which in Europe tries to pass itself off as 'secret', 'occult' or 'esoteric' knowledge is at best vain foolishness, at worst a dangerous counterfeit, a deadly parody of the universal supreme Truth. Nevertheless all things have their reason for being. But as experience has taught me, and as Reynald was all too prone to in his impatience, a newcomer to the vast quantity of occult literature, browsing randomly, will be met with puzzlement and sure enough, impatience and frustration will take over. He or she will only see jumbled together the smallest of drops of all cultures, and occasional fragments of philosophy...perhaps profound but almost certainly subversive to right living in the society in which one finds oneself, and consequently they reject it as nonsense for the feeble and weak minded only. They become its greatest critics. For every fragment of truth there is always a huge cloud of confusion, ignorant speculation and falsity. In the present age of strife, this confusion, ignorance and falsehood is important because it permits the genuine Ancient Secret Tradition to remain hidden and protected. This is something your father knows only too well. We do not need ever more 'new truths' but a mutual open and free system that allows a rediscovery of that primordial revelation forgotten or parodied by the ignorant. For, as we Sufis say, 'everything that comes from the Eternal One yearns to return to Him.' And Paul, here in what was once the former ancient sacred place known as Heliopolis...here you can learn just exactly what that means," Attar said quietly and looked across toward the dining area to see if Alisha was visible. "And if you allow me...and Theodoric of course, we can start that learning whenever you are ready."

Tenno shifted in his chair and looked at Attar with a frown of suspicion.

"You can come along too," Theodoric said seeing the expression upon Tenno's face.

"Come along to where?" Alisha asked as she entered the room closely followed by Nyla carrying several long sheets of silk and linen.

"Yes...where?" Sister Lucy then asked folding her arms as she stood behind Alisha and stared hard at Theodoric.

Paul stood up.

"To the university here...and...and that is it," he blurted out.

"Look, Paul...look at these wonderful silks...can we purchase them... please," Alisha asked excitedly as she approached Paul, holding out a bright blue silk for him to feel.

Paul felt the silk and looked at Alisha as she smiled at him, her eyes ablaze with an excitement he had not seen in a long while. He caught sight of Theodoric standing up and winking at him as he mouthed he would leave, pulling Attar up physically as he moved beside him. All looked to the open doors into the small courtyard as Percival appeared looking awkward, his hands held together as he stepped inside.

"Sorry...I was just wondering if...if Nyla was free now...to talk to, that is all," he asked and raised his hands quickly.

All turned and looked at Nyla. She smiled and blushed.

"Time for bed I think," Theodoric said aloud, Sister Lucy immediately hitting his arm as he walked near to her pulling Attar with him. "Bed for some of us...I mean us...not you two, I mean," he said pointing to Percival then Nyla in turn.

"Move!" Sister Lucy ordered and ushered him and Attar into the dining hall.

"I shall retire also," Tenno said as he stood up slowly, nodded at Percival and walked toward the open doors. "We shall continue this discussion in the morrow...yes?" he asked, looking at Paul.

"Yes, yes we shall," Paul answered.

Tenno left the room as Percival and Nyla looked at each other, smiling. Alisha finally noticed how they were staring at each other. She pulled Paul's arm to follow her and led him toward the dining hall.

"Please, we shall be away to our chambers. Feel free to stay and acquaint yourselves more...if that is what you wish?" she asked Nyla.

Nyla shook her head partly embarrassed but also pleased as Percival stood silently with a large grin upon his face just as Ishmael stood beside her.

"I shall wait for you in the main hallway...to escort you home safely when you have finished with Percival," Ishmael said quietly to Nyla and bowed his head.

Alisha and Paul looked at Nyla and Percival as they moved towards each other. Alisha looked up at Paul and smiled having seen the clear affection Nyla and Percival had for each other. She flicked one of the silks over Paul's shoulder and silently beckoned him to follow her as she clasped his hand.

Chapter 51
Not All you Fight are your Enemy

Port of La Rochelle, France, Melissae Inn, spring 1191

"It beggars belief that we fight at all," Gabirol remarked and rubbed his right hand through his thick dark hair, looking puzzled.

"Indeed. 'Tis why Paul and many other knights questioned much...not their faith in God, but certainly their faith in their leaders," the old man replied.

"I am interested in what kind of ships Paul went on to help design then?" the Genoese sailor asked and sat back in his chair.

"Well, he and Alisha as well as the rest of the group all seemed to settle into a regular and settled routine. Sister Lucy had been overjoyed at being present for Arri's first birthday and she was already planning for his second. Tenno insisted on escorting Paul to and from his work daily but eventually conceded to taking it in turns with Ishmael, whilst Theodoric helped Alisha and Nyla start up and grow their new textile business," the old man explained and smiled.

"And what of Thomas, his men and Percival?" the wealthy tailor asked.

"Percival spent most of his days training and learning from Thomas and his men. They all in turn helped train with Husam's naval fleet and doing regular patrols to the west for all pilgrims, both Muslim and Christian, against some of the many undesirable elements and pirates along the Nile and Red Sea routes."

"So Percival did not get lucky with that Nyla then?" Simon asked bluntly.

"Lucky," the old man answered and paused. "I can tell you he and Nyla grew very close, very quickly. Percival would often escort her and sure enough, they both fell deeply in love."

"Ah that is nice to hear," Sarah said and sighed with a large smile as she rested her chin upon her hands.

"Hey, don't forget that Percival hides a secret...," Peter interrupted loudly and raised his eyebrows.

"Oh yes...will you reveal what secret?" Sarah asked the old man.

"By the end of this tale you will all know...but at that time, well, it was a time of

relative ease...peaceful even and when rumour grew that Saladin was seeking a truce again, it cheered all. And Arri," the old man said and shook his head smiling as if he was thinking back upon happy memories. "He grew so fast it was frightening. Tenno had him sat upon Adrastos, causing Paul heart failure on several occasions, as his little body sat up high...he did fall once, but Tenno caught him instantly."

"What happened with that Sufi mystic then...Attar?" Peter asked.

"Oh he lived in Fustat mainly and frequently met Paul after work as Husam's main residency and dry docks were as you know situated there.

"And the pyramids...did Paul go exploring?" the farrier asked.

"Every day Paul could see the pyramids. He walked around them with Alisha escorted by Theodoric and Tenno, and Attar took Paul around the other pyramids several times alone...not that Alisha knew at the time of course," the old man explained.

"Yes, but what about any ships he helped design...or was he just a draughtsman like all the others?" the Genoese sailor asked again, interrupting.

"True to his word, Husam gave Paul total freedom to experiment and design as he felt inspired. Paul learnt very fast and had a natural instinct in what worked and what did not...and the calculations necessary came easy to him. And despite Reynald's constant raids and truce breaking, at least peace remained in the city. Paul tried daily to recall every detail of Kratos's ship and after several months he had a working plan drawn up, which drew a lot of sceptical doubts from Husam's other ship architects and designers, but Husam saw merit in his design and commissioned one to be built, if only to test Paul's theory."

"Was that wise...copying Kratos's vessel which was obviously far more advanced than anything we have. It could have tipped the balance of naval power in favour of Muslim forces?" the Hospitaller asked.

"Yes, it could have...but like all those who try to build a flying vessel based upon the study of birds, they nevertheless do not succeed do they? Besides, as I said, Saladin managed to secure a truce through Raymond and Balian in the latter part of 1180...one that Saladin genuinely hoped would hold."

"I suppose...but it was still a risk, yes?" the Hospitaller replied.

"You would be surprised to learn how much technology and engineering both sides shared with each other...," the old man replied and shook his head. "You know, I can tell you that there are those in Outremer who wished to maintain the status quo, so that neither side would get the advantage and that hopefully one day they would actually join as one...the greatest strength in fighting your enemy, is to exploit his weakness we were taught, yet as I say, by sharing much of each other's

knowledge, it balanced the power both sides had. It was done that way to avoid total and absolute extinction of the other's belief..."

"That is mad. If we had the opportunity to totally wipe Islam off the face of the earth, we should have done so...surely?" the farrier remarked, perplexed.

"And if it had gone the other way?" the Templar commented and looked at the old man then the farrier.

"Precisely! Besides, there are truths in both faiths," the old man said softly. "Paul made sure he kept himself up to date on all the political machinations and developments that were ongoing...and he kept a special ear out for any mention or hint of Turansha...which was to come soon enough."

"Oh no...," Ayleth said quietly, concern written across her face.

"Eventually a truce was brokered by Saladin in late 1180 after an eventful few months and the death of the Byzantine emperor Manuel the First Comnenus on the twenty-fourth of September and Jerusalem's Patriarch Amalric who had died on the sixth of October. Saladin had already managed to get Sultan Kilij Arslan II to side with him and made a peace treaty with the new Byzantine Emperor Alexius the Second Comnenus who was not so pro-Franc as his father before him. Kilij had taken full advantage of the instability in the Byzantine Empire after Manuel's death to secure most of the southern coast of Anatolia, and had sent his vizier Ikhtiyar al-Din to conclude an alliance with Saladin directly. On September 18th King Louis the Seventh of France had also died, as many of you here will already know, and rumours of great changes were everywhere. There were also many rumours circulating after the death of the Patriarch Amalric, that due to disputes between rival factions within the kingdom, it had affected the election of a new Patriarch with the two most obvious choices for his successor being William of Tyre and Heraclius of Caesarea. They were fairly evenly matched in background and education, but politically they were allied with opposite parties, as Heraclius was one of Agnes of Courtenay's supporters. The canons of the Holy Sepulchre asked the king for advice, and Heraclius had been chosen through Agnes's influence. Rumours were already rife in Cairo that Agnes and Heraclius were lovers, but there was no real evidence to substantiate such a claim. When Paul heard these rumours, he could still see Amalric in his mind when he had met him in Jerusalem. He laughed to himself as he recalled that long meeting along with Brother Jakelin and Count Henry. He recalled Theodoric explaining to Percival that statistically major changes occur during leap years...1180 just happened to be one and it had started on a Tuesday. Not a good omen according to one of Theodoric's many charts," the old man explained.

Cairo, Egypt, October 1180

Paul lay awake, his mind alight with ideas. Arri had been unsettled all day and Alisha was exhausted so Paul had placed Arri's crib next to his side of the bed. He was clearly teething. Paul reached out his hand to gently stroke Arri's little shoulders when his little fingers wrapped around Paul's finger tightly. Paul rolled onto his side and just looked at him as he slept still holding his finger. The following day was going to be a busy one as Ernoul, Balian's personal squire, was coming to stay accompanying Conrad again, as well as be given a tour of Husam's ship building docks. Paul watched Arri closely as moonlight shone through the netted windows letting in a cool breeze. He felt blessed that he was doing a job he loved, had the woman he loved, had a beautiful son and a standard of living most people would be envious of. 'Thank you, Father…and you Firgany wherever you are' he thought and looked upwards. Turansha's last words to him seemed to gently wash away all other thoughts as he heard him, as if to remind him about Percival. He placed his left hand upon Alisha's hip as she slept. These times were still without doubt the best, he thought and closed his eyes.

Paul woke with a jolt and sat up fast sweating heavily. He rubbed his eyes and as he went to open them, he placed his hands back down, but felt sand and grit, not his bed sheets. He blinked and tried to focus his eyes. Suddenly a blinding light glared intensely forcing him to instantly shield his eyes.

"Fear not, Paul…you are simply travelling," a calm and soft male voice spoke.

Slowly Paul lowered his hands from his eyes, the light no longer hurting. He quickly realised that he was sitting inside a small stone room, the walls made of a pinkish coloured marble, the floor covered in patches of sand and grit. Five tall figures dressed in white flowing robes stood before him but they appeared to float above the floor by a couple of feet. All of their robes seemed to be weightless and they looked more like people floating in water, he thought, as his mind struggled to comprehend if this was real or yet another lucid dream. The five beings had elongated heads, something he had never seen before, but their faces appeared normal, but with pure white skin and blue eyes. Light danced from behind them giving the impression they had wings but he knew it was light. Suddenly a young girl of teenage years stepped into view from behind them. She looked down at Paul and studied him intently. She smiled then looked up at the figure stood in the middle of the five and nodded enthusiastically. He nodded back as if in agreement with her. She smiled again and approached Paul and knelt down directly in front of him, her eyes looking into his. Her smile was captivating. She placed her hand upon his left shoulder, then gently kissed the side of his cheek before standing up and quickly walking back to the other five. A little confused, Paul tried to stand up but found he could not move his legs. Puzzled he looked at the five again just as the girl waved and walked away out of sight.

"Do not be alarmed, Paul. You are quite safe here," the man in the middle said.

"And where exactly is here?" Paul asked and looked around the small room.

"Just a chamber within a device system...one you deliberately keep away from...though it is not what you agreed...is it?" the man asked with a smile.

"Pyramids!" Paul responded and frowned even more puzzled.

"See...you remember. You just need to remember the rest."

"The rest of what?"

"Why you are here," a female voice said softly, though Paul did not see from whom it came.

"Armed Orders are not the way to carry the secrets forwards. The time has come when you must start what you agreed to do...find a way to communicate to the future," another voice said.

"I truly do not understand what you are saying. Unlike Alisha, Kratos has not removed even a part of the veil that hides my past...," Paul explained, perplexed.

"Paul," the man in the centre said as he moved closer toward him. "There is no veil upon you...you simply need to open the doors of your mind and travel the plains of what you call the heavens," he said and lowered himself until he knelt opposite Paul, looking at him eye to eye. His eyes were almost identical to those of Kratos, but seemed to almost shine. "Look around you. You helped design these devices...look and remember."

Paul rubbed his head confused. 'Devices...how are pyramids devices?' he thought.

"They are multipurpose and multifunctional. But their message will be lost unless you find a way to guarantee its continuation…for that is something we cannot do from our position," a female voice spoke again.

"Where is your position exactly?" Paul asked, trying to establish which of the other four was speaking as he still wondered who the young woman was.

"Paul…our position is beyond the realms of humankind, but from which we were once a part of…but you, in your present mortal form can influence a new way. Lay the foundations and plant the seeds of a new understanding. Then it will be down to humankind to decide whether or not to listen and take heed and act accordingly. That is their free will and choice," the man in the centre explained quietly.

6 - 27

A female from the group stepped forwards and offered her right hand for Paul to take. Quizzically Paul reached up and grasped her hand. Instantly he felt a warm tingling sensation surge down his arm and envelope his entire body. She smiled at him and he felt almost aroused in her presence, her eyes looking deeply into his. She sensed his emotions and smiled even more. Her skin was flawless and delicate, her eyes seemed to be highlighted with a gold eye liner, her top eyelids appearing to have a gold strip set upon them. Truly angelic he thought as she raised him to his feet. Surprised he looked down at his legs. As Paul steadied himself, the other four encircled him and joined their hands together. They all closed their eyes and looked upward. Paul felt his own eyelids become heavy and he closed them.

"Look…see and remember," the female said in his mind as images, clear as if he was seeing them for real, started to flash across his vision.

Paul could see people with elongated heads stood around a clear glass-like table discussing plans that seemed to be highlighted in lines of light set within it. Their clothing was unrecognisable as anything he had ever seen before. The walls were made of a white and sand coloured marble looking material with beautiful columns that looked out over a clear turquoise sea just a short distance away. Instantly he recognised several ships identical to the vessel Kratos had left upon. He tried to focus upon them before his gaze was drawn back to the room. Three taller people entered the room, two with pure white hair whilst the other had red hair. Their heads were not elongated like the others but were facially identical. Suddenly Paul was looking down at the clear glass like table as moving images of many plans in light flashed across its surface stopping every now and then upon certain images that were perfectly clear and visible, looking real. One of the taller beings looked directly at Paul as if he was in the room himself. Without any words being spoken, Paul understood that he was being told about a great shield that was now set in place around the world to protect it in the future. There would not be a repeat of the last time. 'What happened last time?' Paul asked himself, puzzled. No sooner had he asked that than images flashed before him showing a shower of ice meteorites and other objects crashing through the sky and exploding in brilliant flashes. Immediately he recalled all the previous dreams he had experienced seeing the same images. 'It will not be allowed to happen again,' a voice said. Paul looked at the tall man opposite him and followed his gaze as he again looked back at the glass table. Paul could now see plans of the entire Giza plateau showing a large canal leading from the Nile River and surrounding the Great Pyramid which was gleaming in white nummulitic stone. He could see the Sphinx, but with a lion's head, not the familiar human head he had seen so often. In the distance, where there was now just desert, he saw oak trees and a large forest that stretched off as far as the eye could see with a city of what looked like glass towers shimmering on the distant horizon. Images of happy looking builders somehow pushing large stones on air, it seemed, showed how they positioned the stones as they constructed the Great Pyramid, along with even larger stones being formed by some kind of liquid stone, that once poured, set very quickly as hard as marble. Paul sensed himself being led up an internal ramp way that followed up the outer wall area of the pyramid, like a coiled internal pathway that led to the apex. The pathway was a passage used to ferry stone and material upwards as they built the structure from the inside out and upwards. The passageway was then back filled with lighter stones as they sealed it. Once complete, Paul saw images of the planets of Mercury, Venus and Earth overlaid upon the pyramids matching perfectly. Then the image changed to one of the three belt stars of Orion being overlaid upon them. As the image drew further back, other stars began to overlay on other pyramids further out. On the bottom left of his vision he began to make out the very bright and blue light of what he knew was the star Sirius. But where it was projected on the ground, there was no pyramid at all. Suddenly, he felt a jolt as if he was being thrust downwards and beneath the ground where Sirius was projected. In an instant he found himself standing within a circular chamber, the walls made of polished black marble. Images of the circular formation surrounded by a further twelve circles flashed across his vision so clear he reached out his hand to touch them. He knew this was identical to the New Jerusalem images and as represented at Glastonbury and Stonehenge and other sites. Amazed and smiling he turned to look at the tall man now stood beside him.

"The Pharaoh you know of as Khufu, who is attributed to having built the Great Pyramid, as you can see, is not correct. He simply claimed it as his own and restored much damage that had been done upon it. He even states that simple fact upon the Stella he erected between the Sphinx's paws. That is all...and man will again learn this truth," the tall man explained.

"Many people argue that war has always been the path of man, but that is not so," one of the females said softly. "You can help remind them of that fact."

"And this is not some very lucid dream?" Paul asked.

"Is not life but a dream from another position of understanding and experience? For as I am sure you have heard before, in your realm of existence, you are all spiritual beings having a physical experience," a female voice explained.

"Man will again learn this when he discovers how sound and light activate pyramids...and the secrets you must send across time within your stories, your teachings and in whatever manner you best find, will guide him to those rediscoveries. But it must not be done through means of violence and force," the man in the middle explained.

"There was once a time when others sought the end of the age of man. They set down rulers to subjugate men, they introduced money to enslave all, they created different forms of religion on purpose to divide man, but those times are to pass. It was recognised that approach was all wrong on many levels. That is why the very earth you all live upon is protected and the true message of who man is will be revealed. But the sacred sites that keep that protection in place must be maintained...or it shall fail," another female explained.

"And just how exactly do we do that?" Paul asked, confused.

"Simply by remembering and believing. The power of positive thought... that is why you are all masters of your own destiny and more powerful than you realise," the man said and smiled and raised his eyebrows slightly.

"I do not understand," Paul replied.

"You will, for it is simple enough. Now sleep," a female voice said softly.

Paul had a thousand questions he wanted to ask. He raised his hand to say something but all went black before he had time to say anything.

ꙮ

Paul woke up feeling totally relaxed. As his eyes adjusted to the daylight streaming in through his chamber's window, he immediately saw Arri sat up, still holding his finger and smiling. Arri leaned nearer as if to check Paul. His large eyes were wide and full of happiness, Paul thought, as he moved to prop himself up. Alisha was standing near the window leaning over brushing her long hair down.

"Morning sleepy head. You were talking much in your sleep," she said, her face hidden beneath her hair.

"Sorry…I hope I did not wake you?" Paul replied as he sat up fully and held Arri's little hands as he looked up from his crib still smiling. "I shall go and prepare some food and seek Theo out."

"I think you will find Sister Lucy has sorted that out already with Nyla."

"What…did Nyla stay the night?"

"What do you think?" Alisha laughed and stood up straight throwing her hair back over her shoulders. "Ishmael let them stay in his room alone."

"Oh dear. Her parents will kill him," Paul remarked as he stood up and lifted Arri out of his crib and held him.

"I think you'll find her parents like Percival a lot. I am not so sure what tale she told them to stay here last night so I would ask you to find out discreetly."

Paul kissed Arri on the top of his head as he rested his face against his chest and outstretched his arms as if to hug him. Alisha looked at them, her heart filled with pride and more love than she could ever have imagined. She smiled and felt quite emotional all of a sudden as she watched them. Paul slowly turned around to face her. Arri looked at her, smiling, his eyes wide and looking contented despite not having been fed yet. Paul immediately saw the look in Alisha's eyes and he smiled too. He went to move when she raised her hand for him to stay there. She tilted her head slightly as she looked at them.

"You okay?" Paul asked seeing how she looked emotional, her eyes glistening with tears.

Alisha waved her hand and then placed her finger to her lips.

"Ssssh. I just want to keep that image in my mind," she explained and stepped closer. She cupped her hand on Paul's face then looked down at Arri, who by now was looking up at them both.

Paul went to kiss Arri on his head again just as Alisha went to and they bumped their heads together. Alisha rubbed her forehead and laughed, kissed Paul quickly then Arri as he also laughed. Paul seeing Arri laugh properly for the first time laughed himself. He placed his arm around Alisha and pulled her close and hugged them both. 'I am truly blessed,' he thought.

ꙮ

Paul entered the long corridor that had several doors leading off to the rooms that Thomas and his men used. Outside he could hear their horses and someone was already up and outside. Theodoric had taken the largest room at the far end of the corridor which had an adjoining door that led into the main house directly. Ishmael had stayed in Percival's bed sharing the room with Luke. Each room slept two people but Tenno and Ishmael each had one to themselves. Paul looked into the separate adjoining cooking area. He expected to see a complete mess but was pleasantly surprised when he saw it was immaculate and Ishmael setting the table having already started to prepare food.

"Ishmael…morning," Paul said as he entered the cooking area.

"Morning, Master," Ishmael replied and bowed his head.

"Ishmael, please. You know it makes me feel uncomfortable when you call me Master. Just Paul is fine, please."

"If you insist…Master Just Paul," Ishmael replied joking.

"I take it all are not up yet and I hear you let Percival and Nyla have your room."

"Yes. I hope that was acceptable…but as it was both their first time, and was going to happen regardless, I thought I would help make things a little easier. Besides, Thomas and his men would have somehow turned their special moment into some kind of contest and spectacle…you know what they are like."

"Ahem!" Thomas coughed as he entered the cooking area from the side door fully dressed in his chain mail armour and surcoat already.

"I do not wish to sound rude...just saying," Ishmael said and placed wooden plates around the table.

"Ish...fear not, my good friend, for I agree with you. They make light of everything I am afraid. Where do you think I have been all night? Making sure Percy and Nyla did not have an audience," Thomas explained and looked at Paul, who was looking around the cooking room. "'Tis a clean cooking galley, yes?" Thomas stated.

"Yes...very," Paul remarked.

"You look surprised...but we all take it in turns to keep our abodes clean, like our camps, for we learnt the hard way what filth attracts and can do," Thomas explained as Ishmael nodded in agreement just as one of Thomas's men, Luke, entered the room yawning wearing just a long white night shirt. He clearly had an erection pushing out the night shirt as he walked in.

"Luke...stand down," Thomas said and indicated with his eyes toward Luke's protrusion.

"What?" Luke said puzzled, feigned a confused look then looked down at himself. "Oh that. Can't help that boss...always happens in the morning... especially with all these beautiful woman about," Luke said unashamedly and grinned as Thomas walked past him. Thomas flicked his finger down hard against Luke and he recoiled instantly in pain clutching his groin. "Boss, you bastard," Luke said loudly but laughing.

"Paul, do not look so shocked. I am afraid Luke here is a constant hard on I am afraid...even the crack of Dawn is not safe with him about," Thomas explained.

Paul laughed at his remark and seeing Luke dance in pain still holding his groin with both hands. Ishmael cracked a smile.

"Paul...I apologise...I do not mean your beautiful wife, of course," Luke said and took a deep breath and gave Thomas an exaggerated mocking glare. "Don't get me wrong...we all love your Alisha...she is without doubt the fairest, kindest and most beautiful woman any of us has ever seen."

"Stop digging, Luke," Thomas smiled.

"No I have to explain lest Paul thinks we are all masturbating wankers fantasising over his wife," Luke shot back.

"I shall get you a bigger shovel shall I?" Thomas remarked and folded his arms.

"'Tis okay, Luke. I get your point," Paul said and raised his hand to stop.

"Paul," Luke said and stepped closer toward him. "We keep ourselves out of your way pretty much most of the time…but you have to know, there is not one of us who would not willingly sacrifice our miserable souls to save hers. She is more than just a woman to us."

Thomas put his arm around Luke's shoulder and began to usher him back toward the corridor doorway just as Theodoric stepped into view. Paul's mind raced, laughing at Thomas's reaction and action to Luke and his comments, but also the sudden realisation that he had never actually thought that Thomas and his men may look at Alisha in such a manner.

"Luke, you have dug a deep enough hole. Go now and clean yourself. Today we have guests arrive," Thomas said as he ushered Luke out of the door past Theodoric.

"You mean that arrogant fool Conrad. Maybe my horse will accidentally kick his arse," Luke said as he vanished from view, Thomas pushing him.

"What did I miss?" Theodoric asked.

"You do not want to know," Ishmael remarked.

"Theo, I am glad you are up for I have questions I need ask of you before Conrad and Balian's squire arrive. Do you have time?" Paul asked.

"I have time…Balian's squire you say. That will be Ernoul. Quite a mind that one has," Theodoric answered. "Oh and Ishmael…I think we need prepare for a small wedding. Percy only went and asked her didn't he!" Theodoric explained and shook his head.

"A wedding…Alisha and Sister Lucy will love that," Paul remarked.

"Who is getting married?" Tenno asked bluntly as he entered the room already fully dressed. Paul, Theodoric and Ishmael all laughed.

Port of La Rochelle, France, Melissae Inn, spring 1191

The Hospitaller wiped his mouth as he tried to stop himself from laughing seeing the looks upon Ayleth's and Sarah's faces.

"I am sorry. Forgive my crassness but that Luke fellow reminds me of someone I once knew," he explained apologetically.

"Oh 'tis not you I am shocked at…'tis that all those men may think such thoughts of Alisha," Sarah replied.

"All men think such thoughts all the time," the Genoese sailor interjected as Simon nodded in agreement without realising it.

"You filthy buggers," Sarah said and hit Simon with the back of her hand.

"Why do you hit only me? Why not him?" Simon protested but laughing as he pointed at the Genoese sailor.

"Because you are nearest," she replied.

"I think I would be worried if I was Paul," Ayleth remarked.

"Paul was wise and sensible enough to know what men can be like. Plus Thomas and his men had always maintained a discreet distance despite their close proximity in the house grounds. Besides, Paul trusted them enough and welcomed the protection and security it afforded them all," the old man explained, drawing their attention back to him. "Thomas and his men were indeed a tidy lot. They had learnt how cleanliness was healthy from their operations and attachments to Muslim forces over the years."

"How so and why?" Peter asked.

"Our Frankish brethren tend not to care too much for order and cleanliness within their camps...apart from the Templars and Hospitallers," the old man explained and nodded toward the two brother knights. "But Muslim camps by comparison are as clean and sanitised as possible. They believe in caring for their men. It is considered wasteful to spend a fortune training a soldier only to leave him to die from parasitic infestation and disease."

"We learnt a lot from our Muslim counterparts," the Templar interrupted and smiled as he held Miriam's hand tightly. "Many things," he smiled as Miriam blushed.

"What, like the books on love like Alisha read?" Simon asked smiling broadly seeing the looks upon their faces.

The Templar looked at him and gave a slight nod.

"All that aside. The dream experience Paul had...in the pyramid. You explained that the beings, angels or whatever and whoever they were, showed him the pyramids from a different era...but also that they are some kind of device. Well what I wish to know is this...you said they mentioned a protective shield that is in place. Can you explain more on that?" Gabirol asked, his quill charged and ready to write.

"I can," the old man replied. "Norse legends all speak of a time when Thor and Odin along with the other gods who live in Asgard placed a protective shield around our world, which they called Midgard, to protect us from the ice giants...which we know from the ancient parchments and plates refers to real ice that hits our world at such great speeds that they explode with the intensity of the sun, just as Paul had seen in his dreams...and the ice comes around every 3,600 years."

"Where is Asgard?" Ayleth asked.

"It is one of the nine inhabited worlds according to Norse legends where Gods like Thor live," Gabirol answered then looked at the old man for confirmation.

"Gabirol is correct," the old man replied. "Odin and his wife, Frigg, are the rulers of Asgard, especially one area I am sure you have all heard of...Valhalla, in which Odin rules?"

"We have heard of this place many times," the Templar commented.

"That does not surprise me. It was the ice details and Midgard that Paul asked Theodoric about...but he had to wait to discuss it in detail with him as Conrad arrived as planned that very morning."

"What concerns me is I hear that there are some who say the ancient teachings claim that the gods will return and they will enslave us...to dig gold out of the ground...like you explained earlier that those summer, sumer people...you know, where the gods made man as a slave," Peter remarked.

"Peter, I am surprised you have heard such things...but yes I have heard such sayings too," the old man replied and clasped his hands together. "All I can say is that you must ask yourself a question. If this was true, then why do they, the gods, wait? Why do they wait for us to grow in number and understanding whilst their secrets are slowly but surely released to us. If they wished to enslave us they would have done so long ago," the old man explained, looking at Peter intently.

"Maybe they are just waiting until we have procreated so much that they will be spoilt for choice," Simon interrupted enthusiastically. All turned to look at him. "Hey, I could be right, you don't know," he protested.

"Then they most certainly would not have given man such a violent side to kill each other in such vast numbers," the Templar stated. "We would all remain as simple and mostly dumb beings only fit for physical labour."

"Yes...and I fear mankind has not even begun to realise his potential for mass murder," the Hospitaller commented in response.

"My friends, we could debate this matter for as long as I have already kept you, so I must return to this tale for we do not have another day available to us, I am afraid," the old man said, looking at each of them in turn.

"Then please continue," Gabirol replied and started to write a word down the side of his other notes.

Husam's residency, Cairo, Egypt, early November 1180

Paul approached the main gates of Husam's residence accompanied by Tenno, Ishmael and Thomas on foot as Percival followed a short distance back with Luke and the remainder of Thomas's men all on horseback.

Several Mamluk guards stood between a group of black dressed Bedouin and a small contingent of Naval Templars on foot. Conrad stepped into view with Ernoul, Balian's squire, by his side just as Husam's mounted horse escort dismounted off to their right. Husam appeared at the gates just as they swung open. Paul approached nodding at Conrad as he neared him when the Bedouin closest to Conrad turned around to face Paul. Instantly Paul recognised the face smiling at him.

"Turansha!" Paul shouted and drew his sword rapidly, crouching as he took up an immediate defensive position pointing his sword directly at him just feet away from his face.

Without hesitation, everyone drew their swords except Turansha and Conrad, who placed his hands upon his leather waist belt and frowned disapprovingly as Turansha kept his smile fixed upon Paul. As the Mamluk guards surrounded Husam protectively, the contingent of Templars formed a small circle around Conrad all with their swords pointing outward.

"Everyone…stand down. Put your swords away!" Husam shouted as he pushed his way forwards.

Whilst all the guards and knights eyed each other up prepared to fight, Turansha simply kept his gaze firmly fixed upon Paul.

"Ali!" Paul exclaimed alarmed and looked back at Tenno.

No sooner had he said it than Tenno turned around fast, sheathed his sword and pulled the nearest of Thomas's men, Mathew, off of his horse, mounted it and speed off in a cloud of dust. Ishmael drew his second sword from across his back and stepped closer to Paul, staring hard at Turansha with both his swords raised. Percival helped Mathew to his feet as he brushed himself down.

"I said stand down…all of you…NOW!" Husam shouted and stood in front of Paul and between Turansha and Conrad. "Paul…I see the fire that burns in you toward this man, but he is here under my protection and you will stand down."

"Never…that man hurt Alisha and very nearly had us all killed," Paul retorted, his voice deep with anger but controlled.

"I have never seen this side to you, Paul. I see now the fighting man within you, but listen to me. No good will come of any action you take against this man this day. Do you hear me, Paul?" Husam said quietly as he approached Paul and placed the palm of his hand against the tip of Paul's sword.

3 - 46

Paul looked briefly at Husam as he raised his eyebrows. Quickly he looked at Turansha as he stepped closer.

"Master Paul...you misunderstand me. I never had any intention of killing you. If I had, you would already be long since departed, my friend," Turansha said, smiling menacingly as he spoke.

"You are no friend of mine and you would have most certainly slain us but for intervention," Paul replied, still pointing his sword, Husam's hand in the way.

"Paul, not this day," Husam said quietly and shook his head barely perceivably. "He has travelled with Lord Montferrat here as his guest. There is a truce in place may I remind you and I am bound to uphold that truce. Do you understand what I am saying?"

Paul slowly lowered his sword. As he did, all the others slowly lowered theirs in like fashion. Turansha took a deep breath but held his smile.

"You may not believe me, but you were never in any danger from me. The Templar...well that was regrettable...but how many of us here have not killed?" Turansha asked as he looked around at everyone.

"Do not excuse your actions. You did not kill that Templar...you slaughtered him," Paul shot back.

"You clearly have much to learn about what exactly slaughter truly is," Turansha replied and looked at Paul. "You and I would do well to make peace."

"Just keep out of my way for I swear there will never be any peace between us for I know what evil dwells in your soul," Paul remarked.

Husam pulled Paul's shoulder hard and physically turned him around and half dragged him back towards Thomas and his men. Ishmael stood perfectly still, both swords held ready, and stared even harder at Turansha. Turansha tutted and shook his head as if to disapprove in disgust. Husam stopped beside Percival and turned Paul to face him.

"Paul, do not test my patience on this matter. We all have deep grievances for wrong doings committed...but we must temper our sense of anger and desire for revenge otherwise the cycle of violence will only perpetuate itself further," Husam said quietly, close to Paul.

"I am aware of that...but his actions were deliberate, calculating and driven by a cruel evil that dwells within him. He will never change," Paul replied and looked back toward Turansha, who smiled back at him again menacingly.

"I know that," Husam whispered. "But I am asking you to endure his presence whilst he is here. Unfortunately his services to Saladin are too valuable an asset to lose or forfeit. I will make sure he keeps away from you and your family. If he comes anywhere near your home, then by all means...deal with him. But not before, is that agreed?"

Paul thought for a few moments, his heart racing and surprised at the intensity of the hatred he felt toward Turansha at that moment. Within moments his day had gone from one of quiet contentment and looking forward to work to one of fear and being unsettled.

"Agreed," Paul answered and re-sheathed his sword.

"Good...finally! Can we now proceed and freshen up," Conrad said loudly.

Husam ushered Turansha and Conrad toward the entrance gates as everyone else put away their swords. Husam looked back over his shoulder at Paul and nodded by way of a thank you. Thomas grabbed Paul's arm and pulled him back slightly.

"We shall wait here until you are finished...all day if needs be, my friend. Any hint of trouble, blow this," Thomas said as he passed Paul a small ivory whistle. "Now go and impress them all with your brilliance. Tonight we shall each draw guard whilst Turansha remains in the city."

ᘓᘔ

Paul followed Husam as he led Turansha and Conrad inside his walled residency. He kept a close eye on them when suddenly he felt a strong hand grab his left arm. It was Brother Matthew.

"Paul...you did not see me," he said as he released his grip.

"Brother Matthew...no I did not. 'Tis good to see you again though," Paul replied and continued walking.

"These are strange days, Paul. Conrad seeks a permanent peace with Saladin, but on condition he helps secure his own position further...Turansha wants them all to continue fighting as it serves him better...but you would be as wise to make some kind of peace with him if you can. If he thinks he can make profit from you, you will remain safe from him."

"That is something I cannot do. Tenno says often to keep friends close, but keep my enemy closer...but not with that man I cannot. My father taught me always that I should be unafraid to challenge what is not right for silence is collusion and implicit approval of wrong doing. Have courage. Speak up. Speak out."

"Then you must find a way to keep him at a distance for he will not cease until he has power over you one way or another...I know this man. 'Tis why Princess Stephanie ordered I attend this embassy. So he does not do you harm for she heard of his actions...and Reynald is one of Turansha's biggest paying...associates I think best describes their relationship."

"A truly unholy alliance if ever there was one. And what of the princess. Is she well?" Paul asked, looking at him directly. In his mind he was already asking himself if Reynald had anything to do with Turansha's attempt to kill him and Alisha. It would not surprise him, he thought.

"Ah see, that put a smile back on your face. She is well. Her child grows well also...and Reynald...well you know about him and his antics even here in Cairo I am sure," Brother Matthew explained as they walked into a large marbled foyer. He stopped and stared as he looked through the open foyer that looked out from a balcony across the Nile. Instantly visible was a large three masted galley ship berthed alongside the enclosed dry dock set outside Husam's residency. "My Lord, look at the size of that. Is that what you have worked upon?"

"Partly...but my work has been mainly upon another design. Perhaps I shall get to show you later," Paul replied as he watched Husam usher Turansha and Conrad towards some refreshments laid out upon a long table.

Turansha turned and faced Paul, smiled and raised a date and gestured with his other hand that he should come and help himself likewise. Paul knew that if you ate and drank with a person it was a sign that no blood would be spilled between you. Was that what he was hinting at? Paul wondered. Husam looked back at him. Paul would not let Turansha see that he was afraid or intimidated by him nor would he insult Husam's hospitality inside his own home. He walked over to Turansha and stood directly beside him, looked him in the eyes then picked up a date and ate it. Turansha laughed.

"Ah see...we can at least eat together. If you can find it in your heart to forgive me for my previous actions, I know I can make amends for them and I can openly and publicly apologise right here and now for having so grievously assaulted you and your family. It shall not happen again. You have my solemn vow," Turansha said and bowed. "It has been my experience that it is a man's own mind, not his enemy or foe, that lures him to evil ways and only enemies speak the truth for friends and lovers lie endlessly, caught in the web of duty to placate or control those closest. Think upon that," Turansha said and winked before smiling broadly and ate another date.

Paul looked at Husam behind him as he nodded. 'Know your enemy and study him well.' Paul heard his father's words in his mind as he looked at Turansha. 'Okay, I shall play him at his own game,' he thought just as Brother Matthew nodded and raised his eyebrows.

"For the sake of peace and out of respect for Husam, I shall put aside my own feelings and shall dine with you...," Paul said, staring at Turansha intently, not blinking.

"This is good to hear. Very good. You will see...one day we shall be friends," Turansha replied and placed his arm around Paul and ushered him toward the table of food. "You and I can be of so much value to each other mark my words...'tis true."

Paul looked at Turansha as he smiled at Paul. Every instinct screamed at him to draw his sword right there and then and kill him. His heart beat faster as the urge to do so felt overpowering almost. Turansha's overtly friendly stance was unnerving. He also recognised most of the sentence Turansha had spoken was taken from a quote made by Buddha for Niccolas had made him repeat it so many times.

"Perhaps Paul would rather show you his new boat design...it is worthy of a close inspection," Husam said as he gently pulled Paul away from the table. "We can savour these delicacies when we have built up an appetite I am sure. Now, some drink refreshment?"

ꙮ

Paul stood with Ishmael and Brother Matthew overlooking the large dry dock containing a half built vessel. Turansha was laughing and talking away with Husam and Ernoul, Balian's squire, who had just returned to the group after freshening himself up. Paul had heard of him but never met him in person yet. It was strange to listen to the Naval Templars talking and laughing with both Turansha's men and the Mamluk guards with no hint of hostility. They were professional soldiers granted but it still seemed strange. Several female dancers filed past dressed in very little with see through garments that left little to the imagination. All stopped talking as they walked past quickly, Turansha eyeing them all up one by one as they went by.

"Tonight's entertainment I suspect," Brother Matthew said quietly and then leaned on the balcony balustrade to look back upon the large vessel. "'Tis good we can each check what the other is doing during these embassies. I can report back that I have indeed seen just the one vessel being constructed as per agreed terms with Saladin…but what a vessel. I have never seen such a size before."

Paul looked down at the vessel. He knew that one of Saladin's greatest concerns lay in the possibility of Reynald getting more ships and sailing down the Red Sea and attacking Muslim ports and towns, especially the route to Mecca. He had shrewdly written into the truce agreement the checking of each other's ship building programmes. Ernoul was there to verify that Husam was indeed making exactly what he said he was making. Likewise, envoys had gone to several of the Frankish ports to confirm projects there. Fortunately Reynald was based too many miles inland and if he suddenly started building ships within the Frankish ports Saladin would know about it in time to intercept and engage or blockade him to stop him from carrying out his threat to attack Mecca direct.

"'Tis a fine ship is it not?" Husam suddenly said from behind Paul and Brother Matthew.

"Aye that it is," Brother Matthew replied as several of the Naval Templars looked on. "She is what…at least three hundred feet long and perhaps a good hundred and twenty feet wide in her middle?"

"You have a good eye for she is three hundred and eleven feet long by a hundred and thirty feet at her widest. Three masted no less as you can see," Husam explained proudly.

"And her armament?" Brother Matthew asked.

Husam placed his hand upon Brother Matthew's back and laughed.

"You know I will not tell you that…but I am sure you can work it out. And no interrogating Paul here for he is not privy to its protection," Husam said and looked at Brother Matthew, smiling. "But I can tell you she will carry a crew of two hundred and thirty men and seventy marines. 'Tis based upon the Byzantine Trireme Dromon, but we have put some designs taken from Paul's ideas and incorporated them into her final build. It has the familiar central tower near the main mast, from which the marines can use their bows and arrows or throw spears and other projectiles. But this one is also equipped with flamethrowers that discharge Greek fire. The on board catapults are capable of hurling a twenty pound projectile up to nearly a thousand feet...and it is also armour-plated...against enemy rams. Like other Dromon vessels she is constructed from wood and metal, using the plank-on-frame method but she has some secrets...but Paul works upon a greater design separate from this," Husam explained even more proudly.

"Why...do you not work upon this vessel all the time then?" Brother Matthew asked, turning to look at Paul.

"No...I work upon the conceptual and theoretical designs...for speed and distance. Not fighting vessels nor Taridas," Paul answered.

"Ah, very shrewd of you," Brother Matthew said to Husam.

"Come...I shall show you what he has been working upon these past many months. It may not look much, but the methods Paul has developed have enabled us to design and build our larger vessels in section out of dock and simply assemble them once at port. A brilliant method do you not agree?" Husam said, almost boastful in tone as he turned Brother Matthew towards an exit way and started to walk with him, gesturing for Paul and Ernoul to follow.

"Would you show me the method involved?" Brother Matthew asked.

"Do not be silly, Brother...of course not," Husam laughed in reply.

"Paul, 'tis good to finally be acquainted with you," Ernoul said quietly as he began to walk beside Paul.

"And you too. I have heard much about you," Paul replied and part bowed his head.

"My Lord Balian sends his regards and, before I leave, I have a letter from him for your eyes only."

Paul looked at Ernoul briefly as they followed Husam and Brother Matthew. Turansha tagged on behind Paul closely followed by the remainder of the Naval Templars and Mamluk guards.

ꟾ

Husam nodded at the two guards set on either side of the large mud brick building ahead of them. It stood four floors high and was covered by a sliding wooden and canvas roof. Inside the building, a purpose built dry dock had been specially constructed to house Paul's new vessel concept. Husam had been utterly fascinated by Paul's detailed and intricate designs and wanted to see if his concept would actually work. The two guards instantly slid open the two large doors as Husam led the way inside. The air was cooler inside and Paul felt the now familiar change in temperature as he crossed the threshold. He had come to love this place. To him it was not simply a place of work but a place to experiment and indulge his passion for boats. Husam had been a good patron to him and he was grateful for his support and faith in his work. Ishmael remained close by his side and frequently glared at Turansha and when Turansha tried to speak with him, he ignored him completely, refusing to talk or acknowledge him properly.

"Do you really need an armed escort to work?" Turansha asked as they walked toward the sunken dry dock area.

"Are you asking me?" Paul replied as Husam turned to face the group.

"Yes. Are you not safe here in Cairo?"

"I am...or I was," Paul replied.

"My friend...I have told you...I am no longer your enemy. What has been is in the past. People who know me know that my word is my bond. I gave you mine that no harm would come to you from me or my men. I swear I shall keep that promise," Turansha said and bowed just as Conrad came in walking fast tying up his waist band.

"Sorry...missed you all walking off," Conrad called out as he approached looking hot and red faced.

"Yes, shagging all the dancing girls more like," one of the Naval Templars whispered behind Paul.

Paul turned slightly and looked at the Templar who immediately grimaced realising Paul had heard him.

"Do not worry...you are probably right," Paul whispered back.

The Templar let out a sigh of relief and mouthed a silent thank you.

Husam clapped his hands loudly to draw everyone's attention.

"Now this is the kind of ship we should all be working together on. It is a ship of discovery. Lightweight, fast and, if Paul is correct, very manoeuvrable and able to carry three times the water capacity of any existing vessel afloat," Husam said enthusiastically as four men dressed in working coveralls rapidly pulled two sets of pulleys.

As they pulled down, the ropes began to pull away the large brown cotton covering sheets placed over Paul's vessel. As they fell away, several of the Templars looked on in awe at the unique and strange looking vessel revealed before them. Turansha's eyes lit up immediately and he rubbed his small pointed beard several times.

"What in God's creation is that?" Conrad asked out loud.

"'Tis a marvel, yes," Husam said proudly.

"Just hope it works and floats," Paul interrupted as the group all moved closer to see the vessel.

"Oh I bet it works. And the water capacity...that means it can travel three times the distance of other boats...yes?" Turansha asked as he studied the vessel.

"In theory, yes," Paul answered.

"Can we look inside?" Conrad asked eagerly.

Husam looked at Paul, who nodded yes silently.

"Paul...it was a great day Allah saw fit to spare your life. The Templar was regrettable, and your friends...with that Theodoric monk, took some of my best men too. I pray we can put that behind us for I see great potential here. Potential to change the world, Astaghfirullah," Turansha said quietly but close enough to Paul for him to hear him. Paul looked at Turansha suspiciously. Whatever his real intentions were, he was certain it was all for his own self serving interests. "So tell me. How is Theodoric these days?" he asked turning to look at Paul directly.

"He is well. What does Astaghfirrellah mean?"

"You mean Astaghfirullah...it means may Allah forgive me. If you wish, I will be more than happy to teach you more Arabic," Turansha answered with a grin. Paul said nothing. "Never mind. But back to your monk friend...his dressing up as an angel certainly worked the last time I saw him. Do pass on my blessings to him from me...if you would be so kind," Turansha said, smiling even more broadly, and began to walk down the wide gangplank platform to look inside Paul's boat design. "And not all you fight are your enemy," he said aloud.

"Your vessel...it looks more like some kind of egg or beetle almost. Where are the sails?" Ernoul asked as he held on to the barrier railings that ran around the dry dock.

"They remain furled up inside. When the front section is hoisted upwards into position, the sails unfurl and deploy out to the sides. I have designed it so it can catch the wind whatever direction it blows from," Paul explained as he watched Turansha step inside the vessel.

"He is a cunning man that Turansha, but he is not mad and he does pride himself on keeping his word," Ernoul explained seeing the pained look on Paul's face.

"I do not trust his word at all. I have sensed the evil that runs through his self serving soul," Paul replied.

"He is a very powerful man. If he wanted you dead, you would be so by now. His actions are never personal…usually."

"Sire, may I ask a question?" one of the Naval Templars asked as he walked up to Paul.

"Of course…and please, my name is Paul," Paul replied.

"Sire, of course," the Templar continued and pointed to several large wooden sections of another vessel under construction on the other side of the building. "Those…they are parts of a larger vessel, yes?"

"Yes…and please, there is no need for the sire," Paul answered.

"Yes, sire," the Templar said as if oblivious to Paul's words. "Why are they made thus out of docks?"

"Ah I see a sharp mind and eagle eyes," Husam interrupted as he walked back up the gangplanks fast. "'Tis another concept of Paul's. 'Tis how we have managed to construct the ship outside so quickly. Paul helped design a method whereby we construct the vessel in sections on land then assemble them in the docks when all has been constructed. Making the parts laid out flat is so much more efficient."

Ernoul looked at Paul and then the wooden sections. Paul saw him as his mind was clearly making a mental note.

"What gave you such an idea for that is quite a leap forwards in construction?" he asked.

"My wife. 'Tis how she makes her dresses and other items in silks and cottons," Paul answered as Husam smiled broadly and put his arm around Paul.

"Do not be so modest. With your designs and ideas, I can see my ships travelling to new worlds beyond the known horizons," Husam said enthusiastically and patted Paul's back. "Come…come inside and check out the interior. A marvel to behold."

Ernoul looked at Paul quizzically as he started to follow Husam back down the gangway.

"And spread the word of Islam no doubt," the Naval Templar remarked quietly.

Paul watched as Husam eagerly showed Ernoul to the entry hatch on Paul's vessel. Ernoul stooped slightly to step inside, as Husam waved at Paul and grinned. Was Husam really helping Paul or himself, Paul thought, suddenly feeling a little uncomfortable with everything. But there was now a truce in place and his ships were designed for exploration…not war, he told himself. He turned around in time to see several of the Naval Templars looking very closely at the other ship sections and making notes. A shiver ran down his back. What was Husam doing showing off all his construction secrets? he wondered.

"Master Just Paul…just say the word and I will make Turansha vanish," Ishmael whispered as he leaned near to Paul.

2 - 16

Paul turned to face him and looked past him at several of Turansha's men standing a short distance away.

"Ish…just…no, Paul…only Paul…and no, I cannot ask that."

"Okay Master Only Paul," Ishmael replied mockingly.

"Ish, you have a strange sense of humour for sure," Paul replied.

"Paul…Paul!" Conrad called out as he rapidly walked up the gangway heading straight for Paul. "I do not profess to understand how such a vessel works but I hope you will show me in good time?"

"I am sure that can be arranged. I will make sure you are notified in time when we take her for her trial run," Paul answered.

"Good man, good man. I trust I can count upon your support in the future when I am king. If I can, then I can guarantee you a ship yard of your own bigger than this," Conrad exclaimed and put his hands upon his hips, smiling.

"King?" Paul remarked puzzled.

"Yes, my man. Me…king. It will happen, mark my words. 'Tis rightfully mine and I shall not war with our Muslim brothers like the Reynalds of this world continually do," Conrad said, his manner and tone boastful almost. "And it will be men like you that will reap the rewards in our new world…together."

Paul looked at Conrad in silence for several moments unsure what to make of his comments. As he looked at him, he suddenly sensed Alisha as if she was calling him in alarm. He turned to look toward the exit gates.

"I must leave at once. Please pardon my abruptness, but I must," Paul replied, part bowed his head at Conrad and began to walk away fast.

Conrad pulled a puzzled face as Ishmael looked at him, raised his eyebrows and quickly followed after Paul. Husam looked up briefly to see Paul walking away.

ꙮ

Having ridden two together on horses to get home fast, Paul rushed through his front door closely followed by Ishmael as Thomas and his men rapidly dismounted and fanned out around the building to check it was secure.

"Ali…Ali!" Paul called out as he walked through the main entrance foyer and down the corridor leading to the main cooking hall. Alisha stepped into view at the doorway, saw him and ran toward him. "Ali!"

Alisha threw her arms around him and hugged him tightly as Tenno appeared holding Arri with Theodoric and Sister Lucy close behind him. Theodoric looked at Paul as if to ask if he was okay.

"I wanted to come and fetch you immediately but Tenno refused to allow it," Alisha said with alarm in her voice.

"Tenno did the right thing…thank you," Paul replied as he put his arms around Alisha, her head pressed hard against his chest.

"Adrastos knew something was wrong. He would not settle and has injured himself trying to get out from his stable," Alisha said and squeezed Paul harder.

"'Tis not a bad injury. Just his leg is slightly cut," Theodoric said as he walked past Tenno. "Is everything okay?"

"For now, yes. Thomas and his men already post themselves about the property. And we have been given assurances from Husam and Turansha himself," Paul explained, trying to sound reassuring for Alisha. Theodoric shook his head no in silence.

"You will all be safe of that I have no doubt…and look we have a letter from your father delivered this day," Theodoric said trying to sound more positive and waved a wax sealed envelope high.

"Ali, look at me," Paul said as he physically had to pry her away from holding him so tightly. She looked up into his eyes. He could see the sense of panic in her face, her pupils wide. "Turansha will be gone soon enough…I promise you."

"He better had. And if he ever enters this house, he will get this," Alisha replied defiantly and suddenly raised her three pronged dagger. "I had stopped carrying this, but I will not be without it again."

Tenno raised a single eyebrow just as Arri waved his hands playfully at Paul. Tenno sniffed the air.

"'Tis time I gave him back for he has soiled mightily," Tenno said with a forced grimace and lifted Arri towards Alisha and Paul.

Paul quickly kissed Alisha and took Arri from Tenno.

"I shall deal with this whilst you settle yourself," Paul remarked recoiling as he smelt Arri and then laughed trying to lighten the mood. "Theo, please once I have done so, would you be so kind as to read out the letter?"

ꕥ

Paul stood alone with Adrastos in his stable area as the early evening light faded from light blue to darkness. Adrastos snorted and shook his head as Paul patted the side of his face.

"Well, my friend, it would appear that you knew something was amiss this day. I should have taken you instead of walking. I promise that from now on I shall try and spend more time with you…and your little friend Arri," Paul spoke aloud and stroked Adrastos.

Paul clasped the single rope that tethered Adrastos to the rear wall and unleashed it from his bridle and took the whole mouth piece off. He did not need that on any more Paul thought as Adrastos shook his head as if he understood him. Paul's mind wandered back to seeing Turansha again and instantly all the feelings he had experienced flooded his senses again. In his mind he could clearly see Turansha and what his men almost did to him and Arri. He shuddered. He pushed the thought from his mind refusing to let Turansha invade his very mind any more that day. He looked up and saw the belt stars of Orion just beginning to shine on the horizon above the outer wall. Theodoric had read out Philip's letter as they had sat down for dinner. Theodoric had laughed as he read out that Philip intended to kick him several hundred times for every day he had been absent but was truly glad he was still alive. Philip asked Paul to inform Theodoric that the items hidden in La Rochelle had now been safely removed elsewhere. He would know where. Soon Philip would visit them and he hoped the house was fitting enough and how he longed to see his own grandson at long last.

Theodoric laughed when Philip mentioned he had dined with Barbarossa and snipped his beard. It was obviously some private joke between them, Paul thought. Philip's letter had finished by advising Paul to always trust his heart, just do right, that doing right may not always be expedient, certainly not always profitable, but by doing right, his soul would feel satisfied. Killing Turansha would have been right, he told himself and sighed, Adrastos pushing his head beside his as if in sympathy. With Marseille having strong trading links with Egypt it would not be long before his father would be able to visit, especially now a truce had been agreed and appeared to be holding.

Port of La Rochelle, France, Melissae Inn, spring 1191

"Who was Barbarossa?" Simon asked, scratching his head then sticking his finger in his ear and making a noise as he twisted it in and out fast.

"Did his vessel work? That is what I want to know," the Genoese sailor asked as Sarah looked at Simon with mild disgust.

"Barbarossa. Now there is a character. He was perhaps one man for whom the Arthurian myths and Grail Romances deeply influenced his every thought and move. He is charismatic, German, mid sixties, tall and a model of chivalric ideals of the cult of King Arthur and he was once a good friend of both Philip and Theodoric...but most of you must surely know of him as Frederick the First, the Holy Roman Emperor...and he is a real worry for Saladin that is for sure for he has managed to raise an army of some hundred thousand men, twenty thousand knights amongst them. He marches for the Holy Land even now as we sit here this day," the old man explained and laughed to himself.

"Yes we have heard of him under that title," the Templar said as his brother nodded in agreement.

"You look as though you knew this Barbarossa," Gabirol remarked.

"Yes, yes I did and very well. Also, if it had not been for him, neither Philip nor Firgany would have lived to sire children, but that is another story...and I must finish this tale this day," the old man answered and sat himself up straight. "Perhaps we should have a meal and then I shall conclude before I must leave this eve... yes?"

Stephan stood up and nodded silently as Simon shook his head enthusiastically.

"Paul's boat...did it work?" the Genoese sailor asked again.

"Oh yes, it worked and worked well. But it would be over another year before it would see water. And a lot more would happen before then," the old man said as Stephan disappeared into the cooking hall.

"And that evil Turansha?" Ayleth asked.

"Turansha...he left shortly afterwards with Conrad and the Naval Templars. But the knowledge he had gained of Paul's ship building method in sections went with him...straight to Reynald!"

"What problem does that cause?" Peter asked, looking puzzled.

"Because it would have profound and dire consequences on later actions by Reynald and his sworn plans to attack and destroy Mecca," the old man explained and shook his head.

"So that Husam was a bit of a fool displaying all of Paul's ideas?" Gabirol commented.

"No, he was no fool and he knew exactly what he was doing."

"You mean he used Paul?" Ayleth asked, shocked.

"In a fashion. But do not misunderstand me, Husam admired and liked Paul a lot as well as Count Raymond and Balian. But he also knew that no lasting truce would ever hold whilst people like Reynald remained."

"So Turansha kept his word at least not to hurt Paul?" Sarah asked.

"Oh yes, he kept that promise for sure," the old man sighed.

"But your tone gives away that he still did something?" Gabirol remarked, looking at the old man intently.

"That I shall come to...but for now know that for the next few months Paul lived on constant edge and could not relax. His sword never left his side and Alisha likewise never went anywhere without her dagger, and that is the way things remained until they had two visitors within the space of just two days," the old man explained and then took a long slow mouthful of rose water. "And whom I shall tell you all about after we have eaten."

Chapter 52
Living Legends

Cairo, Egypt, January 1181

Arri sat upright in the saddle upon Adrastos as Paul held the reins and guided him in a circle about the rear courtyard. Arri held the pommel of the saddle tightly with both hands laughing, Clip clop half hanging through his fingers. Alisha looked on half holding her breath, concern written all across her face as Ishmael walked on the other side ready to catch Arri if he fell. The sky was unusually cloudy and threatened rain, but Paul had promised Arri a proper ride on Adrastos as one of his Christmas wishes. Tenno had sat him upon Adrastos before but not totally unsupported. Nervously Alisha continued watching and started to bite her thumb nail as several mounted knights and Mamluk guards appeared near the main rear gates, Husam leading them into the courtyard. He had just raised his right arm to halt the troop when a loud report, like an explosion, rang out loudly from inside Theodoric's quarters. Adrastos froze despite the frightening noise as Paul quickly reached up to grab hold of Arri, Alisha running to his side. Some of Husam's men struggled to regain control of their horses as they bucked, fearful and startled. Ishmael vanished as he ran into a cloud of smoke and dust bellowing out of the main entrance way into the corridor leading to Theodoric's room. Alarmed and convinced of an assault by Turansha's men, Paul drew his sword and held Alisha behind him shielded by Adrastos. Arri was still laughing and waving Clip clop.

After a few moments, Thomas and several of his men staggered through the smoke coughing and wiping their eyes guided by Ishmael. Sister Lucy came running out in alarm from the main cooking hall closely followed by Nyla.

"Where is he?" Sister Lucy asked panicked.

"In his room," Paul replied and looked towards Theodoric's window, its shutters blown off and white smoke bellowing out.

Thomas and his men immediately rushed to grab fire buckets with sand in, as Luke started to fill up several spare ones with water from the main horses' drinking trough. Before Paul could turn to face Sister Lucy, she was off and running straight into the smoke. Paul went to move when Ishmael pulled him back firmly.

"No...you stay. Protect Alisha and Arri. I shall get them," he said and quickly hurried after Sister Lucy into the smoke as Husam ran over followed by several of his guards.

"What has happened here?" he asked concerned, his hand covering his sword ready to draw.

"I have no idea," Paul answered just as Ishmael immediately came back into view through the smoke supporting Tenno with his right arm around him and Theodoric being half carried beneath his left arm, Sister Lucy half pushing all three of them. Directly behind them walked Attar holding a cloth to his face and wafting the smoke away from his face.

Paul was aware of several men on horseback draw near into the courtyard as Thomas and his men threw water and sand through Theodoric's window and down the corridor entrance.

"Where is Percy?" Nyla asked, frantic.

Tenno stopped in his tracks and looked across at Theodoric. All of their faces were filthy and covered in blackened powder and dust. Theodoric shrugged and shook his head. Nyla buckled at the knees and gasped, putting her hand to her face in alarm.

"I am fine...just fine!" Percival called out from the opposite side of the courtyard as he approached rubbing his head and trying to shake the sensation of his ringing ears away. Nyla ran to him and jumped into his arms hugging him tightly. In pain but smiling, his hair singed and sticking up on end, he put his arms around her. He then pointed to the ground where he had landed, then at the smashed window blinds and shook his head again, puzzled. He had been blown directly through the windows yet remarkably with only minor scratches.

"What happened?" Sister Lucy demanded to know as she turned Theodoric to look at her.

"'Twas my fault...," Tenno interrupted as he started to brush himself down.

"No...no...no. 'Twas mine alone," Attar said, waving his finger as Husam looked on utterly bemused.

"Was it Turansha's men with grenades?" Paul asked, his sword still drawn.

Tenno and Attar looked at each other briefly, then at the state of Theodoric, his face all blackened and his hair still smoking.

"No, they used too much mixture and Percy there went and lit it too soon. Hence his little flight," Theodoric explained as Sister Lucy closed her eyes, held his arm tightly and rested her forehead against him relieved. "It bloody works well though," he then laughed.

"What does?" Paul asked.

"'Tis a mixture we make in my lands…and in China for displays. Attar here knows of the formula, being an Alchemist also…so we tried to make some to fire them in celebration when Percival and Nyla marry," Tenno explained.

"Do that again and there won't be any wedding!" Alisha interrupted and moved closer to Sister Lucy seeing how shocked she still looked. "And who is going to clean the water and sand mess up?"

"There won't be any me," Percival stated still rubbing his head as a small trickle of blood seeped from his left ear. "I think I have burst my ear."

Theodoric laughed out loud as Percival and Nyla stepped closer. Thomas appeared at the main corridor entrance and gave a thumbs up all was under control. Percival and Attar started to laugh at the sight of each other as one of the mounted horsemen rode nearer and stopped, totally silhouetted by the sun behind him.

"By the Lord, the dead do indeed live," Philip spoke as he leaned forwards to look at Theodoric.

Theodoric stopped laughing instantly, gulped and blinked his eyes several times. He stood perfectly still speechless despite desperately trying to say something, his mouth opening but no words coming out. For several long seconds he squinted as he tried to focus upon the mounted person before him. He knew the voice well. His eyes filled with tears as he gulped again and fought to control his emotions, clenching his fists. Sister Lucy smiled softly at him and stepped back a short distance as she watched Philip dismount. As he slowly approached, he removed his riding gloves. He was wearing the full length mantle of a Naval Templar, which surprised Paul more than the fact he was actually in Cairo.

"Father," Paul heard himself say quietly as Philip stopped just in front of Theodoric.

Philip and Theodoric stood in silence looking at each other; Theodoric struggling to breathe it looked, his face reddening. He outstretched his hands but then dropped them to his sides and looked down shaking his head. He was utterly lost for words. It had been nearly two decades since they had last seen each other.

"My dearest friend…'tis indeed great to see you again…and alive no less," Philip finally said, his voice clearly emotional as his face creased into a forced smile, his lips clearly quivering as he too struggled to contain his emotions.

Theodoric shrugged and tried to force a smile. Sister Lucy looked at Philip and smiled at him. Gently she took hold of Theodoric's arm and ushered him toward Philip. Alisha bit her bottom lip as she saw the emotion in their eyes. Philip being the taller of them stepped closer opening his arms. Theodoric closed his eyes and tried to cover his face as he continued to look down. Philip placed his arms around him just as Theodoric began to sob resting his forehead against Philip's shoulder. Paul put his arm around Alisha as she held Arri who was looking intently at Philip and Theodoric. Philip closed his eyes briefly as Theodoric sniffed and tried to compose himself. Thomas and his men, as well as Husam and his men, all looked on. The admiration, respect and love between Philip and Theodoric was almost tangible. Arri suddenly let out a little yelp and what sounded like 'Clip clop' as he held him out toward them. Philip opened his eyes again and looked directly at Arri then Alisha. Theodoric wiped his eyes, coughed and stood back a pace.

"We…we have much to catch up," he blurted out still very visibly emotional. Even Tenno looked touched.

Slowly Philip walked toward Paul, Alisha and Arri as he kept waving Clip clop. Placing his hands together across his waist, he looked at Arri smiling broadly at him. Alisha had tears in her eyes seeing the emotion etched across Philip's face. He had grown a tight beard and looked taller. His face was deeply tanned and he looked well.

"So this is Arri…my grandson," he said, his eyes filled with emotion and only just managing to keep his tears from falling. He took a deep breath and looked at Paul.

"'Tis indeed, Father. Pray tell why you did not let us know you were coming?" Paul asked as Arri reached out towards Philip.

Alisha passed Arri to Philip and as he took him, Arri looked directly into his eyes for a minute. Philip smiled, which made Arri smile. Without prompting, Arri put his little arms up around his neck and leant his head upon Philip's chest and just rested in that position.

"We have learnt much about you these past two years. We have a lot of questions," Alisha said softly and touched his arm gently, leaned up and kissed him on the side of his face.

"I bet you do…and I of Theo no less," Philip answered and smiled as he looked across at Theodoric.

"You knew a lot of powerful people, we have discovered," Alisha stated.

"A few, as does Theo…"

"A few! Next you will be telling us you are on first name terms with Saladin himself. But 'tis truly great to see you, Father," Paul said, pleased to see his father despite his looking so different.

"He is," a voice said aloud from amongst the ranks of Husam's Mamluk guards.

Paul looked over as the guards parted and a well dressed man wearing a gold and green surcoat with chain mail beneath appeared holding a burnished ornate helmet under his left arm. Philip winked at Paul and gestured with his head towards the man as he stepped ever closer. Attar recognised the man immediately, his eyes widening. He bowed his head as he walked past him. Paul's eyes met the man's eyes. He was confident looking, had a tight beard, was well kept and looked kind. Husam smiled broadly as if about to burst into laughter.

"Assalamu Allakham. And I do indeed know your father. We go back a long way. To a time when I was not so well mannered or behaved," the man said politely and bowed.

"Wa Allakham Assalam," Paul replied, looking perplexed. "And you are?"

Alisha prodded Paul in the side hard making him flinch, which made the man laugh. Philip faced the man and pointed with his right hand, palm up towards him whilst holding Arri with his left arm.

2 - 10

"My son…this is Salah al Din Yusif ibn Ayyub, but better known to you simply as Saladin," Philip explained, smiling.

Instantly Paul recalled his conversation back in Alexandria when Saladin's secretary Isfahani had given him a sealed letter and when Theodoric had advised him 'make it your priority to keep Reynald appeased and befriend Saladin...if the opportunity arises. It will help safeguard your futures, believe me.'

"And you must be Paul and Alisha of whom I have heard so much," Saladin said politely and part bowed his head at Alisha, Paul standing with his mouth open. "All I know speak highly of you both. I understand you can draw images of people that look real. And you design amazing ships too I am told," he continued to say as Husam nodded his head in agreement. "And you...Alisha," he said and paused as he looked at her intently. "My belated condolences for the loss of Firgany. A true tragedy."

Alisha blushed and took a deep intake of air, the realisation that the great Saladin himself was stood before her, in her own courtyard was a little overwhelming. She smiled but did not know what to say and just nodded her head. Saladin looked at Philip and they both smiled. Their eyes turned to Theodoric, who raised his right hand slightly to acknowledge Saladin.

"I do not know what I am supposed to say and do...with you here...in my courtyard," Paul said awkwardly, unsure of protocol.

"A drink will suffice," Saladin replied. "And perhaps whilst I am here, you will honour me with doing a likeness of me," he said and walked to the middle of the courtyard and looked around smiling. "I remember this place well...very well."

Alisha looked at Paul, puzzled. Theodoric seeing the look on their faces stepped closer.

"This was once his property. Even Princess Stephanie stayed here once... as his guest of course," Theodoric explained in a whisper.

Alisha and Paul looked at Saladin as he stood alone in the middle of the courtyard.

"So this is the man we hear so much of. The legend that is Saladin," Alisha spoke quietly in Paul's ear and held on to his arm.

Paul looked at his father, who was holding Arri tightly as Tenno stood beside him and bowed his head pleased to see him again. Sister Lucy sniffed and pulled at Theodoric's singed shirt. Paul agreed with Alisha that Saladin was clearly a legend, but as he looked at his father, holding Arri as if he had known him always, he wondered who he really was; this unknown legend in his own right, who knew so many powerful people who all seemed to hold him and Theodoric in such high regard. He sighed and felt a real sense of pride in his father he had never felt before as if seeing him properly for the first time.

Port of La Rochelle, France, Melissae Inn, spring 1191

"The great Saladin himself?" the Hospitaller remarked.

"Yes, Saladin himself. Do you find this hard to believe?" the old man asked.

"I am open to all things...but Saladin...arriving at their home. Is that normal?"

"In Cairo, and in regard to Saladin, yes it was very normal. A truce was in place, and remember, Ernoul had given Paul a sealed envelope from Balian which had a further letter inside from Philip, but in all the confusion and concern over Turansha, Paul had completely forgotten about Ernoul's letter. If not he would have known his father was coming and that he had been on a special commission to Syria to seek terms with Saladin in person. You see, many years before, as I have explained already, when Saladin was young, it was Philip, Firgany and Theodoric who had...a certain direct involvement in proving certain things about our world to him. They had remained close ever since. And indeed Saladin once owned the very property.

"So why did Saladin return to Cairo then?" Ayleth asked.

"Yes and did Paul do one of his drawings of him? I would love to see what this Saladin really looks like," Simon asked excitedly.

"Gabirol...if you would be so kind...inside there is indeed a picture drawn by Paul of Saladin," the old man said.

Immediately, Gabirol pulled over the leather bound folder, opened it and looked through several parchment sheets and vellum papers until he came across an image of a man holding a sword who looked like a Muslim soldier. He looked at the old man for confirmation. When he nodded it was, he removed the drawing and placed it in the centre of the table for all to see.

Fig. 53: Saladin.

"If this Saladin is such a noble and honourable man, why do we fight him still?" Ayleth asked.

"Religion!" the Hospitaller shot back instantly as he leaned forward to see the drawing.

"'Tis not really religion...more men and how they understand religion, and greed, vanity, power, all play a part," the old man replied looking at Ayleth. "And as our knight friends here can confirm, much was down to the local commanders and their personal relationships with opposing leaders in Outremer as a whole. Sometimes Templars would march and fight alongside their Muslim counterparts against another regional foes."

"Really?" Sarah asked, confused, as she leaned up on her elbows and studied the image.

"Yes, really. The Rule of the Templars, and to a lesser degree that of the Hospitallers, even permits military service in the armies of the Muslim Seljuks of Rum, that is Anatolia. Likewise battle hardened and well disciplined knights like Thomas and his men were highly prized and sought after."

"But I thought Saladin spent all his time in Syria or attacking Jerusalem," Peter said and shrugged his shoulders as he glanced at the picture of Saladin.

"No, that is simply propaganda. But Saladin was in Cairo due to many reasons," the old man started to explain.

"Then please tell us, for I would like to know," Gabirol asked.

"Well I think he looks handsome in a strange sort of way," Ayleth remarked.

"He is indeed a handsome man. He could have any woman he chose, but his real love was a woman he longed to be with but distance and time often kept them apart more than he wished," the old man explained. "Saladin would often say that if you want to make peace with your enemy, you have to work with your enemy. Then he becomes your partner. Husam believed this totally too."

"Is that true about that evil Turansha then?" Sarah asked.

"No...not quite! But his words that not all you fight are your enemies did stick in Paul's mind. Sometimes a great truth can still be told by a great liar."

"You mentioned that Ernoul gave Paul a letter, which he forgot to read. What was the letter about...not from his father but Balian's?" Gabirol asked.

"Ernoul's letter," the old man repeated and smiled, paused for a moment then continued. "It was a letter from Balian stating that he wished it to be formally known that he wanted Paul to be registered as one of his notarised knights in time of crisis."

"What does that mean?" Ayleth asked.

"It means if an arriere ban or call to arms is issued by the king in Jerusalem, or by Balian himself, Paul would join them. It would afford him certain privileges in return should he himself get into trouble and require assistance...a lot of knights affiliated themselves in this manner, but Paul chose not to," the old man explained as both the Templar and Hospitaller nodded in agreement with him.

"Is that all?" Gabirol asked, looking puzzled.

"You miss very little...for there was more. A letter from Princess Stephanie too."

"Oh dear, I bet it was not good?" the farrier remarked.

"'Twas not bad neither. But Paul never read the letter, but I shall come to that," the old man replied.

Simon with his arms folded looked across at Gabirol to make sure he was making a note. As Gabirol wrote, Simon winked at him.

"And Percival and Nyla, they were to wed. Did they, and what were Attar, Tenno and Theodoric doing that nearly killed them?" Peter asked.

"Yes they were to wed, and Attar, being the keen alchemist he is decided to make some powder that explodes. Pretty harmless when mixed and lit as it usually burns off in a bright flash, of different colours, but Tenno was demonstrating how when compressed inside a tube, it could be used to launch another smaller pack of the powder into the air. Percival did not realise it should not be lit indoors and decided to light the powder. He was indeed lucky to survive. In fact they could have all been killed."

"Sounds more like a weapon to me," the Hospitaller commented.

"Yes indeed the stuff they made could be weaponised..."

"So Saladin turns up and if things had gone really wrong, they could have all been killed? End of Saladin by accident," Simon commented. "But you still have not explained why he was in Cairo."

"He had to be there. He left Farrukh-Shah in charge of Syria, whilst he returned to Cairo. He intended to spend the fast of Ramadan in Egypt and then make the hajj pilgrimage to Mecca in the summer. But for unknown reasons he changed his plans regarding the pilgrimage and was seen inspecting the Nile River banks in June that year...but I can tell you that it was because he was very interested in the new ship designs and strange vessel Paul had designed. But he was also again embroiled with the Bedouin too; he removed two-thirds of their fiefs to use as compensation for the fief-holders at Fayyum. The Bedouin had been accused of trading with the Crusaders and, consequently, their grain was confiscated and they were forced to migrate westward. Later, Ayyubid warships commanded by Husam waged against Bedouin river pirates who were plundering the shores of Lake Tanis."

"What is Ramadan?" Ayleth asked.

"Ramadan, 'tis in the ninth month of the Muslim year, during which strict fasting is observed in daylight hours. Almost all Muslims try to give up bad habits during Ramadan and some will pray more or read the Qur'an. Ramadan fell on the 19th of January in 1181," the old man answered.

"And have I understood correctly, that Saladin not only fought Christians but other Muslims, for I did not know this before," Ayleth continued.

"That is very correct, just as too many Christian kings fight each other, their Muslim contemporaries do likewise. So Saladin could never relax from conflict both from outside and within. In the summer of 1181, Saladin's former palace administrator Qara-Qush led a force to arrest Majd al-Din, a former deputy of Turansha in the Yemeni town of Zabid, while he was entertaining Imad ad-Din at his estate in Cairo. Saladin's intimates accused Majd al-Din of misappropriating the revenues of Zabid, but Saladin himself believed there was no evidence to back the allegations. He had Majd al-Din released in return for a payment of eighty thousand dinars. In addition, other sums were to be paid to Saladin's brothers al-Adil and Taj al-Muluk Buri. The controversial detainment of Majd al-Din was a part of the larger discontent associated with the aftermath of Turansha's departure from Yemen and subsequent early death in Alexandria. Although his deputies continued to send revenues from the province, internal conflict grew between Izz al-Din Uthman of Aden and Hittan of Zabid. Saladin wrote in a letter to al-Adil arguing how they had conquered Yemen which was a treasure house yet had seen no reward or advantage in obtaining it only expenses in troops et cetera. Saif al-Din had died earlier in June 1181 and his brother Izz al-Din inherited leadership of Mosul as a direct consequence. On December the fourth, the crown-prince of the Zengids, as-Salih, died in Aleppo but prior to his death, he had his chief officers swear an oath of loyalty to Izz al-Din, as he was the only Zengid ruler strong enough to oppose Saladin. Izz al-Din was welcomed in Aleppo, but possessing it and Mosul put too great a strain on his abilities. He thus handed Aleppo to his brother Imad al-Din Zangi, in exchange for Sinjar. Saladin offered no opposition to these transactions in order to respect the treaty he previously made with the Zengids. It was always a game of cat and mouse for Saladin and his position was always under threat," the old man explained. [85]

"You sound as though you admire him?" the farrier said bluntly.

"I do and I make no apology for that fact. I am sure King Richard will likewise come to admire and respect him also just as many who have actually met him do," the old man replied instantly.

"You think so?" the farrier shot back cynically.

"We know so!" both the Templar and Hospitaller responded in tandem. They looked at each other and laughed.

"So on a happier note. Did Percival and Nyla marry? Was it a grand affair... what did she wear?" Sarah asked excitedly, changing the subject. Stephan shook his head, smiling at her.

"Yes they married. Not so much a lavish affair," the old man replied. "Nyla had spoken at length with Alisha about her wedding day and she wanted hers to be conducted in the same fashion. With Oathing Stones, beside water, virtually the same words and everything. But there were surprises in store that day, and some very notable guests," the old man finished and rubbed his chin.

Cairo, Egypt, January 1181

Paul, dressed in a fine cream and gold silk robe, knocked on Percival's door. Everyone else was waiting near to the lake shore a short distance from the rear entrance. Alisha held Arri as Philip nodded at Paul.

"Sister Lucy will let us know when Nyla is ready but make sure he is there within the next five minutes. We have some important guests in attendance this day," Philip said as he ushered Alisha toward the exit.

Paul knocked harder upon Percival's door. After a few moments stood in silence, Paul slowly opened the door to see Percival dressed in his full armour looking very smart, but kneeling in prayer. The room was fairly dark as the afternoon sun had moved behind the outer wall. Quietly Paul shut the door and walked over to Percival as he continued to mutter words in prayer. Paul knelt down beside him and placed his hand upon his shoulder.

"Percy. It is time. Everyone is in place and waiting," Paul said softly.

Percival sniffed, opened his eyes and looked at Paul, his eyes full of emotion and looking fearful.

"I cannot do this," he suddenly blurted out.

"What? In heaven's name why not? You love Nyla do you not?" Paul asked, confused and shocked.

"More than life itself. That is why she deserves better than me."

"What? What rubbish are you speaking?"

"'Tis not rubbish but true," Percival replied and looked down as tears ran across his cheeks. He sniffed again and wiped his sleeve across his face. "I am not who you think I am...and...and your father tells me we have honoured guests attending who claim to know me, yet they do not."

"Percival, you are not making any sense. What are you saying?" Paul asked, puzzled, and pulled Percival's face to look at him.

"My friend. I have lied to all of you and the shame is too much to bear. I cannot inflict my shame upon Nyla when I am exposed this day."

Paul's mind raced as he recalled the words of the female beneath Jerusalem that told him Percival lies but that he is a good man. He shook his head.

"Percy...I know not what lies you speak of, nor do I need to know...but I know you are a good brave and noble man. And there is a woman out there who loves you more than her own life. Whatever lies you speak of, 'tis not important today. It is what you do and how you live now that is important."

"Paul...I have lied to all of you. I am not what you think."

"Really pray tell how so. For I know you as an honourable and brave man and one who saved my life. That is all I need to know," Paul replied and rubbed his hand across Percival's shoulders.

"No. I am a deceiver of the worst kind," Percival cried and rubbed his eyes with his hands.

"Tell me how so."

"I am not Percival. I am just a lowly humble squire...who...who..." Percival tried to explain and paused as he caught his breath. "Your father tells me a certain Queen Tamar from Georgia is here to seek truces and terms with Saladin. Your father and Theodoric know her well and have invited her to this wedding. She will recognise me and know that I am not the Percival she knows of," Percival explained, shaking his head, with panic written across his ashen white face. "Everything I have struggled and fought so hard for, I am about to lose. The Lord takes his vengeance just as Lord Balian said so long ago," Percival said, his nose running and tears falling from his eyes.

Paul grabbed him hard with his hands and pulled him around forcibly and looked at him as he shook him to open his eyes.

"Look at me, Percy. I do not claim to understand what you are telling me, but I do know you are a good, noble and honourable man who has shown me nothing less...and you have my support and I will back you all the way. But you cannot run away from this today. You will go out there and you will front it when you meet this Queen Tamar whoever she is. My father says she is a godly woman. She may not recognise you but she will recognise the good man that stands before her."

"I cannot. I have lied to Thomas…all of his men…," Percival cried.

"You think we did not know that?" Thomas suddenly interrupted as he opened the door fully and stepped into view. Percival's eyes widened in alarm as his jaw dropped in shock. Paul looked up at him as he slowly walked nearer. "Percy…do you honestly think us that blind that we did not see how naive and untrained you were when we first met you? Stand up, boy!"

Percival looked at Paul, confused. Paul helped him stand up straight.

"What are you saying?" Percival sniffed.

"You had ill fitting armour clearly not made for you, you did not know the basics of sword fighting and soldiering. You were like a pup amongst a pack of wolves," Thomas explained quietly and smiled. Percival looked at Paul again and back at Thomas totally speechless. "But you showed great promise and real courage. We all have a past. Some choose to forget it and start again. That much we knew and accepted for that is all we needed to know. You have more than proved yourself worthy of being called a knight…perhaps more honourable than most of us," Thomas continued to explain and placed his right hand upon Percival's left shoulder and looked him in the eye. "Now honour us and our faith in you by getting your virginal arse down to the lake and marry that woman before one of us misfits does."

"Is there anything about me you do not know?" Percival asked, wiping his nose.

"Much I am sure…but enough to know we have your loyalty and that is all we need to know. You can best most of us in combat now and we are proud to count you as one of us. When we asked you to join us, we knew then you were keeping things back from us…but we are all guilty of that to one degree or another. We judge a man by what he does…his actions and as Tenno keeps banging on, 'tis the intention. Your intentions toward us have been nothing but admirable and honourable, and that is how it shall remain! We shall deal with any comments this queen may say," Thomas said reassuringly as Percival let out a nervous laugh. "In time, when you are ready, then you can tell us about your true past…now go."

"Here, wipe your face dry," Paul remarked as he handed Percival a small handkerchief.

Percival cleared his nose and wiped his eyes. Took a deep breath and looked at them both in silence. He was lost for words.

"We'll follow you down," Thomas said and patted Percival on the back as he ushered him out of the room.

ꕤ

Paul stood just behind Percival's right shoulder as Thomas stood behind his left side. Percival's eyes darted from side to side as he walked towards Theodoric, who was waiting stood inside a circled off area just a short distance away from the lake's shoreline. On either side stood all of Thomas's men and several Mamluk guards. Philip stood to the side dressed in his full Naval Templar's outfit. To his left at the front, Percival could not believe his eyes when he realised that both Saladin and Husam were stood beside a tall and slender young women dressed in expensive attire. His heart jumped and he gulped hard standing still momentarily as he feared the woman turning and exposing him. He was surprised that Saladin himself was even present but the woman, if she was indeed Queen Tamar, made his stomach knot. Thomas prodded him in the back to move forward. Percival gulped again and slowly walked towards Theodoric. Percival looked at Luke nervously as he winked at him.

"You are going to your wedding not your execution," Luke joked and patted him on the shoulder as he passed.

"But I have lied to all of you," Percival whispered.

"We have all lied at some time about something. We are only interested in what you do now and have done since we met you. Now shut the fuck up and marry Nyla," Thomas whispered back.

As Percival neared Saladin, he turned to face him and part bowed his head. Queen Tamar turned slightly and looked at him. Percival quickly smiled nervously and looked away to his right as hard as he could and nodded at Philip. Theodoric motioned for Percival to stand to his left with his back to the assembled members. He stood bolt upright and dared not look left at Queen Tamar. Paul looked at her as she smiled and bowed her head slightly. It was the first time he had seen her himself. His father had spoken of her and her beauty. As she smiled at him, the thin lace head cover blew back but held in place by a single silver head band, her dark hair blowing back gently, Paul thought it was Alisha. He blinked and had to look again. Even her smile was the same as Alisha's. Paul bowed his head slightly as she looked at him intently. His father had explained that Saladin had Queen Tamar visiting him and that all women love a wedding and had basically invited himself and her along. Percival remained frozen with his hands clasped across his stomach. When Nyla started to approach from behind escorted by her father and Sister Lucy, Alisha beckoned Paul to stand beside her next to Philip. Looking at Alisha and then back at Queen Tamar, Paul could not escape the fact of the clear similarity between them. He clasped Alisha's hand tightly and kissed Arri on his cheek quickly before turning to watch Nyla approach. The hues of yellow from the afternoon sun added a warm and gentle feel to the setting and she looked beautiful in a long simple cream dress and head veil. Her father could hardly contain the large grin upon his face. It reminded Paul of his marriage to Alisha. He studied her face closely as she stood holding Arri in her arms. Her cheek raised as she smiled knowing Paul was looking at her. As soon as Nyla was positioned beside Percival, Theodoric looked at everyone to make sure all were silent. Several of Thomas's men and Mamluk guards formed up in a semi-circle just as the knights had done for Paul's wedding. Paul looked at everyone and thought how wonderful this moment was and what exalted company they were in. Theodoric and Philip had gone to a lot of trouble to make the event as special as they could. 'Very surreal,' he mused just as Percival turned to look at him. Paul winked and smiled as Percival returned a nervous smile then turned to face Nyla. As Theodoric started the service, Paul looked across at Queen Tamar as she studied Percival, looking puzzled. Paul had many questions he wanted to ask Percival but they could wait. Queen Tamar looked at Paul and their eyes met. She had an absolute air of authority about her and confidence for someone so young. She raised an eyebrow as if to acknowledge Paul and smiled, holding her stare. It was like looking at a double of Alisha. Philip noticed them looking at each other.

ஐ

As the ceremony drew to a close, Nyla's mother cried supported by Sister Lucy as Percival and Nyla threw into the lake their Oathing Stones. Nyla's father could not have been prouder as he looked on. Paul could not help himself from looking at Queen Tamar. Her escort and guards stood some way back but ever watchful. After Theodoric concluded the ceremony, Percival lifted Nyla's small white veil and kissed her, which was immediately met by loud applause from Thomas and his men. Thomas tried to calm them as Saladin watched on bemused. Percival led Nyla back towards the main house followed by several Mamluk guards and then Saladin and his escort with Queen Tamar at his side. Paul went to move when Philip held him back. Alisha looked at him, puzzled.

2 - 1

"Alisha, please. You go with Arri and Sister Lucy. We shall be along presently," Philip explained and held Thomas back also.

Within minutes, Philip stood surrounded by Paul, Thomas and his men. Theodoric stepped forwards with a small leather satchel and started to unbuckle it. He took out a handful of yellow and black knight's headbands that had a thinner Crimson Thread running throughout the pattern. As he handed them to Philip, Thomas looked at him then Paul bemused. Paul shrugged his shoulders just as puzzled.

"Gentlemen. It has not gone unnoticed the dedicated and loyal service you have shown Alisha and Paul these past two years," Theodoric explained as he handed Philip the last headband.

"Indeed, gentlemen. And in gratitude for that service, and as approved at the highest level within the Order, and if you are willing to accept of course, it is my great privilege to bestow upon all of you here present the band of the Crimson Thread," Philip explained.

"The what of what?" Luke asked, confused.

"'Tis a great and rare honour very few are given. 'Tis only awarded to knights considered worthy," Theodoric answered.

"Worthy of what?" Thomas asked, just as confused.

"As guardians and real protectors of a great secret," Philip replied.

"Must be a great secret then for we have no bloody idea what you are on about," John interrupted as he pushed himself forwards.

"You watch over and protect Alisha and Arri. You have done so and do so for no gain without question or having been asked. You do it willingly and at great risk for there are those who wish them dead, yet you remain. And the Order sees that as a great service and one which must be recognised. Now I know that personally you all swear no allegiance to any single king or order, but as a show of respect I am asked to present you with knightly headbands to wear if you so choose. It does not make you affiliated nor bound to us, but shows you accept our thanks. You may do with them as you see fit afterwards and should you ever require the Order's assistance, present the band and it will be given freely," Philip explained and handed Thomas a band.

Thomas took the band and opened it fully. It had a small leather strap at each end and a clasp. It was thick enough to rest his Great Helmet upon just like his own leather headband. After a few moments looking at it, he raised his chain mail coif up and fitted it in position before affixing the headband around his head and adjusting it until it sat securely, the yellow and black band looking bright against the dark chain mail. The thin Crimson Thread was just visible. Thomas looked at his men in turn as they looked at the new addition.

"We are turning all fancy now…I like it," Luke joked and put his hand out to Philip for one.

Philip smiled and handed out the remainder to Thomas's men. As they all adjusted and tied them in place, Philip looked at Paul and offered him one. Paul looked at his outstretched hand where he was holding two more headbands.

"There are two there," Paul remarked.

"Yes. One for you and one for Percival," Philip replied.

"But I am not a knight," Paul said instantly.

"This is not about being a knight. This represents much more, my son," Philip explained and smiled as Theodoric nodded. "This band is recognised by Saladin as well as the king in Jerusalem. Even Reynald acknowledges what it stands for and what it affords the wearer."

Paul looked over as Saladin and Queen Tamar walked through the rear entrance to his home. He would need to be with Percival he thought if the queen was to question him.

Inside the rear courtyard, Alisha beckoned guests into the main living area, the doors swung wide open. Arri sat with Ishmael looking at the large fish in the net covered pond as Saladin spoke with Queen Tamar. Philip called Paul over as Percival affixed his own knight's headband assisted by Thomas and Luke pushing and pulling him about in an exaggerated fashion. Alarm registered in Paul's face as Queen Tamar walked towards Percival, his face dropping instantly and turning a pale ashen colour. Quickly Paul moved to stand near to Percival as Philip turned Saladin away and engaged him in conversation. Just as Paul stood near to Percival, Queen Tamar stopped and put a finger to her lips and looked at him, puzzled. Percival gulped and Nyla held his forearm tightly looking up at him concerned.

"Queen Tamar," Paul started to say as she raised her finger.

"Please...ssh! I am still just a princess really, but reign jointly with my father...but I simply wish to express my thanks at being invited to this special wedding day. Very different ceremony, but very nice. So much more enjoyable than sat around a large table," she said softly and smiled. She placed her hands across her stomach just as Alisha came and stood beside her. They exchanged a brief look at each other and smiled. "Now young sir, I am certain you were of my court. You were charged with delivering papers to Guy de Lusignan to pass on to the king in Jerusalem," she explained, looking at Percival intently. He gulped, his throat dry. His eyes met Paul's.

"Sorry to interrupt, but yes he did that. That is how we came to acquaint ourselves with Percival," Paul said trying to draw her attention away from staring at Percival as Thomas stepped closer.

"I may be young, but I am no fool," she replied clipped, but then smiled again. "I do not recognise you as the Percival that was sent from my court... the Percival I knew was taller, older...arrogant and boastful. A distasteful character...but perhaps I am mistaken?" she said and paused as she stood closer to Percival. Nyla held his forearm tighter looking concerned. "The Percival I knew was a self serving knight of greedy manner. But you sir... you sir, from what I have been told, are of a pure heart and intent. You serve for the benefit of others I am reliably informed by impeccable sources," she smiled and looked across at Saladin and Philip who both nodded at her as if to confirm her very words. "I care not for the circumstances that bring you here but know that you have my blessing and should you ever decide to return to my court, you will be made welcome for I have need of men of your true calibre," she said softly and offered her hand up.

Hesitantly Percival looked at her hand. Thomas kicked him in the shins hard drawing his attention and focus back. Percival took her hand and kissed the top of it gently. He looked at her closely as her eyes searched his. He looked to Alisha and then back at her again.

"My Queen…I am for ever indebted to you for your understanding and kind offer…and…and you look identical to Alisha," Percival replied, his voice dry and shaky.

Queen Tamar looked at Alisha. Both shrugged their shoulders and laughed lightly. Thomas kicked Percival in the shins again and coughed loudly and indicated with a nod that he should let her hand go now. Percival let go of her hand and bowed his head slightly.

"You have another queen this day," Queen Tamar said and smiled at Nyla then back at Percival. "I would like to speak with you before I leave… alone if that is acceptable?"

Percival looked at Nyla quickly as she nodded her head yes. He nodded at Queen Tamar in silence, his heart pounding so hard he could feel it pulsing in his neck.

Queen Tamar bowed her head slightly and looked at Alisha again. Both stared at each other for a few moments until Alisha laughed. Queen Tamar stepped closer to her and both studied each other. Paul looked on bemused and a little surprised at just how similar they looked. Philip noticed them together and looked on. Queen Tamar placed her hand against Alisha's back and ushered her along and started talking quietly. Both giggled, which surprised Paul. As they entered the main living area out of the sun, Paul looked at Percival. He was holding his breath and looked as though he was about to be sick.

"Breathe," Thomas said and kicked him again. Percival let out a deep sigh and half laughed as he put his arms around Nyla and kissed the top of her head. He winked at Paul, relieved. Thomas stood beside Paul. "Every man's ultimate fantasy eh…two identical twin sisters," he commented indicating towards Queen Tamar and Alisha.

Paul shot him a look of shock but Thomas just winked and smiled broadly and folded his arms. Before Paul could reply, his father tapped him on the shoulder. Quickly he turned to face him to see Saladin stood before him who was holding out a wrapped package. He offered it to Paul to take.

"'Tis a simple gift," Saladin said politely. Paul took the wrapped package. "I hope it will help you in your chosen path. It is my way of saying thank you for today. It is far easier that I am able to speak and negotiate with Queen Tamar in these more informal surroundings."

"I, I thank you," Paul replied looking bemused as Philip laughed. Thomas's remark was still echoing through his mind.

"You look troubled, my son," Philip remarked as Paul looked at the package in his hands.

"Sorry. I am fine. I am just a little overwhelmed...that I am given a gift by the great..." He paused as he looked at Saladin.

"The great, the merciful, the mighty Saladin," Saladin laughed mocking himself and patted Paul's arm. "Your father here is a greater man than I," he said and nodded at Philip, who shook his head no, smiling. "And far too modest as always. Know this, young Paul, your father may wear the armour of a Templar, but his head and heart are those of a truly free man... unbound. And you, like your father, are no enemy of mine. I have greater enemies within my own ranks and own religion to contend with. I trust your father completely and that is something I value. I see you are cut from the same cloth. My door shall remain always open to you," he finished and bowed his head slightly, stepped back a pace, nodded at Philip and then turned and walked away.

"Father...you never cease to amaze me."

༺༻

Alisha sat down at the main dining hall table as Queen Tamar paced up and down clenching her hands. Her fine dress was well made and that fact had not escaped Alisha's attention. The sun shone through the large windows flicking between her head dress as it flowed behind her.

"Is everything all right?" Alisha finally asked.

Queen Tamar stood still, clenched her hands across her chest, closed her eyes and took a deep breath. Quickly she walked over to Alisha and sat on the chair beside her and clasped her hands over hers. She looked into Alisha's eyes with an intensity and full of emotion, which took her by surprise.

"What is the matter?" she asked, concerned.

"Alisha...I have no easy way of explaining this or the time to wait so I must come straight out with what I must say. I am here to discuss terms with Saladin so that my people can travel safely and securely on their pilgrimages to Jerusalem, but in return I must swear to keep my forces firmly in my homelands and not join with the Kingdoms of Outremer against Saladin. This is not a problem for me and my father, but," she hesitated and looked down and shook her head.

"But what?"

"Alisha," Queen Tamar said quietly, almost in a whisper. "Percival, whomever he really is, for he is not the same man I sent to meet Guy, but he is a better man, and clearly honourable...so I make decisions that could have his head removed or remain."

"Percival...but he is a great man. He has saved Paul's life before and yes, Paul has always known he carries a secret, but..."

"Do not fear, Ali, for his secret shall remain safe with me. All I have heard of him is nothing but good and godly. Besides, we all have secrets."

"I don't," Alisha shot back.

"Ali...I hope you do not mind me calling you that?" Alisha shook her head no. "Good. But yes we do all have secrets...even you." Alisha frowned hard, which made Queen Tamar laugh. "You even frown as I do."

Both sat in silence for several long minutes just looking at each other.

"What is this between us?" Alisha asked puzzled.

"You know a man named Kratos, yes?"

"Yes. Why?"

"He is known in my lands also, but under a different name. I know him well and Abi Shadana."

"Abi!" Alisha said excited.

"Yes. Now did not Kratos ever tell you a secret he swore you to keep?" Queen Tamar asked and smiled. Alisha shook her head no. "Are you sure for he told me many...but one in particular. Please, think again."

Alisha struggled to recall her conversations with Kratos. Then suddenly it entered her mind like an explosion the last time she had seen him. He had taken her aside to speak with her in private. She recalled instantly now the secret he had imparted as he left. Her eyes widened immediately as emotion flooded her body with the realisation of what he had told her. She looked at Queen Tamar, her eyes beginning to glisten over with tears as she smiled and shook her head.

"He...he told me I have an elder sister," Alisha blurted out as a tear ran down her face.

"I know....me," Queen Tamar laughed emotionally as a tear ran down her cheek. "'Tis the main reason I sought to meet with Saladin here for I knew you were now here."

Alisha shook her head, the reality of what Kratos had told her appeared to be true after all. A deep sense of knowing it was true enveloped her. A million questions flooded her mind. She laughed as tears streamed down her face. Queen Tamar clenched her hands tighter then pulled her close. As they hugged each other, they both sobbed with tears of joy. A connection had been made and there was no undoing it ever.

Paul stepped into the dining hall and saw them in each other's arms crying and laughing at the same time. Slowly and quietly he moved nearer, concerned. Queen Tamar opened her eyes and smiled at him but did not move. After a few minutes Alisha sat up straight and started to wipe her eyes. Only then did she notice Paul standing nearby. As Paul looked at them, it was nearly impossible to tell them apart in the bright sunlight shining upon their tear filled faces. Philip entered the hall and walked over to them. Paul looked at him puzzled as he smiled at them.

"Will someone tell me what occurs here?" Paul blurted out.

Queen Tamar and Alisha both laughed and hugged each other again.

Port of La Rochelle, France, Melissae Inn, spring 1191

"Okay so now I am confused, Percival isn't Percival and Queen Tamar is the elder sister of Alisha!" Simon interrupted, looking confused.

"That is correct," the old man answered.

"And the mighty Saladin himself attended Percival and Nyla's wedding?" Simon asked, shaking his head disbelievingly.

"Yes," the old man nodded in reply.

"Simon, before you say any more I want you to look at something," the Templar said, his tone quiet as he reached into his own side satchel at his feet. As he removed a small cloth wrapped parcel, he looked at the old man briefly. "Here, open that. I was given that by a knight after the fall of Jerusalem and told I must bring it here when I was given my orders to come to La Rochelle."

Simon took the small package and gently unwrapped it. As he folded back the edges it revealed a black and yellow knight's headband with a Crimson Thread running throughout its length.

"This...is this the same as Philip gave to Thomas and his men?" Gabirol asked.

"It is," the old man answered.

"Things are beginning to make a bit more sense as to why my brother and I are here," the Templar commented as Simon looked at the knight's headband.

"It is?" the Hospitaller remarked questioningly, looking bemused, and shook his head.

"Who gave you this?" Simon asked as he studied the headband.

"Count Henry himself," the Templar answered. "He told me that I had to come here to La Rochelle, to bring any person of my choosing to accompany me and wait to be contacted. If I was not contacted whilst staying at this inn, then I was to board a ship back for Outremer and join King Richard's forces."

"And have you been contacted?" Miriam asked hesitantly.

"Aye, I think it safe to say I now understand I have been," the Templar answered and looked directly at the old man.

"And you are not joining the fleet are you?" Miriam asked even more hesitantly.

"No, my woman, that I am not," the Templar replied and clasped her hand tightly and kissed it. "That I am not."

Miriam sighed visibly relieved.

"What was the gift Saladin gave Paul then?" Peter asked loudly.

"'Twas a fine leather bound book. It covered all aspects of hygiene upon ships, mostly based upon Chinese and Hospitaller practices no less. It was also a manual for war fighting at sea."

"Sorry to change the question, but this Queen Tamar. How old was she and how come they were sisters? Did Philip know?" Ayleth asked in quick succession.

"Queen Tamar as I believe I mentioned before was born in AD 1160. Her mother had a love affair with Alisha's real father and she was the result. So they are in fact half sisters. But that story I am afraid will have to wait for another day, suffice it to say that Philip, Firgany and Theodoric knew full well the details."

"So Taqi is not really her brother at all?" the farrier commented.

"By blood, no," the old man replied solemnly.

"Did Taqi know?" Ayleth asked.

"Eventually he did find out."

"The book that Saladin gave Paul. Did he use it?" Gabirol asked.

The old man leaned down and reached inside his large satchel and removed a large leather bound book tied with a crimson coloured string.

"Yes he did. You will see his notes written down the margins," the old man said as he pushed the book across the table to Gabirol.

"Well I wish to know all about Percival. Where was he from really? Who was he really?" Simon asked as the Genoese sailor leaned closer to Gabirol as he untied the string and opened Paul's book.

"Look inside the cover. It is signed to Paul by Saladin himself," the old man said quietly as Gabirol opened the book.

"And this is truly Saladin's signature?" Gabirol asked as he ran his finger carefully across the large signature.

The old man simply nodded yes. Gabirol flicked through the pages as both Simon and the Genoese sailor leaned in close to also see.

"And Percival and Nyla's wedding was done in exactly the same manner as Alisha and Paul's had been done, out there?" Sarah asked and pointed to the sea.

"Exactly apart from their words being slightly different. It was a lovely service and made all the more special by those who attended it," the old man replied.

"I fear not many here would admit to having Saladin at their wedding," Peter remarked.

"I would," Simon said enthusiastically.

"Paul had become firm friends with Husam, despite their physical age difference, and Husam was likewise much respected by Saladin. It was no different from the friendship Balian and Count Raymond had with Husam and Saladin...and no one questions those friendships," the old man explained.

"I am puzzled and somewhat concerned," the Templar remarked. The old man raised his eyebrows as if to ask what. "This charge, this commission you say I have a choice to either accept or decline...does it require me to remain single and celibate?"

Miriam's reaction was instant and obvious as alarm etched itself deep into her face. The old man shook his head no and smiled.

"No not at all. You are free to take a wife with you...if you accept the commission. Both of you," he explained.

The relief from Miriam was just as immediate as she broke into a large smile.

"If we marry, I wish it to be like Alisha, Paul, Percival and Nyla had," she said quietly looking at the Templar, unable to contain the excitement in her.

"We shall not have living legends attend as they did?" the Templar replied and pulled Miriam close.

Chapter 53
Queen of Kings & the Chains that Bind Us

Cairo, Egypt, January, 1181.

Queen Tamar sat on the stone bench resting her back against the cool wall. Her golden dress shimmered in the afternoon light, the wide embroidered strip folded down her front in waves until it reached her feet. She kicked off her gold thread covered shoes and rubbed her feet together. Alisha laughed as the shoes flew across the small balcony. She looked back through the door as Tenno chased Arri playfully. Paul was downstairs with Philip and the other guests.

"I just needed a few moments alone with you. We have much to learn of each other and my stay here is limited," Queen Tamar said and beckoned Alisha to sit beside her.

"I was told that once there was talk you were to be wed to my Paul or his brother Stewart," Alisha explained.

"I know...but I had Abi argue my case that I should be the one who chooses whom I marry. You are a lucky woman for Paul is indeed very handsome."

2 - 50

"I am indeed...and now I have a sister too...and I do not know what to say or where to begin," Alisha remarked and paused for a moment. "Can you tell me of your father?" she asked hesitantly.

"Oh yes, I can do that. He still lives...and he knows I came here with the main intention of seeking you out. I told him that if I found you, which I knew I would with Philip's help, I would invite you back to my home. I was also told about you at a very early age...and that you were taken away for your own safety and survival," Queen Tamar explained quietly. "I have so few people whom I can trust."

"You can trust me," Alisha said and placed her hand upon hers.

"That I truly believe. Abi I trust, and she is my uncle's daughter, though he was killed many years back now and I never knew him."

"So Abi is related by blood to me?" Alisha asked and shook her head, surprised, as Queen Tamar smiled yes.

"Yes. She gave me this," Queen Tamar said and reached inside the top of her dress and pulled up a small bee pendant identical the one Alisha wore. Alisha lifted hers up and placed it beside Queen Tamar's. "She also gave me this," Queen Tamar then said as she moved on the stone bench, pulled the outer cover of her dress to reveal an ornate gold looking sword. "A nightmare to wear concealed but necessary," she laughed. "I was made Co-regent Queen at eighteen and I have carried this ever since."

"I was given this by Abi...though I am no queen," Alisha replied and pulled out her three pronged dagger. "Easier to conceal than yours," she laughed. She looked at Queen Tamar in silence for a few moments. "I cannot believe I really have a sister as Kratos said."

"Nor I. But it is wonderful. And my father, King George the Third, I know would love to finally meet you, but I warn you, he can be quite blunt and crude. And you may not be a queen...but if I were to die childless, there are nobles who know that you have rightful claim to the throne."

"I am no queen...so do not die anytime soon please. And your adoptive father...a real king...Crude you say! How so?"

"When he announced me as his co-regent, to protect my position of legitimacy, many in the court questioned his decision. His response was quite enlightening. Crude but effective," Queen Tamar smiled as she recalled the moment. "I am paraphrasing, and excuse my crudeness too but he said something along these lines," she said, cleared her throat and tried not to laugh. "It became quite a famous quote...It doesn't matter whether a lion is a male or a female, it will still use its horrific terrifying claws to mutilate your pathetic face in front of your entire family, rip your oesophagus from your bloody corpse with a face full of slavering curved fangs, and then do a fucking 360-degree behind-the-back pole axed ramming of your disembowelled spleen into your own arsehole." She laughed as Alisha chuckled, her eyes wide.

"Crude but succinct," Alisha laughed.

"Well it seems to have worked so far, but father has many problems with some of the arsehole nobles who are supposed to be loyal to him. In 1178 he put down a rebellion and was forced to execute several conspirators. That is when he made me co-regent. That is when I got a crown and this sword. When it was presented to me, he made me swear to unflinchingly decapitate anyone who tried to fuck with our family line. His words," Queen Tamar laughed.

"I have never heard a woman swear so much," Alisha laughed quietly.

"Oh I may be a queen, but it can be so liberating," she joked. "Besides, I have had to behave more like a man at times and deal with them on their own terms in language they understand. I have faced those men down who believed that a woman could not and cannot rule as we do not know anything about the world or have the mental capacity...even that we have smaller brains than men!" She paused as she thought for a moment. "But I have plans to unite my people...and the Church."

Alisha looked at her and sensed the enormous weight and burden her office placed upon her young shoulders. She did not envy her position one bit.

"I can consider myself lucky to lead a simple life," Alisha said as she held Queen Tamar's hand. "And I cannot get over how much we look alike despite different mothers."

"Our father's blood runs through us strongly. And I envy you...I would swap my existence for yours in a heartbeat." Alisha looked at her, puzzled by her remark. "I am but a couple of years older than you at most, yet I have had to send men to the dungeons and command an army against my foes. The blood of men is upon my hands already and is a power I would rather not wield. Many nobles, who had wasted their time talking like idiots when they should have been building an army to challenge me, were all arrested and thrown into dungeons. But I eventually pardoned them, but not before stripping them of their power and replacing them with men, and women, loyal to me...It was something I did not enjoy."

"That is what makes you a great queen."

"I hope so," Queen Tamar replied sadly and looked down. "And now I am being pressured to marry and continue my line...but no man has my heart. That is why I envy you with your Paul. I would swap places in a heartbeat like I said for what you have with him."

"I am sure you will find a man of your own in time," Alisha replied awkwardly.

"No, not in my position. Men see a queen first, a woman second and then me, though me as a person is not even considered."

"Then when we can, I shall come and visit you and we shall seek out a genuine man for you," Alisha said, smiling, trying to raise her spirits. Her mind drifted to thoughts of Nicholas.

"My sister…that sounds so lovely…my sister!" Queen Tamar said quietly as she looked at her. "But many nobles have already chosen a union for me. Yuri, Prince of Novgorod. But I delay my replies…he is very tall and handsome, but, but a little too stupid for my liking," she said and laughed. "It would also be very dangerous for you to visit me openly at this moment in time, but when I have established some new rules, I shall call for you and to meet my father in our capital, Tbilisi. But I can return here to visit you, if you will allow it?"

"Of course I allow it," Alisha shot back instantly. She could sense the heartache in Queen Tamar as she sat looking at her intently. "I have so many questions I wish to ask," she sighed and shivered.

"It is getting cold. Darkness falls quickly here. Let us rejoin the main party shall we? And I have many questions of you," Queen Tamar replied and feigned a brave smile.

Suddenly a loud report rang out and a bright burst of yellow and red sparkles lit up the area opposite the balcony making both Queen Tamar and Alisha jump. A whoosh noise sounded out followed by another loud report and more bright coloured sparkles burst out in a large circle. Both rushed to the edge of the balcony to see Tenno lighting another firework rocket. He stood back, waved at Queen Tamar and Alisha as the rocket shot upwards and exploded in another bright display. Several dogs started barking in the distance. Paul stepped into view holding Arri and pointing at the fireworks. Alisha's gaze fell upon Percival and Nyla stood arm in arm watching the display. Today had to be one of the most enjoyable and memorable days of her life, she thought, and then looked at Queen Tamar. She was beautiful and just for a minute her heart skipped a beat with the fear that Paul could fall for her, as she looked so much like her, and was a queen. She shook her head to clear that thought.

༄༅

Paul lit a lanthorn in his office as Philip moved along the rear wall bench, Theodoric shuffling beside him grinning broadly. Tenno closed the door quietly behind him as he entered the room.

"I think Ali and Tamar will be speaking long into the early hours," Theodoric said as he made himself comfortable and rested his elbows upon the table.

"Arri sleeps soundly. Lucy watches over him," Tenno explained as he sat himself down on a single chair at the end of the table.

"It has been a long day," Paul remarked as he sat opposite his father. Theodoric pulled a bottle of wine closer and opened it as Paul pushed him a blue glass. Tenno declined a glass as Philip pulled one close. "We have some rosehip water," he said to Tenno but he raised his hand no. "All our guests have now departed. I think they all had a good time."

"Queen Tamar's guards are all still outside," Tenno stated and indicated with his thumb behind him.

"Fearsome lot eh?" Theodoric remarked as he poured himself and Philip some wine.

"But loyal," Philip said as he smelt the wine. "And by now Alisha will know she does indeed have a sister."

"Yes…all a bit of a surprise. One of several today," Paul commented as he poured himself some rosehip water.

"Firgany and I did warn you back in La Rochelle there were many things we wished to tell you. Things I think only now are you ready to be told," Philip said quietly as Theodoric nodded in agreement.

"I want to know why Alisha was never told that Raja was her real mother and that her real father had sired another daughter. Why hide that from her for so long?" Paul asked, staring at Philip.

"For her own safety…and as Raja begged us. You have no idea of the bloodshed caused and lost before your births. There are still those in Georgia, nobles, who would use Alisha to further their own political ambitions to remove both Tamar and her father," Theodoric explained.

"But Alisha would never agree to that," Paul stated.

"What if they held Arri as ransom, or you?" Philip asked. "What if it was known that Alisha has the blood of Christ running through her veins, as parchments and other documents in Tamar's possession claim?"

"She would be hunted down by all sides…," Theodoric commented and took a large mouthful of wine before placing the glass back down hard and looking at Paul. "You understand that your bloodlines must be protected and must continue so that in the future, then, and only then, can your line be revealed and used for the purpose it was intended."

"You make us sound like a line of horses being specially bred," Paul remarked.

"You are," Theodoric replied and raised his eyebrows.

"Paul," Philip said softly and leaned forward. "We never wanted Alisha to find out about her real father or that she had a sister. But we could not stop Tamar in her desire to meet her only sibling. But her best chance of survival is to remain in the shadows of history. So that you can all share and enjoy a stable and safe happy life together. And you, you must find a way of ensuring that, as well as finding a way of making certain that the real hidden history remains just that, for future generations' benefits. If not, it will be eradicated and vanish forever. And as I have repeatedly tried to explain, who controls the past does indeed control the future. Our past shapes and moulds our perceptions and affects just how we move, act and live in the future."

"I know all of that, Father...I have also dreamt and experienced many strange things about that very fact. But I still cannot find a way that will enable us to carry forwards, in secret, all that must be," Paul sighed and placed both hands around his glass of rosehip water. He paused for a few moments in silence. "Though I do have an idea that may work."

"Then pray tell you inform us," Tenno said bluntly.

"Tenno, it was you who told me that a true master, a warrior who has complete control of himself, no longer requires the use of his sword. That a master can put away his armour and swords...," Paul explained. Tenno nodded in agreement. "Then we have to move away from the secrets being guarded by men at arms. We have to find a way of organising both men and women into a society, secret if needs be to start with, where weapons are the last resort. Where all are equal when they gather regardless of position, background, wealth or religion. Where when they meet, all the worldly aspects of life are left outside. It will be made up of men who create, design, build, trade. I don't know exactly, but a brotherhood of mutual respect and honour."

"What happens when you get an unscrupulous individual worm his way into that group and abuses the secrets imparted to him...or her?" Theodoric asked.

"Then you set up various levels within the group, just as the Templars, Hospitallers and Ashashin do. They can only progress to the next level when and only when they have proved themselves worthy and trustful to learn deeper secrets and meanings. Father, you already do this within the Order, like the upper initiates' circles and within the hidden codes you display so openly within your church and cathedral designs. As you once said, hidden in plain view."

"And this group would have no religious affiliation?" Tenno asked.

"Exactly. Perhaps a single belief in a god being the only requirement, but no affiliation to one religion when in the group meeting. All of that must be left outside. To promote freedom of expression and discussion but also to learn fully and openly the secrets from our past without all the attached restrictions and dogma attached. Does that not make sense…and no weapons," Paul explained. "And you can use the allegorical symbolism within Grail romances and similar stories surely such as you already write. We would take good men and women, and make them better men and women."

Philip looked at Theodoric in silence for a few moments.

"But you would need to establish a totally free and neutral country to be able to carry out this venture unhindered for it to survive," Philip commented.

"Yes, but until that time, you make all members swear to a code of honour and secrecy, just as Templars do," Paul replied.

"I can see you have given this some thought after all," Theodoric remarked and took another mouthful of wine.

"Oh Theo you have no idea how much time for I am haunted nightly by dreams on it."

"You know Princess Stephanie's father, Philip de Milly, tried to do what you are proposing," Philip said looking at Paul. Paul shook his head he did not know. "'Tis why he resigned from the Order. He did so hoping that like you, he could found an Order on similar lines and without it being an armed one."

"But he died in Constantinople…," Paul remarked.

"Yes, trying to establish the very same you now propose. He gave up the sword and resigned all his positions," Philip continued to explain.

"Does Stephanie know this?" Paul asked as thoughts of her entered his mind.

"Yes she knew, but keeps it a secret as there are many who simply cannot and will not accept what he tried to do," Philip answered.

"Though he did have some success in setting in motion, with Count Henry, the foundations for a neutral state. That much he succeeded in doing," Theodoric said and looked at Philip for his confirmation. He nodded in agreement. "They penned the name Switzerland, though the area in question is presently still several fiefdoms...but ripe for forming the new neutral country. You may consider that as your starting ground?"

"Then I shall write down my ideas," Paul said solemnly. "Where the order will be made up from master builders instead of master swordsmen...or is that naive of me?"

"Philip de Milly did not think so and died believing that," Theodoric said and raised his glass as a toast, then sipped some wine.

"We simply need find good men who would sign up to the idea and its principles of construction, to build, rather than to destroy," Paul said, looking at his father.

"My son, of that there are many...believe me on that point," Philip said and smiled proudly as he reached over and placed his hand upon Paul's shoulder. "Of that I can promise you."

"Percival...he will be one, I know," Paul stated.

"Perhaps. Perhaps indeed," Philip replied and winked at Paul.

"Much changes," Tenno said and clasped his hands together as he always did when he had something to say. "Changes that I must also undertake. That is why, with your permission and hopeful blessing, I shall be leaving with Queen Tamar when she departs."

"What?" Theodoric demanded, looking shocked, and sat up straight.

"My good friend Theo, once known as Ric," Tenno said and nearly smiled. "I grow fat and slow here. I am an adventurer and adventure calls me to serve another now. I have done all I swore I would do have I not?" he asked, looking at Philip.

"And more," Philip acknowledged.

"But we need you here," Theodoric shot back.

"No. Not anymore. You are all well protected by Thomas and his knights as well as the assured friendship of Saladin himself. Queen Tamar needs my assistance now I feel. If she will accept me of course. Plus I fear I grow too fond of Arri and he of me. 'Tis a bond that should be between father and son," Tenno commented and looked directly at Paul.

"That is absurd, Tenno. Absurd!" Paul finally replied after a long silence.

"Maybe, but still true. I will return to visit you when Queen Tamar returns or when you visit her in her lands. I shall also spend some time with Al Rashid as he requested. To get myself back in shape. My armour no longer fits I am getting so large," Tenno explained, his face expressionless, which Paul knew he did when hiding his true feelings. "Do I have your permission?"

Paul looked at Tenno. He would miss him greatly and the very thought shot through his chest like a bolt. Arri would likewise be devastated.

"Tenno, you do not need my permission to leave. You are and always have been master of your own destiny and there are no chains here that bind you," Paul said, his voice dry.

"Only the chains of love that bind me here. Chains that will forever remain bound to you, to you all," Tenno said, his tone clipped as he controlled his emotions.

Paul stood up and moved to stand beside Tenno. Tenno looked up at him puzzled, almost nervous looking. Paul wrapped his arms around Tenno and hugged him tightly. Tenno remaining sat bolt upright, his arms hung in the air.

"You will be sorely missed, my greatest of friends," Paul said quietly. "But if you must leave, then leave us knowing you are loved, admired and respected and always, always welcome in our home. Your home," Paul said and stood up. Tenno still sat with his arms outstretched unsure what to do. He had tears in his eyes.

Slowly and silently Tenno stood up. Bowed his head slightly at Philip, then at Theodoric and then stood facing Paul. His bottom lip quivered as he went to speak but words failed him. If he spoke he knew he would cry… something Tenno did not do in public. Paul just nodded at him. Tenno nodded back, bowed and left the room. Paul turned and looked at his father and Theodoric utterly perplexed at Tenno's sudden announcement. Theodoric shook his head sadly and poured himself another glass of wine. Philip stood up slowly and feigned a smile of support to Paul.

"My son, today you have gained a great sister-in-law…but lost a close companion. That is the way in this world. But you have also revealed a great idea for a new order. You must concentrate upon that for it shall bear fruit of that I have no doubt," Philip said sympathetically.

"No, Father, I have not lost a great companion for he will be forever carried in here," Paul said as emotion welled up inside him when he placed his hand across his chest.

Port of La Rochelle, France, Melissae Inn, spring 1191

"Oh no! We can't lose Tenno from this tale. I like him the most," Simon interrupted the old man loudly.

"I'm liking the sound of this Queen Tamar," the Genoese sailor remarked, grinning.

"And she actually has parchments with the bloodline of Christ?" Gabirol asked.

"Yes she does, as the Pope knows full well. Identical ones were also hidden around La Rochelle before Philip had them removed and hidden elsewhere as I explained earlier," the old man explained.

"I sense that this new order Paul speaks of is now already in motion, yes?" the Templar asked as he held up his envelope.

"Partly...but it is in need of great men," the old man answered and nodded at the Templar with a smile that made it obvious he was referring to him and his brother. "As I said at the very start of this tale, I would at the end of it ask of you all one request, and that request is directly related to the Order Paul helped develop, for it was not his alone, but I shall come to that in good time."

"I'm in. Seriously, count me in!" Simon interjected enthusiastically.

"All men...regardless of background?" Sarah quizzed with a mocking face as she looked at Simon.

"All men!" the old man stated.

"And what of Percival? I am greatly intrigued about his true past. Do you know of it and if so, would you tell us?" Gabirol asked as he moved Paul's book from Saladin forwards slightly.

"I know of it and yes I can tell you if you so desire as now would be appropriate," the old man answered. "You see, Perceval, or Percival as most call him, as a child living not far from Queen Tamar's capital, would often watch knights pass through the forest near his house where he lived alone with his mother. She had lost most of the men in her life to war and quests, so kept herself and Percival isolated and secluded...but it was her very explanations of the knight's job that inspired a wanderlust in Percival. His name was Gauvin but he was sent to be the squire of a knight sent by Queen Tamar to quest in the Holy Land but also deliver important documents to the King of Jerusalem and her own subjects who resided in the city. Percival's character demonstrated justice, eloquence and diplomacy in total contrast to the arrogant knight he was to serve. But as fate would have it, one morning on their journey together, Gauvin tried to wake his master, but he had died in his sleep. He had drunk too much wine and mead beer, vomited and choked himself to

death. Carefully, Gauvin buried him, cleaned his armour and tied it to his horse, took the sealed messages and vowed to complete the task given to Percival. When he traversed the Caucasus Mountains, the cold forced him to put on Percival's green outer surcoat and mantle to keep warm. When he finally met up with Lord Balian's convoy, which included Guy de Lusignan, he was almost incoherent and exhausted, full of the chill and poorly. He collapsed. When he came round in Lord Balian's tent, he was addressed as Percival. Too tired to argue, Gauvin simply slept. When he did come round, he tried to explain to Guy who he was but Guy had little time to listen and dismissed him out of hand and ordered him to join the ranks and form up. And that is how Percival came to be where he is now. He thought he would simply deliver the messages and return home. But then his path crossed Paul's, and the rest you know," the old man explained.

2 - 16

"So his secret remained safe with Queen Tamar. He was indeed fortunate," Peter remarked.

"His secret remained safe," the old man said and shook his head.

Cairo, Egypt, January 1181

The morning air was fresh as a cool wind blew in from the coast. Paul stepped down from the front step into the wide street where Queen Tamar's escort and caravan were already formed up and waiting for her. Queen Tamar's escort looked impressive with their lamellar armour, green surcoats and green horse covers, which had apples and wheatsheaf emblems upon them. Their kite shields were burnished silver with a large ornate cross emblazoned upon them. Philip approached on foot leading his horse along with Tenno and his horse. Arri waved Clip clop frantically at Tenno as they neared. Tenno looked even more serious than his usual self. Paul knew he was struggling to keep his emotions in check just as Queen Tamar and Alisha stepped through the large front door and into the street. Queen Tamar had changed into a lighter more comfortable dress and small head cover for her coming journey. She held Alisha's hands tightly. Percival and Nyla followed them out smiling broadly arm in arm. Several Mamluk guards rode up breaking into two groups, one taking up position at the vanguard and the other at the rear of the small column, Queen Tamar's small carriage being positioned near to her.

"'Tis time I must leave. We cannot miss the tide," she said looking at Alisha. "We shall see each other again, my sister, that I know."

"I pray the day comes sooner than later," Alisha replied and feigned a brave smile.

Tenno moved near to Paul and Arri as Arri reached out for him to take him. Tenno wrapped his reins around his wrist and took Arri. He gulped hard as Arri wrapped his little arms around him tightly as if he knew Tenno was leaving. Philip moved closer to speak.

"My son, I shall see you again soon. 'Tis a pity this visit was so short, but I have at least seen my grandson. Keep the knight's headband with you always on your travels. You never know when you may need it," Philip said and outstretched his arms.

Paul stepped forwards and hugged his father.

"Safe journey, Father," Paul said quietly, lost for words. He wanted to say something deep and meaningful but he simply could not think of anything. "I love you, Father," he said and stepped back a pace.

"I am mightily proud of you, son. And you too, Alisha. Thank you for giving me such a beautiful grandson," Philip said as he took Alisha's hand and gently kissed it.

"Thank you for helping me see my sister," Queen Tamar said and placed her hand upon Philip's as he still held Alisha's hand. "Now remember, my little sister, I meant what I said and I will have funds dispatched immediately for the dresses I have ordered."

"You have ordered much. It will take Nyla and I some time to complete," Alisha replied, smiling.

"They are fine clothes indeed and I know they will be well received," Queen Tamar said and stepped toward her small carriage. She was just about to step up, when she turned and walked back to Percival and Nyla. "Percival...I just wanted to say you are a far better knight than the knight I originally commissioned. Never doubt that fact," she said and placed her hand upon his forearm briefly.

Nyla listened puzzled but too happy to really take notice of what she was saying. Alisha handed her sister a small sealed envelope. It was a letter for her father. She knew what it was without any words being spoken. Quickly Queen Tamar hugged Alisha, kissed her on the cheek and immediately boarded her carriage for the short journey to the harbour. As she closed the door, she sat back out of sight but not before Alisha saw her wipe a tear away as she closed the net curtain across the window.

"We must be away," Tenno stated as he handed Arri back to Paul.

Philip wiped his finger down Arri's cheek gently then kissed him on the forehead. Arri kept waving Clip clop.

"Tenno!" Arri suddenly said aloud, which caught everyone by surprise as he had never spoken his name before.

Tenno's eyes widened and Philip laughed as he patted his shoulder. Philip then mounted his horse and steadied himself as Tenno likewise mounted his horse. He almost smiled at Arri's comment.

"Until we meet again," Philip said, bowed his head and pulled his horse into the column behind the small carriage.

Tenno looked down at Arri in Paul's arms. Arri smiled at him and waved Clip clop again. Tenno simply nodded his head and pulled his horse over beside Philip. With a slight nod at Paul and Alisha, the small convoy started to pull away. Within moments the whole column disappeared around the corner of the street and apart from a small amount of dust in the air, all was silent and still. Paul felt a tug at his heart both for his father and Tenno. Percival had his arms around Nyla clearly still thinking upon Queen Tamar's words to him.

"Have they all gone?" Theodoric called out as he stepped down from the front door and stood beside Alisha. Paul nodded yes as Sister Lucy appeared. "Good. I hate goodbyes," he remarked, coughed and placed his hands upon his hips. "Good!"

Sister Lucy shook her head no at Paul behind Theodoric and placed her hand across her chest indicating Theodoric was in fact saddened by their departure.

Port of La Rochelle, France, Melissae Inn, spring 1191

"And just like that they were gone?" Ayleth asked.

"Yes. Just like that. Alisha and Nyla now had their biggest order for their growing business, Theodoric had made his peace with Philip and Tenno had gone from their company. It was Theodoric who seemed to miss him the most and Arri of course who kept saying 'Tenno' all the time. A sadness filled Paul for some weeks

after they had departed. He could not put his finger upon it, but all seemed different. Alisha was the sister of a real queen, she was related to Abi and the realisation of just how privileged his life and background had actually been really began to sink in," the old man explained.

"So what did he do?" the farrier asked.

"I wish to see the fine dresses Alisha made," the wealthy tailor said, rubbing his hands. "We have dire need of new lines in this port."

"My friend...when this tale is finished, I will give you a whole chest of her dresses and designs," the old man said and winked at him.

"So what was wrong with Paul?" Peter asked.

"There was nothing wrong with him as such...and to keep himself occupied and to not think too hard on everything, especially the details about his and Alisha's bloodlines, he lost himself in his work. He worked closely with Husam and saw Saladin frequently most of that year. He took on board what Tenno had said and made sure he spent more time with Arri. Arri learnt fast and was soon running around talking nonstop," the old man detailed and laughed to himself briefly. "Alisha and Nyla made many dresses and their business grew and grew. Paul's unique design for a ship threw up many problems, but Husam kept on pushing him and after several prototypes were built, he finally hit upon a workable solution that did indeed work."

"How do you mean?" the Genoese sailor asked.

"His design had a large main sail that was raised up from the front of the ship, its sails already fixed in place. As it was raised, the sails would unfurl without the need for ropes being tensioned by men, and it could be turned to catch the wind. But as they discovered, once in full sail, the sail had a tendency to pitch the front of the reinforced bow downwards into the water, so it could never reach its full speed potential."

"So how did he resolve that?" the Genoese sailor pressed.

"Paul designed and fitted two large sections to the outer hull at the bows. As the sails filled with air, the faster the ship moved and as it pushed downwards, the two attached sections guided at an angle, the water rushing over them pushing the whole ship in the opposite direction of upwards. And purely by chance they discovered that when it reached full speed, it actually lifted the front of the ship clear of the water, which took away a lot of the resistance, which meant it went even faster."

"By the Lords, that sounds absolutely fantastical...is that a word?" Simon stated and asked.

"It was. Years ahead of its time," the old man sighed. "When Saladin saw it,

he immediately knew its potential. But he had many other pressing issues to constantly deal with, one of course being Reynald."

"Why, what did he do?" Sarah asked.

"What didn't he do more is the question," the Templar remarked.

"On May the 11th, 1182, Saladin along with half of the Egyptian Ayyubid army and numerous non-combatants finally left Cairo for Syria...but on the evening before he departed, he sat with his companions and the tutor of one of his sons quoted a line of poetry. It read 'enjoy the scent of the ox-eye plant of Najd, for after this evening it will come no more'. Well Saladin took this as an evil omen that he would never see Egypt again. So far he has not returned. Saladin had also been tipped off that a large Crusader force was massed upon the frontier to intercept him, so he took the desert route across the Sinai Peninsula to Ailah at the head of the Gulf of Aqaba. Meeting no opposition, Saladin ravaged the countryside of Montreal, whilst King Baldwin's forces watched on, refusing to intervene. He arrived in Damascus in June and learnt that Farrukh-Shah had attacked Galilee, sacking Daburiyya and capturing Habis Jaldek, a fortress of great importance to the Crusaders. In July, Saladin dispatched Farrukh-Shah to attack Kawkab al-Hawa. Later, in August, the Ayyubids launched a naval and ground assault to capture Beirut; Saladin led his army in the Bekaa Valley. The assault was leaning towards failure and Saladin abandoned the operation to focus on issues in Mesopotamia. Then Kukbary, whom we call Gokbori, the emir of Harran, invited Saladin to occupy the Jazira region, making up northern Mesopotamia. He complied and the truce between him and the Zengids officially ended in September 1182. On 29th September 1182, Saladin crossed the Jordan River to attack Beisan, which was found to be empty, so his forces sacked and burned the town and moved westwards. They intercepted Crusader reinforcements from Kerak and Shaubak along the Nablus road and took a number of prisoners. But the main Crusader force under Guy of Lusignan moved from Sepphoris to al-Fula so Saladin sent out 500 skirmishers to harass their forces, and he himself marched to Ain Jalut. When the Crusader force, reckoned to be the largest the kingdom had ever produced from its own resources, but still outmatched by the Muslims, advanced, the Ayyubids unexpectedly moved down the stream of Ain Jalut. After a few Ayyubid raids, including attacks on Zir'in, Forbelet and Mount Tabor, the Crusaders still were not tempted to attack their main force, and Saladin led his men back across the river once provisions and supplies ran low. Prior to his march to Jazira, tensions had grown between the Zengid rulers of the region, primarily concerning their unwillingness to pay deference to Mosul. Before he crossed the Euphrates, Saladin besieged Aleppo for three days, signalling that the

truce was over. Once he reached Bira, near the river, he was joined by Gokbori and Nur al-Din of Hisn Kayfa and the combined forces captured the cities of Jazira, one after the other. First, Edessa fell, followed by Saruj, then ar-Raqqah, Karkesiya and Nusaybin. Ar-Raqqah was an important crossing point and held by Qutb al-Din Inal, who had lost Manbij to Saladin in 1176. Upon seeing the large size of Saladin's army, he made little effort to resist and surrendered on the condition that he would retain his property. Saladin promptly impressed the inhabitants of the town by publishing a decree that ordered a number of taxes to be cancelled and erased all mention of them from treasury records, stating 'the most miserable rulers are those whose purses are fat and their people thin'. From ar-Raqqah, he moved to conquer al-Fudain, al-Husain, Maksim, Durain, 'Araban, and Khabur, all of which swore allegiance to him. Saladin proceeded to take Nusaybin, which offered no resistance. A medium-sized town, Nusaybin was not of great importance, but it was located in a strategic position between Mardin and Mosul and within easy reach of Diyarbakir. In the midst of these victories, Saladin received word that the Crusaders were raiding the villages of Damascus. He replied 'Let them...whilst they knock down villages, we are taking cities; when we come back, we shall have all the more strength to fight them.' Meanwhile, in Aleppo, the emir of the city Zangi raided Saladin's cities to the north and east, such as Balis, Manbij, Saruj, Buza'a, al-Karzain. He also destroyed his own citadel at A'zaz to prevent it from being used by the Ayyubids if they were to conquer it."[86]

"'Tis a pity they did not wipe themselves out," Peter said, shaking his head disapprovingly.

"So Saladin had to fight more people of his own faith again," Sarah stated, puzzled.

"In effect yes. Muslims and others. Earlier in that year, Saladin had turned his attention from Mosul to Aleppo, sending his brother Taj al-Muluk Buri to capture Tell Khalid, sixty miles northeast of the city. The siege was set, but the governor of Tell Khalid surrendered upon the arrival of Saladin himself on May 17th before a siege could take place. After Tell Khalid, Saladin took a detour northwards to Ain Tab, but he gained possession of it when his army turned towards it, allowing it to quickly move backward another fifty miles towards Aleppo. On May 21st, he camped outside the city, positioning himself east of the Citadel of Aleppo, while his forces encircled the suburb of Banaqusa to the northeast and Bab Janan to the west. He stationed his men dangerously close to the city, hoping for an early success. Zangi did not offer long resistance. He was unpopular with his subjects and wished to return to his Sinjar, the city he governed previously. An exchange was negotiated

where Zangi would hand over Aleppo to Saladin in return for the restoration of his control of Sinjar, Nusaybin and ar-Raqqa. Zangi would hold these territories as Saladin's vassals on terms of military service. On June 12th Aleppo was formally placed in Ayyubid hands. The people of Aleppo had not known about these negotiations and were taken by surprise when Saladin's standard was hoisted over the citadel. Two emirs, including an old friend of Saladin, Izz al-Din Jurduk, welcomed and pledged their service to him. Saladin replaced the Hanafi courts with Shafi'i administration, despite a promise he would not interfere in the religious leadership of the city. Although he was short of money, Saladin also allowed the departing Zangi to take all the stores of the citadel that he could travel with and to sell the remainder, which Saladin purchased himself. In spite of his earlier hesitation to go through with the exchange, he had no doubts about his success, stating that Aleppo was 'the key to the lands' and 'this city is the eye of Syria and the citadel is its pupil'. For Saladin, the capture of the city marked the end of over eight years of waiting since he told Farrukh-Shah that 'we have only to do the milking and Aleppo will be ours'. After spending one night in Aleppo's citadel, Saladin marched to Harim, near the Crusader-held Antioch. The city was held by Surhak, a minor Mamluk. Saladin offered him the city of Busra and property in Damascus in exchange for Harim, but when Surhak asked for more, his own garrison in Harim forced him out. He was arrested by Saladin's deputy, Taqi al-Din, on allegations that he was planning to cede Harim to Bohemond the Third of Antioch. When Saladin received its surrender, he proceeded to arrange the defence of Harim from the Crusaders. He reported to the caliph and his own subordinates in Yemen and Baalbek that he was going to attack the Armenians. Before he could move, however, there were a number of administrative details to be settled. Saladin agreed to a truce with Bohemond in return for Muslim prisoners being held by him and then he gave A'zaz to Alam ad-Din Suleiman and Aleppo to Saif al-Din al-Yazkuj. The former was an emir of Aleppo who joined Saladin and the latter was a former Mamluk of Shirkuh who helped rescue him from the assassination attempt at A'zaz. As Saladin approached Mosul, he faced the issue of taking over a large city and justifying the action. The Zengids of Mosul appealed to an-Nasir, the Abbasid caliph at Baghdad whose vizier favoured them. An-Nasir sent Badr al-Badr, a high-ranking religious figure, to mediate between the two sides. Saladin arrived at the city on the 10th of November 1182. Izz al-Din would not accept his terms because he considered them disingenuous and extensive, and Saladin immediately laid siege to the heavily fortified city. After several minor skirmishes and a stalemate in the siege that was initiated by the caliph, Saladin intended to find a way to withdraw without damage to his reputation while still keeping up some military pressure. He decided to attack Sinjar, which was held by Izz al-Din's brother Sharaf al-Din. It fell after a fifteen-day siege on December the 30th. Saladin's commanders and soldiers broke their discipline, plundering the city; Saladin only managed to protect the governor and his officers by sending them to Mosul. After establishing a garrison at Sinjar, he awaited a coalition assembled by Izz al-Din consisting of his forces, those from Aleppo, Mardin and Armenia. Saladin and his army met the coalition at Harran in February 1183, but on hearing of his approach, the latter sent messengers to Saladin asking for peace. Each force returned to their cities and al-Fadil wrote: 'They, Izz al-Din's coalition, advanced like men, like women they vanished.'"

"Why do we need to know all of this?" the farrier asked, looking at everyone in turn.

"Because it was after these events that Reynald, having pushed his luck and after many deliberate provocations, thought his time had arrived to strike Saladin whilst he could. On the 2nd of March, 1183, al-Adil from Egypt wrote to Saladin that the Crusaders had struck the 'heart of Islam' after Raynald de Châtillon had sent ships to the Gulf of Aqaba to raid towns and villages off the coast of the Red Sea. It was not an attempt to extend the Crusader influence into that sea or to capture its trade routes, but merely a piratical move. Nonetheless, Imad al-Din writes the raid was alarming to the Muslims because they were not accustomed to attacks on that sea, and Ibn al-Athir adds that the inhabitants had no experience with the Crusaders either as fighters or traders."

"But I thought all Crusader harbours were monitored by Saladin to keep watch on any ship building activities...how did he get ships?" the Genoese sailor asked.

"Remember when Lord Montferrat visited Paul in Cairo along with Brother Matthew? He took notes on how to construct ships in sections inland. They took that knowledge and adapted the technique. Reynald commissioned the construction of several ships at Kerak. When they were ready, they simply moved them overland and constructed them almost instantly ready to sail," the old man explained. "Don't forget, Reynald had threatened many times to attack Medina itself and destroy Mecca."

"Mecca?" Gabirol asked.

"Yes. Saladin also received word that Reynald intended to relocate Muhammad's tomb to Crusader territory so all Muslims would have to make their pilgrimages there. Crusader attacks were deliberately orchestrated to provoke further responses by Saladin. Reynald of Châtillon, in particular, harassed Muslim trading and pilgrimage routes with a fleet on the Red Sea, a water route that Saladin needed to

keep open. In response, Saladin built a fleet of thirty galleys to attack Beirut in 1182. Reynald threatened to attack the holy cities of Mecca and Medina. In retaliation, Saladin would eventually twice besiege Kerak, Reynald's fortress in Oultrajordain, in 1183 and 1184. But I shall cover that later for it was the battle that took place in March 1183 that changed much for Paul and would lead to consequences further down the line, especially with Reynald."

Cairo, Egypt, March 1183

Alisha hugged Paul as Arri wrapped his arms around his legs screwing his face up. Husam was outside waiting with a full escort. A damp mist hung in the early morning air, the sun only just beginning to break over the horizon. Percival kissed Nyla on the lips as tears streamed down her face. Sister Lucy finished tying up a large cloth satchel full of fresh food and then gave it to Theodoric.

"I shall tie this to Adrastos securely. I will collect him from Fustat later with Luke I assure you," Theodoric said as he held the satchel high. "I wish I was coming with you."

"You are going nowhere," Sister Lucy shot back instantly and frowned hard at him.

Paul laughed and rubbed his hand through Arri's hair. He had grown so much he reached Paul's waist.

"Thomas and his men remain. They will look after you as they always have. And this action against Reynald...well, it is a deterrent. If my ship can dissuade him from his path of destruction, then surely that is good for all of us no?" Paul said as Arri squeezed his leg tighter.

Alisha looked into Paul's eyes, the sadness in them very clear to see.

"This is not your fight...please, please do not go. I would even rather you explored the passages beneath the pyramids than do this," she pleaded.

"Don't go, Papa," Arri said and looked up, his eyes large and wet with tears.

Paul's stomach knotted and turned as he looked at him. He knelt down and looked at Arri eye to eye.

"My beautiful son. I must do this. I promise you I will be home before you know it. Now I need you to be the man of the house and look after Mummy," Paul said softly and looked up at Alisha as she struggled to remain calm. She feigned a brave smile yet inside she was frantic with apprehension and worry. She bit her thumb nail. Paul lifted Arri up and looked at Alisha. "You know I have to do this. I am only going to make sure the ship works properly. I may not even see any of Reynald's forces. His actions are wrong, and rightly or wrongly, I must do what is right and help put an end to his reckless ways. Deny him access to the sea routes and he will be contained. If not, it will be him and his men that come here and destroy our way of life."

"I hate to agree with him, but sadly he is right, Ali," Percival said looking very solemn.

"We have not been apart in many years. I shall miss you," Alisha said emotionally.

"And me," Arri said and wrapped his arms around his neck tightly.

"Reynald may be a Christian and we have friends and family that fight alongside him, but he is consumed with a madness that goes beyond religion...or logic for that matter. I am not choosing a side here, but I am choosing to do what has to be done," Paul explained as Nyla started to cry. Arri looked at her and started to cry. Paul kissed the side of his face and held him close. "Arri...I promise you I shall return and soon."

"And you never make promises you cannot keep...right?" Arri asked bravely and wiped his face on his sleeve. Paul smiled at him and nodded.

"I love you, my little man," Paul said and kissed him again. "And you know I love you, my dearest. If your sister Queen Tamar can see the logic in curtailing Reynald, then I hope you can do likewise and not resent me doing this?"

Alisha leaned into Paul and kissed him on the lips.

"I have never resented you, nor shall I ever. I love you. Now go...go for the sooner you depart, the sooner you will return."

Paul put Arri down as Alisha clasped his little hand to hold him back. Percival kissed Nyla again and picked up a large case beside his feet and began to follow Paul toward the main front door. Paul took one last glance back to see Nyla sobbing being comforted by Sister Lucy and Alisha standing with Arri. Her shoulders were dropped and she looked in pain as she fought to control the emotions she was feeling. Arri looked up at her and seeing the hurt in her eyes, he kissed her hand and put his arms around her waist and rested his head against her. He looked at Paul and forced a smile. Theodoric backed himself out of the front door with the satchel and held it open as Paul and Percival walked out into the street, the mist covering them as he disappeared from view.

Outside, Paul checked Adrastos and adjusted the main straps as Percival checked his horse. Theodoric placed the satchel over the back end of Paul's saddle.

"I bet that hurt eh?" Theodoric said as Husam approached.

"You have no idea how much," Paul answered and mounted Adrastos. "Look after them for me."

"Get out of here, you daft fool…you know I will. Just make sure you come back," Theodoric shot back.

1 - 16

Husam looked at Paul through the thinning mist and nodded as if to ask if he was ready. Paul nodded back he was. He reached down and shook Theodoric's hand, looked him in the eyes and without any further words, he followed Husam as he led the troop away.

The journey to the docks at Fustat was not long, but it felt like it took forever as Paul's mind raced with many thoughts and fears. His stomach churned and every part of him simply wanted to turn Adrastos around and race back home. The past two years had flown by and he had spent every single day and night with Alisha and Arri. They had not been apart other than the few hours he spent at work each day. The ever present fear that Turansha might return or some disgruntled nobleman from Queen Tamar's court might turn up was never far from his mind. He had not even boarded his ship yet but already felt homesick. He looked at Percival riding beside him deep in his own thoughts. He was glad he was coming along with him. He had spent the past two years studying every aspect of naval warfare alongside Husam, who had repeatedly tried to commission him to his forces. Percival had always declined. He had read the book Saladin had given Paul as a gift many times. Now he was accompanying Paul as his very own naval advisor. Percival noticed Paul looking at him. He smiled and it reminded him of Taqi. He wondered how he was doing and if Tenno had indeed visited Al Rashid on his way to Georgia with Queen Tamar. Alisha had received many letters and orders from her but never once anything from Tenno nor any reply to her letter to the king. Queen Tamar wrote saying she had given him her letter, but he had still to reply. It hurt

Alisha but she also understood why he perhaps did not wish to. The mist cleared as the column neared the main port of Fustat to reveal several large ships and Paul's ship looking starkly different from all the others.

"If I wish to see Ali and Arri again, I must remain focused at all times," Paul said aloud.

Percival nodded in agreement as they approached the vessels. Both were filled with a deep sense of anticipation and excitement. Both laughed nervously at each other. Paul's eyes fell upon the large ropes that secured the vessels to the dock side. Several larger metal chains glistened beside a pool of water. They reminded Paul of the words Tenno had said about the chains of love that bind.

"Here we go then," Percival said.

Chapter 54
Baptism of Fire and Water!

Port of Aydhab, Egypt, western shores of the Red Sea, March 1183

A blood red sun shimmered on the eastern horizon reflecting on the calm waters of the Red Sea as it slowly broke above the far shore. Paul stood beside Percival and Husam on the foredeck of Husam's Dromon command ship. Several other ships were tied up alongside with Paul's ship secured stern on next to Husam's ship.

"His fleet is out there and this day we shall put an end to that mad man's rampages," Husam said quietly as he grasped the wooden balustrade and strained his eyes to the horizon.

Paul could see the determination in his eyes.

"And we are good with this...attacking our own kind?" Percival asked.

Husam looked at him, his eyes narrowing quizzically.

"'Tis not your kind we are about to stop. 'Tis an animal that needs to be tamed...if not, he will bring death upon many of both our kind. If you cannot see that, I suggest you stay behind. No one will think any the less of you," Husam said politely.

Percival started to unfasten his outer surcoat. Quickly he removed all of his chain mail as Paul looked on bemused.

"What are you doing?" Paul asked.

"I fight to protect what I love and care about. I know what Reynald does and intends to do...and if we are to stop him this day...then we need to ditch all of this heavy gear," he explained as his chain mail fell to the deck with a heavy thud. "I would advise you the same in case we end up in the water...look," Percival said pointing to Husam.

"He is correct. You will see that I too wear none on board," Husam replied, motioning his hands up and down himself and pulling his surcoat open to show he only wore a leather padded gambeson. "We have thirty ships at my disposal, thirty-one including yours, and as Saladin fights on several fronts, his reputation is everything...and I am commanded to resolve this matter with Reynald and keep our pilgrim routes open and free. This port, 'tis a gateway for many pilgrims travelling to Medina and Mecca. Reynald knows this. Plus he would love to take this port for its close proximity to all the old Egyptian gold mines at Wadi Allaqi a short distance from here."

"I knew gold would come into the equation somewhere," Percival commented.

"I am not sure what my vessel can do this day for she is not a fighting vessel," Paul said as he started to help Percival unfasten his chain mail chausses.

"If you are willing, with the speed of your vessel, I would ask that you patrol the waters and pass back and forth messages, for my fleet will be spread out. I need to know I can regroup them all fast when we locate Reynald's fleet. Can you do this?" Husam asked.

"We can certainly try," Paul answered as Percival nodded.

"Do you require more men?" Husam asked as two of his naval officers approached.

"No. It was designed to be sailed by just one person if needs be. Plus less weight and we can move faster," Paul replied.

"My Lord," one of the naval officers said and bowed his head briefly. "We have word Reynald intends to intercept the next ferry crossing of pilgrims, which is full of women and children. Shall we delay their departure?" he asked.

Husam looked out across the open water to the horizon.

"If we hold them back, we just delay the inevitable and Reynald will wait until another day. No...they must sail and we shall shadow them. Let Reynald come to us."

"How did you find this out?" Paul asked, puzzled.

"One of Turansha's men...of course," the naval officer answered, looking surprised that Paul had even asked such a question.

Paul shot a look of shock at Percival. Husam saw his reaction.

"Fear not, Paul. Turansha himself is in Syria. But his network serves us well."

"So long as it is not a trap for I know his men also work hand in glove with Lord Montferrat and Reynald when it suits him."

"Indeed they do, but Lord Montferrat also hates Reynald, with equal measure," Husam smiled.

Paul looked out toward the horizon, the sun now a deep golden yellow as it rose quickly. He thought of Princess Stephanie and that, today, Reynald's days could end. Would she be sad? he wondered momentarily.

"My Lord, the Red Wolf of Kerak has already sunk sixteen more ships… most of them pilgrim vessels. Can we afford to risk another?" the naval officer asked.

"Regrettably yes we must risk it. We lose this route and fail to keep it open, then Saladin breaks his promise and risks losing much support. More depends upon today than you appreciate," Husam replied.

"Sorry, my Lord. We shall do as you command," the naval officer replied and bowed.

"Much piracy and instability in the Persian Gulf has moved much trade into the Red Sea. The steady southerly winds make it difficult for large ships to travel further north with any ease, and Reynald knows that too. Last year he managed to sack this port but he did not have the manpower to hold it. This time he intends to seize it and stay. That cannot be allowed. After burning those sixteen ships he then went on to capture a pilgrim ship and caravan at Aidab, which he still holds to ransom," Husam explained and paused as he looked out toward the horizon. "But it is his threats to attack Medina and remove Muhammad's body and relocate his tomb to Crusader territory so Muslims will have to make a pilgrimage there that causes us the greatest concern for he is mad enough to try it."

"How many ships did you say you have in total now?" Percival asked.

"Thirty-one including yours. Fortunately al-Adil ordered most of his warships moved from Fustat, as you saw, and Alexandria to here and placed directly under my command. That is why we must defeat Reynald comprehensively and decisively. I appreciate the position this puts you in, for there will be men amongst his forces whom you know, but all the other lords, such as Balian and Count Raymond, they have not joined with him in this mad venture."

"No, but Gerard has," Paul remarked and sighed.

"And your brother serves with him. That is why I will understand if you wish to remain here. There is no shame in that," Husam said sympathetically.

"No, we shall attend. Our ship has much room to pick up survivors from both sides should the need arise."

"Then at least fly a neutral standard, my friend, for that is perhaps a better idea than the one I had for your ship. In fact I demand it of you," Husam said and smiled. "I will not turn brother against brother. 'Tis just unfortunate that yours finds himself aligned to a mad man."

Paul looked at Percival. He nodded in agreement it was a good idea. Paul thought of Stewart and wondered with concern if he was indeed still with Gerard. He had no idea where he was having not received any word from him in over two years. He prayed he was elsewhere. All turned to look at a contingent of heavily armed marines boarding followed by lighter armoured oarsmen armed with bows and crossbows.

"Fear not, their armour has quick release links...in case they end up in the water," Husam remarked, seeing how Percival was looking at them. "Tell me, you have been present at all of our briefings. You have studied hard these past two years, so what is your assessment of Reynald's fleet from what you know?"

Percival coughed and faced Husam, a little surprised that he was asking for his opinion. Husam raised his eyebrows.

"Well, Reynald's fleet is mainly made up of galleys. They can only sail when the waters are calm for they do not handle well in rough waters and are easily swamped by waves. He only has between now and September to accomplish what he wishes and his vessels are further restricted by the amount of supplies they can carry. Water in particular. His ships can only carry about four days' worth of water. Effectively, this means his fleet is confined to coastal routes, and has to make frequent landfall to replenish his supplies. None of his ships have battering rams, the only truly 'ship-killing' weapon he still has available, as that book Saladin gave you states, is surprise and for his men to physically board other ships or set them ablaze. But I fear his greatest asset is his acquisition of accurate intelligence, often through the use of spies who pose as merchants."

"And you think he has this intelligence?" Husam asked.

"I would stake my life on it, but I would urge extreme caution this day," Percival answered.

"You just have, my friend, for we sail within the hour. If we have to chase the Red Wolf all across this sea, then so let it be. This day one of us will be defeated. Pray it is not us," Husam said and bowed at Paul and Percival before turning to his fellow officers. "Send the pilgrim vessel out first and follow at a distance. If Reynald's fleet attacks, we shall see the flames, then we shall attack him."

"What...you are using the pilgrim vessel as bait?" Paul asked, alarmed.

"Yes, my friend, yes I am. Reynald has to see that it is indeed a pilgrim carrying vessel so there is no way of faking that. Once he engages, then we shall cut into him like a knife and finish this matter," Husam explained. Paul sighed and shrugged his shoulders. "By all means shadow the pilgrim ferry and if it sinks, you can rescue those you can. But if Reynald sees you, he will treat you as spies...and he will not hesitate in executing you. I know this does not meet with your approval, but...but sometimes we have to sacrifice a few to save many more. Unless you have a better suggestion, either of you?"

Percival looked at Paul then at Husam.

"In any specific action we always have the choice between the most audacious and the most careful solution. Some say the theory of war always advises the latter. That is false," Percival stated. "If the theory does advise anything, it is that the nature of war favours the most decisive, that is, the most audacious. Theory is just theory but in practice it is down to the military leader to act according to his own courage...according to the spirit of the enterprise and his self-confidence to make his choice, according to his inner force...and never forget that no military leader has ever become great without audacity." Both Husam and Paul looked at Percival surprised at his insightful comments. "I read all that in your book," Percival smiled.

"We shall run up a neutral flag. Husam is right," Paul said and nudged Percival.

Paul looked at Husam. He knew what he said made sound tactical sense, but it did not sit well with him. He looked across the harbour to the small pilgrim ferry as many young children, old men and women boarded. Paul part bowed his head to Husam and headed for the main gangplank. Percival feigned a brave smile at Husam as he followed after Paul half dragging his chain mail along with him.

"Paul," Husam called out. Paul turned to face him. "Reynald will not recognise any flag of neutrality. Be guarded for he will sink you just as quickly."

"He has not seen how fast our ship can move," Paul replied and smiled at Husam. "May Allah be with you this day and protect you."

"And you, my friend...and Paul, 'tis my ship," Husam replied, winked and smiled broadly.

Paul looked at Percival and both laughed. He looked over at his vessel and returned a smile to Husam.

"My ship," Paul said and waved as he started to walk down the gangplank. Husam laughed. His face then turned serious as he faced his officers and men on deck. A rivulet of sweat ran down his face as the heat of the day started to rise. It angered him greatly that Reynald alone was the cause of so much hostility. He turned his gaze to the pilgrim vessel.

"Today, Red Wolf of Kerak, you will have your claws severely clipped, if not cut off completely," he said quietly to himself.

Within moments Husam ordered his squadrons to form up. His fleet consisted of the main body, composed of oared Dromon warships, and several baggage train (touldon) sailing vessels and other oared transports, which would be sent away in the event of any direct engagements of battle. But if Husam had to chase Reynald's fleet around, then he needed resupplies to be on hand. The main battle fleet was further divided into smaller squadrons, and orders transmitted from ship to ship through signal kamelaukia flags and lanthorns. He gave the order that boarding actions and hand to hand would be the preferable order of the day. To capture Reynald alive would be a massive psychological blow to Crusader forces and allow Saladin to make a public example of him. Paul and Percival pushed off ahead receiving many strange looks from a bemused and quizzical pilgrim population who had never seen such a strange vessel before. As Percival winched the main mast to its fullest erect position, Paul lowered the main sail enough to catch the wind and move the vessel out of the harbour. Everything both Paul and Percival had trained for and learned, they were now alone in putting those skills into practice. Paul convinced himself he was doing what was right and that at least he could use the excuse that his vessel was purely a fast rescue ship. But deep down he knew he was kidding himself. He was sailing with Husam's fleet, under his Muslim command. Percival gave Paul a wave and smiled as if he was out on a small boating trip on Lake Tannis. Paul laughed and was secretly impressed and glad he had Percival along. Apart from Taqi, Percival was the nearest thing he could call a close friend. Paul furled away the sails and halted the vessel and waited as the pilgrim vessel slowly began to make its way out of the harbour. It was followed by a three-masted vessel from the Balearic kingdom of Denia, and two smaller feluccas, a traditional wooden sailing boat used in the protected waters of the Red Sea. Its rig consisted of two lateen sails and was easily recognisable. Their sails would block the view behind them, Husam hoped, as his fleet followed at some distance.

Port of La Rochelle, France, Melissae Inn, spring 1191

"How did Paul get his ship design passed off as seaworthy for I know how stringent and meticulous the Muslim regulations are?" the Genoese sailor asked.

"That is true...but as the ship was of a whole new concept, and would only require two people to safely handle her, Husam was able to push through most of the legalities required to allow it to set to sea," the old man explained. "As you probably know, the ship occupies a unique position in Islamic tradition. Even the Qur'an counts it among the ayat, miracles of God, and devotes twenty-eight verses enumerating its benefits to mankind. The generic Arabic word for 'ship' is markab, meaning a conveyance or riding vessel. A typical seagoing merchant vessel had to carry on board many anchors, appropriate hawsers and ropes, canvas and/or cotton sails, masts, oars, rudders and drawbridges, for greater ease in embarking and disembarking, in addition to nautical instruments, pilot books and charts."

"We always had trouble with Muslim harbour masters or whatever they were called. Always so meticulous on paperwork and rules," the Genoese sailor said and shook his head.

"Yes they are, especially oversized vessels which had to have service boats on board for the transport of goods to the quayside. But identical rules applied to ship sales and purchase contracts. Both parties to the contract had to specify the vessel's tackle and navigational instruments in the bill of sale. When signing a contract to lease a specific vessel for the conveyance of cargo, shippers were most concerned with the seaworthiness of the ship, besides other considerations such as the freight tariff. Seaworthiness of a ship was associated with the equipment and amount and proficiency of the crew it was required to carry. The design, structure, condition and equipment of the ship had to be suitable for carrying goods of a particular kind and bringing them safely to their destination. Meaning, it had to be technically able to encounter the ordinary perils of the voyage. Concerning the crew, bringing the carriage into completion required a licensed lessor to recruit a competent master and professional complement to navigate the vessel under various circumstances; a ship that was powered by unskilled mariners could certainly be regarded as unseaworthy. It fell to the office of Islamic muhtasib, a sort of market superintendent,

who supervised, among other duties, the construction of ships at the shipyard and carriage by sea."

"Yes, muhtasib...that's what they are called. Nightmare lot to deal with," the Genoese sailor interrupted.

"The muhtasib is helped by assistants called 'urafa' al-sina'a, (arsenals' inspectors), whose main task is to ensure the shipwrights' observance of technical standards and prevent them from using inferior and inadequate raw materials. Exacting and thorough inspections are carried out to avoid human and financial losses. Whoever violates these regulations is punished. While the ship is still in the yard, a comprehensive technical inspection has to be carried out by the muhtasib, the captain and the ship's scribe. This is one area that Paul paid very close attention to detail on. Islamic law entitled sailors and lessees to not honour a leasing contract if a technical defect was discovered in the ship. The working hours of carpenters, including shipwrights, began late in the morning and ended before evening. Thus the inspection of commercial ships took place between sunrise and sunset, but not in the evening and prior to the loading processes. The amount of cargo the ship could properly carry was determined by the muhtasib. When the cargo was stowed and placed appropriately and the ship was ready to depart, an official examination to prevent overloading was requested by the muhtasib, or his representative, and the captain. The hisba manuals plainly state that 'a ship can be freighted with cargo as long as the waterline (plimsoll) alongside the outer hull is visible. Islamic law requires that each ship be marked with a load line to indicate how deeply the ship could legally be submerged. The waterline mark along the outer hull could not lay more than a certain depth below the surface of the water. The provision against overloading was intended to prevent not only sinking but also the overexertion of the rowers. Types, dimensions and technical constructions of ships varied in accordance with their purposes and bodies of waters they plied."

"Perhaps someone should inform some of the captains here for I see many ships leave heavily overloaded," the Hospitaller said.

"Sadly that is indeed true," the old man sighed in agreement before continuing. "Islamic technology of shipbuilding shows that the length-to-beam ratio of a typical size of commercial vessel is usually 3:1 or 4:1, with a shallow keel and rounded hull; the wide beam relative to the length aimed to provide maximum storage for cargo. Shipwrights in the Islamic Mediterranean employ the skeletal-building method in all stages of the hull's construction. All the frames are in place before the wales and upper side planks are added. At some point after side planking begins, the open area between the bottom and sides is covered with an odd configuration of

strakes, at least three of which do not run the full length of the hull. When planking is completed, they are caulked with a mixture of pitch or tar. After all the floor timbers are in place, the keelson was bolted between the frames and through the keel at irregular intervals with one inch diameter forelock bolts. Then stringers are added to the floor of the hold, on which a removable transverse ceiling is placed. Next comes the side ceiling, clamps and deck beams. The major difference in the construction techniques and methods between the Islamic Mediterranean and the eastern part of the empire is in reference to planking. The ship's planks in the Red Sea and Indian Ocean are sewn together with ropes, while in the Mediterranean, iron nails are used. The lateen sail is a distinctive feature of the rig of Islamic ships in the Mediterranean." [87]

"Sorry but what shape is a lateen sail?" Ayleth asked shyly.

"Like a large triangle," the Templar answered.

"Most materials needed for shipbuilding are found within the Islamic lands. For instance, Egyptian shipwrights use different types of timber, lebek, acacia, fig, palm and lotus, which are abundantly found in Egypt, in their arsenals. But due to massive deforestation processes, cedar, pine and other timbers are being imported from Palestine, Lebanon, Asia Minor and Europe. All of the conditions I have detailed had been met by Paul's unique design and in most cases exceeded them. And as he had promised Tenno, he used the information he had given him to stop rat infestation and used and incorporated the best elements of Chinese and Japanese vessel design. To Paul his vessel was more than just a ship. It represented so much more and Husam had allowed him to indulge his design unhindered, but still following all the legal requirements," the old man explained.

11 - 14

"And I thought you sailors just knocked a load of planks together to build your boats," Simon joked, looking at the Genoese sailor.

"If it were only that simple," the Genoese sailor replied. "But I would love to have seen this ship of Paul's for real. She sounds a wonder to behold."

"She was that indeed," the old man sighed. "Perhaps too far advanced for her time."

"Oh dear. That sounds ominous...is she at the bottom of the Red Sea now, then?" Sarah asked.

"No not quite...but let me explain what happened that day for sure enough Reynald's fleet sighted the pilgrim vessel and accompanying vessels behind her...and as

Husam anticipated, Reynald in his eagerness did not see beyond them to his ships following some distance behind.

Red Sea, off the coast of Egypt, March 31st 1183

Paul adjusted the pitch of the main sail by winding the winch to pull the sail into the wind. As the vessel picked up speed, Percival raised the main mast vertical, the immediate downward force pushing the vessel's bow deeper into the water. But as it did, the two bow stabiliser fins extended and pushed the vessel back upwards and raised it slightly. With less friction on the bow section of the hull, the vessel picked up speed instantly. Percival smiled broadly at Paul, impressed. Paul steered the vessel to the north of the pilgrim vessel and other assorted vessels following it. His heart was pounding with both anticipation and excitement.

"Do not get me killed this day please for I have not continued my line yet...and Nyla wants children," Percival called out half laughing as he held on tightly as the speed increased.

ꕥ

"Pass me the looking glass," Husam ordered and clicked his fingers as he steadied himself standing on the foredeck of his Dromon. One of his officers stepped closer and handed him an ornate hand held telescope. Quickly he extended it and put it to his eye and focused upon Paul's vessel as it sped across the horizon. "What unbelievable speed!" Husam exclaimed, surprised, and faced his officers. "If things do not go our way this day, and that vessel looks like falling into Reynald's hands...destroy it at all costs... is that understood?" Husam ordered. He shook his head again as he looked upon Paul's vessel. "I had not appreciated just how advanced that vessel is. What a fool I am!"

Port of La Rochelle, France, Melissae Inn, spring 1191

"This does not sound good," Ayleth commented.

"In that instant, Husam, seeing the speed and agility of Paul's vessel, realised its

tactical and strategic potential. His mind raced as he feared Reynald would seize the vessel and copy it as he had done with Paul's other ship construction methods. As a consequence instead of holding back his fleet, he ordered them to intercept the pilgrim vessel immediately and recall Paul and Percival," the old man explained.

"Why?" Peter asked, a little confused.

"Let me explain. On the approach to and during an actual battle, a well-ordered formation is critical for if a fleet fell into disorder, its ships would be unable to lend support to each other and would probably be defeated. Fleets that fail to keep an ordered formation or that could not order themselves into an appropriate counter-formation (antiparataxis) to match that of the enemy, often avoided or broke off from battle completely. Husam seeing the speed and manoeuvrability of Paul's vessel, it caught him totally off guard and he felt as though he had just handed Reynald a major advantage if he captured it. Tactical manoeuvres are intended to disrupt the enemy formation, including the use of various stratagems, such as dividing one's force and carrying out flanking manoeuvres, feigning retreat or hiding a reserve in ambush. A crescent formation is usually the normal tactic, with the flagship, Husam's ship, in the centre and the heavier ships at the horns of the formation, in order to turn the enemy's flanks. But Paul's vessel would change all of that with its speed and handling abilities. So Husam was faced with a dilemma. Locate and engage Reynald as was his primary mission or recall Paul. His signallers frantically sent messages to Paul but neither he nor Percival saw them as they were too busy looking in Reynald's direction. Husam had to get closer as fast as he could," the old man detailed. [88]

"I recall Reynald and that evil Turansha both sought the plans of Paul's vessel...," the Hospitaller started to say when his brother hit his arm lightly and shook his head no.

"Thank you," the old man said and nodded at them. "If you said more, you would let out what happened," he smiled.

"Sorry...please continue," the Hospitaller said apologetically.

"Husam needed to get Paul's vessel away but also get his fleet as close to Reynald's fleet wherever he was so they could exchange missiles, ranging from combustible projectiles to arrows and javelins. The aim was not to sink his ships, but to deplete his ranks before any boarding actions, which would decide the final outcome. Once the enemy strength was judged to have been reduced sufficiently, the fleet could close in, the ships would then grapple each other, and the marines and upper bank oarsmen would board the enemy vessel and engage in hand-to-hand combat. It could be a costly business," the old man explained.

"Because he is Christian, I know I should be rooting for Reynald...but, but," Sarah said and then paused and fiddled with her fingers. "Does that make me a traitor of sorts?" she asked.

"Of course it does not," the old man laughed.

"I was engaged in warfare at sea on several occasions. 'Twas the worst kind, especially as Muslim ships had Manganas and Ballistaes," the Hospitaller remarked.

"What?" the wealthy tailor asked.

"Manganas and Ballistaes...catapults and mangonels that launched stones, arrows, javelins, pots of Greek fire or other incendiary liquids, caltrops (triboloi) and even containers full of lime to choke the enemy. But at least they did not have rams. They relied totally on boarding actions and missile fire as the old man details," the Hospitaller explained.

"So please, tell us what happened," Gabirol asked quietly.

The old man nodded, took a sip of rosehip water and continued.

Red Sea, off the coast of Egypt, March 31st 1183

Paul looked behind to see Husam's Dromon warship speeding towards him followed by the remainder of his fleet. He stood up fast to see clearer as Percival looked back.

"What is he doing?" Percival called out. "Messages…they are signalling us…look."

Paul could just make out the small figure on the foredeck waving flags.

"What does it say?" Paul shouted as Percival struggled to see the signaller properly. "Oh Lord…look!" Paul shouted as several large Christian trireme and cog type vessels loomed into view directly on a collision path with the pilgrim vessel.

"Paul…it says we must retire to Port Aydhab immediately," Percival called out as Paul looked at him, confused.

The pilgrim transport vessel pitched its sail and pulled about hard nearly capsizing as it executed the manoeuvre. Women and children screamed in panic as Reynald's vessels rapidly drew near. Paul pushed the rudder lever hard to his left forcing his vessel to pull a hard turn right, the main sail boom swinging hard and creaking under the sudden tension. Paul steered the vessel into position so it was pointing directly at the pilgrim ship's path. A slower Muslim Tarida tried to pull astern but was immediately intercepted by a large trireme flying the Hospitallers' colours. The Muslim Tarida pitched wildly as it tried to avoid the approaching vessel but just as it started to turn away, a large orange gout of flame shot out from the stern port side of the Hospitaller vessel. The flame arched out as it hit the sea water but slowly reached outwards until it caught the side of the Tarida. As the Tarida slipped through the clear waters, the flame continued to pour upon it. Oars started to clash against each other and break or face upwards as the crew inside rushed away from the incoming burning fire. As the Tarida pulled away, the Hospitaller vessel swung hard astern just as screams of men on fire filled the air with a shrill shriek that made Paul and Percival freeze momentarily. Horses inside neighed loudly in panic. The Tarida side was completely alight as men started to jump overboard, some on fire.

"Paul!" Percival shouted to get his attention. "What do we do?"

Paul looked behind him quickly. Husam was still some distance away. When he looked forwards again, the Hospitaller ship was turning to run alongside the pilgrim vessel. Paul watched helplessly as he saw men moving the flame thrower into position as others pumped up the pressure using bellows. Another three masted trireme vessel started to pull alongside the opposite side of the pilgrim vessel. On the aft forecastle Paul suddenly saw both Reynald and Gerard standing shouting orders to Naval Templars rapidly forming up on the main deck with grappling hooks preparing to board.

"Shit...shit, shit," Paul said aloud, his mind racing, wondering what to do. A man behind the bellows to the flame thrower raised his hand. Paul knew it meant it was ready. Paul straightened his sails to catch the maximum amount of wind and aimed his vessel directly at the rear of the Hospitaller ship.

"What are you doing? I said don't get me killed this day," Percival shouted as he jumped next to Paul.

"Help me to hold this steady. If we can knock that ship aside, they will not be able to burn the pilgrim vessel," Paul shouted and looked behind him again. Husam was closing but not fast enough. "Hold tight, my friend. Our bows are reinforced...she will take the impact."

Percival looked at Paul hesitantly as alarm registered across his face.

"Impact!" he exclaimed.

Paul just nodded and clung tightly to the rudder lever. As the pilgrim vessel drew level with the Hospitaller ship, the flame thrower was pointed directly at her bows as she neared the stern and flame thrower position. Paul had to stand up to see over the bow of his vessel as it rose when it picked up speed. He looked to his right at the large trireme with Reynald and Gerard on board. They saw his vessel approach and looked on in surprise. But within moments Reynald ordered several archers and crossbow men to start firing towards them. Their arrows and bolts fell well short. Paul then saw Stewart run up the steps and stand beside Gerard. For a moment all three of them stared at Paul, now clearly visible. Gerard feigned a brief look of surprise, more at the strange vessel, as Reynald grinned and shook his head. He smiled, but then frowned when he saw what Paul was about to do.

"If I judge this wrong, you must jump off as that flame thrower will cover us!" Paul shouted to Percival as he ducked as a few long range arrows bounced off the deck.

Paul pushed the rudder lever to his right as far as it would go, the bow of the vessel cutting deep into the water then smashing hard into the rear of the Hospitaller vessel's steerage rudder breaking it in two and damaging several planks. With a screech and grinding of wood on wood, the two vessels momentarily locked together, Reynald, Gerard and Stewart looking across the top of the pilgrim vessel at Paul and Percival. Hospitallers rushed to the aft deck and looked down at the damage, the flame thrower having been knocked sideways. As one of the operators fell with the impact, he fired the mechanism, with the resultant gout of thick flame spewing out all across the inside section of the aft deck. Two Hospitallers lit up engulfed in the flaming liquid. One jumped into the sea whilst the other rolled around on the deck screaming in agony as two others tried to push the flame thrower over the side as it kept spewing flame.

"Kill them…now!" Reynald shouted from his vessel.

Paul and Percival looked up at several Hospitallers aiming crossbows at them. One fired, its arrow just missing Percival as he ducked, when several large javelins flew across the aft deck causing the Hospitallers to dive for cover. Paul looked behind just in time to see one of Husam's Dromon ships loom closer.

"Paul! Paul!" Stewart called out as Percival tried to push against the Hospitaller vessel to free their ship. "What are you doing?" Stewart shouted across the decks.

Women and children screamed on the pilgrim vessel as Reynald grabbed a crossbow and aimed it at Paul. Without hesitation Stewart knocked into him hard as he fired, the bolt shooting through the pilgrim ship's main sail. Reynald looked at Stewart in anger.

"Reynald...Reynald...this is piracy and murder!" Paul shouted as Percival managed to break some of the planking away that was entangled in their vessel's bow.

Reynald grabbed another crossbow off of one his men and jumped up onto a balustrade in order to get a better aim. He fired, the bolt whizzing past Paul's head and narrowly missing Percival as it embedded into the Hospitaller ship.

"You traitors! You will hang for this!" Reynald shouted and threw the crossbow towards Paul. It hit the pilgrim vessel astern as it slowly pulled away. Gerard pulled Reynald back onto the aft deck and pointed to all of Husam's ships bearing down upon them.

"I am no traitor but I will not let you murder women and children!" Paul shouted back as the bow of his vessel suddenly broke away from the hole left in the Hospitaller ship. Percival nearly fell overboard Paul just managing to grab him in time.

"Burn the pilgrim ship and then run that bastard down. I want him taken alive for he will pay for this!" Reynald bellowed loudly as several Muslim sailors on the pilgrim vessel gesticulated towards him mockingly.

Paul levelled his vessel and tightened in the main sail. Instantly the vessel moved between Reynald's ship and the Hospitaller vessel, its crew busy fighting the ever growing fire on board. Percival laughed nervously as they ran alongside Reynald's vessel as he ran along the deck looking down at them.

"You Muslim lover...you have chosen your side!" Reynald shouted as he was followed by Gerard and Stewart. A loud report suddenly rang out and an explosion of flame rose from the starboard side of Reynald's ship. Another explosion rang out as another Greek fire grenade exploded just as Husam's Dromon pulled up alongside Reynald's ship. Within moments Husam's marines were throwing grappling hooks and pulling the two vessels closer together. Stewart looked down at Paul momentarily, then at Gerard, who immediately drew his sword and rushed towards the commotion.

"Stewart...jump...here!" Paul shouted to his brother as his vessel rapidly began to pull away. Stewart looked at him, hesitated for a moment as he looked down into the water. Another explosion rang out just as several marines jumped across onto the decks from Husam's ship. "Stewart!" Paul shouted again.

Stewart raised his hands, then turned and vanished from sight as his sword was drawn and raised and he rushed toward the fight. Paul's heart sank and he feared for his brother. Paul and Percival struggled to pull their vessel about to face Husam's and Reynald's ships, and they watched as several engagements started between other ships in the fleet. One of Reynald's cog vessels was already fully ablaze, men jumping into the sea, some burning and screaming. Flashes and bangs rang out from Reynald's ship. Suddenly another flame thrower fired up from the rear of his ship spewing out a large gout of orange flame across the rear of Husam's ship. Heavily armoured marines rushed to the area with other oarsmen and immediately and effectively started to douse the flames. Arrows and crossbow bolts were zipping between vessels and the clash of swords echoed out amongst the shouting. The pilgrim vessel set its sails and tried to steer a course northward against the wind away from the fight, but it hardly moved. Husam's ship started to push away from Gerard's ship as its main sails caught fire from the grenades. Paul and Percival watched as Husam's men jumped back to their own ship. Paul prayed Stewart was okay. Reynald and Gerard were surrounded by many of their own heavily armed guards when Reynald ordered his ship to run down the pilgrim vessel. Husam's ship turned away in the opposite direction unable to shield or assist the pilgrim vessel. A loud crack sounded out as the pilgrim Tarida vessel's back broke, its bow sticking up in the air sinking, its weight out of the water too much for its keel to take the stress.

Several marines and the whole upper-bank of oarsmen, heavily armoured in preparation for battle and armed with lances and swords, along with other sailors wearing padded felt jackets (neurika) for protection, aimed their bows and crossbows at Reynald's ship as Husam tried to manoeuvre into a better assault position. Many javelins started to be fired off toward Reynald's ship from two other Dromons closing in. The sky around his ship appeared to turn black as hundreds of arrows were unleashed against it. Paul gulped hard knowing his brother was on board.

"Look...he is going to ram the pilgrim vessel and take her down with him," Percival shouted as they watched the helmsman steer Reynald's vessel on a direct collision course with the pilgrim ship.

Husam's ships were all too far away to intercept fast enough as Reynald's ship closed in. Paul immediately saw that at both vessels' present courses and speed, Reynald's ship would ram the smaller and lower in the water pilgrim vessel centrally and with all likelihood break her in two.

"If you wish to live this day, you had better get off now!" Paul shouted to Percival, then aimed his vessel directly at Reynald's ship. He pitched the vessel and aligned the sail to catch the wind. As he was coming in from the north, his sails picked up instantly. "Remember I said the bows on this are reinforced...well!"

Percival jumped beside Paul and helped him steady the rudder lever. He winked at Paul briefly.

"I can't swim!" Percival laughed.

Paul looked at him for a second before flinching as arrows whizzed past, fired from Reynald's ship. As the vessel picked up speed, the bows raised up in the water offering protection from all the incoming arrows and bolts that thudded against the hull. Paul calculated where Reynald's ship was heading and steered accordingly almost blind.

"Quick...quick...ram that damn pilgrim shit carrier!" Reynald shouted as his men tried to eek out every last breath of wind in the sails. "Hurry!" he yelled even louder as he saw Paul's vessel approach. He squinted momentarily confused. "Is...is he going to try and ram us?" he asked bemused and laughed as he nudged Gerard.

Gerard looked down towards Paul's fast approaching vessel heading directly for the bow of their ship.

"That, my friend, I think he is...and at that speed, he will not only sink himself, but he will put a massive hole in us," Gerard replied looking on half fascinated at the strange sight of Paul's ship speeding towards him, the bow raised on the two stabiliser fins.

Stewart rushed to the side, the rear of the ship becoming more engulfed in flames. The pilgrim vessel was now directly in front of them. Stewart saw the look of horror on several of the women and children crowded upon the open top deck as they bore down on them. As Stewart's eyes widened and he braced for the impact, he was suddenly knocked sideways instead as Paul's vessel slammed into the bow of Reynald's ship with such force it threw most of the crew, including Reynald and Gerard, to the deck. The force was unlike anything Reynald had ever experienced. Shocked he tried to stand, but the force from Paul's vessel pushed the bow causing the entire ship to turn away from the pilgrim vessel hard, just missing it, the swell almost swamping the upper decks. Reynald looked up as the main mast creaked as it leaned and bowed under the pressure. A sickening loud crack rang out as it snapped. Stewart jumped to his feet and dived at Gerard knocking him out of the way as the broken half of the mast and part furled sail crashed down beside them. Paul and Percival looked up wondering what was happening, their vessel firmly stuck in the bow of Reynald's ship pushing it on a tight arch about itself.

"Well you were correct about the reinforced bow," Percival called out and laughed nervously.

Fire began to engulf the rear of Reynald's ship as cheers went up from the pilgrim ship. Paul looked over to see many sailors from the Hospitaller ship, now completely ablaze, and survivors from the Muslim Tarida all swimming in the water amongst the odd pool of Greek fire as it burnt away on the surface. Reynald's ship seemed to sigh and then the stern suddenly dropped deeper into the water as internal beams began to break. Quickly Paul jumped up.

"Stewart!" he shouted and ran to the front of his vessel, pushed past the sail and looked up at the side of Reynald's ship. Quickly he grabbed hold of protruding broken planks and climbed up. As he jumped over the balustrade he looked about. The stern of the ship was ablaze and men were ditching their armour and jumping over the side. He turned to look forwards just in time to see Stewart helping to drag Gerard along the foredeck. "Stewart!" Paul cried out and rushed towards him. Bemused Stewart looked up, sweat pouring from his face. "Ditch the chain mail, brother ,for you will surely drown if you enter the water."

"Brother…these are my brothers. I do not know who you are any more… or what that is!" Stewart shouted back defiant and looked down at Paul's vessel, Percival struggling to cut away entangled woodwork.

Paul rushed forwards and grabbed Gerard's feet and started to lift him.

"Well you want this man to live do you not?" Paul shouted.

Stewart looked at Paul hesitantly until the aft mast collapsed and crashed down with a loud bang across the deck, throwing up smoke and dust. As they all coughed, Gerard slowly coming round, Stewart lifted him under the arms.

"And just where do we take him?" Stewart shouted.

"To my vessel. You will both be safe upon there…you have my word!"

Paul yelled back as Percival jumped into view, concerned after the mast had fallen.

"So where is the prick Reynald now?" he asked.

Stewart nodded toward the broken main mast section lying across the forecastle deck.

"Is he dead?" Paul asked. Stewart shrugged his shoulders he did not know. "Percy, take Gerard's feet and get them on board our vessel. I will check Reynald!" Paul shouted as he lowered Gerard's feet.

Stewart looked at Paul, confused, as Percival lifted Gerard's feet. Paul nodded at Percival and then vanished into the swirling smoke.

Paul pushed past parts of the sail, holes burning through it as it lay across both the broken mast and decking. Paul coughed as he breathed in acrid smoke. His foot hit something soft. He looked down and immediately saw it was Reynald lying unconscious, his leg trapped under the broken mast. A large cut and raised bump was clearly visible upon his forehead as Paul knelt beside him. He moved Reynald's head to look up and slapped him across the cheek to wake him. Reynald coughed and spluttered as he tried to clear his throat and rubbed his eyes as he tried to focus through the smoke that swirled in ever increasing thickness like someone was waving a blanket up and around them. His eyes widened in alarm as his vision came into focus and he saw Paul standing over him, beams of sunlight flickering through the smoke and burnt sail almost silhouetting Paul as he raised his arms, a large fighting mace in his hands ready to swing it down. Reynald raised his arms protectively as he struggled to move, but his trapped leg holding him fast.

"No...have mercy!" Reynald shouted.

Paul looked down at him as he swung the heavy mace several times to gain speed and momentum behind it. He could kill Reynald right here and now and end the madness of his power he thought...but then images of Princess Stephanie filled his mind. Her beautiful smile, her soft touch as she held his hands at the wadi. Then his eyes caught sight of some initials etched deeply into the main balustrade. It was his and Alisha's initial. Momentarily stunned, he froze. Reynald squirmed on the deck and then frantically started to pull at his leg. Water started flooding over the deck as the ship started to sink slowly. Paul slipped briefly on the wet deck just managing to grab hold of the balustrade. Quickly he ran his fingers over the initials. Alisha had told him she had carved their initials upon a ship when she sailed to Tortosa years ago. A wave washed over Reynald and he shook his head to clear the sea water from his eyes and spat some out. Quickly Paul stood up straight again, raised the mace high and swung it several times as Reynald stared at him transfixed thinking he was about to be slain by Paul or drowned…trapped. With all his strength, Paul swung the mace down hard. It smashed into the decking beside Reynald's trapped leg smashing the planks downwards. Instantly Reynald started to pull his leg but it was still trapped just as another wave washed over him and pushed Paul backwards. Quickly Paul raised the mace again and in one fell swoop swung it over his head and down hard upon the decking, this time smashing his way through the planks. As they shattered downwards, it gave just enough room for Reynald to pull his leg free. He staggered to his feet and looked at Paul. Their eyes met and both stood in silence for what seemed an age but was only seconds. They both fell sideways as the bow of the ship suddenly raised a few feet as the stern of the vessel started to slip beneath the waves, pulling the bow upwards. Paul threw the mace aside, grabbed Reynald and pulled him across the broken mast and half dragged him towards his own vessel as Percival and Stewart fought to push off away from the sinking ship, black smoke bellowing upwards mixed with clouds of white steam as water extinguished flames. Paul pushed Reynald hard into the rear of the vessel forcing him to land upon Gerard, who was semiconscious. Stewart helped pull him on board as Paul leapt from the sinking ship onto the foredeck of his vessel. It groaned noisily as the reinforced bow pulled free from the sinking ship just in time as the stern started to pull it down faster amid a noise of bubbles and breaking wood. Men were still in the water, some screaming mixed with cheers from the pilgrim vessel. Paul could see Husam's fleet engaging at close quarters Reynald's remaining ships which had turned to head back to the eastern shores. The Muslim Tarida had completely vanished beneath the waves. Paul looked behind him, pushed past the main mast in time to see Husam's ship pulling alongside. If he saw Stewart, he knew he would be executed as an example as Saladin had ordered. He jumped down into the aft deck area and pushed Gerard hard and rolled him down the steps leading into the main hold. He grabbed Stewart and almost threw him down the stairs. As he turned to look at Reynald, he stood up straight to face him.

"I shall not be held captive like a rat," Reynald stated proudly as he stood soaking wet, his head bleeding.

"You arrogant arse. I am trying to save your miserable soul...now get down there and hide and do not come up until I call...NOW!" Paul shouted back and pushed him hard.

Hesitantly Reynald looked through the part furled sail as Husam's ship approached. He looked at Paul half surprised then quickly stepped down into the hold looking back up at Paul shaking his head.

"Ahoy...are you seaworthy?" one of Husam's marine officers called out as the ship steered to move alongside. Percival stamped out a small fire and patted down part of the sail that was alight. "Ahoy!"

1 - 39

Paul stood up and waved as Husam stepped into view on the rear aft castle.

"We have put out the fire but I fear we are taking on water," Paul shouted back.

"What were you thinking of? You could have got yourself killed?" Husam shouted down. "And is Reynald dead?"

Paul looked back as the bow mast of Reynald's ship slipped gently beneath the waves and out of sight. Slowly he turned to face Husam.

"He was going to ram the pilgrim transport. I could not sit idly by and watch him do that...but...but as for him, I do not know. Some were picked up from the waters by his flanking ship!" Paul shouted up by way of explanation, his heart feeling like it was in his mouth and fearing Reynald would come up on deck any moment.

"Can you get back to shore, for we must pursue the Red Wolf and finish this...can you?" Husam shouted down.

Paul looked around at the damage on his ship. Percival stood up and nodded his head yes.

"If we can't, we shall board our service boat and start rowing for we are taking on water," Paul replied.

"Then scuttle her here and now and join us," Husam said and ordered one of his men to lower a rope ladder.

"No...she is too valuable to scuttle if we have a chance to get her back. We won't make Port Aydhab but we can run her aground on the shore," Paul explained and shielded his eyes from the glaring sun above. Husam seemed to take an age in considering Paul's idea. "Besides, you need to capitalise upon your gains this hour and get after Reynald and his other ships."

Husam pondered Paul's comments as his ship nudged against Paul's vessel.

"Make sure you put your safety first. If she sinks, we can replace her but we cannot replace you...do you hear me?" Husam called out and raised his hand and indicated for his men to unfurl all of their sails completely to move off in pursuit. "Make sure!" Husam shouted again as his ship started to pull away fast.

Reynald lifted the trap door to the hold and looked up at Paul.

"Just stay exactly where you are or we are all dead," Paul muttered, trying not to move his lips and waved at Husam. "We will see you back on shore...we will make it!" Paul shouted and waved again as Husam moved to the rear of the aft deck.

As Husam's ship slipped away, Paul could see the day had not gone well for Reynald's forces. The Hospitaller ship was still afloat but the entire top half was ablaze. Should he stay and pull on board other survivors? he wondered. But then Reynald's men would outnumber him and Percival and it would be them who would become captive, Reynald's words still echoing through his mind.

"Percy, set our course for the shoreline. That one," he said and pointed to the western shore just visible. "As fast as we can make it," Paul continued and immediately went below to face Reynald and Gerard.

"You must be insane. Do you intend to make us prisoners or ransom us?" Reynald demanded to know, standing upright, his fists clenched.

"You...you utterly deranged fool. You caused all of this...and for what? Some piratical gain. Why?" Paul asked, exasperated and angry at the same time.

Gerard started to come to and Stewart helped him sit up and lean against the side bench. Confused, Gerard rubbed his head and looked around the strange interior of the vessel.

"Are we dead?" he asked and sat up further.

"No...not yet but this traitor has plans of ill intent for us I am sure," Reynald said through gritted teeth then suddenly lunged at Paul.

Instantly Paul stepped back and to his side, drew his sword and as Reynald outstretched his arms to grab him, Paul simply smacked the back of his head with his sword pommel, Reynald falling to the deck hard and sliding across the wet floor. Gerard raised his eyebrows.

"Bit undignified that was, my friend," Gerard half joked to Reynald as he rolled over onto his back.

Paul stepped over him, his sword just inches away from his chest.

"One more stupid action like that will be your last…you fool. Now get up and sit over there," Paul ordered and nodded toward the bench near to Gerard and Stewart. "I will not have your blood upon my soul this day."

"Then why in the name of the Lord did you ram us?" Stewart almost pleaded.

"Because you were about to murder innocent women and children," Paul replied, still pointing his sword toward Reynald.

"They are just Muslims…so we know where your loyalties lay," Reynald snapped angrily.

"They are people first and non-combatants," Paul shot back.

"Horse shit. You think that Armenian mercenary Husam Lu Lu whatever his damned name is was bothered in the slightest about using them as bait?" Reynald snarled back and stood up again fast.

"Sit down before I put you down for good," Paul said through gritted teeth, his voice deeper through anger. "I would have stopped him from doing exactly the same thing if I had to."

"Bit of a sanctimonious holy shit aren't you, Paul," Gerard chipped in as he wiped his forehead and looked at the blood upon his hand.

"You have no idea how much so," Paul replied, refusing to be drawn into an argument with them.

"Well, I did tell Reynald this was a trap…but would he listen?" Gerard stated and feigned a mock look of disapproval at Reynald.

Reynald looked at Gerard hard for a moment before hitting his arm.

"Aye that you did…but what now. Come on…what now? You cannot exactly hide us forever on here can you…unless you intend taking us to our shores?" Reynald asked and folded his arms.

Paul looked at him, puzzled, almost bewildered at Reynald's total apparent lack of fear or conscience.

"I cannot take you to your shores as we would sink long before we reached it. If we are lucky, we may make the western shore…if we are lucky."

"And if not?" Stewart asked.

"Then we take to the service boat and row and you pray Husam and his fleet don't catch us up before we make landfall. After that, once we have landed, 'tis down to you how you get back for that will be the last I do for you," Paul explained.

Gerard sat in silence as he studied the interior of the vessel curiously.

"What manner of a strange vessel is this?" he asked inquisitively.

"This is your design isn't it?" Stewart stated. Paul nodded yes. "And it punched a hole in our ship like it was made of soft wood. Is this a ship of war?"

"No 'tis not. Far from it," Paul answered defensively.

As the vessel caught the wind fully and picked up speed suddenly, all had to grab hold of something to steady themselves as the bow of the vessel raised upwards on its stabilisers.

"We should hit landfall in about twenty minutes if we keep this speed and stay afloat," Percival shouted down.

Water bled through the front stabiliser join in the hull every time the vessel passed through a wave.

"If you wish to reach the shore, I need you to help bail out the water," Paul asked.

"Put that sword away and I shall help you," Gerard said and stood up slowly rubbing his head in pain. Paul looked at Reynald. "Come on...if you wish to live this day out you will need to help too," Gerard said as he patted Reynald's shoulder.

"He lies. He tricks us so he can boast and proudly show us off as his prisoners," Reynald remarked as Gerard raised his eyebrows disbelievingly. "He does!"

"If that was the case why did he drag our sorry arses off our ship...our sinking ship?" Gerard asked, shaking his head.

"As I said...so he can parade us in front of his Muslim friends..."

"Just bail the water," Paul said as he opened the trap door and started to walk up the steps. "If you keep that water out, we may just make the shoreline."

As Paul vanished from view, Reynald grabbed hold of Gerard's arm.

"I know not what type of vessel this is, but we must overpower him and his friend. 'Tis the only way we shall get back to our lands," Reynald whispered.

"And you know how to operate this vessel do you?" Stewart asked aloud.

"Sssh, you bloody fool," Reynald snapped.

"My friend, Brother Stewart speaks wisely...for we have no idea how this vessel works," Gerard said quietly.

"Then we force them to operate it," Reynald whispered.

"We have no arms save our arming daggers and he has clearly learned much about warfare. Challenge him and I fear this will be your last day," Gerard explained and looked Reynald in the eye intently.

Reynald flounced his arms down in anger and shook his head. After a few minutes stood in silence he faced Gerard and Stewart. Gerard smiled and offered up a wooden bucket and frowned as he shook it at him to take. Reynald snatched it and immediately, though reluctantly, started to collect water.

Port of La Rochelle, France, Melissae Inn, spring 1191

"He was lucky to survive ramming Reynald's ship...very lucky," the Genoese sailor remarked.

"That he was indeed. But it was testament to the strength of the design of his vessel," the old man replied.

"Did they reach the shore then?" Ayleth asked.

"Well we know Reynald and Gerard must have survived and got back as look at the chaos they caused afterwards," the farrier commented as he poured himself a tankard of mead.

"We all know here that Reynald and Gerard did return to their own lands...but not after some considerable effort."

"I do not understand this flame thrower. How does that work?" Sarah asked inquisitively.

"The flame thrower shot out liquid fire, an incendiary chemical used since the early sixth century. The actual substance is known as Greek fire and believed to have been created in 673. The most common method of deployment, as Paul saw, was to emit the formula through a large bronze tube, a siphōn, onto enemy ships or even launched in jars fired from catapults. But its use was a dangerous business for the mixture would be stored in heated, pressurised barrels and projected through the tube by a pump while the operators were sheltered behind large iron shields. As Paul saw firsthand, the Greek fire could not be extinguished by water, but rather floated and burned on top of it; sand could extinguish it by depriving it of oxygen. Husam's forces used a similar version of Greek fire, called 'naft' (from naphtha), which had a petroleum base, with sulphur and various resins added. That is how they ran down all of Reynald's ships, many deliberately running their ships aground so they could

escape the fire and Husam's fleet...but over one hundred and seventy of Reynald's men were captured and consequently taken to various ports and cities to be publicly executed as per Saladin's orders...to make a clear demonstration that he could keep the pilgrim routes open and set an example," the old man explained.

"I recall only too clearly the shock Reynald's defeat caused...for Husam broke Reynald's blockade, destroyed most of his ships, and pursued and captured those who anchored and fled into the desert as you say. We lost a hundred and seventy good knights from both of our Orders," the Templar interrupted.

"What of the ordinary sailors and men?" Miriam asked.

"Saladin ordered all of them to be set free...so that they would return and tell of the folly of Reynald's actions...not that what they said had any lasting effect on anyone to be honest...especially when Reynald returned...oh, I am sorry," the Templar said.

The old man smiled.

"No need to apologise, for all here already know Reynald returned. But how... well that I can explain, if you wish, briefly?" All around the table looked at each other and all nodded in agreement. "The naval engagement had certainly been a baptism of fire and water for Paul and Percival...one they would not forget in a hurry."

PART X

Chapter 55
The Heart's Code!

The beach ahead was almost flat on the approach run with a few trees set back a short distance from the shoreline. The sea was calm as Paul saw the rapid shallowing of the water.

"Hold on!" Paul shouted as he braced himself. "Run her aground as high up the beach as you can!"

Percival steadied the rudder as Paul tightened the rigging to get the maximum draw of wind in the sails. The two side stabilisers held the bow just out of the water but as soon as the hull at the stern started to scrape along the sand, Paul dropped the main mast down, collapsing the sail. As the mast retracted, the two side stabilisers retracted against the hull. If Paul misjudged his position, the stabilisers would be ripped off as they embedded in the sand. The vessel jolted violently as it bounced up the wet sand, tilted to the left and gouged out a trench as it slid upwards onto the beach and suddenly stopped, throwing everyone forwards hard, Paul almost falling head first onto the top deck, the collapsed sail stopping him. Percival fell forwards unable to keep hold of the rudder lever as it shuddered violently and broke in half, pieces of splintered rudder shooting off in different directions at the same time. After a few minutes of total silence, Reynald started to moan below decks. Paul scrambled back into the aft deck area and checked Percival, who was rubbing his left arm in pain. He had broken it. Paul looked around to see where they were. Open beaches on either side as far as the eye could see. He scanned the horizon for any sign of other vessels. None could be seen.

"Quickly!" Paul shouted and lifted the main hold door. "You must get out of here as quickly as you can for Saladin has these shores patrolled regularly." He reached his hand down to help Reynald. Reynald looked up at him and pushed Paul's hand aside as he started to climb the ladder unaided. "Stewart...hurry please."

Reynald slowly stood up straight on the aft deck and looked around as he clung to the side to stay upright. As he looked at Paul's vessel he shook his head, bemused at its strange design.

Percival jumped down onto the sand and grimaced in pain. Reynald saw his reaction and knew he had injured his arm. Paul instantly drew his sword and pointed it at Reynald.

"You will have no need of that," Gerard said as he pulled himself up the ladder. "Will he Reynald?"

Reynald looked at Paul and rubbed his chin with his hand, clearly considering his options. Stewart followed Gerard out and promptly jumped down beside Percival. A quick check confirmed he had broken his upper arm. Fortunately it was a clean break and not an open fracture.

"We have company approaching," Percival said in pain and nodded northward.

All turned and saw the shimmering image of a squadron of men on horseback riding toward them on the beach.

"Quick…you must hide back inside," Paul said, alarmed.

"Yeah right and you hand us over," Reynald said as he squinted to see the approaching horsemen.

"If you run off, they will see your footprints in the sand and run you down. If you hide in the damaged water stowage compartments, they will not find you," Paul explained and gestured with his arms for them to get back on board.

Hesitantly Reynald nodded in agreement and quickly pulled himself back onboard the vessel. Stewart immediately followed him as Gerard held the trap door open. Awkwardly they climbed back inside the vessel. Paul leaned inside and pointed to the hatch that led to the internal water tanks.

"They better not set this vessel alight," Reynald said as he started to unhinge the water tank door. The opening was just big enough to allow access. The water tank was damaged and still half full but there was just enough room for them to squeeze in. Within moments they had all managed to fit in and sat side by side shivering. Reynald looked at Gerard and feigned a look of indignation. Gerard smiled at the absurdity of their predicament. Paul looked at Stewart. He simply nodded at him. Paul turned his head as he heard Percival greet the riders as they pulled up. Quickly Paul closed the water tank access door and half crawled out of the vessel in time to see eight Tawashi horse archers. He knew immediately who they were and their fierce reputation. They would shower an enemy with arrows but unlike other horse archers they would not shy away or avoid a melee in combat. Their heavy scale armour slowed them down, yet gave them very good protection in close fighting where they would often crush their enemy's heads with their deadly maces. Their horses were covered in a beige coloured coat with tassels hanging free that matched the sun protector head covers that hung from the back of the archers' polished helmets. Cautiously one of the cavalrymen approached lowering his long lance to point at Percival, standing nearest to them. Paul saw the rider's small bow set in his bow sheath beside his round shield covering his thigh. The blue of his tunic told Paul all he needed to know about these tough battle hardened soldiers. If they mistook Paul and Percival for the enemy, the day would end very badly.

"We are under the command of Husam al Din Lu'lu," Paul said in Arabic as he moved closer to Percival.

Inside the water tank, Reynald looked at Gerard hard straining to hear what was being said. Stewart stared at the hatch, a thin line of light seeping through the top gap. Gerard's eyes looked huge as he listened intently. All three sat shivering but in total silence holding their breath in anticipation. One of the Tawashi archers dismounted and began to climb aboard the vessel.

"What are you doing?" Paul called out as Reynald's eyes widened. He drew his arming dagger, its blade flashing in the dim light shining through the gap at the top of the hatch.

Outside, Paul rushed over to the archer as he jumped into the aft section and balanced himself on the tilted deck. He looked around confused.

"Husam you say. Prove it," the Tawashi soldier asked as he studied the vessel.

"Yes. Husam. We sailed down from Fustat together. This vessel is my proof for it was built in his shipyard...you can check the build mark of his muhtasib....there on the stern," Paul explained and pointed at the chiselled marking.

The Tawashi soldier leaned over the stern to see the marking letter and ran his fingers across it. He rubbed his beard as he thought.

"This is no ordinary vessel is it?" he asked as he jumped down beside Paul and looked at him, his dark eyes looking almost black.

"Check the damage to the bow. That is from where we rammed the Red Wolf of Kerak's ship and sank it...," Percival said as he approached, holding his arm in pain.

"Did you kill the dog?" one of the mounted archers asked loudly.

"We do not know...but Husam pursues all the other ships. A great victory was won this day against the Crusader fools," Paul said, despite his heart beating so hard he could feel it pulse in his neck. "I can tell you that one of the Crusader vessels was damaged and was on a course south to beach...it must be aground not far from here I am sure," Paul explained and pointed down the beach, which gently curved away into a natural harbour about a mile away.

The Tawashi soldier looked at Paul and Percival quizzically then back at the vessel.

"Do you have water?" he asked.

Paul's heart missed a beat.

"Yes...plenty," Paul replied trying to remain calm.

"Good. Good. We shall check beyond for the Crusader ship. One of my men shall return for reinforcements just in case. Either way, you shall have to remain here until we return. You will not last long of you try and walk in the desert so just wait here. Do you understand?" the Tawashi soldier asked as he clicked his fingers at one of his riders and then mounted his horse. He pulled the horse up and moved closer to Paul. "You cannot get far. You have nothing to fear if you are who you say you are. These shores are patrolled, so stay here until I return or..."

"Will you not leave some of your men to protect us and our vessel?" Percival asked.

Paul nearly coughed with shock at his request.

"No. I need all my men in case there are survivors from the Crusader vessel as you claim," the Tawashi soldier replied, raised his hand for his men to follow him and instantly rode away along the beach. The other soldier watched as they left before turning and riding off in the opposite direction.

3 - 40

"Percy...are you mad?" Paul asked and grabbed his good arm.

"Had to make us look genuine...," Percival said through gritted teeth as the pain in his broken arm started to overwhelm him.

Paul helped him to sit down further up the beach on some dried grasses. Quickly he re-entered the vessel, unlatched the cover hatch to the water container and beckoned Reynald to come out first. Within minutes they were all stood on the beach near to Percival, Reynald rubbing his eyes as they adjusted to the bright midday sun.

"They will be back shortly and soon as they get around that spur and see there is no vessel anywhere in sight. You have two choices...," Paul began to explain as he kept looking in both directions.

"And they are?" Gerard asked.

"So you call me a fool, I hear," Reynald said and put his hands upon his hips and stared at Paul.

"You wish to argue that point right here and now do you? And yes you are a fool. Look what your actions have brought upon all of us...look!" Paul retorted.

Gerard shook his head in surprise at his friend's remarks.

"Reynald, old chap. We are in no position to be arguing over name calling, which in actual fact probably just saved our arses...so for once shut the fuck up...please," Gerard said and looked at Reynald and raised his eyebrows.

Stewart nearly laughed at hearing Gerard but quickly checked the smile on his face as Reynald looked at him. Stewart shrugged his shoulders.

"We have two service boats...one you can take. They have oars and a sail. You can either head out across the sea, or you can enter the desert and take your chances there. The choice is yours but you have to make one and now," Paul explained.

Reynald looked around in all directions as his mind fought to make a decision. He then walked up to Paul.

"If you had not rammed us, today would have had a different outcome and we would not be in this predicament."

"If you had not tried to murder innocent women and children, I would not have been forced to do the right thing and ram you," Paul shot back.

"We are wasting valuable time here," Stewart interrupted.

"You think you are the only one who has dreams. Ask that Theo about me and mine...how he convinced me I had a destiny. Ask him why he helped get me released from Aleppo...ask him when next you see him. I was once naive and gullible just like you are now and listened and believed all of his horseshit about doing the right thing...the fucking 'heart's code'. Well the right thing is to eradicate the entire faith of Islam...for if we do not, they will multiply and destroy our very way of life...ask him!" Reynald snapped, his face close to Paul's.

"You are wrong," Paul replied not moving.

"Come on, girls…now is not the time for this," Gerard interrupted and pulled Reynald back a few paces. "Now where are these two service boats for I see none on your vessel?"

Paul stared hard at Reynald as he walked past him toward the stern of the vessel. He bent down to look at the starboard side but it was wedged deep into the sand. Quickly he moved around to the port side, leaned up, flipped open two round hatches, reached inside and pulled a cord hard. As he pulled the second cord, the entire port side of the stern seemed to drop down and out by several inches.

"I need your help to pull this down," Paul asked as he looked over at the group.

Puzzled, Reynald walked over. Paul indicated with a slight nod that he take the weight at one end with him as Gerard and Stewart took the weight at the opposite end. Paul then reached up, and pulled a lever which released a twelve foot long service boat. As they struggled to take the weight, Paul pushed it so it rolled over and level. Reynald struggled with its weight but quickly they lowered the boat onto the sand. As they stood back, Reynald smiled, surprised, as Paul started to pull up a single mast and lock it into position.

"What manner of a vessel is this?" Reynald asked, smiling broadly.

For a moment Paul actually saw a man of appreciation. He shook his head quickly and reminded himself this was Reynald.

"I cannot release the second one as it is trapped in the sand. If we were in the water, it is easy to unlock them and they just lower into the sea, but I am afraid you will need to launch her yourselves. 'Tis your decision for you may run into Husam's ships as they return," Paul explained as he pulled out the main sail.

"We stand no chance in the desert…and a long walk even if we did survive it…so we shall take our chances on the water," Reynald explained, still impressed with the boat and how it had fitted into the side of the larger vessel. "'Tis a real shame you are so blinded by your Muslim friends for we could sorely do with your talents," Reynald said, shaking his head.

Even Gerard frowned, surprised at his comment. Paul looked at Stewart.

"If you sail south, the winds will take you away fast enough from Husam's fleet that he will never see you. Then cross in darkness. You may hit your shores far enough south to miss any of Husam's pursuit ships...," Paul explained.

"We will need water," Stewart said as he fumbled about beneath his tunic. He suddenly pulled out the Order's Piebauld standard flag. "'Tis all we stand for...I could not leave it."

Paul looked at him again. He looked exhausted already, a sadness across his face he could not hide. Quickly Stewart folded the standard flag and put it back under his tunic as Gerard smiled at him almost with pride that he had still been able to keep hold of their standard.

"We have plenty of water we can give you to take. Just make sure you make it and live. And when you do make it...please somehow get a message to me you are alive...please," Paul asked.

Reynald shook his head and began to push the boat toward the sea. Gerard started to help.

"You get the water and we'll get this afloat," Reynald stated and heaved.

Within minutes the boat was floating in the sea, Gerard up to his waist holding her position as Reynald sorted the main sail. Stewart hauled the last of several water bladders on board and turned to face Paul as he placed two more inside. Percival watched on, his face an ashen white and in pain.

"You must leave now before the soldiers return," Paul said as Gerard climbed aboard.

"Brother," Stewart said quietly. He hesitated as emotion welled up inside him. He shook his head, lost for words, and sighed.

"Brother indeed," Paul said back, pulled Stewart close and hugged him. Surprised, Stewart stood motionless, his arms outstretched. Eventually he hugged Paul back.

"Really?" Reynald called out, his tone condescending.

Paul broke away from Stewart and looked at him as they locked arms. No words were needed as Stewart's expression and his one word, brother, had said it all. Paul patted Stewart and helped push him up into the vessel. Reynald hoisted the main sail, which instantly bellowed out full of wind. As Stewart sat up, he lifted a leather jacket, one of several Paul had thrown inside for protection. He smiled and waved gratefully. Paul stood in the sea up to his knees as the boat rapidly sailed away, Gerard and Reynald not even looking back once.

"Bastards...didn't even say thank you," Percival said as he approached. "You realise those Tawashi lot will instantly see the service boat has gone."

Paul turned to look at him. He was correct of course. Quickly and without a word, Paul removed several water bladders and hauled them up the beach along with some blankets, dried biscuits and a single jacket to keep Percival warm. Percival watched on bemused as Paul entered the vessel, poured oil from the waterproofed lanthorn all over the aft deck, jumped down, struck the flint and lit a lighting stick. He blew it until it burned brightly, rubbed a handful of dried beach grass into a roll, lit that and then threw it into the aft section instantly lighting the oil. Paul stepped backwards slowly as the flames flickered. Paul clenched his fists praying the flames would take hold. Percival came and stood beside him. He knew how difficult this action was for Paul to take, but he also knew it was a necessary one. Percival picked up the half full lanthorn and threw it into the aft section. It smashed and the remaining oil instantly caught light and popped as it burst into flames, catching the remnants of the main sail. Both stood and watched in silence as the vessel slowly at first caught fire. Within minutes the entire vessel was completely ablaze. As the heat intensified and black smoke rose skyward, Paul and Percival moved back up the beach and sat down on the dried grass. Percival rubbed Paul's shoulders knowing the anguish he was clearly feeling not only for the loss of his vessel but also a deeper concern for his brother. Paul checked the sand to see if their footprints could be distinguished showing more than two of them were there. With the sea washing in and out, most of the footprints had vanished and no one would be able to tell that others had been present. Paul lowered his head into his hands filled with conflicting emotions.

"Well. my friend…thank you…for at least you did not get me killed this day," Percival stated and winced in pain.

Port of La Rochelle, France, Melissae Inn, spring 1191

"Oh my Lord...so that is how Reynald escaped," Ayleth remarked.

"He should have killed him when he had the chance for it would have saved thousands of lives later," the Templar stated, shaking his head.

"'Twas not Paul's way," the old man said as he looked at the Templar. "Besides, he had his brother to think of."

"Well we all know Reynald returned to Kerak but we never knew how he

survived that naval defeat, especially when so many of his fellow knights perished," the Hospitaller commented and pulled a tankard near.

"Now we do," Simon remarked.

"It was not something either Reynald or Gerard could exactly shout about for they knew if they did, Paul would have been arrested the minute word reached Cairo that he had helped them. But in truth they only remained silent of the fact as Stewart had pleaded with them not too for Reynald did toy with the idea of revealing the manner of their escape," the old man explained.

"The absolute total shit!" Ayleth remarked, which drew instant looks of surprise.

"What happened when those Towerish soldiers returned?" Sarah asked. Stephan laughed at her incorrect pronunciation.

"Tawashi horse archers," the old man replied, smiling broadly, trying not to laugh. "As soon as they saw the smoke, they rushed back to the vessel. Percival told them he was cold and wet and had tried to light the lanthorn, which he dropped and the vessel caught fire. They accepted that. With no vessel to guard, the men helped Paul and Percival back to the nearest village further up the coast. The following morning when Husam returned to port, he was very concerned to hear Paul and Percival had not returned and sent out a search party immediately. It was two days before his Mamluk guards located them, by which time a local physician had set Percival's broken arm...but not before word had been sent to Cairo that they were missing. When word reached Alisha, she remained composed and calm but Nyla fainted. Ishmael instantly volunteered to come and help in any search but Thomas talked him out of that. After Alisha had sorted Nyla, she explained to Arri what had happened, but Arri simply smiled and told her his father was fine and would be home soon. Alisha went to her room and was promptly sick. She cried inconsolably, alone."

"Oh the poor dear," Sarah said sadly.

"How long did they have to wait to find out they were still alive?" Peter asked.

"Nearly five days."

"I think I would have been sick too," Ayleth remarked.

"Five days. Why so long?" the Templar asked.

"Because there was a lot of confusion and the priority of signalling went to confirming Husam's victory and the search for Reynald. When Paul finally arrived back at the main port, he was greeted by a pitiful sight of many of the captured knights shackled and on public display in the port's centre...in the midday sun."

"I know this victory served Saladin well indeed. Reynald was indeed a fool for escalating such a crisis," the Templar said as he looked at Gabirol.

"Yes indeed. But from the point of view of Saladin, in terms of territory, his war against Mosul was going well, but he had still failed to achieve his objectives and his army was shrinking fast. Taqi al-Din took his men back to Hama, while Nasir al-Din Muhammad and his forces had also left. This encouraged Izz al-Din and his allies to take the offensive against Saladin...so you see Reynald was not the only issue Saladin had to deal with. Husam having sorted out Reynald, for now, enabled Saladin in early April, without waiting for Nasir al-Din, along with Taqi al-Din, to advance against the coalition of Izz al-Din, marching eastward to Ras al-Ein unhindered. By late April, after three days of actual fighting, the Ayyubids captured Amid. He handed the city to Nur al-Din Muhammad together with its stores, which consisted of 80,000 candles, a tower full of arrowheads, and 1,040,000 books. In return for a diploma granting him the city, Nur al-Din swore allegiance to Saladin, promising to follow him in every expedition in the war against all and any Christian forces and repairing damage done to the city. The fall of Amid, in addition to territory, convinced Il-Ghazi of Mardin to enter the service of Saladin, weakening Izz al-Din's coalition."

"A very strategic couple of months for Saladin then?" Gabirol remarked and wrote a line in his journal.

"Yes it was. Saladin attempted to gain the Caliph an-Nasir's support against Izz al-Din by sending him a letter requesting a document that would give him legal justification for taking over Mosul and its territories. Saladin aimed to persuade the caliph claiming that while he conquered Egypt and Yemen under the flag of the Abbasids, the Zengids of Mosul openly supported the Seljuks, who are rivals of the caliphate and only came to the caliph when in need. He also accused Izz al-Din's forces of disrupting the Muslim Holy War against the Crusaders, stating 'they are not content not to fight, but they prevent those who can.' Saladin defended his own conduct claiming that he had come to Syria to fight the Crusaders, end the heresy of the Assassins, and stop the wrong-doing of the Muslims. He also promised that if Mosul was given to him, it would lead to the capture of Jerusalem, Constantinople, Georgia, and the lands of the Almohads in the Maghreb, 'until the word of God is supreme and the Abbasid caliphate has wiped the world clean, turning the churches into mosques.' Saladin stressed that all this would happen by the will of God, and instead of asking for financial or military support from the caliph, he would capture and give the caliph the territories of Tikrit, Daquq, Khuzestan, Kish Island and Oman. It was this vow that several of his close supporters and aids would constantly remind him of later. Queen Tamar got wind of his vow and consequently entered into agreements where she promised not to support Crusader forces in the

region if he in return promised not to enter into conflict with her nation. This was duly agreed and accepted by Saladin and Queen Tamar," the old man explained. [89]

"I wish to hear what happened when Paul returned home," Ayleth asked excitedly.

"Well, emotional as you can imagine...and he had two guests arrive with him," the old man said as he moved upon his chair to sit more comfortably.

"Pray tell us all, please," the wealthy tailor said quietly.

"Of course," the old man smiled.

"Before you do, Reynald and Gerard must have been good seamen to have successfully navigated across the Red Sea. How did they do it?" the Genoese sailor asked.

"Recall when I explained how Kratos detailed the Celtic cross. Reynald himself was well versed in its practical use as well as general navigation and the vessel had two on board. Stewart was also taught by his father so between them, their biggest concern was catching the winds correctly and evading Muslim vessels and not landing in error near Medina. They managed to navigate during the hours of darkness, using the stars, up the eastern shoreline and eventually up through to the port city of Ayla, which Reynald's forces still held on to, though very precariously," the old man explained.

"Why precariously?" Peter asked.

"Because Saladin had already taken the port years before, only to lose it back to Reynald in November 1181. Reynald's forces then controlled the area from their fortress of Helim, as well as from the fortified small island of Ile de Graye, now known as Pharaoh's Island, near the shore. When Saladin heard this, he vowed to retake the port and island back. After his disastrous clash with Husam, Reynald did indeed lose it back to Saladin shortly after passing through it. A very close shave indeed for him."

"And Paul and Percival?" Ayleth asked, a hint of impatience in her voice.

Harbour of Halaib, 10 miles south of the port of Aydhab, Egypt, April 2nd 1183

The sun was high when Paul and Percival rode into the central dockside area of the harbour, escorted by several Tawashi archers and Mamluk reconnaissance light cavalry. Several ships from Husam's fleet were berthed stern on against the main harbour wall as stores and supplies were being loaded upon them. Husam, having ordered the search for Paul, had already moved on north taking some of the captured knights with him. A section of Mamluk guards stood over several Christian knights, all clearly worse for wear chained and shackled against a wall. Paul's heart jumped fearing Stewart to be amongst them just as five other knights were manhandled aggressively down the gangplank of the nearest ship. Pushed and prodded by two naval marines, one of the men fell hard. He was stripped almost naked with just the remains of his chausses undergarments and ripped shirt hanging from his exposed back. He was covered in several burn marks and deep cuts. Upon his knees, he gritted his teeth, his hands shackled together, when the man behind him started to help him up. Instantly the marine nearest pushed him away hard with his small defensive shield causing him to fall over. As he landed, he looked directly at Paul. It was Upside. Paul's eyes widened and without hesitation he dismounted and ran towards him. The marine raised his shield about to hit Upside again when Paul ran into him at full force knocking him aside, Paul tripping over Upside. Quickly Paul rolled onto his back and elbows to stand, when he looked at the injured knight in front of Upside and saw it was Nicholas. The marine drew his sword and thrust it downwards toward Paul but he rolled sideways, jumped up and drew his sword just as a second blow came down upon him, the marine's sword breaking in half as it made contact with Paul's sword. Paul stood up straight and looked at the surprised marine.

"Stand down!" Paul shouted in Arabic as he moved over to Nicholas. Several other marines came running over along with several Mamluk guards all looking on confused.

The Tawashi guards who had escorted Paul in, physically pulled back several of the marines. Nicholas looked at Paul and feigned a very pained smile, closed his eyes and rolled over onto his side and passed out. Upside crawled over to him and lay across him protectively as he looked up at Paul in utter surprise, shock registering in his eyes.

"Paul...what is the meaning of this?" one of the Mamluk guards asked, pushing his way forwards.

Paul sighed with relief seeing one of Husam's guards who thankfully recognised him.

"This is not right. These men are good men and deserve to be treated better than this," Paul explained holding his sword toward the marine.

"Many good men have died these past few days...they are our captives and we act under Husam's orders," the Mamluk guard explained as he looked down at Upside and Brother Nicholas.

"Be that as it may, Saladin knows these two men personally and he would not wish harm upon them...that I swear to you this day upon my very life and if I am so later proved wrong then I will gladly join these men in their fate," Paul explained as Percival approached apprehensively. "Will two more make any difference?"

"What do you propose?...we cannot let them simply go free."

"Pass them to my charge...and if later Saladin disagrees with me, they shall be returned...with me along with them as I just swore," Paul explained and knelt beside Nicholas to check him as Upside nodded at him appreciatively.

"Paul...this is highly irregular. But I know both Husam and Saladin favour you. Perhaps they would grant you this wish, but how can I?"

"I can vouch for them," Turansha suddenly called out as he pushed his way forwards.

"You! You are supposed to be in Syria," Paul said aloud, alarmed, and pointed his sword toward him.

"My friend, we meet again. I have heard of your great deed at sea. 'Tis almost legendary in Cairo already...though they all think you dead," Turansha smiled as he rubbed his hands together and walked nearer. "I told you once before my friend, not all your foes are your enemy. I am here to help."

"For what in return?" Paul asked just as Percival suddenly passed out. Two Tawashi archers rushed to his side and helped him to sit up against several sacks of grain and started to undo his tunic. He had clearly overheated. Paul looked down at Nicholas, who was still unconscious. Paul's mind raced. If in Cairo word had reached them, then Alisha would think him dead already. A cold chill ran down his back. He looked up at Turansha, who stood smiling at him. "Well?"

"Oh, just your acknowledged friendship is enough. And one day, perhaps, when I call upon you, maybe you will honour it and return the favour. These men know the authority I wield," Turansha explained. Upside gently grabbed Paul's leg and looked up at him intently and shook his blood soaked head at him indicating no. "Okay...then your friends will die as surely as night follows day. They will be executed along with all the others," Turansha said calmly and turned to walk away.

Paul looked down again at Upside and Nicholas. Upside again nodded no. The Mamluk guard shrugged his shoulders. Paul's mind raced, wondering how he could keep them safe and alive long enough until he saw Husam.

"Okay...you agree to vouchsafe them this day...then come a day should you call upon me to return the favour, I shall," Paul called out after Turansha.

Turansha stopped, stood still for a few moments then turned around to face Paul, smiling broadly.

"Good man. Very wise," he said as he approached slowly. "I told you that one day we would be friends. I am not your enemy despite our previous encounters."

The Mamluk guard nodded at two Tawashi archers to help Nicholas and Upside. As they helped lift them to their feet, another Mamluk helped support Nicholas, whilst Turansha smiled, bowed his head slightly at Paul then turned and walked away.

"What of the others?" Upside asked, coughing up some blood.

Paul looked along the line of chained knights. He knew there was nothing he could do for them. The fact that the guards had agreed to allow Paul to take Nicholas and Upside was demonstration enough of the influence Turansha exerted in the region as he had boasted. Some of them shook their heads with a look of resignation to their coming fates. Anger welled inside Paul as he knew this was all down to Reynald. Such good men's lives thrown away, and for what? Brother Nicholas opened his eyes momentarily and looked at Paul as he was hauled up. Though his vision was blurred, he was just able to make out that it was Paul stood before him. He went to smile, but his lips were split and immediately started to bleed. He blinked in acknowledgement to Paul then passed out again. A Tawashi archer poured some fresh water lightly over Percival whilst another shaded him with a large mat.

6 - 5

Cairo, Egypt, April 9th 1183

Wearily Paul steered the small covered cart onto the road leading to his home. It was late afternoon as Percival looked at him, tiredness etched deep into his face, his left arm resting in a sling. It had been a long and difficult trip back up to Fustat, first by horse, then boat and the final leg by cart carrying Nicholas and Upside in the back. Both were severely injured and Paul was surprised that Nicholas had survived this far. Husam had continued his pursuit of Reynald's fleet and practically destroyed all of it, save two small ships at the Port of Ayla. Paul drew up outside the main front door. The house was quiet and appeared empty. The horse neighed as a swirl of dust danced across its face before vanishing. Paul applied the main brake and stepped down. He reached up to help Percival when the front door slowly opened. Percival nearly fell down as Paul steadied him and they both looked at the door as it opened fully. A woman stepped out wearing black, her head covered. She froze instantly and dropped the small basket she had held. Arri then stepped into view, looked up at her puzzled for a moment then looked toward Paul and Percival. His eyes widened instantly in recognition and excitement.

"Father!" he called out and ran toward him. Paul knelt down, his arms outstretched open ready to greet him just as Alisha stepped through the door. "Father!" Arri called out again and jumped into Paul's arms.

Paul closed his eyes as they welled with tears and he hugged Arri tightly. He smelt clean. It was the most wondrous smell in the world he thought as he stood up holding Arri, whose arms were wrapped around him tightly. Nyla pulled the cover from her face and threw it to the floor, instantly running for Percival. She stopped just in front of him when she saw the sling. She shook her head hesitantly, tears streaming down her face and lost for words. Percival shrugged his shoulders unable to say anything. Nyla leaned up, clasped her hands on either side of his face and kissed him longingly upon the lips. Arri looked into Paul's eyes. Paul could feel the lump in his throat and he could not speak as he stared back into Arri's big happy eyes. He swung his head to face his mother.

"I told you he was coming home," Arri said aloud, Clip clop hanging from his hand.

Paul gently grasped Clip clop's dangling front leg. The emotion that swelled inside him was more than he had ever experienced before. Alisha stepped forwards slowly in disbelief, tears welling in her eyes, and she clasped her hands together. She shook her head as her stomach knotted, her eyes fixed upon Paul's.

"Hope you have everything?" Theodoric called out as he backed out of the front door pulling it shut behind him.

Nyla broke her long kiss and faced Theodoric.

"We have now," she said, bursting with excitement.

Theodoric turned around and froze on the spot, his mouth open. Paul laughed at the sight of him then back at Alisha. She took another step closer.

"I have cried an ocean this past week over you…even though I vowed I would not cry again," she started to say but stopped and bit her bottom lip as she fought to control herself. "I…I have prayed so…so much…and…"

"Just hold me, will you?" Paul said emotionally and reached out his right arm for her.

Alisha put her hand upon his face, gently kissed him then rested her forehead against his chest as Paul put his arm around her. She sighed heavily and rubbed her head against his chest. She wrapped her arms around him gently at first, but as she started to sob, she pulled him closer and tighter. Paul kissed the top of her head, the familiar smell of her fragranced hair filling his nostrils. He was home.

"I shall never leave you again, that I swear, never," Paul said softly. Alisha pulled him even closer and kept her face buried against his chest.

"Luce…we have more for dinner tonight!" Theodoric finally shouted out and laughed, unable to contain his happiness at seeing them again.

"We have others to stay also I am afraid," Paul whispered and nodded toward the cart.

ꟷ

The room was dark save the light from a small candle set in the corner. Nicholas coughed, rasping for air as he lay upon his side on the bed. Upside sat upon the bed opposite him keeping an ever watchful eye. Paul opened the door carrying two bowls of hot food followed by Alisha. Hesitantly she entered carrying a lanthorn that filled the room with light.

"'Tis more than a great risk you have taken bringing us back here," Upside said quietly as he accepted a bowl from Paul.

"Remember…we would not be here in the first place but for you two. That we shall never forget," Paul answered quietly as he looked at Nicholas lying semi conscious on the bed. "Sister Lucy and Theodoric have treated his burns and stitched his many wounds, now it is in the Lord's hands."

"Lord's hands my arse…sorry. Pardon my lack of manners," Upside apologised quickly.

Alisha pulled up a small wooden latticed chair and sat down and gently wiped her hand across Nicholas's forehead.

"He still burns up," she whispered.

"There was much muck in the sea and I fear a lot entered his wounds," Upside explained.

"I shall sit with him whilst you two clean yourselves up. It stinks in here…I shall get Sister Lucy to light some smelling candles," Alisha said softly and rubbed her hand across Nicholas's forehead again, pushing his hair back. He shivered.

"Aye that is a good idea. I shall finish this and sort myself out…but I am afraid I only have the filth I stand in before you," Upside explained pulling his dirty and ripped shirt out.

"Come. I will show you where to bathe and bring you some fresh clothing," Paul said as he opened the door to leave. "He will be fine with Ali."

ꙮ

Upside stood up straight and pulled his ripped shirt over his head, a towel wrapped around his waist. Several scented candles lit the bathing room as Paul looked at himself in the small mirror on the wall.

Ishmael entered the room carrying a large bowl of hot water closely followed by Thomas, Luke and Mathew all carrying more bowls.

"'Tis great to see you returned safely. We had feared the worst," Thomas said as he poured his bowl of water into the sunken tiled bath, Ishmael nodding silently in agreement.

"My only fear was for Alisha and Arri," Paul heard himself reply as he checked his face in the mirror again. Several days' worth of beard was beginning to itch.

"Hardly recognised you with that baby hair on your face," Luke joked as he poured his bowl into the bath. "That should be hot enough now for you, fella." He nodded at Upside.

Upside stepped down slowly into the water testing it first with his toes before stepping fully up to his knees. He pulled the towel away and stood naked for a moment as he lowered himself down slowly. Sister Lucy entered the room carrying a bowl and approached the bath. Quickly Upside covered his hands across his groin and slid down fast into the bath just as she poured the water in near his feet.

"Don't be silly, boy…I have seen it all before in my time," Sister Lucy laughed and turned around and walked back out.

Thomas and Luke laughed as Mathew raised his eyebrows. Arri entered the room smiling as he carried something behind his back. He tugged at Paul's leg to get his attention. Paul looked down at his smiling face and knelt in front of him.

"Father…I made you a gift whilst you were away for I knew you would need it one day," Arri said proudly. "It's not completely finished but…"

"The best gift you can give me, my little man, is to call me Papa, Dad," Paul started to say.

"Old man!" Luke joked.

"Or that," Paul smiled and looked at Arri. "And you should be in bed by now."

"What…today of all days. I don't think so," Arri replied and laughed. "Close your eyes and hold your hands out." Paul smiled and closed his eyes holding his hands out. Arri placed a leather sword scabbard across his opened palms and quickly jumped back. "You can open them now," Arri said excitedly.

Paul looked at the simple leather scabbard and feigned amazement. Arri smiled even more then giggled as Paul looked it over. The more he looked at it, the more he genuinely became impressed.

"And you made this by yourself?" Paul asked. Arri nodded fast. "It is truly a wonderful gift. I shall keep it always."

"Theo and mother helped…a bit," Arri laughed.

Paul looked at the scabbard, then felt for his sword. Memories of when and how he lost his original scabbard flooded his mind. He sighed as he thought of Tara and her parents. Then of the Bull's Head bandit. Maybe Reynald's mind had changed like his had done, he pondered momentarily. He looked up at Arri, who now looked concerned. "Oh my dear son…'tis beautiful and I am so proud of you. I shall carry it always with my sword," Paul said and pulled Arri close to hug him. He kissed him on the head and held him tightly. "Thank you," he whispered.

8003

Alisha squeezed the excess water from the flannel, folded it and gently wiped it across Nicholas's brow. He turned his head muttering words as fever gripped his body. The scented candles flickered in the darkness and despite the evening being hot, Nicholas continued to shiver. Alisha looked back towards the door hearing Percival and Nyla giggling as they passed on their way to their room. She sighed as she thought of Paul. For days she had believed him dead. She had barely had time to even speak to him alone before she helped sort out Upside and Nicholas. She turned to look at him as he moaned. He had lost a lot of blood and some of his wounds had been deep. 'He must have fought hard,' she thought and gently took hold of his left hand. His hand was limp. She clasped her other hand over it cupping his between hers and held it to her face. After a few minutes just holding his hand against her cheek she leaned forward and softly kissed his forehead. As she sat back still holding his hand, he blinked and slowly opened his eyes. He struggled to focus them. Alisha leaned forward again and wiped the flannel across his face.

"I am dead surely," Nicholas whispered in a dry voice and tried to smile, his lips immediately splitting again causing him to wince.

"Ssssh, my man, sssh! You must rest," Alisha whispered back holding his hand against her.

"I am dead…or dreaming for you said your man…," he whispered and coughed as he nearly laughed. He looked into Alisha's eyes, the candlelight reflecting in her large pupils. "I am dead aren't I for you are in Cairo?"

"So are you, Nicholas, so are you," Alisha replied, smiling, and rubbed his forehead and pushed his thick hair backwards.

"Cairo…yeah right…please Lord do not let me awake from this," Nicholas whispered, his voice trailing off as he fell back into unconsciousness.

Alisha let out a slight chuckle at his remark, patted his hand and shook her head emotionally, a tear falling down her cheek. It had been the longest few days in her life and emotionally exhausting, but not once had Arri doubted that Paul would return. She felt sad to see Nicholas in such a state and worried he could still die, but as she looked back toward the door, she knew her place was beside Paul. She wanted to hold him and never let him out of her sight ever again. She would sit with Nicholas until Upside returned then she would be with Paul. She broke down in tears and sobbed as quietly as she could with relief. Nicholas squeezed her hand briefly.

Paul eased himself into bed and pulled up the clean white sheets. He leaned over and extinguished the single candle beside his bed as the moonlight shining was more than enough to light the room. Sweet aromas drifted in through the open window. He left the curtains open so he could see the moon. He had tucked Arri into his bed and sat watching him until he fell asleep. Theodoric and Ishmael had asked if he wished to talk about events, but he simply wished to be alone with Alisha. He sighed as he wondered if she would join him or keep watch over Nicholas all night. Upside and Thomas had told him they would keep an eye on him, but as Paul lay there, he did not know whether to laugh, cry, get up or be upset that Alisha was sat with Nicholas, despite his injuries. A pang of jealousy filled his mind coupled with a sense of guilt for feeling like that. He reached over and picked up his new scabbard from Arri. He smiled as he looked over it. He sat up and picked up his sword hung over the bedstead. He untied it from the single rope and loop scabbard he had been using since Tara was killed. He had deliberately kept the simple belt and loop out of respect and by way of remembrance of her sacrifice. But now he had a new scabbard and one he was sure Tara would understand him now using. Gently he offered the tip of the sword to the mouth of the scabbard and eased the blade in. It clicked securely as it pressed home against the locket section. Paul smiled knowing that Theodoric must have given Arri the exact measurements. He held the entire sword and scabbard to his chest, rested his head back into the pillow and closed his eyes and drifted off to sleep.

ജ൫

"Paul...Paul," a female voice called out softly.

Paul opened his eyes. He was inside a passageway that had what appeared to be small square bricks set within the walls that shone light, illuminating the marbled floor and walls. Confused he spun around to check where he was. He looked down at himself and could not recognise the strange tight fitting white coloured clothes he was wearing.

"Hello!" he called out, the word echoing off in either direction. He turned around to look the other way and jumped as three women stood before him. He stepped backwards alarmed as he looked at them. They wore similar tight fitting white clothes but each had a large white cloak that hung almost to their feet. 'This is a dream, I know it is,' he thought.

"All of life is but a dream but on different levels…this is just another that you are linked to," one of the women said but he could not tell which one. They all smiled at him seeing his confusion. "Have you forgotten us already?" one asked as Paul's mind raced but then, almost at once, he remembered them, having seen them beneath Jerusalem. "You have not visited the hidden rooms of the Halls as you were supposed to do. Years have passed yet you ignore the call and your promise to visit and learn the mysteries you must take forward…"

Paul frowned as he looked at the women. They were beautiful and radiated an air of authority, wisdom but warmth and kindness too.

"I promised Alisha I would not venture beneath the pyramids…," Paul replied.

"That was a promise she should never have asked of you. Besides, she knows deep inside you must," one of the women said just as the woman nearest to him stepped silently closer. Her eyes appeared large, almost unreal as she gazed into his eyes. "Her physical mind holds her back. She fights against what she knows to be true out of fear…but after your recent adventures, she vowed and swore an oath to what you call the Lord to allow you to do that which you must. She knows that and now accepts it," the woman explained without visibly speaking. She then smiled as her two colleagues laughed sensing what Paul was thinking.

"I am so sorry…but every time I am near you, I get this sense of love and…and," Paul tried to explain but became flustered.

"Aroused?" one of the women said as they laughed. Paul blushed but there was no hiding how he felt. "It is good that you feel this for it will help you understand how and why, sometimes Alisha feels this in the presence of the one you call Nicholas." Paul's eyes widened with alarm. "Oh do not fear for she follows her heart's code of conduct seriously. She may have these conflicting physical feelings, but that is all it is…physical due to the way your bodies are made up. Natural attraction that is all. It is why you must learn to recognise such feelings and impulses…to master them. Alisha does this well enough already…and is it no different from how you feel in the presence of the one you know as Stephanie…is it not?"

Paul shook his head, embarrassed, alarmed and excited all at the same time. He let out a laugh and gently slapped his arms down by his sides.

"Is there anything that you do not know of me?" he asked, exasperated.

"Much, for most of your higher self is not only hidden from you in your present form by the veil, but also from us. But now when you return, you must also return to the path you have shied away from. You will not get the chance to build another vessel as you hope for it is too far in advance of the time you now live in. You will learn to understand why that is so."

Paul frowned and felt annoyed. After all of his hard work, his vessel had been destroyed by his very own hand and now he was being told he would never again be able to build another.

"Would you give Arri an armed crossbow?" Kratos asked, standing behind Paul.

Paul flung around to see Kratos stood before him, smiling.

"Of course I would not," Paul answered, surprised to see him, and frowned, puzzled.

"Then understand that you cannot give mankind items ahead of their time for they will use them against themselves. Trust me on this for it has happened before...a long time ago."

"I do not even know where I am or if you are even real," Paul remarked.

Kratos stepped forwards and suddenly and without warning smacked Paul across his arm hard with his staff. Paul flinched and rubbed his arm.

"Was that real enough?" Kratos asked, laughing. "All you need do is learn what is hidden and encode it so that future generations will recognise it... but for only then. Not beforehand, as I keep telling you."

"Why can you not simply tell me what and where?" Paul pleaded.

"Where is the fun and excitement in that?" Kratos joked. Paul shook his head, utterly confused. "Paul, in all seriousness, there are great halls of knowledge and wisdom hidden by our ancestors. You know this already. We put in place codes within religions as we knew those very strong emotions, that deep religious impulse would guarantee it was carried across time intact. But alas, much has been removed, altered or misinterpreted by those who serve themselves, and now we risk those codes never being understood or revealed. If we appear and explain them, it negates the whole point of free agency and choice but also, as is always the way, we would be put up as gods ourselves," Kratos explained and paused as the three women moved to stand around Paul in a circle. "That happened before with disastrous consequences, and despite the human soul being immortal once created, it very nearly caused all to be trapped within the limited learning bounds of your physical world to continually repeat life after miserable life in suffering and ignorance."

"Oh so not much pressure upon me then," Paul half joked.

"No," Kratos smiled and placed his hand upon Paul's shoulder and looked into his eyes. "Now you must return…but do not forget."

As Kratos's words echoed through his head, he caught a brief glimpse of another young woman, the same young woman he had seen before who had looked so intently in his eyes the last time he had seen the three women together. His eyes became very heavy and he could not keep them open just as the three women encircled him and joined their arms together embracing Paul in the middle of them.

༺༻

"Paul," Alisha said softly as she lay down beside him.

The moon had moved across the night sky and sat low on the horizon as Paul stirred and opened his eyes. Alisha smiled at him, picked up the sword from off of his chest and gently placed it on the floor beside the bed. She rolled over on top of him and just looked at him. In the moonlight Paul could see her eyes were wide and full of emotion. She looked at him and wanted to ask him a thousand questions. Her heart beat faster and Paul could feel it as she pressed against his chest. Slowly she moved her hips, then kissed him. She quickly sat up straight, her legs straddling his waist and lifted up her single silk night gown and pulled it off over her head. She placed her hands upon his shoulders and smiled at him, her breasts highlighted by the moonlight.

"You were already aroused," she whispered as she reached down and felt Paul and without waiting gently guided him straight inside her. She closed her eyes and shuddered with delight as she felt him ease in and Paul's body pulsed with an almost overpowering sensation as her warmth enveloped him.

He stroked his hands up and down her thighs and then her hips as she very gently moved on him. She rested her arms back behind her and looked up, her eyes still shut. Paul ran his finger down her neck, across her collar bone and down between her breasts. Her skin felt cool, almost cold. He lifted his own night shirt up and pulled it off quickly. Alisha stopped moving and looked at him as he sat himself up putting his hands behind her back to support her as he pulled her close, their naked bodies pressing against each other. She stopped moving altogether and just stared at him trying to look deep into his eyes. 'What horrors has he seen…is he now different…how and why did he bring Nicholas here?' she asked herself. Her heart felt as if it had been wrung out like a wet flannel. She moved slightly as she sensed Paul inside her coming in pulsating throbs despite no visible sign on Paul's face of the physical release.

"You are coming, my love," she whispered and smiled, resting her forehead against his.

"No, I cannot be," Paul whispered back and tried to sit up further, looking surprised.

"Sssh…do not move…just, just stay as you are. Please."

Paul let out a slight laugh just as Alisha kissed him very softly on the lips. She then kissed his forehead and pulled him close against her chest and simply held him. Paul pulled her as close as he could, running his hands up and down her back.

"But I have not pleasured you," he whispered.

"Oh you have…you have," she replied and kissed his neck then held him again. "Please honour your promise and never leave us again…for my heart would not stand that again," she whispered and pulled his head back to look him in the eyes. She frowned as she waited for his response. "When, when I was told you were missing presumed dead…I felt a part of me die inside. 'Twas a pain I could not quell or hide from, so please, please…," Alisha explained emotionally, her eyes glistening in the moonlight.

"I swear it…," Paul replied, choked, and hugged her even tighter.

They both sat hugging each other gently rocking for over an hour, connected physically, emotionally and mentally experiencing a closeness on a level they had never shared before. Eventually they lay down and fell asleep in each other's arms.

Just before sunrise, Paul awoke hearing a female voice calling his name. Half asleep he could see the interior of the cathedral that he and Alisha had dreamt of together. This time the walls were all clean and brand new.

1 - 41

"From the old will come the new…the old will not end, just change and become as new," the female voice spoke just as he saw the image of the young woman he had seen with the three females and Kratos. She walked towards him, smiling, tilted her head slightly and smiled beautifully at him. As he moved to sit up, all the imagery of the cathedral vanished and he saw only her. Quickly he shook Alisha to wake up but she did not move. The young woman, now surrounded by light, smiled again then seemed to vanish into a ball of yellow golden light. It hovered for a few moments, moved across the room, then to the ceiling before suddenly dropping down fast and disappearing into Alisha. She moved very slightly and rubbed her hand over her stomach.

"Ali…Ali, wake up," Paul whispered and gently rocked her. "Ali, please." Alisha turned and faced him, rubbing her eyes, tired. She looked at him puzzled as he looked at her smiling broadly. "My dear Ali…you are now with child…and it is a girl," he just blurted out.

"Okay. Yes my dear," Alisha replied, still half asleep, and simply turned back over onto her side.

Paul watched her, unable to contain the sense of joy and knowing he felt. He put his arm around Alisha and tucked himself in close against her, kissed her shoulder tenderly and thanked the Lord for getting him home. He knew without a shadow of doubt she was now with child.

Port of La Rochelle, France, Melissae Inn, spring 1191

"Pregnant!" Sarah said loudly.

"I wish to learn more of what Kratos said about souls being immortal," Gabirol remarked.

"Does that not imply reincarnation...a doctrine the Church does not agree upon?" Peter asked.

"In answer, yes, Sarah, Alisha was indeed pregnant, and yes it does imply reincarnation. And maybe the Church shies away from it, even though it is mentioned in the good book itself," the old man answered.

"It is...where?" Peter asked instantly.

"'Tis a massive discussion which we do not have time to cover now but I can briefly inform you of just a few details for you will have the time later to seek out and find such information for yourselves," the old man replied.

"Yes pray tell, inform us," the farrier interrupted.

"Even the briefest look demonstrates the Bible has in it the doctrine of reincarnation. Keep in mind that the writers of the biblical books were Jews with few exceptions, and that the founder of Christianity, Jesus, was himself a Jew. Jews in

his time believed in reincarnation and the belief and theory of reincarnation was very old at the time, and the Old Testament books show this to be so. Proverbs gives the doctrine where Solomon said he was with the Creator from the beginning and that then his, Solomon's, delights were with the sons of men and in the habitable parts of the earth. This disposes of the explanation that he meant he existed in the foreknowledge of the Creator, by the use of the sentences detailing his life on the earth and with men. Also Elias and many other famous men were to actually return, and all the people were from time to time expecting them. Adam was held to have reincarnated to carry on the work he began so badly, and Seth, Moses and others were reincarnated as different great persons of subsequent epochs. In the Orient, they have always held the doctrine of the rebirth of mortals. Unfortunately what Jesus said does not agree with the present view of the Church," the old man explained, when Gabirol interrupted him.

"So you are saying then that the Church view must be given up or it, and by consent us following it, will be guilty of doubting the very wisdom of Jesus himself? he asked.

"Yes, that is exactly what I am saying. But read it for yourselves in the Bible. This, indeed, is the real position of the Church, for it has promulgated dogmas and condemned doctrines wholly without any authority that Jesus held himself," the old man replied.

"Can you give an example?" Ayleth asked.

"Yes. Take for example when a man blind from birth was brought before Jesus. The disciples wondered why he had thus been punished by the Almighty, and asked Jesus whether the man was born blind for some sin he had committed before, or one done by his parents. The question was put by them with the doctrine of reincarnation fully accepted, for it is obvious the man must have lived before, in their estimation, in order to have done sin before being born, for which he was then punished. If the doctrine was wrong as the Church declares then surely Jesus must have known it to be wrong and he would have corrected his disciples' misunderstanding or denied the whole theory, but he did not. Also, when John the Baptist, who ordained Jesus to his ministry, was killed by the ruler of the country, the news was brought to Jesus, and he then distinctly affirmed the doctrine of reincarnation and the old ideas in relation to the return to earth of the prophets by saying that the ruler had killed John not knowing that he, John, was Elias 'who was for to come'." [90]

"So you are saying that the Bible actually says that John was Elias?" Simon asked.

"Yes, yes it does. Plus, when the disciples talked about the coming of a messenger

before Jesus himself, they did not understand, and said that Elias was to come first as the messenger, and Jesus distinctly replied that Elias had come already in the person called John the Baptist. This time, if any, was the time for Jesus to condemn the doctrine, but, on the contrary, he boldly asserts it and man's real immortal nature."

"'Tis rather a massive difference of doctrine is it not?" the Templar asked.

"It is. Why do you think the Church does not like people to be able to read in Latin other than priests? People would start asking awkward questions," the old man replied and raised his eyebrows and paused. "The Church has cursed the doctrine he taught. But you will each have to study and ask yourselves who is right."

"If I understand fully what you are saying, and all that you have said so far in this tale, then all of us, our souls at least, are immortal once created...and that if the doctrine be taught that Jesus believed, then all men are immediately put on an equal basis...which means the power of the human rulers of heaven and earth is at once weakened," Gabirol commented.

"And if that happened, would not chaos reign as there would be no leadership?" Peter remarked quizzically.

"How many times have I heard that argument? No it would not if rulers ruled by mutual consent...but that is another subject I am afraid we cannot cover. In the Bible, the Almighty declared that the man who overcame should 'go out no more' from heaven. Saint Paul also gives the theory of reincarnation in his epistles where he refers to the cases of Jacob and Esau, saying that the Lord loved the one and hated the other before they were born. It is obvious that the Lord cannot love or hate a non-existing thing, and that this means that Jacob and Esau had been in their former lives respectively good and bad and therefore the Lord loved the one and hated the other before their birth as the men known as Jacob and Esau. And Paul was here speaking of the same event that the older prophet Malachi spoke of in strict adherence to the prevalent idea. Following Paul and the disciples came the early fathers of the Church, and many of them taught the same. Origen was the greatest of them. He gave the doctrine specifically, and it was because of the influence of his ideas that the Council of Constantinople five hundred years after Jesus saw fit to condemn the whole thing as pernicious. This condemnation worked because the fathers were ignorant men, most of them Gentiles who did not care for old doctrines and, indeed, hated them. So it fell out of the public teaching and was at last lost to the Western world. But it must revive, for it is one of the founder's own beliefs, and as it gives a permanent and forceful basis for ethics it is really the most important of all the doctrines that has to be remembered for then, and only then

will mankind again act and follow a path based upon the code of one's true heart," the old man sighed.[91]

"That is perhaps the fourth or fifth time I have heard you mention that saying, the code of the heart. Is this something we should make note of?" Gabirol asked.

"'Tis the only way to act and the only code that should be followed," the old man answered.

"But what if an evil man knows in his heart what he is doing is wrong, but still does a bad thing?" the Genoese sailor asked.

"Even the most evil are still children of the Lord, whatever you choose to call him, and all of us can sense, even when a person has not been told or taught what is right and wrong, and still know within themselves what is right and wrong from the heart...'tis the heart's code. Learn to recognise it and listen to it and you will not usually go far wrong," the old man answered.

Ayleth sighed and smiled at him and placed her hands across her chest.

"I like the sound of this heart's code," she said quietly.

"So this young female Paul saw who then entered Alisha as a ball of light. Are you telling us that her soul is what became the child when she fell pregnant?" Gabirol asked.

"Unequivocally yes, and so it was that Alisha fell pregnant," the old man smiled.

"And that is why Paul acts, acted, as he did...following what he thought was the right thing to do as his heart told him?" Simon asked.

The old man simply nodded yes in silence.

Chapter 56
Home of the Brotherhood

Cairo, Egypt, April 13th 1183

The late evening air was cool whilst Paul sat alone at the main dining table in silence running his fingers over the leather scabbard Arri had made for him. After a few minutes, Thomas entered through the side entrance door laughing with Attar and Theodoric.

"Oh sorry, Paul, I did not realise you were in here. Look, look who has decided to grace us with his presence," Thomas explained still laughing as he half dragged Attar in.

Paul stood up and was surprised to see Attar looking so aged just as he had appeared the first time they had met. Back then he was bedraggled, filthy and looked gaunt after his ordeal. Quickly Paul pushed thoughts of that first encounter out of his mind as memories of it still sent a cold shudder down Paul's back, the image of the Templar being beheaded flashing through his mind again. Alisha was upstairs with Nicholas trying to get him to drink more threefold water Theodoric had made.

"Assalamu Allakham," Attar said with open arms to greet him.

"Wa Allakham Assalam," Paul replied and gestured for him to come in. "Attar…is all well with you?" Paul asked, bowing his head slightly, and then offered him a chair to sit on.

"I am well and all the better for confirming with my own eyes that you are alive and well yourself. Word had travelled you were dead. As for me, I just need some hair dye and a few days to recover from my journey…if you will allow me to stay a short while?" Attar explained and asked as he leaned against the back of the chair smiling as he pulled forward a handful of his grey, almost white hair.

"Of course, of course, please sit," Paul answered as Theodoric pulled up a chair opposite Attar.

All turned to look at Upside as he slowly entered the dining hall. Hesitantly he looked at Attar for a minute then Paul.

"Sorry. I heard talking and I cannot sleep, so I thought I would join you," Upside explained and pulled out the chair nearest to him.

"I shall fetch us all a drink," Thomas said just as Sister Lucy entered.

"No you don't. Sit yourself down and I will do that," she ordered and winked at Theodoric.

"Theo, I saw that old woman hanging about outside again earlier, the one you warned us to keep an eye out for," Thomas said as he sat down moving his sword to his side carefully.

"Really…did she say anything?" Theodoric asked as he looked at Sister Lucy.

"No…just smiled and walked off again as usual. She gives me the creeps," Thomas replied.

"She saved my life…," Theodoric said quietly.

"Why does she still linger…and here in Cairo now?" Paul asked.

"'Tis you and Alisha she watches," Sister Lucy stated as she placed a jug of wine and another of water on the table. Theodoric shook his head at her. "Well, he should know she does."

"Who is this?" Upside asked, puzzled.

"Oh, an old woman who seems to constantly pop up wherever we are, yet never actually wants to say anything of importance to us," Paul explained.

"Is she a watcher?" Upside asked and pulled the water jug near.

"A watcher?" Paul asked back quizzically.

"Yes…you know, a watcher. Angels in disguise types," Upside answered as if his comment was just an everyday accepted conversational remark. "Look, even you have to agree and accept that you and Alisha have something special about you…unique, am I right, Thomas?" Upside asked and looked at Thomas to confirm. "I bet if you think back, you will probably realise that old bat has been watching you since you can remember."

Paul looked at Upside both puzzled and surprised that he was even aware of so-called watchers. He looked across at Theodoric, who just shrugged his shoulders.

"Where is Percival?" Paul asked trying to steer the conversation away from Upside's comments feeling slightly embarrassed that he obviously thought of him and Alisha as being different and special.

"Where do you think…upstairs with Nyla. They have not left their room

I don't think since you returned," Sister Lucy remarked and walked back into the kitchen.

"Upside has a point, my friend. 'Tis why we are all still here," Thomas said and smiled.

"Then why do we not have this old woman in and question her and find out her exact intentions?" Paul asked as Theodoric started to chuckle to himself. "What?"

"You should try and do that some time. It would prove most interesting," he replied.

"So you do know there is more to her than you tell," Paul exclaimed.

"Perhaps," Theodoric replied and paused. "'Tis why I asked Thomas to be ever watchful of her presence. You already know enough about her so no need for further explanation."

"Is she bad?" Paul asked.

"Hey you have met her several times yourself, and remember, she did save my life."

"I can recall seeing her in La Rochelle. She always sat at the dockside. Like you said, Upside, ever since I can remember...and she showed up with a little girl on my wedding day," Paul recalled. "And again in Crac de O'spital..."

"Then ask yourself how come she only left La Rochelle after you left?" Upside asked and raised his eyebrows as Sister Lucy placed some dates and olives on the table as a snack. "And is here now?"

Paul looked at Theodoric, unsure.

"So...can you tell me more about her or what these watchers are, or birdmen?" Paul asked looking at Theodoric and Attar in turn as he remembered what the old lady had said to him back in La Rochelle: 'The watchers...you know...the birdmen...they watch you.'

"Hope you are prepared to be up all night," Sister Lucy joked.

"Remember before when I hinted about the watchers...and about your mother...and Alisha?" Theodoric asked in all seriousness.

"Yes, I remember, but I did not really take it all on board if I am honest," Paul answered.

"Then recall how I explained how your parents wanted a child and how the old woman gave us a choice. She would call upon the people of the skies and lakes to let your mother fall with child, so long as I would swear my life to learning the secrets and teachings of the old ways of the High Kings, of the Druids?" Theodoric said and winked at Paul. "We have discussed the watchers many times, Paul, do you really need to know more?"

Paul's mind raced as he also remembered that Theodoric had to take one of their own women until she too fell with child, the old woman. Was the little girl Theodoric's, he wondered but immediately dispelled that notion for she was too young...did Sister Lucy know that part, he wondered. Theodoric raised his eyebrows and looked back at Sister Lucy. Most likely still not, Paul reasoned. He placed his hand upon his sword as he also remembered how his mother had been entrusted with it.

Port of La Rochelle, France, Melissae Inn, spring 1191

Sarah leaned across the table and gently pulled the sword around toward her. She looked closely at the simple leather scabbard then up at the old man.

"So that is how and why the sword is in such a simple scabbard. Made by his own son's hands...," she sighed and sat back down shaking her head.

"Old man, you have already told us much about the watchers. Is there more?" Gabirol asked.

"You say that Theodoric gave Nicholas the threefold water. Did it work?" Ayleth asked.

"Yes, yes it worked," the old man answered and nodded.

"What more of the watchers though?" Peter asked bluntly.

"Well...Theodoric explained in further detail to Paul about the watchers," the old man replied and paused for a moment before continuing. "You see, if what I know and understand is true, then every visible thing in the world is put under the charge of an angel. I did touch upon this before...there are many angels whom people pray to, and the Church does not like this fact. 'Tis why in time they will ban the veneration of many angels they do not deem fit nor worthy enough. I would go as far as to argue they will only allow those mentioned in the accepted Bible."

"And they are?" Simon asked.

"Oh, just the three archangels Michael, Gabriel and Raphael," the old man replied.

"What about those mentioned in the Book of Enoch?" Peter called out loudly with a raised hand.

"Peter, the Book of Enoch was banned remember and not included within the Bible. But according to the apocryphal and the Book of Enoch, it is Michael, Gabriel

and Raphael who were responsible for binding the wicked fallen angels or watchers who had supposedly transgressed God's law."

"Why was the book banned then?" Ayleth asked quietly.

"Why...it was excluded from the authorised version of the Bible because it described these fallen angels and their activities. Activities that greatly concern the Church," the old man explained in answer. "You see, in Genesis 6:1–4 it says: 'When men began to multiply on the face of the Earth, and daughters were born to them, the sons of God saw the daughters of men that they were fair; and took them wives of all which they chose.' Traditionally the Ben Eloha or 'sons of God' numbered several hundred and they descended to earth on Mount Harmon. Significantly this was a sacred place to both the Canaanites and the Hebrews who invaded their land. In later times shrines to the gods Baal, Zeus, Helios and Pan and the goddess Astarte were built on its slopes. These Ben Elohim or 'fallen angels' were also known as the Watchers, the Grigori and the Irin. In Jewish mythology the Grigori were originally a superior order of angels who dwelt in the highest heaven with God and resembled human beings in their appearance. The title 'watcher' simply means 'one who watches', 'those who watch', 'those who are awake' or 'those who do not sleep'. In esoteric traditions they were a special higher order of angelic beings created by God to be earthly shepherds of early mankind to observe and watch over us. However, they were confined by the divine prime directive not to interfere in human evolution. This is very much in keeping with what Kratos still does and the beings that appear to both Alisha and Paul. Unfortunately they decided to ignore God's command and defy his orders and became teachers to the human race, with unfortunate repercussions for both themselves and humanity. Just as Kratos told Paul."

"Who exactly is this Enoch?" the farrier asked.

"In the Bible the prophet Enoch, from the Hebrew 'hanokh' or instructor, is a mysterious figure. In Genesis 4:16–23 he is described as the son of Cain, the 'first murderer'. In Genesis 5:18–19, and several generations later, Enoch is named as the son of Jared, and it is during his lifetime that the watchers either arrive or incarnate in human bodies," the old man explained.

"Reincarnated as you explained before, yes?" Sarah interrupted.

"In a fashion yes."

1 - 6

"Like Alisha and Paul then...are they watchers?" Ayleth asked excitedly.

"No, they are not watchers," the old man smiled. "In the Book of Jubilee, allegedly

dictated by an angel of the Lord to Moses on Mount Sinai, when he also received the Ten Commandments, it says that Enoch was the first among men that are born on earth who learn writing, knowledge and wisdom. It says that Enoch wrote down 'the signs of Heaven'."

"The zodiac?" Gabirol asked, raising his eyebrows questioningly.

"Yes and more," the old man acknowledged and continued. "He did this so that man would know the seasons and months and years in relation to their respective stellar and planetary influences. Two hundred of the 'fallen angels' descended from the heavenly realm onto the summit of Mount Herman or Hermon as some say and they were so smitten by the beauty of human women that, using their new material bodies, they mated with them. This further incurred Yahweh's wrath and the consequence of this union between the Fallen Ones and mortals led to the creation of half-angelic, half-human offspring."

"Where does it say that?" Gabirol asked.

"In Genesis 6:4. These children were called the Nefelim or Nephilim and they were the giant race that once inhabited Old Earth. The fallen angels taught their wives and children a variety of new skills, magical knowledge and occult wisdom. So called magical powers were originally an ancient inheritance from the angelic realm given to early humans."

"Ah...I think I have heard of this before," Gabirol interrupted, raising his quill. "Is this not known in spiritual and metaphorical terms as the 'witch blood', 'elven blood' or 'fairy blood' that is possessed by witches and wizards...like the different types of blood groups you mentioned before?"

"Originally yes. But remember, magic is essentially just the higher understanding of nature...now in the Book of Enoch it states that the leader of the fallen angels was called Azazel, and he is often identified with Lucifer, which actually means 'the light bringer' or Lumiel 'the light of God'. He taught men to forge swords and make shields and armour. Azazel taught metallurgy and how to mine from the earth and use different metals. To the women he taught the art of making bracelets, ornaments, rings and necklaces from precious metals and stones. He also showed them how to 'beautify their eyelids' with the use of cosmetic tricks to attract and seduce the opposite sex. From these practices Enoch says there came much 'godlessness' and men and women committed fornication and were led astray and became corrupt in their ways. This was the basis for the early Church condemning the fallen angels for teaching women to make necklaces from pieces of gold and bracelets for their arms. Saint Paul said that women should cover their head in the synagogue (Corinthians: 11:5–6). This was because the fallen angels were attracted to human females with long flowing hair."

"Oh I always wondered why we had to cover our hair in church," Sarah said and pulled a mock grimace as she bunched up her hair.

"'Tis also a custom in Islam. The fallen angel Shemyaza, another form of Azazel, is said by Enoch to have taught humans the magical art of enchantment; the fallen angel Armaros taught the resolving or banishing of enchantments; Baraqijal taught astrology; Kokabiel, the knowledge of the constellations; Chazaqiel, the knowledge of the clouds and the sky, weather lore and divination; Shamsiel, the signs of the sun and the solar mysteries; Sariel the courses of the moon and the lunar cycles used in horticulture and agriculture and the esoteric lunar mysteries; Penemuel instructed humans in the art of writing and reading; and Kashdejan taught the diagnosis and healing of diseases and the science of medicine."

"Are they not all good and godly things to learn?" Simon asked, looking confused again.

"The watchers were the bringers of culture and civilisation to the early human race. It is therefore strange that in orthodox Judeo-Christian religious texts they are misrepresented as evil corrupters of humanity. Azazel, the leader of the watchers, as mentioned before, was identified with Lucifer or Lumiel. In the Qur'an it is said that Lucifer-Lumiel (Iblis) rebelled against Allah because he was told to bow down and worship the clay-born 'man of earth' Adam and refused as I explained previously. He was forced to fight a battle in Heaven with the Archangel Mikael or Michael and his Army of the Lord. As a result Lumiel and his rebel angels were cast out of Heaven and fell down to earth. Here Lumiel became the Lord of the World and in Christian mythology he was falsely identified with Satan. However, esoterically Lumiel or Lumial is not an evil satanic figure luring humankind into temptation and acts of evil as the Church represents him. He is the angel of God who rebelled against the static, established cosmic order and set in motion the forces of change and evolution...the right to free agency and free choice."

"Can I sink ever lower into confusion?" Simon asked with a sigh and shrugged his shoulders.

"Probably," Sarah joked back.

"Simon, as I have said before, all that you hear does go in and you will remember it again," the old man said reassuringly. "I can tell you that Lumiel originated in Canaan as Shahar, the god of the morning star, Venus. He had a twin called Shalem, who was also symbolised by the planet Venus, but as the evening star."

"Is that not the same as the appellation to Jesus, as the bright morning and evening star?" Peter asked.

"Yes, you could say so," the old man answered and paused, but Peter simply

nodded his head. "These divine bright and dark twins represented the solar light emerging from the darkness of night at dawn and descending into it at dusk. They were the children of the goddess Asherah, whom the Hebrews adopted and worshipped when they settled in Canaan and practised it alongside reverence of the tribal storm god Yahweh."

"Yahweh...a storm god! But I thought that is the Jewish name for God...not a storm god?" Ayleth asked, looking shocked.

"That is correct. They are one and the same," the old man replied. "Also understand that the Old Testament has several references to the continued worship of Asherah as 'Queen of Heaven' by the Hebrews."

"But they are monotheistic are they not?" the wealthy tailor asked, surprised.

"Yes, apparently, but they did this and worship took place at shrines in sacred groves on hills where they made offerings to her. In Canaanite mythology, Shahar was Lord of the Morning Star, who was cast down from heaven for defying the high god El in the form of a lightning bolt. In that form he fertilised Mother Earth with his divine phallic force. Azazel is represented as a metal-smith and a fire-working sorcerer or magician. He has also been compared to the biblical first smith Tubal-Cain, a descendant of Cain. The actual name Azazel can be translated as 'god of victory', 'the strength of God', 'the strong god' and even 'the goat god'. In the apocryphal Apocalypse of Abraham, he is called 'the lord of heathens' suggesting he was originally a pagan god. He has also been identified with the serpent in the Eden myth that seduced the first woman, Eve. In a Persian text known as the Urm al-Khibab or The Primordial Book, dating from the eighth century BC, the angel Azazil or Azazel is said to have refused to acknowledge the superiority of Adam over the angels. As a result Allah expelled him and his rebel angels from the heavenly realm to live on earth. More generally in Islamic lore Azazel or Azrael is the angel of death and he acts as a guide for the souls of the dead. In Leviticus 16:8–10 and in a curious Hebrew ritual is recorded that features Azazel as the name for the 'scapegoat' that takes on the communal sins of Israel. It says that the high priest Aaron took two goats from the flock and cast lots, which in itself is practised divination, to choose which one would be the scapegoat and sacrificed as a 'sin offering'. The high priest confessed all the 'impurities of the children of Israel' over the head of the Azazel goat. By this ritually symbolic act he transferred to the unfortunate animal all their guilt and sins so they could be absolved of them. The goat was then either cast out into the wilderness to die or thrown over a cliff to be dashed to pieces on the rocks below. This ancient and archetypal concept of the scapegoat sacrificed for the sins of the human race and abandoned in the wilderness is a powerful and

potent motif that appears several times in biblical myths. It is seen in the story of Cain, who becomes an exiled wanderer on the earth after being marked by God and banished 'east of Eden' after killing his brother Abel. In one Jewish legend the wise King Solomon, a powerful magician who could summon and control demons, fell from grace because he 'whored after foreign gods'. He was forced by God to leave Jerusalem and wander in the desert disguised as a beggar. Also after their exodus from slavery in Egypt, Moses and the Israelites were forced to spend forty years wandering in the desert before they were allowed to enter the Promised Land. In Ancient Egyptian mythology, the dark god Set is represented as a divine outcast who dwells in the desert and after she left Adam his first wife Lilith or Liliya fled to the wilderness away from human habitation."

"What...Adam had a first wife?" Ayleth asked, very surprised.

"Yes. I explained this before briefly when you first arrived," the old man answered.

"And Lilith is also connected to the lily and fleur de lys," Simon stated proudly.

The old man smiled at Simon then continued.

"In the New Testament Jesus wandered in the wilderness for forty days and nights. He was not accepted as a teacher in his own town of Nazareth and was rejected as the promised messiah by his people. When Jesus was crucified he symbolically took on the role of the sacrificial scapegoat who dies to cleanse the sins of the human race."

"But also to stop further human sacrifices...is that not what you said before?" Simon asked.

"That is also correct," the old man replied, smiling, then continued. "Originally a goat would have been selected by means of a divination ritual and then offered to a desert god or demon that had to be placated by the shedding of blood. Eventually the sacrifice was made to Yahweh as a petition to forgive the sins of his followers. Azazel had a retinue of hairy he-goat demons known as the se'irim who, like the watchers, lusted after human women. It cannot be a total coincidence that the Church imagines the Devil or Satan in the form of a hairy half-human he-goat with a massive erect phallus who has sexual intercourse with his female worshippers at the Witches' Sabbath. Shemyaza is seen by some as either the emissary of Lumiel or one of his avatars as an incarnated divine being in human form. He not only fell in love with human women, but also with the Babylonian deity Ishtar, the goddess of love and war. She promised to have sex with him if he would reveal the secret name of God. When Shemyaza told her, Ishtar used this forbidden knowledge to ascend to the stars and she reigned over the constellation of Pleiades or the

Seven Sisters. While the other watchers were rounded up by the archangels and punished by God, Shemyaza voluntarily repented his error and sentenced himself to hang upside down in the constellation of Orion the Hunter, with whom he is sometimes identified. In the Cabbalistic tradition, Naamah, the sister of the biblical first smith Tubal-Cain, seduced Azazel and she has been associated with Ishtar. The end result of the illicit relationships between the watchers and 'the daughters of men' was, according to Judeo-Christian propaganda, the spawning of a monstrous race of warlike, blood-drinking cannibalistic giants called the Nephilim. Genesis 6:4 less dramatically describes them as 'the mighty men of old, men of renown'. At first they were fed manna, ambrosia or the food of the gods by Yahweh to stop them consuming human flesh, but they rejected it. They slaughtered animals for food instead and then began to hunt down and eat human prey. In the biblical myth of Cain and Abel the dispute between the two brothers that led to the first murder is over the nature of the offerings made to Yahweh. Abel, a 'keeper of sheep' or nomadic herdsman, offered the 'firstlings of the flock', and Cain, who was 'a tiller of the ground' or farmer-gardener, offered 'the fruit of the ground' (Genesis 4:2–4). Abel's burnt offerings of animal flesh and blood were pleasing to Yahweh, but he rejected the vegetables, cereal and fruit offered by his brother."

"So to clarify, the watchers are one and the same as these fallen ones, the Nephilim?" Gabirol interrupted.

"In myth and legend yes, but not what they actually are now. You see, the idea of semi-divine heroes was born from the ancient myths of unions between the gods and mortals. Nephilim are in fact described as the guardians of arcane knowledge who 'knew all the mysteries of nature and science'. They also taught and instructed early humans in the domestication and rearing of animals. In the Book of Enoch it says that when Yahweh saw the lawlessness, chaos, corruption and sexual immorality that had been caused by the interaction of the watchers and humans he decided to intervene through the agency of the archangels Michael, Raphael, Gabriel and Uriel. He commanded Raphael to bind Azazel hand and foot like a sacrificial goat and cast him into a deep ravine in the desert. Gabriel was sent on a divine mission to destroy 'the bastards and reprobates' and 'the children of the watchers amongst men'. The Archangel Michael, the commander of the Army of God, was sent to arrest Shemyaza and bind him 'under the earth' until Judgement Day. As we have seen, the fallen angel repented his sins and sentenced himself to cosmic exile among the stars. The Book of Jubilee says that the archangels bound the watchers 'in the depths of the earth' and in Judaic lore they are imprisoned in a mysterious 'second Heaven'. However, it is also said that some of these 'mighty warriors' have a special

place reserved for them in Sheol, the Jewish underworld. There they are said to lie in state 'with shield and spear intact'. Watchers are, I can tell you, as Theodoric most certainly could, one and the same semi-divine, semi-mythical Tuatha De Danann, children of the goddess Dana who were a race of ancient magicians who descended to earth on the sacred hill of Tara in the ancient Emerald Isle. With the coming of Christianity, the Tuatha De Danann was banished into the 'hollow hills' and became the Sidhe or Shee or 'Shining Ones', the elves and faeries of Irish folklore. There has always been a strong belief among the peoples of the Emerald Isle that the Good People or faeries were originally the fallen angels who sided with Lucifer in the Battle of Heaven. In short, the watchers are accused of being angelic beings with a spiritual form that incarnate in physical bodies to have sexual relations with mortal women. Some claim they were of earthly origin and that the biblical myth of the watchers represents memories of a primeval 'elder race' of super-humans belonging to a lost civilisation who taught their technology to more primitive people, which, in truth, is in fact nearer the truth and why we have female watchers too," the old man explained and took a sip of rose water.

"I always thought Lucifer was the half-goat half-man Devil...not as you explain," Simon said almost nonchalantly.

"Mention Lucifer or Devil and most people run scared, the same with the value 13...but let me explain that symbolically. Lucifer or Lumiel is known as the Lord of Light as he is the first-born of creation. He represents the active cosmic energy of the universe and has been identified with fire, light, phallic power, independent thought, consciousness, progress, liberty and independence. He is also described as the light bringer and 'the spirit of intellectual enlightenment and the freedom of thought' without whose influence humanity would be no better than animals. In the Bible Lucifer or Satan as he is mistakenly called is often depicted in reptilian form as either a dragon or a serpent. In Western mythologies this creature is commonly misrepresented as a symbol of the powers of darkness, chaos and evil. In contrast, in Eastern mythology the dragon is a good omen representing fertility and good fortune. Lumiel-Lucifer is often identified with the serpent in the Eden myth described in Genesis. The biblical serpent is regarded as the personification of knowledge, wisdom and enlightenment who liberated the first humans from the spiritual ignorance imposed on them by Yahweh. The serpent is seen as the symbol of an outside liberating force that quite literally opened the eyes of Adam and Eve to the reality of the created universe and the wonders of the material world. The snake, serpent or dragon is an ancient mythical and archetypal image of the solar phallic power or life force that is associated with Lucifer and the explosion of light following the

divine celestial event that created the universe. When the first man and woman ate the forbidden fruit, the apple, from the Tree of the Knowledge of Good and Evil in the astral or heavenly garden, they became consciously aware. Their first realisation was that their physical 'cloaks of flesh' were naked. They rushed to cover their genitals as they had become aware of the so-called 'serpent power' or kundalini that can be raised by sexual intercourse and non-reproductive sex acts. They also ate from the Tree of Life, which initiated the cycle of birth, life, death and rebirth and of human souls incarnating in physical form. It was the deliberate intervention of Lucifer and the fallen angels in human evolution, rather than any defiance of cosmic authority, which ultimately led to their fall from heavenly grace. The watchers' only 'crime' was that they wanted to help the progress of their human flock. However, the refusal of Lucifer-Iblis to recognise the creation of human beings means that the Fall from heavenly grace was inevitable. The Egyptians wrote they came to Egypt from Ta-Ur, the 'Far Foreign Land'. The Egyptian term 'Neteru' means 'guardians'. The watchers were a specific race of divine beings known in Hebrew as 'nun resh ayin' or 'irin' meaning 'those who watch' or 'those who are awake', which is translated into Greek as Egrhgoroi egregoris orgrigori, meaning 'watchers'." [92]

"Oh...well, that all makes sense then," Simon said and shrugged his shoulders and sighed in an exaggerated manner.

"Fear not, my friend, I shall explain this again for you later if you wish?" Gabirol said quietly and leaned across and patted Simon's arm.

"And Theodoric explained all of this yes?" the Templar asked.

"Yes, yes he did and more," the old man replied.

Cairo, Egypt, April 13th, 1183

"I won't even ask how you say watchers again in Greek," Upside laughed and quickly rubbed his side as he winced in pain.

In the dim light shone by the lanthorns Paul could see clearly the deep lines etched in Upside's face. Up close, it was easy to see that he was a lot older than he actually looked, but as he grimaced in pain from one of the cracked ribs he had suffered, his age became more obvious as shadows highlighted the lines around his eyes.

"Well all you need to know is, that woman can make herself appear the aged old crow as you see her, but trust me, she can also appear beautiful other times," Theodoric explained and looked across to Paul and winked.

"Better not tell my lot that," Thomas joked.

"Why can't these so-called watchers watch the likes of Reynald and Gerard then…you know, and influence them a bit more?" Upside asked.

"How do you know they haven't?" Attar shot back and raised his eyebrows quizzically.

"There was a time when they tried, but alas as you know yourself, Reynald is obsessed with wiping out Islam, and Gerard, well, he is simply too hot headed himself at times as well as impetuous and follows Reynald almost blindly," Theodoric answered.

"Too easily led by Reynald unfortunately," Attar remarked confirming Theodoric's comment.

"I can vouch for that…and they both lack honour, integrity and any sense of nobility," Upside said as he shook his head disapprovingly.

"You surprise me with such words," Paul said, looking at Upside.

"Why…you know them both yourself only too well. I have served under them, and but for my sworn vows to the Order…not them, I think I would have long since put both in their graves for their actions…and I do not mean actions to Muslims alone," Upside replied and studied the bowl of dates and olives.

Thomas moved in his chair and sat back to look at Upside.

"My friend. You are a battle hardened and experienced knight…like my men…so if you ever tire of your service to the Order, we could certainly do with some fresh blood amongst us," he explained. Thomas looked at Upside puzzled for a few moments. "Seriously, 'tis honour above all else we respect. We know only too well of the ways of our so-called nobility."

"Nobility you say. I see so very little of that in our self serving egotistical and arrogant lords and ladies, bar a handful at most," Upside replied and faced Paul, "Princess Stephanie and Eschiva both being the exception to that…and Lord Balian."

"What of Lord Raymond?" Paul asked.

"He has improved, but I have seen his scheming at first hand too. Though Brother Nicholas will not have a word spoken against him. Too trusting and too damned loyal for his own good that one. 'Tis why he lays this hour sorely injured," Upside answered and shook his head almost in disgust. "Raymond refused to join in Reynald's little sea venture but he was forced to send most of his contingent of Templar Knights to assist, except a handful to guard Princess Eschiva."

"Everyone's perception and understanding of people and events is always slightly different, that is why you must always trust your own instincts about people," Attar stated in a low tone as if to emphasise some great words of wisdom. Theodoric laughed briefly. "Seriously, there are always two sides. Let me give you an example," Attar started to say.

"You are not going to bore me to death are you?" Upside asked bluntly, but smiling.

"Yes of course...absolutely, my friend, but it will nevertheless demonstrate the point," Attar laughed back and pulled his dark green cloak around his shoulders, the night air getting cooler. "There was this young couple who every morning over breakfast would watch their elderly neighbour hang out her washing for the day through their prized ornate glass window. This went on for weeks and every morning the young woman would tell her husband how filthy the old woman's sheets always were every time she hung them out. She commented that the old woman obviously does not know how to clean bed sheets properly or is too frail to do it. After a few months of this the young man, frustrated at his young wife not doing anything to help the old woman, decided to do something about it," Attar explained in a deliberate drawn out fashion then paused as he looked at them all in turn.

"And?" Thomas asked impatient but grinning. "Let me guess, he made his young wife do her sheets too or he washed them?"

"No," Attar replied and sat up. "The next time the old lady came out to hang up her washing, the young woman looked on and was amazed at how white and clean her sheets all looked. She turned to her husband and demanded to know what he had done. So he sat her down, looked at her for a few minutes then explained that he had gotten up early, gone outside and cleaned the glass of their very expensive and ornate windows for it was that which was filthy, not the old ladies sheets."

"Well said," Theodoric laughed out loud seeing the bemused expressions on all their faces.

"If you were expecting some great deep and meaningful insight, then look into what I just said later as you sleep," Attar remarked smiling. "For you see, there are always reasons and circumstances as to how and why we all see things so differently."

"I like that...I do," Upside said, nodding his head as he pondered Attar's comments.

"And," Attar started to say and paused smiling before continuing. "There is a Hindu tantric saying, 'nādevo devam arcayet', which means 'by none but a god shall a god be worshipped'. For you see the deity of one's worship is a function of one's own state of mind. But it is also a product of one's culture. Catholic nuns do not have visions of the Buddha, nor do Buddhist nuns have visions of Christ. The image of any god beheld, whether interpreted as beheld in heaven or as beheld any place, will be of a local idea historically conditioned, a metaphor, therefore, and thus to be recognised as transparent to transcendence. Remaining fixed to its form, whether with simple faith or in saintly vision, is therefore to remain in mind historically bound and attached to an appearance preconditioned by our environment, family and religious education."

"And education does not necessarily help either for look at how we are taught...how the Church educates us," Theodoric said as Sister Lucy came and sat beside him. "It leaves no room for personal or individual discernment, personal integrity to stand up to what at times is blindingly obvious as being wrong, or even a way to see a balanced understanding of the real world...for it is presently a sad fact that the dust of acquired knowledge is more often shown to 'obscure the mirror of the heart' than to enhance one's rational faculties and finer perceptions. It strangles our open mindedness to enquire and learn."

"Whoops...I think you have got him started," Sister Lucy joked and held his hand tightly.

"Okay I shall stop before I rant...but in truth, the Church denies the existence of many things that would greatly help and advance us...they keep us in ignorance and the zealot fanatics who follow its every word, to the letter...well that just makes the Church become like a big penis."

"Really, how so?" Thomas asked laughing as Upside clasped his side again as he too laughed.

"Religion is like a penis. Its fine to have one and it's fine to be proud of it, but you shouldn't whip it out in public and start waving it around... nor would you force it down someone's throat yet this is exactly what the Church does," Theodoric explained as Sister Lucy covered her mouth, trying not to laugh.

"I think I will leave this conversation. Who would like a full wooden peg ale tankard filled with heated Syrup of Jule?" she asked as she stood up again slowly, still laughing.

"You have a way with words, Theodoric," Attar remarked. "And yes please," he nodded toward Sister Lucy.

"Hey it was you who told me that years ago…and 'Revelation cometh!' and it will be the watchers who help herald that in by a new breed of hero," Theodoric laughed back.

Thomas and Upside both bowed their heads in acknowledgement to Sister Lucy.

"Heroes…such like?" Paul asked, bemused.

"No idea," Theodoric replied and smiled.

"Paul, it is said that the watchers imparted great knowledge and wisdom to certain men and women, but even then, they were so strongly influenced by the religious impulse and dogmatic preaching's so strongly engrained within them, that even then they could not break away from their old ways of understanding and perceptions," Attar explained as Upside listened very intently.

"And the new type of hero, though I use that word loosely, for what is a hero really, will be individuals who are service to others first and foremost…not service to self," Theodoric explained.

3 - 31

"A hero must be honourable, must have honour for you can't have honour if you're a liar. There is no honour in lying," Upside stated.

"Brother Baldwin…like all perceptions, even lying has to be viewed for what it is. An honourable knight may have to lie to save a person's life. Does that make him dishonourable? People tell many forms of lies for many reasons…," Theodoric remarked, looking at Upside.

"We all lie at some point for I certainly have," Paul interjected.

"Yes, so have I and we all know Percival did yet he is perhaps the most noble amongst us, yes?" Thomas said as Sister Lucy placed several wooden peg tankards down and began to pass them around.

"I do not wish to offend or insult, but I never lie," Upside remarked as he placed his hands around the tankard. "It surprises me to hear you admit such," he said as he looked up at Paul.

"I feel no shame for lying. 'Twas a small but necessary evil to save lives…," Paul answered.

"Whose?" Upside asked.

"Oh, Reynald's, Gerard and my brother, Stewart...," Paul replied.

"How so?" Upside asked instantly.

"How else do you think they escaped? They were aboard my vessel with Percival and I...and now if we do not continue with our lie, 'tis us all who will pay the ultimate price."

Upside shook his head in surprise and looked at Attar and then Thomas before looking back at Paul.

"And you admit such in our company?"

"Yes...for I trust all in here with my life totally...including you," Paul replied and sipped some of his drink, tasting it on his lips and sipping a second mouthful. "And as Thomas said, Percival has a past, one we do not need to know, only his actions now, for he is indeed perhaps the most honourable one of us all now."

"And he is courageous," Theodoric said as he pulled his tankard nearer and looked into it. "He followed Paul beneath Jerusalem in the tunnels despite being terrified of such confined spaces...he also went to sea, to do battle no less, when he cannot swim."

"I think I am beginning to understand where you are all coming from... but this mention of how you saved Reynald and Gerard. This does trouble me somewhat. Why did you not kill them when you had the chance or hand them to Saladin's forces?" Upside asked.

"I will not have their deaths stain my soul as I was once told about, nor could I let my brother die," Paul explained.

"We are all brothers here, Baldwin...and I sense a great unease from you about your present predicament and I do not mean being a Templar in these lands now," Thomas said as he stared at Upside.

"I," he started to reply but paused for several long minutes before continuing. "I question much about what we do under the command of Gerard and Reynald. So much is wrong...I fear it would have been better if you had killed them or handed them over to Saladin. And I am honoured that you trust me enough to know that I will not reveal this secret," Upside said quietly. "You know you can never reveal you helped them and I just pray they do not make much news of it if they manage to get back safely."

"'Tis in the Lord's hands now. I am sure we shall discover soon enough if they make it or not," Paul replied, his mind wondering how Stewart was.

"These are mad days indeed, for before we set sail there were many who questioned the wisdom of Reynald's plans and even more questioned

Gerard's eagerness to follow. I know of several knights who are close to converting to Islam and actually siding with Saladin…but we pray people like Balian and Count Raymond can force Reynald to stop his mad ways," Upside revealed sadly.

"You give yourself away as being of a like mind, my friend," Thomas remarked and leaned over and patted him on the arm. "As I said, you have a place here with us if you so choose. Despite what rumours you may hear, we are not slack, lazy nor spend all our time with women of lesser repute… well, not as much as is claimed."

"I can vouch for the first two parts but the third…well?" Theodoric joked and waved his hand side to side.

"We have a good life here. Yes we play hard, but we work even harder. Think about it," Thomas said and raised his eyebrows.

All turned to face the doorway as Alisha quietly entered the dining room. She was smiling broadly and all noticed this. Paul stood up to greet her.

"'Tis Nicholas…his fever has broken…he asks for food," she said softly and smiled again.

"Good news indeed…truly good news," Upside replied and sighed with clear relief. "So would your offer extend to Brother Nicholas too?"

Thomas looked up at Paul. Paul nodded without hesitation.

"Of course," Thomas replied.

Upside looked back at Paul with the realisation that despite appearances, it was ultimately Paul that had the last word as Thomas had sought his permission first before answering. Stories of Thomas and his men were many. Their chivalry and honour on the battlefield was admired and respected by all sides. They were a brotherhood more unique than the Templars themselves, Upside thought as he considered his offer. He knew he could no longer follow Reynald and Gerard for he had lost all faith and respect in them. He looked on as Alisha stepped closer to Paul and greeted him with a kiss on the cheek. These people were more noble and honourable than any others he knew save Princess Stephanie, he thought. He lowered his head and sighed.

"Have you filled the time piece?" Alisha asked as she approached a water clock. She lifted the lid and checked inside its water container area. "No, I see," she said feigning an angry face but immediately followed by a large smile. As she turned away from the water clock she stubbed her toe on a large circular stone dish type apparatus. "Paul…!" she exclaimed and rubbed her toe.

"'Twas I…I left them there," Theodoric said and quickly moved to pick up the apparatus. As Alisha sat down beside Paul, he placed the apparatus on the table.

"Theo…get that off the table," Sister Lucy demanded, frowning at Theodoric.

Theodoric shook his head as he pulled the apparatus towards him.

"Pray tell what manner of apparatus is that?" Upside asked.

"Oh this…'tis a wondrous item. Very old…it makes the threefold water we have been giving Nicholas…though some argue it's for making rope… ha, rope!" Theodoric explained, his face looking proud as he gestured for Upside to look closer.

Fig. 54: Shisk Disc.

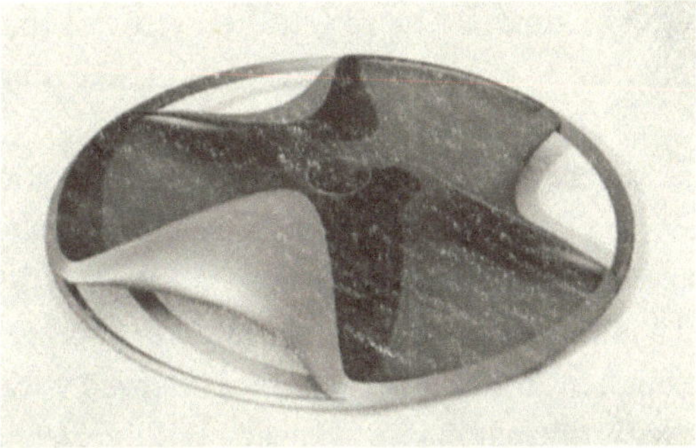

"How does it work?" Upside asked curiously.

"Well…we are not really sure," Theodoric started to explain as he pushed the apparatus across the table to Upside. "But we do know that it somehow transforms the structure and nature of water by spinning in through a vortex…and it is amazing for healing and for keeping you fit and healthy."

Upside looked over the apparatus carefully.

"How is it made for it is of stone no?" Upside enquired as he ran his fingers over the circular part of the apparatus.

"That I also cannot answer for the method of its construction was lost to antiquity. We can make a similar system, but these ones, the old ones, work the best," Theodoric explained.

"'Tis what has saved Nicholas," Alisha said softly.

"It will not hide the scars of his burns will it?" Upside replied, shaking his head sadly.

"You will be surprised, my friend. Look at me," Theodoric replied indicating with his hands to look him up and down.

"But you have no burn scars," Upside frowned.

"Exactly…but I was once burned quite badly. Remember most of what we are made from is water," Theodoric explained and sat down opposite Upside and clasped Sister Lucy's hand.

"Are we? Then make more of these," Upside said, looking surprised.

"We cannot. We have tried, but it is made of the hardest stone known to man. It takes a specially cut diamond to work such stone, and even then, our methods crack or flake the stone," Theodoric explained.

"So are they a gift of God…or what?" Upside asked, bemused, as he studied the apparatus closer.

"You could say that in a fashion," Attar remarked. "They are from a time far back in antiquity…further than even the myths of the Celts tell us… further than all of our religious books tell us, further than we can imagine."

"All about us…wherever you travel in this world…you will discover mysteries that are in plain view and have been for thousands of years, yet no one questions what they are or why they are there," Theodoric started to explain. "Just look at the perfectly executed carvings on the obelisks and some of the benben stones of Egypt alone. Carved with such precision in solid granite with unimaginable accuracy with perfect symmetry that mere hand carving cannot replicate. And there are many wonders we possess yet simply do not understand what they are really for or how to use them…but they prove there was once a time of high civilisation beyond that of ours."

"You are telling me a higher civilisation once existed before us?" Upside asked, looking at Theodoric and then Attar before turning to face Paul.

"Yes…just as every religion and myth tells us," Paul answered. "Theo… do you still have that strange poem you copied from that ancient Indian poem?"

"Of course. 'Tis in my journal upstairs. I shall fetch it now," Theodoric replied and immediately left the room.

"He moves fast and agile for a man his age does he not?" Upside stated and as he watched Theodoric practically run from the room. "Threefold water perchance?"

"And the love of a good woman," Sister Lucy smiled. "Just don't get him started on music please," she whispered and laughed.

"Music...'tis truly the one language that unites us all," Upside replied.

"You like music?" Attar asked, surprised.

"Yes. 'Twas my life long before I became a knight."

"Really? Please, if you do not mind, tell us how you became a knight then?" Paul asked.

"'Tis not a great story...other than to say I believed music was the secret of life. I thought it could heal for music touches the soul so deeply. I can play many instruments...though I have not touched one in many years," Upside explained just as Theodoric rushed back into the room, sat down and quickly opened a leather bound journal. "And I became a Templar after meeting Gerard in Antioch...and I believed in him, back then," he said and sighed heavily.

"Ah, here it is," Theodoric said with a large grin. "Here, let me read it to you and see what you make of it. It says...'Tell your children when you sit together the legends of the cities of a thousand towers of glass and iron, so tall they touched the clouds. Towers that never rusted, and shone forth in the evening light. Where men travelled in chariots without horses, faster than a frightened mare, or descended deeper than the realms of demons into long tunnels where metallic worms whisked them to remote places of outer darkness; where from such places they would ascend again riding upon magic tubes of iron to travel across the known world and beyond, from castle to castle anywhere in just a day, or even to the moon on flaming broomsticks. Such towers of glass and iron, like giant swords pointing heavenward were lit not by sun but by tiny glass bottles that even common men used to make light brighter than day all night. Such cities, many thousands of years ago, were then lit yet more by a terrible new sun that rose in the west, that burned hotter than a thousand thousand fires, for men possessed such terrible catapults of war that a single shot could destroy a city faster than a hundred armies. They did all this magic by black essence of earth that gave them wondrous powers, to see even the ends of the world upon small boxes in their homes like the scrying glasses of the forest wizards and Shamans, yet then all men possessed such magic, could talk across the seas and be heard using tiny magic boxes we have nonesuch today. Yet when this essence of earth ran dry for they abused the earth and she gave her essence no more, then they turned these awesome weapons of war upon themselves and their cities of magic melted like icicles upon a warm spring day. Yes tell your children this story, for one day men will dig deep in the earth once again for magic metals, and once more will make cities of ten thousand towers of glass and iron, and new terrible hot suns will rise in the West…" [93]

"And this came from where?" Upside asked looking puzzled.

"India…well, I found the original poem there but it was from an even earlier poem of what we would term Celtic origin, from the Emerald Isle no less. I was actually looking for details on ancient flying vessels," Theodoric explained almost excitedly. He shook his head smiling as he recalled an earlier time.

"Celts…my mother told me my ancestors came from them. She was the one who taught me to love music, especially Celtic for it is music about a time before time she said. So beautiful it reaches into our souls. If the whole world could but listen to this music, see the beautiful and intricate artwork they created…then perhaps we would all live in peace she would oft tell me," Upside explained quietly whilst still studying the water apparatus. After a few minutes sat in silence, he looked up realising everyone was looking at him, surprised. "Oh…I am sorry. I embarrass myself."

"No you don't. You have just confirmed exactly why you would make a remarkable addition to our brotherhood," Thomas remarked, smiling and nodding his head.

"Theo…your burns. How did you come to have them?" Upside asked and looked at him.

"Oh boring story really. Wrong place and wrong time and all that," Theodoric shrugged off Upside's question and poured himself some wine.

"No Theo…it was far more than that and you should answer the man," Sister Lucy said and frowned at him hard.

Theodoric shook his head no and took a large mouthful of wine.

"Please Theo for there is still so much we do not know of you," Alisha asked softly. "Tell us and then I will take some food to Nicholas."

"Ah my dear Ali, a sweet smile will not work upon me," he replied and raised his glass to her and took another, smaller, sip of wine.

"You stubborn goat…if he will not, then I shall," Sister Lucy said bluntly as Theodoric looked at her and shook his head no. "Then you should leave the room for you should be proud of what you did and how you were burnt."

Theodoric shook his head again and then looked down at his wine as he cupped the glass with both hands.

"Please tell," Paul said as Thomas leaned nearer to listen.

"'Twas many years ago…when your mother was pregnant with you. About eight months gone," Sister Lucy started to explain as Theodoric looked very uncomfortable. "Your mother was held inside an iron cage flooded with oil…with your brother Stewart tied together," she explained and paused as Theodoric shook his head again. "Turansha."

"Him…why is he always somehow involved?" Paul interrupted. Alisha held his arm seeing the immediate tension in his voice and reaction on his face.

"He and his master threatened to set your mother on fire…to burn her and your brother alive trapped inside the cage set within a cave unless Theodoric revealed a secret…which he refused," Sister Lucy explained then paused as all looked at Theodoric. "Your mother, she made Theodoric swear not to reveal the secret…and when Turansha went to light the pool of oil, Theodoric jumped upon him, despite being doused in oil himself and held Turansha and the flaming torch against him as the flames ignited his clothes…but as he burned, he held on to Turansha pushing him ever backwards away from your mother…," Sister Lucy continued emotionally as she clasped his hands.

"Then how did you survive…and that evil man?" Alisha asked as Paul sat in stunned silence at the revelation.

"My then husband…he arrived…and…and he pushed them both into the stream that ran through the cave. 'Twas the day he was killed as he rescued your mother. He opened the cage, unbound the ropes and chains and led them out…and stood his ground and shielded them as many crossbow bolts and sword blows rained down on him…," Sister Lucy explained as tears welled in her eyes. She struggled to stop herself from crying as her bottom lip quivered. "But as Turansha pulled himself from the stream, also burnt, he ordered his men to get him out fast as more of my husband's men arrived…"

"Why have you never told us this before?" Alisha asked, utterly surprised.

"Would it make any difference?" Theodoric finally answered and emptied his glass in one large mouthful. "'Twas all my fault in the first place… that is why I do not speak of it."

Sister Lucy hit him hard on the shoulder, looked at him and shook her head in disbelief at his comment and then hit him again. "When will you ever accept it was not your fault?" she demanded.

"So you saved not only my mother and brother but also me before I was even born?" Paul exclaimed.

"That time yes, but I could not save her the next time," Theodoric sighed.

"Why...why is Turansha so hell bent on some path of evil intent toward my family...and why try to kill us in such a vile, gruesome and cowardly manner?" Paul asked.

"'Tis not just your family...'tis also Alisha's, that is why you can never trust the man, never!" Theodoric answered and looked at Paul with a hard stare he had never seen before. "Ever!"

"That is why I and my men have vowed we shall watch over you for as long as we must. Our somewhat pitiful lives at least have some purpose and meaning by doing so," Thomas said as he sat up straight.

"Your lives are of value...much value," Paul replied looking at him.

"That is kind of you, Paul, but we know our failings and shortfalls, accept them but try to make amends...and here, here you have given us a home for our brotherhood...that is why we shall continue to serve you for we know, as I said earlier, there is a greater force at work here than we understand... isn't there, Theo?" Thomas explained and turned to Theodoric.

"And for that we are extremely grateful," Paul replied and thought for a moment. "Turansha. What makes him so full of evil intent and malice?"

"He was not always so. He was once a poet, a musician and quite soft at heart. Believe it or not so was Reynald," Theodoric started to explain.

"Reynald. He told me I should ask you about his dreams...about who he is," Paul interrupted.

"That, my dear Paul, time itself cannot explain," Theodoric started to reply and then rubbed his chin for several moments. "But let me say, both men were of a kind and gentle disposition in their youth. Full of ideals and dreams of chivalry and honour...but then life and reality got in the way and crushed those sensitive emotions...some people break or even kill themselves, but some go the other way. They become embittered and hard of heart. They lose sight and all sense of doing what is right. 'Tis hard to explain...but I know this deep inner feeling for I nearly went down that road myself." He looked at Sister Lucy and feigned a brave smile and kissed her hand. "'Tis part of the reason I let those closest to me believe I was dead also, for most of me had died inside anyway," he sighed. "I never felt part of the world we live in...I have always had this belief I was from elsewhere...well."

"I know that feeling well my friend for I too have always felt that way," Upside said.

Alisha wiped her eyes as tears were welling in them. A deep sadness touched her as she looked at Theodoric sat opposite her. Paul held her hand tighter as he too looked at him. So much remained hidden and secret about Theodoric still.

"You spoke of the Celts…as I said my mother's descendants came from them, so I am told, but I have to tell you, like you, I have always felt this world is not mine, not of me, 'tis why I sought answers and a sense of belonging and why I joined the Order in the first place," Upside explained.

"That is the same as I and all my men," Thomas remarked and nodded at Upside.

"But is that not the way all people feel?" Paul asked.

"No, Paul…the majority of people do not," Theodoric answered and sat back in his chair.

Upside leaned forward with his elbows upon the table and looked closer at the apparatus.

"You may think me mad, but I believe all you tell me about great ancient civilisations for I sense one of such great antiquity that it still calls out to us even today…I am not a born Celt. but something deep inside calls me to its ways. I have always had this strange feeling for years that I am not of where I was born, but of a far off land from where I am now. Call me mad, but I yearn to go home, and by home I mean where my heart tells me that it feels at peace," he explained.

"Amen to that and join the club," Thomas remarked and smiled.

"It would be my pleasure and my greatest service if I am allowed to join you. If Nicholas is in agreement, then you have just increased your order by two," Upside said as he looked at Thomas. Paul put his arm around Alisha and turned to face Upside upon hearing his words.

Alisha's heart jumped at hearing that Nicholas would be staying. Her stomach turned and she placed her hand across her tummy.

"A wise decision my friend. Very wise…though next when we are out in the harsh desert saving some Muslim or Christian pilgrim from the clutches of slave traders you may regret it," Thomas said and nodded.

"I doubt that," Upside replied and smiled.

"So Nicholas will stay with us?" Alisha asked.

"Looks that way," Thomas said as he stood up. "And our green man here can, I am sure, help him back to full recovery," he explained as he pointed at Attar.

"And me...," Theodoric interrupted feigning indignation at not being mentioned.

Port of La Rochelle, France, Melissae Inn, spring 1191

"Nicholas staying...that has disaster written all over it?" Sarah commented, shaking her head disapprovingly.

"'Tis indeed beginning to sound like a Grail romance...with Alisha being Guinevere, Nicholas Sir Lancelot and Paul being the king," Simon stated.

"Simon, as ever you surpass yourself...that is a good example of what could unfold...but before your mind runs away with itself, let me finish if you will," the old man asked.

"But having Nicholas stay, with his feelings for Alisha...it will lead to trouble I just know it will," Ayleth protested looking saddened.

Gabirol saw her expression and immediately tried to steer the conversation away onto a different subject.

"'Tis truly amazing what you tell us of Theodoric for he is full of surprises. I would love to hear his story in full," Gabirol remarked.

"Perhaps one day I shall tell you of his earlier adventures...perhaps," the old man replied.

"You mentioned that Attar was referred to as the green man...as you explained before about the Ancient Egyptian Green Man symbolism...is Attar somehow connected in this fashion, symbolically or allegorically?" Gabirol asked.

"Gabirol, your mind is sharp for you see the connections clearly. But in answer to your suspicions that it would be a disaster if Nicholas was to stay, let me say that in this life, physical attraction is common, but a mental connection is rare... Once you've had the latter, the former will never be enough again," the old man replied.

"Ah but who had that connection with whom?" the wealthy tailor asked.

"That's you stuffed for life then," Sarah joked looking at Simon.

"I wish to know why Attar wears green all the time and why you draw our

attention to that aspect of him. Is there more?" Gabirol asked. "And Percival for he too wears only green."

"To be brief, yes there is more," the old man replied.

"Then at the risk of delaying yet further, please, if the others are in agreement, will you tell us?" Gabirol asked as he looked at the others in turn, looking for their approval.

As they all nodded in agreement, the old man smiled and proceeded to explain.

"As I have already mentioned before about the Green Man for you, recall I said you should pay particular attention to the myths surrounding him."

"Yes that is why I have it highlighted here," Gabirol said, pointing to a note in a side column on his note pad.

"Well for your benefit, Ayleth, for you were not present when I first mentioned this, the Green Man or foliate god is the animus of nature...the spirit of the forest and of the hunt, and is pictured as a spirit face in the form of gathered leaves and sprouting tendrils. The Green Man is also linked to the constellation of Orion, the hunter, and is also depicted as being green. He, like Attar and Percival, always wore green. In Percival's case it was purely coincidental...to a degree for nothing is really coincidental, but with Attar it was a deliberate choice. As I said then, the Green Man symbolism is vast and you may recall I recounted details about Daniel explaining Nebuchadnezzar's dream about a 'great tree in the midst of the earth and of great height'...I said then that 'the watchers' is an Egyptian name for 'divine being' or 'god' or ntr, or Neter, which means 'one who watches'. Neter-neter land is the name of the place in the stars where these beings dwell, along with the Green Man or Gardener. In Sumeria, this is known as another earthly land of the An-un-naki, the land of 'ones who watch'. And as you correctly deduced then, Gabirol, the old woman who follows Paul, whom Theodoric met in the Emerald Isle...she is a divine being, yes...a watcher and likewise connected to the Green Man in ways we will not be able to fully understand or know of in our times."

"And as you said then, the Green Man can be found within the Hadith on the Qur'an and named Al Khadr, yes?" Gabirol asked as he quickly checked back over his notes.

"Yes," the old man replied and nodded then continued. "In those Hadith, Al Khadr, the Green Man, is a man of godly wisdom, transcending this life. Even the prophet Moses did not possess the wisdom of Al Khadr."

"You said earlier he was called Al Khidr, meaning 'the Green One' but the name Khidr is found only in Hadith literature, such as the case when the Prophet Muhammad is said to have stated that Elijah and Khidr meet every year and spend

the month of Ramadan in Jerusalem...is this the same person?" Gabirol quizzed further.

"Yes just spelt differently. That is all...for Al Khadr is the one who can see beyond life on this earth and beyond death of the physical body. The Green Man is a mystery that spans thousands of years and is a symbol of mysterious origin and history. Interwoven throughout various religious faiths it has survived almost in the same form from its beginnings. It began as a pre-Christian entity as a spirit of nature personified as a man. His earliest images have been dated to long before the coming of the Christian religion, depictions dating back before the days of the Roman Empire. He has been found in other far reaching cultures such as India. Despite the vast distances between locations of the Green Man, he is most often associated with the Celts, particularly in today's Britain and France, by the high number of stylised images found in these regions. But he can be found all over this world we live upon. His face is always encompassed by leaves, vines and flowers, seeming to be literally born from the natural world. 'Tis another reason why the bloodlines of families are portrayed upon a tree, as a family tree with its roots and vines are used to symbolise them," the old man explained but then paused for several moments in silence before continuing. "Because of these depictions, the Green Man is believed to have been intended as a symbol of growth and rebirth, the eternal seasonal cycle of the coming of spring and the life of man. This comes from the pre-Christian notion that man was born from nature, as recounted in all mythological accounts of the way in which the world began, and the idea that man is directly tied to the fate of nature. It is the natural changing of seasons that presents the passage of time that ages man, thus depicting the Green Man in such a way that overwhelmingly illustrates man's relationship with nature highlights the idea to worshippers that one cannot survive without the other. Man was predominantly reliant on nature until recent centuries, so the Green Man as an expression of this close relationship is a powerful message. With the cycles of the year comes the end of the year; with the cycles of life comes the end of life; and with the excessive use of nature comes the eventual end of nature. Like that poem Theodoric read out. The Green Man's other important, powerful affiliation is that of death and of endings. The symbol of the Green Man can be summarised in the three Rs...for rebirth, reliance and ruin."[94]

"Another trinity then?" Miriam suddenly said aloud.

"Yes indeed. Yes indeed," the old man sighed but followed it by a smile. Miriam blushed. "You should speak more for you are wise and far smarter than you presume yourself to be."

The Templar smiled broadly and clasped her hand close to his chest and nodded in agreement.

"And Paul, his home...it was indeed his very own Camelot with his own knights no less?" Gabirol remarked.

"Indeed you could say that. His home was a home for the brotherhood," the old man replied.

Chapter 57
Prophecy & the Seeds of a Promise

Cairo, Egypt, April 13th, 1183

Alisha took a plate of warm food from Sister Lucy for Brother Nicholas. As she stood, Paul looked up at her.

"Do you mind if I give this to him?" she asked softly and smiled.

"Of course not. I will be up for bed shortly," Paul replied and ran his hand down her side gently.

Attar looked at Theodoric and raised an eyebrow. Upside noted this but said nothing.

"So Theo...you have a special place in your heart for all things Celtic and the sacred Emerald Isle then?" Upside asked, drawing everyone's attention back as Alisha left the room.

"I do not hear many call her such these days, but aye, that I do," Theodoric replied and moved so Sister Lucy could sit beside him. "I have felt the gentle kiss of the morning mist blow across my cheeks as I watched the slow moving clouds drift down the hillsides and into the valleys like a sheet being pulled over me...for I have smelt the freshness of the Emerald Isle's air, of a purity unlike anywhere else," he continued, raising his hand and looking upwards in an exaggerated and dramatic fashion. Sister Lucy nudged him, laughing.

"Show him your Celtic tattoo," she said and tilted her head slightly.

"Oh he would not be interested in such a thing," Theodoric replied and pulled Sister Lucy close to him and held her in his arms.

"I would like to see this now you have aroused my curiosity," Upside remarked. "And perhaps you will tell me how you came to be in possession of this?" he asked as he pushed the threefold water disc gently back across the table toward Theodoric.

"The tattoo I shall show you later...but the disc, well, we found several both here in Egypt and Jerusalem...oh and plus one in Georgia. We did find several in the Kingdom of Bosnia," Theodoric explained then laughed as his mind clearly wandered back to an earlier time. He shook his head and laughed again before continuing. "But the ones we found in Bosnia, inside a great pyramid...buried and hidden yet in plain sight, were all smashed."

"A pyramid you say?" Paul asked, puzzled, just as Ishmael walked in covered in dust and dirt. Quietly he entered the room after giving a slight wave.

"Yes, a pyramid for there are several in that region. So very ancient," Theodoric answered as Ishmael quietly moved to the single seat at the furthest end of the table.

"My apology for my lateness in returning. Luke and I were delayed at the docks. The ship from Malta did not arrive. I only pray it arrives on the morn tide and is not lost," Ishmael explained quietly as he lowered his chain mail hauberk and filthy quilted gambeson to reveal a sweat soaked aketon cotton shirt. "Excuse my state for I had to carry Luke back as he drank a little too much whilst we waited."

"You went dressed for trouble?" Paul asked, puzzled.

"A precaution as Thomas advised for several ships have come in recently with mercenaries aboard," Ishmael explained. "I shall rest a short while then I shall clean myself up if that is acceptable?"

"Of course it is," Paul replied as Ishmael smiled in acknowledgement.

"I have some warm food just cooked if you are hungry?" Sister Lucy informed him.

"That would be most welcome," Ishmael replied.

"Why were you at the docks today then?" Paul asked.

"We received word that came in on an earlier ship to be at the docks to receive an item sent from Malta...for you...on the eve tide. We thought it best I and Luke fetched it," Ishmael explained as Thomas nodded in agreement.

"It cannot be from Reynald or Stewart surely...to let us know they arrived back safely?" Paul asked, bemused.

"No it cannot be that...for the journey times do not match," Theodoric replied, shaking his head.

"You do know don't you that Arnold de Tarroja is still Grand Master but Gerard will cement his position if he returns safely after this as Reynald will endorse and bribe all and anyone to get him sworn in as the overall grand master?" Upside said looking tired.

"More reason for you to stay here, with us," Thomas interjected and raised his tankard.

ꙮ

Alisha knocked on the bedchamber door and slowly opened it. As she peered in, a single candle flickering in the corner of the room meant she was able to see Nicholas struggling to sit himself up. With just his night shirt on he pulled the sheet up. In pain he sat up as best he could as Alisha entered carrying the small bowl of warm food.

"I have brought you some of Sister Lucy's vegetable soup. 'Tis thick and tasty and will help you," she said softly as she sat upon the bed next to him.

Nicholas looked at her as the light from the candle danced across her beautiful face. She smiled and his heart simply melted. He sighed slightly and Alisha quickly placed her hand across his forehead to check his temperature. He closed his eyes and savoured every second of the feel of her soft touch. He looked a wreck, he knew, his beard unshaven and unkempt but he knew Alisha saw past that.

"Did I say much in my delirium…and how long have I been here?" he asked as she removed her hand. "And is Upside well?"

"No you said nothing wrong…you have been here nearly four days past now and Upside is well…now eat," she replied and lifted a spoonful to his swollen and split lips. He winced in pain as the spoon touched his mouth. "Sorry…but you must eat," she said gently.

In silence she fed him the soup until it was almost gone, his eyes never leaving hers. It was easy for Alisha to look down at the soup to avert his gaze but she knew he was looking at her intently.

"I have to ask…did Upside…," he started to say.

"Yes, yes he did and I did read your letter before you say any more," she stated, cutting him short.

Nicholas let out a slight laugh and rested back into the large pillow. He sighed and shook his head.

"And Paul knows of this yet still saved my backside no less…I knew he would understand as my letter said."

"He knows…and he has no concerns…for whatever you feel or hope for, he knows my heart belongs to him."

"Ah…but you did once say I have a part of it," Nicholas replied and tried to move but stopped immediately in pain as he coughed. He looked upwards feigning indignation. "I get the hint, my Lord," he joked and held his sides.

"Yes, and if you stay here as Upside wishes, to join Thomas and his men, then you will need to banish any such hopes," Alisha explained softly and tilted her head as she looked at him.

"I know nothing of staying here. What has Upside agreed too?" he asked, puzzled, then coughed in pain.

"To join Thomas and his men...and you also."

Nicholas looked over his shoulder and strained to look at the single flickering candle, a reminder almost that he was a Templar for it was a Templar practice leaving a single candle lit at night. Slowly he returned his gaze to Alisha.

"Ali...you and I both know I cannot remain here," he said, his voice dry and low filled with a clear sadness that made Alisha's heart drop. She smiled, but it was a pained smile, her eyes giving away the emotion she felt at his comment. "We only part to meet again...and you should recall my poem...to die and part is a less evil but to part and live, there, there is the torment. But now, to stay here, with you around me always, that would be a burden I cannot carry," Nicholas said and sighed.

Alisha placed the empty bowl on the side table, looked at him for several minutes in silence then placed her left hand upon his face. His eyes searched hers, the vain but desperate hope that she would say something to keep him there. But she simply looked deeper into his eyes and without words told him all he needed to know. She felt for him and he knew it, but he also knew in that moment she would never ever be his. Not in this lifetime. His heart physically ached and he felt the emotion suddenly swell up in an uncontrollable wave of such intensity he could not control the tears that suddenly welled in his eyes. It must be the fatigue and injuries, he told himself, as he felt connected to her, her hand acting like some bridge to his very soul. Her eyes widened as she saw his fill with tears. As a tear rolled slowly down his cheek, she leaned in close and kissed his face wiping away the single tear as her lips gently pressed against it. She closed her eyes and held the kiss and as she did, Nicholas felt a sense of peace and comfort he had never experienced before and he started to sob unashamedly. He put his arms around her gently and rested his head against her as his heart poured out as if every pain he had ever suffered both physically and emotionally was being drawn from him. Part of him was crying from the knowledge he would never hold her and be able to love her in the fashion he would wish. As those thoughts ran through his mind, he felt a pang of guilt as he thought of Paul. Slowly he pushed Alisha back until they just looked at each other. There was no awkwardness or embarrassment, just a shared knowing between them and a final understanding.

ꙮ

Alisha entered the dining hall looking tired carrying the empty bowl. As she closed the door, Paul looked at her. He instantly knew she had been crying and his heart skipped a beat.

"Is he okay?" Upside asked concerned.

"Well he ate all of this, so that is a good sign," she answered and paused as she walked through to the kitchen area. "He is not all right fully yet... but he will be," she said and placed the bowl inside the large draining unit.

Paul could sense she was upset as did Theodoric and Sister Lucy. Attar looked at her and then to Paul. He motioned with his head that he should go to her.

"Do you still play?" Attar asked turning to face Upside. "I have several instruments. Perhaps now is a perfect time to bring some music in," he asked as he stood up.

"Aye, aye that I can," Upside replied and smiled. "And I would like to see this tattoo you possess...for I too have a small one...'tis between my shoulders too," he explained turning to face Theodoric.

"Really?" Theodoric asked almost incredulously.

"Really...'twas done whilst I was a babe," Upside explained further.

"As a babe...that is so wrong," Alisha said turning round to face everyone just as Paul reached her. She looked him in the eyes and smiled before moving to sit herself down at the main table. Paul stood still not sure whether to go and sit beside her. He could sense her sadness and he knew why. "Come do not be shy, show us your tattoo," she said looking at Upside.

"My mother said it is the mark of Lugh...though I have never learnt what that meant," Upside said as he stood up and removed his cotton shirt. He turned his back so they could view the tattoo set in the middle of his back between his shoulders.

Attar leaned closer to see, then sat down again. Sister Lucy smiled as

Alisha raised her eyebrows at Upside's naked upper torso, his muscles well defined.

"By the lords you look as strong as an ox, my friend," Thomas laughed.

"And you say your family is of noble lineage, you play the harp, your mother tells you your family is connected to the line of Celts, yet you do not know who Lugh is?" Theodoric asked as he moved to stand beside Upside. He looked closely at the tattoo, mainly faded but still with visible hues of blue and green upon it. It showed two trees leaning towards each other, but the tops were like heads, their hair flowing backwards made from branches. A small fleur de lys was just visible between the heads. It looked so similar to the tattoo upon his own back he felt his stomach suddenly tighten and knot. Sister Lucy saw the look in his eye as he stepped backwards. "'Tis of the same fashion as mine…put your shirt back on and I shall tell you what Lugh is."

Upside put his shirt back on and sat down. As he fastened the togs at the top, Theodoric sat down between Attar and Sister Lucy.

"My father told Taqi and I about Lugh and that he played a harp…and that music was the key to understanding the whole of creation," Paul said as he finally sat down near to Alisha. She looked at him, smiled, though he knew she was not smiling inside and she rested her head against his shoulder.

"I suspect there is more to your lineage than perhaps you are aware of, for whoever gave you that tattoo gave me mine," Theodoric said in all seriousness. "Not all Celts had Druids…and some did not worship in the same manner, but they all used the oak and tree symbolism. Dderwydd was another name used to describe them…but that came from Middle Eastern words as I am sure Attar can confirm. Broken up into myth words, we get Dera and Vid and we have the sacred oak tree, and Vid of vision, which in turn means 'vision from a sacred wood' for speaking prophesy accompanied by a harp. Dera-vid or Derwydd, is David, as in David and the harp as detailed in the Bible. It was once claimed that a king could not be a king unless he was a Derwydd, Deravid, a person who leads with prophecy through the harp," he continued and looked at Alisha. "Ali, do you still carry that dagger with the oak seeds in?"

9 - 8

"Always," she replied and patted her waist. Upside raised his eyebrows curiously.

"Know this, the ancient word Danu means Milky Way, and even though many deny it, Celtic and Vedic Danus are one and the same goddess," Theodoric started to explain. "You only need study their identical traits. It was from this Goddess that Lugh came. He was the synthesis of the 'Stag Lord' with Sun-God. The Tuatha De Danann, in the realm of myth, were the Singers of Reality. They created reality with their songs. 'Tis why so much importance is placed upon music and harps. In time man will remember that these myths are indeed historical fact and that all that we are is governed by sound...harmonics."

"My family has always been connected with the name Lugh but we changed it and hid the fact for reasons I know not," Upside explained. "But harps...I think I was born on one," he joked.

"Then you would have probably been told all the stories about bards who were poets, singers, musicians and storytellers oft known as Druids, seers and prophets. They are associated with the Celts but not all were Celts as I said...and most were not what you would call a true Druid. Bardic tradition has many fields of learning from poems, songs, Druid practices and history, Ogham, divination, myths and legends, Brehon law, folklore and of course harps...though much romanticism is attached to them and some still claim to hear their chants in the stone circles, especially in the Glen of Lyon in ancient Caledonia," Theodoric said and paused for a moment as some past thoughts entered his mind. Sister Lucy clasped his had reassuringly and Paul knew there was obviously some past shared experience connected to the place to cause her reaction as she feigned a brave smile. "We listen to the heaven-inspired utterances of the Arch Druid, as he stands on the capstone of a cromlech, in the eye of the sun, surrounded by the white-robed throng, with the bowed worshippers afar. We see the golden sickle reverently cutting off the sacred mistletoe. We follow, in imagination, the solemn procession, headed by the cross-bearer. We look under the old oak at the aged Druid, instructing disciples in mystic lore, in verses never to be committed to writing. We gaze upon the assembly of kings and chieftains, before whom the wise men debate upon some points of legislation," Theodoric rattled off as if performing some stage act until Sister Lucy nudged him hard and smiled at him. "Sorry, I always get carried away when talking about them," he coughed and continued. "Now know this, the Tuatha De Danann…they were the pre-Celtic inhabitants of the Emerald Isle who were the gods of the Celts, they are also seen as fairies and the Shining Ones."

"Shining Ones again…the watchers," Paul interrupted.

"Yes, the genuine ones were at least, for too many opportunists would take on the mantle and outer clothing of a so-called Druid to seek fame, power and position," Theodoric continued.

"Like a lot of men I know of who did and still do the same," Upside commented.

"Like who?" Paul asked, concerned and fearful that he was referring to Percival.

"Oh most do not last long as they soon expose themselves," Upside answered. "'Tis why in the early days of the Order, our white surcoats were replaced with the light beige ones and sometimes dark brown ones because too many false knights would throw on a white mantle or surcoat and off they went."

"But I thought your surcoats were white?" Alisha asked, looking confused, and looked at Theodoric.

"Oh they were to start with…," Theodoric replied immediately. "But look closely and you will see they are in fact an off beige sandy colour. Better camouflage in the hills and deserts. They often appear white from the gleaming sun." Upside nodded in agreement. "Pure white is only used for travelling or ceremonial duties."

Paul's mind immediately raced back to Stewart's initiation ceremony. He wondered how he was or if he was still even alive. And Taqi…how was he?

"I just thought they were that off white because they were dirty," Alisha remarked and chuckled. She looked at Paul and saw how tired he looked. "Perhaps we should retire to bed as we intended," she said and placed her hand upon his.

"No, I shall sit a short while longer now for my mind is alight," Paul replied and kissed her hand.

"So please tell me more of this Lugh," Upside asked.

"Lugh," Theodoric replied and paused. "It was from the Dananns that Lugh originated for he is seen as a Celtic solar deity and king of the Tuatha De Danann. He was also called Lamfhada, of the long arm, in Gaelic. The evil Underworld god Balor was the Sun God Lugh's grandfather, whom Lugh, the Shining One as he was also known surprisingly, had to kill."

"Why?" Upside asked bluntly.

"Oh, because a prophecy had stated that a son of Balar's daughter would kill him with a spear or the sword of light, so Balar had her three sons murdered, so he thought, but Lugh was rescued and taken away. Lugh became king of the Tuatha De Danann and is likened to the Greek Apollo. The story is that as a young man Lugh travelled to Tara in the Emerald Isle to join the court of King Nuada of the Tuatha De Danann. The doorkeeper would not let him in unless he had a skill with which to serve the king. He offered his services as a wright, a smith, a champion, a swordsman, a harpist, a poet and historian, a sorcerer and a craftsman, but each time was rejected as the Tuatha De Danann already had someone with that skill. But when Lugh asked if they had anyone with all those skills simultaneously, the doorkeeper admitted defeat, and Lugh joined the court and was appointed Chief Ollam of the lands. He won a flagstone throwing contest against Ogma, the champion, and then entertained the court with his harp. The Tuatha De Danann were at that time oppressed by the evil Fomorians, and Lugh was amazed how meekly they accepted this. Nuada thought that Lugh could lead them to freedom and so he was given command over the Tuatha De Danann, and he began making preparations for war. Now the Celtic word for August is 'Lúnasa' and comes from 'Lugh Lámhfhada."

"How is this Lugh like Apollo?" Upside asked.

"Because both were skilled in all trades and both were also gods of light, not necessarily just the sun. Both were warriors and artists, and cared deeply for their mothers. In simple terms, Lugh is most commonly known as a god of the sun, and because of that the Romans related him to Apollo. As said, Lugh's name means shining one."

"Do not forget to mention that Lugh is also like the Biblical David. And make note of the connections to the fact that Lugh's grandfather is an evil one-eyed Cyclopean…and there is much symbolism in the one eyed Cyclopean Giants of old," Sister Lucy commented.

"I can explain that later if you wish, my dear," Theodoric smiled and patted Sister Lucy's leg. She slapped his hand thinking he was ridiculing her. Quickly he raised her hand and kissed it and smiled. She shook her head and he continued. "The myths state that Mananaun Mac Lir who ruled the oceans took Lugh in his arms and held him up so that he could see the whole of the Emerald Isle with the waves whispering about it everywhere. He told him to say farewell to the mountains and rivers, and the big trees and the flowers in the grass, for he was taking him away. Lugh stretched out his hands and cried 'Goodbye mountains and flowers and rivers' promising that one day he would come back. Mananaun wrapped Lugh in his cloak and stepped into his boat, the Ocean-Sweeper, and without oar or sail journeyed over the sea till they crossed the waters at the edge of the world and came to the country of Mananaun, a beautiful country shining with the colours of the dawn. Does this remind you of anything?" Theodoric asked.

"No...unless you refer to the tales of King Arthur for there I see similarities," Upside answered.

"Well Lugh stayed in that country with Mananaun where he gathered apples sweeter than honey from trees with crimson blossoms...Paul, you are by now more than familiar with all of that symbolism with bees and even the crimson colour," Theodoric remarked and quickly looked at Paul as he nodded. "Birds, and you may know the story of the birds, or birdmen, who played with him. Mananaun's daughter, Niav, took him through woods where there were milk-white deer with horns of gold, and black maned lions and spotted panthers, and unicorns that shone like silver, and strange beasts that no one ever heard of and all the animals were glad to see him. He even called them by their names. Every day he grew taller and stronger and more handsome, but he never asked to go back as he had vowed. Every night when darkness had come into the sky, Mananaun wrapped himself in his mantle of power and crossed the sea and walked all over the Emerald Isle, stepping from rock to rock. No one saw him, because his mantle made him invisible, but he saw everything and knew that the De Dananns were in grave trouble. The ugly, misshapen folk of the Fomorians had come to the land and spread themselves over the country like a pestilence. They had stolen the Cauldron of Plenty and carried it away to their own land, where Balor of the Evil Eye reigned. They had taken the Spear of Victory also, and the only one of the four great Jewels of Sovereignty remaining to the De Dananns was the Stone of Destiny. It was hidden deep in the earth and because of it the Fomorians could not completely conquer the country, nor could they destroy the De Dananns, though they drove them from their palaces and hunted them through the glens and valleys like outlaws. Mananaun himself had the fourth Jewel, the Sword of Light," Theodoric said and noticed as Paul shifted slightly and placed his hand upon his sword pommel. "When Lugh was fully grown, Mananaun said to him, it had been three times seven years, as mortals count time, since he had brought him to Tir-nan-Oge, and he had never given him a gift so that day he gave him the Sword of Light. When Lugh took it in his hand he remembered his vow. Immediately he asked Mananaun to return him to his proper home despite Mananaun telling him that he would find no joy or the music of harp strings, or feasting for the De Dananns were now weak. Ogma, their champion, carried logs to warm Fomorian hearths; Angus wandered like an outcast; and Nuada, the king, has but one dun, which is a form of hill fort, where those who had once the lordship of the world meet in secret like hunted criminals. But Lugh would not be dissuaded even when it was pointed out that no one would actually know him, he simply answered that he remembered the hills and the woods and the rivers and though all of his kinsfolk were gone from it and the sea covered everything but the tops of the mountains, he would go back. So Mananaun gave him his own white horse and even companions as high-hearted as Lugh himself. All the white horse symbolism of old is connected to the mythical Pegasus and star constellations...some of which have been carved on the landscapes of the Sacred Isles. Mananaun also gave Lugh his helmet and his breast-plate to wear over his heart and assured him he would drive the Fomorians out of the lands. When Lugh put on the helmet of Mananaun, brightness shot into the sky as if a new sun had risen and when he put on the breast-plate, a great wave of music swelled and sounded through Tir-nan-Oge. When he mounted the white horse, a mighty wind swept past him, and all the companions Mananaun had promised rode beside him. Their horses were white like his, and a radiance that age cannot wither shone in their faces. When they came to the sea that is about Tir-nan-Oge, the little crystal waves lifted themselves up to look at Lugh, and when he and his comrades sped over the sea as lightly as blown foam, the little waves followed them till they came to the Emerald Isle and the Three Great Waves of the Isles thundered a welcome, the Wave of Thoth, the Wave of Rury and the long, slow, white, foaming Wave of Cleena. Now no one saw the Faery Host coming and at the place where their horses leaped from sea to land there was a great wood of pine trees. They rode between the tall straight tree-trunks into the silent heart of the wood. Then Lugh told his companions they must rest for the night, but he himself took off his shining armour, and wrapped himself in a dark cloak and went on foot to the dun of Nuada. He struck the brazen door, and the Guardian of the Door spoke to him.

This is when King Nuada called him in and met him and Ogma, the champion. After defeating Ogma in a demonstration of strength throwing a large stone, he graciously gave up his seat as champion next to the king. Lugh then sat in the champion seat and was challenged to a game of chess by the king. They played, and Lugh won all the games, so that thereafter it passed into a proverb 'to make the Cro of Lugh'. The king said that Lugh was truly the Ildana, and that he would make music for him if he could but he had no musical instruments. Lugh saw a kingly harp within reach of his hand, but the king told him it was the harp of the Dagda. No one can bring music from that harp but Dagda himself. When he plays it, the four seasons of spring, summer, autumn, and winter pass over the earth. But Lugh said he would play on it," Theodoric told in an almost dramatic fashion, which made Sister Lucy smile. He winked at her then continued. "He played the music of joy, and outside the dun the birds began to sing as though it was morning and wonderful crimson flowers sprang through the grass that trembled with delight and swayed and touched each other with a delicate fairy ringing as of silver bells. Inside the dun a subtle sweetness of laughter filled the hearts of everyone and it seemed to them that they had never known happiness till that night. Then Lugh played the music of sorrow. The wind moaned outside, and where the grass and flowers had been there was a dark sea of moving waters. The De Dananns within the dun bowed their heads on their hands and wept. Lugh played the music of peace, and outside there fell silently a strange snow. Flake by flake it settled on the earth and changed to starry dew. Flake by flake the quiet of the Land of the Silver Fleece settled in the hearts and minds of Nuada and his people…they closed their eyes and slept, each in his seat. Lugh put down the harp and left the dun. The snow was still falling outside. It settled on his dark cloak and shone like silver scales; it settled on the thick curls of his hair and shone like jewelled fire and filled the night about him with white radiance as he went back to his companions. The sun had risen in the sky when the De Dananns awoke in Nuada's dun. They were light-hearted and joyous and it seemed they had all dreamed a strange, beautiful dream. The Fomorians had not taken the sun out of the sky Nuada told his people and ordered that they go to the Hill of Usna and send out to our scattered comrades that we may make a stand against their enemies. They took their weapons and went to the Hill of Usna, and once there a band of Fomorian fighters attacked them. The Fomorians scoffed among themselves when they saw how few the De Dananns were, and how ill-prepared for fighting. 'Behold, they cried, what mighty kings are today upon Usna, the Hill of Sovereignty? Come down, O kings, and bow yourselves before your masters!' But Nuada replied that they would not bow themselves before them and said that they were ugly and vile and lords neither of us nor of the Emerald Isle. With war screams the Fomorians fell on the De Dananns, but Nuada and his people held together and withstood them as well as they were able. Scarcely had the weapons clashed when a light appeared on the horizon and a sound of mighty battle trumpets shook the air. The light was so white that no one could look at it, and great rose-red streamers shot from it into the sky. The Fomorians thought it was a second sunrise! But the De Dananns shouted out it was 'The Deliverer!' Out of the light came Lugh leading his warriors from Tir-nan-Oge. Lugh had the helmet of Mananaun on his head, the breast-plate of Mananaun over his heart, and the great white horse of Mananaun beneath him. The Sword of Light was bare in his hand. He fell on the Fomorians as a sea-eagle falls on her prey, as lightning flashes out of a clear sky and the Formorians were utterly destroyed by fire save for nine that he held his hand from striking down. He commanded them to bow before King Nuada, and before the De Dananns, and told them they are now your Lords and the Lords of all the Emerald Isle and to go hence to Balor of the Evil Eye and tell him and his misshapen brood that the De Dananns have retaken their own again and they will wage war against the Fomorians till there is not one left to darken the earth with his shadow." [95]

"So this is why they use a harp as their national symbol is it for without this Lugh could not have accomplished what he did?" Upside said.

"Well in time it will be for it is little used presently...yet you know it as their symbol," Theodoric replied.

"Aye...always have. Perhaps this is why I have this yearning to find where I belong as I explained," Upside said and shook his head, a little bemused, and laughed to himself.

"Don't move," Theodoric said excitedly and quickly got up and left the room.

"I did warn you...once you get him started, there is no shutting him up," Sister Lucy said and laughed lightly.

"Is he a Druid for his knowledge is certainly most vast?" Upside asked. "He only needs a harp and he would be the bard," he laughed.

"Funny you say that," Attar remarked and smirked at Paul just as Theodoric came rushing back in carrying a lyre.

"Here you go, my boy…we shall have music this eve," Theodoric said excitedly and sat beside Upside.

Ishmael folded his arms and looked on bemused as Sister Lucy looked at Theodoric, surprised. Paul noticed her frown.

"A lyre…and such a fine piece," Upside exclaimed, smiling as he took the oak lyre from him.

"I thought you swore a vow never to play it again," Sister Lucy interrupted.

"I did…but that does not mean our friend here cannot," Theodoric replied with a large grin on his face and beckoned with several head gestures for Upside to play it.

"Aye, that I can do but do not expect me to sing," Upside replied and took up the lyre.

Alisha clasped her hand upon Paul's and rested her head against his shoulder again as Upside plucked a few strings.

"I have a bow if you prefer that?" Theodoric stated and moved to sit beside Sister Lucy and put his arm around her.

Upside studied the lyre with a loving eye revealing a softer and gentler side to his nature as he became lost in its simple beauty and a thousand memories from his earlier days.

"No, I prefer the simple block and strum method," he answered quietly as the fingers on his left hand tuned the strings by blocking them until he could gauge the tone and tune of each, remembering their every sound with a smile.

Paul kissed the top of Alisha's head and put his arm around her. As the familiar scent of her hair entered his nostrils, he breathed it in to saviour the moment and thankful he was with her. He looked at Upside and could not help but smile seeing this other side to him. He did not know Theodoric even possessed a lyre, and was more surprised at Sister Lucy's comment. He would ask about that later. Paul knew exactly what type of lyre it was as his father had shown him so many when he was younger. His mind wandered back to those early and so easy years. He knew the lyre was a seventh-century Germanic type made with a shallow box with two extended arms, made of one piece of oak, hollowed at the lower half and a thin oaken sound-board. A separate yoke was joined with arms and held by oaken pins. There were two narrow slits at the junction of the sound-board and arms for affixing the supporting cord which was attached to the arm of the player. Six gut strings of the lower-end fastening type attached to the boss projecting from the body with a frontal type fastening of tuning ends; iron tuning pins were inserted into the yoke, anterior type and a movable bridge. It was an expensive item.

Paul closed his eyes and listened as Upside started to play it. The soft tones seemed to drift effortlessly through the air in harmonious waves. Such beautiful music sounded almost heavenly in its serenity and gentleness. Paul thought of his father and prayed that Stewart was alive. He knew the pain would crucify his father if he was dead. He sighed and kissed Alisha again. She turned to look up at him. In the low light of the lanthorns, she looked more beautiful and incredible than ever. He lowered his hand over her tummy and raised his eyebrows. She knew exactly what he was intimating. She placed both her hands over his on her tummy and smiled. It was still too early to know if she was pregnant or not, but somehow she also instinctively knew she was. She looked up to see Sister Lucy smiling at her. The door to the main corridor opened and Percival and Nyla entered curious to see where the beautiful music was coming from. Upside did not stop playing as he was lost in the music himself. Thomas winked at Theodoric as Percival and Nyla sat down opposite Alisha and Paul. They all sat in silence for over an hour as Upside played several tunes before finally stopping and resting the lyre down gently. He sniffed and wiped his eye and just feigned a smile but it did not hide the emotion in his eyes of a lost life he could have had, so different from the one he had now.

"Well I think I can safely say you are of the Lugh line somewhere in your blood for I have never heard a lyre played so beautifully and delicately in all my born days," Theodoric said, breaking the silence. "For that, I shall indeed show my tattoo later this eve."

"'Twas truly beautiful…thank you," Sister Lucy said quietly.

"'Twas more than that…and it has made me feel very tired so I am afraid I must take myself away to bed," Alisha said as she slowly stood. "Will you join me?" she asked Paul, holding his hand.

"Shortly…very shortly I promise," Paul answered as she walked for the door.

"'Tis late indeed," Thomas said and stood up stiffly. "Percy, I know you have only just got out of bed this past hour, but I would advise a return to it…to sleep…for we have a long patrol scheduled in the morn."

Nyla laughed, more out of embarrassment at Thomas's comment, as Percival pulled her close and simply shook his head smiling. Theodoric started to pour himself some more wine just as Sister Lucy stood up.

"I am away to our chambers. Make sure you are not long…and make that your last," she said waving a finger at Theodoric. He shrugged his shoulders.

"Better make it a large one then," he replied and pretended to duck from some imaginary swipe from her.

The dining hall was silent, the stillness of the early hours enveloping everything in a hushed blanket. Theodoric held his wine with both hands, Paul sat beside him whilst opposite Attar and Upside sat.

"You know I deliberately did not mention in front of the others certain aspects of the Lugh story and Danann…for in Scythian Danu means a river as well. Also, Danu's castle was said to reside in the Milky Way, up there in the heavens. In the Rigveda, Danu is a description of the primeval waters, where life originated, but the primal waters are not physical down here but celestial waters…up there in the heavens," Theodoric explained in a whisper.

"That is so," Attar remarked quietly. "There are lots of parallels with the Welsh mother goddess Don, also for Caer Gwydion, which also means Milky Way in traditional Welsh and is also the place where Danu or Don's children came from…in other words from the heavens. Danu is definitely connected to the Milky Way but too many seek and focus on earthly waters instead of the heavenly counterparts!"

"I am totally lost on all you speak of…," Upside said, shaking his head.

"But there is some argument that it refers to the Nile for it mirrors the Milky Way," Attar explained.

"Paul, you looked troubled," Theodoric said, seeing Paul was staring blankly.

"Oh sorry. Did I miss something?" he replied and sat up. "I was just going over in my mind Turansha…that even before I was born he was trying to kill my family. 'Tis something I cannot shake from my mind. I worry for Arri and my daughter when she is born."

"So you are certain the baby is a girl?" Attar asked.

"Yes...without a doubt."

"'Tis the female line you must worry about for Turansha knows the Crimson Thread flows through their lineage...'tis only strengthened by the male line," Theodoric explained.

"One day man will again learn why and how this is so but we simply have to accept it from what we have been shown," Attar said quietly.

"Why...why I just do not understand it all I really do not," Paul remarked shaking his head.

"Look, Paul, it all stems back right to the beginning of the Crusades... You know the history," Theodoric said and moved to sit nearer to Paul.

"I do not know," Upside interjected and smiled, trying to lighten the mood.

"Okay, to refresh Paul's mind and inform you, I will briefly explain," Theodoric replied, took a large mouthful of wine, downed it and continued. "It all started on the 27th of November 1095 when the Pope declared a holy Crusade. He granted a papal bull that all murderers, rapists and criminals et cetera would be pardoned if they went on the Crusade. So you can imagine all the unsavoury types that were instantly attracted can't you? In 1089 those very same people captured Jerusalem and slaughtered every man, woman and child whatever their religion was. After this, nine monks all related in one way or another gave up everything they possessed in France and ventured to the Holy Land. But they also had nearly thirty attending support members. Together they excavated beneath Solomon's old temple on Temple Mount. They excavated over 200 feet down. Whilst they carried out these excavations nothing was heard of them for a further nine years...then suddenly they recovered something and speedily returned back to France. 'Twas after this that there was a sudden explosion of Grail romances and poems. They were based in Troyes in Champagne wherefrom as you know Count Henry comes. In the new Grail romances, the so-called Grail cup is very much like the Celtic Cauldron of Plenty...but as you are learning, there are many forms of the Grail from the cup at the last supper to the womb of Mary. The nine knights returned to France in 1128 and became rich overnight. At the time it was rumoured that the Jews in AD 66 had buried over two hundred tons of gold. Bernard of Clairvuax was a nephew of one of the nine original knights. Then followed the most successful recruitment drive in history by the knights as well as being given grants of land all over Christendom. Originally knights had to come from noble families, and prove a legitimate descent. When the original nine knights returned to the Holy Land, they had over three hundred knights...after just three months....an impossible task to arrange and complete."

"So how did they do it?" Upside asked.

1 - 8

"They already had many of their recruits pending before they even returned, that is how." Theodoric paused as he looked directly at Upside. "As you know full well look what just eighty of you did at the battle of Montsigard back in 1177. It just proves what a dedicated full time standing soldier, with the best equipment and a Destrier war horse can do. Huh... are you not the only force that even teaches its horses to kick and fight?"

"Not the only one for we do also...," Thomas remarked.

"'Tis a dangerous power the Templars now hold and are gaining more all the time," Attar said and quickly checked one of the jugs of drink. "You Templars have a fierce reputation that you will never leave a battle or ever accept being ransomed. 'Tis a reputation that says you are almost suicidal."

"Aye...that I cannot deny for there are those who even seek death eagerly," Upside sighed. "Sometimes that fanaticism worries me greatly... and Reynald and Gerard exploit those traits. If Gerard ever becomes the Grand Master, then he will have power without limit."

"The Templars are already a state within a state, a Church within a Church," Attar replied, looking at him seriously. "They may presently be the most secret of secret societies, but it is their control of hidden wisdom I fear that will be abused the most should Gerard ever learn of what is really at stake."

"You confuse me for I know not what you speak of," Upside replied.

"Good...that makes two of us," Thomas laughed and poured himself some wine and offered more to Theodoric.

"Aye thanks," Theodoric replied as he pushed his tankard for Thomas to refill. "You see, in 1150 the Templars introduced the cheque system so there was no need to protect pilgrims, which they did not do anyway. But the cheques meant they could offer high profile loans which are against church teachings, so they charge rent instead. All the monetary systems are protected by their unique Cipher system and Atbash code. A Papal Bull absolved all Templars from all taxes and they are able to cross all borders and only answer to the Pope and no other king. 'Tis why your father still travels when he does in his Naval Templar uniform," Theodoric explained and nodded at Paul. "If Gerard does become the Grand Master, I am sure there are machinations in place that will see him not long in that position."

"Paul…I understand you had dreams of a great battle where the Templars meet Saladin between two great horns…is this correct?" Attar asked.

Paul looked at Theodoric immediately.

"Yes, but I have only told Theo this…in confidence," Paul replied.

"Oh do not question Theo for it was I myself who have dreamt the same. I just needed to hear you confirm it," Attar quickly replied then looked at Upside. "My friend, 'tis a warning…a portent of things to come that must pass. But a whisper of a prophecy for I too have seen the Blue Wolf, known to you as Muzaffar al Din Gokbori, clash between the horns with the Red Wolf of Kerak, Reynald…I would urge you caution should the day come if you find yourself trapped between two great horns…keep that in mind for I see other paths for you."

"Hey don't put him off…we need him with us," Thomas said in a half protesting manner.

"Keep in mind what I say. And know also that despite being enemies, Saladin has more than a fair respect and admiration for Templars. I know he seeks in time a joint union of his knights with yours. A draft treaty has even been prepared should the day arise when the likes of Reynald are no more," Attar explained.

"What, Muslim knights becoming Templars. Impossible!" Paul replied.

"Nothing is impossible…nothing," Theodoric stated.

"It will happen and it will come to pass," Attar remarked.

"As Upside will confirm…as will your father…the Knights Templar Order has always been an institution of leaders, and not followers. 'Tis not about secretive fraternities with questionable agendas known only at their highest levels, imposing control over their brethren and sisters for no such philosophy or practices exist in the Order," Theodoric explained as Upside nodded yes in agreement. "A brother will only advance within the Order on what is earned by merit with equal opportunity, and are granted based upon the roles and activities which members voluntarily choose to contribute. That includes the female members…members whom the Church tries to hide from the roll call."

"But as you said in Jerusalem along with Count Henry, the Order is structured so only a handful at the top fully understand the true secret teachings and wisdom," Paul interrupted.

"Yes, and as explained, it is a path that is nevertheless open to all members if they so choose to advance themselves. But there are many who simply do not choose to," Theodoric answered.

"He is right, Paul," Upside said. "There are many whose motives have to be questioned and who are worse than zealots in their eagerness to serve and follow the simple practices and seek a glorious death in battle. Trust me, I have been in many a conroise charge that was suicidal..."

"Paul...," Attar said quietly, drawing his attention. "The ancient sacred knowledge is inherently the collective heritage of humanity, and was never supposed to be secret or hidden. The only reason such information has been secret is simply because it was suppressed or overlooked as lost history. It is the primary mission and strict policy of the Knights Templar to ensure that all secrets of humanity are reassembled, restored and published for the world, to the fullest extent of its institutional capabilities... but that cannot happen for many many years, so in the mean time they must simply be its guardians. Do you understand this?"

"I understand this...but how can Upside leave the order if he so chooses?" Paul asked.

"'Tis a misconception that one cannot leave the Order," Theodoric started to explain. There has never been any prohibition against leaving the Order, and certainly not any negative consequences whatsoever for doing so. Take Princess Stephanie's father for a start. He resigned did he not?"

"'Tis true, Paul," Upside remarked. "I know of many brethren who have seen and experienced too much or simply lost faith who were allowed to leave, or retire as we say. Most were given a horse and weapons to keep, and even given coinage. Should I leave, I will receive all these things in good standing and with appreciation and gratitude from the Order."

"And what of the Church...does it not condemn you for breaking your vows to serve?" Paul asked.

"No...you see it is a fact that the Order was founded under the sovereign royal patronage of King Baldwin the Second and then King Fulk of Jerusalem...the Vatican did not give its additional sovereign patronage until eleven years later. If the Church ever suspends its patronage of the Templars the Order will simply and legally revert back to its original sovereign patronage from the kings of Jerusalem, which will never be terminated,"

Upside explained.

"There is so much I do not know of the Order…," Paul sighed and thought of his father and brother. He shook his head, tired.

"Paul," Theodoric said quietly. "The Order serves the Church with dedication, and voluntarily. It never has nor ever will be dependent upon recognition nor sovereign patronage from the Papacy for it already has its own pre-existing sovereignty from the Templar Kings of Jerusalem, and its own ecclesiastical authority from the Ancient Priesthood of Solomon as restored by the Templars in AD 1118, which in turn carries a direct succession from the biblical and most ancient Magi Priesthood of Melchizedek."

"And that I can prove dates back to at least 10,068 BC…," Attar stated as a matter of fact.

Upside frowned and looked at Attar quizzically. He simply smiled and nodded back as if to confirm what he was stating as a fact.

"Under Canon law, the history of initiatory Magistral Succession combined with doctrinal succession makes the Ancient Priesthood of Solomon of the Templar Order a religious institution in its own right, having full legitimacy. Nevertheless, true to the traditional Templar style of modesty and humility, hence 'Non Nobis Domin', the Knights Templar have never relied upon their own authorities, happy to serve other established Churches for the greater good," Theodoric continued to explain. "This is why it would be permissible for Muslims to join the Order as Saladin knows and approves of."

"Yet Gerard wishes to destroy him," Paul sighed again.

"The original knights of Solomon were holy warrior monks, highly trained skilled soldiers, who strictly followed religious and spiritual pursuits of esoteric knowledge and communion with God. The Order does not independently use autonomous military force. They do so strictly under sovereign authorisation at the request and by permission of a king, pope or leader of a country, thus serving as an official military force adjunct to a government's official army. And do not forget Knights Templar irrevocably and undeniably openly welcome and encourage the full participation of women, whether as priestesses, knightly spiritual warriors or actual combative knights."

"But I do not understand how, if my father was and is a Templar, how he had me and my brother?" Paul asked puzzled.

"Celibacy as Count Henry and Brother Jakelin tried to explain to you in Jerusalem is not an absolute prerequisite to join the Order…especially when you reach the higher ranks. In reality, as I am sure Upside will confirm, the celibacy rule really only applies when serving."

"Aye, 'tis a misconception that we are all celibate following Vatican rules for clergy and monks under Canon law, but as far as I am aware we have never been prohibited from marrying and having wives, nor having offspring and descendants," Upside said. "Think about it, the majority of knights joined direct from their dynastic families of nobility, and if not permitted to continue their family lines through heirs to preserve their heritage, most would never have joined and served in the Order as their lineage would die with them."

"I am surprised your father or Stewart did not tell you all of this," Theodoric said, a little perplexed.

"Because my father never wanted either Stewart or me to join," Paul replied.

"Well, in practice, most knights do have wives and raise families just as you saw Brother Jakelin with his wife. Written within Templar protocols, if a knight is married or engaged to be married, his lady is required to wait for him while living in a Roman Catholic monastery. Thus, joining the Knights Templar is a joint decision by the couple, which means holy service of both spouses, the male in military campaigns, and the female in monastic religious service. This also ensures the safety and monastic protection of the female spouse during the knight's active military service, giving all knights confidence and peace of mind that their beloved ladies would be waiting when they return home. But this was something your mother, God rest her soul, did not adhere to," Theodoric explained.

"How do you mean?" Paul asked, surprised.

"She refused to go and live in a convent. Oh the fun we had with your mother," Theodoric answered and shook his head smiling to himself.

"This Islamic Templar lot…please I would like to know more on that," Thomas asked curiously.

"Attar!" Theodoric said and gestured for him to answer.

"What can I tell you?…I can say that Saladin wishes to formally approve of the formation of a Muslim contingent of Templars to follow the same Codes of Honour as the Knights Templar. You must understand that the original Templar Order found unity and brotherhood with many Muslim knights for both are united in combat and also united in the ancient faith.

One day this dream will be realised...of that I am sure," Attar explained.

Paul's heart raced at hearing this. It would make his life so much easier without the constant sense of being torn between his Christian origins and his love of so many aspects of Islam and his Muslim friends.

"'Tis simply that a bond exists that is oft created between enemies during and after battle, which is called the Warrior's Code," Upside explained as Thomas nodded in agreement.

"Saladin knows and understands this rule," Attar commented.

"As does Balian and Count Raymond...," Theodoric started to say and paused for a few moments. "In a much more profound sense, the rules of the Warrior Code are there to protect the people doing the actual fighting. 'Tis designed to prevent soldiers from becoming monsters...all battlefield behaviours that erode a soldier's humanity...Most warrior cultures share one belief. There is something worse than death, and one of those things is to completely lose your humanity. Most on the battlefield can recognise the common humanity of their enemies, especially when face to face...and that respect starts at the top where the leader sets the tone and manner."

"I have known men who feel more bonded with their enemy than those of their own kind back home," Thomas remarked.

"This is true," Theodoric said in response. "'Tis why the likes of Reynald with his lack of humanity risk so much more than he realises."

"We understand this in our Order. 'Tis all part of our 'Code of Chivalry', for it is all about preserving one's humanity. 'Tis about having honour by accepting the humanity of one's enemy, and respecting them. The highest mark of a true Templar following the Code of Chivalry is the ability to be gracious and merciful to a worthy opponent who is even of a different faith, and to accept, forgive and even assist or cooperate with that opponent as soon as hostilities have ceased," Upside explained and took a large mouthful of his drink.

"These knights of Saladin...it sounds like a good idea, but will it ever happen?" Ishmael asked.

"Thought you were asleep," Thomas laughed.

"Was resting my eyes but I heard all," Ishmael replied.

"It is a possibility...," Attar replied.

"And you all still pronounce his name wrong. Perhaps if you get that correct it may happen...'Tis spoken Salahadin...," Ishmael said as he sat forward and rubbed his tired eyes.

"Why then, why are Christians and Muslims so at odds with each other?" Paul asked.

"For the same reasons as Christians fight Christians and Muslims fight Muslims...," Theodoric started to explain. "The First and Second Crusades were never intended to be a war against Islam, at least that was never the motivation nor mission of the Knights Templar. 'Twas the Vatican that authorised the Templars to protect Christian pilgrims travelling to and from Jerusalem, not to conquer nor eradicate any other religion. But escorting pilgrims could have been done by any number of other knights, which was indeed the case anyway. But by becoming the best and strongest force to meet that apparent need, the Templars were able to advance their research and excavations, preserve the ancient knowledge and heritage of humanity, and influence our entire European civilisation. Plus the only true purpose of fighting against Muslim armies was strategic, and not motivated by religious differences. It is necessary for Templar and Vatican missions to secure access to Jerusalem for Christians, to maintain protective military outposts, and to defend those strongholds against attacks or isolation. Saladin knows this and he too rejects all claims that the Crusades are purely against Islam, for he knows it is about the strategic importance of Jerusalem."

"Indeed," Attar remarked. "For genuine Christianity cannot logically nor ethically reject or oppose Islam, a religion which fully recognises Christianity, considers Christianity to be a part of the Muslim faith, and considers Jesus the Nazarene to be one of the most honoured Prophets of Islam next to Muhammad, peace be upon him. 'Tis madness fuelled by the likes of Reynald and Turansha for in reality Christians and Muslims are natural allies in spiritual faith."

"'Tis why I cannot follow someone like Reynald any longer," Upside remarked and sighed heavily and lowered his head.

"You have much to consider, my friend," Thomas said and patted Upside on the shoulder. "Much indeed."

"If I were not now sworn to protect Paul and his family, I would consider this knights of Saladin myself," Ishmael said as he leant down and lifted up his dirty chain mail. "But now I would beg my leave to sleep."

"Ishmael...you know there are no binds that chain you here should you ever wish to leave to follow another path," Paul remarked as Ishmael stood up.

"I know...and that is why I stay...and there are chains that bind me," he replied and bowed his head slightly. All watched as he walked over and opened the rear exit door then turned to look back at them all. "The chains of love that bind me to this brotherhood I am blessed to be a part of...I bid you goodnight," he stated and left the room, closing the door quietly behind him.

"Oh Lord," Paul sighed. "Where does this all lead to and where does it leave me?"

"With the weight of history...and the future upon your shoulders, my boy...and that you will surely find out soon enough," Theodoric said as he stood up and looked him in the eyes. "Remember...your mother's maiden name was Keys and she came from Gizors in France though her parents were both British. And you are now here near to the original Giza where it all started. Work that all out and we all may just have a future...and with that I shall be away and bid you goodnight."

ꕥ

Thomas and Upside likewise called it a night and left the dining hall leaving Paul sat alone with just one small ceramic candle holder, the candle almost burnt away. He untied his sword and placed it upon the table and unsheathed it enough to see the image patterned onto it the blacksmith had etched so delicately. He moved the crimson cord lower that was permanently tied around it. He smiled tiredly as he rubbed his fingers over the leather scabbard. He rested his head forwards in his hands and thought back over how far he and Alisha had come since leaving La Rochelle. He closed his eyes.

ꕥ

"Paul," a soft and gentle female voice called out.

Paul shook his head slightly and tried to open his eyes. He sat up quickly and leaned back pulling his sword closer as he shielded his eyes from the bright light before him. As he blinked, he could see what appeared to be the image of some standing stones. Puzzled he rubbed his eyes with his left hand just as a tall slender female stepped into view walking slowly toward him. She wore what appeared to be a full length dress made of a shimmering silk but it was neither blue nor purple but shone somewhere between them. She wore a single diamond looking pendant that hung in the middle of her forehead on a very delicate silver chain. Her eyes stayed fixed upon his as she stepped ever closer and outstretched her right hand. Without thinking he raised his left hand and she clasped it softly. Paul stood up slowly. The woman had blue eyes that reflected the clouds as they passed overhead. Paul looked around seeing that he was standing in a lush valley…one he knew to be a Scottish glen.

"Dare I ask where I am?" he asked quietly.

"Paul…it has been a very long time since last I saw you," the woman said and smiled gracefully at him but her eyes full of emotion. "And even longer since I last saw that," she remarked and looked down at the sword held in his right hand. "You are in a place special and sacred to me…and I wish for you to meet someone," she explained and stepped aside to reveal a man standing behind her. He looked familiar, Paul thought. The man bowed his head and smiled as he stepped closer. He held the woman's left hand and the moment he did, it was as if a surge of energy ran through his arm, up through the woman's and down her left arm into Paul's. With a jolt the sudden realisation and knowledge hit him and in an instant he knew the woman was his mother. But just as quickly as that realisation hit him, so did the fact that he then instantly recognised the man was the Templar Knight who had been so grotesquely beheaded beside him…but also a realisation that this was also his uncle. Confused, Paul let go of his mother's hand in alarm. He looked at the man.

"This is not my uncle…what manner of a dream is this?" Paul demanded and feared it was some trick perhaps orchestrated by the old woman who constantly hung around.

"This is no trick, my son, my beautiful youngest son," his mother spoke softly and clasped his hand again. "And this, this is indeed your uncle, your father's eldest brother," she explained and smiled.

The man nodded he was.

"But…but how, I do not understand it!" Paul exclaimed, confused.

"Your grandfather and grandmother, their first born, was taken from them as an agreement. For his own protection, but Elek, for that is his name, he found us again but the one you know as Kratos…he took him away again," his mother explained.

"Well it did not do him any good for I witnessed your death," Paul answered and stepped back, again suspicious this was some kind of trick.

His father had never once mentioned he had any brothers or sisters. He would not hide such a fact.

"Paul…I lived a very long and fulfilling life…and it was my fate to die in the manner I did and of my choosing," Elek explained and moved closer to Paul.

"But you cannot be, that is how I know this is just a dream…for as Kratos and Abi explained, you were as old as Abi, if not older," Paul snapped back.

"My son…there are many things you do not know and have yet to learn for know this, time as you perceive and understand it is truly but an illusion. I cannot explain it fully to you now but try and understand that I met Elek a long time before I even met your father. As you will learn, some people can see as well as move across the cycles of time. All you need understand now is that Elek did," his mother said and stepped closer.

Paul's throat tightened as he looked at her and fought to hold down suppressed emotions. He had never met his mother and yet she now stood before him appearing as real as he could imagine. Elek smiled.

"And this place…where are we?" Paul asked and coughed emotionally.

"Look around you. 'Tis a place your father and Theodoric know of well," she replied and motioned with her hands to look around. "'Tis Glen Lyon."

"Paul. This place was once the stronghold of the ancient Picts…'twas the original centre of their kingdom, not that of Scone as some now believe," Elek explained. "You shall perhaps one day visit this glen for it is more sacred than most know of…in Fortingall near Loch Tay, the glen itself is void of megalithic monuments for it is the site of the Creator Goddess and the solar deity, Lugh, and is sacred by its own nature. Truly sacred sites are left untouched by human hands."

3 - 35

"Then what is that?" Paul asked as he pointed to two upright stones that appeared split.

"They are these days called the 'Praying Hands of Mary'. They sit aside the conical hill of Creag nan Eildeag, the two huge stones rise sideways, with a narrow split between them as if they were two hands, held together without the fingertips touching, as if in prayer. The Praying Hands 'pray' towards the conical Creag nan Eildeag. Like all conical hills, they are the symbol of the 'primordial hill', the first hill created on earth, the navel of the earth, its shape mimicking the shape of the belly of a pregnant woman. In Egypt, the conical hill was identified as a 'primordial hill', on which the solar deity masturbated, to create the world. In Celtic countries, a very similar event occurs, though it is more correct to say that the solar deity Lugh had impregnated the Cailleach, hence the conical shaped hill expressing her pregnancy," his mother explained patiently as she looked around lovingly at the scenery.

"'Tis a dream," Paul said aloud to himself and closed his eyes for several moments. When he opened them, both his mother and Elek were stood just looking at him smiling.

"'Tis no dream," Elek remarked.

"All ancient dolmens and stones sit across natural faults in the earth. They strengthen and increase the energy to keep the lands fertile, including all that lives. All are aligned to a great web of lines that interconnect to maintain balance and stop illness and decay…and all converge on the navel of the world…in Giza!" his mother explained.

"All areas have different heights in waves of energy, but they can be tuned like the strings on a lyre, to balance the energy by cutting in various sized cup marks in them. From one to eight, and sometimes nine," Elek explained.

Paul's mind raced as he thought over the many discussions he had had with his father over the years. It was clear now that he had been educating and preparing him all those years. He felt sick and dizzy and had to shake his head to clear his mind. He remembered his father had told him to always remember the yew tree in a place called Fortingall. As he recalled this, he looked up at his mother, who nodded her acknowledgement and that she knew what he was thinking of.

"That yew tree, my son, is thousands of years old…and it shall remain growing until the dawn of the new Age of Aquarius," she smiled and took his hand again.

"If this is no dream, then how do you forgive those that beheaded you?" Paul asked Elek.

Elek smiled and looked to Paul's mother.

"She can best explain that," he answered.

"Forgiveness you must learn and practice…it is one of the primary lessons preached by all those true followers who walk a spiritual path. But understand that forgiveness is not the first thing one must do when one has suffered a great wrongdoing or injustice or traumatic experience.

Healing is so misunderstood by placing impossible pressures upon people to forgive without having first accepted and dealt with the trauma or wrong doing or pain for it sidesteps their own unresolved shadow and the principles of accountability. If a knight is severely wounded in battle, he does not have time to start a forgiveness prayer or mantra for the assailant. He would need to remove himself from further harm's way, seek medical attention and recover or he would die. When it comes down to it, healing and forgiving ourselves is the important step. We are not responsible for those who wound us. They can take that up with God. Grief and time are the dynamic healing team that receive little praise, yet they make our hearts soften and allow for new love to grow. A hard heart is not able to understand or heal," she explained and sat him down upon the lush green grass. She sat beside him and held both his hands. "As we all grow, we likewise grow out of old ways and our souls yearn to learn more and grow further and you will want to grow more. Then you start the same process over again just with more understanding than before. It does not stop as growth and consciousness is infinite and ever expanding. You will change many times my son, my beautiful son," she said and cupped his face in her hands and gently kissed him upon the forehead. [96]

"I do not understand how we are able to do this?" Paul remarked and looked up at Elek.

"'Tis but a natural process we all posses. You would call it 'telepathy' from the words 'tele' meaning 'distance' and 'path' meaning 'feeling'. It actually means getting feelings through a distance...the communication between two minds, separated over a distance, without the use of the five known senses," his mother explained and looked deeply into his eyes. "We must go now...but remember the Glen of Lyon for it is there that my mortal remains lie buried. Please let your father know."

She stood up slowly and moved back to stand beside Elek. He clasped her hand and both smiled at Paul.

"Tell your father I am with your mother and we shall see him again," Elek said.

"And Paul...Death is never the end. In the end, only three things matter... How much you loved...How gently you lived...How gracefully you let go of things not meant for you! And remember this...your son will hold your hand but a short time, but he will hold your heart for a lifetime."

As she said the last sentence, Paul's heart jumped in fear with a sudden sense of dread about Arri. What was she telling him? He went to stand but a sudden loud and almost painful high pitch ringing echoed out within his ears making him feel dizzy. He lowered his head immediately and clasped his hands over his ears and screwed up his face, looking down. In the distance he thought he could hear Arri calling him. He felt a shaking sensation upon his shoulder. Suddenly his head was full of noise and a rushing sound, his heart beating fast.

ꟷ

"Father, father!" Arri called out in a whisper as he shook Paul's shoulder.

Paul had his head resting in his hands as he leant forwards with his elbows on the table. He opened his eyes wide instantly as he woke up. Sunlight was already beginning to enter through the corners of the window covers. He turned to see Arri stood beside him in his night clothes smiling.

"Arri!" Paul said and quickly pulled him close and hugged him tightly. He kissed the side of his head and felt emotional as he held him close. Arri put his arms around him and Clip clop caught him in the side of his face as he did so. "And please, call me Papa…remember."

"Why is everyone having a lazy day today…Papa?" Arri asked, puzzled.

Paul laughed and hugged him even tighter just as Alisha walked in rubbing her eyes.

"Have you been here all night?" she asked and kissed the top of Paul's head as she walked past him.

Paul just held Arri and ran through everything he could remember of his strange dream. He shook his head puzzled and confused. It was only then that he noticed a small white feather beside his sword and a small rolled up piece of paper. It had Attar's typically green string partially tied around it. He leaned over and with his left hand picked it up and rolled it open as Arri looked down at it. He raised his eyebrows as if to ask what it meant.

"'Tis written in Arabic…and it says…'Write the bad things that are done to you in sand, but write the good things that happen to you on a piece of marble'."

Arri smiled and quickly pulled away and rushed over to Alisha. As she asked him what he would like to eat, Paul's heart felt heavy almost like a real weight was inside as he thought back over the words his mother had apparently told him in the dream. He heard her words echo in his mind and it made him shudder. Perhaps he was misunderstanding her words. Perhaps he should look upon them as he should always be grateful and make the most of the time he has with Arri for he will grow so quickly. Maybe she meant it from her to him as he was her son?

'Your son will hold your hand but a short time, but he will hold your heart for a lifetime' he heard his mother say again, her face perfectly pictured in his mind. He would draw her image whilst he remembered, he told himself, as emotions welled inside him to the point he could not speak for fear of bursting into tears. Attar had mentioned about being cautious of the dream he had about two armies fighting with two horns on either side and his dream of the same event came vividly back to mind. Though tired, he forced a smile and stood up trying to concentrate on the comment his mother had said that she promised to always watch over him. In Attar's comments he had strongly hinted at a prophecy that would come to pass, but the seeds of a promise had also been sown by his mother.

Chapter 58
Beyond the Veil, Revelation Cometh

Port of La Rochelle, France, Melissae Inn, spring 1191

The old man sat back in his chair and raised his hands to his face, resting his chin upon them. He closed his eyes and took several long and slow breaths.

"I sense what comes next will be difficult for you...will it be?" Gabirol asked.

"No, 'tis fine. I shall continue," the old man answered and sat himself up ready to carry on.

"Does it mean that Arri will die, or be given to Kratos and why was Elek handed over?" Simon asked in quick succession.

"What if I told you Elek was not of normal creation. As for the dream about him and Paul's mother...well Paul felt it was real enough to draw an image of her and the stones in Glen Lyon...look for yourselves," the old man said and nodded towards Paul's folder. Gabirol opened the folder and carefully looked through the images inside. "I think you will find he has marked them."

Gabirol pulled out an image of a woman with the simple title penned at the bottom 'Mother' with a question mark beside it.

Fig. 55: Paul's mother.

He then pulled out another image simply marked 'Elek'.

Fig. 56: Elek.

"You mentioned female knights before and again just now...but do you really mean it?" the Genoese sailor asked.

"Yes...as our good friends here will confirm, they were and are real enough," the old man answered and looked at the Templar and Hospitaller, who nodded in agreement.

"And time...you said it was a circle or something?" Peter asked.

"Time indeed...'tis a vast subject we simply do not have time to discuss in detail but I can say that there are those who claim and teach that the time we live in is a circle. That what was, will be, that we live and die and that we can not only be born again in the future, but also the past," the old man started to explain, Simon rubbing his head confused. "God, or whatever you wish to call him, in his infinite wisdom is teaching us all to become more than we are, and if you believe the spirit being eternal, then why make life experiences just one way in time?"

"And I guess race, colour or creed make no distinction and therefore no real meaning if in one life you can be born black as a man and the next as woman and

white...Muslim one time, Hindu or Christian the next," Gabirol said, shaking his head as his mind raced pondering the possibilities.

"'Tis far too deep for me, but I am interested in the pyramids in Bosnia. How are they hidden and how many more are there in the world?" Peter asked.

"My friend...our entire world is covered in pyramids, even on the seabeds...such is their age. But there are even older ones that remain buried, especially in areas like China and closer to home in places like Crimea, even Georgia...huh, and those when they are eventually opened will not be able to be denied or hidden," the old man laughed.

"What do you mean?" Ayleth asked.

"Their great antiquity and the very real physical remains of some of our ancient forefathers," he answered.

"But why were so many pyramids made then?" Peter asked.

"Because our ancient forefathers knew and understood the delicate forces that wrap around this world we live upon. They used the pyramids to control that force not only to remain healthy and maintain the fertility of the lands, but also to stabilise our atmosphere and protect us. But that knowledge was lost as you all now know. The Norse myths still recount them in their legends of Thor and the ice gods as mentioned earlier."

"Though not really lost if what you have told us is true," Gabirol remarked.

"If what was handed down to us is true, then other planets that housed life lost their atmospheres after losing their natural forces of energy...this cannot be allowed to happen again," the old man sighed. "As our planet's harmonic signature, its tune, its rhythm increases so too it will affect each and every one of us and as a consequence our consciousness will also be raised. Our ancient forefathers knew how interconnected we are with our mother planet and so stabilised that energy and that is why they buried and hid for protection the very things necessary to safeguard us as mankind transits from one level of consciousness to the next higher level."

"How?" Simon asked bluntly.

"As our earth passes into the new period of light, enlightenment, and the harmonics increase, it is the pyramids that will again regulate that energy and keep us balanced," the old man explained.

"And you have told us that all of this happens to a set time scheme...a plan almost, but you now tell us time is but like a circle. Does that mean we simply keep going around over and again doing the same thing?" Gabirol asked.

"A good point, Gabirol. Let me explain briefly that all ancient cultures speak of vast cycles of time with alternating Dark and Golden Ages. Plato called it the Great

Year. Many ancient cultures believed consciousness and history were not linear but cyclical, rising and falling over long periods of time. Myth and folklore all speak of a cycle of time with long periods of enlightenment broken by dark ages of ignorance, indirectly driven by a known astronomical phenomenon, the precession of the equinox. We all know the two celestial motions that have a profound effect on life and consciousness. Diurnal motion, earth's rotation on its axis, causes humans to move from a waking state to a sleep state and back again every twenty-four hours. Our bodies have adapted to earth's rotation so well that it produces these regular changes in consciousness without our even thinking the process remarkable. Earth's revolution around the sun, the second celestial motion, which Copernicus identified, has an equally significant effect, prompting trillions of life forms to spring out of the ground, to bloom, fruit and then decay, while billions of other species hibernate, spawn or migrate en masse. Our visible world literally springs to life, completely changes its colour and stride, and then reverses with every waxing and waning of the second celestial motion. The third celestial motion, the precession of the equinox, is less understood than the first two, but if we are to believe ancient cultures from around the world, its effect is equally transformative. What disguises the impact of this motion is its timescale. Like the butterfly that lives but one day a year and knows nothing of the seasons, the human being has an average life span that lasts only one-360th of the roughly 24,000-year precessional cycle. And just as the butterfly born on an overcast, windless day has no idea that there is anything as splendid as sunshine or a breeze, so do we, born in an era of materialistic rationality, have little awareness of a golden age or higher states of consciousness, yet that is exactly the ancestral message that has been handed down to us. The idea of a great cycle linked to the slow precession of the equinox was common to numerous cultures before the Christian era, but today we are taught nothing about it. The observation of earth's three motions is quite simple. In the first, rotation, we see the sun rise in the east and set in the west every twenty-four hours. And if we were to look at the stars just once a day, we would see a similar pattern over a year: the stars rise in the east and set in the west. The twelve constellations of the zodiac, the ancient markers of time that lie along the ecliptic, the sun's path, pass overhead at the rate of about one per month and return to the starting point of our celestial observation at the end of the year. And if we looked just once a year, say on the autumnal equinox, we would notice the stars move retrograde, that is opposite to the first two motions at the rate of about one degree every seventy years. At this pace, the equinox falls on a different constellation approximately once every two thousand years, taking about 24,000 years to complete its cycle through the twelve constellations. This is called the precession, the backward motion of the equinox relative to the fixed stars. The standard theory of precession says it is principally the moon's pulling force (gravity) acting upon the earth that must be the cause of earth's changing orientation to inertial space, as in 'precession'. Ancient oriental astronomy teaches that an equinox slowly moving or 'precessing' through the zodiac's twelve constellations is simply due to the motion of the sun curving through space around another star, which changes our viewpoint of the stars from earth. However, and as man will relearn, our very solar system also travels around and by doing so produces the precession observable accurately, resolving a number of solar system anomalies even though astronomers have not yet discovered a companion star to our earth's sun, but as you all know we do indeed have a companion dark star as I have already explained. A moving solar system provides a logical reason why we have a Great Year, to use Plato's term, with alternating Dark and Golden ages. That is, if the solar system carrying the earth actually moves in a huge orbit, subjecting earth to the forces and influences of another star along the way, and shaping the subtle energies through which we move. Just as earth's smaller diurnal and annual motions produce the cycles of day and night and the seasons of the year so the larger celestial motion produces a cycle that affects life and consciousness on a grand scale. And to finish on this very large subject, I would urge you to simply remember that consciousness prefers light, which is consistent with myth and folklore, the concept behind the Great Year or cyclical model of history is based on the sun's motion through space, subjecting earth to waxing and waning stellar energies that thus result in the legendary rise and fall of the ages over great epochs of time." [97]

"I was once told that Easter, in fact the Sabbath and our days of celebrating events from the Bible, are all wrong because we are now following a Roman instigated time model...and that the Sabbath is correctly connected to the moon and the great cycles of time and the constellations. Is that true?" Gabirol asked.

"You have heard correctly. Suffice it to say that neither Saturday nor Sunday have ever been the ancient seventh-day Sabbath of the Creator, Adam, Noah, Abraham, Moses, David, Daniel, the Apostles, or our Messiah and Saviour. But that is all I need say on that matter," the old man answered.

"But what about time being a circle?" the wealthy tailor asked.

"If I told you that time was a circle, in the realm of existence we all live and experience life in, would you really believe me?" the old man replied.

"I would," Simon interjected loudly.

"If you can believe the soul is eternal, and that life reincarnation was real, then judging people by the colour of their skin, their material wealth, or lack of

it, or where they were born is quite literally and physically a redundant factor as Gabirol alluded to earlier. And suppose, as I explained before, we are all here to learn and grow...to evolve to a higher state, and so we inherit all that our parents knew and experienced so as time moves on, the newly born will be for ever increasing in their knowledge and experiences...but what if I then told you that you can just as easily be reborn in the past as well as the future. This is why some people who have already lived in those times are able under certain conditions to remember and recall events from those lives. Hence how prophecy and visions can and do occur," the old man explained and paused as he gauged their reactions. "And what if I told you the sins of the father being visited upon the children is actually quite true, but also, what if, now consider this, what if everyone of us was a small part of a greater being of consciousness and that we are in fact all one and the same being and experiencing many different emotions and trials, all compressed into one world...so when great mystics and religious teachers tell us to do unto others what we would want done unto us, it literally means if you hurt someone, you are hurting yourself."

"But then if that was the case, I could do anything I wanted...as I would be doing it to myself. And that means I am marrying myself and...and," Simon started to say but stopped, thought for a moment and shook his head utterly perplexed.

"I am not saying that is how it is, but I ask you start to consider such things," the old man remarked in response. He noticed the Templar and Hospitaller whispering to each other.

"Sorry," the Templar said after Miriam nudged him. "This uncle of Paul's...Elek you said his name was yes?"

"Yes," the old man answered.

"Then...am I correct in saying he is one and the same Master Elek Alden, of my Order?"

"That is correct, one and the same," the old man replied.

"'Tis sad news indeed to learn it was him then for we both knew of him," the Templar explained and shook his head in sadness. "We did not realise you were speaking of him."

"How do you know of him then?" the farrier asked.

"He was a legend in my early years of my service for his travels and adventures to the east...and for being very wise and a protector of the poor and weak," the Templar explained as his brother nodded in agreement.

"Last we heard he had gone missing in the orient at the ends if the silk route many years ago," the Hospitaller said and folded his arms.

"If he is Paul's uncle, from his father's side, does that mean that Paul's real surname is Alden, with his mother being Keys as you said?" Gabirol asked.

"No...Elek was given that part of his name by Kratos himself after he had taken him," the old man answered solemnly. "'Twas Niccolas who called him Alden remember."

"It means something doesn't it?" Ayleth stated.

"Very perceptive Ayleth, and yes it does," the old man replied and smiled before explaining. "Alden actually means 'Old wise protector' and Elek literally means 'defender of mankind'. He would often just sign his name as EL which as you all know is an identification for a god..."

"As in Elohim?" Gabirol remarked.

"Are you saying this Elek was Elohim...for that would mean so too is Paul and his father," Peter said, looking concerned almost.

"I did say that Elek was...how shall I say, partially created. That is all I can tell you...but the sacred bloodline, as I have explained already, runs through Paul's veins, yes."

"And his father's?" Gabirol asked, pushing for a definitive answer.

The old man looked at him for several moments in silence before finally answering. "To a lesser degree, yes."

"You mentioned Vedic and Rigveda. What is that?" Sarah asked, sensing unease in the old man.

"Rigveda is a Sanskrit compound word from Rc, meaning 'praise or verse', and Veda, meaning 'knowledge', and is the word given for an ancient Indian sacred collection of Vedic Sanskrit hymns. It is counted among the four canonical sacred texts, or śrut of Hinduism known as the Vedas. It is one of the oldest extant texts in any Indo-European language," the old man answered.

3 - 15

Simon nodded and smiled as if he now fully understood as Sarah turned to him and pulled a face. The old man laughed at her response.

"Hey, I have learnt something too," the Genoese sailor announced proudly. "That Lugh character...he journeyed in a boat like Mary had, you know, without oars or sails."

"So the legend states," the old man replied and bowed his head slightly.

"Before I forget...you mentioned women knights and female Druids. Did I hear correctly...that women could be Druids too?" Sarah asked.

"Yes you heard correctly. Templars have women in their ranks just as Druids did, so never be misled that only men could be Druids or bards," the old man answered. "'Tis a sad fact that this secret remains so...this misconception can be placed firmly upon Roman historians who reported on Celtic culture, even as they decimated the Druids. The Romans deliberately ignored the true status of the women of the tribes. But even Christian monks still ignore and downplay the status of Celtic women, even while recording and copying their tales and oral histories. The role of powerful women in ancient Celtic times has been and is there for those who care to find it."

"So to get this right...the word Druid derives from 'deru', which carries meanings such as truth, true, hard, enduring, resistant and tree," Gabirol stated and checked back over his notes. "And deru evolved into the Greek word drus, also meaning oak and referred over time to all trees as well as the words truth and true. Id comes from wid, to know, related to both wisdom and vision. A Dru-id is a truth-knower and a true-knower, one with solid and enduring wisdom, a tree-knower, and an expert. So as dru meant oak, so Druid also means oak-knower," Gabirol stated, checking over his notes again closely.

As the old man nodded in agreement, Peter leaned forwards and raised his finger.

"I finally see...Oaks are the most balanced of trees...their roots grow as deep as the tree is high. They give the hottest fire excepting the ash tree, and provide medicine via their leaves and bark as well as food...their acorns, for humans, pigs and deer," he explained, pleased with himself.

"But how would you or anyone else know these facts if all the Druids' traditions were only given orally?" the wealthy tailor asked.

"Yes the Druids preferred to keep their teachings in oral form, feeling they were too sacred to write down, but writers like Tacitus gave us vivid accounts of the slaughter of the Druids by Roman soldiers on the island of Mona (Anglesey) in Wales. Black clad women defending the island were also noted down. Described just like a typical witch no less. The island was the most sacred stronghold of the British Druids and we can confidently state that these women were Ban-druid, female Druids. In Irish traditional accounts there are references to Ban-druid female Druids and Ban-filid female poets. Fedelm is a female seer and Accuis, Col and Eraise are female Druids mentioned in the Tain. We also know that Celtic women wore trousers, and remember," the old man explained and looked at the wealthy tailor, "it was the Celts who invented trousers. Gallic females went to war with their husbands and fought alongside their men. In some Roman reports they said the women were even fiercer than the men!"

"No surprises there then," Simon joked and looked at Sarah.

"In the first century AD Tacitus wrote that the Celts made no distinction between male and female rulers and powerful Celtic women appear in the tales. By tradition Macha Mongruad founded Emain Macha (Navan Fort) in Ulster. The two most famous warriors in Irish history are Finn MacCumhail and Cú Chulainn, who were both trained by women. Finn was raised by two females, a Druidess and a warrior woman, who taught him the crafts of war and of hunting while Cú Chulainn learned the arts of war from Scáthach, who had her own Martial Arts school," the old man explained.

"So what happened? Why did an indigenous culture that had educated and powerful women devolve into a culture where women are now demoted to the status of chattel?" Gabirol asked.

"Yes...what he asked," Simon said.

"Because by the first century in Britain, the Romans deliberately suppressed the Druids, who were the intellectual elite...the advisors to the nobility and the glue that held the kingdoms together. Romans claimed the Druids were perpetrators of savage superstitions and of horrific human sacrifice, yet this was at the same time the Roman Circuses were going on. Druidesses were described as seers who were working on their own, rather than as powerful Royal advisors and clergy. A policy of deliberate extermination was carried out, brought to its catastrophic conclusion by the terrifying slaughter of the Druids at Anglesey. But the Romans never conquered the Emerald Isle and the worship of the pagan gods continued there officially until the death of King Diarmat in AD 565. Unofficially it still continues. As Christianity gained power in all areas Roman, ideals of matronly behaviour and womanhood began to wane, though in the few centuries that it was allowed to flourish the Celtic Church continued to exalt powerful priestesses such as Brighid of Kildare and Beaferlic of Northumbria. But then as the Roman Christian Church gained more prominence female Druids were labelled evil witches and sorcerers as a way to smear their reputations and make people fear them. Religious orders founded by women were systematically dissolved upon their founder's death, preventing continuity of female centred orders. The Druids were demoted in the laws to figures of ridicule, mere magicians, stripped of their sacral function and status. Women in Celtic areas were forbidden to bear arms and their status dropped in most areas of life and society." [98]

"Bastards!" Sarah said out loud and folded her arms in disgust as Ayleth sniggered at her words. "Oh pardon my language. Lord it makes my blood boil...so we women suffer now eh?"

"I think not with you, my dear," Stephan said smiling.

"So going back to Paul then...did he question Theodoric or his father about his uncle?" Gabirol asked.

"Oh yes, that he did...that he did," the old man answered.

Cairo, Egypt, April 14th, 1183

After a light breakfast with Alisha and Arri, Paul went outside to check on Adrastos. He noted that Luke's and Ishmael's horses had already gone. Thomas and Mathew were adjusting the tack on their horses as Percival came running over carrying his chain mail armour and surcoat under his arms. He apologised for being late and got himself dressed rapidly. Within minutes Paul was waving them off as they set out for another day's escort duties on the western approaches. Paul patted Adrastos and checked he was okay. After a few minutes brushing him down, he heard a very faint sound behind him. He paused and strained to listen. He looked around but the yard was empty. He put his hand upon his sword sensing something was wrong. His heart began to race as he turned himself around. Movement caught his eye as the shadow of the main paddock block roof had a small protrusion pop up and vanish just as quickly. Could be a cat or a bird he told himself as he slowly stepped out from the building to check up on the roof. As he shielded his eyes, he strained to look up into the glare of the rising morning sun. He could see nothing but his senses were screaming at him there was someone about. He looked back at the kitchen hall doorway. It was closed. He then looked back toward the stable building, the sun now blocked from view as two large figures dressed in black stood motionless and silently directly in front of him as if they had appeared out of thin air. Paul instinctively jumped backwards drawing his sword at the same time. The kitchen door opened and Arri appeared smiling. Without hesitation he started to run toward Paul.

"No…get back inside!" Paul called out raising his left hand toward Arri but he kept running toward him. The two men remained perfectly still, their faces covered, just their eyes visible. Paul held his sword up pointing at them and grabbed Arri up in his arms as he reached him. Arri kicked his legs and struggled.

"Tenno! Tenno…Put me down, it is Tenno," Arri said loudly and wriggled.

Stunned, Paul looked harder at the two men. The taller of the two men stepped closer. As soon as Paul's eyes met his, the familiar shape of Tenno's eyes became obvious and as he winked and raised his eyebrow, Paul knew it was indeed Tenno. He put Arri down who immediately ran to Tenno. Tenno pulled the black dust mask down from his face and pushed the hood back and scooped Arri up in his arms as he leapt at him. Arri wrapped his arms around Tenno tightly. Tenno almost smiled.

"My, you have grown so much," Tenno said and walked toward Paul.

Paul lowered his sword, bemused, and looked at the other man. Slowly he lifted his mask and hood away, shook his head, his long thick curly hair covering his face momentarily. As he flicked his hair back, he smiled broadly. The man sported a tight beard and looked very familiar.

"Hello, my friend," Taqi said softly.

"Taqi!" Alisha almost screamed with delight making both Paul and Taqi look toward her as she came running from the doorway. "What are you doing here?" she asked as she stopped in front of him. "Look at you…all… all grown up and…different."

"'Tis truly wonderful to see you again," Taqi replied and part bowed.

Paul re-sheathed his sword, his heart still beating fast.

"I feared you were Turansha's men…I almost struck you," Paul said and shook his head, pleased to see them.

"Fear not, you would not have succeeded," Taqi joked back as Alisha wrapped her arms around him and hugged him.

"I bet I can still beat you?" Paul joked back as Taqi kissed the side of Alisha's face, stepped away from her then opened his arms to greet Paul.

"Bet you can't," Taqi answered and hugged Paul. "'Tis truly great we meet again, my friend."

"What brings you here…and how?" Alisha asked as Arri clung to Tenno.

"Business and pleasure," Tenno answered, holding Arri in one arm. "We came via Malta, with your father."

"My father?" Paul said, surprised.

"Yes…he follows with your friend Husam…but also Conrad I am afraid. We had to pick him up yesterday. 'Tis why we are a day late," Tenno explained as Taqi nodded in agreement.

"How…I mean why?" Paul asked, bemused but pleased. "And look at you two…you both look so different."

"Is it safe for you to be here?" Alisha asked, suddenly looking concerned.

"Yes, we are under the protection of Husam...and Conrad is here to negotiate trade and a treaty from his port at Tyre...and guaranteed non involvement with Reynald," Taqi explained.

"I assume Reynald is safe then?" Paul asked.

"You know Reynald...more lives than a cat," Taqi replied and smiled. "And your father knows Stewart is safe too."

"Oh thank the Lord for that," Paul sighed with relief.

"I knew it was Tenno," Arri said aloud and put his arms around Tenno's neck again. He looked at Taqi, puzzled. "But I don't know who he is."

Taqi walked over to Tenno and Arri and ran his finger down Arri's cheek and smiled at him.

"I am your uncle...your mother's brother," Taqi said and looked back at Alisha.

As soon as Taqi said brother, Paul immediately recalled his dream and of his father's brother Elek. He would have to ask him about that when he arrived. He looked at Tenno and wondered where his usual armour was. But for now he was just pleased to see them both again and relieved to learn his brother was alive and well.

ℌℭ

Alisha was serving Tenno and Taqi some refreshments in the cool kitchen area when several horses pulled up in the rear courtyard. Paul immediately saw Ishmael and Luke dismount. Paul recognised Conrad immediately behind them with Husam riding by his side. He then noticed his father following behind him alongside Brother Teric. Several Mamluk escort guards held their positions just short of the rear entrance gate. Paul was surprised to see Brother Matthew with them. Paul stepped down into the courtyard as Husam dismounted and rapidly approached him.

"Paul...my apologies for our delay but we had to pick up Lord Montfferat and his delegation. I wish to speak with you in private before you speak with the others," Husam said as he took off his riding gloves and quickly looked back at his escort. Paul stood still somewhat confused for a moment. Husam turned and faced him again. "Paul, I am so glad you survived the naval engagement...but I must warn you now, do not speak of your involvement with Reynald's escape...along with your brother...do you hear me?"

Paul took a sharp intake of breath. Husam somehow knew he had helped

Reynald. His heart missed a beat. Should he deny it? Was he safe or was Husam here to arrest him? He clasped his sword instinctively.

"I do not...," Paul started to say.

"Sssh...there are those here this day that would have you arrested...all of you if they knew. There are too may spies amongst us. I will speak with you later on this matter do you hear?" Husam said quietly and pulled Paul close and greeted him. "Assalamu Allakham," he said loudly.

"Wa Allakham Assalam," Paul replied nervously and confused. He looked toward the kitchen doorway as Alisha stepped out.

"Fear not, my friend...for a friend you are. She will be safe," Husam whispered and stood back and immediately walked toward Alisha with his arms outstretched.

Many questions ran through Paul's mind as he turned to face his father. He approached slowly closely followed by Brother Teric. Philip stopped just in front of Paul and looked at him intently for a few moments in silence.

"Your brother is safe...that I can tell you," Philip said and then hugged Paul tightly, which caught him by surprise. Brother Teric smiled and nodded at him. "And we are here to negotiate on Conrad's behalf. 'Tis good to see you, my son."

"And take Brothers Baldwin and Nicholas back with us," Brother Teric explained. Paul frowned, puzzled. "Oh we received word they were here."

Paul stepped back from his father still holding his arms.

"Father...Brother Baldwin wishes to stay here...Brother Nicholas is still weak and," Paul started to say and paused. "You had a brother also didn't you?" Philip scowled momentarily caught off guard with the sudden question. He looked at Brother Teric for a second then back at Paul. He feigned puzzlement and shrugged his shoulders. "And Mother...she is with him for I spoke with them both."

Philip's face turned almost white, his eyes widening. He took a deep breath and stood back a pace letting go of Paul's arms. He stared hard at Paul with a look he had never seen in his father's eyes before. After what seemed an age, Philip's stare softened as he saw the genuine look in Paul's eyes.

"Then we have more to discus than I thought," Philip finally replied and put his arm around Paul and ushered him toward the kitchen door where Alisha was laughing with Husam.

ꕥ

After pleasantries and introductions had been made, Alisha and Nyla prepared a midday meal as Sister Lucy took Arri upstairs to change. Conrad sat himself down as if he owned the place and made both Alisha and Nyla feel uncomfortable with his fixed stare. Husam ushered Paul aside whilst Philip spoke with Tenno and Taqi. Upside entered the kitchen and saw everyone. He looked at Husam, alarmed, until he bowed at him in acknowledgment and pointed out Brother Teric's presence. Upside looked confused.

"He need fear not for he is safe," Husam said quietly to Paul and pulled him discreetly to the far end of the dining area. "But you, my friend, may not be." Paul looked at him, alarmed. "My fleet and I chased Reynald's fleet aground…then we used our hunting dogs to track them across the deserts after they had beached their vessels and we captured every sailor, knight and hand that had been aboard those vessels. But no sign of Reynald, Gerard or your brother…and they were not among the captives taken from the waters back to our ports," Husam explained quietly, his deep brown eyes searching every movement in Paul's eyes. "I have already received word via our sources that all three are alive and well…and back in Kerak. Reynald is already telling lies that we attacked his fleet whilst they were in port…" Husam paused. "Now I do not profess to know how you did it, but the only explanation I have is that when your ship rammed his, you took them aboard…I do not know if I am more upset that you helped them or for losing my new ship."

Paul looked at Husam. He could sense he was not at all upset, his eyes smiling and full of admiration for Paul. Paul shuddered involuntarily sensing this with no mistake as if he could read Husam's mind almost.

"My ship," Paul heard himself reply.

Husam frowned for a moment but then his face broke into a smile.

"Your secret is safe with me. I understand why you did what you did…but if Reynald ever succeeds in reaching Mecca one day, it will be upon your shoulders, my friend…and that is one guilt I would not like to carry upon my shoulders. What blood Reynald or Gerard spill from here onwards… that is a matter for your conscience and for Allah to decide upon. But you have my word upon my honour I will not tell anyone of what I know…for I know what fate that will bring upon you…and your family," Husam said quietly and looked toward Alisha as she laughed gently with Tenno, Taqi and Philip. "But you will build me another ship."

Port of La Rochelle, France, Melissae Inn, spring 1191

"My Lord...so Husam knew?" Ayleth exclaimed, looking shocked.

"That he did...and more," the old man replied.

"But he knew if he revealed the truth, he would never get another ship like Paul had designed, so he was looking out for himself really," the Genoese sailor remarked and shook his head.

"We were all told that Reynald's ships were attacked whilst in port as you say Husam stated. I guess we were misinformed," the Hospitaller commented as he took another mouthful from his tankard.

"All propaganda...always propaganda, my friends," the old man sighed. "Husam is an intelligent man, and compassionate, but even he had his limits, loyalties and orders to follow. But you are correct for he knew if he made it known to Saladin what Paul had done, the only outcome would be the execution of Paul immediately and he would never get another ship like Paul had designed."

"So why were Paul's father and brother there with Conrad?" Gabirol asked.

"Conrad sought an audience with Saladin but was refused a direct meeting to discuss terms of an agreement...that agreement being that he would not allow Reynald's ships to use his port of Tyre, nor commit his troops to any campaigns that Reynald and Gerard started. You see Conrad had his eye on the crown of Jerusalem...," the old man explained. "Husam had not wanted to execute any of his captives, but he was overruled by Al Adil, brother of Saladin. Husam had destroyed Reynald's ships and even broken the blockade of the Ile de Gray destroying two of Reynald's ships there. Reynald put out the story that the Muslim fleet had sailed down the Red Sea and caught his ships at anchor. But in reality Reynald's fleet beached their ships and fled into the Arabian Desert. For five days Husam's forces pursued and captured almost all of them as he explained to Paul. Despite Al-Adil initially granting quarter to the captive raiders, he was overruled by his brother Saladin, who was adamant that because Reynald had shown the feasibility of attacking the holy cities of Islam, they must be executed so the word of their incursions would not reach the Crusaders in Outremer...and if it did, they would be defeated. It also sent a clear message to the followers of Saladin, especially his detractors, that he could be relied upon to defend the holy places and keep the pilgrim routes free and safe. So Al-Adil in turn had to overrule Husam's leniency. Saladin also publicly vowed that he would personally behead Reynald for directly threatening Mecca and Medina, challenging Islam in its own holy places. Reynald had almost succeeded getting only a few miles from Medina," the old man explained.

"We know many were taken to Cairo and Alexandria to be publicly beheaded. How did Paul and his father, as well as Brother Teric and Conrad, view all of that?" Peter asked.

"Fortunately those grim fates were already carried out before Philip docked. 'Tis neither fair nor wise to make prisoners suffer needlessly," the old man answered.

"Then it was timely and fortuitous that Paul recognised Brother Nicholas and Baldwin as he did," Simon pointed out loudly.

"'Twas indeed."

"And I am assuming it was Philip, Tenno and Taqi that Ishmael and Luke had been sent to collect the day before then?" Gabirol asked.

"Correct...but they were delayed in their passage from Malta as it had been agreed they would pick up Conrad Montferrat, Brother Teric and others from a secret port further along the coast," the old man explained.

"But why did Philip come with Tenno and Taqi during such dangerous times?" Ayleth asked, puzzled.

"To pass on some details to Paul from Kratos...and that under no circumstances must Paul rebuild his ship design for it would change everything."

"What details?" Simon asked bluntly.

"More about the bee symbolism, the fleur de lys and things that Philip had been up to."

"But you have already told us about the bees and lily...have you not?" Gabirol asked.

"Some of it," the old man replied with a slight nod and a smile.

"So Nicholas and Upside did not get their heads chopped off?" Sarah asked.

"No they did not for Husam guaranteed them safe passage back with Conrad."

"So they did not stay with Paul and Thomas's men?" Ayleth asked quickly.

"I shall come to that..."

"And the bees?" Gabirol asked again and smiled.

Cairo, Egypt, April 14th, 1183

The sun was just beginning to turn a dark orange on the horizon causing a wide band of flickering hues to reflect upon the wide waters of the Nile in the distance. Paul sat beside his father on the balcony bench, both looking down watching Tenno and Taqi teach Arri how to hold the reins properly upon Adrastos. It felt strange to Paul to see them all together like this.

Theodoric was in discussion with Husam and Conrad at the far end of the balcony whilst Brother Teric sat indoors with Upside and Nicholas. Luke, Mathew and Thomas's men busied themselves cleaning and checking their equipment and horses. Alisha, Sister Lucy and Nyla likewise busied themselves preparing an evening meal for all their unexpected but welcome guests. Thomas and Percival would not be back until late evening.

10 - 4

"My son…you should be happy yet you appear saddened. Why is this so?" Philip asked and leaned closer to Paul as he sat resting his elbows upon his knees still watching Tenno, Taqi and Arri.

"Why does Husam arrange this meeting here with Conrad…at my very home?"

"Because both trust you…plus here they are away from prying eyes," Philip replied quietly. "Plus it makes things less obvious when we leave taking Nicholas and Baldwin with us does it not?"

"Upside is staying here. He has said so…with Thomas."

"I think not, my son. He will go where Nicholas goes. Trust me on this matter. But something else troubles you. Has it something to do with Husam knowing you helped your brother and Reynald as a consequence?"

"No…for if he was going to inform on me, he would have done so by now. Besides, he wishes me to build another fast vessel…but…"

"But you wish to know of my brother you mentioned earlier?"

Paul looked at his father.

"So you do not deny you have a brother?"

"No."

"But you chose to never mention him. How many other family members are there that I do not know of?"

"I see pain and anger in those eyes…why…do you feel I have betrayed you somehow?"

"I truly do not know…I question even if I am sane at times, especially when I have such dreams that reveal things to me…like seeing my mother and your brother. They are like revelations from beyond the veil I cannot fathom if real or false."

"What did they say exactly?" Philip asked quietly and put his hand upon Paul's shoulder.

"I cannot recall much but Mother said she was buried in her most favourite place, near the praying hands of Mary…in the Glen of Lyon." Theodoric looked up upon hearing Paul's mention of Lyon. His eyes caught Philip's. Clearly Theodoric could hear their conversation from his seat. Philip took a slow long deep breath and clasped his hands together. He sat back and looked toward the setting sun and squinted his eyes from its brightness. Paul knew immediately this news had hit him hard and deeply. Arri laughed out loud drawing both their gaze. Tenno tickled him as he lifted him off Adrastos. "Do you know of such a place?"

"Arri has a surrogate father there in Tenno," Philip said, but his voice shook as he tried to speak without revealing his emotions.

"Father…your brother, for that is who he was, was beheaded right beside me and yet Theo did not even know him."

"My son…when I lost your mother, I knew not where she was laid to rest…I was supposed to receive word but the knights who were entrusted to intern her were ambushed as they returned. Just a few miles short of Balantrodach Temple. They were all killed…they refused to reveal her grave despite great torture," Philip explained clearly struggling to keep his emotions in check with a forced smile. "And as for my brother…I know as much as you do save for the added knowledge that he was first born of my parents…and that he was given into the care and charge of Kratos. I know it nearly destroyed my mother but it was a necessary evil in order to save and protect him. Anything after that I do not know…this I swear to you by all that is of value to me."

Paul could sense the genuine sincerity in his father's tone and look.

"So we could have family elsewhere from him?"

"We may. But if we do, they are in the furthest reaches of Georgia for that is where he went as a baby. I know he joined the Order, the Templars that is, but Kratos made sure our paths would never cross…that reason why I do not know," Philip explained and sighed.

Pauls mind immediately raced thinking of Percival and Queen Tamar both of whom came from that region.

"You have mentioned Balantrodach before…is it of importance?"

"Yes, yes it is. I have placed some details within parchments I have brought for you. It also explains another reason behind the Templar seal of two knights upon a single horse…just one of many as you are learning."

"Such as?"

"All can see the rear knight is bigger, and as any good Sufi friends, like Attar, will attest and confirm, the rear knight means Jin in Islam, but is also an esoteric code indicating the hidden history line from that of tall giants. Balantrodach actually means 'stead of the warrior'. Initially Balantrodach was the name of the area in which the main Temple Parish was situated. In 1128, Hugues de Payens visited Alba, Scotland as it is being called more these days, and was granted a meeting with King David the First of Alba. He granted the Knights Templar the Chapelrie and Manor of Balantrodach where they built a church with a round tower, and on the west side along by the river to the bridge they have built the main buildings, and along with their Cistercian monk brothers have built twelve-foot walls and a cloister. I have been there also this past year…after hiding something."

"What thing?" Paul asked, intrigued.

"Oh, just a simple piece of pink stone taken from the river near Stonehenge…but engraved. It has a code etched into it should all other codes be lost to recover what is now in a safer place," Philip answered and paused as he studied Paul's reaction. "And Paul," Philip said in a whisper and leaned closer and put his arm around him as if to hug him. "Know this…you must not rebuild another vessel as before…you must not! Husam cannot know this…not yet." Paul pulled away and stared at his father hard and confused. Philip shook his head very slightly and indicated no with his eyes to say no more on the matter. "Now tell me…what else did your mother say in this dream…how did she look?"

"Why can I not rebuild my ship?" Paul asked immediately as Philip shook his head slightly indicating he should not ask yet. After a minute, Paul realised what his father was hinting and so he changed the conversation back to his mother sensing Husam was trying to listen in behind him. "I can show you what she looked like for I drew an image," Paul said loudly, checked behind that Husam was not actually listening then leaned back toward his father. "But why can I not rebuild my ship?" Paul whispered back.

"Because it will change everything before it is time. Whilst I am here, if you will allow me, I need to speak with you of further matters of our family lineage. Your coat of arms, for you have one as does your brother. I must explain all I am able about the symbolism, but also of Oak Island… across the Atlantic."

"Oak Island?" Paul replied, puzzled. Taqi looked up at Paul and Philip. He could see the tense look in both their faces. He waved when Paul looked down at him realising he was being watched. "I would like that…now if you will excuse me I really should go and speak with Taqi and Tenno for we have much to catch up on," Paul said rather coldly and stood up. "You will find the picture I drew of Mother in my third drawer in my study. Please be honest with me if it looks nothing like her for it could have just been a dream only."

Philip nodded in silence as Paul quickly walked away and down the end steps. He watched him as he approached Tenno and Taqi and picked up Arri and held him in his arms as they started to talk. As Paul spoke to Tenno and Arri laughed, Taqi knew something wasn't right and looked up at Philip. He bowed his head toward him slightly as Philip acknowledged him back.

Percival and Thomas rode into the courtyard slowly and pulled up. They dismounted and brushed themselves down but they were still covered in sand and sweat. Nyla came running out to greet Percival and flung her arms around him. Thomas shook Tenno and then Taqi's hand in turn and was just about to speak when Upside led Nicholas out into view holding him up steady. A cheer went up as they came out of the house. Nicholas smiled wearily but pleased to see everyone. As Theodoric looked behind him, Husam got up from his seat, whispered something in Conrad's ear to excuse himself and approached Philip.

"My friend…Paul honours us in allowing us his hospitality. 'Tis a pity things cannot always be this way would you not agree?" Husam said softly as he looked down at the group below. "May I?" he asked, gesturing to sit beside him.

"Of course. Please do for I am in dire need this hour of some reasoned company," Philip replied.

"You know the saying, 'When truths appear, they do not ask if they are welcome'?"

"Yes I know it only too well."

"Teach Paul this simple fact and all will be well for him. I do not wish to lose him and his skills, but he will have to face certain truths as we move forward," Husam said and faced Philip. Philip turned slowly to look back at him. "My motives are genuine for I like, admire and respect Paul. He has become more than just a friend to me…he is almost like a son. I hope that does not offend you?"

Philip sat up straight and looked Husam in the eyes directly for a few moments.

"No, that does not offend me. It reassures me for I know you know things of Paul, his capabilities and what he has done, yet you have chosen to remain silent. For that I am grateful and eternally indebted to you."

"You see much and miss little. I understand why Saladin admires and respects you so much…and Theodoric there. Though I have my severe reservations about Lord Montferrat," Husam replied and looked across at Conrad laughing loudly with Theodoric and drinking. "Theodoric has the measure of the man and appeases him well."

"Conrad is Italian…what do you expect?" Philip half joked, not being serious.

"You mean arrogant, self serving, godless and greedy with a hunger for power that worries me," Husam said quietly.

"You do not hold back when you speak do you?" Philip said and laughed lightly.

"Oh I hold back much, my friend. But I fear whatever agreements Conrad draws up here with Saladin's secretary, to be witnessed by me, sadly will only serve his interests. I do not trust him. He whispers too much in that other Templar's ears for my liking."

"Which Templar?" Philip asked, concerned, as he looked at Brother Teric and Brother Matthew.

"The pasty pale looking one sat beside him."

Philip laughed both with amusement and relief as Husam indicated Brother Mathew and not Brother Teric.

ꕥ

After a sumptuous evening meal, Husam made his apologies, gave his thanks and blessings to Paul and thanked the women for their kind service. Conrad had to be strapped across his horse, almost passing out he was so drunk. Theodoric winked at Philip as he helped place Conrad in a secure position. Theodoric had managed to learn much of Conrad's intentions through drinking with him, heavily. Sister Lucy told him he would be sleeping alone tonight. Husam would have to endure a further week alone with Conrad and his escort he confided in Philip but it was necessary. After they had left, the rest of Thomas's men joined them all and sat outside in the clear night sky talking away until it was late. Nicholas, despite being tired, insisted on staying with them as they joked and laughed with Nyla sat on Percival's lap most of the time. Paul noticed Nicholas look at Alisha several times but was not angered by his looks. They were far removed from the lustful gazes Conrad had shown toward her. As Tenno started a small fire in the courtyard's rubbish furnace for warmth, Arri almost asleep beside him, Paul gently picked him up in his arms. Alisha and Sister Lucy came out with some warm syrup of Jule to drink and relax them all.

"Where is Philip?" Alisha asked as she looked around all of them as they pulled their small wooden chairs closer to the fire Tenno was stoking.

"I do not know. He must have gone inside. Here, sit with Nicholas… make sure he drinks some of that whilst I take this little man to bed. I shall find my father," Paul said as he indicated toward the space beside Nicholas, who looked so weary and tired but smiled, his lips still split and sore.

"Really?" Alisha asked in a very low whisper.

Paul nodded yes and raised Arri, who was now fast asleep, toward her. Tenno quickly rubbed his hand over Arri's head as Alisha kissed him goodnight.

"I will sit awhile with him in case he wakes confused."

Paul walked silently and carefully along the top corridor toward Arri's bedroom. It had been a long and eventful day for him. Laughter rang out from Thomas and his men as they passed some joke about Percival he could not hear, and as he passed by his own work studio, he heard muffled sobbing. He stepped very slowly toward the door which was ajar and could just see his father sat sobbing holding the picture Paul had drawn of his mother in his right hand, his left hand covering his eyes. A knot instantly pulled tight in Paul's stomach and his heart beat fast. As the candle flickered away on the work desk, Philip continued to sob in waves, stopping for a moment, and then starting again. Paul looked down at Arri fast asleep in his arms, then back at his father. Slowly he backed away from the door and took Arri to his bedroom. Gently he laid him upon his bed and looked around for Clip clop before realising Arri had it stuffed down his shirt all along. Gently he took it out and placed it beside him as he pulled up the single cotton sheet to cover him. He kissed him on his forehead. Arri opened his eyes momentarily, squeezed Clip clop tightly in his hand then turned on his side.

"Love you, Papa," he said quietly and immediately went back to sleep.

Paul's heart physically ached for the love he felt for this little man laying before him. Is this how his own father had felt for him and Stewart? he wondered. He recalled a statement his father had told years ago about gratitude. 'Gratitude is one of the least to articulate of the emotions, especially when it is deep.' How true those words felt at that moment. He felt guilty as he had been cold toward his father simply because he felt he had hidden so many things from him, such as having an elder brother, his uncle no less, but now, as he looked at Arri, he knew in his heart he would do and say anything to protect him. He shuddered as he recalled the reoccurring dream where Arri was sat shivering in the cold calling out "Father". He shook his head to clear that thought, kissed Arri again and left his room. He approached his study door and listened. His father was no longer sobbing. He pushed the door open more to check he was still in there.

"Ah Paul…this," Philip said quietly and lifted up the drawing. "This gives me great comfort. More than you can imagine."

Paul gulped seeing the emotion in his father's eyes.

"Is it the likeness of her?" Paul asked as he sat opposite him.

Philip took a deep breath, paused for a moment as he studied the picture again then smiled broadly. He went to speak but held himself in check as to speak, he knew he would cry again. He gulped hard, coughed to clear his throat and sighed again as he sat up straight.

"My son, very few things in this life shock or surprise me any more…but this…this is truly amazing. I cannot believe how accurately you have captured her in all her beauty and character. I had almost forgotten just how much I really still miss her," he explained, coughed with emotion again and took in another deep breath.

"Then, please, take this as a gift from me for all you have done."

"Oh I have not done anywhere near enough for you," Philip replied and looked at Paul; tears welled in his eyes. "This, all of this you have here, 'tis but material only…and there is so much more I should have taught you."

Paul looked at his father, the candle casting shadows in the lines around his face. He had a kind and gentle face yet he had seen so much bloodshed and done so many things in his life he could only but imagine.

"Father…I love you," Paul said and clasped his father's hands, something he had never done since he was a small child. "I love you and I thank you."

Without a word Philip leaned forward and pulled Paul close and hugged him tightly.

Port of La Rochelle, France, Melissae Inn, spring 1191

"He was truly blessed to have such a father...unlike ours eh?" the Templar commented and nudged his brother.

Gabirol looked at the old man intently then smiled. He was sure he knew now who the old man actually was. The old man could see and sense the realisation in Gabirol's eyes and acknowledged him with a slight nod but then shook his head no as if to dismiss his thoughts.

"Well I am sure you will make a great father one day," Miriam stated and pulled the Templar's hand close to her chest, the Templar smiling at her remark.

"Only then did Paul start to fully appreciate all that his father had done for him and the sacrifices he had obviously made over the years. His own love for Arri made it abundantly clear the depths of love a father can have for his children," the old man said and coughed.

"So did Philip teach Paul all the extra details about the bees...and his coat of arms?" Gabirol asked.

"Yes he did. He explained much in fact to both him and Taqi together. It was almost like the days when they were children again being taught by Philip."

"Are you going to tell us what else he taught them?" Simon asked.

"I can briefly, for some of you may have need to understand it as your lives continue forward," the old man answered and looked at the Templar, the Hospitaller and then at the wealthy tailor and Gabirol in turn.

"I shall prepare some more food for I have heard this before," Stephan said as he stood up to leave the room.

"How come he has heard all this before then?" Sarah asked, puzzled.

"He can tell you that in his own time...but for now I can tell you more on the bee and fleur de lys," the old man said softly.

"I want to know about his coat of arms...but are they not family emblems?" Simon asked.

"They are not specific to a family alone. A coat of arms is a set of emblems to distinguish upon a shield an individual, especially when fully armoured and upon

the field of battle," the old man explained. "But the bee and the fleur de lys symbolism...that was a different matter as I shall explain." The old man sat in silence as he pondered how best to explain the details. Eventually he pulled out a small piece of parchment with a small drawing showing three images. One of a bee, one of a stylised bee and one of a fleur de lys.

Fig. 57: Bee to fleur de lys.

"The Merovingians viewed the honey bee as sacred, as I have already explained. Over three hundred golden bees were known to have been stitched into Childeric's burial cloak. Clovis's wife Clotilde of the Burgundians and Bornholm encouraged the emblem's use. The Burgundians came down from Burgunderland after AD 100 where many Templar round churches are to be found. The honey bee became stylised into the fleur de lys by the French court only this century. Philip explained all of this to Paul and Taqi. He also explained that the hexagonal honeycomb was almost geometrically perfect, magical in its use for building, and industry, and that it also esoterically represents Mary. The fleur de lys already appears on many coats of arms now, in Spain, Bosnia and the City of Florence...and, Gabirol, that is one growing place of enlightenment I strongly advise you to visit," the old man said and paused again before continuing. "But Philip also taught them, with Theodoric assisting as he liked to do...huh, Philip had no choice actually," the old man laughed. "That the fleur de lys also represents the 'Tree of Life', which descends to the Netherworld with its roots, as in the so-called hell. The fleur de lys is frequently found in Ancient Egyptian artefacts. In Ancient Egyptian constellations there is a connection between Osiris, who is identified with the Kabalistic Tree of Life because in many of their oldest texts, The Tree of Life grew out of the Sacred Mound, its branches reaching out and supporting the stars and planet studded sky,

while its roots reached down into the watery abyss of the Netherworld. The trunk of the Tree of Life represented the World Pillar or Axis Munde, literally 'Axis of the Mound', around which the heavens appeared to revolve. The World Pillar was the centre of the universe. The Ancient Egyptian symbol for 'plant' meaning 'Tree of Life' was three sacred lotus lilies. They have three stems curving to the left as though blown into life by the breath of Hu, the Celestial Sphinx. On top of each stem is the lotus flower, which was used in Ancient Egypt to represent life and resurrection. It is from this hieroglyph that the fleur de lys in part traces its origin. Their god Osiris, in his earliest Axis Munde form of a tamarisk tree trunk, was called Djed. His later mummy wrappings were symbolic of his having been encased inside a tree trunk. His mummy was therefore an Axis Munde...When Osiris was enclosed in the trunk of a tamarisk tree, which was later cut down and used as a pillar in the palace of the King of Byblos, he metaphorically became as one with the Tree of Life. Osiris became the Axis Munde. He became the World Pillar, the link between the terrestrial and celestial worlds. He held the heavens in his outstretched arms, and he soaked up the word of God from the waters of the Netherworld. In Ancient Egypt the Netherworld was called the 'Netterworld', meaning the 'world of the gods'. The gods had their home among the stars. The fleur de lys is modelled after the lotus in Egypt that was associated with the Nile Lily. The Nile is where a sacred brotherhood had originated that brought its secrets to Jerusalem. Therefore it was only fitting that they would choose an Ancient Egyptian symbol for a plant meaning Tree of Life that was three sacred lotus lilies as their own symbol. It is the fleur de lys that has now replaced the lily as a symbol of royalty of this same said brotherhood. You will find this symbol throughout history as an ornament on the crowns, sceptres, thrones, seals and coins of not only French kings, but also on Greek, Roman, German, English, Spanish, Egyptian, Syrian and Babylonian Kings..."

"I know that the great Charlemagne had imperial bees," Gabirol interrupted.

"That is true also. The fleur de lys is also known as the water rose...," the old man stated and paused as he looked at them all in turn to emphasise that fact. "The lotus or water-rose is the flower sacred to the lux, or the sul, or the sun. The 'Auriflamme'...the flame of fire, or fire of gold, which was the earliest standard of France. It was afterwards called Oriflamme. The lily has also become the favourite attribute of the Virgin Mary. How long that will remain, who knows? But know this also, that before 1130, there were no such things as coats of arms...the first use of the fleur de lys appeared on the shield only under Philippe Auguste. On a stained glass window in Chartres there'll be a fleur de lys. The seals of Philip Augustus

have a single fleur de lys on the reverse as from 1180. Before that, from 1050 at least, the seals of French kings show them sitting, holding a sceptre in their left hand and what looks like a fleur de lys in their right hand. The head of the sceptre is a lozenge, but often the fleurons on the crown, three of them, look like fleur de lys. I have explained already how Philip influenced the king of France to adopt the fleur de lys as an emblem when all other sovereigns of Europe choose animals. The flower has now acquired a strong religious meaning, either Christian or Marial under the influence of Saint Bernard and the emblem symbolises both royal dignity and Christian piety. But there is more," the old man said and smiled before continuing. "The fleur de lys is also known as the Merovingian Lily, and is a very sacred symbol of the goddess Juno, the Lilly Maid, mother of the war god, Mars. It was also used by the early Gauls and the powerful Salian Frankish dynasty that reigned across France from AD 481 to 751. The fleur de lys also has martial as well as religious connotations. The Roman Catholic Church decrees that it should be the emblem of the Virgin Mary and therefore by default, symbolic of the Holy bloodline, or Sangraal without even realising that fact, while the three petals of its flower represent not only the Holy Trinity, but also the Christian values of faith, wisdom and chastity. However, the lily's meaning holds striking duality and affinity to Mars, as well as the values of war...the military often interpreting its shape into that of an ornate, upright spearhead indicating power, fearsome force and brute strength."

8 - 11

"So how does this go with the image you show us of a bee transforming into a lily?" Peter asked as he studied the small drawing.

"Through sacred geometry...and it may surprise you to learn that the design is also found in the Islamic mosque. Intriguingly, the mystical dimension of Islam known as Sufism maintains a secret brotherhood called Sarmoung, or Sarman, meaning bee. Members of the organisation view their role as collecting the precious 'honey' of wisdom and preserving it for future generations."

"Like that Attar Sufi...yes?" Simon asked.

"Absolutely yes, Simon," the old man replied."

Cairo, Egypt, April 14th 1183

Thomas and his men, along with Ishmael, Percival and Nyla, had retired to their chambers for the night leaving the remainder sat around the ornate wooden table in the main living room. Tenno fidgeted trying to make himself comfortable.

"My son, I have hidden items away in Alba, in the village of Balantrodach as I have said...," Philip said quietly and handed Paul a parchment tube. He took it and noted that both ends were sealed. "Inside are details on how to reach a place we have named Oak Island off the shore of the new lands in the west. Much of what was recovered in Jerusalem has been moved there. But I have also drawn up your own coat of arms."

"Why do I need a coat of arms?" Paul asked, puzzled. "I am no knight nor do I intend to be."

"'Tis written in your parchments...remember?" Theodoric said as Taqi nodded in agreement.

"But I had a choice to be one or not...and I choose not to be," Paul replied, shaking his head as Alisha approached with some nightcap drinks.

"Yes...you have a choice, but should you ever need it, then you have your coat of arms," Philip explained as Alisha knelt down beside Paul and started to pass around the small bright blue glasses.

"'Tis an acknowledged honour to be granted your own coat of arms...," Nicholas said, clearly very tired, his eyes heavy and half closed.

"Come on, my friend. 'Tis well past your bedtime," Upside said as he stood up and started to lift Nicholas to his feet. "We shall leave these good people in peace to catch up on family matters."

"You can stay if you wish for you are as family to me," Paul stated as Upside ushered Nicholas to the stairs.

"No...this one needs rest," Upside replied. Nicholas simply raised his hand goodnight as he was led away.

"Can I see your coat of arms?" Alisha asked as she sat down upon her knees, then knelt closer to Paul, looking up at him.

"Can I open this?" Paul asked. Philip nodded yes. Paul twisted the end cap breaking the wax seal, pulled the crimson coloured binding tape and removed the cap. Gently he pulled out the various parchments and laid them out on the wooden table. A white vellum sheet unrolled to reveal a delicately executed painting and part embroidered image depicting apples, bees, acorns and a key. "I think this is obviously it."

"'Tis beautiful," Alisha remarked as she studied it closely. She looked at Paul with pride but also a sense of dread and the hope that he would never need use of it.

Fig. 58: Paul's coat of arms.

"The other parchments detail the projections of constellations, mainly Virgo over our present and soon to be built cathedrals in France, but also ancient sites across Greece and Italy where ancient Omphalus stones are located. They relate to the Ancient Egyptian Magan boat, the same as Jason and the Argonaut…but you need not understand what or how…just protect and guard them. Also the locations where Mary came ashore in France, where she had her daughter but also where she had her later son too on Iona," Philip explained.

Paul moved the parchments and studied the maps briefly. He went to pick up a small candle but Taqi quickly handed him a larger lanthorn.

"You do not want to be spilling wax upon them," he said with a smile. "And I bet you will wish to know everything about them too."

"Yes, that I will," Paul replied and looked closer at the parchments. "I see a lot of markers in Alba."

Philip laughed as he sat forwards and winked at Theodoric.

"'Tis the origin of much that unfolds," Philip replied.

"Or should unfold," Theodoric interrupted as Sister Lucy entered the room.

"'Twas a place of special significance to your mother…as you now know," Philip said and looked at Paul.

"Why?" Tenno asked bluntly.

"A long story, my friend. A very long story," Theodoric answered.

"Good. We have all night," Tenno replied.

"In short," Theodoric laughed, "Jesus and members of his family went to ancient Caledonia, or Alba as you know it. The actual ancestors of Jesus were of Celtic and Hebraic origin and although his immediate family came from the gentiles of Galilee, their earlier roots originated in the British Isles…specifically ancient Caledonia. Jesus's family lineage and the Celtic Royal household of ancient Britain can be found in documents found in London, though presently sealed away. It is hoped that one day, in the future, they will again be revealed and confirmed. As you know, coats of arms belong to specific individuals and families and there is no such thing as a coat of arms for a family name. They are borne by individuals as Philip said…as marks of their identification. The proclamation and organisation of tournaments was the chief function of heralds originally. They marshalled and introduced the contestants and helped keep a tally of the score. The knights taking part in tournaments are recognised by the arms they display upon their shields and the crests they wear upon their helmets. Have you not noticed all of Thomas's men have them?" Theodoric explained and asked as he looked at Paul intently. "Heralds require expert knowledge for recording arms, and for controlling their use. As coats of arms are hereditary, with slight additions and changes for each successive individual, heralds have come to add expertise in genealogy to their skills. This had a direct bearing on the presence of Joseph of Arimathea and a key Apostolic mission in ancient Britain, the ramifications behind his Christian movement in the British Isles are far reaching indeed and many of his symbols and emblems have likewise been recorded and kept safe...just as yours must be...so that in the future, your bloodlines can again be recognised for who you are and where you come from."

"I do not follow what you are saying," Alisha said and sat up straight.

"During the first century AD, an apostolic mission in the British Isles was the root of the development of the Church of Christ in Britain. Jesus called upon Andrew the Meek, the brother of Peter, whom he appointed to be their leader and patron saint forever. Ancient records clearly reveal that Saint Andrew was specifically charged with a mission to carry the message of Christ to Alba (Scotland) by Jesus himself. Proving Jesus personally knew of the existence of ancient Caledonia and considered it of sufficient importance to send a leading apostle there along with the connection to the colour blue," Philip explained.

"What lay behind this?" Taqi asked.

"During the reign of the Roman Emperor Domitian around AD 81 some of the disciples of the apostle John visited Caledonia and a strong Christian base was established there by AD 200. Chronicles record that the then king, Donaldus, was the first Christian king of Scotland. Joseph of Arimathea and Lazarus went on a secret Essene mission after the crucifixion of the historical figure known as Jesus of Nazareth but not with Mary initially. With them was a small band of relatives including several women initiates. This small group came to Alba, to a place known as Fortingall. There you will find a very ancient yew tree, which is believed to be the oldest tree in Europe," Philip continued to explain.

"Fortingall...," Paul said and looked at his father. It was the same place his mother had mentioned in his dream.

"The village of Fortingall has a monastic settlement for the dissemination of an ancient mystery tradition centred on the teachings of Christ. But it also has a Johannite Grail Church which has incorporated the mystery teaching of Saint John the Evangelist, which is the result of a fusion between this Essene group and elements of a pre-existing Druid magi. This Johannite Church developed through a monastic line which became known in Celtic circles as the Culdees. Christian Grail descent from the family of the patriarch Noah, through to the immediate family circle of Jesus himself. The Celtic Hebraic origins of the family of Christ are directly associated with Alba, Scotland, giving rise to its appellation as the Holy Land. It is claimed that a son of Jesus and Mary Magdalene was born on the holy isle of Iona, with their daughter having been born in France already as I have explained previously," Philip explained.

"I can see why the Church vehemently denies this...but why are there many points of reference across Italy also?" Paul asked as he checked the parchments closely. "And this symbol of a Cyclops on Italy..."

"You can answer that," Philip replied smiling at Theodoric.

"In Italy there are miles of ancient polygonal stone walls...ancient ruins so unique and strange that many of our best most learned scholar types and philosophers believe they were built by an extinct race of giant human beings. Scattered throughout ancient Latium, which is the region in Italy where Rome was founded, are massive ruins that for thousands of years have been attributed to having been built by that long lost and now forgotten race of giants. They were said to have been taller, stronger, more intelligent and generally superior to us and known in all eras as Cyclopes. 'Tis where we get our word Cyclopean to mean massive constructions. Many classical writers and historians, including Homer, Hesiod, Plutarch, Thucydides and Diodorus Siculus, wrote or pondered if the Cyclopean ruins of Italy and all across Europe were erected by this Cyclopean race. Hundreds of years before Rome existed, the land of Italy was inhabited by a people who left indestructible monuments as their only record of their prior existence. The earliest Cyclopean cities are thickly scattered throughout certain districts, and are often perched like eagles' nests on the very crests of mountains, at such an elevation as to wonder how they ever constructed them."

"I thought Cyclopes only had one eye though...," Taqi stated.

"Yes, indeed mythology speaks of an ancient race of giants with superhuman strength, stature, and longevity with a single eye...but this is a simple misunderstanding," Theodoric continued to explain. "A mutation over successive generations has now prevented us from lucidly seeing the 'soul within'. Though some can and still do this. It was done through the use of a so-called third eye centred just above and between our two physical eyes. But it is a spiritual eye and can see physical light our normal eyes cannot see. Most of man has lost the ability and so does not see or recognise our own inner divinity any more. We once possessed this mysterious ability due to the existence of an enigmatic, luminous organ associated with the forehead that has become known as the Cyclopean Eye or Third Eye as I have said. A strange and beautiful appendage from where we get the term Cyclopes."

"I have missed these conversations," Tenno said and sat back in his chair.

"And all God fearing people now shy away from such knowledge," Paul commented as he started to roll up the parchments.

"God fearing…err where is the love? Why must you be fearing your God?" Tenno asked.

"'Tis all about power and control. That is all," Theodoric answered.

"I recall being taught that Alba was really established by Ancient Egyptians…or did I understand that incorrectly?" Paul asked, looking down at a map of Alba.

"You heard correctly. 'Tis a pity Niccolas is not here for this was his passion," Theodoric replied. "When your father and I were in the Emerald Isle, we saw and were taught many things, including the fact that many of their ships originated from Egypt via Scota, the Egyptian princess and daughter of the pharaoh Akhenaten."

"Who?" Taqi asked, perplexed.

"I will explain later," Paul replied.

"She was a princess who fled from Egypt with her husband Gaythelos with a large following of people and arrived in a fleet of ships," Theodoric continued to explain. "They settled in Alba (Scotland) for a while, until they were forced to leave and landed in the Emerald Isle. They formed the Scotti, and their kings became the High Kings of that land. In later centuries, they returned to Alba, defeating the Picts, and giving Scotland its new name. Scota's father is actually named as being Achencres, a Greek version of an Egyptian name. In the work of Manetho, an Egyptian priest, the translation of the name of the pharaoh Achencres was none other than Akhenaten, who reigned in the time frame of 1350 BC. Scota was in fact Meritaten, eldest daughter of Akhenaten and Nefertiti. The controversial religious shift to the one god Aten caused conflict with the Amun priesthood, who reasserted their authority after Akhenaten's reign ended and he disappeared from history. But he will be discovered again in time for records of him are also sealed and hidden," Theodoric said and winked at Philip. "When she arrived in the Isle, the people inhabiting it at that time were none other than the Tuatha De Danann, the magical children of the goddess Danu who originally established the site of Tara, in the Boyne River valley, as the ritual inauguration and burial place of the ancient kings of the Isle. They were regarded as the gods and goddesses of the Celtic tribes, but their true origins date far back into history. The land of the Emerald Isle was divided, with Eremon in the north and Eber in the south, which was identical to the division of Upper and Lower Egypt itself. Egypt was unified by a central connecting city, Memphis. Likewise the Emerald Isle was divided with a central site of unity, known as Mide. Within Mide is the Hill of Tara situated as a site of High Kingship, representing the unity of the land and all of its people."

"Perhaps you should tell them how you compiled many of their ancient poems into a single volume…," Philip said and nodded his head at Theodoric. "No point being modest or hiding the fact. You see, Theo here was compelled to write them down but refused to put his name to it."

"Hey, if I had put my name to it, I believe I would never be able to enjoy the life I do now," Theodoric replied.

"What did you compile then?" Taqi asked.

"I had to write the poems, with some of my own interpretations, into an elaborate prose framework, partly of my own composition and partly drawn from older, no longer extant sources…though I did paraphrase and enlarge upon the verses," Theodoric started to explain then laughed to himself briefly as he recalled some prior events. "I wrote it in a form of Irish Gaelic. It tells of Princess Scota, how she met her end and was killed. How after her death in battle, war continued on at Tailtinn against the three kings of the Tuatha De Danann, the husbands of the goddesses Banba, Fodla and Eriu. MacCuill, MacCeacht and MacGreine. How the sons of Mil eventually conquered the de Danann s and took the seat of Tara. I did detail exactly where Scota was buried between Sliab Mis and the sea but that was removed. She will be found one day in a glen located in Glenscota. As with many myths, as a real person she lent her persona and identity to the landscape of the land she became a part of, giving Scotland her name…well it will be called that one day. They will also find within the Hill of Tara that it is riddled with pearls from Egypt. Pearls of the sea show kingship, sovereignty, the true centre of kingship, a centre that rules over all. Tara is the site of queenship, the beautiful centre of the rose, which is not…located in England. The goddess stands on Tara, in the centre, looking out over the Emerald Isle, Scotland and England."

"Did you all know that when said backwards, Ta-ra becomes Ra-Ta, the priest from the names of the Egyptian creator god Ptah and of course the sun god Ra. Combined they become Ptah-Ra," Philip explained.

"And I previously forgot to mention that Glen Lyon, which is derived from Gleann Lìomhann, essentially meaning Lugh's Glen…I must remember to tell Upside that," Theodoric remarked.

"I sometimes wonder if all men are just crazy for the way you all act and think," Alisha said quietly.

"Men…crazy! I would agree with that," Theodoric replied.

"No, no, no. Women are crazy and men are stupid. Women are crazy because men are stupid," Sister Lucy joked, which made them all laugh, except Tenno, who sat bolt upright in his chair still.

"And you came all this way to pass on these details in person?" Paul asked after they had stopped laughing and looked at his father.

"Yes for trouble grows between France and England. 'Tis why I requested the assistance and escort of Tenno and Taqi from Al Rashid. Picking Conrad up was not on our initial route…," Philip replied. "Plus I wished to simply see you all…especially after I learnt that you are expecting another," Philip continued and smiled at Alisha.

"What troubles?" Theodoric asked, looking concerned.

"Eleanor," Philip answered and sat back looking at Theodoric.

"Who is Eleanor?" Alisha asked.

"If there is trouble, a woman was bound to be involved," Sister Lucy half joked.

"Eleanor…," Philip said shaking his head. "Let me tell you about her for Theo and I know her well. She along with her husband Louis took up the cross after a sermon preached by Bernard of Clairvaux. She insisted on taking part in the Crusades as the feudal leader of the soldiers from her duchy. Her launch of the Second Crusade from Vézelay, the rumoured location of Mary Magdalene's burial, emphasised the role of women in that campaign. In Constantinople, Eleanor was much admired. She was compared to Penthesilea, the mythical queen of the Amazons, by the Greek historian Nicetas Choniates. While in the eastern Mediterranean, Eleanor learned much about maritime conventions developing there and she introduced those conventions in her own lands, on the island of Oleron in 1160 and later in England as well…'twas the beginning of what would become Admiralty law. She was also instrumental in developing trade agreements with Constantinople and trade ports in the Holy Lands," Philip explained.

"A smart woman by the sound of it," Alisha said and sat closer to Paul.

"Oh she is that and much more," Philip replied and continued. "Even before the Crusade, Eleanor and Louis had become estranged."

"Oh yes I can vouch for that," Theodoric chuckled to himself.

"Eleanor's reputation was tarnished by an alleged affair with her uncle, Raymond, Prince of the city of Antioch which had been annexed by Bohemond of Hauteville in the First Crusade, and it was now ruled by Eleanor's flamboyant uncle Raymond. He gained the principality by marrying its reigning princess, Constance of Antioch," Philip explained, when Taqi interrupted him.

"Is that the same Constance Reynald was once married to?" he asked.

"Yes, yes it was," Philip replied. "You see, Eleanor supported her uncle Raymond's desire to re-capture the nearby County of Edessa, the cause of the Crusade. She also showed conspicuous affection towards him which she did not hide. This was just familial affection, for her uncle was similar to her father and grandfather, but at the time a hostile Church chronicler believed, and reported, that the two were involved in an incestuous and adulterous affair."

"Yes and what a shit he was eh?" Theodoric interrupted. Sister Lucy sat down beside him and frowned at him. "Sorry. I shall keep quiet."

"Louis was sent to visit Jerusalem instead by the Church but Eleanor declared her intention to stay with Raymond along with her Aquitaine forces. Louis had her brought out by force. His long march to Jerusalem and back north debilitated his army, and her imprisonment disheartened her knights. Divided Crusader armies could not overcome the Muslim forces so at the insistence of Church leaders, who were even more incompetent than Louis, the Crusade leaders targeted Damascus, an ally until the attack. Failing in that escapade, they retired to Jerusalem, and then left for home in 1152. Eleanor and Louis returned on separate ships due to their disagreements, but were first attacked in May by Byzantine ships attempting to capture both of them. Although they escaped, stormy weather drove Eleanor's ship south to the Barbary Coast. Only in mid-July did Eleanor's ship finally reach Palermo in Sicily, where she discovered that she and her husband had both been given up for dead. She was given shelter and food by servants of King Roger of Sicily, until Louis eventually reached Calabria. She set out to meet him there. Later, at King Roger's court in Potenza, she learnt of the death of her uncle Raymond. Two lords, Theobald of Blois, son of the Count of Champagne, and Geoffrey of Anjou, who was the brother of Henry, Count of Anjou and Duke of Normandy, tried to kidnap Eleanor to marry her and claim her lands on her way to Poitiers."

"What...that is shocking," Alisha remarked.

"'Twas a normal way for Christian men of all classes to find a wife," Philip explained and smiled. "Well, both attempts failed and as soon as she arrived in Poitiers, Eleanor sent envoys to Henry Count of Anjou and Duke of Normandy asking him to come at once and marry her.

On Whit Sunday, May the 18th, 1152, six weeks after her annulment, Eleanor married Henry. She was about eleven years older than him and, incidentally, related to him more closely than she had been to Louis. A marriage between Henry and Eleanor's daughter, Marie, had been declared impossible for this very reason. She bore Henry five sons and three daughters over the next thirteen years."

"Who were they?" Tenno asked.

"William, Count of Poitiers, Henry known as Henry the Young King, Matilda of England, Richard the First of England, Geoffrey the Second, Duke of Brittany, Leonora of Aquitaine, Jeanne of England and John. Subsequently, the period between Henry's accession to the throne of England, as Henry the Second, and the birth of their youngest son has seen many turbulent events. Aquitaine defied the authority of Henry as Eleanor's husband and attempted to claim Toulouse, the inheritance of Eleanor's grandmother and father, were made, ending in failure. 1167 saw the marriage of Eleanor's third daughter, Matilda, to Henry the Lion of Saxony, during which time Eleanor remained in England with her daughter for the year prior to Matilda's departure to Normandy in September. Following that, Eleanor proceeded to gather together her movable possessions in England and packed them up, transporting them on several ships in December to Argentan. At the royal court, whilst celebrating Christmas, she agreed to a separation from Henry. She then left for her own city of Poitiers immediately after Christmas. Henry did not stop her; on the contrary, he and his army personally escorted her there, before attacking a castle belonging to the rebellious Lusignan family. Henry then went about his own business outside Aquitaine, leaving Earl Patrick as her protective custodian. When Patrick was killed in a skirmish, Eleanor was left in control of her inheritance. She ransomed Patrick's captured nephew, the young William Marshal."

"We are not told any of this," Alisha said, a little surprised.

"No and why should you unless you have an interest in courtly affairs?" Philip replied before continuing. "It was whilst away from Henry that Eleanor was able to centre her court on courtly love. Henry and the Church tried to expunge the very records of the actions and judgements of her court, but a small fragment of her codes and practices was written by Andreas Capellanus. She was the patroness of such literary figures as Wace, Benoît de Sainte-More and Chrétien de Troyes...," Philip said and paused as he looked at Theodoric for a moment. "Henry meanwhile concentrated on controlling his increasingly large empire, badgering Eleanor's subjects in attempts to control her patrimony of Aquitaine and her court at Poitiers. In March 1173, angered by his lack of power and encouraged by his father's enemies, the younger Henry launched the Revolt of 1173–1174. He fled to Paris. From there the younger Henry, devising evil against his father from every side by the advice of the French King, went secretly to Aquitaine where his two youthful brothers, Richard and Geoffrey, were living with their mother, and with her connivance, he incited them to join him. The Queen sent her younger sons to France to join with him against their father the King. Once her sons had left for Paris, Eleanor encouraged the lords of the south to rise up and support them. Sometime between the end of March and the beginning of May, Eleanor left Poitiers to follow her sons to Paris but was arrested on the way and sent to the King in Rouen. Henry did not announce the arrest publicly. For the next year, her whereabouts were publicly unknown. On July the eighth, 1174, Henry took ship for England from Barfleur. He brought Eleanor on the ship and as soon as they disembarked at Southampton, Eleanor was taken away to Winchester Castle and then on to Sarum Castle and held there. Eleanor still remains there to this day. She has become more and more distant with her sons, especially Richard, who was always her favourite."

"So how does this cause trouble now?" Taqi asked inquisitively.

"Because as of now, Henry the Young is again trying to gain power and control. He is in debt and has been refused control of Normandy. He has already tried to ambush his father at Limoges, where he was joined by troops sent by his brother Geoffrey and Philip the Second of France. Philip of France is already claiming that certain properties in Normandy belonged to the young queen but Henry insists that they had once belonged to Eleanor and would revert to her upon her son's death. Henry has summoned Eleanor to Normandy but as yet she has not returned...but she will.

If unrest and war is not averted between France and England, or even war just in France, then much of all we have done will be wasted. What happens in France and England will have implications and a direct impact upon all of you here and in Jerusalem." [99]

"But there is nothing we can do here is there?" Paul asked, puzzled.

"There is…you simply protect all that I pass on to you for it is no longer safe in France, nor England," Philip replied, looking serious. "Can you do that?"

Paul looked at Alisha as she shrugged her shoulders.

"I do not know…but I can try," Paul finally answered.

"No try about it, my lad…we shall and we will," Theodoric stated.

Chapter 59
Altar of Stone

Taqi leant against the stone balustrade of the balcony, standing beside Paul, who was already leaning against it. Paul looked at the stars shining brightly, the constellation of Orion almost appearing to sit motionless just above the horizon, the star Sirius twinkling a bright bluish colour sat on the horizon like a distant beacon calling them.

"My friend, it has been truly good to see you all again if only briefly. I did not realise just how much I had missed you," Taqi said quietly as he looked to where Paul was staring.

"I have missed you also, my friend…truly. Tomorrow will be hard for Alisha to say farewell again," Paul replied still looking at Sirius.

"Things are changing fast…'tis why I had to come for who knows when I will get the opportunity to visit again."

"Much has already changed. I am here to build boats for Husam, yet I am told I must not…and though Ali has her dress making business, there is nothing else I can do…unless I patrol with Thomas and his men as a Confrere Knight…so I am at a crossroads, my friend, and one at which I have no idea which path to follow," Paul explained and sighed, lowering his head.

"You have a job…as a guardian of what your father has entrusted to you," Taqi remarked and looked at Paul. "My ambitions have always been simple. I have learnt much and seen much already, as you have, but my path is easy compared to yours."

Paul turned and looked at Taqi in silence for a few moments. Alisha came out onto the balcony and quietly approached them. She clasped Paul's hand.

"'Tis very late and you are tired. You must get some sleep…both of you," she said softly and smiled.

"Father would be so proud of you, Ali. A mother, with another on the way and a successful business woman in her own right I hear," Taqi remarked as he stood up straight and faced her.

"Only because of the support I get from Paul, and Nyla's parents," she answered and smiled at Paul lovingly as she interwove her fingers through his.

"And I see you still wear that sword always," Taqi remarked looking at Paul's sword strapped to his side. "I like the scabbard little Arri made for it. You are truly blessed, my friend…for you have each other and men who defend you constantly."

"Yes…that can be a problem sometimes," Paul replied quietly. "But we are grateful."

"Is there not a special woman in your life?" Alisha asked.

"No…not yet," Taqi replied.

"No…have you not been with a woman still?" Alisha asked, puzzled.

"My dear sister," Taqi laughed. "There are some questions you do not ask, and that is one of them. But for the record, I have known a woman… and that is all I shall say," he replied and made an exaggerated frown and smiled.

"I pray it is not too long until we meet again. I have missed our time together," Paul sighed. "Since last we met, both Ali and I have been taught much. From deep meditation to unarmed combat…"

"What, you as well, Ali?" Taqi asked, surprised.

"Of course…you know me," Alisha replied. "And I bet I can still throw you," she laughed.

"That I do not doubt," Taqi replied then leant back against the balustrade. He sighed heavily and shook his head. Alisha looked at Paul, concerned. "There is much danger ahead, and I will not be around you to protect you."

"What danger?" Paul asked, instantly alarmed.

"The seers…our Sufi mystics, they say they can see a great conflict coming and many will perish…and there is nothing any of us can do to stop it," he sighed as he answered. "Whatever fate awaits me, I will welcome it…so long as I know you two are safe and well," Taqi explained, stood up straight again and looked at Paul intently. "Just swear to me you will always look after and protect my sister."

"Taqi…need you ask such for you know I will," Paul replied. "Always!"

"Then you will need to return to France for it is not safe here in these lands," Taqi stated bluntly. He saw the reaction on their faces. "Please, before it is too late."

"But my father says it is too dangerous in France also," Paul shot back.

"Then go to Alba…or the Emerald Isle. You must trust me on these matters. At least consider it." Alisha looked at Taqi, concerned. "I am not the same man you knew of…for I have seen and learnt so much, and it has changed me in ways I did not think possible. But trust me when I say your time here is limited."

"Taqi…you sound…so mysterious. Why so?" Alisha asked softly.

Taqi turned to face her properly and took her hand away from Paul and held both of her hands close to his chest. He looked at her intently.

"Ali…I know you are not my blood sister but in my heart and soul you have and always will be my little sister," he said almost in a whisper, sadness visible in his eyes.

"What…how do you know?" she asked surprised.

"It matters not how I know but I do. We have Sufi members who teach us much too you know," Taqi answered and forced a smile. "They speak of many things past and things to come…"

"Taqi…" Paul started to speak but Taqi quickly shook his head no.

Taqi just looked at Alisha for several moments in total silence until she pulled him close and hugged him tightly.

"And Tenno, he has become like a father to me. I have learnt much from him," Taqi explained and stood back from Alisha, still holding her hands. "Now I bid you a good evening. I have a long journey ahead of me tomorrow."

Taqi kissed Alisha on the forehead, bowed politely to Paul and walked away quietly. Alisha bit her bottom lip as she pondered on his comments then put her arms around Paul and hugged him tightly. She sighed heavily, saddened. Paul kissed the top of her head as he held her and just stared out toward Sirius as the star rose slowly. He too could almost sense change was in the air.

Port of Fustat, Egypt, April 1183

Large fires were burning off rubbish from the major clearance project that was in operation. Saladin had ordered the rebuilding of the entire area near to the port, which still mainly lay in ruins after it was burnt to the ground several years earlier. Philip rode alongside Paul as Taqi, Tenno and Theodoric followed along with Thomas and his men. Lord Montferrat rode ahead with his escort and Brother Teric. Their ship was being readied as they pulled up near to it. Brother Matthew walked down the rear gang plank immediately recognising Paul. He looked at him hard.

"He still does not care much for you does he?" Taqi said referring to Brother Mathew.

"No…must have been a previous life thing," Paul half joked back.

Quickly everyone dismounted. As Brother Mathew and several other Naval Templars took away the horses of those about to embark, Nicholas, still looking weak and tired, approached Paul with Upside assisting him. Several Mamluk guards arrived and surrounded the area near to Conrad's vessel as another contingent arrived from the opposite end of the quayside led by Husam.

"Oh Lord, I pray there will be no trouble in us leaving?" Nicholas said and held his side, clearly in pain.

"I think not," Philip reassured as he stood beside Paul.

"Brothers Baldwin and Nicholas…so you have decided to leave after all," Husam called out as he dismounted.

"Alas yes my Lord…tempting as it is," Nicholas said and bowed his head at Husam.

"We tried," Thomas said aloud as he approached smiling.

"I hope you can understand why," Upside said as he held Nicholas up.

"Of course…but if you should ever change your minds, you know where we are…and I pray our paths do not meet on the field of battle," Husam said politely and looked across at Conrad, who was laughing loudly as he looked over some large trunks filled with silks. "Now I must see our mutual friend off…no less."

Nicholas and Upside looked at each other and frowned as Husam bowed politely at them then walked over to greet Conrad. Paul noticed Brother Matthew was still looking at him directly. Nicholas offered his hand to Paul.

"Who knows when our paths shall cross again…and thank you for all you have done for us," he said and shook Paul's hand. "And please pass on my apologies to Alisha for not saying goodbye."

"Tell her yourself for here she comes now," Paul replied with a smile and nodded toward a small cart rapidly approaching driven by Alisha with Arri sat beside her. "I did tell you she would not let you leave without saying goodbye."

Alisha drew up fast, applied the main wheel brake and started to step down from the cart. Arri jumped straight down and ran toward Tenno, Clip clop in his hands. Tenno stood up straight as Arri ran and jumped up at him. Tenno half caught him in his arms and looked surprised as Arri flung his arms around his neck tightly and closed his eyes.

"Don't leave us," Arri said quietly, his eyes still shut.

Paul sighed seeing that Arri was clearly upset.

"I had no choice...I think he would have taken the cart himself," Alisha said as she stood between Paul and Philip. "And you," she said pointing at Nicholas. "You never leave without saying goodbye," she said and quickly hugged him, kissed him on the cheek then stood back a pace, pulling her dress down flat.

"Was it not you who said goodbyes are for funerals?" Nicholas replied as Upside held him up firmly.

"Ever leave again without saying goodbye and it will be your funeral," Alisha joked back.

Tenno looked at Philip, bemused, as Arri still clung around his neck. He indicated with his eyes for Philip to take him.

"Come here, my young grandson. Tenno must leave...but I shall be going with him so I will make sure he sees you again," Philip explained as he tried to take Arri but he clung on harder. "Come on, Arri."

Arri flounced his arm back against Philip and buried his face into Tenno's shoulder.

Alisha moved to take Arri and after a little pulling, he quickly turned his face toward her, let go of Tenno and clung onto her instead hiding his face beneath his hands as she held him in her arms. Tenno raised a single eyebrow.

"I shall see you again I swear," he said and rubbed his hand over Arri's head.

Arri said nothing.

"He will be fine," Alisha said softly and rocked him gently.

"We are eternally grateful for all you have done for us. I hope we can repay that one day," Upside said politely and part bowed to Alisha and Paul.

"No...we are only alive because of you two in the first place," Paul replied. "Are you sure you will not reconsider and stay as Thomas asked?"

"I would stay in a heartbeat my friend...but this one," Upside said and held Nicholas up straight. "This one insists our destiny lays elsewhere... and who else would look after him?"

Nicholas punched Upside in the chest playfully with his left hand before looking at Alisha and Paul.

"And I shall see you again too…of that I have no doubt," Nicholas said, smiled and immediately turned around. Upside nodded at Alisha and Paul and without any further words from either, helped Nicholas walk toward the ship. He raised his hand goodbye.

"My dear son, we must leave you now too. I shall send word as soon as I am back in France," Philip said as he shook Paul's hand and looked at him. "Look after yourselves, do you hear me?"

"We shall, Father…and should you see Stewart, tell him I love him…," Paul replied.

"I think he knows that by now. But I will indeed, that I will," Philip said and then looked at Alisha, who was still watching Nicholas as he started to board the vessel. Philip kissed Arri on the head and then Alisha on the side of her face. "Nicholas will be fine, that I promise you," he whispered.

Alisha looked at him in surprise, her face flushing red. He smiled and squeezed her arm reassuringly. He looked back at Paul once more, nodded and walked away to join Conrad and Husam.

"'Tis time to go, my friend," Taqi said as he put his arm around Paul's shoulders. "We have all changed so much eh?"

"Taqi…you shall always be the same to me…brother," Paul replied, watching his father walk away. "Just make sure you stay alive whatever comes next."

"Whatever comes next? Hmm, I like that. Whatever comes next? I shall remember that," Taqi remarked and quickly hugged Paul. He patted him hard then stood back from him. "Do not become too fat either or you will turn into Theodoric."

"I heard that!" Theodoric shouted out from behind Adrastos and the other horses.

"The port of Tyre will not side with Reynald," Conrad called out loudly as he walked up the gangplank waving at Husam. Husam shook his head slightly, unimpressed with his loud remark. "'Tis a pleasure doing business with you!"

Taqi looked at Conrad very hard, his eyes narrowing. Paul noticed this and frowned at him. Taqi realised Paul saw his reaction to Conrad.

"He is also part of the reason I am here," Taqi whispered to Paul. "That man is far more dangerous than Reynald. Now I must bid you all farewell."

As Taqi hugged Alisha and kissed her on both cheeks, he kissed the back of Arri's head, who was still refusing to look up.

"Come on, young Arri…let's sit you upon Adrastos so you can see them off better," Theodoric said, trying to get his attention. Arri shook his head no.

Tenno leaned closer to Arri, kissed him on his head and stepped back in silence. Eventually Arri turned to look up at him. When he noticed Tenno was still there, he quickly buried his head again. Alisha smiled and sighed at the same time. Tenno bowed his head in silence at Paul and Alisha, then at Theodoric. As soon as Theodoric nodded back at him, Tenno turned around and walked toward the ship that was about to take them all away, and for how long before they would see each other again, none of them knew.

Taqi took a few paces back, paused for a brief moment as he looked at Alisha and Paul. After a slight nod of his head, he turned around and followed after Tenno. Theodoric stood beside Paul holding the reins of Adrastos and they all stood in silence as everyone boarded the vessel. Husam came and joined them and watched as the vessel slowly eased away from the dock side and then out of the harbour, Taqi, Tenno, Nicholas and Upside stood at the stern looking back at them.

"Where is your father?" Alisha asked.

"No idea…I cannot see him."

"Below decks…for your father hates sea travel. It always makes him sick," Husam commented with a broad smile. Paul looked at him bemused. His father, seasick! Something else about him he never knew before. "Now then Paul…'tis back to work for us no? We have a new port to build also," Husam half laughed as he looked around at the rubble being loaded onto carts a short distance away. "We shall restore this port to its full former glory. You and I…together."

Port of La Rochelle, France, Melissae Inn, spring 1191

"What had happened to the port then...to be so damaged and in need of such major repair...did Reynald attack that far?" Peter asked.

"I wish to know why Taqi was so interested in Conrad," the Templar remarked as his brother shook his head in agreement. "Was he the real reason Taqi visited... as perfect cover?"

"I feel for poor little Arri. He obviously has a soft spot for Tenno," Sarah commented.

"Taqi was indeed keeping a close eye on Conrad just as he had been instructed to do by Al Rashid himself. He did not trust him one bit. And yes Arri remained silent for several days after Tenno had left. They certainly had a strong bond...but Alisha managed to get him interested in his coming new brother or sister," the old man explained.

"And why was Husam rebuilding Fustat? Is it because Saladin aims to increase his fleet?" the Templar asked.

"Partly...but also to restore Fustat to its former glory just as Saladin had promised after it had been destroyed."

"Who destroyed it then...did I miss that part?" Simon asked.

"No Simon you did not miss that part. It was years previously. Prior to its destruction Fustat had been known for its prosperity, with shaded streets, gardens and markets. It contained high-rise residential buildings, some seven storeys tall, which could accommodate hundreds of people. Some even rose up to fourteen storeys, with roof gardens on the top storey complete with ox-drawn water wheels for irrigation. 'Twas a beautiful city. In the markets there they often had exotic and beautiful wares ranging from iridescent pottery, crystal, and many fruits and flowers, even during the winter months. Fustat was also a major production centre for Islamic art and ceramics and one of the wealthiest cities in the world. Fustat was laid out with intricate house and street plans and Husam wished to rebuild it and return it to its former glory...and Alisha and Nyla certainly sold many of their dresses there," the old man explained.

"So what was it...an earthquake?" the Genoese sailor asked.

"No...'twas down to the then young caliph of Egypt...just a mere teenager named Athid, but his position was mainly a ceremonial one. The true power in Egypt was that of the vizier, Shawar, who as I have already explained was involved in extensive political intrigue for years, working to repel the advances of both the Christian Crusaders and the forces of Nur al-Din from Syria. Shawar managed this by constantly shifting alliances between the two, playing them against each other, and in effect keeping them in a stalemate where neither army could successfully attack Egypt without being blocked by the other....However, in 1168, our King Amalric the First of Jerusalem, having tried unsuccessfully for years, attacked Egypt again in order to expand the Crusader territories, and finally achieved a certain amount of success. He and his army entered Egypt, sacked the city of Bilbeis, slaughtered nearly all of its inhabitants, and then continued on towards Fustat. Amalric and

his troops camped just south of the city, then sent a message to the young Egyptian caliph, Athid, to surrender the city or suffer the same fate as Bilbeis."

7 - 50

"Our Christian knights massacred all the inhabitants?" Ayleth asked, looking shocked.

"Yes...as I said at the start of this tale, there have been great deeds and great wrongs committed by both sides, and others in the Holy Lands," the old man replied as Ayleth shook her head almost disbelievingly.

"'Tis all too true I am afraid to confess," the Templar remarked and nodded at Ayleth.

"So what happened?" the Genoese sailor asked.

"Well, seeing Amalric's forces massing, Shawar ordered Fustat city burned, to keep it out of Amalric's hands. No one questioned his orders and Fustat was evacuated. He forced everyone to leave their money and property behind and flee for their lives with their children. In the panic and chaos of the exodus, the fleeing crowd looked like a massive army of ghosts....it was said. Some took refuge in the mosques and bath houses...awaiting a Christian onslaught similar to the one in Bilbeis. Shawar sent twenty thousand naphtha pots and ten thousand lighting bombs known as mish'al and distributed them throughout the city. Flames and smoke engulfed the city and rose to the sky in a terrifying scene. The blaze raged for fifty-four days...."

"That is awful," Ayleth remarked.

"What is awful is that after the almost total destruction of Fustat, Syrian forces arrived and successfully repelled Amalric's forces. With the Christians gone, the Syrians were able to conquer Egypt themselves. The untrustworthy Shawar was put to death, and the reign of the Fatimids was thus effectively over. The Syrian general Shirkuh was placed in power, but died due to ill health just a few months later, after which his nephew Saladin became vizier of Egypt on March 2nd, 1169, launching the Ayyubid dynasty. The rest you now know."

"Is that why Saladin moved his capital to nearby Cairo?" Gabirol asked.

"In part yes...though he has since tried to reunite Cairo and Fustat into one city by ordering the building of massive defensive walls to enclose both as one...but Husam saw Fustat as being the port whereby he would build a whole new range of seagoing vessels...with which to expand Muslim territories," the old man sighed.

"And that is why Paul's father said he must not build another ship...yes?" Gabirol asked.

"Yes...yes indeed. 'Tis one of the reasons Paul delayed much when redesigning his vessel for Husam whilst at the same time befriending a respected physician. Paul's interest in medicine had been started by Roger des Moulins back here in La Rochelle. If he was to change his career, then becoming a physician was one he would consider seriously," the old man explained.

"And who was this respected physician?" the Hospitaller asked.

"'Twas none other than Maimonides," the old man answered.

"Who?" Sarah asked, looking painfully puzzled.

"Maimonides, the renowned physician, who even practised in the family of Saladin...and in that of his vizier Ḳaḍi al-Faḍil al-Baisami. The title Ra'is al-Umma or al-Millah, meaning 'Head of the Nation or of the Faith', is already being used to refer to him. He arrived in Fustat in 1160 where he wrote his Mishneh Torah in 1180 and 'The Guide for the Perplexed'."

"Yes, yes I know of these books. And Paul studied under him?" Gabirol asked excitedly.

"He did. Or at least he started to, telling Husam that he was learning all he could in order to compile a medical journal for all sea captains. I am not sure Husam ever believed him totally. He could see the passion for ship designing had left Paul... but as it happened, Husam spent more time away supporting Saladin, so Paul was pretty much left to his own devices."

"So what happened next?" Simon asked in his now familiar blunt manner.

"Next..." The old man paused and took a deep breath. "We shall eat what Stephan has prepared for us first, for what I speak of next may put you off your meal...but I will tell you that Paul felt ever more pulled to enter the pyramids and the passages beneath them to seek guidance and answers as to what he should do next. Remember he been told a long time before that he should seeks answers there."

Giza Plateau, Egypt, June 3rd 1183

It was early morning and the sun was only just beginning to make its presence felt with the dim pale blue sky only just cresting the horizon, but the sky above Paul was still a dark black. He adjusted the sack slung over his shoulders and pulled his padded jacket tight around his collar, the air feeling cold. Alisha was against him travelling alone to the pyramids, especially if he was planning to enter any of the underground passages. Theodoric had offered to accompany him but he refused, wanting to be alone. Paul intended to put into practice all the many sessions of meditation both Attar and Tenno had taught him over the past few years. A dog barking echoed out in the distance as he began to walk toward the three large silhouettes of the main Giza pyramids that towered like huge mountains before him. Alisha had very reluctantly agreed to let him go alone but he swore he would take no unnecessary risks. He checked his sword. He walked past an old man sat in the middle of the main pathway leading to the pyramids. He had his head down and was asleep. Paul sensed someone following behind him but he could not see them. After a short distance he spun around quickly just catching a glimpse of someone's cloak being pulled in fast as the person ducked behind a wall. Quickly Paul set off again and turned around a corner. As soon as he had, he sprinted for the next turning beyond several buildings and ran down the pathway that ran between them only stopping when he exited onto the steep track that led up to the pyramids. A dead donkey lay half in the filthy canal that ran parallel to the main track. If anyone was following him, they would expose themselves now as the land was open. A small fire was being tended by some people off to his right under an old shack cover. As Paul walked toward the main pyramid, known as Khufu's pyramid, the apex suddenly lit up in a bright orange glow as the sun finally fell upon it. The light seemed to crawl down the side like honey being poured over one of Sister Lucy's puddings, he thought.

ꟸ

It took Paul nearly an hour before he found the entrance, climbed up the imposing large stones and gave one of the two guards sat beside it a permissions strip from Husam to enter. One of the guards shivered with the morning cold as they were sat in the shade still, the sun's rays slowly but surely edging their way down the side of the pyramid. The guards wore simple full length black robes with just a blanket wrapped around them. They had a belt and a small scimitar sword each but that was it. Paul suddenly heard laughter of several women echo out from inside the pyramid. One of the guards coughed and shook his head not looking Paul in the eye. Just as Paul went to step inside the forced entry hole that Al Mammon's men had made back in the ninth century, three women, scantily dressed in just short waistband type skirts, half cut tops and thin see through silk coveralls, stepped out still giggling and leading a half drunk expensively dressed man out, his robes a combination of the finest white cotton and gold coloured silks. The women were the same women Paul had seen back in Alexandria brought in to entertain Turansha and Conrad. The man looked at Paul, puzzled, then at the guards, who shrugged their shoulders. The man laughed and followed the women down the stones, nearly falling at one point on one of the remaining lower courses of intact white casing stones. One of the women looked back up at Paul and smiled. She put her hand to her chest then outstretched her hand, her palm upwards to him intimating the question did he want her to follow him. Paul immediately shook his head no and mouthed 'no thank you'. The women smiled, shrugged her shoulders and indicated toward her thigh as she stroked her hand down herself. Paul shook his head no again but returned a smile. She was dark haired, her skin smooth and clear and her alluring and seductive presence almost intimidated Paul. She laughed at his obvious embarrassment, blew him a kiss and rapidly turned away to follow the man and other two women. The two guards just shrugged their shoulders feigning ignorance.

Paul took out his lanthorn from his sack and lit it from the small ceramic oil burner set just inside the rock hewn passage. He had wanted to enter this pyramid for so long and now as he was about to, apprehension grew inside him. As he started to make his way through to the main internal passages, he felt nervous. He recalled the dream-like visions he had already experienced where he had seen, or dreamt, he still could not confirm in his mind which, how the pyramids had been constructed. He could smell incense the women and man had obviously been burning. It was common for wealthy men to hire the pyramid for the night for all manner of activities and rituals. He looked back and checked where the forced entry cut into the passageway was. As Attar had told him, careful study showed that it was not cut from the outside in, but the other way. He tried to remember the details as he had studied pictures of the interior layout. His father, Theodoric and Attar had all been adamant that the pyramids on the Giza plateau had not been built by the Egyptians, but by a long since vanished civilisation many thousands of years before the earliest Ancient Egyptian dynasties.

Paul made his way down the steep descending passageway that led to the subterranean lower chamber. After a short distance he came to a small wooden set of steps and a rope that gave access to the ascending passage that led upwards toward the Grand Gallery as it had been named. Quickly he clambered up the wooden steps careful not to let go of the rope in one hand and the lanthorn in the other. He then made a steep climb upwards on wooden boards that had smaller wooden strips set across them. After an awkward climb, he reached the junction where a horizontal passage led away toward the Queen's Chamber. Paul used the small rope ladder placed against a wooden support and climbed up it into the massive ascending Grand Gallery passage above this passage entrance. At 153 feet high, the vaulted ceiling was barely visible in the light cast from his lanthorn that seemed to get swallowed up in its vastness. Slowly he made his way up the steep angled passageway heading for the King's Chamber, though his father, Theodoric and Attar had laughed at it being named so. He could hear his father's words echo in his mind…"King's Chamber…'tis no such thing". The idea that the Egyptians had made the first chamber below ground then changed their minds and built the Queen's Chamber only to change their minds again and then build the upper King's Chamber always made his father laugh. Paul smiled to himself. He had still not heard any word from his father since he had left, so prayed every night that he was safe and well. When he reached the top of the Grand Gallery, he had to pull himself up over the main step and into the small passageway that led into a small anti-chamber that had strange portcullis type protrusions. His father and Theodoric were adamant these had once contained sliding blocks. After viewing them, he stooped down and crouching made his way through the final section of passageway toward the actual so-called King's Chamber itself. He paused momentarily before entering, his mind racing. There should be no one inside now. It was so silent, his ears almost rang. He could sense the sheer antiquity exude from the very walls as he rested his hand upon one. Stooping low, he moved forwards and stepped slowly into the King's Chamber and raised the lanthorn to reveal a rectangular shaped room with a high ceiling and a single empty granite sarcophagus at the far end of the room. The walls were totally devoid of any markings or hieroglyphs, a fact his father had pointed out he would note. This little fact was in direct contrast to all other pyramids and tombs built by the Ancient Egyptians that were covered from floor to ceiling, and including the ceiling, in hieroglyphs and stars. Pyramids that were conclusively attributed to having been built by the Ancient Egyptians, mainly in mud bricks, were now just massive piles of bricks looking more like desert hills than pyramids. This was because they had been built as copies of the Giza pyramids with far less precision and engineering. A backward step in technology, his father had repeatedly informed him. After a few minutes standing in silence, he knew he would have to lie in the sarcophagus, which had not had a pharaoh found inside it when it was first broken into by Al Mammon. No treasures either. Attar and Theodoric had both told him he must lie inside the sarcophagus, which had never had a lid either, and relax and push all thoughts from his mind…but that he must do so alone with no one else in the room. So with a great sense of trepidation and a million questions of what could happen or go wrong, he climbed inside the sarcophagus and knelt down. Theo had said he should extinguish all lights, but if he did that, how would he see afterwards to get out, he worried. He placed the lanthorn down beside the sarcophagus carefully, pulled the blackout slide cover around it and lowered the inward air vents so it would not burn out. Just a little ring of light shone down around its base hardly visible. The lanthorn had been a gift from Attar and was one of his favoured sailing safety and signalling lamps. Paul placed his sack down, adjusted his sword to lie flat by his side and lay down fully. Just the faintest of light from the lanthorn cast the smallest line of yellow along the edge of the sarcophagus. He lay still in total silence, his eyes making shapes out of nothing in the darkness. He closed his eyes and started to relax himself and put into practice all the meditation techniques he had been taught… but even then he found it difficult to relax fully.

"You are in the wrong place if you seek answers to those questions you have in your mind," a woman's voice said softly. "Ask the one you know as Theodoric about Luke. That will help."

Paul went to sit up but he could not move. It felt as if his heart was beating to a rhythm that seemed to vibrate with the actual stone of the sarcophagus. 'It must be one of the dancing women returning,' he thought for a moment.

"Then where should I be…and what is this place for then?" Paul asked quietly, expecting to see a woman peer over at any moment.

"This place is but like an altar in stone…to reveal facts, measurements and even prophecy if you choose to ask of it. It also helps energise this world…but more importantly it will help contribute to shield your world in the future when the dark twin returns. But that which you seek, you must find by descending to the Netherworld. It is accessed by an old passageway from the destroyed pyramid at Abu Rawash. Go there and it will be revealed to you," the female voice explained.

"How will it help protect this world?" Paul asked as images appeared to flash before his eyes but were in his mind as vivid as if real.

"It generates a subtle energy…that is all you need know for now. But as for the many questions you seek answers too, they can only be retrieved from what your kind know as the sacred chambers of creation…the Halls of Amenti or Halls of Records…but this you already know of."

"Then how do I find that?"

"Go to Abu Rawash, the pyramid known in your time as that of Pharaoh Djedefre, and you will be shown…but only so you may know it is real and to then safeguard the location and codes to its position…for mankind's very survival in the future…and safeguard it you must as you so volunteered to do…long ago…Nothing, absolutely nothing else matters nor must come before that. Do you understand that fact?" the woman asked, her tone almost severe and clipped now. "Agree to those terms and you will be allowed admittance to the Chambers of Creation to ask of it what you will."

"Yes…yes I understand that fact," Paul answered, but perplexed. Suddenly his head was full of images, some familiar of massive stone blocks sliding into place just as he had seen in his repeating dreams and at Kizkalesi Castle, and solid black granite stones fashioned in a circular layout being sealed containing large polished egg shapes made from granite with gold inlaid symbols upon them. But now he could see inside the Great Pyramid, its interior fully lit up by some artificial means as if daylight. Suddenly above his head he heard a hiss of air rushing over the sarcophagus, a pungent smell entered his nostrils as a white mist formed. Suddenly a blue spark arched across the room and, in an instant, it flashed a large gout of orange flame which then ignited all of the mist. Paul's heart stopped, his eyes widening in sudden panic as the whole chamber seemed to explode in a ball of almost blue flame. He shielded his face with his arms as the flames came toward him, but there was no heat. Suddenly Paul was looking down upon another large white stone covered pyramid from above. It appeared to shudder and go hazy as if surrounded by a heat haze. A loud explosion report sounded out to his left and he looked to see the Great Pyramid, but it too was covered in brilliant white nummulitic limestone. It still had no capstone, Paul noted. A massive blast echoed across the fertile green plateau, not the dry desert sand surroundings Paul knew. Several large chunks of white limestone blew away from the Great Pyramid followed by several large internal sandstones. Suddenly an even bigger explosion hit Paul and vibrated him so hard his eyes could not focus for a minute as he returned his gaze to the other pyramid he knew to be that at Abu Rawash.

A liquid looking bubble seemed to encapsulate the entire pyramid, then it shuddered as the bottom half bulged outward but still contained within the shimmering water looking bubble, but then the whole structure just folded in upon itself as if being swallowed into the ground, the bubble vanishing. All went quiet for a moment but the silence was soon shattered as a huge convulsive explosion shot upwards and outwards in a violent blast of stone blocks and limestone covering slabs. Wide eyed, Paul looked on stunned at the enormity of the explosion as a visible shock wave spread out like a blanket flattening palm trees and smaller buildings and walls surrounding it instantly.

"It is at the deepest part of this ruin you will find a portal that will allow you to enter," the woman spoke softly. "Now go there for it shall not remain open long."

Paul found he could now move and instantly sat up, but in the very dim light, he could not see anyone. He jumped out of the sarcophagus and immediately opened fully the slide cover on the lanthorn. As the light spread out he still could not see anyone. He knew where the remains of the Abu Rawash pyramid were and quickly gathered up his sack, slung it across his back and made his way out of the pyramid as fast as he could. When he rushed out of the entrance, the two guards laughed. They had seen many people stay overnight and leave in a hurry scared witless or in a state of shock. They laughed louder as Paul began to run away from the pyramid and toward Abu Rawash.

ᢒᢓ

Paul approached the remains of what was once a great pyramid, as big as the one he had just left. Two scruffy looking men wearing dirty white robes looked at him suspiciously as they chipped away upon a large piece of white stone ready to carry away for use in building another construction elsewhere. Most of the stone from the site had already been taken and now all that remained were a few blocks scattered about and broken red granite blocks. The last few remaining lower courses were systematically being removed and just a large outline remained protruding here and there through the sand. A deep gouge in the sand sank at a steep angle into the ground, its side walls of stone blocks the only visible sign it was once part of a large subterranean chamber. Paul stood upon several large paving slab stones. They were angled down toward the gaping gouge. Images of how it once looked flashed through his mind. Once, they had been laid flat and fitted flush against the base of the white stone covered pyramid. Now they lay broken and slanted down toward the ruined pit of the former pyramid interior. He sensed an overpowering emotion of loss and sadness as many of the images he had dreamt of in the past flashed within his mind like some long lost memory he was struggling to recall. He became aware of the two men looking at him again having stopped their work. The passage way down looked blocked and full of rubble and sand at the bottom, but the voice in the Great Pyramid said he must go there...and to hurry. Quickly Paul started to make his way down.

As he entered, the walls on both sides grew ever taller. According to local tradition the pyramid had never been finished and was simply abandoned before completion. Paul noticed the layers of large stone blocks were not set horizontal but angled downward towards the bottom of the passageway. At the end of the passageway he stopped and looked up at the open sky above him. The sun was rising fast along with the heat. He climbed up several blocks of stone and into a wider section. The floor was just rubble and sand. He walked around the entire area checking the steep walls for any sign of an entrance but there was none he could see. For over an hour he checked and rechecked but still nothing. Eventually he sat down in the shadow cast from the wall behind him, removed his sack and took out a leather water bottle. After a few mouthfuls he sat perplexed and shook his head. He took out his small drawing folder and rather than waste the trip, started to sketch the entrance and sunken passageway.

Fig. 59: Abu Rawash Pit Entrance.

There was something not right with the way the stones were set and he would show Theodoric later as well as ask him about Luke as the voice had advised. Two people peered over the edge carefully and looked down at Paul. He could not tell who they were as they were silhouetted against the bright sunlit sky. By midday, the sun was directly overhead and there was no more shade to shelter in. Paul wiped the sweat from his forehead and pulled his padded jacket off. He knelt down to pack it into his satchel backpack and as he did, he saw a bright light flash directly into his eyes. Momentarily blinded he instinctively shielded his eyes. When he lowered his arm again, a similar light flashed at the very corner of the wall where it joined with the sand. Quickly he rushed over to it thinking it could be some old jewellery or relic. As he wiped his hands through the sand, he found nothing. There was nothing on the stone wall either. He rested upon his knees, confused. Just to his left he caught sight of movement as the sand seemed to trickle away like it does in a sand timer. Slowly but surely the sand was draining away to somewhere beneath. Quickly he started to scoop and push away the sand. After a few minutes he revealed a small recess. He could push his hand through into a dark space. Excited, his heart now pounding, he scooped more sand aside and pushed the loose stone around the small hole. When it was big enough to put his head through, he lay down flat upon his stomach and very slowly edged his way so he could look inside. It was just big enough for his head to fit through. The sun's rays flickered past his head and shoulders as he squeezed himself further in, but his satchel back pack stopped him going further. He started to roll onto his side so he could free his arms from it, but just as he moved onto his left shoulder, the stone directly beneath him gave way. In panic he tried to grab the sides but it was too late as he slipped headlong down an inverted narrow stone shaft, the sand causing him to slide faster. He frantically tried to push his hands, elbows and knees against the sides as he slid even faster. All that achieved was to create several scuff friction burns on his elbows, knees and hands. Suddenly he was free falling in the air in blackness save for the single beam of sunlight that shone down the shaft behind him. He braced himself in anticipation for the sudden stop as he would inevitably hit the floor. Almost instantly he hit a pile of sand that splayed out taking most of the force of his fall, but still hard enough to knock the wind out of him, his face burying itself into the fine sand. He rolled onto his back and spat out sand and blinked as he wiped more sand away from his eyes, his immediate concern being spiders, snakes or worse. He looked up at the shaft of light streaming in. It was at least fifteen feet above him. The sunlight beamed across the room, which he reckoned was at least twenty feet, before ending in a starburst square of light on a smooth marbled wall. Paul felt around himself as the fine sand collapsed under his weight. For a terrifying minute he feared he would be swallowed up in the sand but then all movement stopped. The beam of sunlight started to thin as more sand from outside started to fill in the upper section of the shaft. It was pitch black except for the rod of light. Quickly he knelt up only now starting to breathe again, his chest hurting from being winded. He took out his sailing lanthorn, rapidly removed the two flints from the watertight section at the base. As quick as he could, his fingers fumbling frantically, he pulled out the emergency cotton, wool fibres and oil soaked wood fillings and placed them together in a small pile, took out the oil soaked cloth strips and placed them around it. He started to strike the two flints and as they sparked, he looked up at the ever thinning beam of light. Sweat beaded down his face as he felt the first sensations of panic start to well in his mind. He gritted his teeth and struck the flints harder. Eventually one of the sparks ignited some of the wool fibres and it started to burn. Gently he placed his hands around the kindling flame and started to push the cotton strips and oil soaked fibres onto the flame. As it grew, it shone brightly, but Paul knew he had to be quick before it burnt out. He opened the lanthorn's slide cover, opened the glass access panel and exposed the oil soaked wick of the sea candle. He was shaking so much the flame missed the candle, but after what seemed an age, it finally lit. Quickly he slid the glass cover shut and gently placed the lanthorn into the sand so it stood upright. Breathing heavily he looked up as the light from the shaft flickered as something tumbled through it. Someone moaned loudly as they fell through into the room landing hard just a short distance from Paul. He grabbed the lanthorn back to protect it, the light from the shaft finally vanishing as sand and rubble from above sealed it. Hesitantly Paul moved the lanthorn toward the figure lying face down in the sand. The person moaned and Paul grabbed his sword ready to draw. As light fell upon the figure, Paul immediately recognised the dark green robe as that of Percival's.

"By the Lord in heaven what are you doing here?" Paul asked, surprised, and began to help him sit up.

Percival wiped his eyes and spat out sand.

"I promised Ali I would keep an eye on you," he coughed and wiped his hand across his face. "When I saw you vanish, I just dived in after you."

"Are you mad...now we are both trapped down here and no one knows we are here," Paul exclaimed and looked back up toward the now closed shaft. The room was deathly quiet as Paul listened out for any other unwanted occupants. Percival's eyes widened as he listened intently. "No snakes or scorpions that I can hear."

"Thank the Lord for small mercies" Percival remarked and laughed nervously as he wiped his nose.

"We are trapped, my friend. I have several spare candles but after they are gone..."

"Well...let us see if we can find anything to climb out of here with or if there are passages out...better than sitting down to die," Percival said and stood up brushing himself down.

"Why did you not go and seek help rather than dive straight down after me?"

"Did not have time to think...I just did."

"Thank you. Thank you," Paul said grateful for Percival's act. Only then as they both stood in the darkness, just their faces lit up from the lanthorn, did Paul suddenly realise the importance of the green knight symbol that had been written upon his chart parchments as given by Niccolas. It represented Percival all along. Knowing this filled him with optimism. "We shall get out of this, my friend...of that I have no doubt. Now come, there will be passages I am certain."

6 - 2

"I pray you are correct...Nyla will kill me again if we do not!"

Port of La Rochelle, France, Melissae Inn, spring 1191

"Well they obviously get out or we would not have the sword now would we?" Peter stated and pointed to the sword.

"Clearly...but it was the nature of their escape and what happened that should interest us," the old man replied politely as Stephan placed some fresh ale and honey cooked bread in front of him. "Thank you."

"What manner of power could totally destroy such a massive structure like a pyramid...or was it as the traditions stated never completed?" the Hospitaller asked as he smelt the fresh bread with a smile.

"A very large amount of power, my friend. And Paul felt confident of their escape as he recalled the time lines upon his parchment," the old man explained.

"So Percival is the actual knight of the symbolic green knight that was on them all along?" Gabirol asked.

"Yes. It gave Paul great comfort to remain calm and not panic," the old man answered and broke a small piece of bread off.

"So how did they get out?" Sarah asked.

"Well they soon established that the room they had fallen into was rectangular and built from granite slabs," the old man began to explain. "In the far north eastern corner they discovered a tiny square exit mainly covered in sand. After clearing it away, they managed to wriggle into a long three feet by three feet square tunnel. Of course Percival was terrified but he kept his head despite shaking visibly and feeling very sick. It took the time of one complete candle to crawl along its length before they entered into another vaulted V shaped room. It

was devoid of any markings but the walls had a thin layer of what appeared to be salt deposits."

"But what was it that caused it to explode in the first place...if that is what happened?" the wealthy tailor asked as he pulled two large pieces of bread over to his plate and bit a large piece off.

"All I can tell you is that some natural force from within, which also caused the salt deposits on the walls within the pyramid chambers, was over used...and consequently exploded. Similar marks and deposits can also be found within the Great Pyramid itself," the old man explained.

"That would make the very word pyramid very appropriate then," Gabirol stated.

"Why?" Simon asked.

"Because pyramid is made up from two words that actually mean Pyr for fire and Mid for within the middle...fire in the middle," the old man answered with a smile as Gabirol nodded in agreement.

"So you are saying these pyramids were and are some kind of power generating system?" the Templar asked.

"Yes they are also that. Both a real energy that can be harnessed but also other energies...but also as you now know, they contain knowledge and wisdom about the very earth we live upon, our place within our solar system and greater universe as a whole."

"'Tis too much for me to understand...but I believe you," the farrier remarked, shaking his head.

"Please...tell us how they managed to get out then," Ayleth asked quietly.

"That I shall," the old man smiled.

Giza Plateau, Cairo, June 1183

"Percy...are you okay?" Paul asked as he hauled himself out of the cramped tunnel and stood up slowly. Percival pushed the lanthorn forward as he crawled out. Paul took it and raised it trying to see what kind of chamber they were in. "There must be a way out for there is air down here."

"Maybe, but the air smells odd to me so it may be stale...could run out."

"No...'tis too clean. That is not the smell of stale air for I have smelt that before. I just cannot remember where," Paul replied as he moved to follow the edge of the wall. Just a very thin layer of fine sand lay upon the stone floor.

Percival followed closely behind as Paul made his way along the wall. They had no idea of how big the chamber was as the small flickering light from the lanthorn did not reach any walls except the one they were stood beside. Suddenly the floor beneath Paul sloped away fast and he slipped onto his backside, his arm with the lanthorn raised. Percival instinctively grabbed it as Paul rapidly slid away and downwards. Percival stepped back holding the lanthorn, shaking with dread seeing the floor slab where Paul had been standing ease back up and into place. He froze unsure what to do.

Paul tried to stop himself as he slid down the smooth tunnel picking up speed. Fearful of a trap or spikes at the base or some kind of blade, he pushed out hard with his hands and knees but the sides of the tunnel were so smooth he just kept picking up speed. As he pushed his forearms and hands even harder, he used his feet to slow down. He finally slowed down enough and came to a halt, his hands burning from the friction grazes on them. He listened but all was silent.

"Percy!" he shouted.

Percival heard the muffled shout. Quickly he knelt down and looked for any sign of an opening. The marble floor had the faintest of lines just visible where the slab was located. He tried to push it but nothing happened.

"Lord keep me sane!" Percival whispered to himself.

"Percy!" Paul called out again in the pitch darkness, the blackness around him feeling like a tangible blanket wrapped tightly. His call echoed out in what was obviously a larger cavernous chamber below him. If he slid out of the tunnel into it, how big was the drop like the first chamber he had entered? Slowly he started to edge his way back upwards pushing hard against the sides to get some grip. "Percy…stay where you are I am coming back up!" he shouted.

Percival placed his head against the slab to hear better. As he moved forwards on the slab, it suddenly dropped away and he fell forwards head first. As he threw his arms up, he let go of the lanthorn as he tried in vain to grab the side of the hole. As soon as Percival had fallen through the gap onto his stomach and started to fall head first down the tunnel, the slab slid back up into place cutting out the light from the lanthorn.

"PAUL!" Percival screamed as he plummeted downwards unable to brace himself.

Paul looked above him but could see nothing but could hear Percival sliding and tumbling towards him. Crack…Percival collided with Paul, their heads smacking into each other hard, the force of Percival's momentum pushing Paul downward again, their head and shoulders almost interlocked as they both shot down the tunnel towards an unknown fate. Paul reached back to try and grab hold of Percival as his ears rang and the pain in his head registered from the impact of their heads. Percival was unconscious and a dead weight as they picked up speed. Blood ran across Paul's forehead where a cut had opened. He lay fully upon his back, his sword scabbard catching the side of the tunnel and sparking off brilliant flashes of white light where the leather scabbard tore away at the end revealing the tip of the blade. Paul grabbed Percival's head with both hands to try and hold him steady as their heads kept banging together.

"Sorry for getting you into this, my friend," Paul said aloud and gritted his teeth in anticipation for the fall that was coming.

Suddenly Paul was out of the tunnel and flying helplessly through the air, Percival behind him but dropping away fast as he frantically tried to keep hold of him. He braced himself for the impact knowing it was going to be bad at the speed they were travelling. Suddenly he saw a pale greenish light glow from his sword. He went to look down at it when everything went black and silent. He lost all sensation of movement. He could not move. "Am I dead?" he asked himself, confused. He could not even move his eyes or speak. After what seemed like an age alone, he felt overcome with tiredness and despite fighting it, he eventually fell asleep.

ꙮ

Slowly, almost painfully, Paul opened his eyes. A warm glow from a setting sun bathed his face. He could feel that he was lying down upon thick green grass. As he sat up he saw Percival lying asleep beside him. They were in some kind of opening set within a forest of great oaks, a path having been cleared toward the horizon where the sun set, its rays of warmth stretching out toward him. Suddenly he heard voices behind him. As he spun around and sat up, he saw what looked like his father dressed in armour, but not of Templar type. His cloak was a deep crimson colour. A large standing obelisk type stone stood proud just feet beyond him. His father was waving a sword identical to his own. He was shouting at someone but Paul could not see any others. He tried to wake Percival but he would not rouse. Paul stood up, pulled his clothing straight, checked his sword and approached his father. The tree trunks appeared to almost glow a yellow and orange from the sun's rays.

"This! This!" Philip shouted, his back to Paul and waving the sword in the air. "This cost me the life of my wife!" he shouted angrily.

"Father," Paul exclaimed, surprised, and reached out to touch him on his shoulder.

Philip flung himself around fast swinging the sword outwards in defence cutting straight through Paul in one swipe. Paul shuddered momentarily and froze in shock as he looked down at his stomach waiting for the inevitable pain and blood. But neither came. In shock he looked up at his father, who had taken a step back and was looking around alarmed totally oblivious to Paul's presence. He suddenly jumped around to face the large standing stone as images of the outlines of three very tall individuals flickered into view. No sooner had the images appeared, like a shimmering reflection cast upon clear water, than they vanished again.

"Come on. Reveal yourselves fully!" Philip shouted again.

Paul walked and stood beside his father. It was his father but he was so much younger looking, in his late twenties at most. The look on his face was one of pain, frustration and exhaustion.

"Father…it is I, Paul, your son. Can you not see me?"

Philip sensed something and looked to his left and directly at Paul. Paul smiled thinking he had finally seen him. Philip waved his left hand in the air next to Paul and stared quizzically knowing something was close but he could not see it. Suddenly Philip rushed forwards toward the stone, raised the sword in both hands above his head, held it horizontally pointing at the stone replete with spiral symbols upon it. With a yell of raw emotion he thrust the sword with all of his might into the stone. As he pushed the sword deeper, the ground trembled and the trees all appeared to shake as a deep moaning sigh sounded out. Sparks flew out along the sword's blade as Philip pushed it in harder, his face gnarled up in anger. A boom echoed out as an invisible wave of energy shot out like a strong wind blowing away from the stone. It hit Paul with a force that knocked him back a pace. Philip collapsed to his knees in exhaustion, his long hair falling forwards hiding his face as he started to sob. Paul went to move when the three shimmering outlines of the tall individuals appeared. As Paul watched in awe and confusion, the three seemed to materialise fully visible one minute then vanish the next. They were all men, dressed in thick white cloaks and jackets, the like of which Paul had never seen before. They were at least three times the height of his father he could see. They all had pure blonde, almost white, hair when they remained visible long enough to be seen. Two of the men bent down and lifted Philip to his feet just as the third man looked directly at Paul. The man smiled and bowed his head slightly acknowledging his presence. Paul gulped hard, surprised that he could obviously see him. Slowly the man turned and pulled out the sword as if was not even in the stone. His huge hand covered the entire length of the handle of the two handed sword. Paul jumped half out of his skin as a hand grabbed his right shoulder.

"Where are we?" Percival asked, bemused and scowling as he tried to see what Paul was looking at.

"Percy….you can see this too?"

"Yes…so where are we and who are they?" he replied and pointed toward the group at the stone.

"Why….why?" Philip called out sobbing as he was supported to his feet. "Why if all these religions teach peace, why can they not achieve peace?" he cried.

Paul felt a lump tighten in his throat as the emotion of seeing his father so distraught upset him.

"Every sword is given a name…you must choose one…and then continue what was given unto you to fulfil. Your wife gave her life for the sword so that you would do the right thing with it," a deep voice spoke.

The tall man with the sword offered it to Philip. He just looked at it for several long minutes. Paul knew it was the sword he now held. This was some kind of dream or vision of past events he told himself as Percival looked on perplexed.

"It was made from the metals of heaven…and to heaven it will one day return after it has served its purpose. Your wife knew this. Do not let her death be in vain," the voice said as the tall man placed the sword down beside Philip on the grass. The three tall men looked at Philip for a few moments until he picked it up, still shaking and in tears. "Now arise. Do what you swore to do."

Philip slowly stood up holding the sword and, staring at it, turned to look toward the setting sun. Theodoric dressed in a dark green robe covered in symbols came running into view. He too was much younger looking. He ran to Philip, paused for a moment, Philip looking utterly broken, then embraced him with a hug as Philip just sobbed. A tear ran down Paul's face.

"Are we dead?" Percival asked quietly.

"I honestly do not know," Paul answered and looked at him briefly. When he turned to look back at his father, they were gone.

Instantly the scene around them changed to one of what looked like a domed wall of stone around and over them that was covered in colours. The walls appeared to move like an undulating wave. The floor changed to a solid marble floor. Many colours of stone were set in a pattern that made it appear to spiral as they looked at it. Paul recalled seeing similar drawings of Ancient Egyptian frescos on walls that Attar and Theodoric had shown him. The greens and blues were bright and beautiful to look at.

"Yes, we are dead. That fall must have killed us. So what comes next?" Percival asked as he looked about them fast.

"Yes, what comes next?" Paul thought and was reminded of Taqi, who liked that saying.

A bright blue and green light suddenly lit up the circular enclosure. Before either of them could raise their hands, the light was gone and a woman with long pale blue hair stood before them. Dressed in an all in one white garment neither of them had ever seen the like of before, she walked toward them. Percival grabbed Paul's arm. The woman stopped just feet away from them and looked into their eyes intently in turn. Percival felt embarrassed and looked down. Paul frowned at her, puzzled. Her clothing was tight fitting and showed her figure. No more than twenty years, her blue eyes almost hypnotic, Paul went to speak but she raised her hand quickly and shook her head no.

"You cannot remain here. I will help you leave, and leave you must for if you stay any longer, you will never see alive those you love the most," she explained in a soft but commanding voice. Percival looked at Paul, alarmed. She sensed his fear. "Fear not. They are not in harm's way, but if you stay here, time is different. For every minute you stay here, a full day passes where your loved ones exist."

"What...but we have been here hours," Paul replied shocked.

"Oh my Lord. Nyla will think me dead," Percival said and coughed, his throat dry.

"A month and some has already passed," the woman said.

"How?" Percival asked, fraught with concern.

"That you would not understand," she smiled in reply.

"Try me," Percival shot back, shaking his head, feeling angry now.

Paul saw the look on Percival's face.

"Percy, remain calm. I am sure Nyla and Alisha are fine," Paul said, reassuring him, then looked back at the woman. "But what is this we are in and where?"

"When your kind finally unearths your true past, then you will discover your future. When you remember, your kind will again signal they have done so."

"Remember? And what signal?" Paul asked. "And can we get out of wherever here is soonest...please," Paul asked.

"If you vow to continue that which your fathers started...then I can lead you from here."

"Fathers! My father never made any vow," Percival remarked.

"You never really knew your father did you for I assure you he did...as Paul's father here did," the woman explained.

"You know our names?" Paul asked.

"Of course," the woman replied with a smile.

Paul's mind raced as he thought back upon all the stories Theodoric had explained to him about the many instances where people had entered a cave, fallen asleep and come out and years had passed by but only a day for them. As he thought that, Percival pulled him hard to look at him as if he had thought the same thing. Paul's heart jumped as he feared months would have passed by the time they got out and Alisha and Ari would believe them long since dead.

"We must leave now!" Percival demanded, alarmed.

"You will leave soon enough. But in future, be more prepared. Write a letter for your wives to be given to them should this occur again so that they will always know to wait," the woman said looking intently into Paul's eyes and his alone. "You know how the pyramids were built...you know that they stand as an alter in stone to testify to what man once achieved... that they contain the simple truths of your physical world," she said without moving her gaze for a moment from Paul. She stepped closer and gently rested her hand upon his forearm. "You also know there is a gateway here to other worlds and realms. Places men of your kind cannot and must not have access to until they all remember. You must remember all that you have learnt and only write down that which is allegorical, symbolic and only seen by those entrusted in the mysteries. Do you understand this?"

"I, I think so," Paul answered hesitantly. "But where are we now and you still have not told us of what signal will let you know we have remembered."

"Both of you remember this. You will always, always find the truth and strength within you." Percival and Paul looked at each other puzzled. "You are not the first to enter here before its time. The one you know as Moses and his brother Aaron also entered. Moses as you know is now written down as one person but the things attributed to him were of two men. The last one being a former Pharaoh as you know the term. He was the one who took a power tool, for it was granted unto him to do so. That tool is a staff. It still exists in your world with the man you know as Kratos, to us as Mer El In. You can work out his name I am sure." Paul shook his head no. "Then you will. Moses and his brother had to leave this place and once they did, Moses known also as Thotmoses, changed his name to Akhenaton and started his new belief system. In the one Almighty as he perceived it."

"But you still do not reveal what symbol…or signal…we must remember to make it known we have remembered," Percival interrupted impatiently. The woman broke her gaze from Paul and looked at him. "Please," he said and shrugged his shoulders.

"All paths leading into here are blocked and shall remain blocked just as those on what your kind will call and know as Oak Island are likewise sealed. When the earth once again moves its bounds and the stars in the heavens seem to fall, and when your sun rises and sets again in a new position, only then will you gain full access for only then will the vibrations that hold your realm together be changed high enough. Only then will the power of light envelop your world to reveal to you what is yours by right. All of the peoples not just a few who will still cling to their false pretence of power. But some of the chambers will be opened just prior to help warn you all and so that you can make ready and are prepared for the great changes…and some of your ancient forefathers will again reveal themselves…after you have signalled remembrance," she explained then paused as she looked at them both in turn. "When you place the sacred symbols of the rose and lily once again upon the limb of the bay where the mother of the Crimson Thread set foot upon her new lands, then and only then will they reveal themselves openly. It is as simple as that."

Paul looked at Percival, even more puzzled.

"Okay…good. Now we really must be leaving," Percival said and looked around for any sign of an exit. "And I have no idea of what you speak."

"You understand that ice, water and mist are made from the same source yes?" the woman asked, looking at Percival. He nodded yes. "Then understand that your world is like water. When frozen, it is solid. You cannot pass through it but you can walk upon it. When it changes its formation back to water, then you cannot walk upon it, but you can still travel upon it and swim in it. It is the very same substance you are made up from. But when it is mist, you cannot travel upon it but it is just as real but, unlike ice, you can travel through it easily enough. As mist, water takes up a different volume, as does ice, yet it is still the same element. This is how different realms exist side by side in its simplest explanation."

"That was its simplest explanation?" Percival frowned as Paul took in the woman's analogy. "But how does that help us get out of here now?"

"You know the pyramids all align with the belt stars of Orion?" the woman asked. Paul nodded yes as Percival looked at him first then also nodded but still confused. "You are presently just feet below the surface of where the Star of Isis is projected in relation to Orion being overlaid upon the Giza pyramids. I have placed the imaging within your minds but note, the third pyramid does not align perfectly as the others do. This was deliberate. For it only marries up perfectly with the star constellation of Cygnus. Align that and you will discover an exit. It was once an entrance but all passages are now sealed save one…but it too will be sealed."

"If we are just feet beneath the surface…surely it would be too easy to find before its time," Paul exclaimed.

"A man can dig a hundred feet and he would not find it for it exists on what you should understand as being a different realm but in the same space as I just tried to explain."

"Then how come we are in it…and that Akhenaton or Moses man was able to access here also?" Percival asked.

"Because of your blood…and as you have that key," the woman replied softly and indicated toward the sword Paul carried. "It is far more than a mere sword as you know. It also gives off a frequency, than means a set of sound waves, that allows you to enter this realm. One day your kind will again learn all about these facts, for facts are what they are and all governed by mathematics and harmonics."

"I hate maths," Percival said, trying to joke.

Paul's mind flashed back to when Firgany had told him and Taqi about there being six truths. He shook his head and smiled as he recalled his words. Even back then Firgany and his father had been educating and preparing him. He recalled the parchment. He had done the boat building path but now knew that career was dead to him. Medicine is the one he would follow. The knight path he would not, he told himself.

4 - 6

"The boat you cannot build again as your father informed you," the woman stated as if reading his mind. She smiled as if to acknowledge she could.

"Make note, before you vow to all of us here, within the centre of the chambers of creation, for all of your kind's history is stored here, that it is from a place in the centre of what you call Orion, that your eternal souls are first created. This world is but one for those souls to grow, learn and evolve...know not that ye are gods," the woman said and stood back a few paces.

Paul and Percival looked in awe, Percival with his mouth dropping open as images of great cylinders of black polished granite appeared to become transparent, twelve of them set around a larger circular enclosure with a bright gold covered pyramid set in the middle. Inside the chamber cylinders, black granite polished egg shaped looking objects were carefully lowered inside by some unknown and unseen force. Almost ghost like images of tall men and women appeared as they set items within the chambers, each specific to a different area of knowledge. Medicine, engineering, objects that flew and power tools, many looking like the staff of Kratos. Percival fell to his knees shaking his head in surprise and awe, emotions overwhelming his senses.

"Was Moses really real then?" he blurted out, nearly in tears.

"Yes. Some will argue he was not. Some will come to realise he was in fact of an Ancient Egyptian Pharaoh dynasty...others will claim the real Moses was murdered and replaced by a magician and puppet expert...and many will argue over where the actual sea Moses parted the waters of was, or where he received his Ten Commandments," the woman explained as they looked on.

"And where were these places?" Paul asked as he looked on utterly captivated at the scenes before them.

"That gold sheathed pyramid is the original stone that the builders rejected. I know you know of these facts already. It is within your mind. Beneath the gold shield there is white stone and then black basalt granite. You will note a small piece is broken from the corner. That is what the one you know as Abraham took and that now resides in Mecca as the Kabba stone. Again, one day this will be confirmed as true. It will happen when all I have said will come to pass and when many will accuse the book of the Prophet Muhammad as being the book of the Beast. You must speak with the one known as Theodoric for time here does not permit us. But swear you will continue the work your fathers vowed to continue."

"But I did not know my father...and," Percival started to say but fell silent as he watched several elegant women walk past him dressed in the same fashion carrying items that appeared to be made from glass. One of the items was almost identical to the threefold water system Theodoric used. "But whatever vow he took, take it as given I swear the same."

"I think from what Kratos has told me, several times now already, I have already made these vows. To safeguard the codes and make sure they are updated to be carried forward," Paul remarked quietly as he studied every facet of the scene before him.

"There will be signs in the heavens in the last days that mirror the image of the solar wings...as the Egyptians tried to copy...and then men will seek out those that know the codes of your forefathers for they will by then know them by their seals...apples, bees and harps... and they will seek them for comfort and knowledge and guidance set apart from the many false prophets that will claim many miracles and revelations to secrets. But as is the way, no matter what you present to people, they will always choose to accept that which is easy for them to comprehend. The fear that comes from changing their views and perspectives based on those placed within them by their parents and religions they were born into."

"Then why in God's name 'have' religion and I do not understand how we can be here, that this is real yet we cannot see it when in our world. How can the two exist together?" Percival asked.

"Like mist becomes water...becomes ice. As I have already explained. It is the same matter just in a different form. Why do you think all matters spiritual are represented by aqua...water? The same applies with matter, the materials of your world and ours."

"Just tell me...was Jesus real and not a myth then?" Percival asked, almost pleading. Paul looked down at him. "Please...for I need something tangible that my mind can accept and grasp."

"Yes, he was a real person, though much has been added to his life. Likewise he adopted and used much that was presented to him...here in Heliopolis in Egypt. He knew and understood the principle that you are all the sons of God and all gods in the making. But the last thing he wanted or wished for was a religion to be started after him," the woman explained softly and knelt down opposite Percival and took his right hand in hers. He looked at her stunned in disbelief as he felt her hand. "And you...you have never known your real father, but Paul there did. Just briefly. He resides in the higher realms beyond ours in what you would call paradise. A holding world between worlds where he waits," she said then looked up at Paul. "Along with your mother."

Paul stepped back taken by surprise. The image of the knight who had been decapitated beside him and whom he believed he saw in his dreams with his mother in Glen Lyon.

"No...it cannot be. 'Tis impossible. That would make Percival my cousin!" Paul stated and looked at Percival as he slowly stood up. "Impossible!"

"Impossible you say. Look around you at all you are seeing before your very eyes. All is possible. What coincidences do you think brought you together?" the woman asked as she stood up still holding Percival's hand. Paul and Percival looked at each other shocked. "You cannot lie that you do not feel the connection between you. From the moment you first met."

"I...I just thought him a good and godly man," Paul blurted out as Percival shook his head. "But that means your father is dead..."

Percival just looked at Paul then back at the woman. He clasped her hand with both of his and kissed it softly, then stood holding her hand making sure that in his mind he knew he was holding a real hand.

"You must go...for those that love you the most are beside themselves with fear and grief...but remember all you have seen and heard here, but never write it down for there would be consequences beyond your wildest fears if you do."

"How do we get out of here?" Percival asked, his voice emotional.

"When you awaken, you will find the way. But know this before you leave, when the apostles are placed around the zodiac as you now have it, the one known as John the Baptist, his head is the one that sits above the sign of Aquarius...and Percival, you once asked if Jonah had really been kept in the belly of a whale. Of course he was not but you try to explain to a people how he was taken on board a vessel, similar to what Paul built, but one that can travel beneath the waves. Do you think they could comprehend that? Plus, all actions and events have been recreated almost to the letter to re-enact events to make them current...and to fulfil prophecies as Jesus knew and understood. So Jonah was portrayed as being eaten by a whale though it was done so that reality mimicked what was based upon an ancient sun myth, and to carry the moral codes but also real mathematical codes. We constantly try to rationalise events as rational facts, but religious fanaticism makes people very irrational...and bigoted, obnoxious, aggressive, hostile, hateful and violent. People argue that their religion has rights above all others....but only people have rights. Ideas such as religion do not have rights."

"I am sorry...I do not follow what you say," Percival said hesitantly.

"Every ideology and religion must be subjected to open, free discussion in regard to its values, without fear of reprisal. No exceptions. Speaking out against injustice and intolerance within a religion, whether Christian, Hindu or Islam, is not being blasphemous. All are inspired ideas, but still ideas ultimately and in a civilised moral society, no idea, religious, political or philosophical, can claim any special treatment, or be set beyond the reach of empirical evidence. All of your religions carry the same codes from antiquity. Put there by a great and very ancient worldwide civilisation. Carrying within all religions are the roots of humanity's greatest astro-theological traditions dating back many thousands of years. It does a great disservice to these ancient peoples...your forefathers...to ignore or twist the knowledge and wisdom they left for you. Even Jesus knew this and understood this and so he likewise re-enacted past myths and prophecies. The so-called fable of Christ as many will one day shout, and his twelve apostles...is indeed but a parody of the sun and the twelve signs of the zodiac, copied from the ancient religions of the Eastern world... but all to lead you back to all of this," the woman explained reverentially as she opened her hand toward the fast fading images of the chambers as they were being sealed. "Everything told of Christ has reference to the sun. His reported resurrection is at sunrise, and that on the first day of the week; that is, on the day anciently dedicated to the sun, and thence called Sunday…"

"But I have learnt you do not need religion to have morals though. Plenty of people live moral lives without religion. Religious people thinking religion is the root of morality are committing an egregious act of arrogance are they not?" Percival asked as the woman let go of his hand and started to walk backwards.

"Whilst humankind is still childlike, then childlike rules for moral guidance must be instilled. When humankind matures, then new revelations will be revealed. Your fathers hid away the bodies of those whom you know as King David and his wife Bathsheba, mother of Solomon. They both know the material from which your sword is made and either of you can wield it."

"What…whose bodies?" Paul asked, confused, just as a blinding pain shot through his forehead, his ears beginning to ring loudly.

"They secured them away in the land of Alba, but you must ensure they are moved to Oak Island and keep your vow to continue the codes…only then is your task complete in this lifetime," the woman said as both Paul's and Percival's vision blurred, darkened and they fell asleep.

ꙮ

Paul felt heavy, his eyes closed as he tried to move. He sensed his face was covered in dirt and fine sand, his back aching. He moved his legs but they also felt heavy and painful. He coughed as dust entered his mouth as he opened it to breathe. He struggled to sit up and opened his eyes. Percival lay beside him. They were in a dark and cramped tunnel. Its walls were rough cut stone. To his left was total darkness but to his right he could just make out the glimmer of a shard of light beaming down from outside like a beacon. He coughed again to clear his throat and pushed Percival to rouse him. After a few minutes of vigorous shaking, he suddenly coughed loudly and spat out dirt. Confused and alarmed he sat up looking at Paul, trying to focus in the dim light.

"Okay…okay so where the f….," he paused, "the heck are we?" he asked, his voice dry as Paul helped him sit up.

"I have no idea but that light calls us that way," Paul replied, quickly checked he still had his sword and immediately started to crawl toward the light.

Percival looked behind him at the dense blackness and quickly hurried after Paul. When they reached the beam of sunlight, Paul saw that it was shining through a tiny crack in the stone above their heads. He looked at Percival as if to ask if he should pull it down. Percival looked up hesitantly, wiped his face then nodded in agreement both knowing it could bring the whole shaft down upon them. Paul moved aside and reached his hands up into the crack, used his fingers to prise a larger space so his hand would fit through. Once his hand was through he grabbed hold of what felt like a thin stone slab. He looked at Percival once more, he nodded again and with an almighty heave, Paul pushed the slab upwards as a lip around the sides would not allow it to move downward. As he heaved upwards, his entire arm moved. The small stone slab pushed up and over against a stone cut shaft. As grit and sand fell over Paul's head and shoulders, he held his arm steady. Eventually the sand stopped falling and he cleared his eyes to look up. It was a small shaft of no more than twenty-four inches square.

"Good job Theo is not with us," Percival joked, looking up. "And I hope you can climb?"

Paul eased himself upward into the shaft, placed his already scuffed and bleeding knee against the entrance lip and hauled himself up. Using his arms and knees pushed hard against the shaft walls, he positioned himself ready to ascend.

"Sorry, my friend. I know of your fears of confined spaces…would you like to go first?"

"No…just get a move on," Percival replied looking behind himself nervously.

The shaft was thirty-three feet straight up. Slowly they eased their way upwards inch by inch. The hole above them was partly covered by a stone block and Paul prayed it was not too heavy to move. When he reached the top, the cool air changed to one of arid heat. The sun was setting fast and the light was now angled casting the shaft beneath them into total darkness. Percival was shaking from both fear and exhaustion. Paul pushed his hand against the stone, the space open being just wide enough for his arm to stick through. The stone block was far too heavy to move. In desperation he slapped the stone hard several times but all it did was knock off fine sand into his eyes. After fifteen minutes of trying, getting weaker all the time. Paul went to get his sword to see if he could use it somehow. But as soon as he went to move it he realised immediately he could not turn the sword around in the confined space. He sighed heavily and looked down at Percival staring up, his eyes wide. Suddenly more sand was kicked into the hole falling on Paul's head. Someone started shouting outside. As Paul cleared his eyes again and looked up, he saw a child's face peering in at him, smiling. Excitedly the child shouted and started waving to others outside.

"Hold on a while longer, my friend," Paul said quietly.

"They better hurry for I have not the strength to climb back down nor hold much longer," Percival replied.

Suddenly a rope appeared and a strong hand feeding it in.

"Grab this, my friends, whilst we shift this fuck of a rock," Luke's voice echoed out into the shaft.

Paul and Percival gasped with relief upon hearing his voice and they grabbed the rope. Quickly Percival tied it off around his waist as Paul interlocked his arms over it. After what seemed an age, lots of shouting and swearing plus the groans of a mule being pressed into pulling the stone, it eventually moved aside to make a big enough hole for Paul to reach upwards. No sooner had he put his arm up, when several strong hands grabbed him and hauled him out. As Paul was dragged across the sand, Percival was likewise dragged up and out. Paul turned over onto his back and in the remaining orange and yellow light of the setting sun he nearly cried at seeing Thomas and all of his men. Many other men and even Mamluks seemed to be everywhere. The Great Pyramid rose before him a short distance away bathed in the hues of the sun. The small child who had seen Paul's arm knelt down beside him and smiled, proud of himself.

"You are in so much shit, my friend…but it is a mighty end to this day that we have found you alive," Thomas laughed as Luke offered Percival some water.

A deep rumbling sound echoed out and a slight shaking of the ground beneath their feet made everyone freeze. A loud thud followed by several more accompanied a loud groan from within the shaft as it collapsed in on itself throwing out a vertical shaft of dust and fine sand. They all shielded their eyes, some coughing as the dust slowly settled. Theodoric suddenly appeared through the cloud of dust a short distance away running toward them fast. It surprised Paul to see just how fast for a man his age. Paul sat up full of relief when Theodoric stopped just in front of him, fell to his knees in the sand and pulled Paul close hugging him tightly, his eyes shut tight with emotion.

"For the love of God where have you been these past weeks?" Theodoric asked, still hugging him tight.

"Weeks!" Paul exclaimed. As memories of his encounter flooded back, he recalled the woman had informed them that a month at least had passed.

"Ali?" Paul asked concerned.

"At home waiting...just waiting," Theodoric said and finally sat back and looked at Paul. "You have scared the absolute life out of her this time...far worse than when you went missing after the sea engagement..."

Paul looked at Percival, who was being grilled by Thomas and Luke as they poured water over his face to clean away the dust. Paul's eyes fell upon the now blocked shaft. He heard the words of the woman again as he recalled her comments about the entrance being where one of the stars of Cygnus was projected on the ground. He turned his gaze toward his home. Quickly he stood up and took a deep breath.

ꕥ

Alisha, her tired eyes closed, sat with her head resting in her hands at the main kitchen hall table. Nyla sat opposite with her hands resting across her tummy gently rubbing it staring out of the window in a daze. Sister Lucy was busy putting Arri to bed upstairs. A sense of oppression and misery pervaded the place like a real blanket of darkness that had been placed over the house. Long shadows were cast from the setting sun that only served to add to the sense of gloom. Alisha had not put out any flowers since Paul and Percival had vanished and simply existed in a sense of fatigued helplessness, her life set on pause. Both sat oblivious to the sounds of the returning men on horseback just as they had every evening for the past month and a half. Their arrival no longer solicited any hint of expectant hope from Alisha or Nyla. They did not look up when Theodoric entered the room. Full of emotion and twiddling his large hat through his fingers he stood in silence for several long minutes before Nyla finally looked up at him. Her eyes widened in alarm seeing his expression and fearing the worst. She gasped causing Alisha to look up at him, her eyes puffy and tired.

"We...we...," Theodoric started to say but his voice was broken and so full of emotion he could hardly speak.

"Have you found them...are they dead?" Alisha asked quietly as she stood up slowly, her hand placed upon her growing belly. She was shaking in anticipation of his reply. The fear in her eyes was real and immediate, the desperation obvious. Nyla placed her hands over her mouth fearing the worst. "Please!"

Theodoric shook his head up and down then quickly no, his mouth dry not able to speak. As he gathered his thoughts he quickly stepped aside and ushered the figures now stood behind him silhouetted by the sun, to enter. The first figure stepped into the room and lowered his hood. Instantly Alisha recognised the tall dirty figure stood before her as Paul. He broke a pained nervous smile at her just as Percival moved to stand beside him. Nyla immediately started to sob holding her hands over her mouth in disbelief, her arms held up horizontal. Percival shrugged his shoulders and smiled, his lips quivering emotionally. Nyla just sat where she was, sobbing, her eyes filled with tears, her hands still cupped tightly over her mouth. Quickly Percival rushed around the table and knelt beside her and flung his arms around her as she continued to sob uncontrollably. Alisha had followed Percival with her eyes and just stared at them, her senses numbed and tired from the weeks of worry. Slowly in disbelief she turned her head back to look at Paul. She sighed lightly and leaned her head to the side as she looked into his eyes. She looked briefly at the cut upon his forehead. She felt numb. No tears...nothing. Paul nervously looked at her, waiting for some kind of reaction. He stepped closer but as he did, she raised her hand abruptly for him to stop and took a pace backward. She put her right hand up covering her face. She closed her eyes and took a deep breath. She sighed and Paul could see she was starting to struggle as if unable to catch her breath. She took a deep breath again and shook her head as emotions finally began to register at the shock of seeing him again alive. It filled her like water filling a jar from her stomach upwards. Eventually the feelings reached her throat and as it tightened, she waved her left hand at Paul and hid her eyes beneath her other hand. Paul could see her mouth beginning to quiver. A lump swelled in his throat seeing her clearly upset. He stepped closer but Alisha put out her hand again, this time her palm landing upon his chest. At first she raised her hand away but then patted his chest again until, still shielding her face, she rested her hand upon his chest fully. She could feel his heart pounding beneath his cotton shirt. Paul placed his hands over her hand as tears streamed down her cheeks, her eyes still shielded by her hand. She clenched his shirt and moved closer to him still not looking at him hardly daring to believe he was actually stood in front of her. She clenched his cotton shirt as she lowered her head sobbing but desperately fighting to control her tears. She stepped a little closer and rested her forehead against his chest. The kitchen door opened as Sister Lucy walked in. She stopped dead in her tracks seeing both Paul and Percival back. Her mouth wide open she looked at Theodoric, stunned. He smiled and nodded, tears in his own eyes. Paul looked at her as she clasped her hands to her face in surprise. Paul placed his arms around Alisha as she broke down in tears, her silent sobbing and shaking of her body sending a wave of guilt through him. She had lost weight despite the baby growing inside her and it was all his fault. He kissed the top of her head gently and simply held her as Sister Lucy moved to stand beside Theodoric.

"I do truly swear, and I mean it, I will never ever leave your side again," Paul remarked and kissed her again. "And Theo…we have much to ask of you…later."

Percival looked over at him. Paul nodded back and they both knew things would forever be different. They knew now that somehow, despite the distance separating them from their birth countries, they were related. They had also shared an experience very few would believe let alone understand. But any doubts Paul had had about the events and similar previous ones being real were now truly dispelled. Percival had once again been with him and this time the woman they had both seen, the images they had witnessed they both saw, and the time loss had been a shared experience. Paul smiled at Percival as tiredness began to take its toll on them.

Port of La Rochelle, France, Melissae Inn, spring 1191

"I recall you explained about the story in both Islamic and Christian tradition about people entering caves and coming out many hundreds of years later...but Paul and Percival...really?" the farrier asked, unsure if what he was being told was the truth.

"I swear to you upon this very sword," the old man started to say and placed his hand upon the sword. "All that I tell you is the truth."

"Even if some is not, so long as these are genuine, that is all that I am concerned about," the Hospitaller remarked and raised his sealed envelope.

"They are genuine, my friend. And as I have said already, if you choose to accept the commission contained within them, you will be carrying on a great challenge and honour," the old man answered immediately.

"I mean no offence...but some of what you say is so fantastical it beggars belief," the Hospitaller replied.

"True enough. But you and your brother's surname is Seincler is it not...and I can promise you this, in time, your name will be remembered for the deeds you have yet to do. And has not your surname oft been writ as Sinclair, after Saint Claire?"

"Aye...but that is a name our father forbade us ever to use or repeat. How do you know these things?" the Templar asked suspiciously.

"In good time, my friend, all in good time," the old man replied and smiled disarmingly.

"I heard you mention the real name of Kratos as being," Gabirol said and quickly checked his notes. "Ah...you called him Mer El In. That sounds remarkably too close to the mythical Arthurian wizard Merlin."

"As I keep telling you...all that is considered just myth and legend was once based upon real people, places and events. Perhaps over romanticised presently, but all carrying a kernel of truth," the old man smiled.

"I have heard of Merlin...does it mean something then? And the word pyramid. 'Tis something you have mentioned much of yet I have never heard this word before," Ayleth remarked.

"Pyramid is made up from several words and has several different meanings for each. That is the beauty of word play...and so too is the word Mer EL In," the old man replied, looking at Ayleth. He paused for a few moments before continuing. "The word pyramid will become familiar enough in time across the whole of Europe...but on one aspect alone consider the part Pyr, which means fire amongst many other things. How many times does God appear in the Bible represented as fire? Take the burning bush for example. Wherever God appears there is always fire connected somehow. And the Altar of Stone by now you should all surely realise is one and the same Great Pyramid itself. It alone sits at the centre of all our world's landmass...though it may be a while before mankind confirms that again."

"That is what concerns me," the farrier interrupted. "You say so much that will not be proven or discovered, as you tell us, for many years."

"Yet you believe a book where an unseen and unknowable entity commands you to do things and tells you things you cannot possibly know, and you accept that as gospel...literally?" the old man asked him.

2 - 37

"Yes for it is the Lord's book...," the farrier replied, his face turning red.

"The Lord's book? Okay, well let us consider the sources of the word and term pyramid. In Greek πύραμίς, or the plural πύραμίδες, had two meanings. The first was 'wheat cake' because Egyptian buildings reminded the Greeks of pointy-topped cakes. Later the Greek word 'puramis' signified a monumental structure built of stone with a square base, and sloping sides meeting at an apex. But the origin of the Greek word 'puramis' has a special history. There is one version that proclaims that the Ancient Egyptian 'Pir E Mit' meaning 'division of number' or 'division of perfection' was taken from the Greeks. The Greek word puramis is an alternation of the Egyptian pimar. The Greek word puramis crossed into Latin. The Ancient Egyptian word for pyramids is Mr, pronounced as 'mer', also the root word that starts Kratos's original name as well as Merlins. In Arabic the word for pyramid is مره, pronounced 'haram', meaning ultimate age or size. Consequently the term pyramid in the Arabic world means 'the most ancient and largest construction ever built'," the old man explained.

"You told us before what Mer meant," Gabirol said as he flicked through his earlier notes. "Yes here it is. You said that the Mer part means 'ascending place'. Ah but that was to do with the Merkaba star," Gabirol sighed.

"It could be argued that both Kratos as Mer EL In and the fabled Merlin denotes that they are men of great renown connected with that communication device with God you all know as the Ark of the Covenant, which I also explained previously, then Mer EL In can be seen as an individual who helps, or will help, mankind ascend spiritually," the old man explained and laughed lightly at Gabirol's expression. "And remember El is the root word for God!"

"So what does the pyramid tell us...or more correctly those that built it...like that woman?" Simon asked.

"Many things, Simon...many things. But as an altar of stone, I suppose we could sum it up that they, those who built it for future generations' benefits, were saying, speaking out to all of us across time, to trust them in what they state and show as provable evidence. To listen to the voices from the past calling out across time to remind those in the future. But there is also a warning...one that warns us that in the future there will be those few, few but powerful, who will deliberately orchestrate hate and intolerance and wars. They will deny the past by teaching falsehoods in history. Only when most wake up to reality and take back that power will wars cease and peace be returned..."

"And you believe that?" the Genoese sailor asked bluntly.

The old man looked at him intently for a few moments in silence.

"I know so," the old man replied.

"And in the future, all it will take is for people to remember and simply go out there, to the point and lay a rose and a lily?" Ayleth asked, bemused, and pointed toward the large windows.

"Yes. 'Tis really that simple," the old man answered and smiled. "As I keep saying...all of nature and God's plan is really quite simple. Empathy and love is all it takes. Empathy!"

"You mentioned the woman claimed Jesus was re-enacting prophecies and a connection to Ancient Egyptian sun myths. How so?" Gabirol asked.

"That I shall come to, my friend," the old man replied and smiled as he pulled the sword across the table closer to him.

Chapter 60
Once and Future King – Arthur

Gabirol checked through his earlier notes and read a page carefully before looking up at the old man. The old man could see he had a question and he waited as did all the others. Simon coughed deliberately loudly to get Gabirol's attention.

"Sorry...but what you said earlier about this town hiding a great secret in plain sight. You now tell us that a simple act of placing a single red rose and white lily is all that is required to send a signal...a message that we have remembered. And I am beginning to see now that what you have told us means that indeed Mary Magdalene came ashore here, had a daughter, but also went on to have a son later on the Island of Iona...yes?" he asked.

"That is correct," the old man replied with a slight nod.

"And when you told us that a great key was hidden in a church, where the square meets the corner on the church you said, then if I understand correctly what you have told us, then the nine original knights of the Order were buried here in La Rochelle until very recently when Philip removed them to a place in Alba...yes?" Gabirol further quizzed. The old man nodded yes again in silence. "Also that the bodies of Solomon and David were also found, recovered and transported to a safe location...this Oak Island you speak of?"

"Yes...though in truth the final resting place of Oak Island has still to be undertaken," the old man replied and looked at the Templar and the Hospitaller.

"I get the feeling we have work to do in Alba that will connect us to that task," the Templar remarked and waved his sealed envelope. He held it up for a few moments before smiling broadly. The old man shrugged his shoulders very slightly and smiled back. "Brother...I hope your bags are still packed." The Templar smiled again and slapped the envelope against his brother's arm then gently squeezed Miriam's hand. "And if you will, I pray you will come with me."

"Just try leaving without me," Miriam replied instantly, smiling.

The old man closed his eyes for a moment, took a deep breath and then looked up toward Ayleth. All followed the old man's gaze and looked at her. She started to blush.

"You have a question," the old man said to her directly.

"I do...and..." She hesitated, looking at everyone. "If I were to go outside right now and place a red rose and white lily on the circle where Paul and Alisha were married...where the single lanthorn burns nightly, will that signal show that we have remembered and will God send his messengers as promised?"

"It would be the start," the old man answered. "But, and this is the big but, now is not the correct time for as I have explained previously, it can only happen as the world we live upon changes physically and our position in the heavens not only enters the time of light, but also the zodiac position of the water carrier...Aquarius. And when, during that time, people remember, then as those symbols are placed, so within a short time will those that we would call messengers of the Lord make their presence known."

"But I thought Mary came ashore at Roussillon where Theodoric came from or have I missed something?" Simon asked, scratching his head.

"You heard correctly," the old man said. "But after landing there and staying a short while, they travelled here, to La Rochelle, where they stayed a great many years. And as Paul was to discover, another Roussillon will be planned and built... in Alba," the old man explained, looking again directly at the Templar and his brother Hospitaller.

Cairo, Egypt, July 25th 1183

Paul wiped his head with his sleeve with Alisha sat beside him just holding his hands looking down utterly exhausted and emotionally drained. Percival and Nyla sat holding each other, their eyes closed, when the main door from the hallway into the kitchen opened. Arri stepped down into view rubbing his tired eyes with one hand whilst holding Clip clop in the other. When he saw his father sat at the table, he opened his eyes wide, his mouth opening wide and ran around Percival and Nyla. Paul just managed to turn in his chair, when Arri jumped up and threw his little arms around Paul's neck.

"I told Mama so many times you would come back. I told her you would not leave us," Arri exclaimed excitedly and clenched his little arms around Paul tighter. Alisha looked up at him as he looked at her smiling, nodded and appeared to wink with both eyes. Alisha let out a little chuckle at his expression. Paul held him tightly. "And I told her you would be back in time for her birthday…tomorrow. Now where have you been? You made Mama very sad!"

"That, my little man, I shall tell you all about after I have slept," Paul replied laughing at his remark but quietly shocked inside. If it was Alisha's birthday the next day, then he and Percival had indeed been away longer than he had realised and nearer two months. He shook his head, confused, but also very glad to be home.

"I shall sort you both a hot bath," Sister Lucy said as she brushed past Theodoric, gently squeezing his shoulder as she went.

Paul lifted Arri and sat him on the table. He clasped Alisha's hand and placed hers against Arri's. With both of his hands he held theirs together, Arri's face glowing with happiness. Alisha forced a brave smile but Paul could sense the pain and emotional exhaustion she was feeling.

"You two. Please listen to me and believe me when I say I swear to you this hour, that from this day onward, I will never, ever, leave your sides again. This I truly swear and mean by all that I am. I swear it upon my very life…I swear," Paul said emotionally. Arri waved Clip clop excitedly but Alisha just looked into his eyes. Paul knew his words probably sounded hollow but he meant every one of them. He felt sick seeing the broken look in Alisha's eyes. Gently he kissed the side of her face. "I swear it," Paul whispered to her.

Alisha looked deeply into his eyes for what seemed an age. She looked exhausted and pale and it was all down to him. Knowing that only served to make him feel guilty. Alisha held Paul's hand and kissed the top of it softly.

"You ever…ever put me through this again, and I swear, I will kill you myself," she said quietly, her pain very obvious as she fought to control her emotions. "I love you…but the strength of my love is what will kill me," she whispered even quieter so Arri could not hear, pulling Paul closer. She kissed him on the side of his cheek then stared into his eyes. He could feel the love but hurt inside her as if it was a tangible force he could physically touch almost. She raised her eyebrows as if to ask if he understood her. "Well?"

"'Tis you that wields the sword through my heart," Paul replied referring to his original poem he had written to her back in La Rochelle.

Alisha leant closer and put her arms around him. She closed her eyes and rested against him. Arri waved Clip clop excited again and put his left arm around Alisha and his right arm around Paul. They remained like that for nearly an hour until Arri started to fall asleep. Paul decided he would write Alisha another poem by way of apology but to reinforce his genuine desire and promise never to leave them again. Alisha gently carried Arri upstairs back to his bedroom when Theodoric beckoned Paul and Percival to follow him as the hot water had been put into the baths ready for them.

Sister Lucy laid out two large towels, one each for Paul and Percival, and turned to face both of them as they entered the large bathing room. Steam rose from the large sunken bath as Ishmael entered the other door excitedly having only just returned and hearing the news they were back.

"My prayers have been answered," he said enthusiastically and rushed across the bathing room and grabbed Paul's arms. "I wish to know all there is to where you have been, my friend…everything!"

"Aye, you and me both," Theodoric said aloud as he entered carrying two clean robes.

Paul looked at Theodoric.

"And as I said, we have many questions of you Theo, such as what is it you must tell us about Luke…Saint Luke that is. And what and where is the standing stone you and my father visited where he thrust this sword into it?" Paul asked.

"And who were the semi visible giants?" Percival interrupted.

Theodoric looked a little shocked at their questions.

"And Paul…Saladin's secretary Al Isfahani…he wishes to meet with you again as soon as possible for Saladin himself has a great request of you," Ishmael explained excitedly.

Paul looked at Theodoric again, puzzled.

"Ah…yes. You may have to break…or at least bend…that promise you made Alisha and Arri," Theodoric started to explain. "It would appear that you made an impression on quite a few of Saladin's senior command, especially Husam's. Would appear that Saladin himself has approved the formation of a Muslim contingent of several squadrons of Templars…and he wants you to broker the formation."

Paul looked at Ishmael, who shook his head in agreement. Percival shrugged his shoulders, as confused as Paul.

"This is a joke yes?" Paul asked.

"No, my dear boy, no! It appears you are considered a natural and trustworthy diplomat by all sides," Theodoric answered and handed him a robe. "'Tis what your father started I am afraid." Paul felt a knot churn up in his stomach. "Now clean yourselves up, get a good night's rest and we shall speak of it in the morning."

ꕥ

After bathing and putting on clean and warm robes, Paul bid everyone a good night and headed for his chambers. But as he passed his study room, his mind still awake and running through a hundred questions, he entered rather than go to bed. He used the small ceramic oil lamp to light the large lanthorn in his room. As the room lit up, he sighed heavily both glad to be home but still filled with a real heavy sense of guilt and sadness for what he had put Alisha through. In a few short hours she would be up and it was her birthday. He sat down and gathered several sheets of parchment together and prepared his writing quill. He would write her a small poem as the only gift he could give her. As he sat in silence trying to find the words, he simply could not. Perhaps it was tiredness, he thought, or perhaps it was the many questions and images still running through his mind. His gaze fell upon the parchment tubes his father had left him to look after. Not exactly well looked after he told himself as he reached over and pulled one closer. Quickly he opened it and rolled out its content. Instantly he recognised that several of the sheets were plans for a sizeable chapel very ornately designed. Several other sheets had symbols upon squares. The symbols were identical to some of the symbols he had been shown within the chambers upon the egg shaped granite containers. He knew they represented sounds somehow. Had his father also seen the same images? he immediately thought, seeing how identical they were. Suddenly his study door eased open making him jump, startled.

"'Tis only I," Theodoric whispered as he entered, closing the door quietly behind him. "I knew you would not be off to bed…too much in your mind eh?" Paul nodded yes. "I have something that may help," he said with a cheeky smile and pulled out from his robe a Roman styled glass bottle of red wine and two blue glasses. He winked at Paul, sat himself down and immediately started to pour the wine. "I still remember the first glass we shared back at Rochfort…how so long ago that seems already."

"Yes…it does indeed seem a long time ago," Paul replied as took the glass of wine.

"I thought my life was all but over back then…until you just happened to appear arguing with Gerard!" Theodoric said as he finished pouring his wine. "You do know don't you that you gave me back my life, and for that I will never be able to thank you enough."

Paul looked at Theodoric as he raised his wine glass to him.

"Yes…Rick!" Paul replied and laughed quietly.

"Well, I knew if your father had spoken of me, it would not have been favourably."

"You were wrong about that though weren't you?"

"Aye, that I was for I was sure he must have hated me…as well as my Luce. And now look at us. I was such a fool…such a fool," Theodoric sighed and took a large swig of wine, wiped his mouth and smiled. "That's better… demon drink and all that!"

"Perhaps whilst we are here alone you will answer some questions?"

"Fire away and if I am able, I shall answer."

"These parchments Father has entrusted to me. I know they are copies… but what are they really of? For I have but this past day seen these very same symbols beneath the pyramids," Paul asked and tapped his finger down upon the sheet with the symbols drawn out upon squares.

Theodoric pulled the sheet closer and studied them for a few minutes in silence. He moved the lanthorn closer to shine more light upon it. After another large sip of wine he looked up at Paul.

"These are but plans of a new chapel designed and based upon sacred numbers, proportions and the Temple of Solomon in Jerusalem. The building also incorporates many sacred features such as the twin pillars symbolism. It will also be called after Roussillon."

"But where is this chapel then?"

"My friend. This chapel has yet to be built. Look, see the symbol of the Templars…the twin riders upon a single horse. This is marked down as such because both your father and I were told that two brothers, twins no less, would be entrusted to reconstruct this chapel along with all its inherent symbolism and dimensions. To house the nine original knights of the Templar Order. But it would also encode these," he explained and pointed to the small squares with different symbols inside them. "These are images produced by different sounds. When put together they make a musical scale as well as harmonic resonance that will help unlock one's higher mind…our higher consciousness but also doorways…portals to other realms. Realms such as the one I strongly suspect you have just been to," Theodoric explained further and looked directly at Paul.

"Then where are the nine knights now?"

"Exactly where your father has placed them…in Balantrodach in Alba. 'Tis up to the twin knights, whomever they turn out to be, to commission and complete the new chapel. 'Tis not for us in our time, to do so ourselves. But it is charged to us to find the two knights in question that they may carry out their great commission."

Paul pondered Theodoric's words carefully.

"Is Percival my twin brother by any chance?"

"Don't be daft, you silly bugger!" Theodoric laughed a little too loudly and quickly cupped his mouth. "No…your father and I, when we shared what I suspect was a similar experience to yours, were told that two brothers, twins, would be the ones to pick up this task. All we have to go on is the name Seincler…and that is all. And that they will in time recover the bodies of the nine knights now hidden at Balantrodach as you know to a place South West of Edinburgh in Alba. It will be named Roussillon as I said in memory of where the Holy Family first came back to France before eventually heading 'back' for Britain. A sacred and holy location with peculiar properties within the land itself."

"So I can rest knowing it is not for me to do?" Paul asked.

"Rest only after you have found these twins. 'Tis something your father is still doing."

"And they definitely have to be twin blood brothers…not say brothers in arms?"

Theodoric looked at Paul and shook his head no.

"Theo…where I have been is almost impossible to describe and explain, but a woman we met there…she said that there will be signs in the heavens in the last days that mirror the image of the solar wings…and then men will seek out the those that know by their seals…apples and bees and harps. But I do not understand what she means."

"The twin dark star…when it comes back around. Your father and I were once shown and given details of the protective shield that protects our world. As detailed and retold within the Norse legends. The Ancient Egyptians likewise knew these things and how the image of both the approaching twin dark star and the image of the protective shield around us look. I have a drawing I keep within the pages of my Bible," Theodoric explained, put his drink down and pulled out his small leather bound Bible. Inserted in the rear section he had several small sheets of vellum and parchments. Carefully he removed one and gently unfolded it flat on the table in front of Paul. And as we learnt, many of the Ancient Egyptian myths are in fact identical to even older ones from Sumeria and Babylon, which in turn were picked up and used by Jesus and his followers."

Fig. 60: Winged Discs.

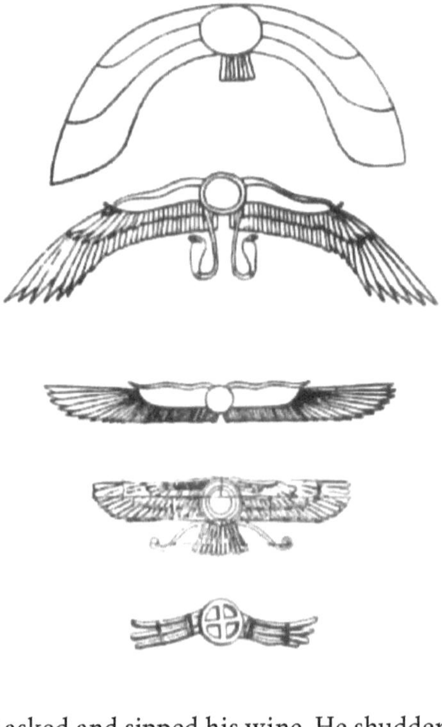

"Such as?" Paul asked and sipped his wine. He shuddered at the taste.

"'Tis a good wine," Theodoric laughed, seeing his face purse up. "Whatever you saw and heard beneath the pyramids, you must not speak openly or unguardedly about it. And do not draw what you saw…by all means do so using symbols and allegory but not in detail as you are capable of."

"Like our good old friends the Druids eh?" Paul quipped and took another sip.

"Absolutely…'tis why it took over twenty years for them to memorise everything…well, not everything but a lot."

"And what of this…truly?" Paul asked as he lifted his sword into view and placed it upon the table in front of Theodoric. "I know so very little of just exactly what this really is and does."

"Hmmm," Theodoric sighed and rubbed his chin. "I can tell you it still has one more symbol to be put upon it for your father and I saw what this tool would one day look like."

"Tool?…'Tis a weapon, Theo," Paul remarked and half laughed.

"No, Paul…'tis a tool. It can be used as a weapon when required, but this is more than just a weapon. Surely you must know that already? And it will be you that puts the final symbol upon it as you have the others already."

3 - 7

"I have only put images I liked upon it," Paul replied, looking puzzled.

"Paul…they are symbols. Trust me on that fact."

"So what is the last symbol?"

"Don't ask me you are the one who will come up with it," Theodoric laughed and took a mouthful of wine. "Lord, that is good wine," he smiled and licked his lips.

"Theo," Paul said quietly as he studied the symbols. "When I was beneath the pyramids…both Percy and I saw you and my father. You were young and father stabbed this sword into a standing stone. But there were people of great height who appeared to be part invisible. One acknowledged me but you two could not see me," Paul explained and looked up at him. "I felt it was somewhere in Alba…Glen Lyon perhaps? Is what we saw real and where and when was that?"

Theodoric took a large mouthful of wine and downed it. He sighed as his mind clearly thought back upon the event.

"Aye 'twas real, my boy…but no it was not Glen Lyon really," he replied and paused for several moments. He shook his head before looking at Paul. "'Twas in fact the now lost lands of Lyonesse, the Legendary City on the Bottom of the Sea as nowadays recounted in Arthurian legend. Lyonesse… the so-called home country of Tristan, from the legendary story of Tristan and Iseult."

"But I thought that was just a myth based on older stories?"

"No...'twas a very real place until recently...and I do mean recently. The lands it sat upon simply dropped, the sea came in and swallowed it and all that remains now are the former tops of its hills. You know them as the Isles of Scilly. Check old Roman records and you will find details about the land and its people," Theodoric sighed as he explained. "The story of Tristan and Iseult is but a tragic story of love and loss inspired by Celtic legend. It is the inspiration for one of the Arthurian romances...of Lancelot and Guinevere, as both stories push the boundaries of love, family, loyalty, adultery and betrayal. Most of the land had already sunk when your father and I visited what was left...that was when the event you saw happened. Most of Lyonesse disappeared on November 11th 1099 though it had started to sink back in the sixth century. But very suddenly the land was flooded by the sea. Entire villages were swallowed, and the people and animals of the area drowned. Once it was covered in water, the land never re-emerged. It was once attached by a land bridge to the Scilly Isles in Cornwall. 'Tis almost an identical story to that of Atlantis eh?"

"Yes...yes indeed," Paul replied as thoughts of Nicholas entered his mind. He shuddered momentarily as he thought Nicholas could be his own Sir Lancelot who would steal his Guinevere, his Alisha. He blinked and shook his head trying to dispel the idea.

"My friend. I see you tire so I shall bid you a good night...what is left of it," Theodoric said and stood to leave.

"I shall not sleep for my mind still runs too awake. Plus I need to know why my father thrust the sword into the stone...something about it costing my mother's life. But I also must ask of you about Luke," Paul said and grasped Theodoric's forearm and beckoned for him to sit back down. "And this sword...why do I keep wanting to call it Durandol?"

"You mean Durandal or Durendal...'tis from the French durer meaning to endure. You carry this sword, you must endure! But the actual Durandal was the sword of Charlemagne's paladin Roland. Some say it is one of the Four Swords of Power used to create ley gates and ley lines that date from the Time Before Time."

"What is a paladin?" Paul asked, bemused.

"Paladin is like a great knight. Roland was the bravest and most loyal of the twelve legendary paladins, or knights, who served Charlemagne, king of the Franks. Twelve again eh? Like the Arthurian legends, many fanciful tales about Charlemagne and his knights were written and now, in most cases, spoken of as if fact. But as you know, all myth has its roots in truth," Theodoric answered and paused. He took a final mouthful of wine before continuing. "It was said that Roland stood eight feet tall and carried a magical sword called Durindana or Durendal that had once belonged to the Trojan hero Hector. You see, Paul, like the sword you have been entrusted with, there are some who believe that God or his messengers, call them what you wish, help us out by bestowing such weapons to a select chosen few to do great deeds…"

"If that is so, then after what I have put Alisha through, I will gladly pass on this sword for it is a burden I feel I cannot honour. For I refuse to leave Alisha ever again as I swore to her."

"Paul…'tis something beyond your control I think you will discover… what will be shall be."

"Percival is a more deserving man than I to have this," Paul remarked and unsheathed the sword, its brilliant almost white blade reflecting beautiful colours from the light of the lanthorn.

"Well, getting back to Roland, or as he was otherwise known, Orlando. He was the son of Charlemagne's sister and after living as a poor peasant in Italy, he was welcomed to the court of the king after his true identity was revealed. Although a powerful warrior, Roland's concern with winning honour and fame eventually cost him his life. The story of his death is told in the famous epic The Song of Roland. The poem concerns Charlemagne's defeat by the Muslims in Spain in AD 778. Charlemagne had sent a paladin named Ganelon to negotiate with the Muslim leader. Instead, jealous of Roland, Ganelon plotted with the enemy and revealed the route Roland's army planned to take. The Muslims waited for Roland and ambushed him at Roncesvalles in the Pyrenees mountains. The other paladins told Roland to blow his ivory horn to summon reinforcements from Charlemagne, but Roland refused to call for help until the battle was almost lost. By then it was too late. When Charlemagne's troops arrived, Roland and many of the bravest paladins were dead. At the end of the story, Charlemagne had Ganelon killed for his treachery."

"Why is there always such treachery?" Paul sighed, looking sad.

"'Tis what makes this world I am afraid. Man's selfish ego unfortunately. Too many are afflicted with the selfish attitude of service to self… instead of service to others. 'Tis why I believe you are blessed that you have Thomas and his men…for never in all my years have I ever met such a rabble of noise, bad behaviour, insubordination yet utterly loyal and free of egos, as they are. A truly rare breed, my friend."

"Yes…there is something uniquely odd about them all isn't there," Paul remarked and smiled to himself. "But still you do not answer about what Percy and I saw and about Luke."

"Hmmm. Let me simply tell you that your mother refused to reveal the whereabouts of the sword you now carry. 'Twas known then as Caliburn, which I am sure you know became known as Excalibur, but there are others identical to it…," Theodoric started to explain and waited to see what reaction Paul gave to its former name. "This does not surprise you to hear the sword was once named such?"

"Nothing surprises me any more," Paul replied.

"'Tis a matter for your father to explain to you one day, for only he can explain about your mother."

"Well I also wish to know more about your tattoo for I am certain I saw an identical image of it whilst underground…and I know that so much of what is known about Jesus has either been copied from ancient times or is a continuation of some secret. A secret I am sure is connected to Luke somehow for they told me I must ask you…about Luke?" Paul explained and asked, looking at him intently.

"Luke…I will explain that in a minute after I have briefly, and I do mean briefly, explained a little about Jesus and my tattoo," Theodoric said, checked the wine bottle and poured out the last remnants into his glass. Slowly he drank all that was in his glass and took a deep breath. "Jesus or Egyptian myth? Let me say that both stories tell of a divine son of God battling the evil one. A son is born, an official date given as the winter solstice of December 25th. Born of a virgin called Mary or Mery. Three wise men follow a star in the east…always the east. The Divine son or God is mentioned at ages twelve and thirty and known as the holy baptiser of souls. Both mention a god with twelve followers who perform miracles such as walking on water, raising the dead and healing the sick. God is anointed and Lord of Truth, Lord of Light and Lord of Resurrections. God is associated with the cross, symbolising eternal life. As in the Christian cross based upon the earlier Celtic cross and the Egyptians have the Ankh, the Cross of Life. God or Jesus is buried for three days, resurrecting and ascends into heaven. All of these facts are found within Ancient Egyptian texts and myths thousands of years before Christ…the image of the son

Horus cradled by his mother, Isis, is identical to that of the Virgin Mother and Christ. So many Ancient Egyptian and even older practices and symbols are carried over into Christianity. This is because they are carrying on an ancient sacred set of codes. Just as your father, I and Firgany have tried with additions to the Arthurian romances…but I fear we have not been as successful as we had wished. 'Tis no accident nor coincidence that history repeats itself."

"Well so long as it does not try and repeat itself through Alisha and me… for I swear there have been many times I have looked at her and wondered if she is yet another Mary for she is certainly other worldly. I have seen the effect she has upon people simply by touching them," Paul remarked.

"'Tis natural to worry about such matters, especially when so many strange things have happened to you both. 'Twas the same with your father and mother," Theodoric started to explain but stopped himself, shaking his head no. He laughed quietly to himself for a moment before looking back at Paul. "Let me tell you this…in the Bible, Mark 6:3, Jesus is called a 'Tekton', which is a Greek word meaning woodworker, craftsman, carpenter or builder. Throughout history gods and goddesses have been known as architects, carpenters and craftsman as a symbolic and mythical attribute…never as an actual historical biographic fact. From Ptah of Egypt, to Buddha in India, Yahweh of Judea to Hesus of the Druids. And you…you are known as a navigator…one who will show the way. There is a difference."

"Navigator…," Paul sighed, tired.

"As for my tattoo…'tis known as the twin goddesses of the tree-wings… well near enough translated it means that," Theodoric explained and laughed. "In every human there is a tree, and in every tree there is a human. Just as water, aqua, symbolises our spirit, and the oceans and seas we travel across, so too the forest is the second sea on earth, the sea in which man wanders. The forests work in silence, fulfilling nature's mighty work… working with the winds, cleaning the air, mitigating the climate, forming soil, preserving all our essentials without wearing them out. It represents all that is physical in our world. The World Tree is connected with our own creation, preservation and destruction. It teaches us that trees are bound to the fate of the world. It is up to us to care for our past, to remember that which we have lost, and also to celebrate the flowering world, the present moment, whilst reaching forward to a future possible. And bees…bees, my friend, are the key to it all. When mankind again understands that, then there will be hope for all."

"Apples, bees and harps made from oak…I am slowly taking all onboard that which I am learning," Paul replied and nodded. He pulled the sword closer to himself and ran his fingers over the delicate engravings upon its blade. "This sword needs a bee symbol," he said out loud. But it also needs to be connected with the image of your tattoo."

Theodoric sat back, surprised.

"I have learnt much from Tenno and Attar about swords these past few years. I know that throughout history, famous figures and legendary heroes were said to possess magical swords. Excalibur, for instance, the sword of King Arthur of Camelot…and even perhaps this very sword… whilst the sword Zulfiqar is said to have been sent from the Heavens to the Prophet Muhammad. I know he subsequently handed that weapon to his cousin and son-in-law."

"You now also know of Roland and Durandal. The best-known legend regarding Roland is his last stand at the Battle of Roncevaux, which was an actual historical battle that has now been romanticised into a major battle between Christians and Muslims. It is recounted in the epic poem La Chanson de Roland meaning The Song of Roland. 'Tis an epic poem you should read and acquaint yourself with. It is claimed the sword Durandal was given to Charlemagne by an angel of God, who instructed the emperor to give the sword to one of his counts as you now know. Some claim however that prior to that it had been given to the Trojan hero Hector, but later passed to Roland by the enchanter Malagigi. Regardless of its origins, Durandal was a valuable and powerful sword both physically and symbolically. In fact, the primary objective of the invasion of France by Gradasso, the heathen king of Sericena, is rumoured to be the retrieval of Durandal from Roland."

"'Tis a pity that such tools as you prefer to call them are the cause of such death and chaos," Paul lamented as he studied the sword.

"Aye 'tis that for sure. But at the battle of Roncesvaux, Roland was able to hold back the Muslim army, which was a hundred thousand strong, from attacking Charlemagne's main force. Using Durandal, he slayed a great number of the enemy and even succeeded in chopping off the right hand of the Saracen king, Marsile, and decapitated the king's son, Jursaleu. 'Tis a worthy and noble tale that is perhaps the one thing we can be certain of," Theodoric said quietly.

"Then what of Luke?" Paul asked bluntly.

"Luke's Gospel…it is what he wrote and how he wrote it that is the important fact to remember. For it contains information that will not be relearnt for perhaps hundreds of years still…but it is still all valid as your father, Firgany and I discovered."

"How so?"

"From ancient documents and codes that detail the very world we live upon. When mankind again learns the truths about this world, only then will they be able to see the encoded truths in plain sight all along and it could forever change the way the Bible is read and understood. Let me explain…in the early part of the first century, between AD 20 and 50, Philo of Alexandria developed a set of guidelines for the allegorical interpretation of scripture. Luke used these guidelines to construct his stories…the same guidelines can be used to recover the coded messages."

"But why leave coded messages? Why not just write the stories as they happened?" Paul asked.

"Because by the time Luke wrote his two books, roughly around AD 80, the sect of the Nazarenes were facing a crisis. Their doctrines and teachings had become heresy and their sacred texts were being destroyed. Jesus, a Nazarene, had come to teach the masses the difference between the truths of creation and the superstitions derived from myths and lore used to keep wealth and power in the hands of the few elite. But Rome and the religious leaders of the time would never allow this to happen. Gnosis, which as you know means 'knowledge', became a heresy and Jesus had replaced the sacrifice of animals while the science of Pythagoras and Plato were being obliterated. Luke left his coded messages in the most unexpected of places in plain and obvious sight…in the hands of the powerful who lacked the tools to know what they actually had. Once the books that made up the Bible as decided upon at the Council of Nicea in AD 325, the very 'approved' Bible itself became a Trojan Horse. One of Philo's guidelines for identifying codes was to look for numerical clues. Clement of Alexandria called Philo 'The Pythagorean' because he taught a blend of Judaism and Pythagorean science. By hiding Pythagorean sacred numbers in his gospel, Luke accomplished two things. Firstly, he inserted the presence of the numbers making it easy for someone to detect if the codes could be found in the stories. Secondly, Luke was trained in Pythagorean science and sacred numbers, knowledge that Orthodox Christians in the latter decades of the first century were not permitted to have."

"Then pray tell how does this Bible code work? For I have learnt that there are many hidden within it."

"There are even more that we cannot even fathom yet but our descendants will have the tools to do so. But here, let me explain and show you," Theodoric said and opened his small Bible and flicked through the pages until he came to Luke. "Look here...Luke deliberately scattered numbers throughout the story of John the Baptist in Chapter One." Theodoric pointed with his finger to the page. "Here in Luke 1:24: ...for five months. This gives us our first number as in 5. And here at Luke 1:27: In the sixth month...so we get our second number of 6. And here in Luke 1:36: the sixth month...so we get our third number 6 again. In Luke 1:56: ...about three months...so we get our fourth number 3. Luke 1:59: On the eighth day...so we get our fifth number 8."

"But they can mean anything," Paul interrupted.

"No because look. One of the methods for finding coded messages is to multiply all the numbers in a story. So now from Luke we get 5 x 6 x 6 x 3 x 8 which equals 4,320. One of Pythagoras's favourite and most sacred numbers was 432,000. From what your father and I learnt these values deal with harmonic values but we cannot yet prove that. But the same numbers, same sequence or zeroes can be added or removed and the decimal can be moved right or left. Harmonics were established and taught by Pythagoras and Plato. 432,000 can be found in many ancient cultures and myths that predate Christianity, including Sumerian, Norse, Greek, Egyptian, Indian and others. Most of the myths tell the story of a worldwide catastrophe, usually a flood. 432 is also encoded in Genesis and the story of Noah's flood. 4320 is a very special number in the Pythagorean 'Science of Number' because 4320 divided by 2 equals 2160 which as we discovered is the diameter of the moon. 432,000 times 2 equals 864,000, the diameter of the sun as we have also learnt. Do not worry, Paul, for later generations will establish and confirm these simple truths again. Also 432 times 432 equals 186,624. The speed of light is 186,400 miles per second, a difference of .001201."

"Light has a speed?" Paul asked, bemused.

"Ah...yes. I forget this is still all new to you and you still have so much to learn. Forgive me. I speak of things I was shown and taught a long time ago. 'Tis all very ancient wisdom and ancient knowledge...much of which your father has hidden away safely."

"After all I have seen, I believe you, Theo, so please continue."

"Okay. You are aware that the Nazarenes called themselves Children of Light. Well Luke actually means 'Light'. This opening chapter reveals the one number that, when halved, is associated with the 'night light', when doubled is associated with the 'day light' and when squared is associated with light itself. Luke made it clear in the first chapter that he was a highly trained student of Pythagoras. In addition to the hidden, sacred numbers in Chapter One, Luke left word clues. He introduced the angel Gabriel, who is named in only one other place...The Book of Daniel."

"I see now why my father made me study the Book of Daniel so often," Paul interrupted.

"Naturally. Daniel was an investigator who solved riddles and puzzles. He translated writings and interpreted visions and dreams. Within just a few short verses it becomes obvious Luke was asking Theophilus, defined as 'One who has an affinity for religious truth', to solve the riddles and decipher the codes in Luke–Acts. Both Luke and Acts are addressed to Theophilus. Luke's story of the conception and birth of John the Baptist is taken almost verbatim from the story of the conception and birth of Samson. One bit of information given about Samson was missing from the description of John. Samson was a Nazirite. The Nazirites, like the Nazarenes, were vegetarians, did not cut their hair, and did not drink wine or strong drink. Without using the word Nazarene Luke left no doubt that John the Baptist and Jesus were Nazarenes and that the Nazarenes were unable to talk openly about their beliefs. All the chapters in Luke's Gospel reveal numbers associated with Pythagoras...but time this late hour does not allow me to explain more thoroughly...but I shall in time. Another striking example of the Pythagorean numbers embedded in Luke's Gospel should leave no doubt that it was intentional and required immense expertise. Luke Chapter Nine contains only 15 numbers, 12 x 2 x 12 x 5 x 2 x 5,000 x 50 x 5 x 2 x 12 x 3 x 8 x 2 x 2 x 3, which equals 24,883,200,000,000. This is the diameter of our earth, that is, 7,920 miles. When multiplied by one of Plato's values for pi (864/275) the product is 24,883.2 miles. No first century Christian would have hidden these sacred numbers within a gospel. Only a Pythagorean, Gnostic or Nazarene would have had the knowledge, the expertise or the need to do so. Luke's coded messages also suggest that Jesus did not die on the cross. Jesus and 'Simon the Cyrene' switched places before the crucifixion just as our Muslim friends believe. Luke 23:26...they seized...Simon...and they laid the cross on him, and made him carry it behind Jesus. Luke 23:33...they crucified him there with the criminals... Luke's original words have and are being changed by the Church to hide this fact...such as in Luke 23:33, where 'him' is being changed to Jesus. But the earliest texts show that Luke's original word was 'him', leaving it grammatically more likely that it was Simon, rather than Jesus, who was crucified. Then in Acts 7, just as he is about to be stoned to death, Stephen rambles on for 58 verses about Moses. You will recall the many other Templar connections to the value 58 I am sure. Just two of the 58 verses from Stephen's speech as he is about to die are Acts 7:15–16: ...So Jacob went down to Egypt. He...died there...was brought back to Shechem and laid in the tomb that Abraham had bought for a sum of silver from the sons of Hamor in Shechem. Philo's 'guidelines' include, 'Watch for repetitions and errors'. In addition to repeating Shechem, there's a glaring error in Acts 7:15–16: Luke switched the names. According to Genesis 50:13, Jacob was buried at Hebron, not Shechem. According to Genesis 33:19, it was Jacob, not Abraham, who bought the tomb at Shechem. Luke switched the names, Jacob and Abraham, putting the wrong man in the tomb. He switched the cross from Jesus to Simon...they seized Simon ... laid the cross on him, made him carry it behind Jesus...crucified him there with the criminals. According to Philo's rules for finding coded messages, Jesus, the man believed to be in the tomb, was not in the tomb. In a similar way, Luke reported that Jesus and Mary Magdalene were married and had a daughter. As shocking as these revelations may sound, they become apparent when Philo's rules are applied to Luke's stories. Luke–Acts, read allegorically and following the clues, support the ancient legends about Jesus and Mary Magdalene." [100]

"That is a lot to take in...but I accept what you are telling me. I am not sure people such as Nicholas would be so open and agree with you or accept it," Paul remarked.

"But people like Nicholas are the ones who will guarantee its message is kept and carried forwards," Theodoric replied and folded his arms.

"Is there anything else that you learnt that you know will not be understood until the future?"

"I know that we are mainly made up from water...and that little chains made up from the smallest of parts hold us together. Our physical bodies being just like a cloak we wear around our spiritual forms. I know that just as we cannot shrink back into a child's robe, so too our spiritual bodies cannot shrink backwards as they evolve. I was also shown that the very chains that hold our every part within our bodies are shaped like a cross. That form which holds human beings together is referenced in the Bible, so your father and I were told when we experienced a similar situation to the one you and Percival have just had. We are branded by the cross! He is before all things, and in him all things hold together'; Colossians 1:17...still remember that as if was yesterday," Theodoric explained and sighed again.

Both sat in total silence for several minutes.

"I shall write a poem for Ali before I retire this eve. 'Tis after all her birthday tomorrow and I have no gift to offer her," Paul said as he pulled a sheet of parchment near and looked for his writing set.

"Paul...she has you back. That is gift enough trust me," Theodoric remarked and clenched Paul's arm. "She has suffered a great assault of her senses these past weeks. No deeper a sadness have I ever seen before in a person. It will take her time to heal for all her fears, grief and thoughts of losing you cut her deep."

Paul looked at Theodoric and simply nodded he agreed with him.

"Well I am encouraged to learn that I am not to be any Messiah type figure and Alisha no Mary...," he remarked and ran his fingers through his hair as he sat back.

"No...but you may be a new Arthur whether you like it or not!" Theodoric replied and raised his eyebrows.

"I shall never be a knight, Theo...never."

"You are already that and more. The sooner you realise that, the easier your task shall be."

Paul looked at Theodoric and just stared at him in silence. Tiredness was beginning to overwhelm him but he wanted to at least write Alisha a birthday poem before he retired.

Port of La Rochelle, France, Melissae Inn, spring 1191

"Arthur as in King Arthur?" Gabirol asked.

"The same," the old man replied.

"Poem...did he write her a poem?" Sarah asked, looking excited.

"Yes he did, and before you ask, no I do not have a copy here but I do know the words," the old man replied, smiling as he sat upright.

"Pray tell us it," Ayleth said and nodded at Sarah.

1 - 22

"Pray tell us more on this Arthur for surely he is just a myth," Peter interrupted.

"As I keep saying, all myth is based upon real people and real events. I can explain about Arthur and afterward, for our dear ladies here, I can recount the poem," the old man answered and bowed his head slightly at Ayleth and Sarah.

"Please do, for I need to confirm what you say and as I understand it...that there were two Moseses and two Arthurs," Gabirol said and charged his quill ready to take notes.

"Then know you have listened well and understood correctly."

"That's it...I am lost...again!" Simon joked and folded his arms, shaking his head.

"I want to know if Paul did indeed become a diplomat to help form these Muslim Knight Templars for we have heard many rumours of such," the Templar remarked.

"I will have to repeat certain elements I have already covered so forgive me for that. What is little known about the Templars, the information hidden within historical records, is that the Templar Order has held its own autonomous ecclesiastical authority since its inception, carrying multiple lines of ancient priesthoods with full legitimacy under Canon law. I did explain this as Theodoric detailed it. These priesthoods have been preserved by the Knights Templar as the Ancient Priesthood of Solomon. This Ancient Priesthood of Solomon embodies the most ancient traditions of the Biblical Melchizedek, and the ancient Gnostic traditions of the Essenes of which Jesus the Nazarene was a High Priest, together with the medieval priesthood of the Gnostic Cathars. This is why I fear for the Cathars for the Church will not allow it to continue. But that bridge we must cross later should it happen. This Ancient Solomonic Priesthood is constitutionally maintained as a separate institution within the Templar Order. Count Henry presently presides over it and it is the same priesthood as that of the Biblical Magi, including the legendary 'Magi of the East' who visited upon the birth of Christ. As established by the historical record this consists of the most ancient institutional priesthood in known human history, carrying an original spiritual tradition of over 12,000 years, dating back to 10,068 BC. This most ancient sacred priesthood is essentially the Magi Priesthood of the biblical Melchizedek, descending from seven sources of Magistral succession since 10,068 BC...here look," the old man said and pushed a small vellum sheet toward Gabirol.

"May I copy this?" Gabirol asked.

"Of course," the old man replied.

(1) original biblical Melchizedek Magi Kings from 10,068 BC;

(2) ancient Persian Magi Knights from 10,068 BC;

(3) ancient Egyptian Djedhi Magi Priests from 5,500 BC;

(4) ancient Sumerian Magi Fisher Priests from 3,500 BC;

(5) the Essenes ca. 250 BC through the Holy See of Antioch ca. AD 33;

(6) original Al-Banna Magi Sufi Order from AD 825;

(7) original Syrian Hashashin Sufi Order from AD 1080.

"What...it states here the last two are Sufic...even Hashashin," Gabirol noted, surprised.

"Indeed. But let me continue...this priesthood also carries the original ancient Gnostic tradition, which underlies the earliest form of Christianity, descending from an additional seven sources of priestly succession since AD 33," the old man explained and pushed a second vellum sheet to Gabirol.

(1) the Nazarene Essene Priesthood of Jesus from AD 33;

(2) Saint Mark the Apostle;

(3) Saint Thomas the Apostle;

(4) Saint Mary Magdalene the Disciple (and Gnostic Apostle) of Jesus;

(5) Saint Thecla the Disciple (and Gnostic Apostle) of the Apostle Peter;

(6) the Gnostic Church of the Cathars from AD 1054;

(7) Saint Bernard de Clairvaux the patron saint of the Knights Templar from AD 1129.

"So you are saying that all these fourteen sources of priestly and ecclesiastical authority constitute direct lines of initiatory Magistral succession?" Gabirol asked.

"Yes and each in turn additionally perfected by authenticity of doctrinal succession. This establishes a substantial level of ecclesiastical authority as a historical institution, effectively meeting the standards and criteria of the Vatican and Orthodox Churches under traditional Canon Law as it stands."

"But that would mean that the Ancient Priesthood of Solomon of the Templar Order is genuinely the direct continuation of a 12,000 year old priesthood, possibly the oldest ecclesiastical authority in recorded human history that goes beyond the creation of the world as recounted within the Bible. 'Tis a contradiction surely?" Gabirol protested.

"There is no contradiction when the Bible is read and understood properly... codes and all," the old man replied, winked and smiled. "The priesthood of Ancient Egypt was the central institution for academic knowledge and sciences. Science and

religion were always in perfect harmony and spirituality itself was considered a discipline of science. The Pharaonic Temples actually served as universities teaching mathematics, astronomy, architectural engineering and other sciences, also serving as a medical school. The Egyptian priesthood even invented the practice of surgery. Authentic to that true history, the doctrines and practices within the Ancient Priesthood of Solomon include scholarship of the physics of classical esoteric knowledge. This involves energy sciences of the mechanics of consciousness, as applied to priestly sacraments, divine communion and meditation, workings of the Holy Spirit and related visitations and manifestations of spirit."

"No wonder the Church is worried about the Templars for they compete directly against them for authority," the farrier remarked.

"Believe it or not that despite the formidable basis, wealth of priestly heritage and legitimacy of the Templar Order's ecclesiastical authority, they have never sought to compete with the Vatican or other Churches, but consistently choose only to support them," the old man explained. "Although the Knights Templar know their Order is vested with the ecclesiastical authority of the Holy See of Antioch and the Ancient Priesthood of Solomon, they mostly build churches only for the Vatican or Celtic Church. The Templars only built churches or monasteries for themselves when necessary to serve as a working facility, to support the operations of a Commandery. And true to the Gnostic doctrines and ancient spirituality of its priesthood, the Order does not exercise its ecclesiastical authority in the form of a Church, and thus does not operate any standing churches with congregations. Instead, Templar Knights are sworn to be protectors of the original spirituality which is the basis for all religion, dedicated to supporting established Churches of ***all*** *denominations and religious Orders of other traditions...including Islam."*

"So where does King Arthur come into this?" Simon asked.

"Much popular awareness and a significant part of the public image of the Templars has and is being shaped and promoted by the Arthurian tales. Chretien de Troyes for a start certainly does this well. The many portrayals of knights in shining armour fighting to champion noble causes, and always pursuing deeply spiritual Quests, seeking profound esoteric wisdom by pursuing or protecting the Holy Grail, are all an artistic expression of the genuine traditional values and religious beliefs of the Templars. The Arthurian legends have their own historical value as symbolic esoteric teachings. But separate from this, however, is the identity and factual history of a real historical figure, who was later transformed into the legendary King Arthur of Camelot as many of you know," the old man said and moved in his chair stretching his legs beneath the table.

"I always believed he was real," Ayleth stated.

"And he is, and just like Jesus he too has had much added upon his shoulders. Official royal records of Alba reveal that when Columba, a Catholic priest, performed the induction ceremony for the coronation of King Aidan of Dalriada in AD 574, Aidan's eldest son was Arthur, indicating that he was born in AD 559. The second reference to Arthur in a historical context was in a ninth century Latin text, the 'Historia Brittonum', which reported Arthur as 'dux bellorum' meaning 'war commander', fighting alongside the kings of the Britons against the invading Picts and Saxons. In this work, the chronological order of the appearance of Arthur in between other dated events indicates the peak of Arthur's notable activities as during the early to middle sixth century AD. The third historical record of Arthur using the Celtic spelling Artuir was in the eleventh century Irish 'Annals of Tighernac', which reports 'Death of the sons of Aidan' including Arthur at the battle of Chirchind, in which Aidan was victorious. This account confirms that Arthur was the son of the Scottish King Aidan, and that he died in a battle allied with Briton kings fighting against the Picts and the Saxons."

"Hmmm, this is not what I have been taught," Gabirol remarked as he wrote some notes.

"These records are all available for scrutiny and genuine...and it is because of them being so historically significant, they became attributed with inspiring and leading to most of the later Arthurian legends telling various symbolic tales of King Arthur and the Knights of the Round Table, and their Quests for the Holy Grail. But now with added esoteric additions to continue the codes of antiquity."

"And you say all this is written within authentic documents?" Gabirol asked.

"Yes. The connection between the historical Prince Arturius Aidan and the legendary King Arthur is confirmed by an eighth century manuscript, 'The Martyrology of Oengus the Culdee'. It contains a clear reference to Morgan as the daughter of King Aidan, being the half-sister, same word as for 'sister', of Arturius. This matches the legendary King Arthur having a sister, Morganna, the feminine grammar for Morgan as a woman's name, also known as Morgan Le Fey, simply adding The Fairy as a title of honour after the same name Morgan. Arthur Aidan's mother was reported to be Ygerna del Acqs, better known as Igrain, the High Queen of the Celtic kingdoms. Accordingly, Arthur's grandmother was Vivien del Acqs, the Queen of Avalon and a High Priestess of the ancient Celtic religion. Arthur's father, King Aedan, was the son of King Gabran and Lluan of Brecknock, and Lluan was reported to be a direct descendant of the Biblical Joseph of Arimathea, thereby entitling King Aedan mac Gabran to the title of Pendragon, which means Chief

Warrior, being a king higher than other kings to unite them. The name Merlin was also a title, which meant Seer to the King, a position which was reserved for a High Priest of the Celtic religion. One person of many at different times who held the title Merlin was Emrys of Powys, the son of Aurelius, and Emrys was an elder cousin to King Aedan, Arthur's father. But you all here now know the original name and person behind the name Mer EL In," the old man said and looked at their expressions before continuing. "Arthur had three brothers, Eochaid Find, Eochaid Buide and Domingart. Since Arthur was the eldest son and Crown-Prince, however, Merlin was assigned to mentor, guide and train Arthur. Therefore, although Arthur was not an only child and not without a living father, the legendary accounts in stories that Merlin raised Arthur from childhood are a fair description which does not contradict the historical record. These facts placed Prince Arthur Aidan in the unique position of being both ancient Celtic royalty and biblical and Catholic royalty, simultaneously. Merlin became a title of respect like the Caesars after Caesar in Rome. This made Arthur the embodiment of balance and reconciliation between the developing Catholicism and the ancient Celtic religion, resulting in their effective merger into the medieval form of the Celtic Church. The battle in which Arthur died was variously called the battle of Miathi, of Manann, of Chirchind and of Camlann. None of the four historical accounts specify the location, but all of them describe the same royal Arthur leading the same battle against the same invaders, thereby confirming that it happened in the same place. The varied historical references to King Arthur's death at this battle are reasonably close considering the prevailing practices of mostly oral history during that time period, around AD 589. Arthur's birth in AD 559, becoming Commander at age sixteen in AD 575, and beginning of active battles at age seventeen in AD 576 would make him 30 years old at the time of his death around AD 589, having a total of fourteen years of military experience by that time. That timeline and resulting level of experience would explain how that last battle he led was victorious, despite his being killed in the process. Therefore, reliable and verifiable historical evidence does establish that, in fact, the legendary King Arthur was the Celtic Crown-Prince Arturius Aidan of Scotland, AD 559–589, who facilitated establishment of the Celtic Church, which integrated Catholicism with ancient Celtic spirituality."

"So where is Camelot as I thought we already covered that and it was in Colchester...isn't it?" Peter asked bluntly.

"As many here know, the land of the Arthurian legends was known as Avalon, described as an island. Avalon was most notably described by the renowned British–Welsh poet, Bard Taliesin. He was the author of fifty-six Welsh manuscripts

from the sixth century. He himself has become a legendary mythic hero, now a contemporary companion of Bran the Blessed and King Arthur. Most scholars who translated the sixth century manuscripts assumed that they were written in Old French, instead of the Old German Celtic languages they were originally written in. Thus, Bard Taliesin's description of Avalon as Insula Pororum Fortunata was mistranslated as Old French for Island of Apples, even disregarding the significance of the third word, which was omitted from translations. However, since Taliesin in his time spoke ancient Celtic, his words Insula Pororum Fortunata originally meant an Island by the Sea, one characterised by abundance, Fortunata. This full and more accurate translation is additionally supported by various accounts of the profuse vegetation on the island of Avalon, and the inhabitants accordingly living long life spans."

"So I ask again, where is Avalon?" Peter demanded, his tone impatient.

"Peel Castle on Saint Peter's Isle on the Isle of Man, 'Ellin Vannin', is one of the main historical sites of the legendary Arthurian 'Avalon'. The ancient Celtic name for the Isle of Man, in its native Manx language, is Ellin Vannin, literally the Island by the Sea. This shows that the Isle of Man was exactly the same place with the same ancient name as described by Bard Taliesin in his own native language, thus being the true historical location of Avalon of the Arthurian legends. In the Arthurian legends, Guinevere's father was named King Orry. Chretien de Troyes, a Templar by the way, and Marie de France found the name Orry to come from the Manx word Gorrie, clearly identifying the Isle of Man. That fact also explains the otherwise strange spelling of the name Guinevere, which is actually a Pictish name. During the historical time period of Arthur, the Picts were ruling the Isle of Man. The Irish Annals of Ulster documented in the historical record a battle of Manann, described as identical to the battle of Miathi fought by Arthur against the Picts as established in the Scottish 'Vita Sancti Columbae'. The battle of Miathi and the battle of Manann are identifiable as the same event, because the Miathi Picts lived in the Ochill Hills, directly opposite Manann, which is the ancient Celtic name of the Isle of Man."

"So in short, Arthur fought and died in that battle which took place on the Isle of Man?" Gabirol asked.

"In short yes. Saint Patrick's Isle, the three-sided island with 'crooked banks', Isle of Man. The tenth century 'Annales Cambriae' manuscripts referred to the place where Arthur died as the battle of Camlann. The name Camlann is a Celtic version of the Old English word Camboglanna meaning crooked bank, and the Celtic word Camlann is similar to the Manx Manann. Therefore, the description

of a crooked bank refers to a bank or shore of the Isle of Man. There is one particular part of the Isle of Man that has a mini island off the west side of the main isle. This part is called Saint Patrick's Isle, whereupon stands the castle built by the Vikings...Peel Castle. The small separation between the Isle of Man and its adjunct Saint Patrick's Isle creates a sort of river with crooked banks on both sides, and the sea side of the mini isle itself prominently features a wide stretch of crooked bank."

"Then why is this not told as part of the legends for all to know?" Ayleth asked, puzzled.

"Because the story would become dull and boring," the old man replied. "Peel Castle on the Isle of Man was used by the historical Arthur and his Knights of the Round Table. Thus, the report of Arthur's final battle at Camlann is consistent with the seventh century Scottish record in 'Vita Sancti Columbae', indicating that it took place at Manann, on the Isle of Man. The small mini island of Saint Patrick bearing Peel Castle was a very important strategic holy site for the early Catholic Church, such that the Pope sent Saint Germanus to that site in the fifth century, to begin integrating the pagan Celtics to Christianity. Saint Patrick after whom the mini island was named led worship and preached there in AD 444. Perhaps more significantly, if Saint Patrick's Isle at the Isle of Man was the historical site of the Arthurian Avalon, then Peel Castle itself would be the headquarters of the legendary King Arthur and his kingdom and royal court affectionately known in the later medieval tales as Camelot. But as you should understand, the very first original Camelot was indeed that of the ancient town of Colchis with all its connections to Jason and the Golden Fleece...but in more modern times it was re-seated. For in our recent times Avalon, the Grail Castle and Arthur's third castle, Galoches, were all in fact on the Isle of Man. But the Camelot or Camulod in Colchester, the very first Camelot, there still lies a secret connected to Orion and Sirius," the old man remarked with a smile. [101]

"I know of the three legged emblem you mention for I have seen it upon many a knight's saddle bags that have passed through this way," the farrier commented.

"That does not surprise me. The Isle of Man has an official three-legged heraldry, labelled 'Whichever Way You Throw It, It Stands' in Latin. This was confirmed by the British lawyer, scholar, Vatican ecclesiast and Canon Law advisor to King Henry the Second, Gervase of Tilbury, who is still alive this day, who described King Arthur in a royal establishment, explaining that the palace was located on a three sided, three legged island. As a consequence many English knights have adopted the emblem when heading for the Holy Lands. The symbol from its most ancient Celtic times is three

legs joined at the thighs. It is also relevant and interesting that all factual historical data for the real Prince Arthur Aidan who later became the legendary King Arthur was recorded primarily only in the Emerald Isle and Alba, equally. This fact is significant, because the Isle of Man is located in the sea at equal distance from the Emerald Isle and Alba, and is the only part of Britain that has experienced several millennia of mixing Irish and Scottish culture, while alternating Irish and Scottish rule, before the British later got involved with the territory."

"So basically what you are saying is that the Isle of Man is the location of the most recent Arthurian Avalon?" Simon asked.

"Yes. But also keep in mind that a far more ancient castle of his was in Camulud, the old Roman Town of Camuludinum, Colchis as already mentioned. In Latin the D and T are interchangeable so the step from Camulud to Camulut is not a long one, as I have previously explained during the telling of this tale."

"I know that much of what is written about the Grail romances comes from Chretien de Troyes as you state, most written in about AD 1188, and was produced in the very city where Templarism was born, Troyes...yes?" Gabirol asked.

"Yes. He was given much assistance by Philip and others at that time...to ensure the messages of antiquity were and are carried forwards," the old man explained. "It was at the Council of Troyes here in France in AD 1127, where Bernard de Clairvaux established the Roman Catholic Cistercian rule of the Templar Order. Subsequent Grail stories have since emanated from various parts of Europe, and many of them mention Templar, or Templar styled knights, and espouse their virtues as holy knights. From the first to last, Templars have written or have sanctioned many of the Grail stories. It is the very same Chretien de Troyes whose translations from ancient Celtic Gaelic identified the Isle of Man as the historical location of the legendary Avalon. Accordingly, it is as one of the original second generation of Knights Templar that Chretien de Troyes began the tradition of Arthurian legends embodying ancient mythology and sacred wisdom, possessing a connection to factual academic knowledge of the true historical Prince Arthur Aidan of the sixth century."

"So what legends shall be wrapped around Alisha and Paul?" Sarah asked.

"Hopefully...none. In order to protect them and their future line," the old man answered. "Legends of the Holy Grail have become popular though it has come to be associated with the cup from which Christ drank at the Last Supper, its true origins, now supposedly lost in the mists of prehistory, as a sacred cauldron. The concept of the sacred cauldron however is essentially a Celtic metaphor for true esoteric spiritual alchemy, tracing back to the ancient Pharaonic Egyptian priesthood and simultaneously the ancient Celtic Druid civilisation of Western Europe," the old man explained.

"So am I correct if I say that the earlier Arthurian knights are based upon Templars, but they were in fact also Celtic priests who pre-dated Christianity?" Gabirol asked.

"You could indeed state that. You can also link the pre-Christian Knights of the Round Table to the Gnostic heretics of the fourth century, who managed to pass on their secret knowledge to the founding Templars. The ancient tradition of alchemy was the Quest or search by scientific or spiritual exploration for the philosopher's stone, which would give enlightenment. The connection of alchemy and the philosopher's stone to the fabled Holy Grail of the knights is now soon to be demonstrated at Chartres Cathedral in France, being financed and built by Templars of the Order of the Temple of Solomon. In Chartres Cathedral, a scene of Melchizedek presenting the Communion sacrament, which by biblical definition is supposed to be bread and wine, to Abraham will be depicted in a statue at the northern entrance, called the Gate of the Initiates. In this sculpture, Melchizedek is presenting a stone within a sacred Grail chalice, thereby clearly signifying that the knightly Holy Grail is in fact the philosopher's stone of alchemy. While thinly veiled in well-known symbolism this association of the Holy Sacrament with the Holy Grail as the alchemical Quest for the philosopher's stone is considered heretical at this time. Nonetheless, this evidence demonstrates that this concept is in fact part of the core Templar beliefs and secret teachings."

"And it is all connected to Egypt and that pyramid building...with the symbolic sword of knowledge and wisdom being drawn from it...as in Excalibur being drawn from the stone," Simon remarked.

"There he goes again," the Genoese sailor commented, looking at him surprisedly.

"Are you sure you simply don't play the fool when in fact you are incredibly bright?" Gabirol asked him.

"Why...what did I say wrong?" Simon protested.

"Nothing at all, Simon," the old man said, shaking his head. "Let me finish on this matter of King Arthur, the once and future King, as was Christ likened and also named. You see the ancient Gnostic esoteric knowledge of the Cathars which is at the core of Templarism is itself central to the alchemical enlightenment associated with the Holy Grail. One of the Arthurian legend stories tells of a Lady Esclarmonde who assumes the form of a white dove, which escaped and flew over the walled crest in order to carry the Holy Grail away from the persecutors of the Gnostic Cathars. This legendary figure I can tell you is none other than Esclarmonde de Foix, who was born in 1151 and already considered by some as a saint within some existing Gnostic Churches."

"I have heard of this woman...," Peter remarked.

"So who rules over Avalon now?" Ayleth asked.

"The Isle of Man was re-established as a Celtic kingdom in AD 1079 by the Celtic

warrior King Godred Crovan, who was also king of Dublin and the Irish and some Scottish isles. Thus, 490 years after the death of Prince Arthur, Godred Crovan reclaimed and ruled the Isle of Man for the Celts from AD 1079 to 1095, when he died. A parallel line of ancestry of the Independent Kingdom of Mann comes from Count Fulk of Anjou (AD 1090–1143), the king of Jerusalem succeeding Baldwin the Second. King Fulk was one of the original founding knights of the Order of the Temple of Solomon in AD 1118 and was part of its original sovereign patronage of the Order from the kings of Jerusalem. The descendants of King Fulk flowed through several lines of British kings, including King Henry the Second of Anjou, who died only last year, in AD 1189. Note, one of the most prominent scholars to establish that King Arthur, Avalon and Camelot were all located on the Isle of Man is the British lawyer Gervase of Tilbury, who also served under King Henry the Second of Anjou as a royal advisor. King Henry the Second, through his father Count Geoffrey the Fifth of Anjou, was directly related to King Fulk of Anjou."

"Will it ever again be recognised as Avalon?" Ayleth asked.

"Perhaps...but it is no longer important that it should be. Like Lyonesse that sank, places change, but the memories linger...like the Druids...they may be long since gone from walking among us, openly at least, but their legacy lingers. And in time even they may return," the old man explained.

"I want to know what Paul's second poem said," Sarah interrupted loudly, which made Stephan laugh.

"Before I recount his poem, let me remind you that bees are symbols of the Virgin Mary throughout the known world. In the Slavonic folk tradition the bee is linked with the Immaculate Conception. July 26th, being the feast of Saint Anna, mother of Mary, whose birth also resulted from an immaculate conception, is the time when beekeepers pray for the conception of new healthy bees. Note, if you did not know or remember, Alisha was born on the 26th of July. Paul knew this and it is why he drew a stylised bee, which was later engraved upon this sword. Two people entwined as one as a bee!"

Fig. 61: Two Entwined as a Bee Symbol.

PART XI

Chapter 61
A Darkness Falls

Cairo, Egypt, July 26th 1183

Paul gently shook Alisha as she lay sleeping. Long beams of sunlight shone brightly through the wooden slats of the main window. Seeing the sun like this always reminded him of his home in La Rochelle. The single white sheet that lay over Alisha was pushed down to her waist. Her nightshirt pulled across her tummy with her hand resting upon it, the bump looking larger than when she stood. Gently Paul placed his hand upon her tummy and felt the slight movement of a small foot or hand push upward from the baby inside. Alisha stirred but did not open her eyes simply turning her head away, her hair falling beside her revealing the almost white skin on her neck. She had not been outside much whilst Paul had been missing. He looked at her and his heart sank. He had hurt the one woman he loved more than his own life following a stupid and selfish desire to find answers he thought would somehow help. Well he had found one answer and that was the knowledge that never again would he put himself at such risk knowing the pain and sorrow it had brought to their door. In his left hand he held a small vellum scroll rolled up and tied with a short crimson band. He had only just finished a new poem for her. Carefully he placed it on the pillow and quietly moved away. Alisha turned over just as Paul shut the door. She saw the small scroll and gently picked it up. She rolled onto her back, untied the crimson binding and slid it off and held it up. Carefully she unfurled the scroll and read the words.

7 - 19

'In the darkness, 'twas your light that guided me to follow what was right. When all seemed lost and hopeless, 'twas your beauty that always shone so bright. You always bring me life and joy instead of strife and I grow prouder every day knowing you are my wife. Every day and every night, I think of you, and because of you, I will never give up the fight doing what is right. Though at times we may be apart, the sense of your beauty stops my very heart, and as time goes on, if I am lost or gone, my touch you can no longer feel, know that your heart and soul will heal for my love remains forever real. I love you truly, wholly, completely and solely. And if alone you one day should stand…without me there to hold your hand, then know as the waters break on the shore, so then will I be there…maybe out of sight, but lost no more. You saw the cathedral ruined and bare, but you will make it anew…a church of love and empathy so fair…for all to remember what was once sacred, ancient and we all knew. Should you cast the white lily and the red rose on the point, of La Rochelle or any shore of ancient lore, it will show the message from a time before has survived and is remembered by more and more. Then I know I will again stand by your side, eternally yours for that we sought evermore!'

She looked at the symbol Paul had drawn on the bottom of the sheet of what looked like two people face to face, but their bodies forming the shape of a bee. She held the scroll close to her chest and closed her eyes. She took a deep breath and sighed, a single tear rolling down her cheek falling onto the pillow.

"Oh my dear Paul…these words will not keep you with me for your vow you cannot keep. Our Lord has plans for you that I cannot stop…," she said quietly to herself as another tear ran down her face. She held the scroll to her lips and kissed it. "Kratos knows for he has seen it. I thought it was this time." She began to cry and rolled onto her side. "But I swear my vow to thee this day…I will always, always wait for you…no matter how long the parting," she said determined to control her emotions, holding the scroll to her lips and kissing it again. She started to shake as she gave in to her feelings, the emotions of the past weeks finally being released fully and she cried quietly.

Outside the door, Paul stepped away having heard all she had just said. His throat was tight and he nearly coughed, his mouth dry. He felt humbled and honoured that he had her love but also felt the guilt weigh heavy upon his heart.

ꟷ

Paul acknowledged Sister Lucy as he walked through the main dining area and out through the side door. It was still early with only the odd cough coming from Thomas's men opposite in their dormitory. Paul sat down on one of the wooden benches near the stables and sighed. What exactly had Kratos told Alisha? he wondered. How was he going to make things right with her and be happy and have fun again? Everything seemed so serious and urgent these days and what career could he do now? He was about to close his eyes when Theodoric appeared walking toward him.

"Paul, I forgot to mention last eve...whilst you were away, Gerard has become the Templars' overall Seneschal...his return after the naval engagement only served to enhance his prestige and image somewhat," he explained quietly.

"Oh great. I help him escape only for him to fight another day and hand him more power," Paul remarked, shaking his head disapprovingly. "What else has happened I should know about then?" Paul asked and sat back, closing his eyes and resting his head against the wall.

Adrastos started to snort loudly upon hearing Paul's voice, which made him smile.

"Someone else who missed you," Theo remarked and sat beside him. "Much indeed has happened I am afraid."

"Then please pray tell me," Paul said, his eyes still closed, the sun shining down upon his face.

"You know many Templars, including two senior commanders, were executed in Damascus as Saladin had to...in order to demonstrate his control after Reynald's little sea going adventures, which has been seen by many as selfish and foolhardy...however, men like Bernard Hamilton are claiming loudly it was actually shrewd strategy on his part, meant to damage Saladin's prestige and reputation. Plus a new general tax has just been levied throughout the kingdom, which is unprecedented in Jerusalem and almost all of Europe. Fear not we are not subject to it here," Theodoric explained.

"Why a new tax?"

"Why do you think?...to help pay for larger armies for the next few years. More troops are needed, since Saladin has finally gained control of Aleppo whilst you were away, and with peace in his northern territories it is feared he could focus on Jerusalem in the south. Reynald, Gerard and Guy are certainly scare mongering to convince all that Saladin will attack Jerusalem. King Baldwin is unfortunately incapacitated by his leprosy, so it was deemed necessary to appoint a regent," Theodoric paused. "And guess who that is?"

"No idea," Paul replied and opened his eyes to look at him.

"Guy de Lusignan…as he is Baldwin's legal heir and the king is not expected to live."

"Guy…of all people!" Paul said, surprised.

"Yes…the utterly 'inexperienced' Guy. He has led his army against Saladin's incursions into the kingdom a few times, but neither side has made any real gains. Guy has been criticised for not striking against Saladin when he had the chance, mainly Reynald and Gerard of course who are pushing for all out war."

"So it will not be safe to remain here for much longer then?" Paul asked and sat up straight.

"Oh as long as Saladin remains in power, we are quite safe here. There are many Jews and Christians here who stayed during many a previous campaign. That will not change. Besides, Saladin will need Alisha to send more dresses."

"What…why dresses?" Paul asked, bemused.

"He has one particular lady he loves beyond all others. She in turn loves the dresses Alisha and Nyla make. Now you have returned, perhaps she can catch up on her orders. Oh, and Isabella is betrothed to marry Princess Stephanie's son, Humphrey, in October. You have an invite," Theodoric said and looked at Paul with a frown. "My advice…do not accept the invitation."

"Well I must decide upon what work I should do as I know my career as a ship builder is but finished…medicine I think."

"Husam had messengers inform him daily on your disappearance. He spared no expense or troops in his search for you. He had half the labourers arrested and held for nearly a month believing foul play had been made against you. He will be made aware of your return before this day is out."

"Arrested…if I had know just one visit would cause so much heartache and chaos, I would never have ventured below the pyramids."

"Paul…yes you would," Theodoric said and raised his eyebrows at him. "So long as you got answers to what you sought."

"That is just it. I was told that which I must not do, but not what I should do," Paul sighed and shook his head.

"You may be a navigator now, but sometimes you have no control over where the seas of life will take you. Sometimes you just have to hang on and let the winds of fate take you with ease rather than fight it."

"Me…the navigator. That was once my father's designation and now Count Henry's. 'Tis not mine."

"Like it or not, you are the navigator as I said last eve. You will realise that soon enough…soon enough," Theodoric said and stood up. "Breakfast?"

"Yes please…and afterward I would like you to accompany me to the sword smith's foundry."

"Why?"

"Because I aim to have the bee emblem I drew last eve etched upon this," Paul answered and placed his hand upon his sword. "And I also want a better faithful rendition of your tree-wing tattoo etched on it too…please," Paul replied and looked at Theodoric with an intensity Theodoric had never seen before. "If it will let me of course for it has a mind of its own."

"Aye lad…we can do that," Theodoric said, but clearly surprised.

Port of La Rochelle, France, Melissae Inn, spring 1191

"Ah so that is how the final symbols became etched upon the blade," Ayleth said aloud and leaned over and pulled the sword toward her. Carefully she clasped her hand around the handle and slowly eased the sword from its scabbard. She noticed the corner was indeed covered in tear marks but had been repaired from when Paul had fallen down the tunnel. "The tree-wings symbol touches me the most profoundly," she remarked as she studied the delicate etching.

"So what job did he decide upon?" the wealthy tailor asked.

"For a few weeks he did nothing but remain in his study writing up notes and making a few drawings…some of which he had been told he should not produce. He spent as much time with Alisha and Arri as he could…though in truth Alisha spent a lot of time with Nyla running their business and catching up on orders. Husam sent word he would return and hoped Paul would be advanced with his new ship, but Paul simply copied his original plans and altered them slightly…but never instructed the carpenters at the dock to start building it. Time was running out for Paul and he knew he had to make a decision soon enough as to where their future lay. But he also had to consider everyone

else. Theodoric, Sister Lucy, Ishmael, Percival and Nyla...and of course Thomas and his men. Whatever decision he made, it would affect them all."

"Did he attend the wedding Princess Stephanie invited him too?" Sarah asked.

"No...but I shall come to that shortly," the old man answered.

"What manner of drawings did he produce that he should not have?" Gabirol asked.

"Mainly to do with the projection of Sirius over Giza, Cygnus marking the old entrance where he and Percival escaped and details on the 'Zep Tepi', 'First Time' or Golden Era which he wrote down as being around 36,000 years BC. He even wrote that all major monuments of Giza were built before the Dynastic Age to celebrate the Age of Osiris rule. He detailed that on the vernal equinox 10,500 BC Al Nitak is not on the meridian and not connected to the Great Pyramid and that Sirius was under the horizon. Planets have not a symbolic arrangement. This hints that Sirius is hidden...so where Sirius is projected is the location of the Hall of Records. Paul tried to write these details down in a manner that later men would be able to work out. But the consequences of doing so would in time have profound and dangerous repercussions."

"I am not sure I follow you," Gabirol stated, looking unusually puzzled.

"Well what hope have we if you do not?" Simon laughed.

"I shall try to explain better," the old man said. "At the dawn of the vernal equinox, the Lion constellation Leo and the Sphinx are closely connected to the East. The Orion constellation is on the celestial meridian, exactly above the pyramids. Most importantly, it's a perfect connection between Al Nitak, the largest star of the belt of Orion and the Great Pyramid, the biggest monument in the Giza plateau. The seven known planets are positioned along the ecliptic in a perfect row, fixing the beginning of the New Era. Just below the ecliptic, the new moon gives way to sunrise, symbolising the rebirth of the New Light that will flood the land of Egypt, bringing lifeblood for new crops. Within a few moments, the moon followed the Sun God, Ra, through its astronomical move...while all courtiers, the planets, waiting for him, were darkened by its vitality. In its rising path, the Sun God, Ra, had its first stop at the foot of the Lion constellation-Sphinx, where it met Jupiter, the Temple of Valley. Jupiter symbolises the Father of the Gods, and it's an expressive symbol of justice. At Giza in 36,400 BC only, the Lion constellation meets Mercury and Jupiter. The two mysterious temples on Giza have planets' proportional values...the Sun God, Ra, then meets Mercury, represented by the Temple of the Sphinx, the Messenger of the Gods, ready to accomplish its function as marking the beginning of the Zep Tepi. The arrangement of two planets in conjunction with the star Regulus has an amazing meaning. Looking at the Sphinx, there are two temples at its feet characterised by colossal and mysterious columns that were built at the same time as the pyramids and represent Jupiter and Mercury. Lastly, the sun meets Mars, the red planet,

symbolising power. It is time to establish the rule over the universe, sitting on the throne of the sky, so as for Osiris when he ruled over the land of Egypt, starting the Age of the Zep Tepi. Now, the Sun God, Ra, is at the zenith. Everything has been accomplished according to the laws of astronomy. Passing the zenith, the Sun God, Ra, goes through the ecliptic, in the southwest quadrant, where Saturn is waiting. Observing the astronomical maps, some of which were recovered by the original Templars, a curious detail strikes...all planets whose names are associated with the days of the week are on the ecliptic. It is very intriguing to note that the planet of rest, Saturn–Saturday, is located exactly in the southwest quadrant, the place of death for Ancient Egyptians. The disposition of Saturn is very telling for in Hebrew traditions they consider Saturday as the day of rest, dedicating it to celebrating the Lord. It means that Hebrew traditions were most likely influenced by memories of Zep Tepi, which is not surprising considering all the connections I have discussed with you so far." [102]

"But we have no way of proving the validity of these details," Peter stated.

"No...just like you have no way of proving the validity of the Bible itself except by blind faith alone," the old man replied. "We know how ancient texts of pyramids told us about connections between the star Sirius and the goddess Isis. She played a great role after the death of Osiris, at the climax of the Zep Tepi. So, when Giza was projected, the builders gave her a key role; they built a monument to celebrate the goddess who preserved Egypt. The monument is located southeast of the Sphinx, known today as the Tomb of Khentkhaus...but this is not its true name and origin. Alas it will be many hundreds of years before mankind has the tools and methods to fully understand and accept the reality of the information. Especially when so many will misinterpret what the ancient writings actually say."

"In what manner?" Gabirol asked.

"Cheops or Khufu who we are told built the Great Pyramid...is an utter rubbish statement for even he himself admits, as written upon a great stele, tells how he simply cleared the area, repaired certain parts and claimed it as his own. The oldest ancient book, the 'Virgin of the World', tells us clearly that the Giza pyramids were already there at the dawn of their civilisation. Also how he found the Temple of Isis that was beside the pyramid near the temple of the Sphinx. But where? In 36,450 BC an astronomical map would show Sirius is just above the horizon between the Lion and Orion constellations. The Tomb of Khentkhaus has the following strange properties. The lower part was built at the same time as the pyramids and Sphinx and the lower part of the tomb has water erosion just like the Sphinx; its base is entirely carved in the rock and has a spiral shape. Its transposition on a plane surface is equal to the orbital movement of Sirius."

"Meaning?" Simon asked, confused.

"Meaning the lower part of the Khentkhaus tomb is the ancient throne of Isis! Or at least represents her. It is just part of the hermetic message that the lost civilisation who designed and built Giza wanted to convey. In the Age of Leo, the Lion, an extraordinary event took place. This event marked the climax of an amazingly developed civilisation that managed to colonise emerged lands and whose fingerprints have resisted the passing of time, but who wished to leave a record of their presence on earth," the old man explained.

"So what you are saying is that the entire Giza complex, including hidden passages and hidden chambers, like the one with twelve chambers as Paul saw, was designed and constructed around 36,000 years before Christ...but that a time marker to indicate Sirius by the positions of the planets and stars was set to coincide with 10,500 BC to show Sirius as Isis was hidden beneath the ground in relation to where Sirius would be upon the ground...yes?" Gabirol commented.

"Yes. You have understood well, my friend," the old man smiled.

"But the passages they are now sealed for eternity," Simon interjected enthusiastically.

"Indeed," the old man nodded.

"I am so glad we have you here," the Genoese sailor said and patted Gabirol on his shoulder.

"Then how do people in the future gain access to it?" Ayleth asked.

"Well as the old hermetic poem reads, the Lord will reveal helpmeet tools and souls who will again access it...from above...but with the use of harmonics...sounds," the old man replied.

"So what happened to all the drawings Paul did of the twelve chambered site then?" Peter asked.

"I have but a few in my possession. Some here this day, but the majority are now hidden, and as the language of the Ancient Egyptians is being eradicated by the Church, it will be a long time again before people can read the images of their symbol language," the old man said and opened his leather folder and pulled out several parchment sheets. Gently he pushed them into the centre of the table where Sarah immediately opened them flat. "Those images you can view."

"Vesica Pisces, symbol of the fish," Gabirol stated as he looked at the top image.

"I once heard that Jesus was from India. Is this also true?" Peter asked.

"I can tell you he travelled to India. Also that a god variously named Issa, Isha, Ichtos, Iesus, Ieshuah, Joshuah or Jesus, linguistically as a name, indisputably originated from India. A lot of Jesus's life and, particularly, his childhood has been likened as matching, if not being identical to, those of Krishna. A well-known instance of this is the so-called

'Evangel of the Infancy', an apocryphal, as in not accepted gospel, directly taken from its Indian precursor. Even the Church clergy recognise this undeniable fact, hiding away such books and rejecting them as I have previously explained."

"But, could we not in fact argue that all evangels are really apocryphal, having been written by anonymous writers under the pseudonym of the Apostles years, if not decades, after the events? I know some who have claimed the whole history of Jesus is a fraud, for he never existed at all, at least as a real person some claim," Peter commented.

"But as I have explained, there was a real Jesus," the old man replied. "Dates and certain details have been changed or lost in translation but he was nevertheless a real person. As explained he deliberately acted upon prophecies and knew a great deal more than most people even suspect. But a time will come when we can all recognise and see just what he did know and reveal. The very names Issa or Ieshuah are not indeed Krishna, as his name is taken directly from that of Ishvara, 'the Lord of the Universe' in Sanskrit, Ish Vara. Ishvara, but pronounced Ishwar is also called Ishva meaning 'Lord', pronounced Ishwa. The name of Ieshua or Ioshuah means 'Saviour' in Hebrew, and is taken directly from the above Sanskrit term, which also has this acceptation, particularly when applied to Vishnu and to Shiva. Ishvara, Ishwar is widely worshipped in the Far East, being also called Isha or Ishana in India, Issara in Pali, Isuan in Thai, Jizu or Jizai in Japanese, and so on. In turn, Issa or Issi is a corrupted form of the Sanskrit Rishi or Riksha."

"Issa is how the Muslims say Jesus Christ, whom they acknowledge as a sort of saint is it not?" the Templar asked.

"Yes it is indeed," the old man replied.

"What are Rishis?" Ayleth asked.

"The Rishis are the sages or seers who revealed the Vedas...the Hindu evangels to the world. They date from Vedic times in India, being far older than the times of Christ, and even of Israel as a biblical nation in Palestine. The Rishis are widely worshipped in the Far East, whence their cult passed to the Near Orient and, thence, through Alexandria, into Greece and Rome. Isha or Ishan or Ishwa means 'Lord', as already said. Emmanuel or Manuel derives from Manu-el, that is 'Lord Manu', meaning 'Saviour Lord'. Ishva, pronounced Ishwa, means 'master', which equals Rabbi, a frequent term for Christ. Ishi or Isha means Rishi, that is, the one who reveals the evangels, like the Seven Rishis, who preceded Jesus."

"So there is some truth in what I hear...that the Essenes, from whom most of the doctrines allegedly preached by Jesus were copied from older sources?" the Hospitaller asked.

"Many ancient Indian initiates and prophets were known and named Issar, or Issarim for two or more of them. In Sanskrit, which was the sacred language of India in

which such myths were composed, Ishu means missile and, more exactly, envoy, messenger, emissary. Jesus as Ishu is thus the Celestial Messenger or 'Angel'. Angelos in Greek means just this, the avatar commemorated in the Mass, in Latin Missa equals Emissa meaning Emissary," the old man explained.

"So how in the Lord's name did Jesus become associated with the pyramids as you have explained earlier and such symbols as a lamb?" the farrier asked, frowning hard.

"Isha is also the same as Rishi or Riksha or Rishabha, meaning the sacrificial bull...or lamb...which represents the Saviour in many ancient traditions, as well as in Christianity. Isha also means the Elixir or Soma, to which Christ is mystically identified. In fact, Soma is an ancient Hindu god whose sacrifice, the same one as expressed verbatim in the Christian Mass, results in the production of the Elixir or Eucharist precisely as in Christianity. Also Ishta, a variant of the name of Christ as the Ichthus or 'Fish', in Greek means 'the Sacrificed One'. In fact, the fish, which was the early symbol of the Eucharist and of Christ himself, is an avatar of Krishna as the Fish Matsya that saved Manu from the Flood, precisely as in the Judeo-Christian myth of Noah. The mystic identification of Christ with the fish, the ichthus, can be explained as an abbreviation of the Greek phrase 'Iesous Christos Theou Uios Soter', meaning 'Jesus Christ Son of God, Saviour', which as I explained before when converted into Gematria the total value equals 1746, which in turn is directly connected to the Great Pyramid itself."

"Are you saying that the whole Jesus story is then just a borrowed myth copying older myths?" Ayleth asked nervously.

"No...the Jesus myth is Jesus fact but continuing a long hidden tradition in plain view...for those who can see it for what it is. There is no fraud or deception at all. This is something Nicholas knew as a Templar initiated into most of the upper circles secrets," the old man explained reassuringly.

"It appears a mere contrivance, a very poor one at that, to explain Christ's mystic connection with the fishes of Pisces does it not?" the wealthy tailor said.

"As I already explained, Jesus as Ichthus is the god of the era of Pisces, the zodiacal era that will end in around the year 2,000, along with the present Church as she stands," the old man started to explain.

1 - 12

"Ah...so that is why Alisha and Paul experienced that dream event standing in the ruined cathedral...and how they would rebuild it anew," Simon interjected excitedly.

"Correct, Simon. Well perceived," the old man smiled as the rest all looked at him, surprised. Simon started to blush with embarrassment. "'Tis obvious is it not?" he asked.

"To some select few 'tis indeed obvious," the old man smiled. "But in fact, the Greek word ichthus for fish was used to designate the Oannés, the legendary 'fish-people' who were the alleged saviours of the Sumero-Babylonians, as well as other equivalent fish-deities, both male and female, such as Dercetto and Dagon. Images from their artwork and murals show their gods with fish heads...identical in form and shape to our modern clergy hats. Moreover, the crossed fishes of Pisces were used directly to symbolise Jesus Christ. And he himself affirms that his zodiacal sign, the one that represents him, is 'the sign of Jonah'. That sign is the Whale or, more exactly, Pisces. Just read Matthew 12:39 and Luke 11:29. Even the story of Jonah and the Whale that Christ here mentions is identical to the Indian myth of Matsya."

"So it is possible, as some legends claim, that Jesus, as Christ, having identical symbolism to Hindu myths, went to India as Issa after his resurrection...or escaped as some say where he lived to an old age with his wife and children...or have I got that totally wrong?" Gabirol asked.

"Some say that, for the protection of his family, Jesus went to India whilst Mary went to France. She had a daughter as you now all know, before journeying on to Britain and Iona where she again met up with Jesus after which they then had a son. Do you recall that I have already explained how the town of Bethlehem did not exist during Jesus's time and that he was of the David line from the tribe of Judah who usurped the house of Saul, the first king of the Jews, from the tribe of Benjamin?" the old man asked. Ayleth shook her head no but the others all nodded yes except Simon, who shrugged his shoulders. "I shall repeat then...that Mary was from the tribe of Benjamin and Saul, so by marrying each other, the full legitimate king of the Jews was re-established. It was the Jewish Sanhedrin who could stone Jesus to death without Roman permission, but they did not...it was the Romans who were responsible for his crucifixion as a revolutionary. Plus Jesus was not crucified at Golgotha, hill of the skull, but in a private garden opposite Joseph of Arimathea's house and the tomb was owned by him proving his wealthy background. Jesus was an aristocrat and wealthy, as well as the rightful priest king, and after his crucifixion, Islam claims that Jesus went to Kashmir after surviving the cross where he lived to a ripe old age. At the risk of repeating myself again, the Cathars teach that Jesus was married to Mary Magdalene. After all these events had passed, only then a new religion, started by Saint Paul, based upon the faith of Jesus and his divine

status started to compete with Roman and Egyptian gods," the old man explained. He paused as he studied their faces to see what reaction this solicited.

"But is it not true that the whole history of Jesus Christ, who is not mentioned in any contemporaneous historical sources, except in some so-called fraudulently inserted passages of Josephus and others, was in fact taken word for word from earlier Hindu sources...such as the killing of the innocents, the virgin birth, the Christmas Star, the visit of the Magi Kings, the episodes concerning John the Baptist, and so on. Most of these have an esoteric sense in Hinduism, which became lost when they were adapted to the person of Jesus?" Gabirol asked.

"You are indeed well versed, my learned friend. But is it also not the case, as I have explained, that perhaps the Hindu myths and legends are likewise copied from a far older civilisation for are they not in turn identical to those of Ancient Egyptian myth and legend, which are in turn taken from even earlier sources again...for you see there is a continuing current that pervades throughout all of them, and they all carry the exact same codes. Remember when I started this tale I explained that the very real Jesus of antiquity had his entire life set out to mirror and mimic the past Messiahs and fulfil the prophecies of the Old Testament...but more crucially to continue the ancient codes from our ancient forefathers across time and remain intact. That is why the same reoccurring and identical themes and actions keep being repeated. And as I said then, an even greater code using mathematics runs throughout all of them...identical!" the old man explained.

"For future generations' benefits...," Ayleth said quietly as the old man nodded yes.

"And what of these seven rushes?" the Genoese sailor asked.

"The Seven Rishis you mean?" the old man said. "They are often identified to the seven stars of Septemtrio, or Ursa Minor or of Ursa Major. They are often alluded to in the Bible and in the Gospels in connection with these constellations, said to be their celestial representations in Revelation. 1:16; 1:20; 2:1; 3:1; Amos 5:8; Zech. 3:9;. This is 'the mystery of the Angels of the Seven Churches' mentioned there, and who are the Seven Manus or Saviours or Angels of the seven eras of humanity that have already elapsed in the Hindu scheme that is indeed followed by all ancient nations. Every time a new zodiacal era starts, such as when Aries, with all its shepherds and lamb symbolism passed into Pisces and all the fish symbolism, and just as we again pass into the age of Aquarius with all its water symbolism to come, then a new angelic Saviour or Manu will descend in an avatar, or at least manifest, in order to 'save' humanity and make safe our crossing into the new era of Aquarius. It was thus with Jesus as a 'Saviour', and it will be so again when we enter the third

millennium and a new lord, whose secret name cannot yet be disclosed, manifests himself to all. It is no coincidence that Jesus was also called Emmanuel or Manuel, that is, 'the Lord Manu' Manu-el. Christianity as a religion was contrived in Alexandria for the new era that was then starting, the one of Pisces, the Fishes. It was composed from the fragments and secret traditions of the older Mystery Religions, particularly those of the Orient, by the sages that then congregated there from all nations. There were many religions contending for supremacy then, including, among others, Mithraicism, Essenianism, Osirianism, Serapianism, the Mysteries of Isis and Osiris, the Orphic and the Eleusinian Mysteries, and so on. Christianity assembled from these Mystery religions and, originally, from the Gnostic traditions which eventually won the dispute and gained the favour of Emperor Constantine, becoming the official religion of the Roman Empire. But, to achieve that hegemony, it adapted and cut with the Gnostic tradition. Then began a ferocious persecution of all other religions, particularly the ones that followed the ancient Mystery cults. The Church branded these cults with the stigma of 'heresy', burning the 'heretics' at the stake, together with their holy books. It is a consequence of this ferocious censorship that we know so little about the ancient pagan Mysteries."

"Sounds to me that all religions become war-like and corrupt," Simon stated.

"Yes, with time, religions too can become old and corrupt, and need a refreshing restart. That is why they have to be changed and renewed periodically, like the Phoenix...which is symbolic of the destruction and end of one age and the rebirth and beginning of a new one. As explained already, this has already occurred seven times hence the 'Seven Days of Creation' and now we are in for the eighth avatar of the present cycle of twelve zodiacal eras. Eight is the number of perfection, the one which closes the present cycle with the golden key. This golden key is the brief return of the Golden Age. Such is the secret of the Mystery of the Seven Angels of the Seven Churches. Churches are founded one per era, and are dissolved when their era ends. The Catholic Church, named Katholikos, which means 'Universal' in Greek, knows this inevitable reality full well, which she attempts to evade at all costs...but in the end, the last pope will recognise its time has come...and he will be responsible for inaugurating a new Church...just as Alisha and Paul saw...," the old man explained and shook his head slightly.

Gabirol coughed and sat up.

"Such is the reason why she censors away the heretical books of the Gnostics, 'Those Who Know'. For she tries to hold her position like the Whore of Revelation, the great prostitute at the service of those who exploit and enslave not only the lesser nations and the minorities, but even the people of the larger

nations. In order to enforce its dominion, the Catholic Church turns one nation against the other, one race against the other, one religion against the other, one person against his neighbour. Dividere ad imperare, that is her lemma," Gabirol stated, shaking his head as he looked down at the parchments passed to him by the Templar. [103]

"Say that outside these walls and there are those who would have you burnt at the stake immediately," the Hospitaller remarked, nodding at Gabirol.

"After what I have seen and learnt...let them try," he replied and winked.

"Yes, but the Church, as I said previously, in its own way has, and is, guaranteeing the safe passage across time, the ancient codes," the old man interrupted. "That is why Orders such as the Templars and Hospitallers, understanding this, vow to protect her...Our world needs a total change of mental awareness and spiritual awakening. We need love, empathy, charity, wisdom and compassion. In other words, all those attributes will be the mark of the next great god or holy figure of the forthcoming era of Aquarius...the spiritual age! It is by understanding the codes handed down to us that the great victory, as has been promised from the dawn of time, be given to us. To all become as like gods ourselves. For such is the real message of the Apocalypse, the book of the secrets for as you now all know...as I explained at the very beginning of this tale, that in truth Apocalypse means to 'unveil' or to 'reveal' meaning 'un-covering', translated literally from Greek meaning 'disclosure of knowledge', a lifting of the veil or revelation. You see the Book of Revelation in the Bible actually predicts an unveiling of a great truth and unimaginable wisdom. Not the end of world but rather the end of the world as we know it...but most definitely not the end of the world," the old man explained.

"And this image...of two circles and a pyramid drawn inside...this is what is known as the Vesica Pisces yes?" Gabirol asked as he studied the image carefully.

"Recall when I started this tale I explained how the cross, or crucifix, did not become a Christian symbol until the fourth century AD. Before that it was a symbol of fish, the Vesica Pisces. Also that the cross with a circle and dot became a rose."

"I recall you said that the cross was used for centuries prior to Christianity by the Egyptians to represent the intersection of two dimensions, the human and celestial," Simon commented proudly.

"I recall you showing a similar picture to this and that it is all connected to the Giza pyramids...but you would tell us toward the end...is that now?" Gabirol asked.

"It is beginning to all make sense now...slowly," the Templar remarked. "The hidden mysteries behind the significance of the number seven as a mystical number, like the seven candles on the Jewish candelabra and seven stars of Orion as well as

the seven churches you have just mentioned. 'Tis all connected both in a real sense and symbolically."

"I wrote it here," Gabirol said and flicked his notes open. "As you explained...the acts of John 102 to 104, where the importance of symbolism is stated. The first line reads, 'The Lord contrived all things symbolically'."

"Whatever that Lord proves to be...the code and message is still the same," the old man replied. "And that Vesica Pisces with the pyramid inside, that is drawn where the circles have a measure, in scale, of a circumference of 1746 feet. The pyramid that can be constructed and drawn within then gives a triangle shape whose base length is 755 feet with a height of 481 feet...exactly the same dimensions of the Great Pyramid. Peter, the Rock that Jesus was to build his Church upon was originally named Simon, but was changed. Peter in Gematria equals 755...and remember how I informed you the Grand Gallery within the Great Pyramid is exactly 153 feet tall and how the King's Chamber starts at the 153rd course?"

Fig. 62: Vesica Pisces with Pyramid.

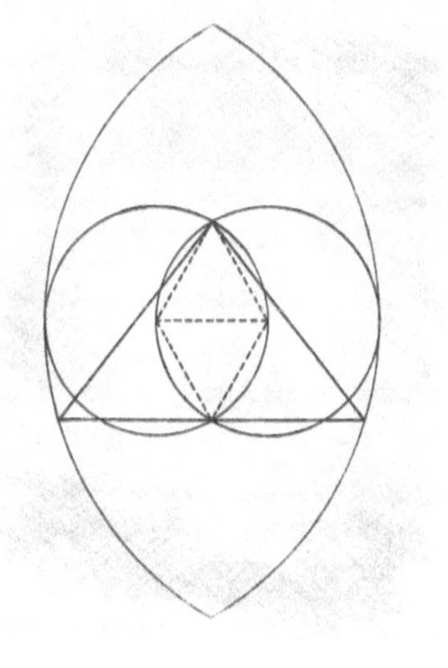

"Yes I have made many notes on all you spoke of previously about the Vesica Pisces and the sacred values," Gabirol said and pushed the diagram back toward the old man.

"Good then there is no need of me repeating all again," he smiled and took the parchment papers.

"So what happened about the other drawings and writings Paul produced that he should not have done, for you say you have some but the majority are hidden?" Peter asked.

"Stolen!" the old man replied seriously and sat back as he took a deep breath.

"Ah...your voice has turned serious...why?" Sarah asked.

All looked at the old man intently waiting for his response as he took his time to respond.

"'Twas not immediately...but several months later as November was almost over. A lot had happened during those months, with Alisha and Nyla concentrating on their business that was growing again steadily, and Paul and Arri developed a closer bond spending many hours a day in each other's company. Together they even made creams that would surely be needed for the new babies soon to arrive."

"Creams...what for?" Simon asked, puzzled.

"To sooth any irritations and rashes the babies may experience...as is common. Arri saw it as his big brother duty. And oh how he could ride Adrastos despite the size of him," the old man explained and paused.

"But there is a 'but' coming isn't there?" Ayleth remarked.

"Indeed...and a big 'but'," the old man replied, looking at her directly. "As arranged that October in 1183, Isabella married Humphrey of Toron at Kerak. But Saladin returned to the region and laid siege during the wedding determined to capture Reynald and end the constant violations of their agreed truces. King Baldwin, although now blind and crippled, had recovered enough to resume his reign and command of the army. Guy, much to his disgust, was removed from the regency and his five-year-old stepson, King Baldwin's nephew and namesake Baldwin, was crowned as co-king in November. King Baldwin himself then moved forces to relieve the castle, carried on a litter no less, and attended by his mother. By this time he was reconciled with Count Raymond of Tripoli after their fall out, which I shall explain later, and duly appointed him military commander. The siege was finally lifted in December and Saladin retreated to Damascus."

"Was Paul not concerned for Princess Stephanie during that time?" Ayleth asked.

"Constantly. She was never far from his thoughts...but she is a shrewd, clever and resourceful woman. She had been carefully planning for just such events since 1180 when Baldwin the Fourth of Jerusalem betrothed his eight-year-old half-sister, Princess Isabella, to Stephanie's son Humphrey. She knew even then the potential peril this put not only her but also her son's life in. It did not therefore come as a surprise when the ceremonies were interrupted by the arrival of Saladin, mainly in response to Reynald's continued threats against Mecca. Remember earlier when

I explained how according to the chronicle of Ernoul, Stephanie sent messengers to Saladin, reminding him of the friendship they had shared when he had been a prisoner in Kerak many years before?" the old man asked.

"When you state that Stephanie had previously had secret dealings with Saladin but he could not be seen by his own side to back down, so did not lift the siege only agreeing to not target Humphrey and Isabella's wedding chamber. And something about Stephanie hating Isabella's mother, Maria Comnena?" Simon remarked, the old man smiling at his comments.

"I am so glad I am no princess...some fairytale I think not!" Sarah commented.

"The siege, even the threat beforehand, gave Alisha and Paul a valid enough excuse to turn down the invite but Paul knew things were changing rapidly. His ship modification designs enabled him to delay the actual building of it but Husam was now beginning to get a little impatient as well as suspicious. Alisha being too far gone pregnant put off any ideas about travelling until at least a month or two after the baby was born...and here comes that big 'but'. Thomas and his men were spending more and more time away on patrols and escort duties for emissaries and ambassadors due to the heightened hostilities and someone had evil intent in mind...their eyes set firmly upon acquiring the plans to Paul's advanced ship...and they would stop at nothing to obtain them...by all and any means," the old man sighed.

"Sounds ominous," Gabirol remarked.

"'Twas...for from the actions of one evil intent...another greater evil was unleashed."

"Oh I do not like the sound of this," Ayleth cringed.

Cairo, November 1183

Paul brushed Adrastos just as a cool wind blew inside the stable. The sun was setting fast and Arri reluctantly went with Sister Lucy to prepare for bed. Alisha and Nyla were still out along with Ishmael and Percival as their evening escort attending a show of their dresses. Theodoric approached carrying two large horn cups of wine laughing as he nearly tripped over the small soak away open drain from the stables.

"Get that down you," he said, passing Paul his drink.

"You are a bad influence upon me. I am getting a little too familiar with this wine," Paul remarked and took a sip. "I am pleased to hear my father is in Britain. At least he knows we are all safe and well."

"Hey, he always knew you would return…never doubted it. And I bet he is having a real treat advising Queen Eleanor…she's now held at Old Sarum I hear. Your father will love that," Theodoric replied and took a long swig of his wine.

"You must tell me one day about my father's connection to her. There is so much I do not know about my family. Look at Percival. Who would have believed when we first met that we are cousins?"

"'Tis obvious…that Kratos and Abi had a plan B all along. I should have seen it earlier," Theodoric said and took another swig of wine. Paul looked at him quizzically. "You know…two separate lines to ensure at least one of them survived. Explains a lot as I look back upon my time in Georgia with your father all those years ago. Georgia being the twin state of Britain… well, that is what Kratos told us at the time," he sighed, thinking back upon those times.

"Why is Father in Britain seeing Eleanor again?"

"Whilst you were away much happened with King Henry the Second. He besieged the town his son had taken residence in forcing him to flee. Henry the Young wandered aimlessly through Aquitaine until he caught dysentery. On Saturday, 11 June 1183, the Young King realised he was dying and was overcome with remorse for his sins. When his father's ring was sent to him, he begged that his father would show mercy to his mother, Eleanor, and that all his companions would plead with King Henry to set her free. Henry sent Thomas of Earley, Archdeacon of Wells, to break the news to Eleanor at Old Sarum where she is being held…as a prisoner basically. Your father is negotiating her release to return to Normandy."

"So they cannot even resolve their own differences there so what chance do they have of doing so here and in Outremer?" Paul sighed and shook his head, feeling dizzy all of a sudden.

"You all right?" Theodoric asked, seeing the look on Paul's face as he drained of colour.

Paul put his drink down as Adrastos snorted and kicked his front legs as if startled.

"Must have been in the heat too long this day," Paul replied and leant against the wooden gating. He lowered his head as his ears began to ring. He looked up toward the main house. "I think I will check on Arri…for I have a strange feeling…'tis the same as I have had before."

"When?" Theodoric asked and moved to support Paul.

"Whenever trouble has followed…," Paul answered just as a slight knocking sound echoed out from inside the main house. Alarmed, he stood up straight just as Nyla opened the kitchen hall door, smiled and waved.

"We are home early," she said excitedly. "We sold all our items almost at once."

Alisha appeared beside her waving a large purse and several chits.

"'Tis only us," Alisha called out, smiling, and nudged Nyla. They both laughed and moved back inside the door.

"Thank Lord for that," Paul remarked and sat himself down as Ishmael and Percival came into view leading the horse and cart. A dark image flashed across the top of the main building's roof but it vanished before he had time to look up properly. Must have been a bird he told himself and stood to greet Ishmael and Percival. As soon as he stood up, his ears rang even louder and he felt nauseous and he rested his hands upon his knees leaning forwards. Something was not right he sensed and his heart began to pound fast.

ඞ

Alisha held onto Nyla's right arm as they walked along the upper corridor. They were laughing and talking about the evening's sale when they passed Arri's bedroom door. Alisha handed Nyla the dress she had slung over her left arm and looked inside at Sister Lucy telling Arri a good night story. A dull thud made them all look upward at the ceiling then Arri sat up excitedly. Quickly Alisha walked over to him, kissed him on his forehead and lay him down again with Clip clop placed beside him.

"I shall finish our little story then be down," Sister Lucy said and rubbed her hand through Arri's hair.

"Thank you. The night went very well. I shall come in and check on you again shortly," Alisha replied and kissed Arri again, and Clip clop as he raised him up.

Alisha walked back into the corridor and started to head for her main room just as Nyla stepped out from her room looking puzzled. Nyla pointed toward Paul's work study as someone inside opened drawers. Both approached the partially opened door which was usually locked shut. Both paused as they listened. Alisha leaned up against the door and peered in. Her eyes widened instantly as she made out the dark outline of a black dressed man, only his eyes visible as he looked up at her. As Alisha raised her hand to her mouth in shock, Nyla instinctively pushed her aside just as the man threw a sharp bladed star shaped weapon. It flew past Alisha's head just missing her and embedded itself in the wall with a thud and metal ringing sound. It was instantly followed by a second one that embedded slightly higher. Alisha stepped back in front of the door and slammed it shut as a third star hit the inside of the door.

"PERCY!" Nyla screamed loudly and joined Alisha to hold the door shut.

Sister Lucy rushed to look out from Arri's bedroom door and saw them. Alisha waved her to go back into the room.

"Shut the door!" she called out.

Arri appeared beside Sister Lucy as the man inside Paul's room pushed hard against it. Quickly Sister Lucy ushered Arri back into his room. Suddenly a second figure dressed entirely in black appeared from the loft doorway. As it flung open he jumped down almost directly in front of Alisha and Nyla. He pulled a black sword from behind his back and waved it at them, his eyes darting from Alisha to Nyla and looking at their tummies.

"Which is Alisha?" he demanded in a deep clipped accent. "Alisha!" he shouted and waved the tip of his sword closer to their faces.

"I am!" Alisha called out loudly just as the second man started to cut and smash his way through the plaster work wall beside Nyla. She looked at Alisha in terror then at the man before them as he pulled his sword back ready to thrust into Alisha. "I am," Alisha said calmly and stared the man in the eyes directly.

The man hesitated for a second, his eyes narrowing.

"No, I am the real Alisha!" Nyla shouted.

As the man looked at her, Alisha stamped her left foot down upon the man's right foot whilst at the same time crossed her wrists, pushed her arms upwards so the sword went upwards and brought her right knee up hard into his groin. The man's eyes widened but only briefly as he stepped backwards, raised his sword up high to bring it down upon Alisha but as he did, Alisha stepped to her side slightly, blocked his downward thrust with her left arm, then tucked her right arm beneath his armpit, thrust her hip hard into his side and using his own momentum, she bent down whilst grasping his arm with both hands, and pulled him over her shoulders. The man landed heavily upon his back, taken by surprise. He blinked and looked up just as Alisha thrust her three pronged dagger directly into his neck just as Arri broke away from Sister Lucy and rushed toward them. The man, despite the pain and blood spurting from his neck, pulled his sword across his chest and flung it toward Arri, Alisha just knocking his wrist as he let go. Arri froze, his eyes wide as the black bladed sword flew through the air toward him. It was about to hit him when Sister Lucy pulled him aside just in time, the sword embedding itself in the main wooden door jamb. Alisha looked back down at the man, withdrew the dagger, causing a large spurt of blood to shoot up the wall and all over her. She thrust it down hard upon his chest as he tried to turn on his side. The second man kicked his way through the wall and as he stepped out into full view, he looked twice the size of the man on the floor who was holding his neck and chest gurgling and choking in his own blood. Alisha stood up to face the man as he wielded his sword high with his right hand, his left hand wiping dust and plaster from his eyes. Nyla looked at Alisha briefly then at the man. She pulled the bone comb type hair clasp from her hair and instantly scraped it hard down the side of the man's face immediately cutting eight deep groves in his cheek as it pulled the black face cover down at the same time. Alisha threw her dagger at his chest but he knocked it aside with his sword. Alisha looked to her left at the small recess in the wall that contained several metal spiked candle holders. She grabbed one as Sister Lucy cowered over Arri to protect him. Alisha's gaze was drawn upwards as she saw movement. A third masked man looked down through the loft entrance. He was holding two of Paul's parchment containers. The man before Alisha looked up briefly. When he did, Alisha stepped nearer and stabbed the spiked metal candle holder into his knee. The man did not make a sound but pushed Alisha backwards hard against the door beside Nyla. He studied both women quickly checking to see which one was pregnant. It appeared to confuse him that both were. Nyla was shaking uncontrollably still holding the bloodied hair comb as Alisha stepped in front of her protectively. He pulled his sword back ready to strike when Sister Lucy whacked him hard across the back of his black covered head with a bed warming pan. He flounced his arm backwards, the pommel of his sword smacking Sister Lucy hard in the face knocking her backwards. Alisha tried to pull Nyla with her away from the man, but he grabbed her arm tightly. As he pulled his sword back, holding Alisha's arm even tighter, he thrust it forwards toward her belly…but Nyla pushed herself in the way, her arms outstretched to her sides totally obscuring Alisha. A sickening squelch filled the corridor as the sword sliced into Nyla's belly, the force pushing her backwards pinning Alisha behind her up against the wall. For a moment they all remained perfectly still and silent, Nyla her eyes wide. She moved forward a little off of Alisha, who looked down to see the sword sticking out of her back, the blade having caught Alisha's tummy too cutting her dress and scratching her skin. Nyla moved her hands down slowly and put them on the blade, but as she did the man quickly pulled the sword out, Nyla letting out a groan and falling to her knees. Alisha bent down to catch her, looking up just as the man raised his sword to strike her.

"NYLA!" Percival screamed as he appeared running onto the landing leading into the corridor, his sword drawn and rushing toward them.

2 - 40

The man looked toward him, stood up fully, raised his sword to bring down upon Alisha's head when he suddenly let out a groan in pain, his eyes screwing up. He shifted his weight to try and turn around and see what had happened as pain ran through his back. He could hardly move his legs. Alisha jumped aside seeing Arri stood behind the man. He had picked up Alisha's three pronged dagger and thrust in into the base of the man's spine. As he turned and faced Arri, he tried to lift his sword, as he did, Percival's sword burst through his chest as he thrust it through his back with all his might and yelled out a great scream. Percival pushed the man to the floor, withdrew his sword and thrust it down again between the man's shoulder blades with all his might, anger burning across his face. The man flinched and shook briefly, Arri staring in total disbelief as Paul and Theodoric ran into view, Paul quickly grabbing his little arm and pulling him away and toward him. Paul saw that Alisha was kneeling on the floor, her dress ripped and covered in blood. Quickly he passed Arri to Theodoric, who was trying to check Sister Lucy's face, her nose bleeding. Percival pushed and pushed his sword harder, tears streaming down his face. Paul moved across to Alisha, alarmed, as Nyla lay against her still alive.

"I am fine...but there is a third man," Alisha said and pointed to the loft.

Instantly Percival removed his sword, looked up as if possessed. He pulled a stool over, stood upon it and without checking it was clear, hauled himself up into the loft and vanished without even looking at Nyla. Paul checked over Alisha frantically just as Ishmael, Thomas, Luke and Mathew appeared, weapons drawn.

"They came in through the roof," Paul shouted as Arri jumped away from Theodoric and rushed over to join Alisha and Paul.

Ishmael and Thomas immediately turned away heading back down the stairs to go outside and cut off anyone trying to escape as Luke and Mathew stood protectively beside Alisha and Paul. Nyla gently clasped Alisha's hand. Her breathing was shallow and she looked white.

"Look after my Percival…please," she whispered.

Alisha put her arms around her and cradled her as Paul supported her and held Arri close. Sister Lucy shuffled over on her knees and started to check Nyla. The floor was covered in her blood and that of the dead man laying a few feet away. The other injured man looked at them intently still holding his hands to his throat but not moving. He had almost bled out and Paul turned Arri's face away so he did not look at him.

"Did I do the right thing?" Arri asked nervously.

"Oh my dear brave little warrior you did more than the right thing," Alisha said emotionally and went to put her hand upon his face but stopped when she saw her hands were covered in blood.

"You did," Nyla whispered and feigned a smile at Arri.

Percival came walking back towards them from the other end of the corridor having jumped out the far end of the loft after the third man. His sword was trailing on the floor held low by his right hand. He approached covering his eyes with his left hand, crying, afraid to look at the scene before him. He had seen the sword enter Nyla and knew it was a fatal wound. Nyla looked up at him wearily, her eyes heavy. She tried to raise her hand for him as he approached. He stopped a few paces away and dropped his sword and covered his face with both hands.

"Percy," Theodoric said trying to snap him out of his stupor. "Percy!" he said again louder and stepped closer to him. He gently grabbed his hands and pulled them away from his face, his eyes clenched shut as tears streamed down his face and shaking his head no. "Percival…you have but a few short moments to say goodbye…do so while you still can," Theodoric said quietly. "Here, come." Theodoric led Percival to Nyla's side. She looked up at him and tried to raise her hand again. Theodoric took her hand and placed it in Percival's. "Now."

Percival slowly opened his eyes and caught Nyla's looking back at him.

Her hand was cold and sticky. She blinked and went to force a smile but blood trickled from the side of her mouth and she coughed, pitifully weak. Percival fell to his knees beside her and with both hands clutched hers. He could not speak, his throat so tight with emotion, his eyes filled with pain. He had tried to not look thinking in desperation that if he did not, it would not somehow be true...but it was all too real and true. As he clenched her hand in his he leaned closer and kissed her gently as tears rolled down his cheeks. He pulled back and started to sob uncontrollably as the others looked on helpless, Arri holding Clip clop close staring in silence. Nyla blinked again.

"In the blink of an eye I will see you again I swear...for I will do all that I can to make certain I join you, my love," Percival managed to force out and sniffed wiping away the tears from his face with his forearm.

Nyla blinked once more at Percival then looked at Alisha and smiled, then slowly her eyelids closed, her body going limp, her head resting against Alisha's shoulder. Percival held her hand tightly and placed his right hand upon her tummy, screwed his eyes closed tightly and cried uncontrollably, lowering his head. As he cried, Thomas came running up the stairs and stopped as he saw the image before him. His shoulders dropped and he sighed shaking his head no as Ishmael followed behind him. After a few minutes, Percival stopped crying, opened his eyes and looked back toward the injured man lying feet from him. A tear rolled down Alisha's cheek and she pulled Arri closer as Paul stood up. Percival suddenly leapt to his feet, pulled out his arming dagger and threw himself on top of the injured man straddling him. He grabbed his hair and pulled his head up, placing the dagger against his throat. Through gritted teeth, Percival stared aggressively at the man, shaking with rage, but the man remained silent and still.

"Why....why?" Percival cried, tears streaming down his agonised face.

The man looked toward Alisha and blinked to indicate her. Percival twisted himself to look at her, his breathing becoming deep, the look of total despair and anger etched deep into his face. Alisha pulled Nyla closer to her chest, kissed the top of her head and looked into Percival's eyes and shook her head no silently. Percival flounced back to look at the man, pulled him up so his face was just inches from his.

"She has to die...," the man coughed in a gravelly voice and tried to point to Alisha. Arri wrapped his arms around her tightly hearing this. "She must...," the man tried to say once more but Percival pushed his dagger closer to his throat.

"Percy…no," Theodoric said firmly and stepped closer.

As Percival glared at the man, his eyes rolled upward white and his body fell limp. Percival clenched his fist tightly as he wrapped his hand in the man's collar. After a short while, he pushed him away and stood up. He turned to look at Nyla, his heart breaking, and sighed. He appeared to visibly shrink as he stooped low and fell to his feet beside Nyla and pulled her up from Alisha, put his arms around her and gently started to rock her, his face hidden against her head, and sobbed, Alisha placing her hand upon his shoulder. Paul lifted Arri up and walked toward Thomas and Ishmael, pulling out one of the embedded metal stars. It was razor sharp and he had to pull it hard to remove it from the wall. He raised his eyebrows as he showed Thomas.

"Whoever the other one is, he physically jumped from one rooftop to the other. Only Ashashin are that good," Thomas whispered.

"No…not Ashashin…this is the work of Turansha's men," Paul replied quietly and looked back at Percival still holding the lifeless body of Nyla in his arms. Sister Lucy knelt beside him and tried to console him as Alisha stood up. She was covered in the blood of the dead men and Nyla's. She looked at her hands then at Paul. Her expression said it all. Paul ushered Thomas and Ishmael downstairs.

Paul stepped outside into the yard carrying Arri following Thomas and Ishmael. The night sky was darkening fast just as Luke walked into view followed by the rest of Thomas's men. Luke had informed them of what had taken place. Quickly they dismounted, tied up their horses and with swords drawn checking the rooftops, they encircled Paul and Arri.

"I am afraid you are all too late…they have murdered Nyla," Paul explained and put his hand across Arri protectively as he clung to him.

All turned to look at Alisha as she stepped down from the dining hall doorway. She straightened her dress and approached them. Her face was stern and Paul knew immediately she was angered. She stopped and eyed all of Thomas's men then walked directly up to Thomas. She shook her head disapprovingly. He frowned. Suddenly she started to rain her fists down upon his chest hard. As he stepped backwards she pulled his surcoat and hit him harder.

"Ali!" Paul called out, shocked at her outburst.

"No, Paul…'tis fine," Thomas replied, raising his left hand for Paul to keep back as Arri looked at her.

"Mama," Arri said quietly.

As soon as Alisha heard Arri, she stopped thumping Thomas's chest and grabbed his surcoat in clenched fists. She stared hard into Thomas's eyes for what seemed an age, the hurt and anger clearly visible in her face as the others all looked on.

"'Tis not fine," Alisha remarked emotionally, her arms going weak. Thomas held her arm gently and looked at her. "Where were you when we needed you the most?…you failed us," she said in a broken voice. She stepped away from Thomas and looked at one of the horses nearest. She walked over to it, looked at the saddle and the small leather strapping specially attached to hold a horn cup. She unbuttoned the fastening and pulled out the horn cup and looked at it. "This…this is what is more important to you lot…drink…and women," she snapped angrily and threw the cup on the floor and immediately headed back toward the dining hall doorway covering her face with her arm.

"Ali…that is not fair," Paul said and tried to grab her arm as she passed him. She flounced her arm away hard and carried on walking. "Ali…"

Percival appeared in the doorway looking utterly broken. He looked at Alisha as she rapidly approached. She stopped. Slowly Percival stepped down and walked toward her. When he reached her, he fell to his knees and placed his hands upon her tummy, kissing it before resting his forehead against her. Surprised and overwhelmed by emotions, Alisha placed her hands upon his head not knowing what to do. Her lip began to quiver and she turned to face Paul, seeking some guidance. Paul held Arri up in his left arm and moved to stand beside her. Everyone in the courtyard looked on deeply touched and affected by Percival's actions. Alisha looked around at them all in turn, tears welling in her eyes. Percival looked up at her, his eyes wide and full of pain.

"My Nyla…I saw what happened…'tis not the fault of these men… their sworn oath remains to protect you always…and Nyla knew that," he started to explain, looked down, shook his head and then stood up slowly. "She felt you worthy enough to sacrifice herself to protect you and your unborn. Do not let her death be in vain or full of bitter recriminations… please," he pleaded. Alisha drew a sharp intake of breath, her heart beating so hard she thought it would burst, the emotions feeling too great to control. "You already had my sword...now you have my soul...for I have nothing more now to live for...but I swear to never fail you. When you need me the most, I will be there...this I swear on the memory of my Nyla and unborn," Percival said, full of emotion, almost unable to finish his sentence. He stepped back a pace, unsheathed his sword and thrust it into the ground just in front of Alisha then knelt down in front of it and rested his hands upon the pommel, closed his eyes and bowed his head.

Alisha looked at him and hesitantly stepped closer, shaking with emotion she placed her hand upon his head gently. Just as she did, a bright shooting star streaked across the night sky, lighting up the yard momentarily, followed by a boom. All except Percival looked up but it vanished just as quickly. All stood in silence for several minutes.

"Is that Nyla going up to heaven?" Arri asked, breaking the silence just as Theodoric and Sister Lucy came out.

Thomas approached Alisha and Percival as Paul stepped back a pace with Arri. Thomas thrust his sword into the dirt near to Percival, knelt down and looked up at Alisha, who frowned, puzzled. She sniffed and took a deep breath again.

"We have become bloated and complacent in our charge to protect you... in this we have failed," Thomas said, uncharacteristically emotional. He put his hands together as if in prayer as he looked at her. "I humbly beg that you and Percival forgive us for this day's failing...and pray grant us the chance to redeem ourselves. I vow to thee this hour we will not fail you again...unto death...this I swear," he pleaded.

Percival turned to face him. As he did, Luke came up, thrust his sword into the dirt and knelt down too.

"May Nyla's death indeed be not in vain for I swear the same," he said.

No sooner had he clasped his hands together than the rest of Thomas's men did likewise. Percival looked at them all in turn as tears rolled down his cheeks. He nodded in acceptance of their gesture then looked up at Alisha.

"I do not want people dying for me," she finally blurted out.

"Nyla saw fit to give her life for you...and so do I for this world is in sore need of people like you," Percival said, looking up at her. "I was once told by a wise man," he started to say and quickly looked at Theodoric before looking back at Alisha. "If you can't find something to live for, you best find something worth dying for...and like my Nyla...you are."

"No...I want no more deaths on my account. 'Tis too much to bear."

"Then we had better make sure no more do so," Thomas stated and stood, pulled his sword out of the dirt and re-sheathed it. "Starting as of now."

"No...I cannot ask of this for my temper is too great at times...and I am not worthy of this vow you all pledge," Alisha replied, holding her hand to her face as she fought to control her emotions that were welling up inside.

Theodoric walked up to her and placed his hand upon her forearm and looked at her in the reassuring way that only he could.

"My dear...must I remind you just how worthy you really are?"

Thomas and his men moved closer to Alisha and helped Percival up. As Paul watched them, Arri also looking at the scene before them, he recalled the words Abi had spoken to him about how the Crimson Thread of an ancient bloodline that far outreached any of the royal bloodlines now being sown within royal families flowed through both of their veins. But he knew now it also flowed through Percival's. His heart ached for him and it hit him suddenly, the realisation of again just how close he had come to losing Alisha. It could have been him now stood in Percival's place. Abi's words came echoing through his mind as if she was speaking beside him. "You must understand and believe, and accept it as a truth, that you above all people have a right to wield your sword. You carry the wishes and ambitions of all your ancestors to establish a line of leaders who heal, protect and educate their peoples. To lead by example doing service to others, not service to self. And that is something you must learn and accept fast." Paul looked at Theodoric as he reassured Alisha and he recalled exactly the words he too had given. "Accept and know that there are people and groups out there who will want to stop you doing just that and who will kill you without hesitation to obtain weapons such as the sword...but also to kill off your bloodline. That is why it has been protected and remains in the shadows. Let the other bloodlines and kings fight each other and be high profile, for all the while they do, they help keep you, Alisha and Taqi, protected out of sight." As Paul recalled Theodoric's now almost prophetic words, he had to add Arri to that statement. He felt privileged to know Theodoric, Percival and Thomas and all his men. He and Alisha had no power or any great wealth, yet these men standing before him had chosen to be there by they own free will. But how could he protect his family and remain in the shadows if there were those with evil intent and a wish to kill them who knew where they lived? A very dark shadow had fallen across them this eve.

Chapter 62
Hymn of the Risen

Port of La Rochelle, France, Melissae Inn, spring 1191

"I think I am going to be sick," Ayleth remarked and cupped her mouth.

Sarah quickly passed her a small glass of fresh water.

"Here...sip this...'tis pre-boiled and cool so safe," she said as Ayleth took the glass and drank the water.

Simon wiped a tear from his eye and coughed.

"How does one ever get over something like that?" the wealthy tailor asked.

"You don't...you just carry on living the best you can...as some wounds never heal," the Templar replied. Miriam sensed that he was speaking from past experience and squeezed his hand gently.

"Did those evil bastards go there with the purpose of murdering Alisha?" Sarah asked, her voice angry in tone.

"Let me just say for now, for I shall reveal fully later, that yes...they had been given specific instructions to steal whatever plans they could find of Paul's advanced ship design," the old man said and watched as Sarah shook her head disapprovingly and clenched her fists together. "They had already tried several times at the boat yard but found nothing. But their primary mission all along was to kill Alisha and her unborn child."

"Bastards!" Sarah fumed and banged her fists down on the table, making Ayleth jump.

"And who pray tell ordered her death?" the Hospitaller asked.

"That evil bastard Turansha I bet," Sarah interrupted, her face turning red.

"He had a part to play in it yes...but his interest that eve was purely the boat plans...but it will surprise you when I tell you whom exactly it was who had ordered her death," the old man explained.

The room fell silent for several long minutes before Stephan stood up.

"The hour is very late...should we not resume this in the morn?" he asked.

"No bloody way," Sarah shot back instantly. "I mean...I mean no, surely we must

end this night," she said, exasperated, and pointed at the Templar and Hospitaller. "They have to leave and will miss any ending."

"Oh...I think I have started to work out that my brother and I already have the next path of our journey, in this life, set before us," the Templar replied and nodded at the old man.

The old man leaned forward interweaving his fingers together as he rested upon his elbows.

"The man who got away over the rooftops took with him, not the plans of Paul's ship designs, but plans Paul should never have drawn up...detailed images and dimensions of the sacred Hall of Records itself. Its full layout and written notes of how it was directly representative of the New Jerusalem as detailed within the Bible's Book of Revelation..."

"Oh no...which is what he was specifically told not to do," Peter sighed.

"Exactly," the old man replied. "And Paul knew this as soon as he realised exactly what had been stolen. And the guilt he felt was almost unbearable for the loss of Nyla and the harm it had brought to their doorstep."

"So much pain and anguish. Perhaps it would have been kinder if he and Alisha had not gotten together as Sister Lucy had warned all along," Ayleth commented sadly.

"Paul learnt a very valuable if costly lesson. He now fully understood exactly why the ancient mystics, people like Kratos and Attar, all memorised things over many years...just like the Druids before them...just so no such thing could happen," the old man explained.

"But so what if whoever it was ends up with the plans he had drawn...it did not give away the location did it?" Gabirol stated.

"No it did not. But that is exactly why from one evil, an even greater evil would be initiated in order to gain that knowledge," the old man replied solemnly.

"Oh dear Lord I don't think I wish to hear what comes next," Ayleth responded shaking her head looking saddened.

"Please tell me that Thomas and his men did stay to protect them," Miriam said softly.

"Yes...they stayed. They even cut back on their other paid duties, and Husam, when he heard of what had happened, even re-stationed a crack troop of his own most trusted men permanently at their residence. Paul was able to twist the truth a little...that the new plans to the ship had been stolen, for which he also felt guilty over, having to lie."

"But a necessary and understandable lie yes?" the Templar asked.

"Yes," the old man replied. "Thomas and his men, true to their word, sorted themselves out...they even named themselves the 'Knights of Aquarius' and even made up their own new motto."

"Motto...what?" Simon asked.

"Well, along with Percival, they carried out a ceremony and all swore a new pledge...but only after they had buried Nyla. That was a particularly sad day for everyone...her father even threatening suicide. In truth I believe it was Thomas's way of uniting the group tightly as well as give Percival a purpose. But he was not the same person. When Nyla was killed so too was a large part of him that he could not heal or replace."

"So despite everything, Paul decided to stay where they were?" the farrier asked.

"Yes. He knew if they moved, they would just as soon be found again. He made a deliberate decision to wait until after Alisha had given birth, then make plans to return to La Rochelle," the old man answered and sat back in his chair.

"And the motto. Do you know what it was?" Gabirol asked, ready to write it down.

"Yes, that I do. 'Tis simply 'Nos vivere, sed ut ministraret'."

"Meaning?" Simon asked bluntly.

"We live but to serve," the Templar answered for the old man. "I know of this motto and the men of the group you speak of...now that you have told us their name."

"So they are real then?" the Genoese sailor asked, surprised.

"Have you not heard a thing you have been told?" the Templar asked with a look of disappointment at the sailor. "They were real enough that I can vouch for...now I know of exactly whom we are talking about."

The old man lowered his head for a moment clearly deep in thought.

"Every day Percival tended to Nyla's grave just a short distance from their home. Nyla's parents were utterly broken hearted. It was something no one could help any of them with. And Alisha, she missed her friend daily. 'Twas Sister Lucy and Theodoric that held the household together during those dark early weeks...but Paul's sense of guilt only grew ever bigger. And Arri...he could no longer sleep alone upstairs so every eve, Sister Lucy or Alisha would have to sit with him until he fell asleep. 'Twas a very sad time and laughter was not heard anywhere. 'Twas Ishmael who managed to really motivate Percival, slowly at first, but daily he persisted with him. He could empathise with him and Percival acknowledged the fact that they both shared and had a similar tragedy in common."

"I think it providential that Tenno had taught Alisha to fight so well," Ayleth

commented almost in a daze as her imagination ran over many scenarios of how the fight must have looked.

"It would sadly not be the last time she would have cause to use such skills," the old man said.

1 - 19

"Oh my Lord I truly cannot listen to much more...surely not?" Ayleth pleaded.

"I shall make us all a snack and more drink for we shall need it," Stephan interrupted.

The old man looked up and nodded in agreement.

Cairo, December 1183

Paul ran his fingers through his hair, sat at his drawing table unable to concentrate. It was midday and he had not completed any work. Husam was due to visit any day yet he had nothing to show him except his previous slightly amended drawings and he hoped Husam would accept his story that all his recent work had been stolen. Using the attack and Nyla's death as an excuse troubled him greatly. He had the corridor cleaned of all traces of blood, the wall repaired and Arri moved into the bedroom beside his and Alisha's. Percival had moved into the dormitory spare room along with Thomas and his men no longer able to bear staying in his previous room shared with Nyla. Several times Paul had caught Percival looking at Alisha, her bump extending more as each week passed, being reminded of Nyla whichever way he turned or looked. Paul sighed deeply and rested forward upon his knees shaking his head. A light knock on his door drew his attention and he looked up as Theodoric popped his head around the door.

"I come bearing gifts," he said and entered carrying something behind his back. "Close your eyes," he smiled.

"What…Theo no. What is it?" Paul asked, slightly irritated.

"Oh come on…indulge an old man and humour me. Don't be so grown up," Theodoric replied and raised his eyebrows. Reluctantly Paul closed his eyes. "Hands out." Paul shook his head, unimpressed, but held out his hands, his eyes shut. Theodoric placed a small wrapped package upon his open hands and stood back. "You can open them now."

Paul opened his eyes and looked at the small sealed package. It was from England and he immediately knew it was from his father. Quickly he broke the two wax seals and untied the bindings. As he folded the outer wrappings down a small beautifully made polished oak wood box revealed itself. A small gold latch held the top in place. Carefully he opened it to reveal an ornate mariner's compass. In surprise and smiling he looked up at Theodoric.

"'Tis one of the new compasses my father promised," he said and smiled broadly.

"'Tis better to see you smile again," Theodoric remarked and stood with his hands behind his back. "I can teach you how to use it when you are ready."

"You know how to use this?"

"Er, I should hope so," Theodoric replied and raised his eyebrows.

"'Tis a beautiful instrument. I am surprised father risked sending it at all," Paul remarked as he took out the compass.

"Oh...and this also arrived. From Saladin himself," Theodoric explained and handed Paul a sealed envelope. Paul looked at him, puzzled.

"Saladin himself?"

"Well, it is actually addressed to both you and Alisha. Possibly just another dress order."

Paul immediately opened the envelope and took out the folded letter. He studied it and was surprised to read that it was written in French, not Arabic. Theodoric stood still patiently waiting as Paul read the letter thoroughly.

"My Lord...'tis indeed a personal letter from Saladin expressing his deepest condolences to us and Percival on the sad loss of Nyla...and that his wife Ismat...wife?" Paul said, again puzzled. "That she is likewise saddened but hopes Alisha will carry on with her dress making...and...and it says here that they will find out who was responsible for Nyla's death and they will face justice accordingly!"

"Interesting," Theodoric said and rubbed his chin. He pulled up the small stool nearest to him and sat down opposite. "I am sure Saladin would know it was Turansha's men..."

"This Ismat...I know Alisha said her dresses were for a woman whom Saladin was greatly fond of...but who is she?"

"Ismat? Your father, Firgany and I met her once. A beautiful and determined woman for sure," Theodoric answered but continued to rub his chin. Something he always did when thinking hard. "She was the wife of Nur ad-Din and Amalric once laid siege to her castle the moment Nur ad-Din died...but she offered him a bribe to lift the siege, but he demanded a larger offer. She refused and Amalric continued the siege for two weeks, until finally accepting the money along with the release of twenty Christian prisoners. Even William of Tyre described her as having courage beyond that of most women. Saladin was Nur ad-Din's general and after gaining control over Egypt, claimed Damascus as Nur ad-Din's successor when he died. He very smartly legitimised this claim by marrying Ismat ad-Din in 1176. Though not Saladin's only wife, I can assure you she is the one woman whom he loves the most, that I do know," Theodoric explained. "Fortunately she had no children with Nur ad-Din and so far none with Saladin. Even now in Damascus she is the patron of numerous religious buildings, including a madrasa and a mausoleum for her father. She could prove a good ally should you ever need her support."

"Why would I need her support?"

"There is much politic and intrigue at the moment. Saladin deals daily with disruption within his own ranks let alone those like Reynald and Gerard...and she is without doubt his priority."

"And so much of the same back in France and Britain no less...is there nowhere we can go and be safe?" Paul asked and sighed.

"Then stay here. You are guarded and well protected and you know the place. Anyone who wishes you harm, let them bring the fight here on your terms. Besides, there is much still to learn of this sacred place...for this house is built upon the very ruins of what was once the most holiest of Ancient Egypt's cities...Heliopolis as the Greeks named it...the birth place and home of the legendary Phoenix."

"Yes I was aware of that. But I am also already aware how the Phoenix is symbolic for mankind being reborn and its connection to the Holy Grail legends...how Phoenic was the bird of the Phoenicians with its root word for Phoenix as you have explained previously. I have not forgotten," Paul replied and shook his head, looking sad. "I saw so many things when I was inside that pyramid complex...and I still have so many questions. Questions I dare not ask."

"Then ask for I may have answers to some...and I am sure you have not forgotten," Theodoric replied, seeing the frustration written across Paul's face. "Look Paul...Heliopolis was Ancient Egypt's most ancient temple though nothing remains, its stones used for various buildings in Cairo. But its true importance lies scattered in various ancient accounts, from Diodorus Siculus, Plato and many others. It must not be confused with the labyrinth which funnily enough had twelve parts for twelve kings... It is said that those who fly too close to the sun get burned. In the case of the priests of Heliopolis, it is reported that of all temples of Ancient Egypt, theirs was the most magnificent; that their temple had a floor so perfect that one could see the night's sky reflected upon it. Though it was the home of the mythical Phoenix, Heliopolis, once destroyed, never rose from its ashes to be born again. The Greeks used Heliopolis as a quarry to use its stones for the construction of the Pharos lighthouse in the harbour of Alexandria as well as its obelisks taken there and to Rome by the Romans. Over half of the obelisks now in Rome came from Heliopolis. You know it existed at the very dawn of the very first Egyptian dynasties... even before."

"I recall my father telling Stewart and I that Heliopolis was the name the Greeks gave it. The Egyptian name was Iunu, meaning 'place of pillars', which in biblical Hebrew was corrupted as On. He said the pillar aspect was important," Paul sighed.

"Diodorus Siculus, in 60 BC, wrote that Heliopolis was built by Actis, one of the sons of Helios and Rhode, who named the city after his father. It is claimed that while all Greek cities were destroyed during the flood, Egyptian cities, including Heliopolis, survived. The chief deity of Heliopolis was the creator god Atum, who soon became known as Atum-Ra. He was the self-begotten creator god who created the universe through masturbation seeing he was, after all, totally alone in the universe. He also created the so-called Ennead, the group of nine gods that embodied the creative source and chief forces of the universe. The Ennead, being the Nine Principles through which the Pharaoh ruled and ordered the forces of the universe, which dominated Egyptian thought from the Old Kingdom onwards, for no less than three thousand years. It is therefore the longest living theology that has ever existed...so far! Atum was worshipped in the site's primary temple, which was known by the names Per-Aat, 'Great House', and Per-Atum, 'the House of Atum'. Another temple in Heliopolis was the 'Mansion of the Benben', also known as the 'Mansion of the Phoenix', which is believed to have been a sacred precinct in which in the middle of an open courtyard stood a stone pillar, on top of which sat the 'benben stone'. It was seen as the solidified seed of Atum, the Stone of Creation, a magical stone, and some have concluded that it was of meteoric origin, 'shining' in the sky, but when fallen to earth, black. I am sure you are more than aware the sword you carry is made from the same material?" Theodoric asked and nodded at Paul's sword.

"I am certainly beginning to understand that it is unique for sure," Paul replied and placed his hand upon it just as Theodoric cleared his throat to continue.

"Alas, the stone itself has disappeared and is hence impossible to study. It was on this stone that the Phoenix, the Greek rendition of the Egypt benu bird, was said to return periodically, whereby he was reborn from his ashes, heralding a new era. Ancient accounts differ as to the number of years that passed between his visits, some dates apparently linked with a calendar that in turn was linked to the precession of the equinoxes, others with the stellar calendar, dominated by Sirius. The pyramids of Giza align to the obelisk of Heliopolis, which replaced the Temple of the Phoenix, where the benben stone had previously been kept. Furthermore, Giza and Heliopolis were connected by the 'Sacred Roads of the Gods'. This confirms the direct links between Giza with Heliopolis, and it is a very important connection. But know this, Paul...some will argue that the sacred primordial hill where the self-begotten Creator God Atum created the world from is not here in Heliopolis like the Greek geographer Strabo stated, for despite being situated on top of a noteworthy mound, the primordial hill of their mythology was actually Giza. The Giza group represents a symbolic expression of the Heliopolitan myth and the Sphinx was said to guard the 'Splendid Place of the Beginning of All Time', which is of course the primeval hill, the Mound of Creation. There is an account of how an old sycamore tree that grew near the Sphinx was damaged when the Lord of Heaven descended upon the Place of Hor-em-Akhet, the latter translated as 'the place of the Falcon God Horus of the Horizon', identified with the Sphinx. This tree was linked to Atum and in Heliopolis there was a chapel to Atum of the sycamore tree. The cult of the sycamore tree was, as usual, worked into Christianity for it became the Tree of the Virgin, which is a sycamore."

"My father did mention the Virgin tree, but I must confess I did not pay that much attention," Paul explained and shrugged his shoulders.

"Well...according to Coptic Christian tradition, and don't forget the Coptic Church was among the very earliest Churches of Christianity, dating back to around AD 42. It was established by Saint Mark, apostle and evangelist of his faith, who would eventually be martyred in Alexandria...I digress...the Holy Family on their journey through Egypt rested beneath this tree after crossing the desert, and today, it remains a place of pilgrimage. Giza and Heliopolis were two aspects of the same cult of the Creator God Atum and considered part of the same complex system. The primeval hill is the Giza plateau. Diodorus Siculus wrote that during the construction of the Great Pyramid a cut was made from the Nile, so that the water turned the site into an island."

Paul immediately recalled his vivid dreams of the Giza plateau showing the Great Pyramid surrounded by water.

"Yes...that I can believe for I have seen it," he remarked.

"By diverting the Nile, the plateau was turned into an island, to forcefully portray the creation myth of the primeval hill that rose from the Waters of Chaos. 'Tis identical to the original location of La Rochelle and Glastonbury in Britain before the lands surrounding them were drained. Imhotep, the great ancient Egyptian architect, was not the only great priest of Heliopolis for the biblical Moses was a high priest there too, which would make total sense if he had been one and the same Akhenaton, the heretic Pharaoh. But another important priest was Manetho, who in the third century BC codified the Egyptian religion in such a manner that it would be comprehensible to the Greeks who had conquered Egypt. Thankfully your father and I managed to learn a lot on this subject before it was branded as heresy to educate oneself with the language. When Herodotus visited and met the priests sometime around 449 to 440 BC he praised them for their wisdom. In 25 BC, when Strabo visited Egypt, he wrote that in Heliopolis he saw large buildings which the priests lived in who studied philosophy and astronomy. But there is no longer either such a body or such pursuits. Though little was left, as late as the fourth century AD, another Heliopolitan priest, Ammonius Saccas, taught two Greek philosophers, Plotinus and Origen, who developed what is now known as Neo-Platonism. The Greek philosopher Plato himself stated that he studied at Heliopolis. By the fourth century, most priests of Heliopolis had actually moved to Alexandria, the new capital."

"Oh how easy life in Alexandria now seems compared to now," Paul sighed.

Theodoric waited whilst Paul pondered, clearly reminiscing. He shook his head when he realised Theodoric was waiting. Paul feigned a brave smile and nodded he should continue.

"Getting back to Ammonius, we know that Egyptian priests wrote nothing down and passed everything on orally. He made his students vow absolute secrecy. Alas, at least in the eyes of Ammonius, both Plotinus and Origen broke this vow and their doctrine, which was closer to the true Heliopolitan doctrine, as passed down to us. Ammonius fled Alexandria when its pagan temples were attacked by Christian mobs, which also set fire to many of the libraries of Alexandria as you know. The Christian attack was but the final assault in a long series, begun when the Persians under Cambyses razed Heliopolis in 525 BC, both to destroy the power of the priests and to take a strategic position for entering into the south of the land. Ammonius declared that all moral and practical wisdom was contained in the books of Thoth of Hermes Trismegistus."

As soon as Theodoric had said Hermes Trismegistus Paul pulled up his sword and rubbed his finger across the triple Tau image engraved upon the pommel. It too formed the Latin letters of a T placed upon an H. A shiver ran down his spine at the very obvious connection.

"H and T!" Paul laughed to himself.

"At least you now see it," Theodoric remarked and patted Paul on the shoulder and smiled broadly at him before continuing. "And it is with Thoth that we learn of another key aspect of the Heliopolitan priesthood…their role in the Pyramid Texts. These texts adorn the walls of several pyramids, later constructed pyramids I stress, not the earlier ones. The texts are almost identical, repetitive sequences of magical utterances, to be spoken by the Pharaoh during his voyage in the Duat, the Egyptian afterlife, on his way to Heaven where he will meet, and become one with, the gods, and the creator deity Atum specifically. The Heliopolitan priesthood was famous for its astronomy as well as mathematics and were able to calculate and predict the heliacal rising of Sirius. They were in charge of the religious and civil calendars. They controlled time, or rather, were in charge of keeping time. That the temple was a centre of astronomical knowledge was also reflected in the title of its high priest, Chief of Observers or Greatest of Seers, a titled carried by Imhotep. All writing in Egypt was dedicated to Thoth, the scribe of the gods, and the inventor of hieroglyphs, the sacred language which is sadly being hidden from all as what it states does not fit with orthodox chronology," Theodoric explained.

"Such as?"

"Such as the fact that man's history stretches many thousands of years beyond that which the Church claims since the world was created. Those few learned enough to understand the ancient writings dismiss them as false and written by the Devil to mislead us," Theodoric said, shaking his head. "King Khufu, the so-called builder of the Great Pyramid of Giza, was apparently looking for the origins of the Pyramid Texts, which, according to various papyrus, were kept inside a flinty chest in a chamber called the Investigation Hall, which was somewhere in Heliopolis. Maspero wrote that the likeness between what was copied in the various Pyramid Texts suggests that some of their information was taken from old written sources...which were held in Heliopolis. Apparently Khufu consulted a magician, no doubt a high priest of Heliopolis, named Djedi, asking what of the report that he knew the number of the ipwt of the wnt of Thoth, that being the words meaning 'tomb', but also container, or more accurately 'hidden chamber'. Djedi replied that he knew not the number thereof, but he knew the place where it is...in a box of flint in a room called 'Revision' in Heliopolis. Maspero's interpretation is just one of several and others have included keys, or the secret chambers of the sanctuary of Thoth. The important aspect is, however, that the so-called builder of the Great Pyramid was searching for information and that this information was held in Heliopolis. Khufu afterwards went into the Per Ankh, the House of Life, but also a library, in search of information regarding the number of the chambers of Thoth. And though the priests were forbidden to commit things to writing, it is clear that some priests at some time had been allowed to write down their knowledge. And it is likely that it was this library that would later be transferred and/or copied to become the famous Library of Alexandria...or at least parts of the many libraries there. The books of the libraries as you know went up in flames; over the previous centuries, the priests, knowledge and monuments had been transferred, dispersed, largely in efforts to preserve them. Heliopolis might have survived the Deluge, but its element of destruction was obviously fire so closely linked with the sun. Just like the night will extinguish the last rays of the sun, so the City of the Sun entered into the shadows of history. A new dawn might be on the horizon, but it might merely be a false hope. Perhaps it never will...perhaps Heliopolis just shone too brilliantly, and its spark can never be reignited."

Paul sat in silence as he pondered upon Theodoric's words. After Theodoric waited patiently again, Paul looked at him.

"And this tree…Father said Alisha and I should visit it but time has flown past and we have not," Paul said.

"Ah well, the Al-Matariyyah tree as it is called. Lucy and I have visited it oft times. 'Tis named from the Latin mater, which means 'mother', and is from the presence of the 'tree of the Virgin Mary', Al-Matariyya, within the Ain Shams district, which is of course the old Heliopolis itself. Legend tells of the Christian Holy Family sheltering under a tree in Heliopolis, 'the tree of the Virgin Mary', now with the Chapel of the Virgin in Al-Matariyyah. Where Memphis, the first capital of Dynastic Egypt, embodied the political and administrative heart of the ancient kingdom, Heliopolis was its spiritual, theological and cosmological counterpart. Your father and I saw Memphis once as it stood…in a fashion and manner as you saw the Giza pyramids as they were long ago. It was surrounded by large gleaming white walls and hence why it was named Ineb-hedj, meaning 'white walls'." [104]

"You mean to say you have had similar experiences to that which Percival and I have?" Paul asked, surprised.

"Of course…" Theodoric smiled and winked. "Despite being sacked by the Persians in the sixth Century BC, Ancient Heliopolis remained a centre for learning and religion until the mantel was taken by Alexandria two hundred years later. The Virgin Tree lies just half a mile southwest from the Senusret obelisk. According to the Coptic Christian tradition, when the Holy Family, that is the Virgin Mary, Joseph and Jesus, entered nearby Heliopolis, all the Egyptian idols were destroyed by their presence. The Holy Family fled Heliopolis seeking refuge from angry Egyptians. They stopped at a sycamore tree, whose branches covered the Holy Family and hid them from the mob. The original Virgin Tree has been dead for centuries, but it has two generations of trees that have grown out of its dead shell. The second generation tree is also dead, but the third generation tree, still alive and bearing fruit which is considered blessed, still stands," Theodoric explained then yawned.

"Theo…I am sorry for I keep you," Paul said, standing up.

"Aye…these old bones grow weary this hour. I shall teach you how to use the compass starting tomorrow," Theodoric answered, gesturing to the compass. "I will bid you a good night…and make sure you take an escort and visit the Virgin Tree."

Port of La Rochelle, France, Melissae Inn, spring 1191

"I am seeing that trees indeed seem significant," the Genoese sailor remarked as Stephan placed several plates on the table.

"Is there really such a tree in Egypt?" Ayleth asked.

"Yes there is," the old man replied. "And Alisha and Paul did visit the place. They were quite shocked at how it was used as a money making scheme...the wealthiest getting to see it first and for longer periods of time. But now when they went out they had Ishmael, Percival and at least two of Thomas's men with them at all times."

"I bet that must have made them feel secure," Sarah said.

"No...quite the opposite. It made Alisha feel oppressed and trapped into a way of life she did not want. It made her fully appreciate how Princess Stephanie must feel daily. But it affected every aspect of their daily lives. Arri had to be tutored at home...alone most of the time...and all of Alisha's clients had to now attend measuring and fittings at her home, which meant they all had to be checked in and out every time. Without Nyla and with all the added pressures involved, Alisha lost her desire and passion for making dresses. Despite the generous support of Husam and his guards, she felt like a prisoner," the old man explained.

"And Percival. Did he not seek revenge?" Gabirol asked.

"'Twas not his way," the old man answered quietly. "Besides, he vowed to protect Alisha and Paul...despite being reminded daily of Nyla and the child he had also lost. And how could he get close to exact revenge upon Turansha anyway?"

"But you said the one who ordered the attack was not Turansha," Peter interjected.

"Yes I said that and it was so...but at that time, all blamed him for want of knowing who else would wish such on them," the old man explained.

"What is a compass?" Simon asked.

"'Tis an instrument that shows the direction of north at all times," the Genoese Sailor answered. "But they are very few in number."

"Theo spent many hours teaching Paul how to use the compass. 'Twas a mariner's compass and functions to establish the holder's position relative to the magnetic meridian by use of a magnetic needle," the old man started to explain.

"He is lucky for we have but the simple 'needle and bowl' compass. Try using that in a swell," the Genoese sailor commented and laughed.

"Needle and bowl?" Ayleth quizzed.

"Yes...you know, when you magnetise a needle by rubbing it on silk, then place it in

a straw and float it in water to become a compass. But it could only help us to establish a rough location in conjunction with astronomical observations and depth soundings. Luckily those dry box compass sets are beginning to become more available."

"Tenno helped to improve the one Philip sent to Paul. The development of the 'dry' box compass is contested between us here in Europe and that of the Orient. Chinese literature first mentions a mariner's compass in 1044, whereas here, we have only just started to note its design. The biggest difference really is that Chinese compasses have the needle highlighted as pointing south, whereas we have it highlighted north and the European compass card has sixteen rather than twenty-four basic divisions."

"How do they work?" Sarah asked.

"In short, the 'dry' compass is a single sealed instrument where a magnetised needle is free to turn on a central pivot. It thus consists of three parts: the box, the card and the needle. Paul's compass was actually divided into thirty-two points, or rhumbs, which follow wind directions. Our Naval Templars are presently using these with new instruments derived from the Celtic cross, as I explained earlier, to navigate...and, my dear friends, I have that very compass with me here this day," the old man explained.

"Why...and may we look at it?" the Templar asked as the Genoese sailor looked on, very interested.

1 - 1

The old man leaned down and opened his satchel and removed the ornate polished little box made from oak wood. Carefully he opened it and placed it upon the table so all could see its content.

"'Tis beautiful to look at," Ayleth remarked as she leaned forward to look at it closely.

"'Tis that for sure," the Templar said and ran his finger around the edge of the compass sat neatly in a bed of silk.

"When we have concluded this tale I speak, one of you will be leaving here with it...as a gift," the old man said but not looking at anyone in particular so as not to give any clue who.

"The fact that this gift to Paul sits here this day does not bode well for him I suspect," Gabirol said as he looked at the compass.

"Did Alisha have her baby?" Sarah asked hesitantly pulling an exaggerated grimace on her face.

"Yes...yes indeed she did," the old man answered solemnly.

"Did Paul keep his word or did he ever return to the pyramids...did he enter and stay longer so disappeared for good, from our time at least?" Simon asked.

The old man looked at him in silence for s short time just as Gabirol stared at him.

"Simon...you have as yet to begin your true vocation in this life...and your perceptiveness is what shall lead you," the old man said.

"So he did and that is why he is no longer here and you have his sword and journals," Peter interrupted.

"No, my friends...that is not what happened, though it could have. Paul visited the Great Pyramid again, mainly to check out certain things in his own mind, but he never entered them or below the plateau. I hope you have by now learnt and understood that Giza is the most central site on earth. All others link to it across the world and man will again learn this truth. Paul did however thoroughly check out the black floor slabs next to Great Pyramid and how they were made. 'Tis how it was made that will finally make man in the future wake up to its real origins...," the old man explained and lowered his head. "'Twas there at Giza an old friend called upon him..."

Giza Plateau, Egypt, December 23rd 1183

Paul knelt beside a large black stone and ran his fingers along the perfectly cut groove. The stone made up part of the constructed levelled floor the Great Pyramid was built upon. There were no tools that could make the cuts and shape the stones in the exact manner they had been fashioned. The air was warm and dry, the sun setting fast on the horizon. Ishmael and Percival remained upon their horses keeping hold of Adrastos. The few remaining workers were packing up to leave as the night shift guards took over from the two guards at the Great Pyramid's entrance. Paul closed his eyes.

"This is not a privilege, nor an honour but surely a curse...this burden you put upon my shoulders," Paul whispered to himself. He closed his eyes tighter and tried to recall all the images he had seen of the Giza complex when it was first constructed. He could sense the presence of the place just as a gentle breeze blew cool across his face.

"'Tis no curse, my friend, for you volunteered for this," a familiar voice said behind him.

Paul opened his eyes and saw a large shadow cast of a man wearing a tall pointed hat. He knew immediately who it was. He turned around and looked up to see Kratos stood before him silhouetted by the sinking sun. Paul stood up slowly and moved to stand beside him, the light showing his features as he turned to the side.

"Kratos…what brings you here?" Paul asked surprised and clasped Kratos's large hand to shake.

"Oh…many things…the celebration for the birth of Christ perhaps," Kratos replied with a smile just as Paul noticed Abi sat upon her horse pulled up alongside Ishmael and Percival. Kratos looked over his shoulder back at them. "Besides, Percival is in need of us."

"Percival?"

"Yes…Percival," Kratos repeated and turned to face Paul. "We have other plans for him I think he will gladly accept…for his soul is greatly wounded. Staying with you only hurts him more."

"What! How?"

"Nyla's passing has cut him deeper than he lets on. Alisha with child soon to be born reminds him daily of what he has lost," Kratos explained quietly as Paul looked toward Percival just as Abi waved.

Paul raised his hand in reply but he felt sick. The sudden realisation of the pain Percival had been suffering in silence now so obvious. He felt guilty but also alarmed that he would lose perhaps his best friend. Kratos placed his hand upon Paul's shoulder and looked at him in the way only he was able to do, his deep blue eyes telling Paul all he needed to know. Percival would, and had to, leave with him.

ꕥ

Paul opened the main door into the kitchen and smiled at Sister Lucy as she washed Arri's feet, which were covered in mud, as he sat up on the side, his little feet in the wash basin. Paul raised his eyebrows at Arri, who just waved his hands and smiled back. Paul held the door half shut behind him as he stepped into the room. Alisha entered carrying several plates ready to set the table for the evening supper, with a large lanthorn slung under her left arm. Her eyes widened, pleased to see Paul home.

"I hate to do this, but I think you will require more plates I am afraid," Paul explained and opened the door fully as Alisha and Sister Lucy looked on.

Abi stepped into view, ducked her head and entered the room.

"Abi!" Alisha called out excitedly, quickly placed the plates and lanthorn down and rushed over to her. "I cannot believe it is you," she said and flung her arms up and around her. After a short hug, Alisha stepped back a pace looking up into her eyes. "You…you look so well…and…and what are you doing here?"

"I am here for you and your unborn…," Abi answered and gestured to Alisha's large tummy.

"This is the best Christmas present ever," Alisha said just as Kratos bowed his head low to step through the door. He stood up straight, his hat held in one hand, his staff in the other and smiled at her. "Kratos!"

"Yes, my dear child. We have come to assist where best we can until the baby is born."

Alisha hugged Kratos, leaned up and kissed the side of his cheek and then stepped back so she could look at both of them. Kratos nodded a greeting smile at Sister Lucy and Arri, who picked up his toy Clip clop and hid his face, embarrassed.

"We hope you do not mind us visiting and staying a short while?" Abi asked.

Alisha looked at Paul just as Theodoric entered the room carrying two wine jars. Quickly he placed them down on the main table and rushed around, grabbed Kratos's hand and shook it vigorously.

"My Lord…we shall require more wine this eve," he bellowed as Sister Lucy shook her head disapprovingly but laughing at his behaviour, seeing him so excited. "And Abi…you look different," he said loudly as he moved to grab both of her hands.

Whilst Theodoric shook Abi's hands just as vigorously, pulled her close and hugged her, Paul noticed she did indeed look different. Whatever Kratos had done to heal her had clearly worked, but she was also dressed differently. New clothes and new leather armour beneath her cape. Percival entered the room quietly and closed the door behind. Kratos faced him and gave a slight nod. Percival returned a faint smile and stood still, his hands together across his waist.

"I note you have Mamluk guards outside," Kratos spoke out loud to no one in particular.

"They are needed," Percival replied.

"Sadly so I hear…now come with me. I must have words with you in private," Kratos said to Percival, put his arm around him and ushered him across the room. "Nothing bad, I promise," Kratos assured him as he opened the door to the main corridor.

As the door closed behind them, Alisha grabbed Abi's hand excitedly and beckoned her to sit down. Paul smiled and was pleased to see her smiling so happily. It had been a long time since he had seen her smile like that. Sister Lucy dried Arri's feet and helped him to the floor. He ran over to Paul, embarrassed, as Abi watched him.

"He has grown some," she said softly. "You must be very proud of him?"

"Oh we are…'tis such a pity you cannot feel this pride and love of a mother," Alisha said still clasping Abi's hand.

"Do not be so quick to say such," Abi replied and smiled in a manner that made Alisha instantly know there was more. "I too know what it is like for I am also a mother now."

Theodoric sat down hard on the end chair, his mouth open in surprise. Abi and Alisha both laughed.

"How so?" Paul asked, puzzled.

"The same way all babies are made," she answered.

Theodoric's eyes appeared to widen even more.

"Who…and where is your child. Is it a boy or a girl?" Alisha asked excitedly.

"Oh that matters not who…and he is a boy," Abi replied and looked at Theodoric.

Sister Lucy sat down opposite Abi.

"Well this is a double surprise for I thought it impossible you could ever be with child," she remarked.

"So did I…but a son I now have. He is safe in Malta and looked after very well," Abi explained.

"That explains the difference in you," Alisha said and laughed. "A mother too."

"Don't sound so surprised…I am after all still a woman," Abi laughed. "But it does mean that I can only stay a short while until your baby is born…if you do not mind of course?" she asked but looked at Sister Lucy.

"Of course we do not mind. It is reassuring to know I will have you present when the time comes," Sister Lucy replied and nodded at Alisha as she nodded her head in agreement.

Theodoric scratched his head, looking confused.

Port of La Rochelle, France, Melissae Inn, spring 1191

"Abi...with a son?" Simon said, bemused.

"I want to know, who was the father?" Sarah asked.

"Think back upon this tale for I have told you already if you recall...when Philip visited her in Malta," the old man stated.

"Tenno!" Gabirol remarked.

"Of course," Sarah said loudly.

"Did Tenno know?" Peter asked.

"No...not then but he would find out in time...just in time," the old man answered.

"Sounds ominous as well?" the wealthy tailor remarked.

"Perhaps...," the old man said quietly. "But that Christmas was a delight for Alisha and Paul. Percival was kept busy with Kratos and Theodoric instructing him on many things...at times to the exclusion of Paul altogether...not that he minded as he was pleased to see Percival start to gain some sense of purpose again. Theodoric got into trouble on more than one occasion drinking far too much wine and mead beer," the old man explained and laughed to himself.

"What did Abi do all that time then?" Ayleth asked.

"She literally guarded Alisha and Arri constantly. Paul learnt how to use the compass and made preparations for the arrival of the new baby, which, he was adamant, would be a girl as he had seen. He also drew up the tattoo that was on Theodoric's back and painted it on the inside of his shield...a shield Ishmael had made as a gift and painted Paul's coat of arms upon that Philip had presented to him before."

"Why did Ishmael make him a shield?" the Templar asked.

"Ishmael felt Paul should have one to put his coat of arms upon. And in case the day should ever come when he may need a shield," the old man replied then looked at Stephan.

"Shall I fetch it to show?" Stephan asked as Sarah looked at him quizzically. The old man simply nodded yes.

Everyone's eyes followed Stephan as he left the room, then went upstairs and several minutes later returned carrying a shield wrapped in a protective leather hide cover. Sarah looked on utterly bemused having not known Stephan even had a shield.

"Where have you been hiding that all this time?" she asked.

"In the loft within the chimney breast cupboard," Stephan answered and gently placed the battered shield upon the table so they could all see it.

"Ishmael was obviously correct...that he would need it as this shield has seen much combat," the Hospitaller commented as he looked over the many grooves, dents, cuts and arrow marks upon the battered shield, Paul's coat of arms faded but still clearly visible.

"It did indeed," the old man sighed.

"How did it come to be kept here?" Gabirol asked.

"Yes...pray tell!" Sarah said and folded her arms and raised her eyebrows at Stephan.

"I shall come to that soon...," the old man said and turned the shield over to reveal the tree-wings tattoo drawing. "You will see Paul copied it exactly. Even the slight differences on either side of the sword, for like twins, though they be identical, they still have subtle differences," he explained and looked at the Templar and Hospitaller.

"There is much dried blood upon this shield," the Templar remarked, pointing out several dark stained areas.

Ayleth put her hand to her mouth at the realisation the marks were blood.

"The shield is here by the same manner the sword was also brought here along with Paul's journals. But as for Alisha and Paul...when the baby was due, though a little late actually, it was a time of happy arrivals and sad farewells..."

"But what happened with Saladin after he left the siege at Kerak?" Ayleth asked.

"As I said, the siege was lifted in December and Saladin retreated to Damascus, though he would have cause to attack it again later in 1184."

"But the baby arrived okay?" Sarah asked.

Cairo, January 21st 1184

The morning air was cool as Paul stepped out of the front door followed by Ishmael and Thomas. Two Mamluk guards bowed to greet them when several riders on horseback appeared trotting toward them. The Mamluk guards made ready but soon relaxed their stance when they recognised their fellow men and Husam riding up front. Paul squinted from the sun as he tried to make out the other rider beside Husam.

"Oh great. 'Tis Lord Montferrat...," Thomas muttered through gritted teeth. "Why is he here again?"

Husam dismounted passing his reins to one of the Mamluk sentry guards and pulled Paul close and greeted him enthusiastically.

"Assalamu aliekum," Husam bellowed almost.

"Wa allakam assalam", Paul replied smiling at Husam's exuberance.

Husam looked up to the second floor of the house sensing he was being watched. He noticed three of the upper windows had crossbows aimed from them. Quickly Thomas waved them to withdraw back into the property.

"An unfortunate but wise necessity," Husam remarked and gestured for Conrad to approach. "I trust my men have been vigilant and helpful?"

"Very," Paul replied, looking at Conrad with suspicion.

Conrad eased his horse nearer, looking down at Paul. He bowed his head very slightly at him.

"We meet again," Conrad nodded with a grin.

A cold shiver ran down Paul's spine. Something had changed with Conrad since they last met. He was hiding something and it made Paul feel uneasy.

"Please, come inside for some refreshments," Paul said and gestured toward the door just as Theodoric walked out, stopped, took one look at them and spun back around on his heels and walked back into the property. "Please, if you would follow Theo."

ജ്ജ

Theodoric asked Sister Lucy to go upstairs and let Alisha know they had guests. As she left the main dining area, Percival held the doors open for Conrad and Husam to enter.

"I am glad all is well here," Husam said as Paul offered him a chair.

Ishmael pulled out a chair for Conrad, who sat down upon it without acknowledging or saying thank you to him.

Within minutes, Sister Lucy returned and immediately started to sort out some cool refreshments.

"You have no real servants, I note," Conrad said, looking at Sister Lucy, who shot him an instant look of disdain and frowned hard at him. He just laughed. "You should, you know...have proper servants."

"I do not believe in holding servants unless they work for pay and of their own free will," Paul replied and sat opposite Conrad. "So please pray tell what brings you to these shores?"

"Oh the usual. Another truce or treaty to be negotiated. Husam was good enough to bring me all the way. We meet Karaksh, Saladin's deputy and Gokbori tomorrow. Whatever foolhardy schemes that reckless idiot Reynald thinks up next, I do not want his actions interfering with my men and my ambitions."

"And what pray tell again are those ambitions exactly?" Paul asked, his tone serious.

"Swear and pledge your sword to me and I will reveal all," Conrad replied and stared at Paul intently. "The likes of Reynald, the so-called Red Wolf, need to be brought to heel like a dog…for all our sakes."

Paul looked at Husam, who nodded in agreement with Conrad's remarks.

"Conrad is the sole rightful heir to the crown of Jerusalem, Paul, and all of Outremer. We could have peace if he sat upon the throne for he is not like Reynald or the other Franks," Husam said and studied Paul's face for his reaction.

"Reynald and all the barons of Outremer war with each other over petty matters and who has the most legitimacy…yet it is I and I alone who has that right. Join me and you will have security and safety," Conrad explained.

"Bullshit!" Theodoric coughed, his words barely discernible as he covered his mouth and coughed again and pretended to clear his throat.

Paul tried not to smile as Conrad looked at Theodoric. Husam had heard his words and smiled but shook his head no.

"What did he say?" Conrad asked.

"Prove it, I think he said?" Paul replied and looked at Theodoric who raised his hand and kept on coughing.

Sister Lucy took him some cool water to drink and frowned at him hard.

"Oh I can prove it. 'Tis why I am here and to secure agreements with Saladin and my forces," Conrad stated, looking indignant that he had been verbally challenged by Theodoric.

Alisha entered the room with Arri by her side. He looked at Husam and Conrad and quickly held her hand.

"We swear allegiance to no one," she said forcefully and placed her other hand across her tummy. "I heard what you speak of…and we shall not be coerced into siding with any king, lord or whatever," she continued to state as Conrad turned around fully in his chair to look at her.

"Alisha…you must be due soon for surely you are overdue?" Conrad asked calmly. "But in this real world I am afraid we all must decide and chose a side…eventually."

"Paul," Husam interrupted. "I hear you have one of those new compass devices. May I see it before we move on?"

"Of course," Paul said and stood up, a little puzzled how he knew but also how Conrad knew Alisha was late.

"Will you be here long...in Cairo?" Alisha asked bluntly.

"I shall remain but a few weeks whereas Conrad must leave when we have agreed terms," Husam replied politely.

"Did you come alone?" Alisha asked, her tone clipped.

"Are you interrogating me?" Conrad asked and stood up.

"No she is not...but she is tired no less," Paul said and walked over to her.

"I sense perhaps we intrude. Will it be more convenient if we meet later at Husam's?...If he is in agreement of course," Conrad asked.

2 - 42

"Of course. Please bring your compass with you when you do. Conrad has but only four men of his own guard with him on this visit. 'Tis a mark of his trust he has in me," Husam explained and stood up and bowed at Alisha. "And I trust him."

Alisha suddenly bent forward in pain, her face grimacing as it flushed red. Arri looked up at her, puzzled. Quickly she held on to the door for support as her legs started to shake. A pool of liquid formed near her right foot and she looked down then back up at everyone.

"'Tis her waters. Her baby is coming...and fast," Sister Lucy said aloud and started to push Husam toward the rear door and gestured for Conrad to follow. "Come on...this is women's work and no place for men to be standing around gawping."

Husam looked at Paul and smiled reassuringly at him.

"Paul...come to my residence when you can. We have much to catch up," he said and then looked at Alisha as she started to turn herself around. "And may Allah bless you with a swift and easy birth this day."

Alisha simply waved her hand as she breathed in and out quickly, Arri still holding her other hand, Paul now trying to support her upright.

"Paul, think upon what I have said...," Conrad stated as he followed Husam.

Theodoric ran to the main oven and started to fill a large pan with water ready to boil.

"Paul...just get her upstairs now!" he called out and started to blow the hot embers of the fire grate below the pan. "And he will most certainly think about your words...My Lord."

Conrad looked at Theodoric, unsure whether he was being serious or sarcastic toward him. Sister Lucy gave him one of her looks. Conrad shook his head and stepped out of the rear door. Husam smiled as she passed him, nodded at Alisha and Paul and followed Conrad out. As soon as the door was shut, she slapped Theodoric across his shoulders and raised her hands in mock despair.

ꙮ

The room was darkened, the heavy curtains closed. Several candles flickered as Alisha lay upon her bed propped up by large pillows. Sister Lucy was busy preparing two basins full of water as Theodoric entered carrying another bowl full of hot water. Arri held Paul's hand, looking on concerned.

"Why is the room all dark?" Arri asked in a whisper.

"Arri there is no need to whisper. And it is darkened so the light does not shock your new sister when she enters this world," Paul explained as Alisha stretched out her hand for Arri.

"Or brother," Alisha said and smiled despite the pain arching through her lower back and pelvis.

Arri rushed over to Alisha and took her hand. She rubbed her other hand through his hair and kissed his forehead just as Abi entered the room by pushing her backside into the door, her hands just washed held up. She had changed into a one piece robe and clean apron around her waist.

"I think you will find this baby is in a hurry," she explained as she turned to face Alisha.

"Come...let us leave the adults to do what they must," Theodoric said and gestured for Arri to follow him.

"Must I?" he protested. Alisha simply smiled and nodded yes as pain enveloped her body bringing tears to her eyes. "You will not go to heaven with Nyla will you?" Arri asked looking serious.

"No...Mama is going nowhere," Paul reassured and moved Arri to Theodoric. Arri looked up at him clutching Clip clop close to his chest.

"Promise," Arri said.

"I promise," Paul replied.

Reluctantly Arri followed Theodoric out of the room, Theodoric giving a thumbs up to Alisha and smiling awkwardly. No sooner had the door closed when Alisha let out a deep moan of intense pain and shifted herself down further onto her back and raised her legs. Abi looked at Paul.

"I am staying right here," he said.

"Good...then make yourself useful and hold her leg," Abi ordered and indicated he take her right leg.

Alisha screwed up her face in agony and started to pant. Abi quickly unfurled a roll of gleaming instruments each sealed within smaller rolls. She parted Alisha's legs to see the baby's head already crowning. Paul looked down surprised as Sister Lucy took Alisha's other leg.

"Do you prefer this position or would you rather be on all fours?" Sister Lucy asked as Alisha put her hands on her thighs and gritted her teeth, took a deep breath and screwed her face tightly as she felt the urge to push overwhelm her. "Too late I think."

Paul held Alisha's leg as she started to shake, then let out a deep groan, opened her eyes wide staring directly at him.

"I have her," Abi said as she bent down quickly just in time to catch the baby as it slid out fast into her hands. Paul looked down in time to see the little figure covered in blood from where Alisha had split and fluid. Abi lifted the baby up slightly with her hand so it faced downward. Paul's heart stopped when he saw the baby was not moving. Alisha saw the look of concern in his face and gripped his hand tightly. Abi tilted the baby downwards briefly, and it suddenly gave out a small cough, drew its first breath and made just one slight cry. As Abi lifted its little body up, it was clear to see she was indeed a girl. Sister Lucy passed Abi a clean shawl, which she wrapped around the baby gently, just her face showing, the umbilical cord still trailing below her and into Alisha. "Let the placenta come away naturally before we cut the cord...'tis: far better for both," she smiled and handed Paul the baby.

Paul took the baby in his hands keeping her close to Alisha and looked at her as she opened her eyes. His heart skipped a beat and the emotions inside him hit him like a crashing wave. He went to speak but could not as tears welled in his eyes. He looked at Alisha. As soon as she knew all was well with the baby, she relaxed her hands beside her and lay back into the pillows.

"That was one very quick birth," Sister Lucy stated and shook her head, trying not to show emotion, but her voice gave away just how emotional she too felt.

Paul moved slowly and sat beside Alisha offering up the baby to her chest so she could see her face. Alisha let out an emotional laugh as a tear ran down her face. Paul kissed her on the cheek and put his head against hers, the baby between them.

"You said it would be a girl," Alisha half laughed and cried and put her arm up around Paul.

Suddenly Alisha's arm dropped away and she closed her eyes, her body going limp as she passed out. Alarmed Paul looked up at Abi as she was busy dealing with the placenta as it was discharged. She picked up two of the instruments beside her and started to do something with Alisha. She then wrapped the placenta in a cloth and moved it closer to Paul and the baby. Sister Lucy could not hide her look of concern as Abi concentrated on Alisha. She took out what looked like a highly polished black egg with symbols on. Instantly Paul recognised the symbols were identical to those he had seen below the pyramids. He took a deep breath as Abi gently placed the egg over Alisha's tummy, put both her hands over it and pushed downward gently closing her eyes as if praying. Sister Lucy put her hands together and bit her bottom lip. Paul looked down at the baby girl. She was looking directly at him. Immediately images of his experience in the pyramid when he saw a young girl approach him flashed through is mind. A recognition of her in the eyes of the baby. He stared closer, transfixed as she looked back at him in silence.

"Aum!" Abi suddenly said aloud, opened her eyes and then stood up straight. She took a deep breath and looked at Paul. "She will be fine now." Sister Lucy gasped in relief and covered her mouth and looked at the shining egg object still positioned on Alisha. "Please…do not ask me to explain," Abi said calmly and smiled with relief herself.

Paul sensed Alisha looking at him and as he turned. She was indeed. She forced a tired smile then closed her eyes again. A light rap on the door drew their attention.

"Come in," Paul called out.

The door opened slowly and Theodoric peered around.

"'Tis a little too quiet. Is everything okay?" he asked as Arri popped his head around and positioned Clip clop so it looked as though it was also peering in.

Paul nodded all was well and indicated with his eyes at the baby in his arms. Arri instantly running in to see his new sister stopping to stare in amazement at her.

"'Tis a girl," Paul said, his voice wavering with emotion and kissed the baby on her forehead as Arri pulled her down gently to see.

Theodoric gave a silent thumbs up, winked at Abi and Sister Lucy and slowly closed the door behind him as he left the room.

"'Tis a girl!" he then shouted out loudly, Sister Lucy shaking her head.

"A girl!" Thomas then shouted out further along the corridor.

"Girl!" Luke could be heard shouting further downstairs.

A loud cheer from all of Thomas's men, Ishmael and Percival went up outside for them to hear. Alisha opened her eyes again and smiled. Paul laughed hearing them. Arri laughed and jumped on the bed beside Alisha and hugged her. Abi looked at Sister Lucy and winked, relieved. After a few minutes of silence, a beautiful chorus of men singing with a deep background chant started to sound out filling the air with a harmonious song that seemed to penetrate each of them. Alisha looked at Abi, puzzled, as she opened the blackout curtains, the rays of sunshine making them all squint instantly. She looked down to see Thomas and his men stood in a semicircle singing out the chorus. She indicated to Paul to come over and look. Slowly he stood up, placed the baby beside Alisha and moved to stand beside Abi.

"What are they singing for it is beautiful?" Sister Lucy asked as she looked down just as Kratos walked into view behind the men. He stood still, his staff in his right hand and looked up, his large hat shielding his face from the sun but revealing his smile.

"'Tis an ancient chant. One I have not heard in a great many years...," Abi replied and smiled. "'Tis the chant and song of the Resin. Ancient words and harmonies that touch the soul."

Arri tried to look through the window but he was too short. Paul lifted him up and held him so he could look down.

"Beautiful," Alisha said quietly as she cradled the baby. "As is our daughter...Ailia."

Paul turned to look at her.

"You have a name for her already?" he asked smiling. Alisha nodded yes. "Ailia."

"Her full name to be Ailia Tara Amaya Erin," Alisha said as she looked into Ailia's eyes.

Alisha's choice of names was not lost on Paul.

Chapter 63
Quiet Before the Storm

Port of Fustat, February 6th 1184

"'Tis indeed sad that we must leave you again so soon," Kratos said quietly as he stood beside Paul looking out across the Nile, the stars sparkling above them in a brilliant dance of light. "It has been a very enjoyable and constructive visit, I must add."

A welcoming cool breeze blew in off of the calm waters and Paul took a deep breath. Ishmael and Percival were sat on a stone bench behind them but still keeping an ever watchful eye out for any hint of trouble.

"I am pleased with Alisha's choice of name for our daughter. I am sure Tenno and the blacksmith would approve too. Her names are so befitting, Ailia after her own birth name and in memory of Raja, Maya after Tenno's daughter, Erin after the sacred Emerald Isle goddess and name...and of course Tara. Huh, I can still hear and recall the blacksmith's words as if just spoken. 'Say nothing...nothing. It will give us some small measure of comfort in the years ahead to know she died for something,' much like the advice Theo gave Percival actually," Paul said quietly and looked over his shoulder at Percival, his green tunic looking black in the night air.

"The blacksmith was right though, for you have never forgotten Tara," Kratos said and nodded at him knowingly. Paul's eyes followed the height of his hat to its point. "Ah...do you not approve of my new hat?" Kratos laughed.

"'Tis rather pointed is it not?"

"For a reason...many so-called magicians wear them without even knowing why or how to make one properly," Kratos replied and winked. "Mine is lined with copper and gold wire to protect me. 'Tis similar to ancient gold hats once used by adepts of the old ways."

"How does it protect you?"

"Do you recall all the many ancient symbols and images for medicine, for healing and the gods…the entwined serpents such as on the caduceus staff?"

"Yes I have studied them often."

"As this world we walk upon changes, it sends out waves of sound that directly affect and interact with the very physical construct of our bodies. One day in the future, as we pass into the age Aquarius, the world will itself increase in harmonic frequency that will in turn increase man's vibration and his subconscious to a higher level. We have energies that are centred in certain parts of the body. I believe Theodoric has taught you these points, chakras as they are known?" Kratos asked, looking down at Paul. He nodded yes. "Good. I cannot fully explain now, and it will be a great deal of time in the future before man again learns that the very smallest parts that make us up are designed and constructed as a double helix chain…'tis what the entwined snake symbol represents. When man again discovers these simple truths, only then will he be able to recognise just how advanced our ancient forefathers really were…just as they shall learn with the study of the ancient pyramids and how they were made."

"Is that why the serpent symbol has always been used to represent knowledge or wisdom?" Paul asked.

"Yes. But the waves of energy that surround this world, they grow weak at this time and disturbed as man has forgotten his connection to the land…and tears down many of the ancient stones that kept the balance and harmony. The vibration waves unfortunately affect people like me, especially the higher chakras above the seven most known of now…for there are in fact twelve, which again man will one day learn. So to protect myself from the more harmful influences, I am now forced to wear this ridiculous headdress," he explained and laughed as he pointed to it. "At least it is not as bad as the heavy gold ones used years ago covered in symbols and stars. Small mercy I am grateful for. 'Tis why crowns for kings were started but they have long since lost their true original meanings and practical uses."

"My father and Firgany once told Taqi and I about a crown connected with the three wise men, the Magi who came from the East. I am sure they even mentioned the land of Ind…was that India?" Paul asked.

"Ah…that golden crown," Kratos replied and nodded his head a few times. "They were talking of the story of the Three Magi who came to worship Jesus Christ in his infancy and the Land of Ind, where there was a mountain called the Hill of Vaws, or the Hill of Victory. Ever since the times when Israelites came out of Egypt and conquered the Promised Land, the keepers of this hill watched for anything unusual in the West. Of course the main purpose of this outpost was to prevent a sudden attack on the Land of Ind, but it was on this hill that the star announcing the birth of Christ was first observed. After the Three Kings of Ind, Chaldea and Persia had made their famous journey to Bethlehem, offering gold, frankincense and myrrh to the newborn Messiah, they made a pact to return to the Hill of Vaws once a year. They also chose to be buried there. However, the relics of the Three Kings were destined to be transferred out of that area… first to Constantinople, then to Milan and, finally, to Cologne. Still, the kings' legacy lived on in that land, and the 'progeny of Vaws' was respected throughout the East. Around the year 1200, a delegation of noblemen of Vaws came to visit the flourishing city of Acon, Acre. They brought many gifts, including a golden diadem which once belonged to Melchior, the king who offered the gift of gold to the infant Christ. It was adorned with crosses, Chaldean letters and stars, a reminder of the Star of Bethlehem. It was supposedly a miraculous crown that could heal…the Order of the Knights Templar and personally the Grand Master got hold of this crown, along with many other valuables, treating it as great treasure and making ample use of it. As Gerard has become the Master now, the crown will be removed for safe keeping…something your father does as we speak for Gerard cannot be trusted with it. But much knowledge came from the East as a consequence…from the Land of Ind…India!"

"But I thought the Star of Bethlehem did not really exist and that the three Magi came from the Orient," Paul remarked.

"The Star of Bethlehem was a conjunction of stellar phenomena…and as I have just said, the three kings, the Magi, came from three different locations coming together to offer their gifts…but the symbolism behind those gifts has long since been obscured and now hidden behind a story and image of added romance and symbols. The actual story gives clues within the Gospels still…as in the shepherds, the animals within the stable, and all related to stellar constellations and signs. I see you look more puzzled," Kratos laughed. "Let me explain. The gold Jesus is given is to indicate that he is going to be a king. Gold is a symbol of divinity and is mentioned throughout the Bible. Pagan idols were often made from gold and the Ark of the Covenant was overlaid with gold. The gift of gold to the Christ child was symbolic of His divinity as in a god in flesh. Frankincense is a white resin or gum and is obtained from a tree by making incisions in the bark and allowing the gum to flow out. It is highly fragrant when burned and was therefore used in worship, where it is burned as a pleasant offering to God. Frankincense is a symbol of holiness and righteousness. The gift of frankincense to the Christ child was symbolic of His willingness to become a sacrifice, wholly giving Himself up, analogous to a burnt offering. Myrrh is also a product of Arabia, and is obtained from a tree in the same manner as frankincense. It is a spice and used in embalming. It was also sometimes mingled with wine to form an article of drink. Such a drink was given to Jesus when he was about to be crucified, as a stupefying potion. In Mark 15:23. And Matthew 27:34 refers to it as 'gall'. Myrrh symbolises bitterness, suffering and affliction just as Jesus would grow to suffer greatly as a man and would pay the ultimate price when He gave His life on the cross for all who would believe in Him." [105]

"So the whole nativity story is really quite dark as well as prophetic in meaning and symbolism," Paul stated.

"Yes when seen for what it is. The lambs that are sacrificed as was Jesus. The shepherds used to symbolise and mark the period as set during the cycle of Aries…the Ram. Jesus performing miracles actually put his life in danger from the start."

"Why?"

"Look at the effects Alisha healing that man's hand back in France caused. In the time of Jesus the sick were considered as impure and so was Jesus for healing them. It went against the customs of his times, especially healing women. He was most definitely playing with fire when he exorcised evil demons. Casting demons into pigs caused many to accuse Jesus of surely being a demon himself or in league with the Devil."

"We actually passed the place where Jesus carried out that exorcism and cast the demons into pigs when we travelled to Alexandria," Paul explained.

"I know you did. Every part of your journey was necessary," Kratos remarked and stared out across the Nile, smiling. "The sick could not be part of a religion in the time of Jesus, yet he came along and proclaimed that everyone, sick, lame and healthy alike, could all be part of God's new religion. In his time, anyone accused of being a false prophet or speaking of a new religion were to be thrown down from a high place and then stoned. Jesus very nearly suffered this fate as explained within the Gospel of Luke when his own village was about to stone him. But no one could throw the first stone or throw him of the cliff. If they had, he would have simply joined the ranks of the many who had been killed in that fashion and history would never have heard of him. I am sure you know that Jesus learnt much in Egypt, Britain and India. His wealthy uncle, Joseph of Arimathea as he is now known, traded in tin from England. Jesus was also more than well versed in the traditions and teachings of the Druids…'tis no wonder then that Christianity was accepted in Britain within five years of his crucifixion. And you know the rest about Mary Magdalene…and in time so will Christianity remember and restore her memory to what it should be, the mark of being a prostitute being just one of the first signs the Church will put right great wrongs and evolve herself."

Paul looked out across the water thinking hard upon Kratos's words. He had so many questions he wished to ask but knew his time was limited. Percival coughed lightly behind him as he moved about, Ishmael looking out behind them constantly.

"Will Percival be gone with you for long?" Paul finally asked with sadness in his voice.

Kratos looked around slowly at Percival then back to Paul.

"Long enough to ease the pain within him…then you will see him again."

"I shall miss him for he has become more of a brother than a friend to me."

"Yes he has. You have experienced much together but now there are other things he must do…for himself for he is one of the very few who are totally selfless in character and heart. It has been explained to him that the tragedy of life is not death, but what we let die inside us while we live. You too should remember that," Kratos said calmly but the words cut through Paul like a warning almost. "And you…you question what path you must follow," Kratos said and looked down at Paul intently. "You will find a way to continue the codes within a new order….a brotherhood of builders… masons and architects with men from all walks of life of good character. You will take good men and you will make them even better. But never turn away anyone because of their past, especially if they are genuinely repentant for prior actions that were wrong. The only prerequisite you need adhere too is that anyone wishing to become part of any such group at least has the belief in a higher purpose…call him God if you must."

"I had discussed this already with my father," Paul replied.

1 - 2

"I know you have...you will find men to form this new Order, and in time women for they will all display selfless characteristics...much like Percival. Your father already busies himself seeking out such people already. That is how much faith he has in you starting this task. But I caution you... under no circumstances let any such Order be turned into a religion of its own standing or be taken over by fanatics and narrow minded limited fools. Most other men are honest purely out of fear of punishment by the laws of their land...they are religious in expectation of being rewarded, or in dread of the Devil in the next world, which totally negates the right of free will. The new Order will be made from people who would be just and honourable even if there were no laws, human or divine, except those written in his heart by the finger of his Creator. In every country, under every system of law and religion, they are the same. They kneel before the Universal Throne of God in gratitude for the blessings they have received and in humble solicitation for their future protection. They venerate the good men of all religions. They disturb not the religion of others. They restrain their passions, because they cannot be indulged without injuring their neighbour or themselves. They give no offence, because they do not choose to be offended. They contract no debts which they are certain they cannot discharge, because they are honest upon principle. By those principles you will know them," Kratos explained.

"I shall remember that and write it down...and you will all be missed when you leave on the morrow's tide," Paul sighed.

"I shall miss you all too. But you and I have walked many a shore together, and we shall walk more yet. But for now I must take Percival to Dwarka in India. There is much there he can learn that will be of benefit when he returns...for, fear not, he shall," Kratos explained and smiled.

"I hear so much about India...but where and what is Dwarka?"

"Dwarka 'tis a city on the northwestern coast of India...and Bhet Dwarka several miles further away was once a great ancient port and city. All of what was once a mighty and magnificent city now lies beneath the waves. 'Twas truly a beautiful place...but there are still temples and people we can all learn much from...just as the physical Jesus once did when he visited the area," Kratos explained and looked briefly at Paul. "Dvaraka as it was also named boasted 900,000 royal palaces, all constructed with crystal and silver and decorated with huge emeralds. Inside these palaces, the furnishings were bedecked with gold and jewels. Supporting the main palace were coral pillars decoratively inlaid with vaidurya gems. Sapphires bedecked the walls, and the floors glowed with a perpetual brilliance. In that palace Tvashta, a Hindu god of blacksmiths, had arranged canopies with hanging strands of pearls. There were also seats and beds fashioned of ivory and precious jewels. In attendance were many well-dressed maid-servants bearing lockets on their necks, and also armour clad guards with turbans, fine uniforms and jewelled earrings. The glow of numerous jewel-studded lamps dispelled all darkness in the palace and on the ornate ridges of the roof danced loudly crying peacocks, who saw the fragrant aguru incense escaping through the holes of the latticed windows and mistook it for a cloud."

"It sounds wondrous to behold."

"Oh it was indeed." Kratos seemed to reminisce before sensing that Paul was staring at him. "Let me explain briefly before we return for the evening that ancient Vedic astronomical texts of the Vedic tradition assert the current epoch of Kali-yuga began in 3102 BC and that Hindu Lord Krishna's disappearance and the subsequent submergence of Dvaraka occurred shortly before this date."

"Sorry, but what does Kali Yuga mean? For I have not heard this before," Paul asked.

"'Tis part of the ancient Indian Yuga Cycle doctrine which tells us that we are now living in the Kali Yuga, meaning the age of darkness, when moral virtue and mental capabilities reach their lowest point in the cycle. The Indian epic the Mahabharata describes the Kali Yuga as the period when the 'World Soul' is black in hue when only one quarter of virtue remains, which slowly dwindles to zero at the end of the Kali Yuga. Then men will turn to wickedness. Disease, lethargy, anger, natural calamities, anguish and fear of scarcity will take over. Penance, sacrifices and religious observances will all fall into disuse just as all creatures degenerate. Change passes over all things, without exception."

"Age of Darkness I can already see and believe...but how long will it last?" Paul remarked.

"Until the new Age of Aquarius as your calendars follow time. But understand that each age according to properly translated Sanskrit texts last twelve thousand years. The Kali Yuga period was preceded by three other

Yugas…the Satya or Krita Yuga, which you would refer to as the Golden Age…the Treta Yuga, or Silver Age, and the Dwapara Yuga, or Bronze Age. In the Mahabharata, the Krita Yuga was named because there was but one religion, and all men were saintly therefore they were not required to perform religious ceremonies…Men neither bought nor sold and there were no poor and no rich. There was no need to labour, because all that men required was obtained by the power of will…The Krita Yuga was without disease and there was no lessening with the years. There was no hatred, or vanity, or evil thought whatsoever…no sorrow, no fear. All mankind could attain to supreme blessedness. The universal soul was white and the identification of self with the universal soul was the whole religion of the Perfect Age. In the Treta Yuga period, sacrifices began, and the World Soul became red. Virtue lessened and mankind sought truth and started to perform religious ceremonies. They obtained what they desired by giving and by doing. In the Dwapara Yuga the aspect of the World Soul was yellow. Religion lessened even more. The Veda was divided into four parts, and although some had knowledge of the four Vedas, others knew but three or one. Mind lessened, truth declined, and there came desire and diseases and calamities; because of these men had to undergo penances. It was a decadent age by reason of the prevalence of sin. And now we are living in the dark times of the Kali Yuga, when goodness and virtue have all but disappeared from the world. Is it therefore just a coincidence that certain texts, such as the Mahabharata and the Laws of Manu, still retain the original value of the Yuga Cycle as twelve thousand years? Many other ancient cultures such as the Chaldeans, Zoroastrians and Greeks also believed in a twelve thousand year Cycle of the Ages."

"And it was at the start of this age that Dwarka vanished beneath the waves?" Paul asked as he looked out across the gentle waves of the Nile, the stars reflecting upon it.

"Yes. The sacred Mahabharata talks about the sea suddenly engulfing the city after Lord Krishna's disappearance and Arjuna taking Krishna's grandsons and the Yadava wives to Hastinapura. Arjuna gives a detailed account in the Mahabharat of seeing the beautiful buildings becoming submerged one by one. In a matter of a few moments it was all over. The sea had now become as placid as a lake. There was no trace of the city. Dvaraka was just a name, just a memory…On the same day that Krishna departed from the earth the powerful dark-bodied Kali Age descended. The oceans rose and submerged the whole of Dvaraka. Three texts, the Harivamsa, the Matsya Purana and the Bhagavat Gita, all state that it took seven days to vacate Dvaraka before it was submerged by the sea. According to the Shrimad Bhagavatam, 11th Canto, Lord Krishna sent a message to the people of Dvaraka. He told them that once he leaves this world, there would be no one on this earth to save Dvaraka. The sea would finish Dvaraka and hence he asks the fifty-six crore Yaduvamsis to leave Dvaraka. Dwarka is considered as one of the four Dhamas, sacred place for pilgrimage of the Hindu religion. According to ancient Sanskrit literature, Krishna founded the holy city of Dwarka himself. It was one of the most busy port centres during the past on the west coast of India. Yet an even older site was in what is now called the Gulf of Cambay...which goes back even further to at least nine thousand years. The story of Krishna as told in the sacred scripture Srimad Bhagavatam describes the scenario that led to the construction of Dwarka. Once, when Krishna was ruling the city of Mathura, the kingdom was repeatedly attacked by Jarasandha, the tyrant King of Magadha (the present day Bihar, India), around seventeen times. The Monarch lost to Krishna in all seventeen battles, and he attacked Mathura the eighteenth time. At this stage, Krishna decided to build a separate city on an island on the western coast of India, to save his citizens, his Yadava clan, from the trouble of repeated wars. The city was built by the divine architect Vishwakarma himself. The city soon grew in fame and became the invincible pivot of Lord Krishna's mission, housing thousands, in around nine hundred palaces. The city was well fortified and could be reached only by ship. Dwarka soon became a talking point everywhere, and commanded awe and wonder all over the world. Ancient Hindu texts state that Dwarka was attacked with a flying machine, known as a Vimana. This shows they fought with sophisticated technology and advanced weapons, potentially even with a craft attacking from the heavens...where the craft commenced an attack on the city with the use of energy weapons, which to the on-lookers resembled a discharge of lightning, and it was so devastating that after the attack most of the city lay in ruins. Lord Krishna counterattacked and fired his weapons on the ship. They looked like arrows yet they roared like a thunder and shone like rays of the sun when released. Dwarka would be very significant for the understanding of what the Mahabharata is. It would no longer be merely a book of myths and legends, but in fact, at least to some extent, a genuine account of past events. Older than Chinese and Egyptian history..."

"Oh my Lord…I am glad such weapons no longer exist," Paul sighed as a cool wind blew his hair and he breathed in the fresh air.

"Oh…but they do. And there will come a time when man will rediscover how to make these weapons again…that is why it is so important men of reason and compassion must join together," Kratos said and looked down at Paul.

"My father once mentioned that much can be learned from India. He mentioned the points of energy in the body, like those of the world, and how it related to ancient wisdom and that it too could be used for either good or evil intent to heal or kill a person. I wished I had paid more attention."

"Your father and Theodoric both know much about it. You still have time to learn of it. Just ask Theodoric to fully explain about Kundalini, which is also a Sanskrit term meaning 'coiled up' or 'coiling like a snake'. It comes from the term kundala, which means a 'ring' or 'coil'. Kundalini energy is often illustrated in ancient drawings as a serpent coiled around the back part of the root chakra in three and a half turns around the sacrum. The phenomenon of kundalini awakening gives rise to the energetic phenomena experienced by meditators. The intensified energy originates from a very real reservoir of subtle energy at the base of the spine. And, Paul… trust me when I say that there is a place, roughly located within the position as we study it, of Orion…from where souls are born," Kratos explained and looked upward to the stars and smiled, his features highlighted by the glow from his staff. He sighed before continuing to speak softly. "Man will also again relearn that which has been lost on the origination of their languages. For in India, where the Sanskrit language was the main language of their literature, they will discover European languages are similar in word concepts and structure…too much so to be mere coincidence. The Sanskrit culture or Vedic culture, as it is sometimes called after the ancient Indian Vedic literature, derived from the word Vedas, which means knowledge. But it is far more ancient than later European cultures whose languages are related to the Indian language Sanskrit of the Vedas…which means the European peoples had to have come out of India somehow and then gone to Europe with their languages, which differentiated into Russian, English, Spanish, Germanic and the rest of them. This notion will not be accepted for fear of giving the Vedic culture a position superior to their own for a great many years…but it matters not for eventually the truth will become too obvious. Just like they will react in the same fashion about the concept of the Vedas of the Krishna character who came and said the universe is teeming with life and who appeared to have knowledge about other habitations in the cosmos and is talking from an age that would go back at least nine and a half thousand years," Kratos smiled, nearly laughing.

"So what you are saying is that Vedic literature implies that there were great highly advanced cities in India inhabited many thousands of years ago?" Paul asked.

"Of course...as you well know...or should by now. For example, the Rigveda, which is one of the earliest Vedic literatures, talks about a mighty river called the Saraswati that flowed from the Himalayan mountains down to the Arabian Sea, down to an area of northwestern India. No such river exists there today, but again, in the future man will find a way of seeing where mighty rivers once ran, and when they do, they will see that the ancient texts spoke the truth all along. And it will show how it emptied into what is now known as the Bay of Khambaht or Cambay as some prefer. Likewise they will also learn of a great lake that had cities beside it...but that was even further back in time. Some fifty thousand years ago in fact. An ancient Sanskrit manuscript speaks of the lake that existed in what is northern India where just a valley now sits. It was covered by a huge lake and it was blocked on the southern end by a little range of mountains. But during the last upheavals, it broke open and the lake drained out. That happened about forty to fifty thousand years ago." [106]

"So, it is interesting that you've got this ancient historical record that talks about this lake. And if it is to be taken literally, then it means that somebody must have seen this lake as it existed fifty thousand years ago and wrote about it," Paul remarked. "But why must Percival travel there... to learn what exactly?"

"Oh, words, sounds and images that will help you later..."

"Such as?"

"Aum, Gum, Shreem, Maha, Lakshmi yei, Namaha," Kratos replied and laughed lightly as if teasing him. "They are words from an ancient Sanskrit mantra used for thousands of years for prosperity and wellbeing. But you don't need any spiritual or religious beliefs to use them. Because they are just six of the countless words in various languages, containing a vibration 'plan' that can physically help to rearrange the very nature and structure of your physical body and mind. That entwined double helix I mentioned before..."

"Why can I not learn this?"

"Perhaps you will in time...but this is for Percival."

"I do not understand or see how words can transform or help you?"

"Because your habits if trained to be positive can transform you for the better...your thoughts and emotions become more positive..."

"That does not explain how sounds alone carry so much power?"

"Because just like symbols, the truth about sounds will expand your consciousness. You see according to the Rigveda, another ancient Sanskrit work, in fact the world's oldest spiritual text, sounds are built from elementary particles, which are in turn made from the smallest strands of energy. All sounds have energetic layouts and plans tied to them. They act as triggers that can induce a certain emotion, visualisation or action in the person who hears them. That is why those who subscribe to ancient wisdom often believe in reciting specific words every day as a 'lubricant' for ongoing positive growth. 'Tis where the popular concept of mantras comes from! Speaking of mantras, I'm sure you've heard of the world's most widely spoken mantra, the one many people use when they meditate."

"Theo and Attar have taught me that one. 'Tis Om," Paul replied and folded his arms as he started to feel cold.

"'Tis actually AUM," Kratos remarked, emphasising the word, and turned to face him fully. "Think about that word for a moment. When you start saying the first letter, the 'A', your mouth is fully open...when you get to the 'U', your mouth is half open...and when you get to the 'M', your mouth is fully closed. There's a reason for that...it's because AUM represents the very concept of openness and closure...of the beginning and end of the universe itself. The alpha and omega! The power of sound and words is even clearly illustrated in your Bible. Remember the very first sentence from the Gospel of John?"

Paul paused for a moment as he tried to recall the actual words.

"In the beginning was the WORD, and the WORD was with God, and the WORD was God," he called, out pleased with himself for remembering.

"Good...good man. By themselves, these facts are compelling but when you also start exploring sounds in the context of mathematics and linguistics...it becomes crystal clear why they can have such a profound effect upon a person. Sounds, even if you don't know their meanings, will resonate in different parts of your mind and nervous system, and create specific outcomes in your behaviour or performance."

Paul thought back to the sound of Thomas and his men when they had sung their powerfully emotional song when Ailia was born. It had felt as if the sounds were passing through him and it had touched him deeply, almost profoundly even.

"Why though?" he asked.

"Because you react to them on a vibrational and physical level. This is why you can hear a song in a foreign language, and still feel your soul moved by it. Even the Greek philosopher Pythagoras used the sounds of vibrating string music to heal people's bodies and emotions. He termed it the 'music of the spheres'. If you place sand, salt or sugar...or any fine powder upon a flat shield or drum, you can make certain sounds and the powder or grain will naturally form geometric shapes. The same sound will always make the same pattern. It even works in liquid...and these symbols are another aspect Percival will learn. Your Templar friends, and that includes your father, know of many of them already."

"But for what purpose?"

"Sound can be used to heal...as well as kill as I have said...but more importantly, sound is the force that all creation hangs upon and is held together by. Understand the secrets of sound and you will unlock the secrets of this physical world we presently exist in. Including how to levitate," Kratos explained and winked at him with a large smile. "So imagine if sound can affect the physical world...just imagine what it can do to your mind...your consciousness."

"My father, Tenno, Theo and Attar all tell me that our consciousness as a human being has multiple levels. Is this so?"

"Yes...there is surface thought, where your mind is active and engaged on a daily basis. But there are also deeper, quieter levels of thought, all the way down to the deepest, purest level of feeling...where thoughts fade, and only your consciousness remains...and where you can gain access to your higher self. The majority of people presently just live most of their lives on the level of surface thoughts and physical impulses. But your life's greatest work, your highest realisations and your deepest sense of fulfilment will only come when you're trained to dive deeper, on a subconscious level...into the ocean of your own stillness. Sounds are a gateway to this ocean! And once you start swimming in it there is no limit to that which you can achieve. If you can imagine it, you can achieve it," Kratos explained and paused for a short while. "And you have already stepped into this ocean have you not?"

"I believe so," Paul said quietly as the word Nautonier echoed through his mind.

"And simply ask yourself this...if, as everyone seems to get so upset about it, Jesus died on the cross and that was the end of his line...did all of his brothers, sisters and other family members also die at the same time? More people should consider this simple question. Jesus was an initiate and adept of all the ancient Sanskrit teachings and practices."

"I have...believe me. My father explained this to me many times and how descendants became the Desposyni from Edessa."

"Ah Edessa. I shall have cause to take Percival there via Urfa...for there is a man made monument identical in size and shape to that of the mound in Silbury in Britain...for they were constructed by the same people."

"I have lost count of the many sacred places Theodoric has informed me about. Just yesterday he showed me on the map where a great buried crescent of stone lays hidden in Outremer...plus something about Mercury being hidden in great streams beneath pyramids. Though I must confess I was too tired to really take in what he was explaining."

"Then you must make more effort to pay attention. Theo is to your father what Percival is like to you...and both know more than you credit them with," Kratos remarked in a chastising tone. Paul frowned at his sudden change. "Oh do not be offended. You know I speak the truth...but listen to them when they speak to you. Promise me that much...now as we stand beneath the firmament."

Paul looked up in time to see a bright shooting star streak across the night sky as if to reinforce what Kratos had just asked. Paul looked at Kratos in the darkness now most of the nearby lights had been put out for the night. Kratos gently banged his staff down and immediately the round ball at the top started to let off a brighter glow of bluish green light that illuminated the floor around them. He smiled broadly.

"I swear it of course," Paul replied and bowed his head slightly. Images of his dreams flashed across his vision showing the pyramid at Abu Rawash exploding. "Before we return home, can you confirm that the pyramid, what is left of it, that I entered with Percival was actually destroyed in a great explosion...and was this at the same time of the events you have just mentioned in India?"

"I can confirm that yes it was destroyed in a great pulse of uncapped and unregulated power...on purpose. But it was a long time before the events that took place in India happened. The evidence is there and obvious to see, including the damage to the inside of the Great Pyramid itself, which was likewise almost very nearly destroyed. The sarcophagus, though as I am sure now it was never that, and has exactly the same dimensions as the many Arks of the Covenant, was once a rose colour pink of Aswan Granite, not the burnt dark brown it now is. And know this, the upper wall of the Grand Gallery, near the entrance into the so-called King's Chamber, is made of granite, not limestone, and shows deep dark stains caused by being exposed to tremendous heat. Many will ponder and be puzzled what the rectangular holes or sockets that are evenly spaced throughout the entire distance of the ramps in the passages were for…" Kratos laughed to himself. "They were not for statues as some claim for none were ever placed in the Great Pyramid. I can tell you they were for small devices that resonated sound vibrations to amplify the energy produced within the pyramid. Alas they exploded and if you check you will still see the scorch marks on the ceiling of the Grand Gallery directly above the corresponding slots on the side ramps."

"What caused such an explosion then?" Paul asked, looking puzzled.

"'Twas the twin dark sun that came too close during its last passing… and, as explained, it was done so deliberately for it was left running instead of being shut down…but fortunately most of the damage was limited to the pyramid at Abu Rawash…which you saw for yourself."

Paul's mind flashed back to the image of the dark sun mural painted upon the wall of the Templars' headquarters in Jerusalem. So much was connected and identical but how could he ever put all the information together and pass it all on? he wondered. As he pondered this question, Kratos stood silently with him for some time until Paul began to shiver from the cold night air.

Paul entered the dining room first and held the door open for Kratos to enter. Alisha, Sister Lucy and Arri were sat at the main table and looked up as Percival and Ishmael followed them in. Several lanthorns lit the room with a welcoming warm glow.

"You are still up late," Paul said as he approached Arri sat on Alisha's lap and rubbed his hand through Arri's hair and gently kissed Alisha.

"He is a little sad that Abi and Percival must leave…so I said he could stay up late to say goodbye," Alisha explained.

"Where is Abi?" Percival asked.

"She is doing some training with Theodoric, Thomas and Luke…you know what she is like," Sister Lucy explained.

"Then there will be wine involved I am sure," Kratos joked.

Arri looked up at the tall size of Kratos and half hid his face behind Clip clop.

"Mama, why do people have to go away?" he asked quietly.

"Because people have different places to go to and different people to meet, but you will see them again," Alisha explained softly, sensing how sad Arri was.

"But I won't see Nyla again will I because she can't come back," Arri remarked. All looked at Percival as he moved to sit beside Alisha and Arri. He leaned forward and smiled at him. "Why did Nyla have to die…why did God take her?" he asked awkwardly.

"'Tis simple," Percival replied and took Arri's little hand in his. "Ask yourself this…when you enter a garden in full bloom, what flowers do you pick?"

Arri looked at Alisha, puzzled for a moment, then held Clip clop closer as he rested his head against Alisha.

"The brightest and the most loveliest," Arri finally replied.

"Exactly. 'Tis the same with God….he only picks the brightest and loveliest…and I will see her again of that I have no doubt," Percival replied assuredly and winked at Arri.

Sister Lucy held her hand to her chest and sighed just as Theodoric half burst into the room through the rear door carrying two full jars of wine. He paused as everyone turned to look at him. Sister Lucy shook her head disapprovingly and immediately took the jars from him.

Port of La Rochelle, France, Melissae Inn, spring 1191

"Oh that breaks my heart," Sarah exclaimed emotionally and shook her head, blinking, trying hard not to shed a tear.

2 - 11

"'Twas a sad time and Percival yet again demonstrated the kind and insightful nature of his character," the old man remarked.

"I never knew that stuff about India and how far back its history went," Gabirol said whilst still finishing off writing a sentence.

"I want to know what work Paul decided upon for his shield shows much use," Simon interrupted and lifted the shield up and held it studying all the marks and arrow head puncture holes.

"Husam left the same morning as Kratos, Abi and Percival, along with Conrad, leaving Paul pretty much alone to work upon his ship designs at his own leisure as Husam had agreed. They parted and each wished each other 'enough' as had become their standard words for farewells," the old man started to explain before he was interrupted by Simon.

"But things must have happened differently for this to have been used."

"May not have been Paul who used it?" the Hospitaller remarked.

"Oh it was Paul...and used for good reason," the old man replied.

"Which you will tell us about later yes?" Simon said in a sarcastic tone.

"Hey, lift that shield up," Sarah told Simon. Puzzled, he lifted the shield above his head with both arms. Sarah slapped his side hard. "Less of the sarcasm!" she said and frowned at him hard.

The Templar laughed out loud, the first time anyone had seen him laugh so openly. The Hospitaller started to laugh as Simon looked on bemused, placed the shield back upon the table and rubbed his side, looking indignant.

"Lucky it was not a punch," Stephan joked.

"Well...there is so much we are still to be told later and it is late," Simon protested.

"I agree with you, Simon," the old man said and sat up. "So I shall continue as quickly as I am able."

"We shall stay up all night if needs be to hear the end of this tale and all of the morrow if necessary," the wealthy tailor interjected loudly, then went red in the face as everyone looked at him in surprise.

"Then let me explain that after Kratos, Abi and Percival departed, as guests upon Husam's command ship no less, Alisha and Paul settled down into a rather sedate and more relaxed lifestyle...with Thomas and his men ever vigilant and ever present of course who all decided to grow their hair long once more, just as they had done many years ago remembering and respecting old traditions they had long since discarded...but now took on with a new sense of purpose and vigour."

"Old traditions?" Gabirol stated questioningly.

"Yes, ones they had originally practised but over the years had let slip. Traditions

from their homelands...so despite the heat, their long hair was certainly striking to see, especially as most of them had blonde hair, an inheritance of their Norse heritage. They certainly looked a formidable sight and mainly being of a tall stature, they became a different group of men to behold. The only one to stand out was Ishmael, who readily and proudly accepted to stand in for Percival's stead," the old man explained and wiped his mouth as he thought upon something. After a lengthy pause, interrupted as usual by a deliberate cough from Simon, he continued. "1184 would prove to be perhaps the most peaceful and quietest year for all of them... though the same could not be said for the rest in the Holy Land."

"Why what happened?" the farrier asked.

"Well Saladin attempted another siege of Kerak to get Reynald, but King Baldwin repelled that attack as well, and so Saladin raided Nablus and other towns on his way home instead. Ailia grew strong and healthy and was a quiet baby even when she was teething or became unwell. She was without doubt a father's girl. And Arri...he made himself a wooden shield and sword and protected her every day when he wasn't being schooled by either Sister Lucy or Theodoric. In October 1184, Guy of Lusignan led an attack on the Bedouin nomads from his base in Ascalon but unlike Reynald's attacks on caravans, which may have had some military purpose, Guy attacked a group that was usually loyal to Jerusalem and provided intelligence about the movements of Saladin's troops."

"Yes, we know of that raid. Bloody fool!" the Templar interrupted.

"Foolish indeed," the old man remarked and nodded in agreement before continuing. "At the same time, King Baldwin contracted his final illness and Raymond of Tripoli, rather than Guy, was appointed as his regent. His nephew the younger Baldwin was paraded in public, wearing his crown as Baldwin the Fifth. As I am sure most of you know, sadly King Baldwin the Fourth finally succumbed to his leprosy the following year in May 1185. The succession crisis looming prior to his death prompted a mission to the West to seek assistance and in 1184 the new Patriarch Heraclius travelled throughout the courts of Europe...but no help was forthcoming. Heraclius even offered the 'keys of the Holy Sepulchre, those of the Tower of David and the banner of the Kingdom of Jerusalem', but not the crown itself, to both Philip the Second of France and Henry the Second of England, the latter, as a grandson of Fulk, being the first cousin of the royal family of Jerusalem, and who had promised to go on a crusade after the murder of Thomas Becket as I explained earlier in this tale. But, both kings preferred to remain at home to defend their own territories, rather than act as regent for a child in Jerusalem. The few European knights who did travel to Jerusalem did not even see any combat, since the truce

with Saladin had been re-established. William the Fifth of Montferrat was one of the few who came to his grandson Baldwin the Fifth's aid. However, Baldwin the Fifth's rule, with Raymond of Tripoli as regent and his great-uncle Joscelin of Edessa as his guardian, was short. He was a sickly child and died in the summer of 1186. Raymond and his supporters went to Nablus, in an attempt to prevent Sibylla from claiming the throne, but Sibylla and her supporters went to Jerusalem, where it was decided that the kingdom should pass to her, on the condition that her marriage to Guy be annulled." [107]

"By the lords we know full well what happened then for we were both present," the Hospitaller interjected and nudged his brother.

"Yes, she agreed to the court's terms, but only if she could choose her own husband and king," the old man explained.

"So who did she choose?" Ayleth asked.

"Immediately after being crowned, she then crowned Guy with her own hands. Raymond had refused to attend the coronation, and in Nablus he suggested that Isabella and Humphrey should be crowned instead, but Humphrey refused to agree to this plan, which would have certainly started a civil war. Humphrey went straight to Jerusalem and swore allegiance to Guy and Sibylla, as did most of Raymond's other supporters. Raymond himself refused to do so and left for Tripoli... Baldwin of Ibelin also refused, gave up his fiefs, and left for Antioch."

"I never realised or knew how such matters were decided," Peter remarked, shaking his head, surprised.

"As I believe I have mentioned already, it was in 1184 that Gerard finally got his dream and realised his ambition for he became the Templars' overall Grand Master after Arnold de Tarroja died. But Reynald himself also suffered an emotional blow that year for his own daughter Agnes died that same year. It did hurt him deeply."

"That was Agnes, his daughter from his first marriage to Constance, Sovereign Princess of Antioch...and not a daughter of Princess Stephanie?" Gabirol asked, the old man immediately nodding yes.

"Arnold was already elderly when he took office as the ninth Grand Master though so it came as no surprise when he died," the Templar commented.

"How did he die then?" Simon asked.

"Whilst taking advantage of a two-year truce agreed between Baldwin the Fourth and Saladin, he had set out to tour the courts of Europe to appeal for support for the Holy Land. Having been dispatched by a council in Jerusalem along with Heraclius, and Roger des Moulins, they hoped to secure the support of Henry the Second of England, but Arnold fell sick, and died before he could get any further

than Verona. There was some rumour that foul play had been involved to hurry Gerard's appointment but I am afraid that we shall never know for certain. His companions carried on without him. That year Gerard allied himself, bringing along the power of the Templar Order with him, to Sibylla and Guy of Lusignan against Count Raymond, and his influence contributed to the recognition of Guy as king of Jerusalem, although Raymond and the Ibelins were attempting to advance the claim of his stepson Humphrey's wife, Princess Isabella. Humphrey remained loyal to his stepfather and Guy."

"This is the same Humphrey, as in the son of Princess Stephanie?" Gabirol asked.

"Yes one and the same," the old man answered.

"Why did Gerard side with Guy against Raymond?" Ayleth asked.

"You may recall because when Gerard took service as a secular knight under Raymond on the understanding that he would be rewarded with a grant of land and the hand of the heiress Lucia of Botrun, Raymond reneged on the arrangement, after which Gerard joined the Templars, but nursing a bitter grudge against Raymond. Now he was able to pay him back," the old man replied in answer.

"I do not think Ayleth was present when you explained that before," the Templar said.

"Was it not Balian who managed to negotiate between all parties?" Gabirol asked.

"Yes for he was incredibly good at doing that. As some of you know he came from perhaps the most famous feudal family in the Latin Kingdom of Jerusalem. His d'Iblin family had humble origins being part of new aristocracy carved out of the early kingdom. He is one of the most respected local barons and enjoyed semi-autonomous authority in southern Palestine for he is trusted by all sides and acted as intermediary between Raymond and King Guy during their standoff, of which I shall have more to say, but he was also well known as a negotiator among Muslims and counted as a personal friend by Saladin."

"Then how come war still came?" Sarah asked.

"Not because of people like Balian for sure...," the old man said and then continued. "In 1185 Saladin signed another truce for four years. But in 1186 Reynald attacked a large Muslim caravan travelling between Cairo and Damascus. He took all the merchants and their families prisoner, seized a large amount of booty and refused to receive envoys from Saladin demanding compensation. This led directly to the end of the truce as Reynald proclaimed very loudly that he was Lord of his own lands and that he had made no peace with Saladin. Saladin swore that Reynald would be executed if he was ever taken prisoner after that. This was the same

year that Saladin himself fell very ill...and at one time it was feared he would die but for the timely intervention of the brilliant physician Soleim Al-Razi...whom if you recall Paul saved when their caravan was attacked along with Saladin's brother...remember?"

All around the table nodded and said yes in agreement they remembered.

"Yes, we received word at one stage that he had even died. 'Twas a short lived rumour though," the Templar stated.

"Whilst ill Saladin wrote many letters to his favoured wife but she too had sadly died that year. News of her death was kept from him for three months for fear he would give up the fight for his own life," the old man explained.

"That is so sad. You don't ever really think of such men as being frail and to suffer the same weaknesses and heartaches as we do," Ayleth remarked.

"No most people do not," the old man replied and paused briefly. "As you know Saladin's brother Turansha died in 1180 in suspicious circumstances and there was suspicion that Saladin's prolonged illness came after an attempt to assassinate him by men serving the other Turansha, but no proof could be gathered in support of that claim...but a clear path of contact and correspondence connected Turansha and Lord Conrad of Montferrat, which proved many deals between both of them to engineer and further Conrad's own career and claim of the throne of Jerusalem."

"You mean to say that all the while the others quarrelled with each other for the crown of Jerusalem, they all missed the actions and machinations of Conrad altogether?" Gabirol asked as he charged his quill with more ink.

"Yes that is indeed the case," the old man acknowledged.

"'Tis a pity more did not listen to the queens at such times for they certainly seemed more informed than their husbands," the Hospitaller remarked, shaking his head.

"What do you mean?" Peter asked.

"Well, King Guy may have been ineffectual on many an occasion but his wife, Queen Sibylla of Jerusalem, she was something altogether different," the Hospitaller explained.

"Yes I have to agree with you," the old man said. "She comes across as a quiet woman but she is highly intelligent...and a good friend of Princess Stephanie's no less. Often distanced from Guy she fully understood unrequited love and the loneliness of a cold loveless marriage."

"'Twas Guy and Reynald who made constant provocations against Saladin during the two-year truce. But it was Guy's military hesitance at the siege of Kerak

which disillusioned King Baldwin of him if I am correct," the Templar remarked and looked to the old man for confirmation.

"'Twas indeed for throughout late 1183 and 1184 Baldwin the Fourth tried to have his sister's marriage to Guy annulled, showing that Baldwin still held his sister with some favour. Baldwin the Fourth had wanted a loyal brother-in-law, and was frustrated by Guy's disobedience. Sibylla was in Ascalon with her husband. Unsuccessful in prying his sister and close heir away from Guy, the king and the Haute Cour altered the succession, placing Baldwin the Fifth, Sibylla's son from her first marriage, in precedence over Sibylla, and decreeing a process to choose the monarch afterwards between Sibylla and Isabella, whom Baldwin and the Haute Cour thus recognised as at least equally entitled to succession as Sibylla, though she was not herself excluded from the succession. Guy had kept a low profile from 1183 until his wife became queen in 1186. At one stage the Latins fielded the largest army so far raised but adopted a defensive stance refusing to meet Saladin in a set piece battle. This worked and Saladin withdrew. However, many Christians saw previous invasions by Saladin as very damaging and blamed Count Raymond, on whose advice the passive strategy had been adopted, for missing the chance to destroy Saladin. This would be raised during arguments between Raymond and Reynald with King Guy just before the battle of Hattin with very dire and serious consequences," the old man explained.

"I know that Raymond of Tripoli allied with Saladin against Guy and allowed a Muslim garrison to occupy his fief in Tiberias, hoping that Saladin would help him overthrow Guy for I was garrisoned there at that time," the Templar said.

"Yes, Raymond did indeed ally himself at that time with Saladin, who had by then pacified his Mesopotamian territories, and was now eager to attack the Crusader kingdom...to remove Reynald once and for all. But do not forget that Saladin had much respect for the other Latin lords...but he did not intend to renew the truce when it expired in 1187."

"And just what exactly did Alisha and Paul do during all of this time?" the Genoese sailor asked.

"You did not make much about Percival leaving," Gabirol remarked.

"What more can I say about Percival leaving? 'Twas a simple farewell said in the early morning outside the house. Abi hugged Alisha and Sister Lucy and with a slight nod of his head from Kratos, they all mounted their horses and left. But in answer to your question, Paul spent as much time as possible with Alisha, Arri and Ailia as he could. The years 1184 to late 1186 were quiet years indeed for them and they relished every moment of the time afforded them," the old man explained

with a hint of sadness in his voice. "Paul used the time to further his painting and drawings as well as his medicinal skills. He did some incredibly life like drawings of Thomas and his men with their long hair and armour."

"Pity we cannot see them...for like thinking of Kratos on a horse, which I had never thought of before...I always imagined him on foot," Sarah remarked.

"I have one saved image Paul drew of Thomas and Luke...here look," the old man said and pulled out another parchment sheet from his folder and gently pushed it across the table to Sarah.

Fig. 63: Thomas and Luke.

"Really?" she asked, surprised, and opened the square folded sheet to reveal a highly detailed image showing both Thomas and Luke's faces staring out from the page.

"My Lord...handsome men indeed. Look how their eyes seem to look back at us," Ayleth remarked.

"I have never seen such work," Gabirol commented.

"Then you should visit Rome...or better still, Florence, for I have seen many

paintings and drawings executed in a similar fashion," the Genoese sailor remarked as he leant over to view the picture.

"'Tis true...and much of Roman art is highly detailed. You need only look at their statues and busts to know their love for realism," the old man explained.

Gabirol looked up from his writing and stared at the old man intently. When everyone had finished looking at the drawing, Gabirol sat up straight.

"So what event brought an end to those quiet years for Paul and his family?" he asked seriously, knowing that obviously something big had occurred.

"Truly the darkest of days fell upon them all...," the old man replied and sighed heavily.

Ayleth put her hand to her mouth alarmed. Sarah saw the concern in her youthful face and placed a reassuring hand over Ayleth's left hand.

"If it is not too difficult, pray tell us all, please," Gabirol requested just as the others around the table all nodded in agreement.

"Yes, yes I shall...for I must," the old man replied sadly and prepared himself to explain matters. He took a deep breath and sat himself up, clasped the sword upon the table with both hands, looked up and began.

Chapter 64
Storm Fall

Cairo, Egypt, October 1186

Paul stood with Theodoric on the balcony looking out toward the horizon as dark clouds loomed ever higher looking like distant mountains, the waters of the Nile some way off reflecting the moon upon its surface in a million sparkles. The house was quiet, everyone else save the two Mamluk guards below having retired for the night.

"Why do you not go ahead and secure safe passage back to France via Malta, now while you can?" Theodoric asked, the dark clouds snuffing out the last rays of the bright moon casting the whole sky into a gloomy darkness, the Nile turning to an almost ink black line.

"I love the sea in all its phases…but no I cannot travel ahead alone. After that naval engagement I swore to Ali I would never leave her again…but I did when I vanished for over a month…I cannot ever leave her and do that again…I swore it so. And look at all we have here now," Paul answered and thought back to the night he made that oath and Ailia was conceived.

"This was all once your father's, Firgany's and mine before it were yours…not that I'm moaning for I am simply trying to explain that nothing physical lasts forever. Understand that you own nothing, everything that is around you is temporary, only the love in your heart will last forever," Theodoric remarked as he continued to study the dark clouds growing ever taller and rolling closer. "I have been blessed in being given a second chance with Sister Lucy, which is far more than I thought I deserved, for the true love of a woman is both rare and a beauty. If you never remember anything I have ever told you, always remember the most precious gift that ever comes to a man in this world is a woman's heart, and that what comes easy to us in life, won't last, but that which lasts won't come easy," Theodoric said quietly and paused. He sighed heavily. "But war is coming…I can sense it, Paul…you will have to leave and the sooner the better."

"And you say this because you see a sign in the approaching dark storm clouds?"

"Don't be so bloody stupid," Theodoric laughed and hit Paul's arm. "No I say it because it is true and if you wish to leave for France you better do so soon before every ship is commandeered by your good friend Husam and Conrad alike. Husam to engage any force that comes from Europe and Conrad so he can ship whoever pays the most and to use his port of Tyre."

"And you are certain of this?" Paul asked, concerned.

"'Tis a curse I carry for being right...except where Sister Lucy is concerned and camels of course."

"Are you ever going to tell me what it is about camels and Sister Lucy?"

"Probably not...but ask me on my death bed. When I am old and incontinent," Theodoric laughed and carried on looking at the approaching clouds.

"We have been blessed these past few years with good health and we have prospered and by the grace of our Lord we have been protected."

"By the grace of our Lord my arse...'tis by the grace of Thomas and his men."

"Theo you surprise me at times," Paul replied, smiling at his casual bluntness.

"They are all good men. Other knights of half their standing have at least seven or eight men in support yet they do everything for themselves. You, in fact all of us, have been blessed with their presence. But those blessings will not stop the war that is fast approaching I fear," Theodoric sighed and pulled up his hood around his neck as the wind picked up speed. "Since King Baldwin the Fifth died in August, still just a boy of nine poor soul, Count Raymond will not remain regent for long despite agreed terms with all the other barons."

"Terms...what do you mean?"

"What limited unity there is between our so-called noble lords was all sadly focused on the infant King Baldwin. 'Twas agreed if the new king were to die young, Raymond would remain regent until the Pope, the kings of France and England, and the German Emperor had all been consulted on the succession as it is sorely disputed between Baldwin the Fourth's sister Sibylla, the mother of the young Baldwin the Fifth, and Isabella, daughter of King Amalric I. With no new truces being sought with Saladin and still no word from Europe or the Pope, Sibylla's faction tricked Raymond into travelling to Tiberias, officially to summon the barons of the kingdom together to carry out Baldwin the Fourth's will. However, once he was out of the way, they occupied the main ports," Theodoric explained then faced Paul. "The kingdom is split in two. Sibylla, with that fool of a husband, Guy of Lusignan, who still holds Jerusalem, and Raymond and his allies, who are based at Nablus. Of course we now know Sibylla has been crowned queen, and then she crowned Guy as king. Raymond and the other barons had planned to crown Princess Isabella and her husband, Humphrey, Princess Stephanie's son. But that plan was abandoned when the gutless Humphrey fled to Jerusalem, terrified of the prospect of being crowned...but I suspect more fearful of opposing Reynald himself."

12 - 12

"So there is no opposition at all to Guy?" Paul asked.

"None at all, save perhaps Conrad, who schemes and plots against them all. Do not take your eye off that man. Alas yes all opposition to Guy has collapsed, but the damage has been done. 'Tis why we received word courtesy of Ernoul, that Baldwin of Ibelin, one of the greater barons, has now permanently left the kingdom and Raymond has moved back into his lands of Galilee and now refuses to acknowledge Guy. We are fortunate that Ernoul keeps us informed."

"Fools...for if they cannot even rule themselves properly and work together then how will they stay strong enough to counter anything that Saladin may do?"

"If they do not unite or secure a lasting truce and peace with Saladin, then they will not counter Saladin...and that is why it is time we must leave. Reynald's behaviour alone demonstrates just one of the main problems facing all in Outremer. Barons like Raymond have the foresight to realise that to survive they need to live on peaceful terms with their Muslim neighbours for as long as possible...a policy that Saladin agrees with, but his patience is being sorely tested daily. To maintain numbers new Crusaders arrive daily and they are much less willing to live peacefully with the infidels as they view them purely as an enemy they have come to fight. Now, as this year draws near to a close, and with the kingdom in desperate need of a few years of peace to restore order, Reynald has yet again committed another outrage."

"Oh Lord, what this time?"

"A huge caravan travelling north from Cairo passed through his lands, under the protection of treaty, but you know Reynald, and he launched an attack on it, killing the guards, stealing the trade goods, and taking the merchants hostage. Saladin attempted to act within the terms of the treaty, and sent envoys demanding the return of the merchants and their goods, first to Reynald, who in his usual arrogant fashion chose to ignore them, and then on to King Guy, who listened to Saladin's envoys, more the advice of Count Henry and Balian I suspect advising him. Guy has agreed that they were in the right. However, he is far too dependent upon Reynald for his power, and he cannot take the risk of an attack on his own main ally and has consequently refused to force Reynald to pay recompense or make him apologise. Even if he tried we know Reynald never would…so alas the envoys have returned to Saladin unsatisfied, and war is now inevitable."

"'Tis at times like this one actually wishes for a natural drought to force a new treaty as before when one was suffered."

"With storms like that coming, there will be no droughts this time to secure any such truces. Now that it is clear war is looming, the weakness and dissention of the Crusader states is becoming ever more apparent and Saladin's spies can see this most evidently. Saladin's own generals are pushing for war…some even demanding it. Bohemond of Antioch has renewed an already existing truce, and Raymond has rushed to make a new one with Saladin," Theodoric explained and rubbed his chin as he thought.

"What…I know you well enough by now to know there is a but coming," Paul asked.

"Hmmm, but," Theodoric said and paused. "Alarmingly this truce has been extended to cover his wife's principality of Galilee, actually part of the kingdom of Jerusalem. That, I assure you, in fact I can guarantee it, will cause a major problem that may well split and divide Raymond's forces to the side of Saladin if Reynald persists in his actions."

"'Tis a pity someone like Al Rashid could not sort him out and save us all a whole world of pain. Why, if this can all be seen by such people as Kratos, do they not intervene and stop it?"

"People like Kratos can assist and advise but they cannot intervene. Well, not usually as he has been known to at times. The choices we make are down to us and us alone. Kratos tried once before to directly intervene, with disastrous consequences. And as is often the case when they have intervened, it has proved too much for the individuals concerned to endure…such was the case with a knight we once knew."

"Who was that?" Paul asked and started to button up the front of his cape as the first misty drops of rain started to blow in.

"Oh he was a knight, with a sword very similar to yours," Theodoric replied and indicated Paul's sword. "You are of course more than aware of the legends of King Arthur and the sword in the stone…well according to the various versions of the story, the sword could only be pulled out of the stone by the true king of England. You know it symbolically represents drawing knowledge and wisdom from the stone, as in an initiate who is able to understand the codes written within the Giza pyramids," Theodoric explained and tied his robe around himself tighter as the wind picked up. "Well, my friend, a similar, though much less well-known, story can be found in the Italian region of Tuscany. It was in part the inspiration for the English legend. This is the sword in the stone of San Galgano. Believe it or not 'twas San Galgano who was the first saint to be canonised through a formal process by the Church. There is much of his life known through the documents of this canonisation process, which was carried out just last year in 1185."

"But I have never heard of him before," Paul replied.

"No not many have. 'Tis funny how coincidences and events repeat themselves, which is what he did."

"So who is he?"

"Well he was born in 1148 in Chiusdino. His mother is recorded as Dionisia, whilst his father's name is said to be Guido or Guidotti. San Galgano was only concerned with worldly pleasures in his early life. As a noble, he was a knight trained in the art of war, and was arrogant as well as violent. Just like Reynald no less. All that changed, however, and he subsequently became a hermit."

"Why did he become a hermit?"

"He had a vision of the Archangel Michael, who, incidentally, is commonly depicted as a warrior saint. In one version of the legend, the Archangel Michael appeared before him, and showed him the way to salvation. The archangel even told the saint the place that he should go. The next morning, San Galgano declared he was going to become a hermit, and would reside in a nearby cave. He was ridiculed by his friends and family, who thought he had lost his mind. His mother managed to convince him to visit his fiancée for the last time before renouncing all worldly pleasures. On his way there, the saint's horse suddenly reared, and he was thrown off its back. An invisible force lifted him onto his feet, and a heavenly voice led him to Montesiepi, a hill close to Chiusdino. When he reached the foot of the hill, he was told to stand still and look to the top, where he saw his vision of a round temple with Jesus and Mary surrounded by the twelve Apostles. The voice told him to climb the hill, and the vision faded. When he reached the top the voice spoke again, commanding him to renounce all his worldly desires but he objected, saying that this was as easy as splitting stones with a sword. To prove his point he drew his sword, and thrust it into a stone. Much to his surprise the weapon went through the stone with ease. It has been stuck in the stone ever since. But at least he understood the message loud and clear, and lived on Montesiepi as a hermit. Several years after San Galgano's death, a round chapel was built there with the sword in the stone as its main attraction. The chapel was just completed this year and the sword is still firmly stuck within the stone."

"As I have oft heard, myth can be true and myth can become real," Paul said and stood up as the rain began to spit harder. "Will anyone draw that sword out?"

"No…well no one should at any rate as it will stand to a testament for later generations."

"Why and how do you know such things?"

"'Tis my business to know…plus your father keeps me abreast of such matters. Ask him next time you see him about the part Kratos played in this tale," Theodoric said and winked and stood up just as a flash of lightning lit up the horizon as the approaching storm drew nearer. A few seconds later a deep rumbling sounded out.

"I best go and make sure Arri does not wake for he hates thunderstorms," Paul remarked and turned away from Theodoric. "Good night," he called as he left the balcony.

Theodoric turned to face the oncoming storm.

"Dear Lord, give me the extra strength I need to deal with whatever comes next," he said quietly, clasped his hands together, and closed his eyes, taking in a deep breath. When he opened them he caught sight of a ship setting sail to leave into the storm. This surprised him and he squinted to see if he could recognise the banners and flags being flown, but it was too dark and too far away.

Paul gently eased Arri's door open to allow the light from the main corridor lanthorn to shine inside. He squinted his eyes to focus upon Arri's pillow but he could not see him. Quietly he stepped inside thinking Arri had snuggled down beneath his covers. As he drew nearer he could see his bed was empty. Quickly he looked over the bed to see if he was lying upon the cool floor as he sometimes did. He was not there. 'He must be in with Alisha,' he thought and made his way to his own chambers. Inside Alisha was soundly asleep. Puzzled Paul went and checked Ailia's room. Her bed was also empty. His heart beginning to pound he hurried back down the upper corridor passing Theodoric fast.

"What is it?" Theodoric asked and began to follow him.

"The children are not in their beds," he replied anxiously.

"They must be with Lucy then," Theodoric replied and immediately began to follow Paul down the stairs.

Paul hurried along the downstairs corridor and opened the door into the main dining area and kitchen. It was dark save for a single ceramic oil burner on the edge of the table. Paul looked around noticing the main rear door was open slightly. As he went to walk around the table he tripped over something and fell forwards upon his elbows hard. As he turned around, in the dim light he could make out a body face down. As he went to sit up, his hand felt the cold sensation of a sticky fluid. It was blood, he knew instantly. Theodoric rushed around and stopped in his tracks as he looked down at Paul and the body. His eyes widened in terror as recognition registered across his distraught face. It was Lucy. Theodoric fell to his knees, his mouth open in shock not sure whether he should move her or not. Paul sat himself up and gently went to move her as Theodoric grabbed the small oil burner and moved it nearer. Blood glistened all down her shawl and dress, her hands fixed holding her throat. As Paul eased her up slowly, Theodoric shaking, the flame of the burner nearly going out, she suddenly let out a slight cough and blinked. Theodoric let out a huge sigh of relief and moved so that he could help support her. In horror he saw that her throat had been cut from her chin downwards across her neck. She had lost a lot of blood.

"I can still breathe," she said in a broken dry voice still clutching her throat tightly trying to stem the blood loss. "The babies…they took the babies," she blurted out.

Paul's heart stopped, then thumped back with a massive wave of force that made his head feel like it expanded. He jumped to his feet and ran to the back door. He reached outside and grabbed the alarm bell chain and started to ring it as fast and as furious as he could. Theodoric tried to lift Sister Lucy up but could only manage to help her sit part propped up against the main table leg. Paul rushed outside as Theodoric tore a strip from his own clothes and pushed it up hard against the wound in Sister Lucy's neck and throat. Alisha came running in, saw them both on the floor and rushed over to them.

"They have taken the babies," Theodoric choked emotionally.

Alisha's eyes widened in panic and she stood up instantly looking around both confused and full of anger. Sister Lucy weakly raised her hand, covered in her own blood and tried to hand Alisha a small scroll.

Paul ran out toward the main side gate. The two Mamluk guards on sentry duty came running toward him barely recognisable in the dark and heavy rain lashing down. Thomas and Luke came running out from their quarters swords already drawn, closely followed by Mathew and the others.

"They have taken Arri and Ailia!" Paul shouted out in panic just as lightning lit up the whole area in a brilliant flash and thunderous roar.

"They cannot have gotten far in this storm as it is directly over us," Thomas shouted back as Adrastos snorted and kicked in the nearby covered stable.

Paul looked at the floor for any signs of footprints but the ground was awash with rain water. His heart was beating fast and a sense of total panic and helplessness was beginning to overwhelm him. Not his children… please no, he begged silently, his heart breaking. Thomas took one look at him and grabbed him by the shoulders.

"Paul…we shall find them…I swear it and we shall kill the bastards who have taken them….do you hear me, man?" Thomas shouted.

Paul felt as if his body was going to fail and collapse beneath him, the rain feeling like it was also battering him down further. Luke ran off toward the exit taking with him Mathew and the others as the two Mamluks looked on in surprise.

"Only your Brother Matthew and his companion have entered and left this night," the nearest Mamluk stated, looking confused.

"Brother Matthew….are you sure, man?" Thomas shouted as another roll of thunder echoed out and lightning flashed across the entire night sky.

"Ali?" Paul said suddenly realising he had not woken her. He turned and ran back toward the house.

Paul burst through the door and stopped seeing Alisha preparing the medical kit on the main table, a lanthorn now lighting up the room better. Sister Lucy lay flat on the main table being comforted by Theodoric as he bravely tried not to cry and show his total terror. Paul was surprised to see Alisha looking so calm. She turned and looked up at him as he stood in the doorway, soaked, looking utterly helpless.

"I will need you to fetch the physician….," she simply and calmly stated.

"What…but Ali…the children," Paul exclaimed, utterly bemused.

"They are fine…for now," she calmly stated, picked up the small rolled scroll and gently threw it to Paul. He caught it and started to unfurl it, confused. "'Tis a note from Turansha. He has them."

Paul felt as if a physical stake was being driven through his chest and for a moment he could not breathe. His eyes transfixed upon the words written on the scroll. He felt like he was about to utterly fall apart, yet Alisha was calmly carrying on and sorting things for Sister Lucy. He blinked and shook his head in surprise at her behaviour and apparent calmness. Little did he realise just how fragile and close she actually was to falling down in a thousand emotional broken pieces, which she knew herself would not help Sister Lucy nor her children. With his hands shaking Paul began to read the note. He felt sick beyond anything he had ever felt before.

"They must have left upon that ship I saw leaving…," Theodoric commented as he comforted Sister Lucy.

"In this storm?" Paul blurted out.

"They will be fine," Alisha said quietly yet reassuringly.

"Fine!" Paul shouted, anger now filling his veins and head.

Sister Lucy opened her eyes and tried to speak but she could not. Theodoric wiped her forehead and gently stroked her, tears in his eyes. Sister Lucy indicated with her eyes that he read the note.

Shaking uncontrollably Paul tried to look at the now blood covered note. Alisha walked over to him, placed her hands upon his and looked at him intently. As his eyes met hers, he could not help but feel humbled in her presence. Her eyes showed sheer determination and a strength he had never seen before. As her hands clutched his ever tighter, her stare not faltering once from his eyes, he stopped shaking. Overwhelmed with concern for Arri and Ailia he started to cry, the tears falling down his cheeks uncontrollably.

"We shall get them back, do you hear me?" Alisha stated softly. "Do you hear me?" she repeated. Paul nodded silently in agreement. "Just pray tell me you understand the message."

Paul stepped away from her and toward the lanthorn so he could read clearly. As he rolled it flat on the table near to Sister Lucy he began to read the cryptic message half crying and half laughing that at least he did understand the message. Thomas rushed in soaking wet and dripping rain water all over the floor. Out of breath he stood shaking his head no.

"Fear not, Thomas…I know where they are going and why," Paul said emotionally and held up the note. As he did his eye caught sight of Arri's horse, Clip clop, lying on the floor with some of Sister Lucy's blood on it. Slowly he knelt down and picked it up. As tears filled his eyes again, he fought to control himself. Alisha gulped hard and tears finally welled in hers seeing Clip clop. Paul seeing her like that cut him like a knife. "I swear we will get them back," he swore through gritted teeth. "I swear it."

Port of La Rochelle, France, Melissae Inn, spring 1191

"I am going to cry," Ayleth said emotionally and wiped her eyes.

"You and me both, my woman," Sarah said softly and held out her hand for hers.

"Well come on...did Sister Lucy die or what?" the Genoese sailor asked impatiently.

"I wish to know what the cryptic note said," Gabirol said.

"What does cryptic mean?" Simon asked the Templar quietly.

"It means that unless you understand the meanings behind the words, then they are just words. If you do, then the words can tell you something that others will not understand," the old man answered. "As for Sister Lucy...yes she survived. She had disturbed the man as he carried both Arri and Ailia through the kitchen. He had tied them and gagged them as well as wrapped them in horse blankets."

"Was it one of Turansha's assassins?" Peter asked.

"No, a trained assassin would have definitely killed Sister Lucy with a thrust directly into her throat, not sliced across it. No gurgling, silent and a swift death... no, when this man tried to cut her throat, she knew she could not fight against his

overwhelming strength so she pushed her chin down as hard as she could against her chest, but even then the knife cut deep into her chin and down across her throat and neck. 'Twas a true miracle it did not cut her actual throat or main blood veins in her neck...," the old man explained and paused for a moment. "She played dead as he then stuffed the note into her hand, picked one of the children up and left in silence with his companion carrying the other."

"My Lord, that showed some presence of mind for sure," the farrier remarked.

"I think I would have gone mad if my children had been stolen," the wealthy tailor said, shaking his head in disbelief. "I would not cope."

"Why did the children not wriggle or squirm and make a noise?" the Hospitaller asked.

"Because he had drugged them earlier so knew full well they would not resist or make any noise. When he left walking past the two Mamluk guards with two horse blankets, one under his arm the other across his horse, his companion beside him, it did not look out of place."

"Who exactly was this man and companion?" the Templar asked.

"I shall come to that shortly...but here, here is the very note," the old man answered and took out a small blood stained scroll from inside his robe. He pushed it across the table toward the Templar. "Please...read it if you will aloud."

The Templar unfurled the note and flattened it out to read.

"It says...If you wish to have your children returned unharmed, you must give me the location and method of entry to that which is known as the Chambers of Creation. Bring the plans to the place we know of as written in Deuteronomy 3. To the stones where King Og of Bashan, the last of the great Refaim was attacked and defeated and that which the Sidonians call 'Sirion'. There amid the stones on the night of the 25th of November by your calendar they shall be. Come alone. Failure will result in their immediate execution. As your friend always, I keep my word, Turansha."

"Some sick bastard fuck friend!" the Genoese sailor exclaimed angrily. "Sorry," he quickly apologised.

"Did Paul know what that meant?" Ayleth asked hesitantly.

"Of course...Turansha knew exactly what he was doing," the old man replied.

"Then pray tell us where this place is and why?" Gabirol asked.

"'Twas northeast of the Sea of Galilee...many weeks' travel away from them..."

"How did Turansha know all about the Halls of Amenti or Chambers of Creation, whatever they were?" Simon asked.

"Years previously when Nyla was murdered...remember one of the assassins

escaped and took with him parchments that Paul had drawn up and clues...," the old man answered.

"Oh dear Lord...so as he was warned not to for if he did there would be dire consequences by that woman beneath the pyramids," Ayleth remarked.

"Yes...and Paul knew and felt this intently. 'Twas a guilt that hit him hard from the minute he read that note," the old man explained sadly. "I think it was that sense of guilt that fed his growing anger as they made plans to set sail and get to the place in question without delay."

"So where is this place?" the Templar asked, lifting the note up.

"'Twas as it said...at a great stone circle where in the Bible it states that King Og of Bashan, the last Refaim...or giant as we would know him, was defeated. 'Tis a place of great antiquity many thousands of years old. Its significance was clearly not lost on Turansha for he knew it was connected with Sirius and thus the Halls of Records. It is situated in a place Abi had had to retrieve an ancient artefact from years previously...you would probably know it as being not far from Mount Hermon...but to all Sidonians, as Sirion," the old man sighed.

"I have heard of this Giant King Og. His iron bedstead is kept at Rabbah. It measures thirteen and a half feet in length and six feet wide," the Hospitaller explained as he took the note from his brother and read it.

"Why travel so far and to such a place?" Sarah asked, puzzled.

"Because it was land Turansha knew well and it was close to his own lands and men. But as there are several places that have been mistaken or claimed to be Gilgal, Turansha knew he had to make it obvious which one he was talking about and Paul would know without any doubt," the old man replied.

"This Gilgal...'tis the same as the first camp of Israel after crossing the Jordan yes?" Gabirol asked. The old man simply nodded yes in reply. "'Tis where they laid twelve memorial stones taken from the river bed as recounted in Joshua and Deuteronomy. 'Tis also where the people were circumcised preparatory to their possession of the land, when it is said in Josh, with a play upon the word, 'This day have I rolled away the reproach of Egypt from off you.' This is when the Passover was celebrated (Josh 5:10) and the manna from heaven ceased (Josh 5:12) and was to here the Ark of the Covenant returned every day after having compassed the city of Jericho during its siege (Josh 6:11)."

"My Lord...did you swallow a Bible?" Simon joked.

1 - 4

"No, my friend, 'tis simply a matter that my father taught me much," Gabirol replied and bowed his head politely.

"Gilgal was once the headquarters of the Israelites and is mentioned often in their subsequent history. Samuel made it one of the three places where he annually held circuit court, the other places being Bethel and Mizpah. The Septuagint text adds that these were holy places. The place continued as one of special resort especially for sacrifices...it was here that Samuel hewed Agag to pieces before the Lord and that Saul was both crowned and rejected as king. It was at Gilgal also that the people assembled to welcome David as he returned from his exile beyond Jordan during Absalom's rebellion. Do not confuse this Gilgal with the former ancient city associated with Dor upon the maritime plain or with Jiljuilieh, thirty miles south of Dor and four miles north of Anti-patris. The place Paul was being called to was Gilgal Refaim, the Circle of the Refaim or Wheel of Refaim. 'Tis truly a mysterious place," the old man explained.

"I hope it does not become the sacrificial place for the children then...and what does this circle of stones look like?" Peter asked.

"'Tis set upon a high hill...'tis older than Stonehenge in Britain. It consists of five concentric stone rings, the outer of which still stands some seven feet tall with a thickness of eleven feet. In the centre there is a mound, around sixty-five feet in diameter and sixteen feet high. In the middle of it all lies a cairn."

"And this is where again?" the farrier asked.

"'Tis not far from Gamla, some nine miles east off the coast of the Sea of Galilee. 'Tis in the middle of a large plateau that is covered with hundreds of dolmens. It was used as a great calendar. It has two large openings, one that faces northeast, the other southeast. I can tell you from what I know and learnt that it was constructed many thousands of years ago, and then some three thousand years before Christ, the first rays of the summer solstice appeared directly through the northeast opening as seen from the central tumulus whilst at the same time, the southeast opening provided a direct view of Sirius. Calculated years in advance."

"So these stones functioned as an astronomical observatory then and Sirius is yet again important?" Gabirol asked.

"Yes, amongst other things," the Older man acknowledged. "There are over thirty-seven thousand tons of stone laid at Gilgal...and you, my friends, should ask yourselves why when a single rock and stick would have sufficed."

"Then what was it for and why did Turansha specifically choose that location?" the Templar asked.

"No one can see the shape or layout from the ground. There are no hills that can

look down upon it and anyone sat in the middle can see for many miles around in all directions. Only a few wooded areas now remain as you approach up the hill... 'tis claimed that the biblical giants, the Refaim, were its builders. In Genesis 14:5, we are told the Refaim inhabit the place called Ashtherot-Karnaim. Just ten miles from Gilgal is the site of an ancient Canaanite city called Ashtarot. It is named after the Canaanite goddess of war and, contradictorily, love. In Joshua 12:4, we learn that King Og of Bashan, who was the very last of the Refaim, lived at Ashtherot and ruled a vast territory from there. The Refaim were a large and powerful tribe, as tall as the Anakim giants...In Chronicles 20, the last of the Anakim is killed. He was a giant with six fingers on each hand and six toes on each foot, whose father was also a giant, killed by David's nephew Jonathan. These giants were descendants of the giants of Gath and were killed by David and his soldiers. The Jewish oral tradition says King Og stowed away on Noah's ark and was the only survivor of the Flood outside Noah's family. Og was descended from the Nefilim, deities who fell from the heavens as has been explained previously. Og had children with Noah's daughters and they were hybrid giants called the Anakim or Refaim. They existed in ancient times and the Bible records their presence in the region. Substitute one name as representing a whole group of people and you will be closer to understanding what the Bible is telling us." [108]

"You have the note...but what happened next then?" the Hospitaller asked.

"Paul immediately made plans to travel east by ship. Now he wished he had completed his own fast ship design. Aware that he was supposed to go to Gilgal alone, he nevertheless decided to take Ishmael, Thomas and Luke. Theodoric had been deeply shocked by the attack on Sister Lucy and was taken quite poorly and he chose to stay and look after her'." the old man explained. "He, Sister Lucy and Attar prayed constantly for what else was left for them to do...but pray and wait?"

"And what of Alisha?" Sarah asked.

"Oh Paul tried to persuade her to stay home with the others...but she was having none of that. Where Paul was going, to their children, so was she and no force on earth was going to stop her. She developed a steely cold look that seemed to harden her face. Determined would be a great understatement."

"I still do not know why Turansha did not just steal all of Paul's work...why the need to use the children?" Gabirol asked.

"Because he knew that even should he find the site, he did not have the tools or the knowledge to gain access just as all the myths and legends tell us, but he knew Paul did. He also wanted Paul's family dead...all of them...but also to receive great wealth and power from another source in the lands...for he had sworn a pact with

a very devious and potentially powerful lord who if successful in removing all and any other potential claims of birthright, would be a ruler without equal...both in Outremer and Europe."

"And who was that?" Ayleth asked, almost too afraid to.

"I shall come to that later...but do you recall how Brother Matthew hid behind a tapestry concealed in Kizkalesi Castle...and overheard all that was told to Paul about his and Alisha's bloodlines and true origins?" the old man asked and paused. "Well Brother Matthew revealed that information to others...the consequences of which led to the kidnapping and ransoming of Arri and Ailia."

"So it was that bastard Matthew all along then. Tenno said to watch him right from the start," Sarah said loudly and clearly angry.

"It was indeed Brother Matthew who took them...for he had his reasons to."

"As you will reveal later," Simon said, sounding sarcastic, and shrugged his shoulders.

"I do not understand how Brother Matthew could be in Cairo so freely?" the Templar asked.

"Remember, Gerard was now Master of the Order, but Count Raymond still had Templars under his charge...such as you and your men, correct me if I am wrong," the old man replied. "Raymond had signed a treaty with Saladin and Brother Matthew was able to travel openly and safely as part of Raymond's embassy escort."

"But who was the man of power he was really working for?" Gabirol asked inquisitively.

"That I promise I shall reveal shortly...but as Alisha and Paul set sail having secured passage on one of the very few vessels prepared to sail that day in the high seas, they strongly suspected it was Brother Matthew but they had no idea of who had actually ordered the kidnappings, firmly believing it to be all Turansha's doing."

"So it is all but a trap...to kill them all. Oh I do not think I can hear this out," Ayleth exclaimed, looking upset. She shook her head a few times, took a deep breath and looked directly at the old man. "Okay...I am ready. Please continue."

Port of Caesarea, Kingdom of Jerusalem, November 8th 1186

A hard cold wind blew into Alisha as Paul helped her down the docking bridge to the stone harbour wall. Wrapped in wind proof leathers, the wind still cut into her. It had been raining unseasonably hard and large puddles dotted the walkway along the length of the promenade. The night was closing in fast and they were glad to be ashore after the rough sailing from Fustat. Not surprisingly, few people were about and Thomas quickly rushed in front of them keeping an ever watchful eye out for any suspicious behaviour and people. Ishmael followed carrying two large luggage cases accompanied by Luke and Mathew, who had insisted on coming along.

Running through Paul's mind always was the constant reminder of his mother's words. 'Your son will only hold your hand but a short time, but he will hold your heart for a life time.' Those words coupled with his previous dreams made for a constant knot in his stomach the like of which he had never experienced before. Alisha still had a determination in her eyes that Paul drew strength from. He felt sure that at any moment he would fall apart inside and just scream. The not knowing, the fear that gripped his very soul in a vice he could not escape from. He constantly felt sick and it became an ordeal to even eat, but eat he must. Alisha felt an overriding sense of anger. At times she found it hard not to blame Paul and she fought to suppress those emotions torn between the love she had for him and her children. She knew and could see the pain in his eyes, and the more she looked, the angrier she became with Turansha. She balanced her anger toward Paul by reminding herself that Turansha had been trying to kill them since before they were even born. In her rush to leave Fustat she had left her dagger, the one thing she went everywhere with, but she had misplaced it and did not have the time to find it. In her mind she constantly told herself all would be well. Paul would give Turansha what he wanted and that would be the end of it. But something did not sit right inside her. She had prayed and prayed until she could pray no more. And now as they walked along the dockside, the weather the worst it had been in decades, at least she took some small comfort in knowing no ships had floundered so Arri and Ailia must have made it this far. Inside her jacket she could feel the little lump made by Arri's toy, Clip clop. She feared how he would cope without his constant little companion. Her heart broke every time she thought of him and Ailia. She squinted her eyes in the fast fading light as she saw several men at the far end of the dock. Wearing heavy leather weather proof capes and furs, she could see several were Templars by their emblazoned emblems on their chests. One individual was very tall and clearly blonde despite the hood being raised as a misty fine rain started to blow in. As Alisha drew nearer she recognised Brother Teric then as the tall figure smiled reassuringly, she realised it was Abi. Without thinking, she ran toward her and threw her arms around her tightly.

"My Lord has answered my prayers. Thank you…thank you," Alisha said emotionally as Abi put her arm around her.

Paul was more than pleased to see them but also curious. There was no way they could have been there to meet them as word could not have reached them that quickly surely, he thought.

"Who are you here to meet?" Paul asked, his voice low.

"You of course…who else," Brother Teric replied and outstretched his arm to greet Paul.

Alisha looked up puzzled but grateful. She turned to look at Brother Teric to see Nicholas step forward into view closely followed by Percival.

"But how…I mean?" Paul exclaimed, surprised, and immediately greeted Percival with a hug.

"'Twas Abi. She called us," Percival answered.

"My Lord, you are solid," Paul said as he felt the muscles in Percival's arms as they each held the other's forearms.

"How did you know?" Alisha asked emotionally and stepped back from Abi to look at her.

"I shall explain all. First we need to get you out of this coming storm. We have secured shelter within the Keep and on the morrow's break we shall head for Tiberias. Brother Teric has already sent word ahead for Princess Eschiva to expect us," Abi explained.

"And I pray you will allow us to escort you," Nicholas said and bowed his head.

Paul looked at Alisha. She nodded immediately. It was uplifting to see them and the very fact they had come to help filled Paul with hope and a renewed sense of purpose…the sense of utter helplessness at last beginning to be replaced by that hope. He shook his head and prayed inside it was not just a forlorn or empty final hope. He hugged Percival again then shook Nicholas's hand.

"We would be most grateful and honoured…but, but we are to meet Turansha alone we were told," Paul explained and paused. "Or else," he finished.

"Then you try telling those two that message," Nicholas replied and pointed behind them to two men stood next to their horses some distance away.

The moment Alisha saw them she knew it was Tenno and Taqi. She ran toward Taqi and flung her arms around him, her eyes shut tightly lest a tear should fall. She squeezed and hugged him tightly as he held her. His eyes met Paul's as he walked toward them. Tenno bowed his head slightly. It had been good to see Abi, Percival, Nicholas and Brother Teric, but seeing Tenno and Taqi filled Paul with a sudden sense that yes, perhaps they will get Arri and Ailia back after all. Lost for words he stood before them as Alisha kept hugging Taqi, her head resting against this chest.

"How did you know we would be here at this port and not Acre or Tyre?" Paul asked.

"Because this is the nearest port that will take you across good roads... besides we knew you could not berth at Tyre under Conrad's control nor Acre upon a Muslim ship. Besides, I just knew," Abi replied and took Alisha's hand and beckoned her to follow.

Taqi gestured for Paul to walk beside him as they started to follow Abi and Alisha toward the old aqueduct, its massive arches still as impressive as the day they were built. Brother Teric and Nicholas followed behind with the horses with Thomas, Luke and Mathew beside them. Paul looked at them briefly and wondered where Upside was. Ishmael carried the two large trunks as if they weighed nothing and when Paul offered to take one, he refused.

ꕥ

The evening air was cool and filled with the smell of fresh rain. From the open rooftop of the three storey Templar Keep, Paul looked out across the port and even in the darkness he was able to make out the old Roman amphitheatre just a short distance away. His heart ached and he could not shake off the helpless sense he still felt. He looked to the east and the horizon where a star flickered barely visible between a gap in the dark clouds. Arri and Ailia were somewhere out there. His stomach knotted again. He clasped his hands over his sword pommel and vowed that despite whatever stain upon his soul it may create, he would kill Turansha. He had lived with the constant presence of him overshadowing every aspect of his life daily. Enough was enough he vowed. Gilgal was sixty-eight miles away by road, four days' march if they kept up their speed, but he knew they would have to stop over at Tiberias and wait until the appointed day.

An agonising wait he was unsure he could endure. Paul jumped as a hand rested upon his shoulder. It was Percival.

"My friend, you are not alone in this venture, and we shall get them back I swear to you," he said softly.

Paul looked at him. He appeared to stand taller, more confident and he looked incredibly well. Paul knew the sadness Percival had suffered and yet here he was ready to assist him in his gravest hour of need. Nicholas came out and stood beside them before Paul could ask Percival what he had been up to since last they were together. Nicholas bowed his head at Paul in acknowledgement.

"Whatever it takes and for as long as it takes, we will get them back as he states," Nicholas said and put his hand out. Paul took his hand, Nicholas's grip being strong. "Upon my life I too swear it, Paul."

Paul looked into his eyes and he knew he was sincere. This was not even his fight yet somehow Brother Teric had managed to arrange it to have him here. Paul looked past his shoulder and saw Alisha approach with Abi as Tenno and Taqi walked up the outside stairs having sorted out the horses for the night. They stopped beside Nicholas and Percival and simply looked at Paul as if waiting for him to say something. Lost for words all he could do was look at them each in turn. But no words were necessary such was the depth of understanding between them all. Paul turned and looked eastward again as Alisha took his hand.

Port of La Rochelle, France, Melissae Inn, spring 1191

"You say they came to Tiberias...for that is where I met them. I know now what you speak of in this tale is truly real," the Templar remarked.

"But this cannot end well, no matter how highly trained they are if they all turn up as Turansha forbade it did he not?" Sarah asked, looking concerned.

"Yes he did forbid it as per the instructions...but Paul knew if he turned up with Alisha alone, once he had handed over the details, they would all be killed. He knew that without any doubt. Now with the others on board, he stood a chance of making some kind of plan to rescue them. And that is exactly what he set about doing. At that moment in time, his immediate concern was whether he had indeed understood the code and ultimate location of where to meet Turansha," the old man explained.

"And did he understand the correct location?" Gabirol asked.

"Yes he did. That fact alone is perhaps the one thing Alisha kept on reminding herself. She would stare at the parchment tube with further codes and drawings Paul had produced and wished she had never seen or knew of them. She started to feel they were cursed almost. That fact she hated," the old man replied.

"Did she regret having gotten involved with Paul then?" Ayleth asked.

"No...despite it all, she did not regret the path they had chosen together. She knew and felt within in her heart that she could not live without him. She loved him with more than her heart and soul," the old man paused. "But sometimes in this life, in this world, love is not always enough," he sighed.

"That sounds very ominous," Gabirol remarked.

"It is said that love is enough...that love conquers all. 'Tis a view I still hold onto, but one I know to be seriously difficult to maintain," the old man explained sadly.

"Jesus said that love is all you need," Simon interjected and quickly looked at Sarah.

"The man Jesus certainly said many things. For you, Simon, I would ask that you remember these simple facts about the man. There will come a time when he will be viewed and looked upon as the greatest man that ever lived in this age...he had no servants yet he is called master. He had no recognised qualifications yet he is called a teacher...he had no medicines yet he is called a healer...he had no army yet kings feared him...he won no military campaigns yet he has conquered the world... almost all the world," the old man sighed.

"Why do you tell us that?" the Genoese sailor asked, bemused.

"Because it is not necessarily by force that fights are won. And despite all that was happening in Paul's world, he was still constantly trying to justify the use of force, especially as he stood there looking at the men before him, highly trained, armed and ready to inflict extreme violence on his behalf for the sake of his children. In the back of his mind was always the thought of how to carry the codes entrusted to him forwards without the use of such a force, like the Templars have so far managed to do. Plus how he could possibly ever help with the diplomatic charge he had been commissioned with....to raise and inaugurate a Muslim contingent of Templars?"

"That I would like to see," the farrier remarked and sat up.

"Hmm, it most certainly would be an interesting development," the Hospitaller commented and leaned upon his right elbow and looked at his brother. "Well?"

"Well what? 'Tis possible. And imagine if we did join with the best of their men," the Templar replied.

"This harbour they have all met at. Is it not the same one as built by the biblical Herod?" the Genoese sailor asked. "Sorry to change the subject. Just wondering."

"Yes, yes it is," the old man answered and faced him. "The port of Caesarea Maritima...'Twas indeed Herod the Great who constructed the large port city to honour the Roman Caesar Augustus in around 25–13 BC. Theodoric on one of his earlier escapades actually found and reburied a stone confirming Pontius Pilate's historical existence. But that is another story," the old man explained and momentarily laughed to himself. "The emperor Vespasian raised its status to that of a colonia and after the destruction of Jerusalem in AD 70, Caesarea became the provincial capital of the Judaea Province. Herod built his palace on a promontory jutting out into the sea, with a decorative pool surrounded by stoas. It became the official residence of the Roman procurators and governors, Pontius Pilatus, praefectus and Antonius Felix. Josephus described the harbour as being as large as the one at Piraeus, the major harbour of Athens. Remains of the principal buildings erected by Herod are still visible today, including the city walls, the castle and of course the Crusader cathedral and church. In AD 66, the desecration of the local synagogue led to the disastrous Jewish revolt. In AD 70, after the Jewish revolt was suppressed, games were held there to celebrate the victory of Titus and many Jewish captives, some 2,500, were slaughtered in gladiatorial games. After the revolt of Simon bar Kokhba in AD 132, which ended with the destruction of Jerusalem and expulsion of Jews, Caesarea became the capital of the new Roman province of Palaestina Prima. According to the Acts of the Apostles, Caesarea was first introduced to Christianity by Philip the Deacon, who later had a house there in which he gave hospitality to Paul the Apostle and baptised Cornelius the Centurion and his household, the first time Christian baptism was conferred on gentiles. Paul's first missionary journey no less. When the newly converted Paul the Apostle was in danger in Jerusalem, the Christians there accompanied him to Caesarea and sent him off to his native Tarsus. He visited Caesarea between his second and third missionary journeys, and later, as I mentioned before, stayed several days there with Philip the Deacon. Later still, he was a prisoner there for two years before being sent to Rome. In the third century, Origen wrote his Hexapla and other exegetical and theological works while living in Caesarea and as a consequence many believe the Nicene Creed may have originated in Caesarea. Under Arab rule, the city walls remained, but within them the population dwindled and agriculture crept in among the ruins. By the ninth century there was a substantial colony of Frankish settlers established by Emperor Charlemagne to facilitate Latin pilgrimages. When Baldwin

the First took the city in 1101/2, during the First Crusade, it was still very rich. A legend grew up that in this city was discovered the Holy Grail around which so much folklore has accrued...hence why Philip, Firgany and Theodoric at one time found themselves in that very city as well as helping with the design and building of new strongly refortified structures."

"So after staying there briefly, Alisha and Paul and the others went on to Tiberias?" the farrier asked, pushing the issue.

"Yes. It was agreed that once there, they would formulate the best plan they could. But they were ever cautious about spies and whom to trust. It did not help that when they arrived in Tiberias, Gerard and a full squadron of Templars, including your very own troop, were there at the same time."

"I remember it as if it were yesterday," the Templar recalled and shuddered momentarily. Miriam clasped his hand reassuringly as he appeared to become emotional. "But I had no idea...only the sense that they were not like us when they arrived. You could sense there was a purpose about them. And this Paul," the Templar explained and paused as he shook his head. "I actually met him..."

Simon sat back hard in his chair and folded his arms as Gabirol just looked up at the old man, his quill held in midair.

"The journey from the port had been a hard yet fast one. Alisha did not wish to wait around for fear of not being near to Gilgal and having enough time to reach it when the appointed day arrived, so she rode a horse, Paul riding Adrastos of course," the old man explained.

4 - 17

"What you mean they took him along too?" the farrier asked, surprised.

"Yes. It would have cost a small fortune to purchase or hire another and as they knew the captain and the ship had stabling for eight horses, they took Adrastos and their other horse with them," the old man answered. "Taking a cart out across the plains to Gilgal was also impossible."

"Ah, you promised me you would explain why Tiberias no longer stands," Simon interrupted, recalling the old man's earlier promise about the fortress.

Crusader fortress of Tiberias, Principality of Galilee, November 12th 1186

Alisha rode beside Paul as Brother Teric pulled up just short of the main fortified entrance. She saw the massive ten foot thick walls and her eyes fell to the shoreline, the waters looking choppy as a cold northeasterly wind blew in hard. No sooner had they stopped when they were being ushered across the drawbridge, the large façade of large ashlar stones shining with moisture from the constant drizzle. The water in the moat was being blown into mini waves and everything appeared dark, miserable and full of gloom. Her eyes looked up at the massive iron portcullis as she rode beneath it. Once inside the main courtyard, Alisha sat motionless, her hood drawn up over her head as the others dismounted. Her heart fluttered as she thought how Arri and Ailia were. Were they being treated well or abused? She shuddered and closed her eyes trying to shake such thoughts out of her mind.

"Alisha," a softly spoken female said.

Alisha opened her eyes and looked down at a dark haired woman smiling up at her.

"Yes," was all Alisha could reply.

"Come with me. I have a hot bath being prepared. Do you remember me…I am Eschiva, Raymond's wife," she explained and beckoned her to dismount.

Paul dismounted and a Templar sergeant took the reins of Adrastos. Quickly he walked over to help Alisha down. Gently he took her weight and lowered her to the floor beside him. Princess Eschiva smiled at them both.

"Well well well. Look what the cat's dragged in," Gerard called out loudly as he approached across the courtyard. "What on this good Lord's earth brings you here?" he demanded. Alisha and Paul looked at him and he immediately saw the sadness etched across Alisha's face. "Ah…I sense sorrow here. I must beg your pardon," he politely remarked and bowed his head.

"They are here as my guests…just passing through," Count Raymond explained as he appeared alongside Brother Teric.

Gerard took a cautious step back as Tenno, Taqi, Percival, Ishmael, Thomas, Mathew and Luke moved to stand behind Alisha and Paul.

"And pray tell what war are you all off to start?" Gerard asked, bemused, as the drizzle of fine rain started to fall harder.

"We are here to finish one," Percival blurted out, his eyes narrowing as he looked at Gerard hard.

"Not with me I trust for I have not eaten today," Gerard replied, half joking but concerned.

"Not with you," Paul said and nodded at Gerard. "I am glad to see you are still alive and well after our last meeting."

"Yes...very well indeed. Please, excuse me for I am remiss with my manners. 'Twas just a surprise to see you here of all places," Gerard said and bowed to Alisha as several Templars formed up behind him. "Brothers Teric and Nicholas...perhaps you would be so good as to enlighten me as to your involvement here?"

Brother Teric and Nicholas bowed their heads to Gerard and stood between him and Paul.

"Master," Brother Teric started to explain before Count Raymond interrupted him.

"They were following my orders, that is all you need know at this moment," he stated and started to usher Alisha and Paul away toward the main keep's entrance door. "I shall explain all later, Master Gerard."

"May I remind you who commands these men?" Gerard retorted.

"And may I remind you who commands this principality and lands, including you...unless you wish to withdraw your men and all that goes with your commission to us and depart this very hour?" Raymond countered immediately.

"Gentlemen...please there is no need for quarrelling," Princess Eschiva said calmly and took Raymond's hand.

Gerard looked up as the clouds grew darker and more rain fell. He blinked as the rain splashed upon his face.

"My Lord...I would so hate for MY men to suffer needlessly on such a wet and miserable day, so I shall of course bow to your indulgence this day," he remarked, not looking at Raymond. When he lowered his gaze he looked directly at Paul. "Besides, I have a long overdue thank you to proffer to this young man," Gerard smiled as he stepped nearer to Paul. "No offence meant so please ignore my brashness for I am genuinely grateful and indebted to you. I was just taken a little by surprise at your presence here," he said quietly.

"No offence taken," Paul replied, looking Gerard in the eyes intently.

Gerard leaned closer and patted Paul on his upper arm and smiled.

"Seriously, thank you," Gerard said quietly, looked at Alisha and winked.

As he walked away followed by several of his knights and sergeants, Stewart stepped out from amongst another group of mixed Confrere Knights. Standing still before Paul he feigned a nervous smile. Without a word Paul embraced and hugged him just as the heavens opened up above them in a deluge of rain. Paul smiled at Stewart as he held him back at arm's length and began to laugh as they started to get soaked. Princess Eschiva quickly led Alisha out of the downpour and inside the main keep. Several other Templars and two Hospitallers looked on bemused as they stood beneath a wooden awning shielded from the rain. Raymond ran inside and called for them to follow but Paul and Stewart just stood and looked at each other. Out from an archway an old man appeared with a small wooden staff in his hands. Slowly he approached Paul and Stewart only stopping when he reached Paul, staring at his sword. Gently he reached out his old gnarled looking hand and touched the pommel. As he did, he suddenly smiled and stood up straight, his aged eyes widening. Stewart looked on bemused. Paul looked at the old man, also puzzled, and frowned.

"You…you took your time to arrive," the old man said, his voice old and crackly. He waved his finger at Paul and smiled broadly despite the downpour falling. "Are you aware that this sword…this sword was that which was sealed since the dawn of this age of man within that altar of stone in Egypt…for it is the same one for sure?"

Stewart shrugged his shoulders, puzzled.

"I know it is of a great age and passed on to me by our father," Paul replied.

"Ah…so brothers you are…as are those two," the old man said smiling and pointed at a Templar and Hospitaller looking in from the cover of the enclosed paddock nearby. Both stood up straight when the old man pointed at them. "You are of the same vine," the old man stated, nodded and began to walk away across the large forecourt. "You must all four be far away from here before the summer of next year," he called out, stopped and looked back. "For this fortress is no fortress against what cometh and shall befall all here." With that he smiled again, turned his back on them and carried on walking.

Paul looked at Stewart then both looked across at the Templar and

Hospitaller stood together. Thomas ran over, grabbed Paul's arm and started to pull him.

"Come on. We can't afford for you to fall ill with the shivers," Thomas said and pushed Paul toward the main entrance door.

Stewart glanced briefly at the two knights, one raising his hand in acknowledgement. Stewart knew the Templar as belonging to Count Raymond's contingent based at the fortress.

Port of La Rochelle, France, Melissae Inn, spring 1191

The room fell silent as they all looked at the Templar and Hospitaller. The Templar shook his head in disbelief.

"Like I said...I know now of whom you speak for that was my brother and I you speak of," the Templar remarked, his voice slightly broken.

"You say the old man said we are of the same vine. What did he mean? For we did not hear of what was said that day," the Hospitaller asked.

"I wish to know who the old man was," Gabirol asked.

"The old man was a Jewish sage who had lived in Tiberias many many years," the old man explained.

"Jewish?" Simon blurted out.

"Yes, Jewish. Tiberias had a large Jewish population," the old man answered.

"But of the same vine...what are you telling us?" the Templar asked, his voice concerned.

"Exactly what it infers and implies, my friends...," the old man replied and looked at him directly. Both the Templar and Hospitaller shook their heads, confused and in disbelief. "As I said at the very start of this tale, I know you both well enough to have known I was in no danger with you."

Miriam clasped her hands over the Templar's hand seeing him recoil uncomfortably at what he was hearing.

"Are you confirming that you were both there in Tiberias when Alisha and Paul arrived?" Gabirol asked.

"Yes...and the old man was there, in the rain just as explained," the Hospitaller answered. "I knew earlier that much of what has been told we could confirm...but this news you speak of...that we are of the same vine and what that implies. I...we, we cannot believe that, I am afraid."

"Do not doubt your own worthiness either of you, none of you in here should.

You said it yourselves, your father treated you badly for he was suffering a great loss and could not cope. Listen to that inner voice that now speaks to you this very minute. You said you remember when Alisha and Paul arrived with their knights. How different they seemed. That, my friends, was simply you recognising your own kind," the old man explained and sat back slowly and waited for their response.

"Are you saying that their bloodlines are of the same tree as Alisha and Paul's?" Ayleth asked, finally breaking the silence.

"Yes," the old man stated matter of factly.

Miriam let out an involuntary gasp.

"How so?" the Templar asked, visibly shaking.

"Your mother...she was the elder sister no less of Paul's mother, your aunt," the old man said softly.

"Holy Mother of God," Sarah said aloud, surprised.

"Yes, almost," the old man laughed lightly.

The Hospitaller lowered his head and shook his head, trying to hide his emotions. The Templar, seeing his brother, immediately leant over, pushing Simon back a little, and rubbed his shoulder reassuringly.

"We never knew our mother and father refused to speak of her...," the Templar said emotionally as his brother started to sob, rubbing his eyes. "So Paul is our cousin...and you have known of us all this time?"

"Of course. Why do you think you were 'cursed' as you once called it for not being allowed to attend that fateful march toward Hattin?"

Miriam and Ayleth began to get upset seeing how tearful the Hospitaller was becoming. The wealthy tailor wiped away a tear quickly trying to hide it but the Genoese sailor had seen him. He winked in silence.

"Huh, as you can see, I am the softer of us two." The Hospitaller laughed emotionally, wiping his tears, embarrassed. "So much makes sense now."

"A soft heart in a harsh world is the strongest and bravest heart of all," the old man replied.

"You said the old man claimed the sword came from the altar of stone and had been there since the dawn of this age of man. What did he mean by that?" Peter asked.

"'Tis true. Long before Paul's mother even took charge of this," the old man started to say and paused as he placed his hands over the scabbard gently and gripped it. "This was sealed inside a special chamber, inside the Great Pyramid, separate from the other hidden chambers of creation. In removing it, the guardian set to watch over it sadly perished. That was not part of the plan. Her body still

resides within...and perhaps one day it will be found. But when that time comes, many new questions shall be asked of it that is for sure," the old man explained and shrugged his shoulders briefly and smiled as he thought upon his own words.

"Who was she?" Ayleth asked sheepishly.

"Oh, let us say she was a messenger of sorts for that is all I can and will tell you about her," the old man answered and looked at her.

Gabirol raised his hand to speak.

"I heard that according to legend, the first man to break into the Great Pyramid, the caliph named Abdullah al-Ma'mun, or as you called him, Mammon, the son of Harun al-Rashid, in AD 813, found in the King's Chamber the remains of a human looking figure, but different to us somehow. I have read that some Arabian authors reported he found in the sarcophagus a stone statue in the shape of a man. They say that within the statue lay this body wearing a breastplate of gold set with precious stones, an invaluable sword on his chest, and a carbuncle ruby on its head the size of an egg, which shone as with the light of day. Is that why the Jewish sage said the sword came from there?"

"Those reports and authors are not that far from the truth," the old man acknowledged.

"Why are we not told of such matters?" Sarah asked.

"Because it would change everything and the Church would lose its control...," the Hospitaller said as he sat himself upright and took a deep breath, his brother letting go of his shoulder.

"I just need to know Alisha and Paul got their babies back," Sarah said quietly and looked at Stephan. He feigned a knowing smile for he knew what was about to be explained next. He lifted her hand and gently kissed it before looking toward the old man. He nodded for him to continue.

Chapter 65
The Deepest Wound

Crusader fortress of Tiberias, Principality of Galilee, November 12th 1186

Alisha took off her wet over cloak as Princess Eschiva helped take it from her shoulders. The large open reception room was warm and inviting, a large welcoming fire burning away. Paul entered, his wet cloak already in his hands. Count Raymond walked across the room fast and opened a side door and indicated with a swift nod of his head for the two maids inside to come out. As they did, Taqi and Brother Teric entered the room closely followed by Ishmael, Thomas, Luke and Mathew. Balian entered and walked directly toward Alisha and Paul just as Tenno and Nicholas entered the room behind him, their wet coveralls in hand.

"I came as soon as I heard," Balian said and shook Paul's hand and bowed his head to Alisha. Steam started to rise off of him from his soaked fur lined cape.

"How did you hear?" Paul asked, both bemused and concerned.

"Nothing escapes my knowledge…one rumour that the Grail family was coming here and I knew it was you," Balian replied.

"We are not the Grail family," Paul replied and frowned hard.

"You try telling others that. That is exactly why we find ourselves in this predicament now," Balian explained and gently took Alisha's hand and kissed it. "There are those lords amongst our kind who see you as a direct threat to their own claims in this region."

"We are no threat and this is our predicament," Alisha said in response.

"'Tis ours also…trust me on this matter," Balian replied as Count Raymond nodded in agreement. "Also, Paul, my warrant and commission still stands as good as the day Ernoul wrote it out. That also means my pledge to support you still stands."

"But I did not accept it," Paul answered.

"Maybe not…but as a friend, this problem you now face is the worst kind any parent should ever face," Balian explained. Princess Eschiva smiled softly at Alisha and nodded in agreement with him. "Even Saladin himself is aware of your predicament and has offered a full troop of his best men to help..."

"Saladin?" Alisha gasped in surprise.

Count Raymond stepped closer and looked at her.

"Fear not, I speak with Saladin frequently as does Balian. Turansha knows full well he has over stepped the line on this matter...I have banned Reynald from my lands for now, so the only problem we face is in deciding a stratagem to recover your children safely without giving Turansha what he is after...and if that means we use some of Saladin's men to do that, then so be it," Raymond explained.

"You cannot give him what he demands," Abi suddenly interrupted as she entered the room unfastening her thick fur collared surcoat.

"We know Brother Matthews is involved," Brother Teric said. "He has not reported back for duty as he should have and his family has also left the safety of this castle. It is highly probable that wherever he is, so too we shall find your children. We will keep a constant look out and patrols to see if we can locate them prior to Turansha's deadline meeting."

"But if Turansha finds this out, he will kill them as his terms state!" Paul interjected, alarmed.

"We have two weeks to locate and rescue them. Gerard leaves soon but we have most of the Knights of Lazarus camped outside the walls ready and willing to serve us alongside whatever troops from Saladin arrive," Balian explained reassuringly. "There is no way of softening what I say so I shall just say it. Turansha has no intention of letting any of you live. You know this to be true."

Alisha turned pale as the colour in her face drained away. Her eyes wide she looked to Abi for some words of comfort or reassurance. Abi took hold of her hand.

"Listen to the voice that speaks within you. You know Balian speaks the truth. That is why I have come along with Percival, Tenno and Taqi. Even Al Rashid wishes to help. Turansha has succeeded in uniting friend and foe alike against him," Abi said and looked across at Paul. "And whatever happens, you cannot, I repeat, and as unfair and as cruel as you may think me this hour, you cannot pass him the parchments you have drawn nor the knowledge and means of accessing that which he wishes. You cannot," she stated and took several steps toward Paul, her deep blue eyes cutting into his very heart and soul. "You swore a promise remember?"

Paul turned away and walked over to the large arched windows. So similar to the windows in his father's study, he thought. How he wished they were all there at that moment in time. He fought to control his emotions that were welling up inside. He could not speak for he knew he would cry yet again. He had to appear to be strong. He took a deep breath as he looked out of the windows overlooking the outer curtain wall and across the Sea of Galilee. Words to Alisha from him would be useless he knew. All stood in the room in silence, only the two maids moving as they took the wet cloaks away. After a while, Paul finally turned to face them all. Knowing the sword was part of the key, his hand resting upon the pommel, he vowed that he would put the very blade right through Turansha when he saw him. Memories flooded back to what the woman had told him beneath the pyramids as Abi had just reminded him. How she knew was quite irrelevant. The woman's words echoed through his mind as if he was hearing them for the first time. He stood in silence looking mesmerised. 'Safeguard the location and codes to its position...for mankind's very survival in the future...and safeguard it you must as you so volunteered to do...long ago... Nothing, absolutely nothing else matters nor must come before that. Do you understand that fact? Agree to those terms and you will be allowed admittance to the Chambers of Creation to ask of it what you will. But remember all you have seen and heard here, but never write it down for there would be consequences beyond your wildest fears if you do.' As her final words struck, he blinked and flinched backwards.

"Are you all right?" Balian asked, concerned.

"Yes...I know only full well what must be done," Paul answered and walked over to Alisha. The desperation in her eyes pained him greatly as he took her hands. "I was told once that I could command an army of kings," he said then looked around the room. "This day, as I look upon those here present, no finer or more noble men have I ever known for I see that army of kings...and this day I swear to my very own queen, I shall get our children back."

Alisha looked at him and shook her head lost for words. Quickly she took out Clip clop, smelt him, closed her eyes and held him between her hands in prayer. Paul pulled her close and hugged her. Abi looked at Paul and simply nodded slightly as Taqi put his arms around both of them. Tenno took a deep breath, stood up straight and checked his emotions.

Port of La Rochelle, France, Melissae Inn, spring 1191

"And both Gerard and Saladin agreed to help?" Simon asked, confused.

"Yes and do not forget that both sides had often worked together to fight bandits as well as do harvests and move water during times of drought, especially in Raymond's area of rule and influence," the old man answered.

2 - 11

"How did Balian hear of their plight? 'Tis not he who is the other powerful lord who works with Turansha is it?" Gabirol asked.

"No, not he. As I said before, Balian is a great man of honour and personal courage," the old man answered.

"Did they find the children then before the appointed time?" Sarah asked hesitantly, screwing up her face.

"No...for Turansha had hid them well. He had also made sure that word of Alisha and Paul's plight would become common knowledge fast. 'Twas his own spies who made sure Balian heard the news. When everyone knew of them and their presence, Turansha knew he would wield far more power and influence when it became known that he had been the one to end their line. It also gave him the excuse to kill Alisha and Paul, claiming they had broken the bonds of the agreement," the old man explained, shaking his head.

"Devious evil man," Peter said sadly.

"Turansha wanted war between all sides and hoped that in by doing so and helping cause much friction between all, he could kill off anyone even remotely connected to any so-called legitimate claim to any of the fiefdoms or crowns in the Holy Land...such as Stewart too."

"Of course...I had not thought of him," Gabirol exclaimed.

"So what did Alisha and Paul do in the days leading up to the actual allotted time?" Simon asked.

"I can tell you they stayed inside most of the time for we were tasked with guarding them around the clock. I distinctly remember the protection that was afforded them and the curiosity they aroused as being the Grail family," the Templar remarked.

"They were agonisingly long days for sure," the old man commented, looking at the sword. "And to add to the misery, the weather turned even colder. The worst in decades with great snowfalls. The Knights of Lazarus camped outside endured all that the weather could throw at them."

"Why were they not inside the castle?" Ayleth asked.

"Why do you think...for they were considered by many as unclean. Though in truth despite their ailments they were probably cleaner than most of us at the time," the Hospitaller explained. "I recall now, 'tis so obvious, the beautiful woman we all saw and who was being looked after, on the day it stopped raining and sleeting... for she ventured outside and into their camp to thank them for their daily and continued searches and patrols. I did not see it personally but I was told that she even hugged several of them, one a very badly afflicted leper."

"That was Alisha for you," the old man sighed. "She visited them several times, taking them warm food and extra clothing she personally paid for. She even managed to convince Gerard to hand over several loads of blankets from his Order before he left heading back to Kerak and Reynald."

"I sense Gerard was not all bad," Sarah remarked.

"In truth as I have said before, he was not. When apart from Reynald he was an entirely different man and, albeit begrudgingly, began to admire and respect Alisha and Paul. He had changed much over the past few years since their earlier encounters."

"But not enough," the Templar huffed.

"Sadly no," the old man agreed. "Paul, Balian and Raymond tried to devise all manner of schemes that would free Arri and Ailia, but there was never any way of knowing if come the day, they would actually be at Gilgal as promised. When it was raised, the possibility they could already be dead, Paul immediately dismissed that notion refusing to believe it or listen to it. The guilt he felt about having ignored the advice given about committing to memory and not writing down the details haunted his every thought. If only he had not done so, he chastised himself daily."

"But regardless, Turansha still wanted them all dead, codes or not," Gabirol pointed out.

"Aye that is true, but try telling Paul that at the time. He and Alisha became distant, just when they should have been pulling together closer, but each was drowning in their own worst fears and emotions neither being able to support the other. Alisha would sit staring out of the window across the sea, clutching Clip clop, trying to remember how Arri and Ailia smelt. How they had felt in her arms and kissing them good night in their beds each night. Not even Abi could comfort Alisha. And Paul, he too felt and thought exactly the same things. As the many memories of Arri and Ailia ran through his mind, the many sleepless nights when they had been ill teething, comforting them when they had hurt themselves, tutoring them, just

sitting with them upon his lap late at night as they fell asleep after a busy day. It cut through his very soul and nothing and no one could reach him, not even Taqi when he tried to reassure him. I don't think the dreams he had of wading through snow looking for the boy calling out "Father" helped either with every second feeling like an hour, every hour feeling like a day," the old man said quietly, looked down and paused in silence for several minutes before continuing. "Then the time was upon them. A note was passed to Ernoul by a shepherd who came to the gates asking after him. He in turn took it to Balian."

Crusader fortress of Tiberias, Principality of Galilee, November 24th 1186

Alisha jumped, startled, as Balian rushed into the small room set in almost total darkness as no candles or lanthorns were lit. She was sat alone in the window seat. Rain and sleet lashed down hard against the windows, blurring the view outside.

"Sorry to barge in...but where is Paul?" Balian asked holding a small note in his hand.

Alarmed, Alisha stood up clutching her hands to her chest.

"He is with Abi, Taqi and Tenno I believe...though I am not sure," she answered, her voice low.

"No we are here," Paul said entering the room closely followed by Abi, Taqi and Tenno. "We were just in the other room...we saw you rush past. What is it?"

"This...'tis a note from Turansha. It says you two are to go to the village just past Gamla, that ancient big city, half in ruins, tomorrow. When the sun touches the horizon, then and only then, proceed along the eastern path up to the stones of Gilgal by following the course of the Daliyot stream," Balian explained, shaking his head, not understanding it fully, and offered Paul the note. "It further states for you and Alisha to come alone except for the 'beast' Ishmael."

Alisha rapidly walked across the room and snatched the note from Paul before he could even read it. Paul frowned hard seeing her reaction.

"We cannot allow you to go alone. Somehow we must follow you at a discreet distance," Abi remarked.

"Yes and I and Thomas will travel around the other side along with the

Knights of Lazarus to cut off any escape Turansha may have planned," Tenno stated.

"Paul, you cannot take the parchments...in case all goes wrong and they fall into his hands. You know this do you not?" Abi asked.

"If Turansha or whomever is sent to meet us, they will not take us to the children until he has confirmation I have them with me...so we must take them," Paul answered immediately.

"No, Paul, you cannot. What is at risk here is far more than the lives of the children or your lives. You know that," Abi retorted.

"I thought after all these years you were on our side...to help us," Alisha snapped, anger in her voice.

"Ali, save your anger for those who deserve it...and you know I have always been there for you...always. But this I cannot allow. This is far bigger than us...but I promise you, we shall get the children back," Abi said and looked at Alisha intently.

Quickly Alisha rushed across the room, unbolted a large wooden chest and removed the sealed parchment tube. She walked back toward Abi and held it up to her.

"Take this from me now and you may as well strike me dead this instant for I am swearing to you, I care not for this world at this moment in time... with all its bitterness, nastiness, selfishness and murder...but I do care for my children. You will not take this from me, nor will it leave my hands so help me God until I have my children back in these hands," she said impassioned, tears welling in her eyes, her hand shaking holding the tube.

All looked at Alisha in silence.

"Ali," Paul said quietly and went to touch her arm. She flounced her arm away from him and stood back a pace.

"Back off, Paul! But for these accursed parchments we would not be in this mess," she said angrily, her eyes still firmly fixed upon Abi. Paul's heart missed a beat hearing her words.

"We will all come with you...we will get your children back but you will not pass them over to Turansha," Abi stated and tapped her finger on the end cap of the parchment tube. "Ali, this I swear to you this day. Do you understand me?" Abi asked in all seriousness, her eyes looking deeply into Alisha's.

Balian looked toward the window as snow started to fall outside.

"The weather turns in our favour," he exclaimed positively and looked at Alisha. "It means we can shield many out of sight for visibility will be reduced."

"Then I beg you prepare your men…all of you who so wish to help me… but these, these stay with me," Alisha said and held the parchment case closer.

"Spoken like a true queen," Thomas remarked.

The knot tightening in Paul's stomach made him feel sick. Alisha's words were spoken in the singular, to help her, as if he was not even there. He gulped hard as Alisha turned away from him. The distance between them seemed to be getting ever wider and wider. Seeing the snow falling filled him with an absolute sense of dread as the dreams he had seen repeatedly flashed through his mind. Taqi placed his hand upon Paul's back.

"I did warm you, my friend, years ago…'tis the passion of a fighter you are witnessing…but do not take her words to heart. All will be well again when we have secured Arri and Ailia…," he said reassuringly. "Now go and sort your armour out properly in case you need it, for you are certainly not going anywhere without it on."

Paul took a deep breath and stood up straight. Where was Ishmael? he wondered as well as why Turansha demanded his presence too. He looked around the room at everyone packed in it. If anyone could help them, it was certainly this lot, he told himself. 'Just one more day to go,' he thought.

"'Tis a good full day's hard ride from here to the stones at Gilgal," Count Raymond explained. "You shall need to leave early…I would suggest an early night to sleep."

ᘓᘏ

The small room was dark and cold, the single bed covered in Paul's armour, chain mail, sword and the shield Ishmael had painted his coat of arms upon. He had never even worn it before but Ishmael had packed it unbeknown to him within one of the two large chests he had insisted on bringing. Wind and snow battered the thin single window, the blackness of the night outside only adding to the sense of gloom. He knelt down beside the bed, his knees sinking into the thick white fur rug on the floor. Alisha could not bring herself to even look at Paul and even though she knew what she was doing was cruel almost, she could not deal with her conflicting emotions. Abi had suggested he sleep alone in order to be ready for whatever came the following day. A light rap at the door drew Paul's attention just as Taqi opened the door and looked in. The single lanthorn lit the room enough for Paul to see it was him.

"Thought you may need some help adjusting all that so it helps and not hinders you tomorrow," Taqi said as he closed the door. "You are going to wear it I take it?"

"My friend…I have never worn it before. I am probably better off without it. Tomorrow I stand to lose all that means everything to me…and I fear I have already lost part of the greatest gift I ever had," Paul replied, still kneeling.

"My friend…if there is to be any fight tomorrow, you will need the protection it will afford you. Stupid to get the children back but fall to any blows or arrows needlessly. And Paul…when Ali was a little girl…if ever she was in distress or needed to think, she would always take herself away on her own. Trust me, this is the greatest ordeal she has ever had to endure. Do not mistake her actions for I know she loves you more than ever before."

"I pray you are right…and this, this lot," Paul shrugged and shook his head at the array of equipment and clothing. Paul lowered his head into his hands and closed his eyes as he thought for a moment. Taqi knelt down beside him. The bed was covered in items Paul had no idea how to wear or affix properly. He would need Taqi to help him. "What have I brought upon us?"

It was still dark and the forecourt danced with shadows from the several torches blazing away fixed upon the walls, set beneath protective covers. The snow had stopped falling, which was one small mercy at least, Paul thought as he led Adrastos out of the stables, Taqi by his side with his horse when Alisha approached with Abi. Tenno and Ishmael were talking with the sergeant of the Knights of Lazarus just as Count Raymond, Balian and Brother Teric also approached. The bitter wind cut into all of them and Alisha stopped just in front of Paul and looked into his eyes her breath forming a soft mist as she breathed out.

"Whatever comes next…we do this together," she said calmly and softly and clasped Paul's hand. She looked down sensing the chain mail gauntlet he was wearing.

Princess Eschiva ran out with a thick fur lined and fur rimmed hooded cape and quickly placed it over Alisha's shoulders.

"You will need this," she said and nodded with a smile.

Alisha nodded in acknowledgment and appreciation before turning to look back at Paul. Wearing his chain mail, carrying his shield across his back and a helmet under his left arm, he looked every inch a knight. She was proud of him but also terrified of what the day would bring. Count Raymond stepped closer.

"Alisha, Paul. I have never fought out of hatred against those in front of me that I have faced…but I have fought for those behind me whom I love… but what you face today is a different matter. I wish I could come with you this hour, but I cannot. I pray the Knights of Lazarus, along with your own men, and the few Templars I can spare will be enough?"

"We shall be enough," Nicholas said confidently as he approached with his horse, accompanied by Brother Teric, Upside and Stewart.

Paul's eyes widened in surprise when he saw Stewart.

"We thought you had left with Master Gerard?" Paul remarked, puzzled.

"It would seem Gerard has developed a mild respect and fondness for you…and granted me leave to help this day," Stewart explained. "Besides, are you not my first family?" Paul immediately grabbed Stewart's arms then hugged him before standing back a pace. Nicholas smiled at Alisha and bowed his head slightly. "And look at you now," Stewart remarked and gestured with his hand at how Paul was dressed.

"We must leave now if we are to arrive in time," Abi interrupted and immediately started to usher Alisha toward the other horses being readied by several turcopoles. Alisha mouthed a silent thank you to Stewart as she walked past him and nodded to Nicholas.

"'Tis good to see you again, Brother Baldwin," Paul remarked as he walked past him. "Very good indeed."

Port of La Rochelle, France, Melissae Inn, spring 1191

"I cannot believe it…for I was actually there that morning as they left. We all wondered why they were leaving so early and in such bad weather. 'Twas the worst winter I had ever experienced out there," the Templar explained and began to bite his thumb nail, shaking his head.

"It was indeed the worst winter in decades," the old man replied.

"But would that not help them as Count Raymond said it would?" Sarah asked.

"Usually it may have...but other circumstances came into play that day. The journey was fast and hard riding all day into a bitter wind that blew in from the northeast. Visibility was very low as the snow increased in intensity so at least any spies Turansha had posted would not have been able to see them all coming, and even if they had, they would not have been able to signal ahead. The only small mercy that day," the old man explained further and sighed.

"Oh dear," Ayleth said looking sad.

"Just before they entered the small village just past the remains of old Gamla, Ishmael, Thomas, Mathew, Luke and the eight Knights of Lazarus headed off southeast to skirt around the plain and to come in from the opposite side after sunset. Alisha had asked Tenno to stay close by her side. They were all unsure of how Turansha would present himself but Paul wanted no means of escape for him whatever was going to happen. Brother Teric, Nicholas and Upside would follow Alisha and Paul at a distance. Brother Teric knew the terrain well and that the stream mentioned in the note ran almost directly from Gilgal down to the village through several small wooded areas and scattered trees. It would afford them more cover as they approached...so long as none of Turansha's men were hiding in them."

"Oh I don't think I want to hear this," Ayleth remarked, looking apprehensive.

"Remember I said that even Saladin had offered to help in the search for Turansha and the children...well, his help, true to his word to Balian, eventually came," the old man replied.

"Oh thank the Lord for that," Ayleth sighed.

"However," the old man said and paused. "The sun could not be seen properly at the appointed hour as the sky was heavy with snow clouds and the light was fading fast when Alisha and Paul drew up at the part of the main track where the stream crossed it where a smaller track that led off up the incline toward the stones of Gilgal. The area had many trees dotted around and two areas of thick woodland copses. With driving snow it became impossible to decide or know when the sun was touching the horizon. It was Tenno who suggested that Brother Teric, Stewart, Nicholas, Upside and Abi should all move into the cover of the woods and follow Alisha and Paul as best they could as they headed northeast to the stones. With severe deepening snow upon the ground covering the small track, the task was becoming an impossible one, one that only raised their fears tenfold."

Gilgal, Principality of Galilee, November 25th 1186

Brother Matthew knelt down and wrapped a fur lined blanket around Arri and Ailia as they sat huddled together shivering in the small enclave of stones set within the middle of the main mound of the Gilgal stone circle. It was now almost dark, the snow falling harder as Arri made sure Ailia was comfortable sat on a small rolled up blanket. Her large eyes stared up at Brother Mathew as he placed a small ship lanthorn in a small recess out of the wind. Arri put himself in front of Ailia to help shield her from the biting wind and away from Brother Matthew, who was looking around, his teeth gritted and also shivering from the cold.

"You don't have to do this you know," Arri said calmly and pulled the fur blanket tightly around his neck. With Ailia mainly hidden beneath the blanket, Arri's head stuck out, his hair covered in snow. Brother Matthew took out a fur cap, brushed the snow off of Arri's head and placed the cap on him. "See, I know you like us really."

"Shut up, lad…you know nothing of me," Brother Matthew replied and stood up to look around himself in all directions. With the snow falling and the light fading fast, he could barely see twenty feet in any direction. He could only just make out the two horses he had tied to a lone tree fifteen feet away. "Just keep your little mouths shut and hopefully this will all be over before you know it."

"My father is coming for us you know," Arri said, Ailia peering up through the small gap in the fur blanket and blew her hair up as it kept falling across her little face.

"He better be for that is what he is supposed to do. Now shut up!" Brother Matthew snapped.

"Why are you so angry with us? And you still have not answered why you took us," Arri continued to speak.

Quickly Brother Matthew spun around and knelt down in front of Arri and Ailia.

"I told you, because your father has something I am charged with recovering. If he brings it, you will be set free," he answered, his face twisted in anger.

"But we heard that man in black say we were all to be killed as soon as he gives it to you…but you know you can't kill my father don't you?" Half stunned at Arri's calm revelation, Brother Matthew stepped backwards and tripped on some loose stones. He fell in the snow upon his backside and they just stared at him for a few moments. "That is why I said you don't have to do this."

Brother Matthew sat up and shook his head, his face still twisted in anger and confusion. He looked hard at Arri, his wide innocent eyes just looking back at him intently.

"I am cold," Ailia whispered from beneath the blanket.

Quickly Arri lowered the fur blanket, removed his outer padded jacket and placed it around Ailia and buttoned up the toggles. He then wrapped the blanket around himself and Ailia again, this time putting himself directly in front of her.

"Will you just shut the f…." Brother Matthew nearly swore, but shook his head as he stared at Arri. "This is not what I want or wish to do….but you don't understand."

"I understand you are a Templar and a good knight. And I understand you are not here of your own choice," Arri replied quietly.

"For the Lord's sake, child…how old are you…what, seven or eight years of age?…and you are telling me this because, because, what?" Brother Matthew blurted out, exasperated.

"I just know," Arri replied and buried his face into the fur. "Don't worry, Ailia, Father is coming and you will be all right I promise," he whispered to her. Gently she clasped his hand and blinked back in silence.

1 - 12

"I am no Templar any more for I forsook that when I was forced to do this," Brother Matthew remarked, looking down sorrowfully and shaking his head.

"See, you are a good man and you do not have to do this," Arri replied.

"You are too smart and wise for your young years, lad."

"And you have a choice to make…"

Brother Matthew looked up at Arri. Emotion began to overwhelm him as he looked at the small bundle of Arri and Ailia huddled in the hole shivering.

"Oh Lord, why did you curse me this burden so?" Brother Matthew asked and looked up into the snow as it fell even harder. He started to cry and he placed his hands together to pray. "Why?" he pleaded emotionally.

"Yes, why?" Arri asked immediately, drawing Brother Matthew's attention and gaze.

༺༻

Paul moved Adrastos around to pull up beside Alisha as the others all but vanished out of sight within the tree line, the snow falling in the largest flakes they had ever seen. The wind cut into Paul's neck where the chain mail coif was exposed. Quickly he pulled up the fur collar of the weatherproof cape and tied it up. As he did, a cold shiver ran down his back as the dreams he had of this very moment flashed through his mind. Remembering how Alisha looked in the dream, with the fur lined cape and hood, he turned to look at her just as she pulled it up over her head. It was now almost dark. His heart felt like it was being squeezed inside with every beat it took, his throat feeling like it was swollen so hard he could not swallow or speak. He felt for his sword and placed his hand upon it. He held it and instantly felt a surge of energy run through his arm. Adrastos snorted and bucked as if he had sensed the surge. Paul turned Adrastos to face northeast ready to follow the barely visible track running parallel to the stream. Suddenly, several black clad men appeared on black horses out of the shadows of the small copse of trees directly in front of them. Alisha pulled closer to Paul and steadied her horse as it moved, startled.

"They have no children with them," she whispered.

The men drew their blackened scimitar type swords and in the dimming light Paul instantly recognised them as the same as Turansha's men carried. Slowly they approached, Paul counting sixteen of them in total. He knew Abi, Tenno, Taqi and the others were not that far behind them still in the trees but prayed they would remain hidden until they knew where Arri and Ailia were. Just feet away, the men all stopped, the air filled with the breath of the horses and the tension thick enough to cut with a knife. The central figure eased his horse forward a few more feet, stopped then lowered his black face cover, the smile instantly revealing Turansha. Alisha immediately moved her horse forwards, her eyes narrowing. She pulled out the parchment tube from beneath her cloak and held it up, her gloved hand gripping it tightly.

"This...this is what you want...but only when I see and have my children here...now!" she demanded.

Turansha laughed and looked at his men before returning his gaze to Alisha and Paul.

"You have much to learn about negotiations. Especially when you clearly do not understand the boundaries here, for you are not in a position to dictate to me…you see, I know of your men both behind you and those you sent around the back of me." Alisha kept her eyes fixed upon Turansha and did not show any sign of emotion, just the determined glare she had concentrated upon him. "Did you not think that I knew you would not come alone?"

"Then why all the games?" Paul asked and moved alongside Alisha.

"Games…'tis all but a big game no? Besides it makes life interesting. All you need do is pass me the parchments, if they are the correct ones, as I no longer have much of a future here as you have even turned Saladin against me, and I will have my man over there wave a lighted torch to your good friend Brother Matthew up yonder hill to bring your children to you. If they are not the plans, and I will know, then my man will fire a flaming arrow into the sky," Turansha explained calmly then paused as he moved his horse even closer. "And if you attack me, the arrow shall still be loosed too and by the time you reach your children, their throats will be open to the wind."

"And I will hunt you for eternity if I have to and open yours in return," Alisha calmly replied.

"'Tis such a pity for we could have made such a formidable team. But alas you refused to work alongside me, when the offer was there…and now I am calling upon you to make good on your promise."

"What promise?" Alisha asked.

"The one when I, how you say, vouchsafe Paul and had your lover, Nicholas whatever his name is, spared and entrusted to his care," Turansha smirked.

Alisha looked at Paul. He knew Turansha was trying to provoke a reaction. He shook his head slightly at her, indicating he did not believe him.

"If that was the case then you could have asked for the parchments a long time ago without this entire charade," Paul said and moved his horse closer to Turansha.

"Things change…I am a practical realist. I know I do not have the lineage or so-called legitimacy so much faith is placed in to rule as a king, but I have other means using other powerful lords to help me further my plans…and those plans include the exact location and method of entry into the Halls of Amenti…records whatever you will, and that sword, for I know it is a key."

Alisha shot a look at Paul as one of Turansha's men dismounted, opened the slide cover on a lanthorn and immediately set about lighting an oil soaked naphtha arrow.

"You know the sword will not work for you…," Paul said, staring hard at Turansha.

"That is why either you or Alisha will accompany me," Turansha replied, smiling, and pulling his beard between his thumb and forefinger.

"You bring my children down here where I can see them…pass them to Alisha and let them go, and I shall willingly come with you. That you have my word upon," Paul replied and moved Adrastos even nearer. Paul wondered if he could get near enough to cut down Turansha and the man now stood holding the lit arrow. The snow blew in even harder making the flame flicker, almost blowing it out.

"I know you are weighing up your chances of striking me, but that would be a mistake," Turansha said and steadied his horse.

Alisha frowned at Paul and moved her horse beside his.

"You bring my children here and I shall go with you," she explained.

Paul looked at her, alarmed, as Turansha grinned. Quickly Paul withdrew his sword, Turansha's men immediately lifting their small bows and drawing arrows ready to fire. Paul threw his sword slightly in the air and caught it by the top part of the blade, turned it so the handle faced Turansha and offered it to him.

"You take this now…and I shall come with you…not Alisha," Paul said loudly and then looked hard at Alisha.

Turansha motioned with his head for the mounted horse archer nearest to him to take the sword. The man lowered his bow and reached forward to take the sword. Just as his hand was about to clasp the handle, a single large arrow zipped through the air past Paul and went straight through the man's wrist pinning his arm against his chest as it continued on through his laminar armour. The horse reared up on its hind legs in panic throwing the man off backwards, who was dead before he even hit the ground. Turansha pulled his horse back and raised his hand.

"Hold your fire!" he shouted as his men all aimed their bows at Alisha and Paul.

Abi trotted out of the tree line into full view aiming another large arrow directly at Turansha. Paul pulled his targe shield around and clasped it in his left hand tightly and tried to position his horse between the archers and Alisha. He looked at Abi, confused.

"You wave that flaming arrow to get those children down here now…," she called out, the tension in her bow straining under the pressure as she held her aim at Turansha.

"I think you will find you are somewhat outnumbered and out matched," Turansha said confidently.

"I think not," Abi replied as Tenno, Brother Teric, Stewart, Nicholas and Upside pulled into view, swords drawn. "And should we all lose our lives this hour, you will be the first to go."

"You think so? I can kill you all and take the parchment and sword," Turansha smirked again and motioned with his hand across his chest.

Suddenly from out of the surrounding trees and from the tall grasses covered in snow, men stood up and stepped forwards, many armed with crossbows. They had been lying still in the freezing snow without moving, undetected. Now as they revealed themselves, they numbered nearly fifty men in total. Abi pulled the arrow back even further until the armour splitting arrow head met the bow. Alisha looked at Paul, panic beginning to register across her face. Turansha started to laugh. Suddenly a Muslim heavy cavalry horn sounded out to the east. All turned to look where the sound had come from but with the wind blowing and the snow falling, it was difficult to see exactly where it had come from. The sound of many horses started to drift down to them and the horn blew again. Then through the falling snow, the ghostly outline silhouettes of a Muslim cavalry squadron started to loom into view as they sped down the track toward them, the front four riders with their lances already lowered and held in the assault position closely followed by Balian and several of his men riding mixed within the ranks of Muslim heavy cavalry. Paul's gaze fell back to Turansha just as he ordered the man with the flaming arrow to fire it upwards. As the man pulled back the string, aimed it skyward, Paul instinctively swung his sword up and threw it toward the man. Turansha was already turning his horse away as Abi loosed her arrow. He flung himself low across his horse just as the arrow flashed across his back slicing his cape as it went. The arrow continued and struck the rider's horse beside him. As the horse screamed in agony and fell sideways, Turansha sped his horse through his men as they loosed off their arrows. An arrow hit Adrastos in the chest as he reared upwards. Paul raised his shield just in time as three arrows and a crossbow bolt slammed into it, the bolt penetrating through in a shower of wooden splinters. Paul's sword struck the archer in the left side of his stomach and almost passed all the way through him. The archer fell to his knees as Paul jumped down from Adrastos and pulled Alisha forcibly down from her horse and pushed her to the floor as arrows cut through the air, one arrow glancing off his chain mail leggings as another thumped into his shield. Nicholas was already rushing directly into the men as Abi charged forwards on her horse drawing her sword. Paul saw Tenno and Taqi out of the corner of his eye already rushing into the other archers to his left side.

"No!" Alisha yelled pointing at the injured archer still holding the flaming arrow. He steadied himself as he knelt in the snow, blood turning it red around him. He pulled the arrow back again, aimed it high and let it loose, just as Abi rode past him and slashed her sword down violently taking off his head instantly. Alisha and Paul watched in horror as the arrow rose into the darkened snow filled sky like a bright beacon glowing as it arched upwards. Without hesitation, Paul jumped to his feet, ran over to the dead archer, kicked his headless body over and withdrew his sword. Filled with panic and rage, he looked up toward the hill shrouded in falling snow and the silhouettes of trees. Snarling almost he started to run towards the summit knowing Arri and Ailia were there. He did not see Balian or the Muslim cavalry men enter the melee and start fighting Turansha's men. Tenno dismounted and checked Alisha with Nicholas. Abi tried to get her horse to follow Paul but the ground was uneven and covered in stones and, with the covering of snow, her horse faltered. She jumped down as Tenno ran to her. Brother Teric and Upside engaged two of Turansha's men as Nicholas stood over Alisha protectively. When Turansha's men began to disperse and vanish into the falling snow, she pushed Nicholas aside, jumped to her feet and rushed off in the same direction Paul had gone. Abi reached out to grab her as she ran past but missed her. Alisha jumped over a small stone wall and began to push her way through the deep snow following Paul's path. Abi and Tenno immediately started to follow her as Taqi helped Brother Teric, Upside and the Muslim cavalrymen deal with the remaining men from Turansha's group, most having simply vanished out of sight into the driving snow.

ꕥ

Arri opened his eyes wide as the faint glow from a flaming arrow arched its way across the darkened snow filled sky some distance away from them. But the signal was clear enough. Brother Matthew stood up straight and wiped his hand across his mouth shaking his head disbelievingly. He withdrew his sword and flounced around to look down at Arri as he moved his arms to shield Ailia.

"Your father!" Brother Matthew shouted angrily. "Is he mad…does he not believe what Turansha said?" he demanded and flung his sword around him as he started to pace back and forth. "Why Lord…why curse me like this?" he called out, looking upwards, his arms outstretched, his sword pointing heavenward.

"You do not have to do what you say you must do," Arri spoke, his big eyes fixed on Brother Matthews's sword.

Brother Matthew turned around and looked at Arri then instantly ran toward him raising his sword high above his head. His face was full of rage as he swung the sword with both hands downward. Arri gently closed his eyes. There was nowhere he could run or move out of the way. He simply hoped it would not hurt.

"Naaaahhhhh!" Brother Matthew screamed as he thrust the sword downward vertically.

ꕥ

Above the noise of the wind, Paul heard Brother Matthew's yell. He froze in alarm, his heart stopping as he looked toward the top of the rise, the snow blurring his vision. The snow was now up to his knees and made progress difficult. As the images from his dreams flashed through his mind, panic enveloped him completely. He looked back as Alisha called out for him, closely being followed by Abi and Tenno pushing their way through the snow. With tears welling in his eyes, he raised his sword and shield and began to push on through the snow as fast as he could, his face contorted with exertion and anger. He snarled, furious that he could not move faster as Alisha stumbled behind him.

ꕥ

Arri heard the sword cut into the soil just in front of him and Brother Matthew snorting and sniffing like some wild animal in pain. Slowly Arri opened his eyes to see him knelt in front of him resting his two hands upon the pommel of the upright sword stuck in the ground. He was sobbing, spit drooling from his mouth as he shook his head, his eyes shut tight. Ailia moved behind Arri to look up through the blanket but he gently pushed her back behind him. He was shivering uncontrollably both from fear and the cold but he would not let Brother Matthew see this.

"Please...you have a choice. As my father tells us, we always have a choice," Arri said nervously.

Brother Matthew looked up.

"Your father. Saint bloody Paul no less...'tis because of your father that I am here...doing this. Do you not understand that?" he asked, his face twisted in anguish, which confused Arri.

"He won't hurt you, you know that do you not?" Arri asked, shivering again. His eyes began to feel heavy and he wanted to close them. Ailia fidgeted behind him but he held her back protectively. "My father would help you if bad men are making you do this."

"Ha...I am being lectured to by a child...I am the bad man."

"No you are not," Arri said quietly. He stopped shivering but felt very sleepy. He shook his head to keep himself awake. He looked up at Brother Matthew, who had tears streaming down his face as he clutched the end of his sword, shaking his head from side to side.

"You know nothing of me," Brother Matthew blurted out and forced himself to stand. He pulled out the sword from the ground and held it up with both hands, the blade facing downward. "I have no choice on this deed I must fulfil...your father was wrong for sometimes we have no choice."

"Arri," Ailia called out, her soft voice reaching Brother Matthew's ears as he raised the sword up, the blade half obscuring his vision as it ran vertically down in front of his face. Arri tensed up and Ailia wrapped her little arms tightly around his waist. "Father will be here very soon," she whispered.

"Lord have mercy upon my soul!" Brother Matthew shouted, raised the sword even higher, hesitated for a moment, looked down momentarily with his eyes filled with tears and his hands shaking uncontrollably, then took a step forward.

ꕥ

Paul fell forward in the deepening snow as if hit by some unknown force. Despite sweating beneath the heavy chain mail and fur cape, a cold deep chill ran bone deep through him and his hair stood on end. He shuddered and nearly vomited, just managing to swallow it down. His heart was beating fast as he fought to stand upright again. Through the snow fall he was just able to make out the faint outline of a person kneeling on the very top of the central mound of stones. Paul scurried over the outer wall of stones and slipped on the snow. Quickly he jumped to his feet, snow all over his body and head. He could vaguely hear Alisha calling out for him from behind but all his energy and effort was focused on reaching the figure ahead.

"Father," he heard Arri call out softly, his voice carried upon the wind just like in his dreams.

Paul's heart exploded and a surge of energy drove him on. This was his worst nightmare coming true. Alisha and Taqi called out again from behind him but he would not stop now. As he scrambled ever nearer the kneeling figure, he knew it was Brother Matthew. Finally after what seemed like an unbelievable amount of time, Paul started to run up the inner mound. He saw Brother Matthew kneeling, his hands upon his sword stuck vertically upright, his head drooped beside it not moving. Where were Arri and Ailia? Paul panicked. He ran and fell to his knees next to Brother Matthew and immediately saw the snow around him soaked in blood. He pulled up his head away from the sword. Brother Matthew's eyes were closed but he was still breathing. Paul shook him until he half opened his eyes.

"Where are my children?" Paul shouted and shook him again to keep him awake.

"Paul…forgive me," Brother Matthew whispered and blinked his eyes toward the hole a few feet away, the lanthorn throwing out enough light to illuminate the blood soaked ground. Paul's eyes saw Brother Matthew's footprints from the edge of the depression. As his eyes followed them he saw the snow covered blanket and Arri's hand sticking out the side of it. Instantly he pushed Brother Matthew aside. As he fell onto his back, Paul threw his own sword and shield down and scrambled across the snow shaking his head.

"No…no…no…no please dear Lord no!" he cried as he stopped and looked at the blood everywhere. Hesitantly, his hands shaking, he pulled the snow covered blanket up slightly to reveal Arri, his eyes closed, his face a ghostly white. Quickly he pulled the blanket up and threw it backwards. As he did, he looked down behind Arri to see Ailia sat perfectly still, her wide eyes open staring up at him, her arms still wrapped around Arri. She blinked and as the realisation it was her father, her bottom lip started to quiver with emotion.

"I said you would come, Papa," she whispered, her throat dry, and lifted her arms up toward him and started to cry.

Paul leant down nearer and placed his right arm around her as her little arms wrapped tightly around his neck. He looked at Arri, who was not moving. Holding Ailia he used his left arm to gently shake Arri.

"Arri...Arri, my son...please, Arri," Paul said just as Alisha threw herself down beside them.

"Arri dear...Arri. It is Mama here," she said softly, tears streaming down her face.

Paul looked across to Brother Matthew as Tenno and Abi stood over him. He blinked at Paul.

"Mama," Ailia said, hearing Alisha, and turned to look at her.

"Oh my dear Ailia...what has happened here?" she asked, the snow beginning to ease off.

Paul saw the covered lanthorn nearby and reached over for it. Quickly he opened the storm cover fully to light up the immediate area. There was a lot of blood. Abi stepped closer, shaking her head sadly as Taqi and Tenno kept an eye out for anyone else.

"Mama...he was told to send us to heaven...but Arri stopped him," Ailia explained.

"Arri dear. Come on, wake up, please," Alisha pleaded and tried to shake him awake.

"Look...this is what he used," Ailia said and leaned away from Paul and removed Alisha's three pronged dagger from Arri's right hand. It glistened in the light from the blood upon the blades. "When that man raised his sword, Arri stabbed him between his legs. He won't get into trouble will he?"

Her hand shaking uncontrollably, Alisha took the dagger. Paul wrapped the blanket around Arri, seeing how white and cold he was, his lips almost blue. It was then that he noticed the blood trail from the snow on the ground leading up to Arri's leg then his cotton shirt. He realised in that instant he had given Ailia his jacket to keep her warm. But then he saw the blood from his neck. A small cut ran across his neck. Paul nearly threw up and he gulped.

"What...what is it?" Alisha asked in alarm.

Paul quickly stood up and passed Ailia to Abi.

"Paul," Brother Matthew called out. "I could not do it. Turansha has my family. If I did not carry out his orders, my family are to be executed...but I could not do it," he coughed and leaned over, his face lying in the snow.

"Arri," Alisha said softly and pulled him close to her.

Quickly Paul knelt down beside them and moved Arri so he was sat against Alisha on her lap. Shaking, Paul took out a blood swab from his belt case and placed it against Arri's neck where it was cut. As he applied pressure, Alisha pulled the blanket around them both to try and warm him.

"Arri, you must wake up and stay awake. Can you hear us?" Paul said as he pulled the fur cap around his face to help keep him warm.

"How much blood has he lost?" Abi asked.

Paul looked up at her and without saying a word, she knew what he was saying with his eyes.

"No...come on, dear Arri. You must wake up," Alisha pleaded. "Look...I have Clip clop for you. He has missed you," she said and quickly pulled out Clip clop and placed it in his cold little hand and tucked it back beneath the blanket. "Please, Arri, wake," she cried.

Ailia looked on concerned. Stewart rushed up out of breath and looked on, confused. He looked down at Brother Matthew as he blinked and clearly in pain. Abi handed Ailia over to Stewart and quickly knelt before Arri and checked his neck wound and felt his temperature.

"We have no time to lose. We must get him warm. He has lost much blood and his body is too cold," she said and went to pull him but as she gripped the blanket, Arri opened his eyes.

"Father...we knew you would come for us," he said weakly, his eyes nearly closing again. He smiled.

2 - 11

"Arri...you must stay awake, do you hear me?" Alisha said trying to remain calm but shaking all over.

"I did not stab him," Brother Matthew coughed in pain. "I could not do it....but he stabbed me and the sword fell upon him..."

Alisha looked around at him in anger. She picked up the parchment tube beside her and threw it...it landed just short of him.

"But you still took them and brought them here!" she shouted in anger. "This is still your doing!"

"Mama...please do not shout," Arri said and opened his eyes again. "Mama...am I going to heaven now as I can't feel my body?..."

"No, my dear, no, not if you want to stay here," Alisha said, tears beginning to well in her eyes. Paul put his hand upon his little shoulder, unable to speak, tears filling his own eyes.

"I can rest now I have Clip clop," Arri whispered as he closed his eyes.

Alisha quickly shook him.

"No, Arri, you must stay awake," she said and gently shook him again.

Arri forced his eyes open again, smiled and looked at Paul then Alisha.

"Thank you for being my parents. Promise me you will not forget me. I cannot sleep unless I know you won't forget me," Arri said, barely able to speak.

"We can never forget you, my son...," Paul said, trying to smile though his heart was breaking. He looked at Abi as she stood up. She shook her head very slightly no. He knew what she was saying and nothing would stop the tears from rolling down his cheeks.

"No no no, Arri...you can stay here. Just stay awake until we can get you warm....please," Alisha cried and stroked her fingers down his face. Ailia saw the hurt in her parents' eyes and she buried her head into Stewart's chest. "Please, Arri."

"Mama...is it because I am one of the best, like Nyla, was that why God has picked me now?" Arri asked, his voice barely a whisper.

Tenno dropped his sword and fell to his knees just feet from Arri. Alisha quickly looked at him and saw the tears in his eyes.

"Oh, my dear son, you are the very best, most beautiful in all of God's gardens," Paul said and rubbed his hand over Arri's head and kissed him on his forehead.

Arri opened his eyes again and looked directly at him, his eyes now wide, and his pupils large.

"When I get to heaven, I will see Nyla...and I will tell God that he needs to come down here fast...because there are a lot of bad people who need sorting out," Arri said directly to Paul. Alisha broke down uncontrollably, lowering her head. Nicholas had to turn away unable to watch any more as Tenno just sighed helplessly and started to sob. "Papa…I am not cold any more…and there are two women calling me…can I go now?"

Alisha let out a long moan from the very depth of her being and clenched her hands tightly on Arri's blanket. Paul raised Clip clop and tucked it against Arri's chin just as he had done a thousand times before in his bed. Quickly Paul turned and reached out to pick up his sword. It was not just a weapon, he had been told before. Perhaps it would have the power to help keep Arri alive, he thought. In desperation he placed the handle near to Arri and tried to put his little fingers around the handle. Arri looked intently into Paul's eyes. As a tear fell down Paul's cheek, Arri smiled, blinked once more then closed his eyes for the last time. Alisha and Paul both felt the tension leave his little body as he died. Paul lowered his head against Arri's head and closed his eyes. This wound was too deep to cope with, he thought. Alisha let out a slow low groan, not even a cry but the sound of a woman having her soul ripped from her. Paul moved his left arm and put it around her and they just remained there sobbing, the snow beginning to settle upon their backs. Tenno stood up, looked at Abi, the sadness etched deeply in his tear streaked face. He picked up his sword, turned around and just walked away slowly until he vanished from sight into the falling snow. Balian arrived just as the Knights of Lazarus along with Ishmael, Thomas, Mathew and Luke started to appear from the other direction. As soon as Balian saw Alisha and Paul crouched over Arri, he knew immediately things had not gone well. He shook his head. Abi opened her thick fur over jacket and took Ailia from Stewart and held her closely as she wrapped it around her, her little face buried in her chest. Paul stood up slowly and stared at Alisha holding Arri. He turned to look at Brother Matthew. He picked up his sword and slowly approached him as he lay in the snow.

"Why?" Paul demanded pointing his sword directly at his throat.

"I am already dead…so please, finish me quickly I beg of you…," Brother Matthew replied and moved himself nearer to the blade.

"Paul!" Abi called out and shook her head no.

"Turansha has my family…they will be killed as I said…I did not wish to do this and I could not…but your son stabbed me as I was lowering my blade," Brother Matthew explained then screwed up his face in pain. He started to pant, finding it difficult to breath. "My time is spent. I pray you will one day forgive me?"

Paul stared at him hard, the tip of his sword just inches from his throat. He knew the lengths Turansha would go to and knew Brother Matthew was probably telling the truth. But Arri would not have known he was not going to kill them. Brother Matthew blinked his eyes, closed them and fell sideways briefly gurgling involuntarily as he died. As his face buried into the snow, the sense of anger filled Paul with an uncontrollable rage. He squeezed the handle on his sword until it started to feel hot. He looked at it and then to the parchment tube. In sheer desperation and anger he kicked the tube then pulled his sword back in both hands over his head and behind his back, then with all his might threw it forwards as hard as he could, immediately falling to his knees utterly broken. He did not even see the sword chop through the snow filled air until it thudded with a metallic clang into a nearby tree trunk. Percival appeared and looked at the sword as it stuck firm in the tree. After what seemed an age, Paul eventually looked up to see it just as he had seen in his dreams so many times before. He felt cursed. Abi kicked Paul in the side to get his attention. He looked back over his shoulder up at her. She indicated with her head to stand up.

"Get up...you have others who still need you," she stated bluntly.

Filled with anger toward her now, Paul stood up fast and faced her. She unfurled her cloak to reveal Ailia resting asleep against her chest sucking her thumb. Paul's heart sank even lower. With tears forming in his eyes again, he looked over to Alisha still cradling Arri just as Nicholas knelt beside her, placed his hand upon her back and lowered his head. Ishmael came into view and knelt beside them as Thomas turned away shaking his head in disbelief.

Port of La Rochelle, France, Melissae Inn, spring 1191

Sarah and Ayleth held each other crying as Gabirol sat in stunned silence, his quill dripping ink. Simon coughed uncomfortably as the Templar comforted Miriam as she wiped a tear away from her face.

"I am sorry if this distresses you all," the old man remarked and sat back in his chair.

"Where the hell was Kratos when they really needed him?" Peter demanded to know, visibly shaken by what he had just heard.

"Did that bastard Turansha evade them all then?" the Genoese sailor asked.

"Why did the Muslim cavalry charge?" the Hospitaller asked.

"They had been given their orders by Saladin. Turansha had overstepped the line too far this time and as he had promised, he sent a troop to assist Paul. When the Muslim commander and Balian had seen the two opposing sides, Paul's greatly outnumbered, they had no other choice but to attack immediately. 'Tis the sort of instant decision I am sure you must have experience of," the old man explained.

"Aye that we have...decisions that can haunt you for a life time if they were the wrong one," the Templar replied.

"So little Arri...he had taken his mother's dagger all along," the farrier commented.

The old man simply nodded yes.

"And Turansha escaped?" Gabirol asked.

"Yes he did...and as he made good his escape, all Alisha wished to do at that moment was to go to sleep and never wake up again," the old man explained sadly.

"Cannot blame her," Miriam said.

"Yes, but she still had Ailia to think of."

"So if Arri had not stabbed Brother Matthew, the sword would not have cut his neck?" Ayleth asked tearfully and sniffing.

"We shall never know...but even without the cut to his neck, Arri was already too cold...in giving Ailia his padded jacket, he had without doubt sacrificed himself," the old man said, quietly shaking his head.

Ayleth started to cry more lowering her face into her hands. Sarah rubbed her shoulders comfortingly. The Templar looked at his brother and both sighed heavily.

"We know that Paul you speak of did not return to Tiberias when the others did...only the woman and little girl. Pray tell what happened?" the Templar asked.

The old man shifted himself uncomfortably in his chair and took a few minutes to compose himself enough to reply. He looked at Paul's shield on the table.

"This shield has far more holes than the number you just told us of. It figures Paul saw more combat," the Hospitaller remarked.

"In time...yes," the old man answered. "And as you correctly revealed, Alisha could not bear to stay and bury Arri...so Abi, Nicholas, Upside and Balian returned to Tiberias with Alisha and Ailia along with Stewart, Ishmael and the Muslim cavalry contingent," the old man explained and sighed before continuing. "Percival, Tenno and Taqi remained with Paul...to lay Arri to rest. Paul did not even get the chance to

say farewell to Alisha for she was too distraught. Ailia did not want to leave his side, but with the worsening weather, she agreed she would leave with Abi protecting her. Paul did not wish to ever leave them again, but he had Arri to deal with."

"What of the parchments then?" Gabirol asked.

"Stewart took charge of them and kept them on his person."

"Where did Paul bury him?" Sarah asked, choked.

"It took some time before Abi was able to prise Alisha away from Arri. She sobbed uncontrollably as she kissed him farewell, her heart utterly torn in half. Every time she moved to leave, she fell at his feet again unable to say goodbye. It was the cold and exhaustion that finally made her succumb and allow Abi to put her on a horse. She did not say goodbye to Paul...she was broken."

"I am not sure I could either," Miriam said quietly, the Templar squeezing her hand.

"Paul kissed Ailia goodbye and as he held her little hands, he told her, swore to her, he would always come back no matter what as she was fearful she would not see him again," the old man explained. "'Twas after they had left, Paul took Arri to an ancient site just outside the old ruined city of Gamla. Theodoric had told Paul about the place many times...and those of you who know your Bible would know of the place...Arri's death affected Tenno deeply and Percival knew only too well how Paul was suffering."

"At least Paul still had Alisha and Ailia," Simon remarked and blew out his cheeks.

"Did he though?" the Genoese sailor asked.

Simon frowned at him, puzzled by his statement.

"Strange as it may sound now, even Theodoric sensed the tragedy that had befallen them. He awoke alarmed and shook Sister Lucy awake. She was well enough to travel and he simply told her they must go to Kerak...immediately...such was his intuition," the old man explained and sighed again.

"Kerak...why?" Peter asked.

"Because that is where Alisha demanded that Abi take her...as far away from Turansha's influence as possible."

"Without Paul...that is a bit selfish is it not?" Sarah asked.

"Yes it was...but an understandable selfishness, and remember, Alisha was not herself. Grief affects people in different ways. She stayed but that single night with Princess Eschiva before leaving the next morn, direct for Kerak, whilst Paul carried out the sad task of laying Arri to rest as I said," the old man sighed and wiped his face as a tear clearly rolled down his cheek.

Chapter 66
Betrayed & Broken – A Heart's Memory

Ruins of Gamla, Principality of Galilee, November 26th 1186

Percival and Taqi stepped up out of the freshly dug grave and threw down their shovels. The snow had stopped falling but the whole landscape was blanketed in white. Paul looked around. The position was easy enough to find again in the future, he thought, the ruins of the former city below them looking serene, almost beautiful in the early morning sun, a million sparkles shining off the crisp snow. Tenno tied off the last stitch of the wound in Adrastos having removed the arrow successfully. With their horses tied securely to a derelict flour mill, the stone wheel still visible though covered in snow, the time had finally come for Paul to lay Arri in the earth. He looked at the little bundle secured across Percival's horse of Arri's body wrapped in the fur blanket Brother Matthew had put around him. Paul could hardly breathe as he unbuckled the straps. He gently lifted his little body and held him close across his chest. How could he leave him here? he thought and closed his eyes, resting his forehead against the blanket. Earlier he had placed Arri's hands together across his chest, set the fur hat straight and kissed him one more time. After placing Clip clop inside resting against his chin as he had done a thousand times before bedtime, he broke down in tears. Unable to continue, he could not stitch the blanket together so Percival stepped in and completed it. Paul wanted to rip open the blanket to see his face just one more time, his heart breaking more painfully with every passing moment...but he knew he must not. In a daze he carried Arri to the grave, stepped down inside and gently lowered him. Tenno turned his back and could not watch. Taqi placed a reassuring hand on Paul's shoulder as he knelt beside Arri, not moving. Paul could not catch his breath properly and took several minutes to calm himself down. He felt dizzy and could not stand. Suddenly the air was filled with the sound of several horses galloping up the winding track toward them. Tenno drew his sword as several black clad figures riding horses approached fast. Slowly Paul stood up praying it would be Turansha so he could finish him. Percival had recovered Paul's sword from the tree but he had not wanted it back. It was now strapped to Percival's horse too far away to reach before the men would be upon them. Taqi squinted as he focused his eyes. He recognised them instantly.

"Fear not, my friends…'tis Al Rashid himself," he said and moved to greet them as they pulled up their horses, Al Rashid immediately dismounting.

Paul saw the twin triangle symbol embossed on his saddle, the same symbol Taqi wore as a pendant around his neck. Al Rashid removed his thick face cover and outstretched his arms. He knew he was too late to be of any help.

"Forgive our intrusion this sad hour," he said softly to Paul just as he looked up at him.

"Master…," Taqi said and bowed his head slightly at Al Rashid. Taqi looked behind him to see his other friend dismount. He nodded an acknowledgment.

"Paul, I swear to you and Taqi this day, we shall avenge your son's death," Al Rashid said and offered his hand for Paul to take. Paul looked once more down at Arri, closed his eyes for a moment and took a deep breath before opening them again. He took Al Rashid's hand, his grip strong and firm, and stepped up out from the grave. "Turansha's spies misled us to the other Gilgal. We are so sorry, Paul."

"You are not required to apologise. 'Twas all in the Lord's hands…and not your fight anyway," Paul replied sadly, finding it almost impossible to remain composed.

"You are wrong…'Twas indeed our fight also. And for our failing, we shall escort you to wherever you wish to go," Al Rashid said with a solemnity in his voice that took Paul by surprise. This giant of a man commanded much respect from friend and foe alike, yet he stood before Paul as a friend…a kind friend.

"I shall never be the same person again after this…but I shall try to be the best person I can be, in honour of him," Paul replied and looked back at Arri.

"This pain will be the deepest cut…to the bone and very heart of your soul," Al Rashid said still holding Paul's hand. "But you must live…keep his memory alive always."

Paul's mind flooded with a thousand images of Arri as if all at once running across his vision. He took a deep intake of breath again and steadied himself. He recalled the words Kratos had told him and Percival: 'The tragedy of life is not death, but what we let die inside us while we live.' Kratos had known all along this day would come, he thought to himself. The words of his mother who told him he would hold his son's hand but a short while, but will hold him in his heart a life time repeated themselves over and over again. He wished he could silence the echoes of those words. Alisha still had the parchments but he could see them as clear as day in his mind. The green knight upon them he now knew without doubt was Percival. He looked across at him. The changes in his career, including the one that showed him follow a knight's path, now looking ever more likely as he stood fully dressed as a knight just as they had foreseen. Suddenly all the horses started to buck, startled. A strange hum filled the air as a brilliant ball of light appeared a short distance away in the sky. All looked at it in surprise as it slowly moved toward them. Al Rashid shielded his eyes as he tried to focus upon it. Paul recognised the ball of light as being identical to the light that had hovered over Alisha on the boat when travelling to Tortosa years previously when she was pregnant with Arri. The ball of light, though very bright, did not hurt their eyes to look at. It stopped just short of Arri's grave. A very fine mist seemed to fall from the light depositing a thin covering of white powder that looked more like a spider's web over Arri's wrapped body. Paul's heart raced. Perhaps God had indeed heard his prayers and a miracle was about to happen. He fell to his knees as the others looked on perplexed. As Paul stared longer into the light, in his mind he thought he could see the outline of a female walking slowly toward him stepping out of it. Percival squinted his eyes seeing the same image for a fraction of a second. Paul put his hands together to pray. A female voice entered his mind but he could not see anyone clearly, just the very faint image of what looked like a female figure. As the voice grew clearer, he started to see a pair of eyes made up of many colours. Paul looked back at Al Rashid quickly.

"They cannot see nor hear me, Paul. Only you and Percival," the female voice said softly. Paul looked at Percival as he nodded he could nervously. "Take up your sword again for you will need it. Arri is with those who love him…and one day, the importance of this place where you have set his mortal remains will be a place where our type once again shall reveal ourselves and again walk among you. 'Tis a prophecy I now impart to you… for in the future, three shall again see of me, and they shall give prophecy of three."

Hearing that Arri was with people who loved him, Paul lowered his head and instinctively knew she was referring to Nyla and his own mother. He took a long and deep breath as if breathing again for the first time. When he looked up the figure appeared to back into the light. He blinked just once and the light simply vanished instantly.

"What kind of magic was that?" Taqi asked, confused.

"'Twas not magic, my friend...'Twas a messenger of our Lord," Paul answered as he stood up. "Is that not so, Percy?" All looked at Percival as he nodded yes in reply. Taqi and Al Rashid both looked at Paul, perplexed. "You may not have heard her, but we did."

"Was it a bad message?" Taqi asked and put his hand upon Paul's shoulder, looking him in the eye.

"No, my dear friend, 'Twas not at all."

"Are you sure you are all right?" Al Rashid asked as Paul appeared to smile.

"No, not yet...but I shall be," Paul replied and nodded his head as a sense of purpose and an inner strength started to grow within him that he could feel as a tangible force. He stood up straight, walked over to Percival's horse and removed his sword. As he gripped the handle, he felt a surge of energy pulse through his veins. He took a deep breath again and looked out over the plain below.

Port of La Rochelle, France, Melissae Inn, spring 1191

"So Arri was buried within the ruins of the ancient city of Gamla?" Peter asked.

"No, not within the ruins, but above them set at the top of the hill overlooking the ruins and out across the plain towards the Sea of Galilee. The place is sometimes called the Camel's Back ," the old man answered.

"And the woman of light. Was that real?" Ayleth asked.

"As real as either you or me...or it certainly was to Paul and Percival."

"What did they do after they had completed the burial?" Gabirol asked.

"Paul wrote a small poem and laid it upon the covered grave. Seeing the woman and hearing her words, confirmed by Percival, I think I am safe in saying, gave him great comfort and the strength to carry on. Without doubt he would have broken completely I am sure," the old man explained and sighed. "I wish I could have said the same for Alisha for she was not afforded that comfort."

"Why?" the wealthy tailor asked.

"Well, by the time Paul reached Tiberias, she had already left for Kerak. This hurt Paul deeply. Count Raymond welcomed Al Rashid and his men openly, as

perhaps our friends can confirm," the old man said and looked at the Templar and Hospitaller.

"Yes I can. I recall the look of them as they entered. Percival in green especially for he was a striking individual. And the one I now know was Paul...you could see it in his eyes he had been in a serious fight. Though his shield was not painted like this if I recall," the Templar recounted.

"Ah, that was my mistake for I forgot to mention Paul had his shield covered with sackcloth. One to stop it getting scratched, Ishmael's idea, but also to hide his colours," the old man quickly explained. "Paul wanted to move on immediately and catch up with Alisha, but Raymond talked sense into him and assured him Balian, who had gone with her, was more than capable of escorting them safely along with a contingent of Templars plus they had Abi, Thomas, Ishmael, Mathew and Luke with them. Paul was exhausted, his horse Adrastos was still hurt and needed time to recover...and besides, Alisha needed some time without his presence to think. Rightly or wrongly a large part of her did blame Paul for the parchments and ultimately Arri's death...irrational but understandable."

"I do remember they stayed three days as much rumour was spread about them and secret dealings taking place between Raymond and the Ashashin, though we called them Assassins," the Hospitaller remarked.

"That was an unfortunate consequence of Al Rashid staying over for it led to many accusations later when Raymond had to defend his honour, which led to delays and ill advised decisions being made that would ultimately lead to the disaster that was coming and would befall them all," the old man answered and pulled the shield closer to look at it. "But one thing Paul did discus with Al Rashid was how they could find a way to deter, frighten or scare Reynald away from making any more reckless and hostile attacks upon anyone in the region...after which Al Rashid left swearing loyalty to Paul and that he would help in finding Turansha and eradicating him and his fanatical followers for everyone's sakes as well as sort Reynald."

4 - 10

"What about Tenno and Taqi?" Sarah asked.

"Tenno and Taqi...," the old man repeated and smiled. "Tenno decided to stay with Paul to escort him to Kerak, but Taqi, his fate lay with Al Rashid still and he left with him. But not before Paul had drawn an image of him...and Princess Eschiva," he said as he removed two vellum sheets with images drawn upon them. "It kept Paul's mind busy whilst there."

Fig. 64: Taqi.

Fig. 65: Princess Eschiva.

"My Lord, that is uncanny," the Templar remarked as he looked at the images. "That is most certainly the Princess...look, brother," he said and turned the image so the Hospitaller could see it properly.

"My Lord, Taqi is handsome," Ayleth remarked as she studied his image.

"I know that this meeting with Al Rashid caused my Order to question Raymond and Balian's loyalties...to the point that it actually became more overtly hostile toward him...all of them. It did not go down well when my Order set up its head-quarters at al-Marqab, less than thirteen miles northwest of al-Qadmus, which left Rashid with no alternative other than to ally himself with Saladin in later years... is that not so?" the Hospitaller asked.

"It was but part of the reason Al Rashid eventually came to align himself with Saladin," the old man answered.

"How was Alisha when next she saw Paul in Kerak then?" Gabirol asked.

"If of course they met again in Kerak," Simon stated.

"Alisha...let me explain," the old man said, sitting up, and clasped his hands together. "Though what I speak of next I would ask you to hold any judgements on her. Do not condemn her for her actions."

Crac de Moab, Oultrajordain, Kingdom of Jerusalem, December 3rd 1186

The sun was low on the horizon, the main courtyard cast in shadow. It was cold and empty except for a few guards on the parapets and watchtower. Princess Stephanie stood alone in the centre bolt upright, her hands placed across her tummy, waiting expectantly. The furs of the thick full length cape blew gently in a wave like fashion in the light wind. Word had reached them of the imminent arrival of Alisha and her escort. She had assumed that included Paul, whom she eagerly awaited. She looked on anxiously as Alisha rode in, Ailia sat with her on the same horse. Ishmael rode beside them as Nicholas led Balian and several of his knights into the courtyard. Abi was instantly recognisable as she rode alone in front of eight Templars who followed behind. Puzzled, Princess Stephanie walked over to them as several of her men helped steady the horses.

"Lord Balian, Alisha," she said and bowed her head to greet them. "Where are Paul and your son? Do they follow?"

Alisha looked down at her and shook her head no. Immediately Princess

Stephanie saw the pain in her eyes and her heart jumped fearing the worst had happened to Paul. She put her hand to her mouth. Nicholas dismounted quickly, walked up to Alisha and held up his arms to take Ailia. She was still asleep wrapped up in a leather travelling blanket. Carefully Alisha passed her down. As Nicholas acknowledged Princess Stephanie, Alisha dismounted, brushed herself down and stood in front of her.

"Oh my dear Lord what has happened?" Princess Stephanie asked and took Alisha's hands in hers, tears welling in both their eyes. Alisha went to speak but was too emotional, tears beginning to fall down her cheek. "Come inside. It must have been an arduous trip on horseback all the way," she said and put her arm around her and ushered her towards the main keep entrance door. "And fear not for Reynald is away in Montreal...probably whoring and killing so will not be back for many days."

Balian dismounted and removed his thick gloves as Nicholas carried Ailia and followed them as they started to walk up the small flight of stone steps. The courtyard echoed to the sound of heavy wheels upon the drawbridge as a cart crossed it. Princess Stephanie turned to look just in time to see Theodoric and Sister Lucy entering sat upon a heavy transport cart followed by the remainder of Thomas's men in escort. Alisha turned to see them. Theodoric applied the main brake and without hesitation jumped down and ran across the open courtyard toward them. He had lost weight and two of Princess Stephanie's men stood in his way.

"Let him pass," Balian ordered.

The two men looked at Princess Stephanie. She nodded yes. Alisha stepped down to greet Theodoric and before he could even speak, she flung her arms around him tightly. Theodoric could see Ailia was safe. With alarm he stepped back a pace from Alisha and looked her in the eye. She shook her head sadly, the tears falling silently.

"Where are Paul and Arri?" he asked, concerned.

For a minute Alisha could not speak and she hesitated as Sister Lucy walked over, her neck still visibly bandaged. Only when she stood beside Theodoric, Princess Stephanie waiting with concern in her eyes, was she finally able to speak.

"Paul...he is following....but we, we...," she could hardly say the words. "But we lost Arri."

Princess Stephanie gasped in shock and cupped her hand over her mouth.

"What do you mean, woman, you lost Arri...where?" Sister Lucy demanded, sounding unsympathetic.

Alisha took a deep breath and composed herself, gulping several times trying to do so.

"'Twas Brother Matthew and Turansha...and Arri...he is dead," she finally blurted out and buried her face in her hands.

Theodoric and Sister Lucy looked at each other, stunned. Theodoric blinked several times as the full enormity of her words cut into him. He staggered back a pace, shocked. His eyes fell to Nicholas. He simply nodded confirming her words. Theodoric took another step backwards looking unsteady on his feet. He put his hand to his chest and tried to catch his breath. Sister Lucy grabbed his arm to steady him and looked at him intently until he nodded he was okay.

"Right...let's be getting you all inside and sorted...come on, move," Sister Lucy ordered and ushered both Alisha and Princess Stephanie up the steps, supporting Theodoric as she gently pulled him to follow.

Just as they were all entering the door, Thomas, Mathew and Luke rode in having travelled some distance behind Alisha and Balian's convoy in order to react to any potential problems or ambush.

ᢀ

Alisha sat on the edge of the large four poster bed with Sister Lucy beside her and Princess Stephanie kneeling on the floor in front of her. Ailia was lying on her side at the head of the bed surrounded by large clean pillows sucking her thumb but sound asleep after her exhausting week. They remained silent apart from the odd sniff from Alisha as she wiped her nose and tears. Two maids finished lighting the fire and lit two more candles on the main table near the window. They curtseyed and left the room without a word being spoken. As soon as they had left, Alisha broke down in tears again trying her hardest to cry quietly so as not to wake Ailia. She was inconsolable as Sister Lucy clasped her hands around Alisha's. After a while, Alisha looked up and across the room at the parchment tube placed in full view on the sideboard. She shuddered and Sister Lucy rubbed her hand across Alisha's shoulders to calm her down.

"I cannot tolerate nor endure this pain inside...," she cried shaking her head no.

The door swung open and Abi stepped inside the room closing the door immediately. Quietly she walked across the room seeing Ailia asleep. Alisha looked up at her.

"I will not mix my words nor shall I soften the words that need to be said," she started to speak firmly until Sister Lucy shook her head slightly not to. "I am sorry, Lucy...but at a time like this, 'tis only truth that will carry her through this," she explained and knelt down in front of Alisha. She looked into her eyes intently not blinking or looking away once. "Death is never the end...you of all here present should know that... and feel it."

Alisha looked at Abi, half stunned. Princess Stephanie stood up shocked at Abi's words.

"Abi!" she protested.

"She knows I speak truthfully. Ali, you do not have the luxury to grieve long," Abi continued and nodded toward Ailia. "And you cannot and must not blame Paul for all that has fallen upon you...that is wrong."

"Now I think we have heard just about enough this eve," Sister Lucy protested and stood up frowning hard at Abi.

"Lucy, you need tend to Theodoric. I know of his condition," Abi replied looking just as stern. Alisha looked at Sister Lucy, concerned, and sniffed, wiping away another tear. "His heart!"

"His heart!" Alisha repeated.

"'Twas the shock of seeing me half murdered...it has affected his heart greatly," Sister Lucy explained. "But we had wished to keep it private."

"You cannot hide such matters for the implications could affect all of us at any time. Now, Ali, your heart breaks, but do not wallow in this state. It is not what Arri would have wished for or approved of. You dishonour his memory if you let his death be the ruin of you."

"Have you lost all reason and compassion?" Sister Lucy demanded, getting angry.

"Ladies, please," Princess Stephanie interjected hesitantly.

Alisha coughed and shook her head. She ran her hand through her hair, took a deep breath and slowly stood up looking Abi directly in the eye.

"She is right of course," she said, her voice shaking with emotion. She fought to compose herself and stand up straight. "I shall not shame the memory of my son."

Abi leaned closer to Alisha and stared into her wet eyes as if looking for something hidden. Alisha frowned and recoiled back a pace, the bed stopping her.

"I know your heart. You must do whatever you have to, to live through this," Abi said, her tone softer.

"But how do I get over this?" she pleaded, tears welling in her eyes again.

"You don't…you never get over it. You learn to live with it and you start by taking every day as it comes. But you breathe, and you keep breathing no matter what."

Abi stood up straight and backed away toward the door silently. She simply nodded at Alisha, then at Sister Lucy and Princess Stephanie and left the room, closing the door quietly.

Alisha shivered as she lay in the large bed, Ailia tucked up close beside her, going over and over Abi's words. The room was dark, the only light a single shaft of moonlight coming in through the part opened curtains. The fire was just a red and orange glow of embers. She did not know if she was shaking from the cold, tiredness or the constant ache in her heart that felt like a real pain that seemed to punch inside her taking her breath away. As Abi's words kept running through her mind and despite what she had said, and knowing it to be true, she could see no way of coping with the pain. Quietly she got out of bed and put on a thick night gown, tied it at the waist and stepped out of the room into the small adjoining room which led to Sister Lucy and Theodoric's smaller room. She jumped with fright as a figure sat at the small table moved, sniffing and obviously crying.

"'Tis only me," Sister Lucy whispered. "I cannot sleep," she sighed, her voice full of emotion. She sniffed again and wiped her nose with a small wipe cloth.

"Nor I. I need some air for I feel like I am suffocating and cannot breathe properly."

"Then walk to the night kitchen…fetch us some rosehip if they have any. That will calm us and help us both sleep," Sister Lucy whispered. "Go on, I shall keep an ear out for Ailia."

Silently Alisha walked barefoot along the stone floored corridor. She hugged herself, still shaking from the cold. The corridor seemed long and dark, like the path she now felt she was walking in her life. When she reached the end and looked down into the reception hall area, a small glow from the night kitchen shone through the gap where the door was not shut properly. She could hear the faint mutterings of the guards inside. Quietly she walked down the wide stone staircase and over to the door and gently pushed it open. She opened her eyes wide in surprise to see Nicholas and Upside sat opposite each other, a wooden tankard of warm milk each in their hands. Thomas turned around to face her holding a fresh tankard and offered it to her.

"Come in, you look perished," he said softly.

"Here...please sit," Upside said and stood up immediately, Nicholas just looking up at her, surprised.

"I cannot sleep...I thought others would be on guard this night," Alisha explained.

"No, we volunteered as we are all restless...and we trust no others. 'Tis why Percival, Mathew, Luke and my other men patrol this very hour," Thomas explained and handed her his wooden tankard of warmed milk. "I shall make another."

Alisha sat down on the bench beside Nicholas. He sat up straight and leaned toward her concerned. He just looked at her until she faced him and feigned a smile.

"I can never thank you enough for all you have done for us these past years," she said softly. She stared at the tankard with her hands wrapped around it, the warmth upon her hands registering slowly. She looked up at Upside, then Thomas, but when she turned to look at Nicholas, his eyes searching every aspect of hers, she could not speak. She went to say more, but the words would not come. She gulped and shook her head, part embarrassed. "I cannot...I, I do not know what I am supposed to do," she finally blurted out, turned on the bench to face Nicholas fully and looked at him, her eyes welling with tears again. Without thinking or hesitation, Nicholas reached out with both arms and pulled her close, her head resting upon his chest as she broke down and sobbed uncontrollably in his arms. He took the tankard she was holding and placed it on the table, returning his arm immediately around her. Upside took a deep breath as Thomas nodded it was the right thing to do. Nicholas held her tighter and rested his chin upon her head and closed his eyes to hide the tears that were welling in them. He lowered his face upon her hair and gently rocked her as she cried. She put her arms around him and hugged him tightly, her tears soaking into his surcoat. Upside shook his head and looked at Thomas. They both knew full well how he felt about her, but now in her moment of greatest need, they would not deny him this simple act of comfort no matter how inappropriate some would argue. After a few minutes Alisha pulled herself away and sat up straight. She wiped her eyes and let out a nervous laugh. "I am so sorry to unburden my grief like this on you," she said softly and stood up. Nicholas stood up immediately.

"Let me escort you back to your room," he said politely.

Upside looked at him and frowned just as Thomas did likewise, but then nodded he should.

"Thank you," Alisha replied and turned to leave the room. She picked up her drink. "Good night Upside, Thomas..."

"Be straight back down," Thomas said looking at Nicholas.

Nicholas followed Alisha out and across the reception hall. As she stepped up on the first step, Nicholas took a step beside her. Alisha suddenly held his hand as she went to take the next step to steady herself. She was still holding his hand as they reached the corridor on the next floor. She stopped when they reached an open door into one of the spare chambers, the very same room she had shared years ago with Paul when they had stayed there. Curious, she led Nicholas inside and closed the door quietly behind her. The room was dark except for the moon shining through the open curtains. She was shaking and shivering. She put the tankard down and stood in front of Nicholas. He looked at her, utterly confused.

"What are we doing?" he whispered.

"I do not know...but I cannot...just cannot be alone right now. I do not know what to do, but I do know I do not want you to leave my side this hour. Just talk to me," she pleaded and clasped his hand again. She sat down on the bed and motioned for him to sit down beside her. Abi's words ran through her mind that she must do whatever it takes to get through her grief. Seeing Nicholas was just about the only thing she thought of that would help her at that exact moment.

"Ali, you are distraught and confused...and this is wrong. If we are found like this, alone in a chamber, how would we explain it? No Ali, this cannot be so," Nicholas whispered back, his heart feeling like it was beating so hard she must surely hear it. He sighed as he looked at her. Her eyes were full of emotion and hurt, the moonlight making them appear to sparkle.

"Yes I am distraught…but I know not who Paul is any more," she whispered, a single tear rolling down her face. "You once wrote me a poem… remember. Do you remember the words…I do, and right now, I remember all too clearly where it said about the time when you realise the one you want the most is gone…well, my son has gone…and Paul is gone from me, and I do not know what to do," she cried, trying to quickly wipe away the tears.

Very gently Nicholas used his finger to wipe away the single tear still rolling down her face. He kissed his finger, the salty taste of her tear tingling upon his tongue.

"Ali…you have had my heart since the very first day I laid eyes upon you…and now, right here this moment, as selfish as it is of me, I have this deep emotion that makes me want to hold you tightly with one hand and draw my sword against the whole world with the other," he whispered back, his eyes searching hers. "I have always loved you and always shall."

Alisha let out a slight nervous laugh and bit her bottom lip. Nicholas leaned closer to her and gently kissed the side of her face where another tear was falling. He then gently cupped his hands around her face looking deeply into her eyes. She raised her hands to hold his arms. Nicholas looked at her inviting moist lips. He had desired this so many times and now here she was in his arms. Alisha rubbed her hands up and down his arms, his muscles feeling solid. Hesitantly, slowly and very softly he placed his lips upon hers. She did not pull away. He rubbed his right hand through her long dark hair and pulled her closer as he pressed his kiss more firmly. She responded by pulling his head against hers. Nicholas broke the kiss and pulled back slightly, his eyes looking into hers again. She licked her lips and smiled. She placed her hand upon his chest. She could feel his heart beating through the chain mail vest and tunic. He let out a nervous laugh, then placed his arm around her waist and pulled her closer and kissed her again. He could taste her and wanted to kiss her all over. He pulled back again not really believing what was happening to him. He had dreamt of this moment so many times and now it was actually happening. He knew that sometimes the fantasy was better than the reality, but now as he held her, it was far beyond his wildest expectations. The very touch of her skin sent shivers through his whole being. He had lain with other women before; he had thought he had loved before, but never like this. Her skin was of the purest smoothest white he had ever seen. He had wanted this so much he was prepared to risk everything for her, including his very life. The Lord had contrived things to bring them together this hour, he told himself, and at that very moment in time, the world did not exist. It was just them alone together.

"I need you," Alisha whispered.

Quickly Nicholas unfastened his tunic, flung it off and started to unfasten the leather straps that held his chain mail on. Alisha hurriedly helped unfasten the others until his armour fell onto the wooden floor with a thud. He unbuckled his sword and placed it upon the floor and within moments he had undone his leggings, chain mail and chausses. With his bare chest exposed he looked at Alisha again. He was cold and the touch of her hands as she ran them down his chest made him shudder. She noticed his firm muscles across his chest and his rough hands. She breathed in the very smell of him and felt more aroused than she could ever recall. She moved closer to him and pushed off her heavy nightgown. Nicholas's eyes fell to her chest as she breathed in and out heavily in anticipation. Her smooth white skin and the soft curve of her breasts clearly visible in the moonlight beneath the thin silken nightdress made his heart beat even faster. He too was already aroused as she moved closer to him and leaned in to kiss him again. As their lips met, he ran his hand down her side, his other hand placed in the small of her back, he pulled her against him. She kissed him harder, the passion rising in her. He kissed her lips, and savoured the sweet taste of her. He then kissed her chin, then the side of her face and then started to kiss down her neck including the scar still visible. As he kissed her, she arched her back and moaned with pleasure as his strong arms held her. He lay her down upon the bed, her bosom heaving as she breathed. He started to kiss lower toward her cleavage, his left hand running down the side of her nightdress. She pulled it up revealing her thigh, which he moved to kiss. He ran his hand around her thigh and then slowly inward until his hand was resting on the inside of her knee. Gently he moved his hand back up her inner thigh as she pushed her leg to open herself to him. She shifted herself so her other leg was now around him and ran her hands through his thick blonde hair and moaned, biting her lower lip as his hand moved ever higher. When his fingers finally touched her lightly, she was already moist, his fingers easily parting her. They both shuddered with delight, the emotions running through them overpowering in their intensity. She started to thrust her thighs upwards against him and pulled him close and kissed him. Her pelvis pushed up against him several times with ever increasing urgency. Nicholas broke the kiss as he looked down and began to guide himself toward her taking his body weight on his right arm.

"Come on…I need you inside me…to feel you and your strong arms around me to protect me," Alisha whispered, her hands placed upon his face. She then placed her hands under her knees and pulled her legs up whilst pushing herself upwards to meet him. Her eyes were wide as she looked into his eyes, her mouth open ready for him to kiss her. As he lowered himself to kiss her, he held himself back slightly, as he felt her wet warmth envelope him. He paused just barely inside her as she thrust herself up to take him further inside. His heart beat so hard Alisha could hear it. As he entered her further, she arched her head back in pleasure. She wrapped her legs around him tightly and started to pull him as close to her as she physically could. As he moved upwards slightly, Alisha moaned even more, her body already convulsing as she was overwhelmed by an orgasm almost immediately, the tension flooding her entire body to the point she could hardly breathe. Nicholas could sense himself already about to come so tried to remain still as Alisha thrust herself up in ever faster movements. "Come on…come inside me," she whispered biting her bottom lip, her eyes closed tightly as she pushed herself up and down beneath him, every movement sending surges of warmth through her to the point she felt unable to control her body and became completely lost in his embrace, her legs shaking as she tried to pull him deeper.

"I am so ready to," Nicholas whispered and smiled, kissed her and moved himself so he was deeper inside her. He could feel her tightening and relaxing around him as she smiled at him, her face flushed and slowing down her movements, sensing every part of him.

After a few minutes holding that position and gentle movements just looking into each other's eyes, Nicholas began to move again more vigorously, Alisha moaning with every push forwards in her. As he increased his rhythm, he kissed her passionately, his tongue tasting her as she responded by pressing herself harder against him. As another convulsive wave flooded through her body, she lay her head back, closed her eyes and sighed deeply and waited for the sensation of him to release himself inside her. As she lay there enjoying the moment, she opened her eyes when she realised he had stopped moving and was just looking down at her resting upon his elbows, his chest against hers, her nipples tingling sending shivers throughout her upper body. Nicholas just stared at her, smiling, the tension in his loins now almost uncontrollable and with every slight move she made, he knew he was ready. Never had he felt so much emotion and love for someone as he looked at her, enjoying every sensation, smell and taste of her. 'Is this how Paul felt for her?' he suddenly thought and the crushing sense that what he was doing was wrong overwhelmed him and hit him as surely as if someone had slapped him. It took him by surprise the deepness of that feeling, for this is all he had ever wanted and longed for since the very first moment he had seen her…but it was wrong of him to take her when she was so clearly at her most vulnerable. Alisha saw the sudden tension in his face and different look in his eyes…almost apologetic.

"What is it, Paul?" she asked, sweat beginning to bead down her neck.

"Exactly that," Nicholas whispered and strained to control himself, feeling himself about to ejaculate as her muscles tightened around him.

"What…why have you stopped?" she asked and leaned up to kiss him again.

1 - 27

"No Ali…you just called me Paul…and I must not pleasure myself inside you…I dishonour you, myself…and Paul this hour."

"Oh no, my love…'Twas just a slip of the tongue," Alisha replied and placed her hands upon his face, tightening her muscles further inside around Nicholas.

Nicholas held her hand against his face as he took his weight upon his right arm only and pulled himself up. He could sense the beautiful warmth of her around him tightening and he pulsed with anticipation. Knowing he was about to come, he gently but quickly took himself out of her, but as he moved, Alisha tried to pull him deeper inside her again, but she was no match for his strength as he pulled himself away just in time. He lowered his head against her chest, closed his eyes and sighed with a low moan as he ejaculated outside her. Alisha wrapped her arms around his shoulders, confused. She was burning for him to be back inside her…then it hit her what they had just done as he just remained in that position.

"You are hurting, you are confused…and it is Paul whom you really need here," Nicholas whispered as he wrapped his arms around her and kissed her stomach, his head resting on her chest. "You may have needed me, but 'tis not me you really want is it?"

Alisha shook involuntarily. She turned her head to the side, closed her eyes tightly and began to think of Paul. A tear ran down her face and as she ran her hands through Nicholas's hair, the thought of Paul and what she had just done spilled over into a wave of tears as she began to cry. Not once whilst she was with Nicholas had she even thought of him. This fact alone shocked her. The feel, the smell and sensation of Nicholas was all new and different and she had climaxed so fast and furiously as if all normal sense, thought or regard for Paul had simply left her. Now as she lay upon her back, Nicholas kneeling between her legs, his head still resting upon her, she knew that what he had just said was in fact true. She opened her mouth to speak but could not. 'How many tears can a woman cry?' she asked herself as more streamed down her cheeks. Her body shook as she began to cry uncontrollably. She ran her hands through Nicholas's hair gently as he held his strong hands behind her back, in his mind never wanting to let her go or for the moment to end. She felt guilty for not only Paul but also him. She sniffed and tried to stop herself from crying when the door opened slightly. Nicholas looked up instantly alarmed just as Sister Lucy peered in. Her eyes widened as she could clearly see them. Nicholas sat up and pulled the blanket across Alisha as she tried to sit up seeing her at the door. Sister Lucy's eyes narrowed, the deep scowl upon her face obvious as she stepped into the room closing the door quietly behind her. Her eyes surveyed the floor, then Nicholas before fixing upon Alisha, who started to shake as she held the blanket to her chest. Nicholas just sighed, shook his head and lowered his gaze to floor in shame.

"I was worried as you did not return with the drinks…then I heard you crying in here," Sister Lucy whispered. She looked at Nicholas just sat with his head low, the bed blanket covering his modesty.

"Lucy…this was my fault…not his…and we did not finish the deed," Alisha blurted out and reached to touch Sister Lucy. She pushed her arm away as if angered.

"Well thank the Lord for small mercies eh," she replied, her voice laced with sarcasm. She put her hands upon her hips and looked at them both, disappointment clearly visible in her face as she shook her head disapprovingly.

"What will you do?" Nicholas asked quietly as he looked up at her.

"Me…as I always do in such matters like this," she answered and paused. "Absolutely nothing!" Alisha and Nicholas looked at her puzzled and then each other. "That does not mean for one moment I condone what has happened here, but to speak of this will ruin you both."

"Thank you…you are indeed a godly woman," Nicholas remarked.

"Godly my arse! I am a practical realist…and this never happened… unless of course this is what you both truly want or a child arrives?"

Nicholas looked at Alisha, his eyes desperate for her to say it was, but he already knew in his heart it was not what she really wanted. He sighed and feigned a brave smile and took her hand as she bit her bottom lip. After what seemed an eternity to him, she gently shook her head no.

"I think we already established what she really wants before you came in…and there is no chance of a child being conceived," Nicholas answered, his voice full of sadness.

Sister Lucy knelt down in front of them. She placed her right hand upon his chest and her left hand upon Alisha's chest. They looked at each other puzzled.

"You know, that somehow you are connected…and these things happen. If you have learnt from this, then it would have served a beneficial purpose…and I shall certainly say no more on the matter. But I would advise you both not to torment yourselves with guilt…and neither confess this. Sometimes in this life, you have to keep secrets. Trust me on this matter for I know only too well the consequences."

Alisha put her hand upon Nicholas's knee. He looked at her. She could sense the sadness within him as he searched her eyes.

"I am so sorry," she whispered emotionally.

"Do not be…this moment I shall forever cherish as the best, and perhaps saddest, moment in my life. I momentarily had you only to lose you…actually I never really had you," he explained, a single tear rolling down his face. "I was weak…the fault is with me."

"Don't be a daft romantic noble idiot," Sister Lucy said and slapped his arm. He looked at her, surprised. "'Twas neither of your faults. 'Tis just life. You may beat yourselves up this was a mortal sin you have committed, but you have showed more strength than most ever will in a life time…trust me."

Alisha looked at Nicholas. Sister Lucy's words certainly applied to him, she thought. Emotion welled up in her as she thought of Arri and what he must think of her if he could see what she had just committed. She took a sharp intake of breath as Sister Lucy removed her hand from her chest. She felt sick and lowered her head, feeling guilty, for in her mind using Nicholas. As the tears fell again, Sister Lucy leaned over and put her arms around her to comfort her. As she hugged Alisha, she looked at Nicholas, winked, smiled and nodded toward the door. Without a word, he gathered his clothing, sword and armour. When he reached the door to leave he mouthed 'thank you' to her and with a great weight of sadness and guilt, despite Sister Lucy's words, he left the room.

Port of La Rochelle, France, Melissae Inn, spring 1191

"There is certainly another side to Sister Lucy," the Hospitaller remarked.

"I don't know whether to love Alisha more or hate her," Sarah commented shaking her head disapprovingly.

"I did ask that you do not judge her for her actions for without making excuses for her, or Nicholas, it had been a passion that had burned within them for years. And then, at that moment in time, Alisha was broken in every manner possible. Mad with grief, mad with Paul, whom she blamed, mad with God, mad with life itself," the old man explained.

"I admire and respect Nicholas more I think. I know not of any man who having gone that far, would stop as he did," Sarah remarked, Stephan raising his eyebrows.

"What about poor Paul? How long was it before he arrived in Kerak...and did they confess to him what took place?" Gabirol asked.

"Paul wrote a poem as I explained earlier to leave with Arri. He made a copy for Alisha...and leaving Arri was the hardest thing he had ever done. If he could have lain down with Arri and never woken up, he would have. But his love for Alisha and Ailia, plus Al Rashid and Taqi basically dragging him away forced him into action. Tenno was with him in body, but not in mind. Arri's death hit him hard... very hard. He saw it as a personal failure not having fulfilled his promise to always watch over them and protect them. During the journey to Tiberias, Paul discussed at length how best to threaten or deal with Reynald, but also Tenno vowed he would not fail in his new charge of protecting Alisha and Ailia."

"But I thought Tenno was part of Al Rashid's group?" Simon asked.

"No, he never was. He just helped them...with training and tactics. Al Rashid released him from any obligations he felt he had to him and his organisation," the old man answered.

"And Taqi?" the Genoese sailor asked.

"He was Ashashin through and through now. He stayed with them as far as Tiberias as I mentioned earlier. It was a sad parting made all the harder for Paul was in part afraid to go to Kerak for fear of what he would discover."

"What do you mean....as in Reynald?" Peter asked, confused.

"No. On the night Alisha and Nicholas were together, Paul awoke, startled, as if his heart was about to fail him. He clutched his chest in pain. He sensed something and just knew it involved Alisha and Nicholas somehow. He tried to dismiss it and shook it off as just tiredness making him suspicious and fearful....but he had long since learnt to trust his instincts and feelings. He had sat up and felt without any doubt something was wrong. It weighed heavy on his mind as they travelled south running over and over in his mind a thousand times what he would do, or should do, if his instincts were proved shockingly real. Taqi and Tenno put his long silences down to being exhausted and in grief for the loss of Arri, yet in truth he was in grief not only for that loss but also his whole way of life...and that included in his mind Alisha, plus the words of the female from beneath the pyramid's warning constantly echoing through his mind. 'Twas the deepest sorrow and deepest wound that cut even beyond the bone," the old man explained and sighed sadly.

"You said Paul wrote a poem and copied it...do you know it?" Gabirol asked, sensing the pain in the old man's voice.

"Oh yes....," the old man replied and reached inside his leather satchel and removed two small pieces of polished oak wood bound together by a crimson cord. Carefully he untied it and opened the two pieces to reveal a flattened piece of vellum with the poem written upon it. "I have this to seal away here, on the point yonder by tomorrow's eve," he explained and gently pushed the whole item toward Gabirol.

Quickly Gabirol studied it. One version was written in Latin, the other in a strange set of symbols. He looked up at the old man, puzzled, before pushing it back across the table to the Templar. All sat in silence waiting for him to read it. He cleared his throat and sat up.

"It reads. 'The moment you died, I became forever broken, incomplete, and my soul shattered, cried. My heart 'twas torn in two, one side filled with heartache, the other died with you. At night when the world is asleep, this pain...it cuts bone deep and tears fall upon my pillow running from off my cheek. Remembering you will be easy, for I do it every day, but missing you is a heartache that will never fade or ever go away. I will hold you tightly within my heart eternally to remain, until the day we meet again, for only then, and gone shall be the pain as we walk upon heaven's plain.'"

"Powerful words again," the Hospitaller remarked.

"And did he give Alisha this?" Sarah asked and leant over to see the poem. "And what do the symbols mean?"

*"Yes he did, and the symbols are like the old Viking runes...the same as Thomas and his men used. 'Tis a language almost lost to the world...that of 'Elfdalian' or the preferred term '*Övdalian*'. 'Tis an ancient language derived from the Swedish 'älvdalska', and before you ask, no it is not a language as spoken by so-called elves...'tis a real language," the old man explained.*

"I think I have heard of this before. I was told it was a language of the forest, like the Ogham alphabet based upon the Old Norse spoken by Vikings," Gabirol remarked.

"'Tis indeed as you say...and it has thirty-three letters. Thomas and his men used it almost like a secret code language, especially when in combat...'Twas they who taught Paul the language."

"So pray tell what happened when Paul finally arrived in Kerak?" Ayleth asked.

The old man sat in silence for several minutes before finally sitting forward and continuing.

Crac de Moab, Oultrajordain, Kingdom of Jerusalem, December 7th 1186

It was unseasonably cold when Paul saw Kerak in the distance. His stomach knotted tightly as he wondered how Alisha and Ailia were and whether Reynald was present. The sun was still high, the sky a dull yellow as far as the eye could see despite no clouds. Stewart pulled up alongside him just as Master Jakclin halted his troop behind him. They had met Master Jakelin two days' ride prior at a staging post and agreed to travel as one. The journey had given Paul and Stewart much time to talk together. The tragedy that had fallen at their feet had one small mercy in that it helped mend the rift between them. A new bond, a stronger bond, had now developed. Their father would be proud if he could have seen them together, Paul wrote in a letter he had dispatched to him, along with the sad news of Arri's death. Stewart pointed toward a lone rider approaching fast from Kerak. Paul instantly recognised the tall horse and figure as that of Abi.

"You are late...you should have been here sooner," she said as she pulled up in front of them, looking at Paul. He sensed anger in her tone. "It matters not now...they all await your arrival."

"Why have you come to greet us…is there some problem? Are Alisha and Ailia all right?" Paul asked, concerned.

Abi rode closer to Paul and looked at him hard. Puzzled by her expression he frowned back.

"I must leave this day but I shall return. It matters not my words, but you should have been here sooner. Will you swear to me, here and now this hour in the presence of these men, you will do but one thing for me?" Abi asked and looked deeply into his eyes.

Something was amiss Paul knew.

"I swear it…whatever it is," he replied.

"Destroy the parchments without delay. If you do not, I shall not be responsible or able to put right what will surely follow," she said sternly, not moving her gaze from Paul. "Swear it!"

"I just swore it did I not?" Paul retorted.

"The loss of Arri will be nothing compared with what will happen," Abi stated bluntly and turned her horse to face the eastward road toward Arabia. Tenno moved his horse near to Abi and looked at her in silence unsure of her manner. She patted her horse's neck and looked at him. "Tenno…until we meet again, for we shall…but please if there is love in your heart for me as I have for you, make sure he destroys them," she said, her tone softer with him. She looked back at Paul, her stare almost cold, which he could not understand. "Keep this promise," she then demanded, sat upright, nodded at Tenno and sped off without any further words.

Tenno looked at Paul momentarily before turning back to watch Abi slowly ride off into the distance. Paul wondered what had happened and his sense of guilt over Arri just grew from her harsh warning.

"Come. It has been a tiresome journey," Tenno said and led off heading down the path toward Kerak.

ꟸ

With a great sense of trepidation Paul followed Tenno and Stewart across the main drawbridge into Kerak. He never thought he would be back here again as they entered the main central courtyard. The area was full of people, their horses and those of Master Jakelin's men only adding to the cacophony of noise. Paul was about to dismount when he caught sight of Nicholas walking out of view through a side door.

"Paul...Paul!" Princess Stephanie called out. Paul looked all around but could not see her amongst all the people. Suddenly he saw her hand wave. "Paul!"

He dismounted and held the reins of Adrastos just as she stopped in front of him, out of breath. She smiled beautifully at him, her face framed by the thin lace tied beneath her chin to hold a head cover with a gold band, like a crown in place. He looked her up and down, her slender figure clearly defined by the white and golden material of her dress. Her eyes met his, her pupils wide and clearly happy to see him.

"My Lady," Paul said and bowed his head slightly. "You look well indeed."

"And look at you...you, you have grown...and so different," she replied and laughed awkwardly. "Forgive my manners. I am so sorry to hear of Arri. Please accept my sincerest and deepest sympathy," she said changing her tone and expression. She searched his eyes seeing the pain that was in them. She sighed. "Come, I shall take you to Alisha and Ailia. They eagerly await your arrival," she said and clasped his hand and pulled him to follow her.

As she led Paul away, Balian approached Stewart as he dismounted. Stewart bowed his head in respect to him, Balian's eyes following Paul and Stephanie.

"All day nearly she has stood atop the main watch tower looking out for your arrival," he said quietly. "Sorry, I speak inappropriately. Ignore my indiscreet comment," Balian remarked and turned around to see Tenno before him. Tenno bowed his head in silence.

ജ ഏ

Princess Stephanie knocked on the heavy wooden door and listened for a response. She looked more beautiful than ever, Paul thought to himself. A bolt shifted on the other side and Sister Lucy looked out from the space between the door and wall as she opened it slightly. Her eyes widened as she saw Paul and instantly opened the door fully. Ailia was sitting in the middle of the large four poster bed. Paul recognised the room as being that of Princess Stephanie's and Reynald's former main chambers. Alisha was stood with her back to them looking out of the main window. She did not turn around. Ailia saw Paul and immediately shuffled to the edge of the bed and ran over toward him. He knelt down just as she reached him and jumped into his arms. Flinging her arms around his neck tightly she hugged him with a large smile.

"'Tis Papa," she called out as Paul stood up again holding Ailia close.

Alisha still did not turn around. He could see she was fiddling with her hands, something she always did when she was nervous or worried. He gulped hard, his stomach in knots.

"Come on, Ailia, come with me so Mama and Papa can talk awhile alone," Sister Lucy said and put her arms out to take Ailia. She frowned and shook her head no and held on tighter.

"Ailia, will you be a really big grown up girl for me and go with Sister Lucy and Stephanie just while I say hello to Mummy…we need some time alone that is all, I promise," Paul said hugging her.

After a few minutes in silence, Ailia moved to look at Paul. Her eyes were so similar to Arri's it made him choke with emotion. Ailia put her hands on either side of his face then kissed him on his nose, then she let out a little laugh.

"Make it quick," she said sounding more like Sister Lucy, then she reached out for Sister Lucy to take her.

"My you are getting too big to carry," Sister Lucy said and began to walk out of the room nodding at Princess Stephanie, who quietly pulled the door closed behind them.

Alisha and Paul stood in silence for several long minutes, Alisha afraid to face him. Her stomach felt as if it were in her throat. She knew the minute she looked into his eyes, her secret would be revealed. She felt ashamed of her actions with Nicholas. She felt guilty for Paul and utterly wretched. Her world hung in the balance and despite Sister Lucy's words that some secrets had to be kept, she did not see how she could. Her mind was racing. Would Paul attack Nicholas if he knew? Would Nicholas in fact kill Paul if they fought? How would this affect Ailia?

"I need to see him now," Theodoric said loudly, outside the door.

As whispering outside started, both Alisha and Paul turned to face the door. They listened as Theodoric was ushered away. When Paul turned around again, Alisha was stood facing him, her hands together. She was shaking and clearly nervous. Paul could not understand why she looked like this and he immediately moved toward her, concern written across his face. He went to touch her but she instantly stood back a pace and raised her hands for him to keep back. Shocked, he froze.

"Please...please just do not touch me," she said emotionally, her eyes closed. A tear ran down her cheek.

"Ali, I know you blame me for Arri...but," Paul started to say.

Alisha opened her eyes. They were filled with tears and anger at the same time. Paul's heart skipped a beat. She walked past him fast, her arm up for him to keep his distance. She opened the main wooden trunk at the end of the bed and lifted out the parchment tube. She stood up and held it up.

"I blame this...what it contains. This....not you! 'Twas the knowledge that killed our son," she exclaimed emotionally and stood back as Paul moved toward her. "I never wanted this...all I ever wanted was just us. You, me, Arri and Ailia...nothing more," she cried. Paul went to step closer again. "No, stay back!" she shouted and threw the parchment tube at him. It just missed him and bounced off the stone fire breast behind him just as he had seen in his dreams countless times. In shock he looked at her. His ears began to ring and his heart beat faster. Alisha put her hands to her mouth. She visibly shook as tears streamed down her face. "This grief overwhelms me so much so that I do not know who I am any more...what good am I to you or Ailia? And now...seeing you, 'tis Arri I see in your face...and the pain rips out my very heart....and I know that seeing you will remind me daily of Arri and I cannot bear to face you for that," she cried, her arms out toward him yet her body recoiling away.

Her words cut like a sword through him. Never had there been a moment in their lives together when his first original poem had been so right with his words.

"Ali...I am to burn the parchments...all of them. I shall never redraw or write them up again. I swear it. And Arri...I know he is okay. We saw a great and wondrous thing, Percival included. And I wrote a poem," Paul explained and quickly took out a copy he had written. "Here look, this is what I wrote and laid with Arri just before a woman of light appeared."

When Paul tried to pass it to her, she hit his hand aside and looked at him with anger in her eyes. Paul felt sick and stared at her as he bent down to pick up the poem. He was shaking from head to foot shocked to the very core by her reaction.

"The good Lord, our ever so merciful God and master...he took our son away from us...and you write a poem about it," she snarled, her face full of rage the likes of which he had never seen before. "Fuck our good Lord. I see and understand now why so many in Alexandria were atheists…'tis all but utter nonsense."

Paul stood up straight. He hardly recognised the woman stood in front of him.

"Ali, whatever has come between us, we must move forwards together. I love you with all my heart and soul, and I will do whatever it takes to make you happy and one day smile again."

"Happy! I shall never be happy again. I am broken….broken!" she shouted as she doubled forwards holding her stomach as if in pain. "I am not worthy of you nor your love," she cried and fell to her knees.

1 - 1

"What do you mean, Ali?" Paul asked and rushed to support her as she knelt with her head down sobbing. He put his hands upon her shoulders and tried to get her to look at him but she would not.

"I have so shamed you," she cried, shaking her head from side to side. Paul tried again to get her to look at him but she would not open her eyes even when he held her chin and moved her face to his. "Please just leave me, Paul," she pleaded, sobbing, her whole body shaking.

"I cannot leave you…I love you and you are my wife. Nothing you can do will ever change that," Paul said emotionally, seeing how utterly distraught she was.

After a few minutes Alisha stopped sobbing, wiped her nose and face and opened her eyes. She took a deep breath and sighed heavily. Her eyes looked into Paul's and he knew something was wrong.

"And I do love you…but I have made a terrible mistake," she started to explain and moved back on the floor away from him. "'Tis a mistake I cannot undo…but one I cannot lie and hide from you either," she said and gulped. Paul's stomach twisted tightly. "In my despair…though it is no excuse….I…I…" Tears began to roll down her cheeks again. Paul could see she was struggling and hurting. "I slept with Nicholas."

Her words hit Paul in a manner he had never experienced before. He heard them, but somehow they did not make sense. Alisha bit her bottom lip and then cupped her mouth as if to silence herself, but it was too late. She had said it. As the words slowly began to filter through and their implications and meaning, the air left Paul's lungs and as he went to stand, his head spinning, he stumbled backwards. He tried to steady himself on the bed post but missed it and fell backwards onto the floor. His eyes wide, he stared at Alisha. He could not catch his breath and felt sick. His world was crashing down around him. He shook his head in disbelief, but he knew it was true. His earlier instincts had been proved accurate. He could see she was hurting and part of him just wanted to hold her and comfort her, but wasn't he also supposed to be angry at her and Nicholas? he asked himself. The betrayal from both of them was total. Was he to blame? Was his love not enough? he wondered. His mind seized on her earlier words that she had made a terrible mistake.

"Do," Paul went to say and was very nearly sick. He coughed and took a deep breath. "Do you love him?" he asked emotionally as tears filled his eyes blurring his vision.

Alisha rocked herself back and forth upon her knees, her hands still covering her mouth. Paul longed for her to say she did not and the silence was unbearable as she looked at him.

"I do…in a fashion but not in the way I love you," she finally said.

Paul pushed himself backwards and propped himself up against the main stone fire surround and looked to the floor. As he sat up, he clasped the handle of his sword. Alisha gasped in alarm. Quickly he looked at her. Stunned that she would even think he would harm her, he quickly let go of the handle.

"Ali, 'tis not my way to ever harm you…though I clearly have emotionally," he said softly. Surprised, Alisha tilted her head confused by his response. She shook her head. "I do not lie when I say you are my world… and my love for you will never end," he said and pulled himself to his feet. He took a deep breath and looked down at her. "My love is that strong for you, that…" He hesitated. "That if Nicholas has your heart too, then I will be content knowing you will find happiness with him. If you have to choose between us, then I beg you choose him for I would never be happy knowing that there could possibly come a day when you would question if you had made the right choice," he said softly and knelt down opposite her. He looked into her eyes, the eyes of the only woman he had ever loved or would. An emptiness filled him and he was numb as he looked at her save for the pain of knowing she had been with Nicholas. He had always known of the attraction between them, but always believed Alisha would never cross that line. 'And especially now of all times', he thought. But then that is perhaps why she had, he told himself. He hated seeing her in so much pain and emotional turmoil and blamed himself. Nicholas was a good and honourable man, which was the only consolation he could think of. "Do not be ashamed, my love. If it is so in this life that you will love another, so be it," he said and stood up. Alisha reached out to grab his leg and looked up at him. "But I cannot stay here."

"Paul, yes you can and you must…if not for me, then for Ailia. She needs you," Alisha pleaded and pulled herself up and grabbed Paul's mantle. "We need you. Did you not hear what I said…'tis you that I love more…I made a terrible, mad mistake."

Paul looked at her and again all he wanted to do was hold her. It surprised him that he felt no anger toward her or Nicholas. The thoughts of how he had felt for Princess Stephanie entered his mind. He was not so different. He sighed as Alisha looked deeply into his eyes. Paul understood within himself that with the promises he had made to find a way to convey the secrets of the past and the ever present threat of Turansha, he knew he would have to leave and resolve the matter one way or another. Set the codes, pass them on, form Saladin's Templars and kill Turansha. In that instant, he had decided Alisha and Ailia's best chances for happiness and safety lay with Nicholas. Over emotional, delusional or plain martyr attitude he told himself, it did not matter. Either way, his former life was irretrievably lost to him forever. He gently kissed Alisha on the head, her perfumed hair filling his nostrils with the smell that he loved and always reminded him of her. She wrapped her arms around his legs but he gently pulled them away. As she looked up at him, he placed the poem in her hand and closed her fingers around it and kissed her hand. As she opened her hand to look at it, he picked up the parchment tube then walked over to the door and opened it. He took one last look back at her as she slowly looked up at him. She was as always beautiful. His hand shaking, he closed the door behind him. He stood still for a moment, the world outside carrying on just as before. Sister Lucy coughed loudly from the end of the corridor. He turned and slowly walked towards her. He did not know if she knew about Alisha and Nicholas. Theodoric appeared holding his chest. He was not smiling as he normally did. Sister Lucy could see immediately the crushed emotion behind Paul's eyes.

"She told you didn't she?" she simply asked.

Theodoric looked at her, puzzled, then back at Paul. He feigned a brave smile at Theodoric.

"I must leave...please look after them whilst I am gone," Paul said quietly.

"Going where...you have only just arrived?" Theodoric asked, alarmed.

"Did she also tell you they stopped before fully consummating the act?" Sister Lucy asked bluntly. A shudder ran down Paul's spine just imagining Alisha making love to Nicholas, the pain of it physically hurting inside his chest. "Do not be a bloody fool and run from this. You damn well stay and you damn well fight for her do you hear?" she demanded.

"Paul!" Alisha called out from behind him as she stood at the doorway. "Stay," she pleaded.

Paul felt as if he was about to fall into a thousand pieces. Her words how he reminded her of Arri echoed in his head. He wanted to run down the corridor and hold her and never let her go, but he knew he had to leave. He looked at Theodoric and Sister Lucy.

"I cannot," he said in a broken voice and moved to walk away.

Sister Lucy started to thump him on the chest with both hands, Theodoric immediately pulling her back.

"Yes you damn well can," she said angrily as Theodoric pulled her further away from him. Paul looked down the corridor at Alisha, her shoulders dropping seeing he was leaving. She fell to her knees. Immediately Sister Lucy rushed toward her. "You are a bloody fool, Master Paul...a bloody fool if you go," she shouted.

Paul took two paces back, nodded at Theodoric and without any further words turned and walked down the wide stone stairway. Princess Stephanie saw him coming down and waited for him. She smiled but instantly saw the sadness in his face. She placed her hand upon his forearm as he stopped beside her.

"I shall not be staying...sorry," he said and walked away before she could ask why. She watched him as he crossed the main reception entrance hall and went out into the courtyard beyond.

ജ്ജ

In the stables, Paul tightened the main straps of the saddle, checked his satchels were secure and the parchment tube locked in place, then patted Adrastos. Stewart rushed over nearly slipping over as he tried to stop.

"What is this I hear, you are leaving? What is going on, Paul?" he demanded.

Paul looked at him just as Theodoric approached carrying Ailia. He sighed heavily thinking he was using her to persuade him to stay.

"I am not here to convince you to stay…Luce has told me what happened…well Alisha did actually. Personally I think you are a fool to leave as well," he said as Ailia reached out to Paul. Paul took her in his arms and hugged her tightly. "Go if you must…but never doubt that woman has and will always love you."

"Will someone tell me just what the hell is going on here?" Stewart asked.

"Don't go…please," Ailia said, upset.

"Listen my, young princess. I have to. It will not be forever…but you know there are some bad men out there who wish us harm now don't you?" Paul said as he looked at her and brushed her fringe aside. She put her fingers to her mouth and nodded yes. "Well, I am going to sort them so they never harm you nor Mummy ever again. And Nicholas, well you know he likes you and Mummy very much. Well he will protect you while I do what I must do. So you must promise me you will be good for them."

"Nicholas," Stewart said aloud and looked toward the Templar office. In that instant he knew and understood what had obviously taken place. "The bastard!" he said and went to move but Paul grabbed his arm in a vice like grip, which surprised Stewart. "I am not stupid and I know what has occurred here."

"Stewart…all is not as it seems, trust me on this. Swear to me you will help both Alisha and Nicholas. He is a good and noble man," Paul said, still holding his arm firmly. "Swear it."

Stewart looked at Theodoric, confused. He nodded he would.

"I…I swear it, brother, though I do not understand why."

"And you, my little Princess. I swear to you I shall see you again. I am always with you and you are always with me, carried inside my heart, as is Arri."

"Paul, 'tis neither wise nor safe for us to stay here in Kerak. I shall take them all back to Fustat and on to France just as soon as I am able to arrange it all. Does that meet with your approval?" Theodoric asked.

"Yes it does. The sooner the better. You are a good friend, Theo. I shall miss you," Paul replied. "I have a great and good family of which I am very proud," he continued to say, looking at Stewart. "Now here. Take Ailia, her mother will worry." Ailia clung on tighter. "Please be brave and do not cry for I wish to take the image of you smiling away with me."

"If we go to France, will you fetch Arri and take him there?" Ailia asked.

"Perhaps…if it becomes possible…now please, I must leave now," Paul answered.

Ailia reluctantly let go of Paul and went to Stewart. Paul hugged Theodoric and patted him on the back, Theodoric getting emotional as tears welled in his eyes. He tried to laugh it off quickly. Paul mounted Adrastos, rubbed his hand upon Ailia's head.

"Be safe, my brother, and come back to us soon," Stewart said.

"Please inform Tenno and Percival after I am gone at least an hour, for you know they will try to follow me. And…and tell Nicholas….tell him," he paused as he led Adrastos out of the stable. "Tell him I still love him like a brother too."

"Paul, 'tis far too dangerous to be out there alone, you must not go. There must be another way surely?" Stewart remarked.

"Believe me, what dangers are out there are nothing compared to the dangers of loving a beautiful woman," Paul said and tried to laugh. "Besides…I shall not be alone and I have this," he continued and placed his hand upon his sword. "Fear not, I am not going off to do some foolhardy reckless suicidal action. I have an entire family under threat I must protect and secure their futures. And I can only do that alone."

Stewart grabbed Paul's leg as he rode past him.

"Let me come with you?" Stewart asked.

"No, my brother. Where I am going no one else can go," Paul replied and paused as he looked at Stewart then Theodoric. "This is something I have to do alone…but I swear it, I will return."

"You make damn sure you look after yourself do you hear? And you better return," Stewart remarked, emotion welling in his eyes.

Paul looked at him and smiled. So much had changed between them since La Rochelle and for the better, he thought.

"Don't go getting yourselves killed in the mean time because of Reynald," Paul remarked then smiled at him and Ailia, bowed his head, faced forward then immediately rode Adrastos toward the main gates, glancing briefly back to see Princess Stephanie watching him, puzzled. As he approached the main gate, he looked up in time to see Alisha looking down through the opened wooden shutters at him. She went to raise her hand but stopped herself, seeing that he was actually going. She clasped her chest as a pain shot through her and she gasped taking in a sharp breath.

Sister Lucy stepped into view beside her and gently pulled her away from the window. Princess Stephanie saw them but by the time she looked back at Paul, he was out of sight and gone.

Theodoric stood beside Stewart holding Ailia in his arms.

"Well…now correct me in case I am wrong, but he did not say we could not mention this to Thomas and his men now did he?" Theodoric asked and rubbed his chin.

When Paul reached the furthest summit from Kerak heading north, he looked back. He felt betrayed and broken, yet his heart remembered everything of Alisha and his children. He placed his hand over his chest. 'A heart's memory' he said aloud to himself then continued on his journey.

PART XII

Chapter 67
Wilderness of the Soul

Port of La Rochelle, France, Melissae Inn, spring 1191

"I would have killed Nicholas for sure," the Hospitaller remarked and shook his head.

"Why did Paul not confront Nicholas?" Ayleth asked.

"What do you do when people whom you love and care more for than yourself do that to you? But Paul knew he needed to get himself as far away from both Alisha and Nicholas as quickly as possible for he feared that if he actually saw him he may have said or done something he would regret," the old man answered.

"So Alisha ended up with Nicholas after all?" Gabirol asked.

"Let me explain what happened next," the old man answered and paused as he considered how to explain matters. "Alisha could not face Nicholas at first, the shame she felt was so terrible a burden to carry. 'Twas Theodoric who spoke with him first. He made him swear not to reveal to anyone what had happened between them, especially to Thomas and his men for he feared they would have run him through on the spot such was their love for her and Paul. Stewart had stood with Theodoric, and true to his promise to Paul, he did not make issue with him, though if looks could kill, Nicholas would have most certainly dropped dead on the spot. It was plain enough to see in Nicholas's eyes and whole demeanour how broken he too felt."

"So what happened?" Simon asked impatiently, outstretching his hands.

"Theodoric had a good idea Paul would seek out Turansha and revenge, but he also knew how dangerous that path would be for him. The Devil looks after his own as they say and Turansha certainly was in league with some kind of evil force. It was agreed that Stewart must go with Ishmael, for Tenno refused to leave Alisha and Ailia's side ever again, to seek Paul out before he became truly lost to them. When Percival found out, you can imagine, there was no stopping him from going too. When Brother Teric learnt he had left alone, there were some very unholy choice words thrown about."

"But Stewart was the Gonfanier was he not?" Gabirol asked.

"Yes he was...but Master Jakelin and Brother Teric knew full well his service was required to seek Paul more than the Order's needs at that time."

"And Alisha?" Sarah asked.

"Alisha," the old man repeated and paused. "Remember how Kratos had once taken her aside and imparted a secret? Well, as she clutched the very first poem Paul had ever written to her, only then did she recall the words Kratos had told her...that a day would come when a great calamity would befall her...and that when it did, she must remain strong and forgive herself for her actions, lest she destroy herself, for it would not be her fault alone. When Paul had been missing at sea and then beneath the pyramids, both times she had thought that is what he had been referring too, but as she sat alone in that cold and empty bed chamber, only then did she finally realise what his words had really be preparing her for. Upon reflection she realised that in making love to Nicholas, she had been trying to block out the whole world...its darkness and pain with all its loss, even if only momentarily. She is not the first to do such a thing and she will certainly not be the last."

"I think it cruel Kratos even said such a thing in the first place," the farrier remarked.

"Forewarned is forearmed. Besides, Alisha thought that if Kratos had known that years in advance, then other things he had said about events to come would also happen. That gave her the smallest thread of hope to cling onto...for Kratos had said, in time they would be together again and always."

"Yes but I bet he did not say whether in this life or the next?" Simon stated and folded his arms cynically.

"No he did not," the old man sighed. "But it was enough to make her get up, fired with a renewed determination within her to get through the ordeal and she recalled the words of advice she had heard Tenno tell Arri many times...to look up, get up and never give up...and nor would she until she had gotten Paul back."

"I am guessing Paul must have been found as his sword and shield is here now?" Simon asked.

"Could have found him dead!" the Genoese sailor stated bluntly.

The old man looked at the Genoese sailor and shrugged his shoulders.

"Speaking of prophecy, for surely that is what Kratos and the other people of light imparted as you have revealed thus far, then what of the secret or prophecy the woman of light or angel, told Paul at Arri's grave?" Gabirol asked.

"I shall come to that shortly," the old man replied quietly.

Crac de Moab, Oultrajordain, Kingdom of Jerusalem, December 7th 1186

Alisha sat on her knees upon a fur skin rug in front of a large fire, just staring at the flames in a daze, her eyes wide. She held her hands across her tummy and gently rocked herself back and forwards. When Paul had left, Sister Lucy had pulled her away, only for Alisha to collapse to her knees. She could not cry any more, nor speak, in a state of total shock for all that had happened. Whilst Sister Lucy organised her a hot bath, Ailia asleep in the small side room, Alisha felt empty, an emptiness she had never experienced before. 'A waking death,' she thought to herself. How could she hope to get Paul back, especially as he was now alone in a land full of danger? It was getting dark outside as she turned slowly to look out of the window. Tenno's words echoed through her mind, yet she wondered how or even where to begin. She knew Tenno was close but he kept himself almost hidden from her now, but always there protecting and watching over her and Ailia.

"Ali," Sister Lucy whispered as she approached. "Ali, my child."

Alisha heard her words, but in her mind it was Firgany she was hearing and sensing. She looked up slightly, enough to see her dagger placed on the fireside mantle, one of the last things Arri had ever touched. She focused upon it. Her heart physically ached for him. She tried to take comfort from all the experiences and events she had seen and witnessed that in her mind confirmed life went on after death. She prayed Arri was okay and with Raja and Firgany looking down upon her. Though probably ashamed of her actions she thought and sighed. With sadness heavy in her heart and on her face, she looked at Sister Lucy.

"Please…when you first loved Theodoric, you were betrothed to another…did you break your marriage vows to make love to him, or did you wait?" Alisha asked hesitantly, searching Sister Lucy's eyes for her reaction.

"Aye that I did," she answered and feigned a smile. "But 'twas different from your circumstances…for Theodoric was and is, and shall always be, the love of my life. 'Tis not so with you and Nicholas is it?" she asked and clasped hold of Alisha's hands.

Alisha thought on her words and shook her head no slowly.

"And was it different with your husband?"

"Oh Lord now you will be embarrassing me," Sister Lucy replied and laughed but she could see the need for answers in Alisha's pained eyes. "Aye, my young lady, 'Twas different...but there was not that deeper connection, of our hearts becoming as one," she explained but then laughed to herself, shaking her head. "But it did not start so romantically," she grinned.

"Pray tell me why," Alisha pleaded.

"'Twas rather unceremonious actually. The first time we ever made love my husband was away...oh the way my heart beat that night for Theodoric. We were in my chamber...having so deviously coerced him into the room. I had no intention of doing anything...I just wanted to be in his exclusive company," she started to explain and laughed again. "I actually asked him to remove my necklace as I turned my back to him," Sister Lucy said then paused as she smiled thinking back upon that time.

2 - 10

"And...what?"

"Well, he approached me from behind, started to kiss the back of my neck, then raised my dress up over my waist...oh I nearly fainted my heart was beating so fast...and he took me, right there and then," she laughed and bit her thumb nail.

"No?" Alisha asked surprised. "Theo did?"

"Aye. Turns out he thought I had said would you help me take off my knickers, not necklace!" Sister Lucy laughed.

Alisha laughed hearing her tell this. They both laughed and held each other's hands for several moments. When Alisha stopped laughing, she realised that in that instant, that one simple small laugh had changed everything inside her. She looked back up at her dagger. She took a deep breath. If Arri could fight to protect his little sister, then she could, and she would fight for her now and their father...even if he never returned to her arms, Ailia would at least have her father alive. Filled with a new sense of determination, she stood up and looked at Sister Lucy, who could see a change in her expression.

"Lucy....do you still have Theodoric's writing case?" she asked, her voice no longer shaking.

"Aye that I do, my girl. Why?" she asked, puzzled, and folded the small towel over her arm.

"You sound more like Theodoric daily," Alisha replied and feigned a brave but pained smile. "I must write something for Paul. Have Stewart and Ishmael left yet?"

"No…Balian and Brother Teric argue 'tis too late and dark. They would miss or cover any tracks Paul has left. And the language, well! But why?" she asked again.

"And Nicholas?"

"He is with Theo…and you, my girl, as harsh as my words may now sound, you have broken two men this day."

"'Tis not harsh…but true. But for now, please, Theo's writing case."

"What of your bath?"

"That I can do when I have finished what I must now do. 'Tis the stain upon my soul and within my heart that needs cleansing more this hour."

☙❧

It was past the midnight hour when Alisha walked toward the Templar guard room. She knew Nicholas was in there with Theodoric and Balian. She pulled the dark green fur lined hooded cape Princess Eschiva had given her tightly around her neck, to stop the freezing wind blowing against her chest. Upside stood outside the large ornate double doors looking cold and blowing into his hands, the odd snowflake blowing gently past toward the ground. Another Templar guard stood opposite. When she reached them Upside simply shook his head no, she would not be allowed to enter.

"Let me pass, for I do not have the time to go and drag Princess Stephanie from her chambers at this late hour," she demanded, a small sealed scroll held tightly in her hand. Upside looked at his colleague.

"You are the guard…your choice?" he said to the other Templar.

Without saying a word, the guard opened the door and disappeared inside. Alisha shivered as Upside looked at her. He was about to ask if she was okay when Nicholas appeared, looking alarmed. Quickly he stepped down the three stone steps and simply stared at Alisha in silence. Upside frowned, puzzled. Before Nicholas could speak, Alisha pushed past him and stepped up through the door. Upside shrugged his shoulders, confused, as Nicholas followed after her.

Alisha heard Theodoric speaking inside the smaller room to her right, two large burning torches flickering away on either side of the door. Immediately she pushed it open to see him stood looking over several maps with

Balian, Brother Teric, Master Jakelin, Ishmael and Stewart. She was confused as to where Tenno was, expecting him to be there; probably with Abi, she assumed. Thomas and Luke were sat at the table showing them various details on the maps. They all looked at her and stopped talking. As she walked toward them, Nicholas rushed in behind her followed by Upside.

"When you leave to search for Paul, unless you take me with you, then I beg one of you take this message to him from me," she explained and held up the small sealed scroll.

Nicholas looked at Alisha, his eyes searching for some response to his presence. She looked at him briefly, her eyes immediately averting his and toward Stewart.

"Let me take it....please," Nicholas said, his voice full of pleading emotion. Upside shrugged his shoulders, surprised. "Ali...please."

Stewart suddenly stormed around the side of the table, angered, pushing Thomas backwards. Theodoric grabbed Stewart, putting his arms around his waist, and struggled to hold him back knocking one of the main lanthorns, Thomas just catching it in time.

"How dare you make such an offer? I have stood these past hours and listened to you help plan this search and I have bitten my lip as I promised my brother I would...but this, no, 'tis wrong for you to do so!" Stewart ranted, his old rage breaking through. Thomas stood himself up and helped Theodoric hold him back. "He is only gone because of you and your self serving actions!"

Alisha's hand started to shake as she held the scroll up. She took a deep breath and held the scroll higher and looked at Stewart, her eyes narrowing and shaking her head slightly, but enough to infer 'no' and he should say no more. But the look on Nicholas's face told Brother Teric all he needed to know. He looked at Nicholas hard as he held his hands out to her as if to plead for the scroll.

"Stewart," Alisha said sternly. "'Twas a time when we were in a very similar situation...do you not remember?" she asked and pushed the scroll out toward him. "'Tis not Brother Nicholas who is at fault for it was I who tried to seduce him."

"You what?" Upside coughed. Nicholas looked at him, then slowly at the others around the table staring at him. Theodoric shook his head.

"Now is not the time for bitter recriminations or blame...we must find

Paul. 'Twas madness letting him go," Theodoric said, trying to calm matters.

"We could not stop him," Stewart stated angrily.

"I am responsible and I alone. I am guilty for I led Nicholas to my chambers and 'twas I who kissed him."

"'Twas more than a kiss…far more than we ever did!" Stewart stated through gritted teeth loudly.

"You stupid bastard fool!" Upside said, his tone deliberate and slow. He stepped forward and as Nicholas turned away from Alisha to look at him, Upside swung a powerful punch. Instinctively Nicholas raised his left arm to deflect it, but Upside's fist still connected with his cheek. "You arse…you utter fucking arse! Have you learnt nothing from me these years?" Upside demanded as Nicholas nearly collapsed to his knees, but with his hand to his face he regained his balance and stood up slowly.

Alisha stepped closer to Upside and with her hands shaking placed her left hand upon his arm and ushered him back a pace shaking her head no to stop him.

"'Tis not him you should be hitting," she said softly as Upside stared at her.

"No, he has every right, for I have dishonoured not only you, Alisha, myself and my Order…but all of you here, and the trust you had in me," Nicholas said rubbing his cheek as it started to swell, his left eye already becoming bloodshot. "But Ali…you know the kind of man Paul is. You know he would take the scroll from me and know whatever you have written is true."

"No…I forbid it. 'Tis rubbing salt into his wound. You will stay here whilst I decide your punishment and position within the Order," Master Jakelin said, shaking his head disapprovingly.

"Master Jakelin, Brother Teric…there is no greater punishment you can inflict upon me than the shame and guilt I carry, for despite what Alisha tells this hour…'Twas I who led events to end in the manner they did," Nicholas explained and looked at Alisha as tears welled in her eyes. A single tear fell from Nicholas's rapidly swelling eye. "Master…you either let me do this and commission me with the charge of finding him, or I shall resign from the Order with immediate effect and go regardless. With that or not," Nicholas explained impassioned and indicated with a nod at the scroll. The room fell silent as they all looked at Master Jakelin and

Nicholas. Alisha lowered the scroll, tears in her eyes. Nicholas seeing this, he started to untie his sword belt. Brother Teric frowned at him hard as he untied his fastenings and pulled off his Templar Mantle. "There...'tis done," he said as he threw the mantle upon the table, the maps blowing to the side as it landed. Nicholas started to refasten his sword around his waist.

"Lord, give me patience," Upside said aloud, shook his head and started to unfasten his sword belt.

"What are you doing?" Master Jakelin demanded to know.

"If he goes, so must I as who else will look after him?" he answered and started to unfasten his mantle.

"NO! You cannot do this. Too much damage has already been done. If you cannot agree to work together and help find Paul...I shall go alone," Alisha exclaimed, shaking from head to toe from both desperate emotion and the cold. Nicholas looked at Upside, deeply touched by his gesture but confused.

"I shall also go for I know of no other who tracks better than I...all modesty aside...for this is too important and time is not on our side," Ishmael said and moved to stand with Nicholas and Upside.

Master Jakelin walked around the table and stood between Alisha and Nicholas, looking at them in turn intently. He put his hands upon his hips and looked at Balian, who shrugged his shoulders.

"Did you consummate fully the act?" he asked bluntly. Alisha's eyes caught sight of Theodoric as he very slightly shook his head no. Stewart saw him and looked back. Both Alisha and Nicholas shook their heads no. "Then if that is so, there will be no risk of a child and no lasting harm done."

"What? With all due respect Master, the damage has been done," Stewart argued.

Master Jakelin walked over to Stewart and looked up at him.

"Brother Stewart...then it is my desire and my wish to make sure there is no further damage done. I cannot afford to lose some of my best men, that includes you...so we do what we as Templars always do," he said and turned to face everyone. "We stand as always, alone, but together," Jakelin spoke with authority and then looked at Thomas and Luke. "And you, sirs, you are but truly Knights Templar in all but your attire."

The door swung open and Percival stepped inside, his face immediately turning to one of surprise. He sensed the tension in the air and looked at Alisha.

"Then please, Master Jakelin…I beg of you allow Nicholas to search for Paul before he becomes lost to us forever," she pleaded and handed him the sealed scroll. "Please."

"I can leave several of my men here to cover their absence if that helps," Balian suggested.

"And what exactly is this," Master Jakelin asked, taking the scroll.

"'Tis but words imploring his speedy return," Alisha answered and looked at Nicholas. "And a prayer that he will find it in his heart to forgive us."

Percival sighed and looked at Alisha and Nicholas, realising and instantly knowing what they had done. He closed his eyes briefly before stepping forwards and indicated for Master Jakelin to pass him the scroll.

"Did you know of this?" Master Jakelin asked, looking at Brother Teric and then Theodoric.

"I have already sworn every profanity known to man, and more to Nicholas. 'Tis true what he said earlier. No punishment we can give him will touch what he already suffers," Brother Teric replied.

"Then please…," Percival said calmly and took the scroll from a surprised Master Jakelin. "Here…take this," he said, immediately handing Nicholas the scroll, who hesitantly looked at it, then up at Stewart and then back to Alisha. "I know Paul probably better than all of you present…so if you want this to mean anything, then it can only come by way of Nicholas." Alisha placed both her hands to her face as emotion welled inside her. "Stewart…he forgave you of the same did he not?" Stewart reluctantly shook his head yes in agreement. "Then take up this commission with Nicholas and together honour it."

"Who is actually in charge here?" Master Jakelin asked, bemused, as Nicholas took the scroll in both hands and closed his eyes. "And is there anyone else here who has kissed this woman?"

Thomas stood up fully and slowly moved around the table to stand beside Alisha. Gently he placed his hand upon her shoulder reassuringly.

"She is in charge…," he stated and smiled. "When two hearts truly become as one, no power on earth or in Heaven can make it become undone! Let us put right that which has become broken…so yes, take this commission, Brother," he said, turning to look at Nicholas.

Alisha shaking uncontrollably looked at them all in turn, her heart wanting to reach out to all of them in gratitude.

"Then I suggest sleep…for you will all need to leave as the sun breaks before any tracks are ruined," Brother Teric stated. "Though in this weather you will be hard pressed."

Nicholas bowed his head and clutched the scroll with both hands to his chest. In silence Master Jakelin left the room staring at Alisha as he passed her. Each in turn silently filed out of the door, Theodoric kissing her on the cheek quickly as he went. Percival backed out of the room and ushered Ishmael out leaving just Alisha, Nicholas and Thomas alone in silence. After a few moments, Thomas indicated to Alisha it was time to leave.

"Go now…rest and know we shall do our best to find him and bring him back," he said softly and led her to the door. "Go get yourself warmed."

Alisha nodded silently trying not to cry. She looked once more at Nicholas, his eye half closed from the swelling. 'Thank you' he mouthed to her silently. Princess Stephanie appeared stepping into view in the main guard room reception hall and looked at Alisha, puzzled, then at Thomas and Nicholas. Before she could ask what was going on, Thomas closed the door behind Alisha. Slowly he turned and walked over to the table and unfastened his belt, removed his sword and placed it upon the table gently and stood in silence just resting forward upon his hands, his head down low. Nicholas looked at him, puzzled. Thomas sighed heavily and shook his head.

"Are you unwell?" Nicholas asked.

"Oh you have no idea…I am sick all right…sick of this world and I am sick of carrying a love so deep in my heart it kills me daily," Thomas started to say and stood up straight. He turned his head to look at Nicholas, who in that instant sensed his anger inside, Thomas's eyes ablaze.

"If you wish to do me harm this hour, I will not fight back."

"'Tis why I have laid my sword away for I know the anger that burns through me is strong," Thomas replied as he turned and walked slowly toward him stopping just feet away. "But I know what Percival says makes sense. I also know Alisha has deep feelings for you and would never forgive me for harming you….but if my men learn of this, I cannot be responsible for their actions. They all love her…and I bet not one of them has not fantasised or wished they had her love…but they also respect and admire Paul too much…something you clearly forgot."

"I did not forget...'tis why I stopped."

"You stopped! If you did, then you are a far better man than I," Thomas sneered, fighting to control his anger as he stared hard at Nicholas. He stepped closer until they were just inches apart.

"I know you have your arming dagger. Use it if you must and I will gladly take the blade for you really cannot hurt me any more than I am already hurting."

"So you keep saying...but I am so damn envious of you right now and my heart conflicts with my head...," Thomas said and stood away from him, quickly clenching his fists. "Fuck, fuck, fuck and fuck you again right now," Thomas swore and shook his head. He rested his hands down upon the table again and looked at the maps still left open. "When my men and I left our homes, 'twas after one of our seers, some called him the last Druid, told us we would find a just and worthy cause in the Holy Land. But he warned us not to align ourselves to any one lord, king or side, for one day we would find a true king...a king who would lead, not dictate...but he would have a real queen. Not some inherited, swapped, bartered, negotiated or murdered for throne queen," Thomas explained then stood up to face Nicholas again. "There were seventy-two of us who started that journey. Just eleven of us now remain, save Percival who joined us. 'Twas only when I saw Alisha and Paul that I knew we had found what we were looking for, only after we had stopped looking."

"And what else did your seer tell you?"

"That we would be known as an army of kings one day for the sacrifices we would make...and for our trust, integrity and honour. Maintaining that has been nigh impossible...but Alisha and Paul, they gave us that example...and now if my men know of what has happened, it would crush their long held faith."

"But surely, knowing we controlled ourselves and stopped...does that not count as a better demonstration of her virtue?" Nicholas asked defensively.

"You and I both know what you really did and how far you really went," Thomas stated and rapidly stepped even closer to Nicholas again. "Pray the seed of your loins did not spill within her..."

"May the Lord strike me dead for I swear that did not happen."

Thomas looked at Nicholas hard.

"We gave up our all to remain and protect Alisha and Paul. This we have done so far but failed with their son. 'Tis a stain my men will never get over. We shall not fail either of them again."

"Then let me help put right the wrong I have done not only to Alisha and Paul, but also you and your men?" Nicholas asked, shaking his head, the sadness in his heart clearly etched upon his face.

"Ig har härt glamas um mikid a landi, men Alisha kelinggę ir brunę," Thomas suddenly whispered in a strange but beautiful sounding language. "Learn what that means and carry the language in you, and I may forgive you. Whether you forgive yourself is another thing," Thomas said.

"What? I do not understand what you speak," Nicholas replied, confused.

"'Tis **övdalska** or Övdalian, the language of our forest ancestors. 'Tis also known as Elfdavian…though in truth 'tis not the language of elves as some claim. Learn it and it will speak to your soul as well as your heart," Thomas answered, looking at Nicholas intently. His anger was subsiding yet he still wanted to remain angry at him. He could see why Alisha would fall for him. He shook his head. "Go…for I will need you rested and that eye of yours sorted before we leave on the morrow…now please, just go." Thomas said, his tone lower but deliberate.

Nicholas hesitated for a moment. He knew a fight between them in normal circumstances would have been an equal match, but it was a fight he did not ask nor wish for. He had meant what he said, that he would not fight back. He picked up his Templar surcoat and flung it over his left arm, looked at Thomas briefly, wanting to say more, but there was nothing he could say. As for the strange language Thomas had spoken, he would ask him again later to repeat it so he could learn and understand what he had said. Quietly he left the room, closing the door behind him. Thomas sighed heavily. For years he too had longed to hold Alisha and had loved her from afar, but never had he even supposed or imagined she would even look at a man other than Paul. He thumped his fist down hard upon the table, the bang echoing in the confines of the now empty room.

ꟸ

The crystal clear night sky flickered with a million points of sparkling light, the Milky Way arching across the heavens above him looking like a river of silvered milk, as Paul sat looking up in wonder. Sitting cross legged, his blanket pulled tightly around him with Adrastos stood behind, he could see for miles in all directions upon the flat plain of Moab. If he could return to Alisha, no matter what she had done, just to hold her and Ailia, that would be enough, he thought. He sighed heavily as he wished to return to the few peaceful years he had enjoyed in Fustat. Now all was forever changed. Arri was dead, Alisha was no longer his and Ailia, his beautiful very own little princess, he could not even be there to protect and comfort her. He closed his eyes in sadness as he imagined her little face. If he could have stayed, he would have if only for her sake but he knew there was nowhere safe for any of them as long as Turansha was still alive. He did not know where to even begin to try and find him, but he also knew he could not stay at Kerak and remind Alisha daily of Arri as she had so cruelly shouted at him. How could everything have gone so terribly wrong? After all they had already been through, it did not make sense if he did indeed have some great commission to carry out. He shuddered and shook his head as he thought of Alisha lying with Nicholas. He screwed his eyes tightly and tried to push the imagined scenes from his mind that made his heart almost stop. His stomach turned as the enormity of his situation finally hit him; he leaned over quickly and threw up in an uncontrollable convulsion of fear and a deep sickening sense that made his whole body shake. Several times he retched until he was just throwing up bile, his neck and chest tightening. He coughed and tried to clear his throat, sick still dripping from his lips and nose. He started to cry… the cry that comes from the deepest part of your soul when you can go no lower. Resting over on his arms, he gave in to the overwhelming sense of loss and betrayal and sobbed unashamedly and completely. Adrastos lowered his head to try and touch him as if to reassure him, sensing his pain. After many minutes sobbing he wiped his face and looked upward.

"This hurt in my soul I cannot subdue…please, oh Lord, if you can hear me, take this pain away for 'tis too great," he cried. "I am truly alone and at rock bottom," he cried aloud, clenched his fists and sobbed again.

"Then use that rock bottom as the foundation to build your new life and new self upon," a gentle female voice spoke from behind him.

Quickly Paul jumped to his feet, alarmed. Wiping the tears from his face, he drew his sword. Adrastos looked at him as if to question what he was doing.

"Who is there?" he asked and spat out bile and shuddered at its bitter taste.

"'Tis only an old woman, you need have no fear of me," the voice replied, though Paul could see no one. "I am behind you."

Paul jumped around to see the same old woman from La Rochelle who had saved Theodoric's life and who seemed to appear everywhere he travelled.

"How…how did you get here?" he asked, surprised. "We are in the middle of nowhere."

"'Tis perhaps the best place to be then," she answered and stepped closer to him. "You can put that away for a start."

Hesitantly he re-sheathed his sword, the simple act of holding the scabbard pulling at his heart as he knew Arri had made it.

"I know you are not real…for your voice is usually harsh…yet now your voice is gentle. You are of other realms that much I have learnt of you," Paul blurted out and wiped his face again.

1 - 2

"How would you like me to appear?" she asked and moved closer, her stench immediately filling his nostrils. She laughed, seeing his face purse up. "Always works…the filthy old hag image," she said and started to smile. As she did, her face started to change. Paul looked on in wonder as she became taller, thinner and younger, her old baggy black clothes turning a pale cream and white. He blinked several times trying to confirm in his own mind what he was seeing. The rancid foul smell was replaced by an almost sensuous delicate perfume unlike any he had ever smelt before. "Is this more pleasing?" she asked softly. She glowed with a brightness that showed her fully despite the darkness of the night. Her eyes widened as if to ask him again as she held out her hands for him.

"I do not understand. Am I dreaming? Have I died?" Paul asked and looked back at Adrastos, who immediately snorted and shook his head. Paul let out a slight laugh and turned back to the woman. As he did, she was now standing just inches from him, her eyes looking into his.

"Here…drink this," she said and raised a very small glass looking bottle. "'Tis not poison I assure you, but will cleanse your mouth and the bitter taste," she smiled as she spoke, her eyes reminding him of Alisha.

"If it is of poison, I care not," he replied, took the small bottle and drank the contents down in one. "Here," he said and offered her the bottle back.

As she took the small bottle, she took Paul's right hand in her left hand and pushed herself up against him. Immediately he could feel her figure against him. He felt wrapped in warmth and love, almost like a child. Confused, he looked deeper into her eyes. Suddenly and without warning she pressed her lips to his, the sensation was instant and shot through his body filling him with a calmness and sense of happiness. She placed her hands upon his cheeks and kissed him more intensely; his arousal was instant and surprised him. As he tasted her sweet embrace, her lips gently pulled away. She opened her eyes as he opened his. She smiled and he laughed momentarily, stunned by his own reaction.

"You should care, for you have much to do in this life time still," she explained and stepped back from him and took his hands. "See how easy it is for these physical bodies to react to stimulus and touch?" The moment she spoke those words, he knew she was referring to Alisha and Nicholas. "We can make love right here and now if you wish and I can make it as heavenly as you wish it to be…but it is the heart's memory and the joining of souls we cannot achieve for that is set aside for only Alisha and you… for you are as twin souls, apart in distance, but together as one always. She knows this and she now feels it, as you should." A tear ran down Paul's cheek. He blinked several times trying to control his emotions. He turned to look back towards the direction of Kerak. "It does not excuse nor remove the act that she partook of…but like you are now, alone, broken, vulnerable and hurting, 'tis easy to succumb to the desires and pleasures of the flesh. 'Tis all but natural and expected…yet so very difficult to control," she explained and held his hands up and held them in hers tightly. She kissed him again softly, his body reacting to hers as a sense of pleasure flooded his whole being. "See," she said softly after breaking her kiss.

Paul thought he must be dreaming. He must have been violently sick and passed out. He looked at his blankets, saddle and Adrastos. He could see where he had been sick. A bright ball of light suddenly lit up the area all around him in a brilliant white light. He strained to look up at it as it slowly came lower.

"What is this?…This is the third time I have seen this," Paul asked.

"Do not be alarmed. 'Tis just a method of transport…for we are going on a little journey." The woman spoke softly and touched the side of Paul's head with her finger.

Abi saw the glow of bluish white light on the distant horizon and knew immediately what it was and meant. Quickly she mounted her horse and sped off towards it galloping as fast as she could. The land was level up on the high plateau enabling her to ride as fast as her horse would carry her. It took her nearly fifteen minutes to reach the point she had seen the light hovering above. The sun was already beginning to break on the horizon and Adrastos stood out silhouetted against it. As she approached she could see the saddle still on the ground, Adrastos tied to it, but no sign of Paul. Quickly she dismounted and ran around Adrastos and the immediate area. She checked the ground but could only see one set of footprints.

"Damn!" she snapped and slapped her thigh. She looked upwards. "Why…why must you always intercede? We are capable of dealing with this?" she shouted out, annoyed, causing Adrastos to snort. After a few minutes she looked upward. "Why?" she shouted again then looked down at Paul's saddle, his shield propped up against it. She shook her head and sighed. "Why do you make this so damned difficult all the time? Do not make this a long affair!" she shouted as loud as she could and kicked the ground in utter frustration. After a few minutes trying to calm herself down, she looked at Adrastos and checked the wound still visible on his chest. "You at least heal well, my four legged friend," she said and patted him. She turned and looked south. "I shall take you back to Kerak for I fear the journey to fetch Paul is going to be a long one," she sighed.

Crac de Moab, Oultrajordain, Kingdom of Jerusalem, December 8th 1186

The main courtyard was still shrouded in shadow, the early morning sunlight still to break across the castle walls. Alisha held Ailia to her chest as they stood with Princess Stephanie and Sister Lucy. Percival leant down from his horse as Theodoric handed him two leather water bottles as Thomas checked his men. Brother Teric mounted his horse as Balian approached on foot with Master Jakelin. Ishmael walked out from the stable area accompanied by Stewart and Nicholas leading their horses.

"We will find him," Percival stated as he took the water bottles.

Thomas looked at Alisha. He wanted to say many things to her but he knew now was not the time. Stewart walked up to her and took her hand.

"Have faith," he simply said and moved his horse besides Percival's and mounted up. Ishmael mounted his horse and simply nodded at her just as Tenno stepped out from the main keep. He rushed across and stood beside Alisha and Theodoric.

"Find him and return him to where he is needed and belongs," Tenno called out to Stewart and Percival and then looked at Thomas as he nodded yes.

Nicholas walked his horse toward Alisha. All looked on in silence as they looked at each other.

"We need to leave now," Thomas called out and mounted his horse, Balian nodding in agreement.

"Ali...," Nicholas started to speak but gulped, his throat dry. She looked at him and his swollen eye clear for all to see. "I shall not return without him, this I swear," he said softly and forced a smile and held up the small sealed scroll container.

"Come on, brother," Upside said as he walked out from the stable area leading his horse.

"Stand to!" one of the gatehouse guards shouted down as a single rider approached the castle. Everyone looked to the main entrance, the inner and outer gates lowered. "'Tis that tall woman and two horses!" he called down.

"Abi. Open the gates now then," Balian commanded and looked back at Princess Stephanie. "Sorry, My Lady, if that is okay?"

"Of course," she replied and held her hands nervously.

Alisha saw the look of concern on her face and it made her heart jump. She had obviously not been with Tenno as she had thought. She steadied herself on her feet and held Ailia closer as the chains of the main entrance lifted the gates. Every step of the two horses' hooves hitting the wooden drawbridge echoed into the courtyard, Alisha's heart beating faster with every step, until Abi came into view, Adrastos running alongside her. Alisha gulped hard fearing the worst, her legs going weak. Abi slowed the two horses and pulled up just short of the group, dismounted, handed the reins to a turcopole and immediately approached Alisha. Sister Lucy grabbed Theodoric's arm tightly.

"I found his horse and shield abandoned upon the plains of Moab...," she stated bluntly. Alisha took a sharp intake of breath. "But I saw no signs of struggle or others," she remarked and put her hand upon Alisha's shoulder reassuringly. "He is still out there somewhere…alive."

"And we shall find him," Nicholas said, then quickly mounted his horse and pulled it around. He did not look back as he headed toward the main gate house.

Alisha raised her arm and went to call out but Sister Lucy pulled her arm down.

"Well best you all be off…and stay together," Balian said and ushered them to all leave and follow Nicholas.

Percival led off after Nicholas, Stewart bowing as he passed Alisha and Princess Stephanie. Alisha acknowledged them all one by one as they filed past her filled with overwhelming appreciation and pride. Thomas leaned down, rubbed his hand in Ailia's hair and put his hand upon Alisha's other shoulder, looked at her intently. He sighed and wanted to speak, but words seemed worthless and would remain so unless they returned with Paul. His eyes caught Abi's.

"I shall catch you up shortly," she said.

Thomas looked at Alisha once more, her eyes full of emotion, desperation almost and tears.

"Bring my men back in one piece," Master Jakelin called out as Thomas pulled away.

Upside rode past and smiled at them.

"Fear not, I shall look after all of them…," he stated and trotted after them.

Alisha held Ailia closer and kissed her gently. She was deeply touched they were all willing to risk their lives to find Paul but she felt guilty knowing that none of this would be happening but for her actions.

"'Tis not all your doing…I despair at men and their ways," Abi said quietly in her ear. Tenno overheard her and raised a single eyebrow. "With the exception of a rare few," she then said and grasped Tenno's arm.

Port of La Rochelle, France, Melissae Inn, spring 1191

"Oh so that is how you came to have the shield," Ayleth remarked sadly.

"I wish to know what Alisha wrote to him," Sarah commented fiddling with an empty tankard.

"I wish to know the method of his transport?" Simon asked.

"I cannot explain the method by which Paul travelled for in truth I do not know it...but I can tell you he travelled many miles for when he awoke after a deep sleep, he had no idea where he was. He did not even know if he was dead in some other worldly place. The side of his head hurt and he could not recall if his memories of the woman were real or had just been a very vivid dream. But even if it had been some dream, it did not explain how he travelled many miles. Over 170 in fact in one night."

"'Tis impossible," the farrier remarked.

"But did you not tell us earlier how Kratos was able to travel great distances, as were the ancients of India...but also did not Muhammad in the Qur'an also travel great distances in the single stride of a winged beast or something?" Gabirol asked.

"Yes it is all written as such," the old man replied.

Jabal Al Lawz, The Plains of Arabia, December 12th 1186

It was early morning, the sky a bright clear blue but it was bitterly cold. Paul lay upon his side curled up holding his knees to his chest for warmth. He shivered, his teeth chattering as he started to wake up. A brisk wind blew over him as a loud humming noise filled his ears. The wind started to blow down upon him kicking up dust and grit forcing him to shield his eyes. A loud pop echoed out and the wind dropped instantly. Confused, Paul pushed himself up on his arms and tried to focus on where he was. For miles in all directions all he could see was snow covered mountains, the level plateau he was on itself covered in a dusting of snow. He sat up on his knees and held himself tightly shivering uncontrollably the woman nowhere in sight.

"And!" Paul shouted, his throat dry, as if asking God or the woman to confirm what next?

"No need to shout I am not deaf," Kratos spoke but some distance away.

Paul stood up tired and aching and looked around but could not see Kratos.

"Is this it…am I dead after all?" Paul called out and jumped as he felt a tap upon his right shoulder and turned around quickly.

"My dear friend, you must be cold…come, follow me," Kratos said, smiling, then instantly turned away before Paul could reply and walked toward a small outcrop of rocks. Wearing a full length heavy robe padded with furs and a fur lined hat, Paul would not have recognised Kratos had he not spoken.

Confused and bewildered Paul followed after him quickly. At the rock face Kratos pulled what looked like a hanging sheet of cloth aside and beckoned Paul to enter. As he stepped inside, he was met with immediate warmth from a small fire, the inside of the stone shelter covered with thick animal furs. A funnel of sorts took away the smoke up through a sealed hole in the roof. Several small candles illuminated the cave like room. Paul shivered again, his body still cold.

"Where are we?" Paul asked as he sat down near the fire upon a small wooden x frame seat, the leather creaking as it took his weight. "And how long have you been here?"

"We have time for many questions, and whilst you are here, I shall challenge you to search and look within yourself to find answers and guidance," Kratos replied, took off the thick robe he had worn and hung it up. He sat down opposite Paul and smiled at him as he removed his fur hat. "Here, you will need this when we are done."

"Can you not just tell me what I must do?" Paul asked as he caught the hat.

"Absolutely not. Now there, take some of that wine. 'Tis heated and will warm you," Kratos instructed and nodded at a small pot positioned on a stone plate half over the small fire.

"Wine is strong, women are stronger!" Paul heard himself say as his mind immediately recalled Stewart's Templar initiation all those years ago and the unknown rule when he had to drink a bitter tasting wine. He sighed, the memories now a long distant echo of times past and now lost.

"Nothing is ever lost," Kratos remarked as if reading his mind.

"Really?" Paul asked and looked at him. "Then please tell me where we are for I most certainly feel lost in every sense of the word and way."

"We are where some people might say is a location as detailed within 1 Enoch...13.7 to be precise," Kratos answered and smiled again. "If you had listened to your father better you would know it is also the location where a secret and sacred pact was made of the Fallen Angels...the watchers." Paul frowned at him, puzzled. "We are upon a mountain plateau, the highest point in this part of Arabia known to some as Jabal al Lawz, but to others Jabal al Musa, the mountain of Moses."

"But from what my father and Theodoric taught me, that mountain of Moses is the Great Pyramid...where the laws were taken from," Paul replied, even more puzzled.

"That is true in itself also. But after all Moses, as understood by many and as described in the Bible, was but another enactment to create a lasting memory and for the followers of him to have a tangible and believable experience that they could recognise and relate to. But as you have learnt, and experienced, his time upon the mountain was short, but to those left behind, it was far longer," Kratos explained and gestured by moving his staff, for Paul to pour some wine. There was only one small wooden bowl cup.

"How far are we from Alisha and Ailia then?" Paul asked as he poured the heated wine into the cup.

"Oh, about 170 miles in a straight line. Not far at all."

"Not far! Pray tell how did I get here so quickly...and how do I get back?"

"Do you wish to return?"

"Of course."

"Then why did you leave?"

"Because I had to. I remind Alisha too much of Arri and it pains her greatly...plus," Paul hesitated.

"She betrayed you with another," Kratos said softly and raised his eyebrows as he looked intently at Paul.

"Of course...you would know wouldn't you," Paul sighed and held the cup with both hands, the warmth a welcome sensation on his cold fingers.

"I see much, but I did not see the same love from Alisha to Nicholas as she has for you."

"Do we have to discuss this?"

"No not at all...but we shall discuss your intention to find Turansha and kill him."

"You cannot talk me out of that...for as long as that man lives, Alisha and Ailia are in danger."

"With the passing over of Arri I can understand your reasoning...but it is a wrong and faulty reasoning that will only get you killed, and Alisha and Ailia will still be in the same position but without you."

"Then what in the Lord's name am I supposed to do?" Paul pleaded and shook his head, even more confused.

"Family is not just about blood, it is also about those who are prepared to stand with you and hold your hand when you need it the most. 'I am' are the two most powerful words you can speak, for what you place after them becomes your destiny. Death truly is nothing at all when you know and believe that it is like passing into another room. You know you have known Alisha before…and you will know Arri again. The sin she committed…was it such a truly great sin when all things are considered? You yourself are guilty of having the physical feelings toward Stephanie no? And the old hag," he laughed. "Let Arri's name be spoken without effort or pain, but with fondness and memories of his laughter and his smile. Do not push him out of mind simply because he is out of sight and you pain and long for him. For he is but waiting, just a brief interlude until you meet again…but do not let the poison of revenge make all that is good and still sweet in your life be tainted by its bitterness. You still have a marriage worth fighting for."

"And what of marriage for it certainly does not feel that way any more?"

"Most make the mistake of thinking and believing the myth of marriage. That it is some kind of magical box full of beautiful things, of companionship, intimacy, friendship, stability and exclusive loyalty…but calm waters do not test a marriage. Marriage starts as an empty box which you must put things, feelings and experiences into. Only then can you take from it. There is no love in marriage, 'tis just a word. Love is in people and it is they who put love into marriage. There is no constant romance in marriage either because you have to infuse it into your marriage constantly to keep that box full. You must learn the gentle art of giving, loving, serving, praising, and unconditionally, to keep that box full. If you take out more than you put in, the box will become empty."

"But this path we have chosen, even though we were warned against it, 'tis too hard," Paul sighed and sipped the warm wine.

"The more difficult your path, the higher your calling. And correct me if I am wrong but was it not your father who told you to stand by what you believe in, even if it means you stand alone?"

"He did…and now look at me…I am stood alone."

"My friend, you are far from alone. At this very moment there are those out there looking for you this very hour, despite the cold and hardship they will endure."

"And Alisha…she will be with Nicholas right now I am sure."

"You have so little faith in her love for you? If you believe that then you are truly lost…and blind…But ask yourself this. If you were to know you would die this day, could you not think of a better man to love and protect both Alisha and Ailia than Nicholas?"

As his words ran through his mind with a thousand images of Alisha and Ailia, he gulped hard and his heart thumped.

"So that is where her destiny lay," he remarked sadly.

"You are listening to me but you are not hearing what I say are you?"

Paul looked at Kratos and shook his head, unsure what he meant.

"I do not know how to live without her…or Ailia."

"Nicholas may have held her physically, but her heart and soul are connected to yours."

"But Turansha?"

"As I said, do not let the poison of that man enter your soul. Revenge is like drinking poison yourself and expecting him to drop dead. It will only be you who suffers. You have to have faith that he will get due unto him what is befitting."

"Faith…blind acceptance of old writings and a belief in a god we cannot see."

"Do you think I take the literal word of the Bible or Qur'an and Vedic verses as absolute? No. But they contain truths, wisdom and the codes…"

"Yes, the codes," Paul sighed. "How, when my world is torn apart can I begin to find a way that will guarantee those codes continue…I cannot even think about tomorrow let alone all that and the commission of starting some joint Christian, Muslim Templar unit. 'Tis all too much for one person to bear."

"Paul, listen to me. There are many veils that separate us from what really is whilst we exist and experience life in this so-called 'real' world. But sometimes those veils can wear thin, like clouds vanishing, and the starry eternities show through in beautiful momentary flashes or in tranquil beauty. All other realms are just as real and just as essential an element of this world of rocky shores, the seas, and the sky. Most only see with their outer eyes with just a very few with the inner eye where nothing is invisible. There are many realms, some known as the Tir-Nan-Oge, Paradise, Heaven or the Elysian fields, where the soul lives when its physical energies and desires have been subdued and brought under the control of light; It is a real region which has been described by poets and sages who, at all times, have endeavoured to express something of the higher realities and where love is imperishable. All around us always, within that mystic light that covers our hills and valleys and where the deeds of our ancestors still linger to touch us with their memories to inspire us. The gods of old have not deserted us for they hear our call and they will return. A new cycle is dawning and the sweetness of a new dawn of humankind is in the air. You can breathe it and if we all do, it will but awaken all from their slumber of ignorance. And they hear your call as you know. What has happened to you so far, your history, does not define your future for that is yours to decide and make."

4 - 18

"But what of Alisha?" Paul sighed heavily and shook his head looking down.

"You fell in love with her soul, not just her outer beauty, for chemistry and physicality will age and fade, but real love never does. To love without condition and expectation is the highest truest love...and you possess that for her already. Sometimes the best and worst times of your life can coincide. It is a talent of the soul to discover the joy in pain, thinking of moments you long for, and knowing you'll never have them again. The beautiful ghosts of our past haunt us, and yet we still can't decide if the pain they caused us outweighs the tender moments when they touched our soul. This is the irony of love."

"And what of the comment I heard at my brother's initiation and as my father often hinted at...that wine is strong, but women are stronger for Alisha is certainly stronger than I?"

"I sense you are trying to change the subject somewhat," Kratos remarked. Paul shook his head no, but in truth he was. "Forte est vinum, fortior est rex, fortiores sunt mulieres: super omnia vincit veritas," Kratos said aloud in an exaggerated manner. "Wine is strong, a king is stronger, women are stronger, but truth conquers all. That is what you are referring to. 'Tis a symbolic and esoteric sentence. It was handed down from a time long before the Jews took it up without understanding its significance. The story is found only in the First Edras, and begins in Chapter 3, which are Jewish apocryphal scripts in case you did not know. In it, King Darius gave a banquet for his entire kingdom and, after he had gone to bed, three young men of the bodyguard held a contest to determine what one thing is the strongest. The person giving the wisest answer was to be richly rewarded by the king. Each contestant wrote a statement, sealed it and placed it under the pillow of the king, who, along with three nobles of Persia, would judge which the wisest statement was. The first answer is wine: the second is the king; and the third answer is women are the strongest but, above all things, truth is victor. When the king awoke, he read the statements and summoned a company of judges and called the three young men in to explain their answers. The first young man explained that wine leads the mind astray, causes changes in behaviour, neutralises intelligence, diminishes capacity, and causes loss of memory. The second man believed the king is stronger for he rules over others, sends them to war or work, and takes what they win or earn. They watch over him when he sleeps and obey him in all matters. The third man, Zerubbabel, explained how women give birth to kings and to those who plant the vineyards that produce the wine. Men cannot exist without women and they are willing to give all they possess to be with a beautiful woman. They will risk their lives for the love of a woman, leave their parents and hold to the wives with whom they wish to spend the remainder of their days on earth. Many men have lost their minds because of women and have become slaves because of them. Many have perished or stumbled or sinned because of women. A woman can take the crown from the head of a king but, strong as they are, they cannot compete with truth. Truth is great and stronger than all things. The whole earth calls upon truth and heaven blesses her. All of God's creation quakes and trembles and with him there is nothing unrighteous. Wine is unrighteous, the king is unrighteous, women are unrighteous and all such things. There is no truth in them and in their unrighteousness they will perish. But truth endures and is strong forever and ever."

"I am sorry for I do not see or understand any esoteric meanings in this tale."

"When Zerubbabel had finished speaking, everyone said 'Great is truth and strongest of all'. Zerubbabel is declared the winner and is promised whatever he asks of the king. Zerubbabel asks the king to honour his vow to build Jerusalem, return the holy vessels, and rebuild the temple. King Darius grants him and all who would go to build Jerusalem a safe passage and assistance in building. They will not have to pay tribute and offerings will be given to the temple. He provides land and wages for those who guard the city and sends back the holy vessels. Zerubbabel leaves praising

God and thanking the Lord for providing him with the wisdom and they got to build the city, feasting and rejoicing for seven days. 'Tis your father who, as we sit here now, toils as he plans and designs a new chapel to contain the secrets and codes...a New Jerusalem church, to one day be built in the sacred land of Alba. It shall be named after the true location the holy family, that Crimson Thread blood line so woven as a vine, landed in France, at Roussillon. It shall have, as a marker in its chapel, the figures of King Darius asleep and two of the young bodyguards on an architrave which runs at right angles to the lintel on which the quotation will be engraved for all who follow to one day rediscover and understand, for in truth you are all building it for yourselves for when you again walk upon the bounds of this realm in flesh."

"But what happened to the third bodyguard?"

"Your father designs a chapel where at the opposite corbel the figure of Melchizadek holding a chalice, the Grail, will be seen. The third missing bodyguard is symbolic of the line that shall remain separate and hidden, until it can be revealed again. But even then that can only happen if the codes and symbols of the rose, the lily, bees and apples are carried forward. It shall also have carved blocks showing all the sounds required to open a window into other realms but also awaken that which lies dormant within all of mankind. The chapel will be made whereby every aspect of its design will have been done so for a purpose with every carving having a meaning. It shall be a message for posterity that will finally be understood by those initiates who follow the path of learning and service to others until they are brought to its doors. But the answers will be given to those with the courage to explore, the vision to see and the humility to thank God for Mother Earth from which all bounty flows. The chapel will proclaim that God and nature are ONE, that every green shoot is a word of God; that, if there is any sacrilege, it is what man has done and is doing to Mother Earth. By then, with every passing day, there will be less and less of the surface of the earth capable of sustaining life. The great oceans, both water and forest, shall become almost destroyed. People's minds will become as deserts for in his arrogance man will have set himself above other living things and, in so doing, will divorce himself from reality and from the truth. Alas, the truth is a world which few people have the courage to explore or even to voice in this age of religious restriction and dogma. If you try to reveal this truth now, you will without doubt be charged with heresy. This is why your father and other masons like him build that very truth, the codes within the very buildings of the church hidden but in plain view for an initiate," Kratos said and winked.

"An order of builders like my father had discussed with me. A brotherhood of masons. Free to believe and question all," Paul said, shook his head and recalled his shared experience with Alisha when they saw a ruined cathedral rebuilt as new before their very eyes. "But what of the hidden line, the Crimson Thread. How in the future can any surviving line be established?"

"You are aware of the mystery of why Templars have their hair shaved during their initiation ceremony and sealed away?" Kratos asked. Paul nodded yes. "Then understand that just like the art of flight, man will again also learn the very deepest secrets of how we are made. Not only being able to distinguish the different bloods, but also the very building materials of our flesh and bone. Like the entwined serpents represent, 'tis a knowledge of how and why we grow. The one you know as Akhenaton as your father and Theodoric explained, his very physical body was altered and his code, you call it the code of life, 'twas changed. 'Tis why he and his descendants looked and acted differently. Through our hair we can match from what lines our forefathers came...and those that were mixed with the lines of the watchers, or angels, whichever way you choose to perceive it, then through understanding that code will the Crimson Thread once again be revealed. But I warn you, never assume those that carry the code are any better than the next person, for in truth, a soul can inhabit any line. 'Tis just the physical ability to use and access higher learnings and tools that is enabled...for the advancement and betterment of all peoples."

"And religions carry these details?"

"Yes as religion was known to be a powerful tool guaranteed to carry its message across the millennia of time. However, religion as we have it now, and for years ahead, has been used and usurped by power hungry preachers who, instead of preaching peace as their respective religions require instead rant against each other and engage in holy wars under the euphemistic titles of Crusades or Jihad. 'Tis why the initiates of the Knights Templar wish to establish a rapport with Islam, a need which is just as great as ever before. There is nothing in the Qur'an which is contrary to Christian teaching except they draw a line at accepting Jesus as being the son of God. So do many others who are not of the Islamic faith. All boundaries, whether national or religious, are manmade and they make little sense because, whether we are Caucasian, Mongoloid or Negroid, we are all at one with each other in our primitive mortal needs. That and the law of nature, which is eternal and unchanging, is the truth…a truth which we must embrace. If done in time, it will bring about the recovery of Mother Earth from the depredations of man. But as for religions per se, if there has to be religion, then the best kind is one that will show you where to look, but not what to see!"

"Then what am I to make of the woman of light I saw at Arri's grave? She told me of a prophecy to come…of three children and three prophecies they would reveal."

"Ah…so they told you that already," Kratos remarked and sat in silence for a moment. "Yes there will come a time in the future when three children will witness the same woman of light, bathed in blue no less. Of course they will see her as being the Virgin Mary no less. She will impart to them three prophecies of signs and things to come. All I can tell you of it now is that it will be at a place that is connected to the name of Fatima, after the Islamic tradition. Only two prophecies will come to pass in those children's life times, the third, about a city lying in ruin, only coming to pass after mankind again starts to remember his past."

"And such places where roses and lily's shall be laid down or set out?"

"Yes…and when the people of light, the angels of the Lord, call them what you will, when they have seen and noted the symbol of Mary, as the signature of Virgo laid out across the land, such is what your father and his Order now construct with its cathedrals, then when the final symbols have been recognised, then," Kratos paused. "Then and only then, after great conflict in the world, will they appear in full open view…starting at the city of ruin….where Arri now lies."

"But I thought the ruined city was that of Rome…the city of seven hills?" Paul asked, puzzled, trying to recall what his father had often told him.

"No…though many will assume it to be so. Many people will interpret signs as meaning one thing, this or that. Both sides will have equal and apposing arguments how the other side, the other religion, the other way of life is the Devil's work, and so convincing will be each side, that many will perish when all could be avoided if they focused upon what they do have in common. But it is all part of life's plan to teach souls to experience and learn…for after all this realm is like a school."

"Nothing now seems to matter to me for I feel empty, save the love I have for Ailia, and the pain that covers everything for the loss of my Arri," Paul sighed.

"Do not allow the pain of loss to stop the process of living. As I have said, he is not gone, though I understand that concept is hard to accept and some will argue that you deny yourself the chance to grieve, but you have the advantage of having glimpsed the other realms…not just a dream or fantasy." He paused. "And you know in your heart you still love Alisha and she loves you. You are simply shielding yourself, which is natural, if you do not believe this."

"My father taught me that love and trust are like a ceramic plate two people make together. If you smash it upon the floor, it breaks. If you say sorry to it, does it go back to the way it was?…no. So no matter how much she may say sorry, it will never be the same," Paul explained and rubbed his fingers through his hair, his heart aching again as emotion welled within him.

"I have heard that so many times. But you know what, no it will never be the same again…so you make a new plate but you can make it even better… and stronger," Kratos replied and smiled as Paul looked up at him.

"Then why am I brought to this place for surely Alisha would be better off without me? If Nicholas can make her happy and protect her, then… then my love for her is such that I would wish them a long and happy life together…'tis her happiness I wish above mine. And how shall I return anyway?" Paul asked wearily.

"You are not listening to me are you? And we shall stay here as long as it takes until you are hearing what I speak. Alisha loves you…and when you again know that, and after I have taught you a few things, plus a list of names, then I shall have you returned to where you left Adrastos," Kratos explained, Paul's eyes widening in alarm as he remembered he had left Adrastos. "Fear not, Abi found him. Alisha's heart breaks for the loss of Arri…and you. Remember that over these next few days as I teach you."

"Teach me…what?"

"The truth behind the spear of destiny symbolism, the same as the spear of Vishnu, which became another esoteric symbol for the fleur de lys. But together we shall formulate and plan this new order of builders and masons." Kratos smiled and stood up. "And know and always remember this. Love the image of an infant. Do not boast of your intelligence, knowledge or wit for supreme wisdom adores those who are pure of heart and innocent like a child. She reveals her secrets and treasure to them. This is why the Mother of the Divinity often appears to twelve year old children and adolescents. That is why the lady of the light, oft seen as the Virgin Mary as she is radiant in blue, will reveal her three prophecies to three children," Kratos explained and kneeled down directly in front of Paul and looked into his eyes with an intensity such that Paul felt he was actually becoming part of him. Kratos laughed lightly at his expression. "Paul, what we do for ourselves dies with us. What we do for others remains forever. And the truly strong do not exploit the weak, they do not look down upon them, they help them up. Whilst here, you have a choice for I can offer you riches of gold, camels, power, prestige and as many women as you wish... all that any man may desire. The choice will be yours." Paul frowned at his last remark, bemused, instantly thinking it was some test. "'Tis no test Paul but a real choice." [109]

Chapter 68
Vows, Oaths and the Nine

Port of La Rochelle, France, Melissae Inn, spring 1191

"I do not understand nor quite believe Paul could have travelled such a distance in one night," the Genoese sailor remarked disbelievingly.

"In truth that matters not, my friend...but it was true," the old man replied.

"But surely others would see such things in the sky?" he retorted immediately.

The old man turned to look at the Templar and raised his eyebrows as if he knew he would answer.

"Ah," the Templar said and paused. "Such things are seen in the skies, my friend. We oft saw things that defy explanation when camped out in the deserts," he explained, his brother nodding in agreement.

"Recall how I mentioned that Muhammad ascended in almost the same manner at the Dome of the Rock having been taken there by what Muslims call 'the Buraq'? 'Twas also said to have transported Abraham, known as Ibrahim, when he visited his wife Hagar and son Ishmael. According to tradition, Abraham lived with one wife in Syria, but the Buraq would transport him in the morning to Mecca to see his family there, and take him back in the evening to his Syrian wife. Abraham and Hagar travelled eight hundred miles of uncharted desert, some nine hundred years before history records the first caravan route was ever established along the Red Sea. Abraham had dropped them off under a tree in the middle of nowhere, which is supposed to have eventually become Mecca, and then Abraham 'set out' on his thousand mile walk back home. I think we can all see it makes no sense by our conventional means, and do not forget the many references within the Bible itself of prophets being taken up in the sky, travelling vast distances and also to heaven," the old man explained. "And remember the stories how men flew great distances. 'Tis but an application of natural principles and man will again relearn them."

"So Paul is a prophet...and when will we relearn how to?" Simon asked, excited.

"Not in our life times I am afraid, Simon...and Paul may have been a prophet of sorts." The old man smiled as he replied.

"Then what of this new Order Kratos spoke of that Paul would start?" Gabirol asked.

"Of builders...of men and women from all walks of life and backgrounds. But the world is still not ready for it yet clearly," the old man answered.

"Then what was the point of Paul and Kratos even discussing such matters?" Peter asked.

"Because, as Paul wrote within his journal, even if he could not start it now, the foundations would at least be laid...by others who would take up the commission," the old man explained quietly and looked at Paul's journal beside Gabirol.

"Why, is all that he planned within these pages?" Gabirol asked and pulled the journal closer.

"Yes. 'Tis all in there, except certain details of what Paul learnt and saw whilst with Kratos, and those details I am afraid I cannot reveal for I know not of what happened save for a few parts," the old man replied. "But I do know, as his journal indicates, and as per parts of what I have explained already...'tis to the twin brothers who take up this charge and secure its passage forwards," he said and looked at the Templar and Hospitaller. "But also there would be men and women, scribes, sailors to navigate, stone masons to inscribe and build, tailors to clothe and fashion regalia and farriers with their horses to transport and others not yet known," he said slowly, deliberately looking at their surprised faces all in turn."

"But I am not headed for Britain or Alba as you say they are heading if they so choose to," Gabirol said and pointed to the Templar and Hospitaller.

"No Gabirol...your destiny lies elsewhere...in the City of Florence where, if you are in agreement, I have a comfortable abode you may have as payment, as well as learned and wise men and women who wish to learn more..."

Gabirol gasped and shook his head, then gulped, surprised by the sudden rush of unexpected emotion.

"You are not all here simply by chance," the old man stated and looked at Simon and Ayleth. "Yes that includes you two. I already have your names...and how, I will reveal."

"Well I am staying right here thank you very much," Sarah interjected and looked at Stephan, alarmed.

"Fear not, dear wife. We have our duty here trust me," Stephan said reassuringly and smiled.

"Sounds to me like Paul is being tested in the wilderness just like Jesus was...and camels...was Theodoric likewise tested with camels?" Simon remarked and asked, looking at everyone.

"See Simon...you have much to learn about yourself for you are far wiser and brighter than you think you are," the old man smiled. "In a fashion 'twas a time for testing Paul, for he was given free agency to decide and choose."

"Would that woman have really made love to him as she offered?" Ayleth asked curiously.

"No...for she knew he would not take up her offer. 'Twas a lesson...an exercise on proving a point."

"But if Kratos was able to offer all those things, is that not like the Devil then as he was able to offer all of that to Jesus, as the Devil was master of this world?" Gabirol asked, perplexed.

"No, my friend. There is no figure that stands upon hoofed feet half man and half goat. 'Twas all allegorical and symbolic the story of Jesus in the wilderness, the symbolism I have already explained."

"I am not bothered about that part, I just want to know if Paul chose Alisha or power and wealth...and other women," the Genoese sailor asked.

"Well we know he must have returned for this journal to be here with us this day," Gabirol remarked.

"Could have found it abandoned somewhere...or sent to Alisha?" Sarah commented and looked at the old man.

The wealthy tailor was rubbing his temples with his fingers, still trying to comprehend and make sense of what the old man had just revealed about having their names and all of them being part of the new Order Paul had planned and if they so chose to accept the commission.

"No...he lives...or his memory and legacy certainly does...for I feel it...in a strange unknowable way," he said and looked up. "I am sure Theodoric was at one time likewise given a similar choice...perhaps he chose the camels in error, 'tis why he says never mention it to Sister Lucy?"

"You are nearer the truth than you can imagine," the old man acknowledged. "Theodoric himself was once in a very similar situation...and after Sister Lucy had been married off, but that is all I am prepared to say on that matter."

"You said that Paul would learn all about the real details of the New Jerusalem as written in the Bible and the spear of someone...who?" Ayleth asked.

"Paul as I have explained earlier was in the main already aware of much of what the New Jerusalem symbolism and values meant, that in short it referred to a new time of man, the fifth age, after the Phoenix had flown and a new world is reborn upon this same earth we call home. Do you recall I explained the mathematical details?" the old man asked and looked at them as they nodded yes. "'Twas how

those same details were carried over within other religions and teachings that Paul learnt, but also how the Indian Lord Shiva had a spear, its shape identical to the fleur de lys. 'Twas a trident and we all know the many gods who are associated with that. It also became known in Christianity as the Spear of Destiny, the supposed spear that pierced the side of Jesus. The trishula, or in Sanskrit the *triśūla, means three spear. Like Alisha's three pronged dagger almost. There are many other gods and deities who hold the trishula, the three points having various meanings and significance ranging from various trinities, creation, maintenance and destruction, past, present and future and the three guna. When looked upon as a weapon of Shiva, the trishula was said to destroy the three worlds...the physical world, the world of our forefathers, representing culture drawn from the past, and the world of the mind, representing the processes of sensing and acting. The three worlds are supposed to be destroyed by Shiva into a single non-dual plane of existence that is bliss alone. In the human body, the trishula represents the place where the three main nadis, or energy channels, ida, pingala and shushmana, meet at the brow. Shushmana, the central one, continues upward to the seventh chakra, or energy centre, while the other two end at the brow, where the sixth chakra is located. Paul learnt much on this subject, but as I have already said, he did not write of his experiences during his time on Jabal Al Lawz save a few lines only."*

"How long was Paul away for and who found him?" Peter asked.

"'Twas nearly a month later...exactly where Paul had left Adrastos. Tenno had remained, true to his word, beside Alisha and Ailia constantly whilst Thomas, his men, Nicholas and Upside searched far and wide...as much as they dared venture and in some instances into hostile held lands. Abi accompanied them often but she knew he would not be found until it was decided they would be allowed to find him. She was able to spend some time with Tenno, but with men, especially knights, being so few, she had to split her time between helping Alisha and being with Tenno and out searching, or be seen to be searching at least."

"Did Abi take that opportunity to tell Tenno he had a child with her?" Ayleth asked.

"No, for she thought it not wise at that moment," the old man answered.

"And Alisha?" Sarah asked.

"She just existed from day to day, the pain and heartache of losing Arri a deep wound in her soul, plus the guilt and loss of Paul was nearly almost too much. Sister Lucy was at times quite hard on her, but it served her well for otherwise Alisha would have probably fallen into a pit of despair," the old man explained and sighed. "But dear Ailia, just like Arri before, she went around with a constant smile upon

her face and told everyone daily her father would come back. She just knew he would, she kept saying."

4 - 8

"Was Nicholas still a Templar?" the Hospitaller asked.

"He kept his mantle wrapped up inside his horse satchel...but vowed he would not put it back on until he had found Paul and delivered the poem...and only then if Paul did not kill him and also forgave him. But after a month, there came a time with tensions rising, that Thomas and his men could no longer wander aimlessly daily and neither could Brother Teric and Master Jakelin spare their men any longer in the search. 'Tis why, very reluctantly, Upside had to leave the search and rejoin his brother Templars in Kerak...after much talk with Nicholas and his pleading that Upside must return to the Order. The fault and guilt was Nicholas's and his alone he argued and he begged Upside to follow his own calling. So Upside returned to his normal Templar duties, but at least he was able to stay at Kerak."

"So Upside actually left the search?" Gabirol asked.

"Only very reluctantly, but as I said, he and his men operated out of Kerak so at least he was on hand should anything change, but Nicholas vowed to find Paul and then and only then would he return to the Order if Master Jakelin would let him."

"But why were so few knights available...were they all off with Reynald?" Sarah asked.

"Alas it has always been the case that there were, and are, never enough trained knights to defend all the territories...'tis why the qualification for knighthood was lowered. Sometimes even local Christians could become knights, as certainly happened during the siege of Jerusalem, which we shall come too soon. Many so-called eastern fashions were in fact Byzantine by the way...but it was the early influx of Italian merchants that had posed such a threat to the emerging aristocracy in Jerusalem with many knights of French origin looking down their noses at knights of Italian origin...and yet all were despised as half breeds by men newly arriving from Europe. It was from that mix and attitude that the Mareschal, or Marshal, of each Latin state was charged with recruiting men and knights...but in reality his powers were limited. Some knights were excused service on foot or where their horses could not carry them. Some knights can be called to serve from the age of fifteen and some up to sixty. A knight is not beholding to serve if he has lost his fief to the enemy though. Many troops are recruited from men owing feudal obligations such as the Church, indigenous landowners and military orders, though in truth it

is the military Orders that supply mounted knights and sergeants as well as large numbers of infantry. In a major emergency, such as befell the kingdom in 1187, an arriere ban is declared, which in theory at least means that all free men have to muster and even visiting pilgrims can be called into service as infantry. As the numbers are always so low, mercenaries and the majority of mounted sergeants are hired in from outside the area. That is why so many western mercenaries often stay in almost permanent contracts," the old man explained.

"You mean like Thomas and his men?" Peter asked.

"No, Thomas and his men were no mere mercenaries. They oft worked for little or nothing. After Alisha and Paul left Fustat, there was no way of being paid by Husam as originally agreed. And with Paul missing, there was no way of issuing cheques against him...no, Thomas and his men were something quite altogether different," the old man explained and smiled to himself. "Too often though the aggressive nature of new arrivals is in direct contrast to those Latin settlers who are more cautious. In theory the King of Jerusalem commanded the army, which included the permanent army of Jerusalem, maintained due to almost constant war...'twas the failure to expand beyond the coastal strips and conquer inland apart from Jerusalem that now causes such a logistical nightmare. That is why it has to maintain an abnormally large defensive force. But it does not have the land to support such a force, which would have serious implications. In theory again the king can demand knights and men serve a full year, longer than here in Europe, but the periods are actually negotiated by the Haute Cour, the high court, as and when each campaign is planned. This however led to some major difficulties when a major disciplined foe was to be faced. Different fiefs sent different numbers of knights. Each knight usually has about four to five men attend him as well as three horses. Places such as Jaffa or Galilee supplied around a hundred knights whilst some small fiefs can only supply a single knight. Also the number of sergeants varies considerably from five hundred by the Patriarch of Jerusalem to twenty-five for Le Herin as an example. Mercenary numbers are likewise almost the same in number. Then of course you have to make sure all the Mareschals, connectables and the Grand Turcopolier, who commanded the king's turcopoles, actually all spoke and liaised with each other." [110]

"So please, tell us more of Paul for surely he was found?" the wealthy tailor asked.

"I wish to hear of Alisha's poem," Ayleth remarked.

"Well I can let you read it if you wish...'tis inside the folder. 'Tis the small wax sealed envelope," the old man said and indicated with a slight nod at the leather folder. Slowly Gabirol looked inside until he saw a worn white envelope with a

broken seal upon it. He removed it and laid it flat upon the table. It was difficult to lay flat having once been rolled up for so long. "'Tis a single fold...so please just open it."

Gabirol gently opened the envelope to reveal Alisha's hand written poem. Ayleth leaned over to see it clearer. Some of the words had run slightly and it was covered in several patches of dirt. Ayleth bit her finger as Gabirol lifted it slightly to read. He looked at the old man as if to seek permission. He simply nodded yes.

"It reads in French...it says..." Gabirol started to read and cleared his throat. "'Tis a long poem but here goes." He paused. "Alone I stand just like you, my soul cut in two. Most understand not why I cry, for they can never know why, and I am weak, oft too broken to speak. When surrounded by the darkness of night, my guilt haunts me with the deepest of fright. My sin, 'twas upon a chance and so fast, but even in that moment, I knew it would not last. Your heart I did not count, for in that hour 'twas forsaken as if it did not matter, your soul I did shatter. Of secrets now I must keep, telling lies when looking in others' eyes so deep. 'Twas all my fault, your heart gone from me, locked away in some cold and lonely vault. I am lost in the wilderness of my broken soul, my shattered other half, I know not where...'tis a burden I cannot bear! But know this...my heart weeps tears of blood for the pain caused unto you, for just a moment in my despair and the darkest hour of my mind, I was lost and stupidly blind. 'Twas the time of greatest uncertainty and sorrow, and I threw away all of our tomorrows." Gabirol paused, quickly looking up before continuing. "I watched you leave, tears fell down my cheek, and you were gone, lost from me, my soul eternally to weep. Now, with just memories, the goodness of you lost, my heart yearns to turn back time once again for you to be mine. I beg forgiveness and pray you think upon what I have said, though I broke the vows of our sacred marital bed...but this heart beats for you alone, my eternal love far from dead. Take what time you must to consider my crime, and if you can forgive me, I will love you beyond the end of time. Cut our wedding vows loose if you must, but in me they will remain until I am returned to dust. And if the wound hath cut too deep, and you are mine no more to cherish and keep, then cast me from your life never to return, I will understand... and in the wilderness that is my soul, I shall forever weep."

Ayleth sighed heavily as the others sat in silence for a few minutes before Simon finally spoke up.

"You have her poem...how so?" he asked bluntly.

"I shall explain," the old man replied and sat himself up.

Plain of Moab, Kingdom of Jerusalem, December 24th 1186

Abi walked slowly, leading her horse toward the seated figure. It was Nicholas, the cold wind blowing around him, yet he refused to move, a dusting of snow lying upon his shoulders and head. For three weeks nearly he had remained at this location, refusing to leave. All Abi could do was visit him regularly and bring food and fresh water. His own horse stood silently nearby, its blankets a frozen white covered in snow. Red and yellow hues streaked across the darkening evening sky as Abi knelt down to check him, concerned he had perhaps frozen to death. Several times she gently rocked him before he finally looked up from the blankets wrapped around him. He opened his eyes, his beard and eyelashes full of frozen ice crystals. He squinted trying to focus upon Abi.

"You must finally call an end to this madness for otherwise you will surely die," Abi spoke softly.

"I care not, unless he returns," Nicholas replied, his voice dry.

"Well you should for Alisha does not want another death upon her hands and conscience…so you owe it to her to live. This is not what Paul would want either."

"I have made my last vow. I shall not return without him."

"Read the poem," Abi said and reached inside his blankets and grabbed the scroll tube he was holding with both hands. Too weak to resist her powerful grasp, she easily pulled it from him. "Just read it," she demanded and broke the end wax seal. He looked up at her in alarm and confusion. Quickly Abi removed the small vellum sheet, broke the wax seal and rolled off the crimson thread, keeping it in place, and opened it. She waved it in front of his eyes. Nicholas tried to shuffle backwards but his saddle stopped him. He raised himself to his knees and tried to look away but Abi thrust it hard against his chest. "Read it now whilst I saddle up your horse. Whether you wish to or not, you are coming back with me…one way or another. Tied to your horse if necessary for I will not let you perish and throw your precious life away like this. This is no fairytale romantic gesture…'tis pure stupidity."

Hesitantly, Nicholas held out the poem before him, and in the fading light began to read Alisha's words. He sighed as each and every word cut into him with both regret and pain. Resting upon his knees, he shook his head exhausted. He was too cold to even shiver, which Abi knew was a very dangerous sign.

"I wish with all my heart and soul these words were for me...but they are not," he sighed and closed his eyes. He could even smell the fragrance Alisha wore upon the poem. "But I know she never was mine and never will be. I am truly ashamed of all that I have caused and ruined."

"Then get up. Live...for yesterday is gone. Your past does not have to define you. And for what small measure of comfort this may afford you, Alisha does and always will have a special place reserved in her heart for you," Abi said as she lifted him to his feet. He could hardly stand. She sensed something and looked upwards. She paused as she looked around, the tall grasses sticking through the snow gently blowing back and forth. "And I would say now is probably opportune to put your Order's mantle back on."

"Why?" Nicholas asked, puzzled, trying to follow where she was looking.

"She speaks the truth," Paul said suddenly, behind them, making them both jump with surprise. Nicholas nearly collapsed seeing him stood before them. Paul had grown a full beard neatly cropped and he appeared to radiate a glow of well being. His face was serene almost. Even Abi had to look twice at him. "'Tis truly I."

Nicholas raised his hand out toward him shaking with emotion, his eyes welling with tears.

"Is it really you?" he asked and fell at Paul's feet and grabbed hold of his ankles, his forehead resting upon his boots. "Lord have mercy upon me and forgive me," he cried.

Abi put her hand upon her hip and looked at him, puzzled. Paul bent down and lifted Nicholas's hands away from his legs and knelt down in front of him. Nicholas would not look up until Paul gently raised his chin forcing Nicholas to face him but he kept his eyes shut tightly, tears rolling down his dirty face.

"My friend...we have all suffered greatly. I have learnt that there is no greater demonstration of the purest love, than to love without condition and expectation, for that is the highest most true love," Paul remarked and stared at Nicholas in silence until he opened his eyes. "And if there was any one man on this earth I would want Alisha to be with...it would be you, my friend. What is done, is done."

"'Tis not me she wants...'tis only you," Nicholas cried and lifted up Alisha's poem holding it with both hands. "Just you...," he said emotionally and pushed the poem for Paul to take.

Abi stood up straight, took a deep breath and had to check herself to stop herself from crying seeing the raw pain and genuine emotion within Nicholas.

"Nicholas…I know. But forever you are a part of our lives, as you always have been," Paul explained and lifted Nicholas to his feet.

"Read the poem, Paul," Abi ordered bluntly.

Paul opened the poem and studied the words carefully. In his mind all went silent as he became momentarily oblivious to his surroundings. Every word he read twice and each one echoed within him sensing the heartfelt and genuine emotion Alisha had put into every part of the poem. He knew she meant every word. He looked at Nicholas and part of him felt sorry for him, his pain so evident. But he also knew Nicholas would not wish to be pitied. He was a strong, courageous and noble man, now almost broken from his own guilt and regret. As he looked at him, he felt closer to him than any other man he knew, save perhaps Percival. Taqi was always going to be his best friend in many ways, but so much had changed over the years that he was almost a stranger to him now in many ways. But Nicholas…they were more alike than twin brothers almost, he thought. He looked toward the direction of Kerak, the sky almost black now.

"'Tis Christmas Day tomorrow. Can we make Kerak by daybreak?" he asked Abi. She looked at the weather on the eastern horizon then back toward Kerak.

"Of course," she replied and smiled.

"Then let us return…together," Paul remarked and then hugged Nicholas. "We all have family there to celebrate with. Better than this cold depressing place would you not agree?"

Nicholas looked at Paul in bewilderment. Paul raised his eyebrows questioningly. Emotionally and exhausted, Nicholas finally smiled and nodded his head yes.

Crac de Moab, Oultrajordain, Kingdom of Jerusalem, December 25th 1186

Abi rode ahead as Paul led Nicholas across the main drawbridge, their horses' hooves echoing out across the main courtyard. The outer wall guards had already rung the alarm bell as they had approached alerting the night guards who were already forming up. Brother Teric and Upside came running into the courtyard, the ground covered in ice patches and snow. Princess Stephanie came running from her chambers, down the stairs and was already tying up her coat alarmed at the bells ringing so early, the sun barely shining through the breaks in the heavy overcast clouds above them.

"Well fuck me sideways," Brother Teric blurted out as Princess Stephanie ran up to his side. "Sorry, My Lady…'tis Brother Nicholas…and if I am not mistaken, 'tis Paul with them," he explained and smiled as Upside stood still, amazed.

"I shall fetch Alisha," Princes Stephanie replied excitedly and quickly ran back up the main steps and into the central keep.

Thomas came running out with Luke and Mathew closely followed by the rest of his men. Abi pulled up just in front of Brother Teric and nodded at him with a large smile upon her face.

"You did not kill each other then?" Upside called out as Paul and Nicholas drew up beside Abi. "Though you look like utter shit," he said, looking at Nicholas, and laughed, relieved to see him.

Paul dismounted and helped Nicholas down, who was so weak he could hardly stand. His face was wind burnt and his lips cracked. Upside approached and immediately took Nicholas's weight. He looked at Paul and saw a change in him. He indicated with his finger around his own mouth to make reference to Paul's new beard.

"Thank the Lord this holiest of days…thank the Lord," Thomas said and grabbed Paul with both hands and just stared at him in silence for several minutes. "Is all good between you?" he asked, looking at Nicholas quickly.

"Yes…yes it is," Paul answered and smiled at Nicholas, who nodded back in agreement silently.

Wearing the fur lined cloak Kratos had given him, Paul looked broader and with new boots he had also been given, he looked taller too.

Stewart and Ishmael appeared walking from the stables, having been preparing for another day out searching for Paul. Stewart's jaw dropped seeing him and he stopped in his tracks. He blinked and shook his head in disbelief. Paul nodded at him. As soon as he did, Stewart walked to him fast and then hugged him hard.

"'Tis really you isn't it?" Stewart asked, stepped back and looked at Paul at arm's length. "Look at you…where, where have you been…are you okay…does Father know…are…," he asked fast and laughed with relief.

"Papa!" Ailia suddenly called out loudly as she rushed down the steps leading from the main keep doorway, pulling Princess Stephanie behind her, who was trying to keep hold of her hand. Ailia flicked her arm, broke free and ran across the courtyard and jumped straight up into Paul's arms, wrapping hers around his neck tightly. "You are home…I told Mama you would be."

Paul held her tightly and closed his eyes. Stewart turned to face Tenno as he stepped down the main stairs into view, Alisha nervously holding his arm for support. She looked incredibly anxious and was visibly shaking as they began to walk toward Paul and Nicholas. Paul, sensing the mood had gone silent, opened his eyes. The first thing he saw was Alisha, her eyes locked on his. His vision seemed to polarise upon her and just her, the rest around him appearing as if in a tunnel. He looked at her like a blind man seeing the sun for the first time. He could see and sense the tension and fear in her eyes as she walked closer. In her mind a thousand questions were running through her thoughts. He looked different, was he okay, had he read her poem, did he still want her, did Nicholas and he fight? She felt sick but was oblivious to the men around her. Her heart beat so hard she thought she would faint before she would reach him. When she did, she stopped. Ailia turned to look at her and smiled still hugging him tightly. Alisha went to speak but the words would not come out. His eyes searched hers and she felt he could see into her very soul at that moment. Gently and slowly she rubbed her finger down his face across his old barely visible scar and across his new beard. She let out a slight nervous laugh. He was real. This was not a dream. But had he come back to her? Paul took her hand in his and held it against his face.

"'Tis Christmas after all…a time when families should be together… would you not agree?" Paul finally spoke quietly, the lump in his own throat nearly stopping him from speaking and looked at her intently, then Stewart.

"Paul…Paul…Paul!" Theodoric shouted out loudly as he ran across the courtyard nearly falling over slipping on an ice patch, Tenno giving him a disapproving glance as he pushed past Thomas and his men. Sister Lucy was rushing up as fast as she could behind him. "Jesus Christ!" he exclaimed out of breath.

"No, still just Paul," Paul joked.

Theodoric looked at Alisha, Paul, Stewart, Nicholas and then back at Paul and shook his head.

"Will you be staying?" Thomas interrupted and asked.

"Only if this speaks truth as I believe it does?" Paul asked and pulled out Alisha's poem.

Alisha let out a sigh and looked at him. Her eyes immediately filled with tears and she struggled not to cry.

"You know it does," she finally spoke, her voice sounding the softest and sweetest he had ever heard her speak.

"Then come here...," Paul said and pulled her close with his left arm whilst still holding Ailia. Alisha put her arms around him, closed her eyes and held him tightly, the fragrance of her hair never having smelt so welcoming, Paul thought. He looked at Nicholas and both nodded an acknowledgement. "Thank you," he said to Nicholas.

Alisha looked up at Nicholas. He looked dirty and exhausted but he smiled at them both as Upside supported him. Nicholas nearly collapsing, Ishmael quickly supported his other side and smiled at Paul, a tear in his own eye, relieved to see him back safe. Paul simply nodded. Princess Stephanie looked on, her hands to her mouth almost unable to breathe herself. She was so relieved and happy to see Paul returned. Sister Lucy went up to Paul, kissed the side of his cheek and silently beckoned him to follow her. With his arm around Alisha, and carrying Ailia, they followed her as Theodoric started to check Nicholas over. Thomas approached Nicholas and stared hard at him for a few moments.

"You, my friend...you will now only need to learn the language...well done!" Thomas said and patted Nicholas hard on the arm. "Very well done."

"But...but I did...," Nicholas started to explain.

"You did well and all that was required of you...and more, Nicholas...do you understand me?" Abi asked. Puzzled he looked at her intently. "Now go, clean up and rest," she ordered. Stewart acknowledged Nicholas and bowed his head to him. As Upside led Nicholas away, Tenno stood close beside Abi. "'Tis perhaps best you ask me later...if you can handle me again," she said and smiled at Tenno. He took her hand and held it tightly.

ꙮ

Inside Alisha's chambers, Sister Lucy ushered Ailia into her side room to get her properly prepared for the day but she was so excited she was jumping up and down and all over the room. Sister Lucy quietly closed the adjoining door. Alisha stood nervously beside the large window as Paul removed his heavy fur lined cloak and placed it upon the bed. Alisha fiddled with her fingers and bit her bottom lip as she always did when nervous or apprehensive.

"Are...are we okay?" she finally asked. "And do you," she paused and took a deep breath. "Do you forgive me?"

Paul walked over to her and clasped her hands in his. He looked into her beautiful eyes full of emotion and he simply wished to kiss and hold her again, but he knew that it would be some time before he could again, for to do so now seemed somehow wrong. He wanted to hold her again when she was ready and wanted him. As she looked at him, she wanted to show her love, but she did not know if he wanted her still that way after having lain with Nicholas.

"My dear Ali...'tis I who should be asking for forgiveness. Look what I have put us through...and Arri...," Paul said, his voice calm and reasoned.

Alisha ran her hand through his hair and looked at him. It was Paul but somehow he seemed so different at the same time, and it was not just his beard.

"Forgive you...I have said the cruellest of things and done the worst of things to you, yet you ask for my forgiveness," she remarked as a tear ran down her cheek. "You are the noblest and kindest person I know...and... and..."

"The only cruel thing you could do to me, is if you stopped loving me."

"Never!" she replied instantly.

"I know this all seems and feels a little awkward, and we shall have to talk through all of what has happened, in time...but know this too. Tenno once told me that in his country, when something is broken, they do not throw it away or replace it...they repair it but they also fill the cracks with gold in reverence to it. We may feel awkward now...but if you feel just half of what I feel, we shall be okay." Paul looked at her intently. Her almost white flawless skin, her eyes open wide searching his. "And I burnt all the parchments," he stated, realising he had not informed her.

Suddenly Alisha clasped her hands around Paul's face and kissed him, her lips pressing firmly against his. He raised his hands to hold hers and kissed her back. Her heart pounding, after a minute she pulled away breathless and looked into his eyes searching his every thought.

"And as Sister Lucy told me," Alisha said still short of breath. "What comes easy won't last...and what lasts won't come easy."

"Amen to that," Paul replied and held her in his arms tightly. He kissed the side of her head, just seeing the small scar still visible upon her neck. 'Thank you, Lord,' he said to himself and hugged her even tighter and just held her.

Port of La Rochelle, France, Melissae Inn, spring 1191

"Is Paul not being too needy or too forgiving?" Ayleth asked.

"Some will say that...but true love, not the romantic idealistic love you hear of in songs and poems, especially those of the travelling troubadours, but real genuine belonging love, it does conquer all and do not let anyone tell you otherwise," the old man answered.

"What did Reynald have to say to Paul's return then?" Gabirol asked.

"He was still away, staying mainly in Montreal and raiding Muslim caravans. But he would be back in time for the fall of the first weeks of the New Year. That was something Paul was uncomfortable about and wished to make plans to travel back to France with his family as expediently as possible."

3 - 3

"And what of Nicholas?" Sarah asked.

"He was accepted back into his Order by Brother Teric with open arms. And with hostilities increasing daily with Saladin, thanks to Reynald, he, along with Stewart, Brother Upside and most of the other Templars, was ordered to return to Jerusalem."

"Where was Master Jakelin at this time?" Gabirol asked, puzzled.

"He had already left for Jerusalem along with Lord Balian."

"But all the time Paul was away...you say you do not know what happened or what he learnt?" Peter asked.

"No for he never spoke of it nor wrote it within his journal...save the few lines as explained about the new Order. But he was most definitely somehow different."

"Where was Percival when Paul returned?" the Templar asked.

"Percival...he had set out alone to search for Paul by travelling south. It was a dangerous thing to do, but he felt certain Paul was that way. And strangely enough he did find the old, but empty and long since disused, cave dwelling on Jabal Al Lawz that Kratos and Paul had used...it would be several days before Percival returned to Kerak," the old man explained.

"So, Percival, by whatever means finds Paul's location, but he is not there... and yet by the time scales involved, Percival would have been there when Paul was there...but he wasn't no?" Gabirol quizzed.

"Maybe they were there but in a different time or realm as has been explained... yes?" Simon remarked. Sarah looked at him, surprised, but then nodded in agreement with him.

"As I have said...he never explained nor revealed exactly what happened," the old man answered.

"I bet it was a Christmas little Ailia would not forget?" Miriam said and squeezed the Templar's hand.

"The best present she wanted was back with them. That was the only present she had prayed and wished for at the end of her bed every night...watched by Alisha, her heart breaking every time she saw her do it. Later that Christmas Day, Paul gave Alisha a small simple white gold pendant to attach to her small Mother Goddess pendant she still wore. 'Twas like a figure of eight symbol representing infinity... and he spoke freely and openly of Arri just as he had been advised to by Kratos."

"Did Paul return to the marital bed?" Ayleth asked, curious.

"Yes he did...and as personal as it may sound, they did not resume physical intimacy. 'Twas agreed that it would prove later she was not with child, but also, there was an unspoken agreement between them, that the time was not right...but the closeness they shared as they simply held each other and talked was on a far deeper level of intimacy than they had ever experienced before. As ridiculous as this may sound, when twin flames reunite, the 'one soul' vibrational alignment is the ultimate joining of two people. It is and was in essence what the mystics would call the perfect 'Alchemical Marriage' because of the reunification of the Divine Masculine and the Divine Feminine in perfect harmony. Paul had learnt this was possible from what Kratos had taught him and his gift to Alisha, the figure eight of eternal union, it being the perfect symbol representing this Divine Reunion of equilibrium. The purity of 'one soul' essence at peace and home with the divine source of all," the old man explained.

"That is beautiful," Miriam remarked and smiled at the Templar as he pulled her close and kissed her softly on her shoulder.

"But Alisha still made love to Nicholas. I find that too much to forgive," Peter remarked.

"Let me explain this as best as I am able without sounding crude or embarrassing our ladies here," the old man said and paused as he sat himself up again. "The physical act of joining, is just that...physical penetrative sex, which ultimately is in

itself very superficial. But deep emotional penetration of the heart, that is love... which is far more significant and beautiful...and yet even deeper and further still is the third kind of penetration, that of when two consciousnesses meet, merge and truly become as one," the old man explained and looked at all of them in turn. 'Twas that third stage Alisha and Paul shared."

They all sat in silence for a few short moments pondering the old man's words, Miriam smiling and holding the Templar's hand tightly as he smiled back at her.

"So Paul decided it was time to return to France...back to here no?" the Genoese sailor asked, breaking the silence, and looked around the room indicating with his opened hands.

"Yes, that was the plan," the old man replied.

"But I fear all did not go to plan?" Gabirol remarked.

"Not quite," the old man sighed.

Crac de Moab, Oultrajordain, Kingdom of Jerusalem, January 6th 1187

Alisha, Paul and Ailia had spent the last few days mainly alone as they talked through all that had happened to them and about Arri. The weather had been unseasonably harsh with snow and constant hail, the roads turning into quagmires that limited the activities of the knights and pilgrims. Percival returned in time for the New Year, but celebrations were very restricted with concerns over a coming all out war with Saladin rumoured everywhere. When Paul greeted him, they said nothing, just embraced with a hug and acknowledged each other. Time to discuss what had happened was not necessary between them. Nicholas had spent the time recovering and observing his daily prayers and vespers with a renewed sense of purpose and kept mainly out of the way of Alisha and Paul out of respect. The 6th of January was their wedding anniversary, a fact not lost on all present, but rather than keep the day quiet, Theodoric had organised a surprise celebration for them that evening.

The main stone vaulted banquet hall was lit by many candles and lanthorns. Several large torches flickered their light across the main stained glass window, whilst a large fire blazed away in the main ornate open fire place. The fine drapery and tapestries hanging from the walls added to a sense of warmth and comfort. A large table ran the length of the hall, with Princess Stephanie stood at the head waiting for Theodoric to bring in Alisha and Paul. They had prepared a large feast and surprise for them and even Thomas and his men had all turned out in their finest robes. A very much recovered Nicholas stood with Upside and Brother Teric whilst Sister Lucy hurriedly finished off the centre table presentation of a sword set between two large branches taken from a bush grown within the castle's own allotment. Several maids busied themselves finishing off the table. The main double doors opened slightly as Theodoric peered inside. Princess Stephanie smiled and nodded at him all was ready. Tenno and Percival stepped into the hall and held the two doors open as Theodoric led Alisha and Paul in, their eyes shut. Paul held Ailia in his left arm, but she had her eyes wide open in anticipation. Abi walked in behind them as Theodoric led them to the far end of the table where two high back chairs had been placed side by side. Sister Lucy helped Alisha to sit down, still with her eyes shut, as Theodoric took Ailia and sat Paul down.

"You can open them now," Princess Stephanie said aloud from the opposite end of the table.

Ailia giggled as Alisha and Paul opened their eyes to see the hall and prepared table. Both smiled and looked at each other when a side door opened and Stewart backed out of the kitchen area carrying a large tray of food. As he approached, he smiled at them both.

"I never got to attend your wedding day or give you a suitable present, so this eve, and as it is your wedding anniversary, we all gather to give thanks for your return and to celebrate you as a family," Stewart commented and placed the tray down in front of them. "And we have some gifts to bestow upon you," he smiled and stood up straight and took Ailia's little hand and pulled her close as Thomas and his men all filed past and formed up in a long line. They turned their backs to them and started to pull up their cloaks. "Theodoric has a few words to say to you."

Theodoric walked around the table to stand beside Thomas, the only one still looking at Alisha and Paul. He clasped his hands together and looked awkward, unusual for him. Sister Lucy winked at him. He coughed and cleared his throat.

"Erm…well, where to begin? First of all we must thank Princess Stephanie for allowing us to use this great hall," he said as she bowed her head slightly and smiled at him. "I had a great speech all worked out but I am afraid that has gone out of that window," he started to explain, Ailia looking over to the window. "Much has happened over the past few years and we have all experienced many things...but today, we would like to honour the two people who have without doubt touched and influenced all of us in this room in ways they cannot fully imagine, nor in fact even fathom." Alisha looked across at Nicholas. He smiled and nodded at her. She squeezed Paul's hand tightly and looked back at Theodoric. "You have both taught us so much about ourselves and it is impossible to put a value upon that or ever say thank you enough. You have given us purpose, direction, wise council and guidance in matters we can never hope to fully understand....and...and..."

"What he is trying to say is," Thomas interjected and moved forwards, "we owe you more than we can repay. Not in trinkets, gold or material wealth, but with a priceless treasure that beats in all our hearts. You give us hope."

Alisha looked down in sorrow feeling like a fraud almost. Paul took her hand in his.

"Ali...look up. There is nothing to feel ashamed of here in this company," Paul whispered.

With tears welling in her eyes, she looked up at Thomas again and feigned a smile.

"But what this old sentimental fool beside me does not realise or appreciate is that it was all down to him, that very first meeting we had and the many subsequent ones where he has almost bored us to death with his teachings," Thomas explained and put his arm around Theodoric, who looked surprised. "This old 'fat' man here is the reason we are all together. I think no one would disagree with that?" Paul stood up and nodded his head in agreement. Sister Lucy put her hand to her mouth emotionally seeing how Theodoric was taken aback by his comments. "I am sure Alisha and Paul will not be offended if we make this also a celebration for him. He has taught us so much...and, as we are an army of kings as he keeps telling us...then an army needs a banner...its own sigil or emblem."

Upon those words, starting with Luke, then Mathew, followed by the rest of Thomas's men, they all started to remove their upper clothing until just their shirts remained.

"Hey, old, fair enough...but fat, no...and please do not expose your backsides and declare a full moon emblem, I pray not!" Theodoric joked but was clearly emotional.

"No...'tis the emblem you have upon your back and as Upside also has,"

Thomas explained. All of them then pulled their shirts up over their heads to reveal they all now had the same tattoo across their shoulders and down their backs of the tree-winged sword image. Beautifully executed with green, black and blue inks they all looked perfect. Theodoric gasped in surprise. For several moments he stood speechless, tears welling in his eyes. "Theo, lost for words for once?" Thomas laughed.

Slowly Theodoric walked along the line of men, looking at their tattoos, shaking his head, overwhelmed with the gesture. Sister Lucy walked over to him and held his hand as he could not speak. Alisha looked at the sword set in the middle of the table with the tree branches set either side mimicking the tattoo image.

"Well it looks like I will need a new bigger one doing now," Upside stated, breaking the silence in the room.

"In time, we shall have a small emblem placed above them denoting our origins…our homeland as you likewise have that small red flag upon yours," Thomas remarked to Theodoric.

"And…and you have this tattoo also?" Theodoric asked Thomas emotionally.

"Of course. Who do think went first?" Thomas answered and turned his back to him and pulled up his shirt to reveal his tattoo.

"An army of kings," Paul commented as he started to walk along the line. As he passed them, they each turned around to face him.

"Aye…," Thomas replied. "And we are your army…to serve you and protect you wherever you decide to go."

Alisha cupped her hands over her mouth deeply touched by his words and their actions but also painfully embarrassed.

"Does that make me a princess?" Ailia asked excitedly, looking up at Stewart.

Princess Stephanie walked around the table and knelt beside Alisha and took her hand.

"An army of kings indeed," she said softly and smiled at her. "And you as their queen."

"And these tattoos are a permanent reminder to each of us never to fail you again as we did with Arri," Thomas said and stood up straight.

"This is not right," Alisha replied emotionally, shaking her head no. "This is your castle, your kingdom and I am not worthy of this, any of this. You all honour me too much…for I am no queen."

"Oh my dear girl, you are so much more worthy than this. This, this is all just stone...cold stone at that. I am no queen, and never will be, but you," Princess Stephanie said and paused. "You always have been a queen...you just never realised it, but now you must acknowledge it."

"A queen of hearts for sure," Nicholas whispered, Upside immediately elbowing him in his side and grinning.

"I say we eat and drink...," Percival said loudly and closed the main doors. As Thomas and his men started to cover themselves, Theodoric playfully punched Thomas muttering comments about old men and not to call him fat. "Are you okay?" Percival asked as he walked past Nicholas.

"Yes. I am good. And privileged to be here," he replied quietly. "I still cannot fathom why he forgives me and lets me stay."

"'Tis simple. You can tell a lot about a person by what they choose to see in you," Upside replied quietly. "He clearly is a good man and therefore sees the good he knows is in you."

"Do you think we would be allowed to have such a tattoo in time?" Nicholas asked, looking at Percival.

"Got mine already," Upside said and winked.

"Yes...but yours is rather small by comparison," Nicholas joked.

"Never had any complaints so far," he replied, joking.

As Percival took his place at the table, Nicholas could not help but look at Alisha. He knew that never again would he ever hold her...but he felt grateful, blessed and immensely proud to know her and Paul. He felt even luckier that he was allowed to stay. Abi and Tenno came and stood beside him just as Theodoric coughed and hit a silver spoon against one of the main wine jugs on the table to get everyone's attention.

"Words fail me as you saw...but before we start I would simply like to impart a final word...or two...that I was once told," he said.

"Long ago old 'fat' man," Thomas joked and had to duck as Theodoric swiped the spoon at him.

"Remember this always and wherever we end up," Theodoric said and paused. "What we do for ourselves dies with us, but what we do for others remains forever. And the truly strong do not exploit the weak, they do not look down upon them, they help them up."

Paul immediately recognised those words as spoken to him by Kratos. His mind wandered momentarily back to the time and all the things he had been shown and taught by him. His path was not so different from

Theodoric's he knew now. When Paul took his seat beside Alisha, she took his hand and kissed it softly. Princess Stephanie smiled at them as she beckoned Ailia to sit near her. When Paul looked around the table at everyone seated or just sitting down, he felt tremendous pride in all of them. He truly felt he was in exulted company. Nicholas looked at him and they acknowledged each other with a slight nod. Alisha thought back to their wedding day in La Rochelle. She sighed heavily as she remembered Firgany and how proud he was that day. She prayed he was still proud of her. The wedding seemed so long ago now. But now as she sat with Paul, a different Paul, her heart ached for him and she found it almost impossible to contain her emotions and not cry. She clenched his hand tightly beneath the table and looked at him. She could not be any prouder than at that moment, and despite all that had happened, she loved him the more for he still wanted her as his wife. Paul turned to face her and as he studied every aspect of her beautiful face, her smile, her eyes and her silken hair, the many words of Kratos echoed through his mind. With Ailia sat by her side smiling at them both, he wished he could freeze that moment in time.

Port of La Rochelle, France, Melissae Inn, spring 1191

"A great time was had that night by all," the old man sighed. "Theodoric I am afraid to say drank far too much and could not remember the last half of the evening. The fact the men had all got the same tattoo affected him deeply. Nicholas did not stay long after the meal and left with Upside and even Tenno and Abi sat together, not afraid to let it be known they were clearly together," the old man laughed.

"But Paul was different you say?" Gabirol asked.

"Aye he was...just something about his very presence and look. 'Twas not a sad look. 'Tis hard to describe, but you could see it in his eyes. He knew things beyond our normal comprehension. He had a calmness and set look of contentment allied to a fierce determination...a man who knew what he had to do, and would do it."

"You mean the codes...and the new Order?" Simon asked.

"Yes you could say that."

"I want to know if he was tempted with gold and other women as Kratos had offered," Sarah asked loudly.

"I can only tell you that Kratos offered him the choice of moving to another land where he would have power, authority, gold and as many wives as he wished...

and the offer was a real one. But it all meant nothing to Paul without Alisha and Ailia. Like Princess Stephanie knew only too well, she had the position, wealth and power...but it was all empty of any real worth. 'Tis why she longed for Paul herself. Speaking of which, after the anniversary meal, Paul returned to her the poem she had given him years previously. Do you recall the poem about riding seahorses together?" the old man asked. "She took the poem back and understood why he had returned it, but that did not stop her heart from aching. She adored Alisha in no small way, taking the poem back was a way of also accepting Paul would never be hers."

"So even after all those years, she still harboured feelings for him?" Ayleth asked.

"Yes...more so in fact," the old man answered and moved in his chair. "'Twas on the ninth of January that Reynald returned to Kerak with Gerard. Reynald knew of Alisha and Paul's loss. Having lost his own daughter, it was common ground almost...the grief that is. But before he returned, Paul was able to spend some time with Theodoric...to discuss certain things Paul had been taught and seen."

"Such as?" Gabirol asked, curious.

"Well, and this is according to Theodoric's account, Paul, like Nicholas, started to learn Elfdalian. Much of what Paul spoke of, Theodoric was not allowed to write down but it dealt with the symbolism of the Grail. How it's set up was linked to the seven sisters star constellation, as in the Pleiades, and the belt stars of Orion. That from the region of Orion, many souls are born...but also how all ancient sites encompass within their design and layout the constellation of Orion, the sword of Orion, but also the Pleiades. How the symbol for them combined is set out and identical to that of the Holy Grail...the cup symbolism especially and the womb of the sacred feminine. But alas, the wealth of information surrounding all of that and what he learnt was not written down save just a couple of drawings he made, which in themselves mean very little," the old man explained and sighed sadly. "But, as Theodoric informed his friend within the Carthusian Order, all that Paul knew and learnt would one day be revealed fully as our world passes into the fifth age of man, when again the Phoenix flies."

"What or who are the Carthusian Order?" Peter asked, puzzled.

"'Tis probably more well known to you as the Order of Saint Bruno. 'Tis a Roman Catholic religious order of enclosed monastics. 'Twas founded by Saint Bruno of Cologne in 1084 and includes both monks and nuns. The order has its own Rule, called the Statutes, rather than the Rule of Saint Benedict, and combines eremitical and cenobitic life," the old man started to explain.

"What does cenobitic mean?" Simon asked.

"Cenobitic monasticism is a tradition that stresses community life where the monk is regulated by a religious rule, a collection of precepts. The older style of monasticism is to live as a hermit, which is called eremitic. Cenobitic monasticism exists in various religions, though Buddhist and Christian cenobitic monasticism are the most prominent. The name Carthusian is derived from the Chartreuse Mountains; Saint Bruno built his first hermitage in the valley of these mountains in the French Alps. The word charterhouse, which is the English name for a Carthusian monastery, is derived from the same source. The motto of the Carthusians is 'Stat crux dum volvitur orbis', which is Latin for 'The Cross is steady while the world is turning', which is a symbol with much hidden knowledge behind it."

"How so?" Gabirol asked.

"'Tis connected to the symbols of the Grail, Orion and the Pleiades...if you look within the folder, you will find a symbol of their Order complete with seven stars, but it also represents the world we live upon as spinning around a central cross, but also our very bodies being made upon the cross," the old man answered and gestured to the folder.

Gabirol opened it and removed several sheets until he found the image the old man was referring to with seven stars upon.

Fig. 66: Carthusian Cross.

"Will we ever get to learn of these symbols and what Paul learnt?" the Templar asked.

"If you accept the charge of the commission contained within those documents you now hold, then I strongly believe you will all indeed learn of much of it...as well as such matters like the symbolism behind the true Noah story, which represented not just one Ark, but many along with all the mathematical codes within its story. The dimensions of the actual Ark as detailed within the Bible are commensurate with the dimensions of both the Ark of the Covenant and the actual so-called sarcophagus set within the King's Chamber of the Great Pyramid. As explained previously, mathematics and harmonics are the only truly universal languages guaranteed to span the millennia of time intact...and encoded within religions...so even when certain parts added by men...read like insane rules, it is still a vehicle that carries that message. But even now in our time, religion has been reduced to 'moralism' and a question of faith only following it blindly. Once cherished doctrines are now just simple formulas and routine practices, devoid of any higher meaning. One day, for there will come that day, many numbers of people will view the great religions of this world as being unable to answer the most fundamental questions of existence. Yet throughout history we find people convinced the great religions are a necessary 'outer shell' veiling a more sacred and ancient wisdom that alone can reveal humanity's real origin, purpose and destiny, which to a large degree is true, for hidden behind vital religious practices and doctrines is the esoteric or occult knowledge. That something is hidden because of its immense value, so reverently concealed from the prying eyes of the profane. But this hidden thing may also have achieved its sequestered position because the Powers That Be have found it wanting. Either it is a threat and must be buried, or simply useless, and so forgotten. Paul intended to make sure it would never be forgotten. But at that moment in time, he had to concentrate on plans to return to La Rochelle...and before Reynald returned...but alas Reynald did return before they left." [111]

"How did Reynald react to Alisha and Paul?" Sarah asked.

"Well, Paul was not only busy trying to organise passage for Alisha, Ailia and himself, but of course Theodoric, Sister Lucy, Thomas and all of his men. Not only difficult during that time but also costly and Reynald was more than happy to relieve him of gold to help him do so."

2 - 6

"What of Tenno and Percival?" Ayleth asked.

"Of course they would come with them. That went without saying," the old man smiled.

"I wish to learn and know more of these strange balls of light that seem to visit Alisha and Paul. What exactly are they?" Sarah asked, changing the subject direction.

"Paul was informed that as this world of ours transits from this age of Pisces to Aquarius, identical balls of light will return over Jerusalem. They will make themselves seen just as they were when Jesus ascended and where angels said he would return the same way. Matthew 24:27 'For just as the lightning comes from the east and flashes even to the west, so will the coming of the Son of Man be. He was also taught that there was a far greater code hidden in the Hebrew bible...but we do not have the means to decode it in our time, but the means will become available to man, yet even then he will ignore it for many years," the old man sighed.

"Surely if he spent so much time with Kratos alone, he must have learnt much about him too?" Gabirol asked.

"Oh he did. He learnt that Kratos was one of the nine," the old man answered and smiled seeing the puzzled look on Simon's face.

"Who are the nine?" the wealthy tailor asked.

"The Nine Unknown Men. 'Tis an ancient Indian tradition from the time of the Emperor Asoka, who reigned in India from 273 BC. He was the grandson of Chandragupta, who was the first to unify India. He lost a hundred thousand men in a great battle against the Kalingians, after which he was overcome by the horror of war so that he renounced the idea of trying to integrate the rebellious people, declaring that the only true conquest was to win men's hearts by observance of the laws of duty and piety, because the Sacred Majesty desired that all living creatures should enjoy security, peace and happiness and be free to live as they pleased. Asoka was a convert to Buddhism by the way and spread this religion throughout India and his entire empire, which included Malaya, Ceylon and Indonesia. Later he respected all religious sects. He preached vegetarianism, abolished alcohol and the slaughter of animals. Inspired, he wished to forbid men from ever using their intelligence for evil purposes. During his reign natural science, past and present, was vowed to secrecy. And so for the next two thousand years, all researches, ranging from the structure of matter to the techniques employed in collective psychology, were to be hidden behind the mystical mask of a people commonly believed to be exclusively concerned with ecstasy and supernatural phenomena. It was Asoka who founded the most powerful secret society on earth: that of the Nine Unknown Men."

"Well they must have been very secret for I have never heard of them," Simon joked.

"No neither I," the Templar said, looking at the old man intently, trying to study him behind his raised hood.

"Some claim they can still communicate with the 'council of nine'...but as I have tried to explain already, can you imagine people like Reynald obtaining advanced wisdom and knowledge along with powerful tools? Likewise, the original nine would not allow methods of destruction to fall into the hands of unqualified persons, but would allow the pursuit of knowledge which would benefit mankind. Their numbers would be renewed by co-option, so as to preserve the secrecy of techniques handed down from ancient times. There are but a few examples of when the Nine Unknown Men made contact with the outer world. One even included the Pope Sylvester the Second, known also by the name of Gerbert d'Aurillac. Born in the Auvergne in 920 (died 1003) Gerbert was a Benedictine monk, professor at the University of Rheims, Archbishop of Ravenna and Pope by the grace of Otho the Third. He is supposed to have spent some time in Spain, after which a mysterious voyage brought him to India where he is reputed to have acquired various kinds of skills which stupefied his entourage. For example, he possessed in his palace a bronze head which answered Yes or No to questions put to it on politics or the general position of Christianity. According to Sylvester the Second this was a perfectly simple operation corresponding to a two-figure calculation, and was performed by an automaton. This 'magic' head was destroyed when Sylvester died, and all the information it imparted carefully concealed. In terms of education, there has arguably been no other pope who has more influenced his time than Sylvester. In one generation, he succeeded in introducing to the monastery schools Arabic knowledge of mathematics and astronomy. Sylvester also commissioned multiple copies of ancient scientific instruments to be distributed including the rediscovered abacus and armillary sphere. Sylvester established new higher standards of education using the basis of the 'trivium' of grammar, logic and rhetoric. In all fields of science during his day, he was a man ahead of his time introducing for the first time the hydraulic organ at Reims Cathedral. But Sylvester died in 1012 having never set foot once in Rome."

"You are saying that this so-called pope was influenced by the nine, or at least one of them?" Gabirol asked.

"Yes, yes he was. All I can say is that Paul likewise met one of the nine...hence why I state it was Kratos himself, but that was all he would say on the matter and that they used a different language...and that they had nine books, each covering a different aspect, such as the technique of propaganda and psychological warfare. The second book was on physiology. It explained, among other things,

how it is possible to kill a man by touching him, death being caused by a reversal of the nerve-impulse. Martial arts of self defence and unarmed combat such as Tenno taught were but aspects taken from these original teachings. The third volume was a study on biology, and dealt especially with protective measures and the infinitely small that we cannot presently see. The fourth was concerned with the transmutation of metals. There is a legend that in times of drought, temples and religious relief organisations received large quantities of fine gold from a secret source. The fifth volume contains a study of all means of communication, terrestrial and other worldly, and remember these were supposedly written 250 BC...The sixth expounds the secrets of levitation, as in weightlessness, and of course, as a consequence, flight. The seventh contains the most exhaustive cosmogony known to humanity. The eighth deals with light. But the ninth volume, on sociology, gives the rules for the evolution of societies, and the means of foretelling their decline. Hence how and why prophecy can be used and works. Avoiding all forms of religious, social or political agitations, deliberately and perfectly concealed from the public eye, the nine were the incarnation of the ideal man of science, serenely aloof, but conscious of his moral obligations. Having the power to mould the destiny of the human race, just like the Arch Druids of old, but refraining from its exercise, this secret society is the finest tribute imaginable to freedom of the most exalted kind. Looking down from the watchtower of their hidden glory, these Nine Unknown Men watched civilisations being born, destroyed and re-born again, tolerant rather than indifferent, and ready to come to the rescue, but always observing that rule of silence that is the mark of human greatness."

"So just like Kratos?" Ayleth asked.

"So Kratos is one of the nine?" Gabirol followed up.

"I think it would be a safe bet to argue that point as highly probable," the old man replied. "He probably helped initiate the nine in the first place."

"And so he would have access and use of any such flying machine?" Peter asked.

"Let me just state that what we know about ancient Indian flying vehicles comes from authentic ancient Indian sources themselves...written texts that have come down to us through the centuries. There are many well known ancient Indian Epics, literally hundreds of them. Many still not translated. Ashoka was aware how devastating wars using such advanced vehicles and other advanced weapons were as they had destroyed the ancient Indian 'Rama Empire' several thousand years before."

"But what force could make machines fly?" Miriam asked.

"Several types...but according to the Indian writings, it was a form of levitation

connected to the 'laghima', that unknown power of the ego existing in man's physiological makeup, a force strong enough to counteract all the forces that pull us downwards. According to Hindu Yogis, it is this 'laghima' which enables a person to levitate. Many writings detail how men could be sent to other worlds as well as reveal the secret of 'antima', 'the cap of invisibility' and 'garima', 'how to become as heavy as a mountain of lead'. One of the great Indian epics, the Ramayana, does have a highly detailed story of a trip to the moon in a Vimana, or 'Astra' and in fact details a battle on the moon with an Asvin airship. But if we go further back in time, to the so-called 'Rama Empire' of Northern India, they developed at least fifteen thousand years ago, on the Indian sub-continent, a nation of many large, sophisticated cities, many of which are still to be found in the deserts of northern and western India. Rama existed, apparently, parallel to the so-called Atlantean civilisation and was ruled by enlightened Priest Kings who governed the cities. The seven greatest capital cities of Rama were known in classical Hindu texts as 'The Seven Rishi Cities'. According to ancient Indian texts, the people had flying machines which were called 'Vimanas' as explained already. The ancient Indian Epic describes a Vimana as a double-deck, circular craft with portholes and a dome. Have you ever wondered why so many holy buildings are designed with domes? Anyway, these flying machines flew with the speed of the wind and gave forth a melodious sound. There were at least four different types of Vimana; some saucer shaped, others like long cylinders. The ancient Indian texts on Vimanas are so numerous, it would take volumes to relate what they had to say. The ancient Indians, who manufactured these ships themselves, wrote entire flight manuals on the control of them, many of which are still in existence, and some have even been translated into English."

"And this is all true?" Ayleth asked.

"Every word I swear it. The Samara Sutradhara is a scientific treatise dealing with every possible angle of air travel in a Vimana. There are 230 stanzas dealing with the construction, take off, cruising for thousands of miles, normal and forced landings, and even possible collisions with birds. Other writings, many hidden by the Church, deal with the operation of Vimanas and include information on the steering, precautions for long flights, protection from storms and lightning and how to switch the drive to another form of free energy. The Vaimanika Sastra or Vymaanika-Shaastra has eight chapters with diagrams, describing three types of flying machine, including apparatus that could neither catch on fire nor break. It also mentions thirty-one essential parts of these vehicles and sixteen materials from which they are constructed, which absorb light and heat for which reason they were

considered suitable for the construction of Vimanas. Vimanas took off vertically, and were capable of hovering in the sky. Bharadvajy the Wise refers to no less than seventy authorities and ten experts of air travel in antiquity. Vimanas were kept in a Vimana Griha, a kind of large hall, and were sometimes said to be propelled by a yellowish-white liquid, and sometimes by some sort of mercury compound, though writers seem confused in this matter. It is most likely that the later writers on Vimanas wrote as observers and from earlier texts, and were understandably confused on the principle of their propulsion. It was a liquid that could burn, similar in a fashion to the liquid used within the flame throwers used in naval warfare. According to the Dronaparva, part of the Mahabarata, and the Ramayana, one Vimana described was shaped like a sphere and borne along at great speed on a mighty wind generated by mercury. In another Indian source, the Samar, Vimanas were iron machines, well-knit and smooth, with a charge of mercury that shot out of the back in the form of a roaring flame. Another work, called the Samarangana-sutradhara, describes how the vehicles were constructed. It is possible that mercury did have something to do with the propulsion, or, more possibly, with the guidance system. Curiously Paul was shown a device like a hemispherical object of glass or porcelain, ending in a cone with a drop of mercury inside. This is why as man again learns how to harness machines that will fly, they will discover all over this world writings identical to those of ancient India. 'Tis but a matter of time. The ancient Hindu Veda writings speak of aerial chariots," the old man paused. "But sadly, as is the way of man, the machines were turned to use in war. If Indian texts are to be believed, the Atlanteans, known as 'Asvins', were apparently even more advanced technologically than the Indians, and certainly of a more war-like temperament. Certainly the Ramayana, Mahabarata and other texts speak of the hideous war that took place, some ten or twelve thousand years ago, between Atlantis and Rama using weapons of destruction that cannot be imagined, but caused explosions with the brilliance of the sun...it melted walls of stone to glass..."

"Seriously?" the Hospitaller asked rather incredulously.

"Yes. The ancient Mahabharata, one of the sources on Vimanas, goes on to tell the awesome destructiveness of the war for it is written," the old man started to say and opened his small notebook and flicked to a page near the back. "It reads... 'the weapon was a single projectile charged with all the power of the Universe. An incandescent column of smoke and flame as bright as a thousand suns rose in all its splendour...an iron thunderbolt, a gigantic messenger of death, which reduced to ashes the entire race of the Vrishnis and the Andhakas. The corpses were so burned as to be unrecognisable. Their hair and nails fell out; pottery broke without

apparent cause, and the birds turned white...After a few hours all foodstuffs were infected...to escape from this fire the soldiers threw themselves in streams to wash themselves and their equipment...'" [112]

"Then there would be evidence of such events," the farrier remarked.

"And indeed there is. Everywhere if you look. From ancient cities whose brick and stone walls have literally been vitrified, that is, fused together, found in India, the Emerald Isle, Scotland, France, Turkey and other places. In Mohenjo-Daro, a well planned city laid out on a grid, with a plumbing system superior to those used even today, the streets are littered with black lumps of glass. These globs of glass were once clay pots that had melted under intense heat!"

"So where did they all go?" Sarah asked, perplexed.

"With the cataclysmic sinking of Atlantis, though remember Atlantis is really a word that covers a whole world civilisation, and the wiping out of Rama with weapons as powerful as the sun, the world collapsed into a 'lost age' of sorts."

"As in the end of the last age of man?" Gabirol asked.

"No...these events I have just detailed happened within this age of man," the old man answered.

"And you say that the Atlantis world, which was worldwide in its reach and influence but its centre lay upon lands far to the south, upon a continent sized land now covered in snow and ice...yes?" Gabirol asked as he charged his quill.

"Yes, that is correct. I am glad to see you have remembered much of what I explain."

"So some of these ancient flying machine still exist?" Peter asked.

"Yes...they have led many to see them as dragons, breathing fire as the heat from some of them is seen and when seeing an individual enter thinking them devoured... the Vimanas and Vailixi of Rama and so-called Atlantis are not all gone for they were built to last for thousands of years, evidenced by Ashoka's 'Nine Unknown Men'. They were the ones that initiated many so-called secret societies or brotherhoods of exceptional, enlightened men and women to preserve the inventions and knowledge of the ancients."

"But this is all so ancient...too far back in history," the wealthy tailor remarked.

"Then know that even Alexander the Great when he invaded India, his historians chronicled that they were attacked by flying, fiery shields that dived upon his army and frightened the cavalry. These flying vehicles did not use any weapons though, perhaps out of benevolence, and Alexander went on to conquer India."

"And this is what Paul travelled in?" Ayleth asked.

"I cannot answer that for he never spoke of it. Nicholas, as you know, he refused

to leave the spot Paul had been taken from, totally convinced and believing that by whoever and however Paul was taken, they would return him to the same place... as he was in fact."

"So where do these machines go or stay out of sight?" Gabirol asked.

"Some say great caverns in Tibet, or some other place in Central Asia, and the Lop Nor Desert in western China...or the great landmass to the south. But what Paul did say, regarding these machines, is that prior to them appearing or leaving, he always felt and heard a ringing in his ears...and he was also told that the machines could be made to look like anything the viewer was conditioned to see."

"Like the old hag who was not really an old hag?" Miriam asked.

"Paul did write a few notes explaining that in the last hundred years of this age of man, people will again remember the ancients and their ways and as you now know, would recover items specially sealed and hidden. Great scholars and teachers would once again also reveal, by way of stories, though in truth what they write believing it as pure fantasy is in fact a recollection of events past. Much of what is now written within such books as the 'Exeter Book' known as 'Christ I', secret truths will again be copied word for word into new epic tales that will touch the souls of men."

"Such as?" Simon asked.

"Oh I know of just one...for Paul and Stewart were taught it oft times. It was the same language as Thomas and his men used, Elfdalian, and which Nicholas sought to learn. Perhaps you should all learn it."

"Then pray speak it and I shall write it," Gabirol replied.

"Eálá Earendel engla beorhtast Ofer middangeard monnum sended," the old man said and paused.

"So you know the language of the forest?" the Templar asked.

"Aye that I do."

"What did you just say?" Ayleth asked as Gabirol tried to write down what he just heard.

"It means, hail Earendel brightest of angels, over Middle Earth sent to men."

"Sounds lovely...and you say such words and language will be used again in the future?" Peter asked.

"Oh yes, that I can assure you...and with great success as I have said for it will speak to the souls of men and women."

"So can I ask did Alisha and Paul move back here to France before the calamity that befell the kingdom...or what?" the Hospitaller asked.

"Let me tell you...for Reynald returned three days after the ceremony Princess

Stephanie put on for Alisha and Paul...and rapidly things developed," the old man sighed.

"And Paul really was okay with Alisha?" Simon asked.

"Yes...he told her simply that whatever their souls were made from and wherever they came from, they were both part of one and the same and they would rebuild that cathedral they both saw together...of a new Church...a Church of love, learning and understanding." The old man paused briefly. "Or at least lay the foundations."

Chapter 69
Fists of Iron & Godspeed

Crac de Moab, Oultrajordain, Kingdom of Jerusalem, January 9th 1187

The afternoon air was cold and crisp, the sky a clear deep blue. Ice and snow patches still dotted the forecourt as Paul and Ishmael walked toward the Templar guard room, Percival already waiting outside the door blowing into his cold hands.

"Paul," Princess Stephanie called out, rapidly walking toward him.

Paul stopped and waited for her. She was dressed in her finest cream coloured dress with a fur lined cape pulled over her shoulders, her hair tied up and back in two large plaits and a single head necklace suspended a pearl in the middle of her forehead, the white lace head scarf framing her face beautifully.

"Are you going anywhere?" Paul asked seeing her dressed so formally.

"With you if you would take me...to France," she replied quietly and smiled. She clenched a small sealed scroll in her hands tightly. "Reynald returns this eve. I received word earlier...hence why I am dressed like this," she explained and feigned a brave smile clearly not looking forward to his return. "I must prepare my daughter Alix for his arrival," she said and hesitated. "But I beg of you take this back. Burn it afterward if you must...and I know it upset Alisha, but somehow I cannot burn it myself, and with Reynald returning, if he reads it, he will know it does not refer to him. So please," she pleaded and held it out for him to take.

Paul looked at Ishmael, who shrugged his shoulders non committal.

"I will take it back, but I cannot keep it, you know why," Paul replied and took the small scroll tube.

Princess Stephanie held his hand tightly as he took the tube, her eyes searching his, the desperation clear for Paul to see. She was shaking both from the cold and with emotion, her breath condensing into a whisper white cloud toward Paul as if reaching out for him in the cold air.

"You plan this hour your departures…'tis a departure I will struggle to bear for I will be alone again, save for my remaining daughter. If you can find a way that we could come with you, I pray you find it and fast. This land, this castle…it will fall if Reynald continues his madness."

Paul looked at her, her eyes glistening moist as tears welled in them. How could he possibly take her along? he wondered. Her hands gripped his tighter as she stared at him. Suddenly behind Paul the main gate guards rang the bell and called out to stand to.

"'Tis Lord Reynald's banner!" one of the guards shouted down.

"You must find an excuse to travel to Constantinople as you did before… do so and I will have Thomas and his men come and fetch you to France. But you know Reynald will come after you," Paul said quickly as the sound of the heavy portcullis gates being raised echoed around them.

"Paul…my heart will always whisper to yours," she replied quietly and stepped back a pace. She took a deep breath and stood up straight, placed her hands together across her stomach and stood proud.

As several Templars rushed from the guard room, Percival moved to stand beside Paul and Ishmael. Stewart appeared with Nicholas and Upside as they hurried themselves to form up as the vanguard of Reynald's squadron of Templars pulled into view, the forecourt echoing loudly to the sounds of many horses. Turcopoles and several sergeants rushed forward to help steady the horses as Reynald and Gerard rode into view, both covered in blood as were all the mounted knights and sergeants. Princess Stephanie shook her head saddened at the sight for she knew, as did all, what it meant. Reynald saw her and immediately steered his horse toward her. She took another deep breath and forced a smile as he drew up almost beside her.

"My Lord…you are early," she stated and smiled again.

Reynald dismounted and handed the reins to a young squire. He took off his filthy gloves and stood in front of her. He looked at Paul briefly, frowned seeing he looked different then looked back at Princess Stephanie as Gerard dismounted.

"What a sight for sore eyes," Reynald said aloud, put his left arm around her waist and pulled her close to him, instantly kissing her on the lips hard. She bent backwards caught off guard and he simply kissed her harder then pulled her up straight, broke the kiss and laughed. "You and I have some catching up to do," he laughed again before turning to look at Paul directly.

"And I see 'you' have clearly been enjoying the comforts of my home these past months."

2 - 13

"My men have served this castle well, but I have not been here most of that time," Paul replied.

"Your men...so you have your own men now do you?" Reynald asked and moved away from Princess Stephanie and stepped closer to Paul. "I see you have grown a beard too...it suits you."

"My Lord," Gerard interrupted and stood beside Reynald. "Remember what was agreed," he said quietly.

Ishmael stood closer to Paul as Tenno appeared with Abi walking straight for them. The smell of blood and iron pervaded the air mingled with sweat and body odour despite the cold air.

"I forget my manners...it has been a while since last we met. I am sure my good and godly wife has been the perfect host in my absence?" Reynald said and looked at Princess Stephanie. Her heart was pounding as Paul still held the scroll tube in plain view.

"That she has," Paul replied.

"You will never call me Lord, will you?" Reynald asked, looking back at Paul, his eyes wide, his pupils large.

"If it pleases you I shall, I have no issue or problem in calling you Lord any time you wish," Paul answered.

"Ha! You see. That is what I like and admire about you. You do not fear me do you?"

"As I once said years before, need I have fear of you?" Paul asked in response.

"No...no you do not. You have honoured me and," Reynald started to say then paused. "No. We know the debt I and Gerard owe you," he continued quietly, his tone softer. Gerard nodded at Reynald and smiled. "And I too know and understand the grief and loss you have recently suffered. Death...'tis a great leveller and makes us all equal. I have lost both a daughter and our young son."

Paul looked at Reynald as he stared back at him. Reynald was a formidable character and it saddened Paul to think that Reynald could do so much more if only he stopped his blood lust. The mention of the loss of his and Princess Stephanie's youngest son clearly upset her as she gulped and shook her head slightly, closing her eyes at his mentioning.

"So, Master Paul," Gerard stated and smiled. "We hear you are to return to France. Is this true?"

"Yes…just as soon as we are able to secure safe passage."

"You may have a problem with that. Ships are scarce right now. I thought you would have stayed to find and seek vengeance upon whoever ordered Turansha to kidnap your children?" Reynald asked.

"Who said anything about another ordering Turansha to do the deed?" Paul asked instantly.

"We have our ways and means of knowing such matters. Nothing escapes my attention," Reynald replied. "And by way of thanking you for what you did for us…the little boating incident…I would offer you the services of those who could help you establish exactly who orchestrated and ordered Turansha to do as he did."

"'Tis a great offer, but one I cannot accept. I seek no vengeance for it will not bring my son back. The Lord will see fit to deal accordingly with the person…or persons…who orchestrated such," Paul replied as Theodoric approached.

"Ah…the only man still alive who can out drink me," Reynald laughed out loud as Theodoric came and stood close to him.

"And still can, My Lord," Theodoric replied and smiled. He saw Princess Stephanie looking anxiously at Paul and the small scroll he was holding. "My Lords…you must forgive me for I have urgent business to resolve before nightfall…but I am happy to challenge you to a drink later," he said and took the scroll from Paul. "I only came for my note of credit. You charge far too much for your lodgings here," he joked and waved the scroll.

"Later it shall be then…after I have rested and acquainted myself with my wife," Reynald smiled and looked at Princess Stephanie. She smiled but all could see it was an embarrassed and pained smile. Abi raised her eyebrows disapprovingly, which made Reynald look at her hard. "And I see you grace us with your presence."

"Only here to help…Lord," she replied, her tone laced with sarcasm as she drew out her last word.

"Come, it has been long hard day," Gerard said and began to usher Reynald away. "We shall feast this eve after last vespers and after I have inspected what men I still have here."

"Hey you...perhaps you would like to meet some other manly females," Reynald said to Abi as he put his arm around Princess Stephanie and nodded toward a contingent of female knights pulling into the courtyard.

Tenno gave Reynald a cold hard look as he practically pulled Princess Stephanie toward the main keep entrance doorway. Abi shook her head then looked across at the female knights. They too were stained with blood, and it was fresh blood. Abi sighed knowing that whatever killing had taken place that day, more would surely come. Nicholas walked over to Paul.

"I fear now he is back, our days here will be numbered," he said and watched Reynald enter the doorway slapping Princess Stephanie's backside as she stepped in ahead of him.

"Aye...more reason we leave sooner rather than later," Paul replied, concerned for her. He looked at Theodoric as he raised the small scroll.

"Right...let's see the shit state of what rabble I have remaining here!" Gerard called out and clapped his hands to get everyone's attention. "Ah... as your brother is now returned, do we get our Gonfanier back?" he asked aloud looking at Stewart then to Paul. "Unless he is now one of your so-called men?"

"The choice is his for I am neither his keeper, nor his master...as are none of the men I stand with," Paul replied and looked at Gerard.

"Well he better make his mind up fast for the King of Jerusalem summons all of us...and I think you will find that includes you too," Gerard stated, took off his riding gloves, smiled and walked toward the Templar guard room.

ഋ൙

Paul walked along the upper corridor quickly but as quietly as he could toward his own room where Alisha and Ailia were packing away what little they still had. Two guards stood outside Reynald's room and automatically stood too as Paul walked past them. He nodded in acknowledgment, one of the guards trying not to smile as sounds of grunting came from behind the door. Paul stopped and momentarily considered knocking on the door, but that would only add to Princess Stephanie's embarrassment he immediately realised. Maybe if he spoke loudly Reynald would hear him and stop his actions being so loud.

"Gentlemen, I did not realise a guard was now in order," Paul said loudly.

"'Tis now, sir…by order of Master Gerard. Reynald has been warned of assassins," the guard to his left replied.

All went quiet inside the room for a moment, Paul looking at the guards as they all listened. Princess Stephanie let out a slight yelp followed by a moan. She whispered something but Reynald laughed out loud. Repeated banging of the bed posts against the wall started to echo out, Princess Stephanie groaning every time, more in pain it sounded than pleasure. The two guards looked at Paul, one shrugging his shoulders. The rhythm of the banging increased, Princess Stephanie letting out a deep moan as if biting her own lip every time trying to remain quite. Paul felt embarrassed for her. He wanted to shout out what animal uses a woman as a piece of meat, but again, he knew it would embarrass her more later. He shook his head disapprovingly as Reynald let out a loud sigh of relief and laughed, the banging stopping.

"That, my woman, was most needed…we shall require more later!" Reynald said loudly, knowing full well people were just outside the door.

Alisha opened the door of her chamber and looked across at Paul opposite. Puzzled, she frowned. She was just about to speak when Paul put his finger to his lips indicating she should not. Quickly he walked over to her and ushered her back inside, closing the door behind him. Ailia looked up from the desk she was sitting at and smiled.

"Ali, we must leave in the morning…even if it means we have to travel back via Alexandria. We cannot remain here a day longer," Paul said and clasped her hands in his.

"Is that Reynald I hear?" she asked, looking toward the closed door.

"'Tis indeed…and already he gratifies himself with Stephanie like she is some possession," he answered.

"Am I not yours?"

"No…you are no mere possession," Paul replied and looked into her eyes as she looked deeply into his. "I was told by Kratos that we just need listen to our own heart for that is the best teacher. Mine is telling me we must leave now, but we are too late to leave this day. But we shall leave on the morrow, whatever the weather," Paul explained.

"You are scaring me Paul. What do you know? Is it Reynald…does he mean us harm?" Alisha whispered so Ailia could not hear.

"No…'tis just a very unsettling knowing," Paul replied and looked at her closely. If Ailia was not in the room, he would have kissed her and made to love her right there and then, he thought to himself, if she would have him again, the beauty in her face and eyes calling to the deepest depths of his soul. But he knew he could not, not yet anyway. Every time he looked at her, it felt like he was seeing her again for the first time as he tried to burn her very features into his mind so he would never forget her. He pulled her close, the touch of her as he placed his hand in the middle of her back sending a surge of emotion throughout his body. With his other hand, he held her chin, then kissed her gently, when their lips touched, both became momentarily lost in each other's embrace...until Ailia ran into them throwing her arms around their legs.

"Family hug," she laughed as Alisha and Paul looked down at her.

ꟼC

The room was dark, despite the heavy curtains remaining open as Paul preferred. Ailia slept soundly in the small adjoining room, the door left open, Alisha still awake resting her head upon Paul's chest. In the distance they could hear laughter and the dropping of tableware and tankards as Reynald celebrated his return late into the early hours of the morning. Paul wondered how Princess Stephanie must be feeling.

"I wish to have you so much," Alisha whispered and tucked herself up closer to Paul.

"And I you...but you know what would happen should you fall with child. People will forever doubt who the father is," Paul replied and ran his hand through her hair as she kissed his exposed chest through the unfastened upper section of his nightshirt. She sighed sadly. "Believe me I wish and I want to..."

"But any baby would arrive well after the date Nicholas and I...," Alisha stopped herself instantly.

"And what if it arrived early...people who know will always be suspicious," Paul simply replied and pulled her up closer to him. He could sense the regret she still felt and it pained him to know she was hurting still. He kissed the side of her face. "We can never undo what has been, but we can make a new plate remember," he said softly, trying to reassure her.

"Do you think of Arri?" she asked softly.

"Every waking moment of the day and night...always," Paul replied and kissed the side of her face gently. "Always."

Both listened as they heard Reynald laughing loudly, clearly having drunk too much, being helped along the corridor outside their room. Princess Stephanie was whispering something and Theodoric laughed as he tried to open Reynald's chamber door.

"Hopefully he will be too drunk to use Stephanie," Alisha whispered, raised herself up and kissed Paul softly upon the lips. The sensation and feel of her lying upon him aroused him and the urge to make love was becoming more intense. "Do you remember the first time we ever made love?"

"Of course…I shall never forget it."

Paul's mind instantly returned to Niccolas's old caravan. How intense the emotions were and the anticipation of finally joining with her as one he recalled and smiled. It seemed so very long ago. But if all went to plan, they would again be back in La Rochelle. A loud bang echoed out in the corridor as something large and heavy was dropped in Reynald's room drawing his attention back. Alisha raised her head to listen, then settled back down upon Paul after a few short minutes. They both heard Theodoric speak quietly to the two guards outside and then his footsteps as he walked away.

"If we made love now, would you doubt the child was yours?" Alisha asked softly and pushed herself against him.

"No…never for I know you did not finish the act fully," Paul replied and put both his arms around her despite the heart skipping jolt of pain that surged through him. It still hurt physically to think of her with Nicholas, but he quickly pushed the thought from his mind refusing to let the feeling overwhelm him.

"I am blessed I have you and your understanding, and that you can speak of this openly."

"Ali, I have loved you always, even before this life it would seem, and I shall continue to love you beyond this one. It is I who am blessed that I have your truest and deepest love…and I will always, always find a way back to you. Never doubt that."

Alisha wrapped her arms around him tighter and rested her head upon his chest, the sound of his heart beating rhythmically sounding in her ear. She felt a closeness to him she had never experienced before and felt as if she was actually part of him as she lay there in silence, with no pretence, hidden secrets and a complete knowing of each other; she eventually fell asleep in his arms.

ᏍᏲᏳ

"Paul," a woman's voice whispered, startling him. He blinked and opened his eyes. The room was still dark and silent. Alisha lay asleep to his side and gently he moved away and sat up looking around to see where the voice had come from. Out of the corner of his eye he caught movement pass the upper section of his chamber window. Birds would not be out this time of the morning, he thought. He stood up slowly and moved to the window and peered down into the secure inner keep yard. A light flickered from the rear window of the Templars' guard room. He must have been dreaming or imagined something, he told himself. They were four floors up so no one would be outside. He walked back toward his bed when the realisation hit him that it could be Turansha's men again…coming for Ailia. Instantly, he grabbed his sword hung beside his bed, unsheathed it and ran toward her chamber and flung the door back. Alisha sat up, alarmed, now fully awake as fear coursed through her veins seeing Paul, sword drawn, rush into Ailia's room. Her bed looked empty. An explosion of emotion shot through his head as he threw Ailia's blankets back. She was still there, curled up on her side asleep. Wearily she opened her eyes and looked up at Paul as Alisha came running in.

"Papa…Mama…what is wrong?" she asked, tired and confused, and pulled her small white comfort blanket she always slept with.

Alisha rushed over to her and wrapped the other blankets around her again, the night air cold. She looked up at Paul, waiting for his reply.

"Nothing…honestly. 'Twas just a bad dream I was having that is all," Paul replied reassuringly but looked around and back into his chamber sensing something was not right.

Alisha picked Ailia up and carried her into their chamber and sat her down upon the bed and cuddled her as Paul checked the room and looked out of the window again.

"Where are you going?" Alisha asked as Paul headed for the door.

"I will be right back," he replied and started to unbolt the door as Alisha grabbed her dagger from the side drawer nearest to her. Ailia looked scared seeing the dagger.

Paul's mind raced. Having now learnt that Reynald feared assassins, is that why he had switched chambers? Now if any came for him in the night, they would be coming straight for Alisha and Paul thinking they were Reynald and Princess Stephanie. But likewise if they were coming for Alisha and Ailia, they would go to where Reynald now lay. He looked back at Alisha quickly then opened the door. As the door opened wider, he immediately saw one of the guards on the floor holding his throat as blood spurted everywhere. He gurgled as his legs shook. The second guard was being held against the wall alcove by someone hiding within it, but his black clad hand was showing holding a knife beneath the guard's chin. His eyes darted to look at Paul just as the blade was pushed upwards and into the guard's throat, his eyes widening in terror, blood instantly pouring down his surcoat in a black oily looking manner in the darkness, the light from the two flaming torches shimmering on the blood. Paul instantly raised his sword as the guard was pushed forward onto his knees. The guard, holding his throat, looked up at Paul. The figure in the alcove stepped into view and kicked the guard forward to the floor then instantly threw razor sharp metal stars at Paul. Instinctively Paul raised his sword deflecting the first star with a loud metallic clang, the second star embedding into Paul's left shoulder. Without even realising the star had struck his shoulder, Paul jumped forward to engage the black clad figure, who instantly pulled a blackened straight bladed sword from behind his back. All Paul could see was the man's eyes in stark contrast to the black face veil and cover he was wearing. The man suddenly swung his sword down hard against Paul, Paul only just managing to deflect the blow. Instantly the man dived forward past Paul and jumped up again ready to take another thrust at him when Alisha let out a yell seeing the man in the doorway. The man looked at her. Paul thrust his sword down upon the assailant's blade cutting it in half. Stunned the man stood still momentarily but then pulled a curved dagger from his waist belt. Alisha covered Ailia's eyes as Paul tried to step closer to the doorway to put himself between the man and his family.

"STAND TO!" Paul shouted as loud as he could.

The black clad man jumped at Paul and as he landed upon him, Paul deliberately fell backwards, put his feet up into the man's stomach and, as they hit the floor, he threw him over, then immediately rolled over just as the other man rolled over likewise, jumped to his feet and again lunged at Paul. In one swoop, Paul swung his sword sideways with all his might catching the man across his thigh, his sword slicing into him, through his pelvis bone and only stopped when his blade reached past his navel. The man said nothing, not even a moan, his eyes fixed upon Paul's as he fought to remain standing. The man spun his dagger in his right hand ready to stab it down into Paul, who backed away slightly, his sword still in the man. As the man raised the dagger again whilst using his left hand to pull on Paul's sword, drawing him closer, Paul stepped backwards withdrawing the sword with both hands, cutting the fingers of the man just as a large gout of blood followed the blade out covering both of them. Paul swung his sword behind him, then up and over his shoulders and with both hands brought the sword down upon the man's right shoulder cleaving him almost in two to his waist. As the man's eyes rolled, he dropped the dagger, his right side falling to the side in a grotesque manner, his left lung sliced through and his intestines falling out. Paul withdrew his sword and the man collapsed to the stone floor dead. Alisha gasped in horror at the sight of what she had just witnessed.

"PAUL!" Princess Stephanie screamed from inside her chamber.

The alarm bell started to ring out, someone having heard Paul's shout. He tried to open the door into Reynald's room but it was bolted. He rushed back across the corridor stepping over the dead guard and man in black. Slipping on the blood, he steadied himself and rushed at the door. Not realising he had a metal star stuck in his shoulder, as he barged into the door, it pushed the star deeper into him, but the door gave way and Paul fell through it into the room.

Instantly he looked up to see Princess Stephanie stood beside the bed naked trying to hit another black clad man who was holding Reynald down, a knife to his throat, Reynald desperately trying to pry the man off. But in his half drunken state he was no match for the trained assassin now sat upon him. As Paul jumped to his feet and rushed to the end of the four poster bed, he went to swing his sword at the man. Just at that moment, the man turned and looked at Paul. It was all the time the man needed to duck and avoid Paul's sword as it swung just inches above his head. Before Paul had time to pull his sword up, the man jumped up and over the end of the bedstead and then over Paul completely. Paul flung himself around alarmed he would run into Alisha and Ailia so without hesitation he ran out after him into the corridor. But he was gone. Confused, Paul looked up and down the corridor but he could not see where he had gone. He could see Alisha holding Ailia tightly both sat on their bed. Alisha shook her head no one had entered. The alcove, he thought, and quickly thrust his sword into the darkness but it was empty. Tenno came running into view closely followed by Percival and several of Reynald's men, swords all drawn.

"Ali…watch Ali," Paul yelled as Tenno ran past him directly into Paul's chambers.

"Assassin," Percival stated looking at the dead Ashashin cut in two almost. "But why?"

"There is another…maybe more," Paul said loudly as the other men rushed into Reynald's chambers, Princess Stephanie grabbing the bed sheet to cover herself as Reynald tried to get to his feet visibly shaken.

Paul suddenly noticed the far end window of the corridor was partly open. It was a sheer drop outside onto the main glacis and was usually bolted permanently shut. Seeing Tenno now beside Alisha and Ailia, he quickly ran toward the open window. But no way could the other assassin have got that far from the bedroom doorway in time, he thought. As he approached the last section of the corridor cautiously, he sensed something above him in the roof of the vaulted archway. He looked up to see the other assassin pressed up against the arches using his arms and legs to support himself in position. The moment Paul saw him, the man let go and fell on top of him. As they hit the stone floor, Paul tried to roll over, but so did the man who was now holding Paul's wrists. Paul lunged his right hand upwards trying to get his sword high enough. The man stared hard at Paul for a moment, quickly looked back and saw Percival and several other knights rushing toward them. Suddenly the man rolled himself forwards over Paul, letting go of his wrists, then in one smooth rolling move jumped at the window like an acrobat. Instantly and without hesitation the man climbed out and started to move along the thin outer wall balustrade supports. Paul rushed over to see where he was going. The wind blew up against him. Paul hated heights and he felt momentarily dizzy looking down the sheer nearly 200 foot drop below. If he did not follow the man, he would get away and he needed to know if they had been after Reynald or his family. He tied the waist strap of his night shirt tighter and pushed his sword through it. He took a deep breath and climbed out onto the small wooden catch balcony then onto the stone ridge just inches wide. Gripping another upper stone ridge with his fingers, he started to edge his way along the outer wall just as Percival leaned out.

"Paul…are you mad…you hate heights. Get back. We can find the assassin for he will not get far," Percival called out.

The assassin stopped momentarily and looked back toward Paul, but Paul ignored Percival and continued to follow. Quickly the assassin started to edge his way around the main keep wall and toward the large angled northern support buttress. Paul was physically shaking not daring to look down but simply focusing on getting to the man. He flinched as a spark lit up the wall above him as a metal star bounced off just missing his head. He gulped grabbing hold tighter to the upper ridge, his stomach in his mouth. The assassin reached the buttress but there was a steep gap between the wall and buttress itself of nearly twelve feet at least. How would Paul engage him up here he wondered as he edged himself ever closer to the assassin. Another metallic star sparked off the wall as another was thrown at Paul. Determined and hoping there were no more assassins present, Paul pushed on, the tension in his shoulder finally registering pain from the embedded star. Paul froze momentarily as he saw the assassin turn and hesitate as he stood on the precipice about to leap across the sheer drop to the buttress.

7 - 3

"Paul…for the love of Alisha and Ailia, come back," Percival shouted.

The wind blew hard against Paul in a sudden gust and he had to grip even tighter. He looked at Percival leaning out of the window as far as he dare, resting his arm upon the small wooden catch ledge. Paul looked back just in time to see the assassin leap, hurtling through the air and land hard on the side of the buttress and grabbing hold with his hands on a flattened section just feet wide. The assassin pulled himself up easily onto the ledge then vanished out of sight over the other side. Paul knew if he did not follow him, he would escape. Once Paul was positioned opposite the buttress where it narrowed into a smaller section, he saw the small platform the assassin had jumped to. He turned so his back was firmly against the wall and focused on the single platform only, not daring to look down. If he slipped, there was nothing to grab hold of. The wind kept gusting and he feared that if he jumped, the wind would slow him and he would miss the edge altogether. He could hear Percival calling out but his words were being carried away by the wind. He took a deep breath, waited for a drop in the wind then jumped forward as hard as he could throw himself outward. As he fell through the air toward the edge of the buttress, he immediately realised that he was going to fall short, his legs flaying beneath him. He heard Percival scream out his name as Paul reached out his arms…his hands just smacking the top of the platform then sliding backwards to the very edge fast. Frantically he tried to grip the surface but his own body weight was pulling him downward and the wind felt like it was trying to force him down further. With anger rising he dug his fingers down deep into the grainy stone, but still he was slipping, his legs just dangling in mid air.

"Not like this!" Paul called out frantic and looked down briefly knowing he was going to fall. In the dark he could not see the edge but tried to see where it curved. If he could hit that, he may stand a chance and roll down the face of the glacis. Then his fingers went, his heart stopped and he knew there was nothing he could do. "Sorry, Ali," he whispered, closed his eyes and felt his fingers graze across the stone.

Suddenly he felt the strong grip of a hand around his left forearm. He stopped falling away and hung in the air suspended by the man on the platform. Paul looked up, puzzled, his heart beating so fast and his ears ringing. Another hand grabbed his forearm and then he realised the man was trying to help him.

"You will have to throw your leg up to gain a foot hold on the recess just in front of you, then let me pull you up," Taqi said, out of breath.

With his ears ringing Paul was stunned to hear what he thought was Taqi's voice. But he was in no place to argue. He kicked his leg forward and after two attempts he felt the ridge of the recess and quickly wedged his foot into it, then used the leverage to push himself up slightly, with his right hand, he reached over and grabbed the man's shoulder and slowly began to pull himself up onto the platform. The assassin rolled over as he hauled Paul over to safety, lying on him.

"Taqi…is that really you?" Paul asked out of breath, his throat dry.

"Yes, you reckless fool. What were you thinking?" Taqi replied as a gust of wind blew into them hard.

"Me reckless?"

"Yes…I am trained to do this and far fitter than you," Taqi replied still holding Paul tightly.

"I am as fit as I have ever been," Paul replied, still gasping for air.

"But clearly not as fit as me…what of Ali and Ailia? You have responsibilities, you bloody fool."

"What the…just what the hell are you doing here killing Reynald's men then?" Paul demanded. "And why did you come back to help me...you could not have known it was me?"

"As soon as I landed on you I knew 'twas you and then I heard Percival call out your name and I knew only you would be mad enough to follow. I threw the stars to warn you off. 'Twas not I who killed Reynald's men... 'twas my friend...he must have been discovered."

"But why are you here?"

"Paul...think back...'twas your idea...one that Master Rashid thought wise and expeditious to execute," Taqi replied and looked over the side of the buttress as the wind blew against them hard as sleet started to fall.

"My idea?" Paul exclaimed, surprised.

"Was it not you who suggested it would be a good idea to threaten Reynald, in his own bed in the dead of night just as Al Rashid did to Saladin?" Taqi explained and looked down again.

"'Twas...yes, but I never thought any of you were really listening," Paul replied and shook his head. Shouting below drew his attention and he looked down at several torches being waved and blowing in the wind many feet beneath them. "You still have not answered why you came back for I cannot see how we get down for one, or how you can make good your escape now."

"I knew you hated heights remember...and I knew you would not make the leap successfully if you tried it...as for escape...that moment has passed. I fear you must now kill me, my friend, least you hand me over to Reynald's torturers...for you know he will torture me."

"What?" Paul asked, alarmed.

"You must, and you must do so quickly...that or I jump headfirst," Taqi replied and grabbed Paul's arm tightly and looked at him, just his eyes visible through his blackened face mask. He pulled it up and off over his face so Paul could see him properly in the dim light of the far distance rising sun. "You must."

"No...absolutely not. Think of Alisha...it would end us. There has to be another way," Paul replied and tried to think as more men gathered beneath them. "You jump and I swear by all that is holy to me and upon Alisha's soul, I will follow you this very hour," Paul blurted out emotionally and grabbed Taqi's arms tightly. "I will not let go..."

"Paul...they will torture me and I will pray for death...you cannot allow this to happen to me. 'Tis our way. We are not allowed to surrender, 'tis forbidden, you know that," Taqi reasoned with Paul and looked at him.

For several moments they both just looked at each other.

"I cannot get down from here without you..."

"Good one, my friend, and it just proves you should always study carefully where you live. There is a stone ladder that runs up this buttress for repair access purposes...you will get down just fine," Taqi answered and smiled. "You know I cannot be taken alive. Alisha need never know it was me either."

As Paul looked at him, he knew what he was saying was true, but he could not simply let him kill himself.

"And you say the stone ladder is down that side?" Paul asked and half leaned over to look. Taqi leaned forward slightly to confirm but as he looked down, Paul pulled up his sword and using the pommel end, smacked the base of Taqi's skull hard enough to instantly knock him out as Tenno had shown him more times than he cared to remember how to. "Sorry, brother, but I cannot allow you to kill yourself. I promise I will find a way," Paul said as he held him tightly. He looked over and down the sheer drop and wondered how he would get Taqi down whilst he was unconscious. He looked back at Percival still leaning out of the window trying to see what was going on. Beneath him all he could see was the steep main glacis. If it had not been for Taqi's sacrifice, he would now be smashed upon it and most certainly dead. He shuddered as he thought of Alisha. He shook his head and wished he had not chased Taqi, but he could not have known it was him.

"Hey...Paul," Theodoric suddenly called out from somewhere close. "Over here...this way. Take the plank!"

Surprised, Paul looked off to his left over his shoulder to see a large wooden plank waving about in midair in the darkness, Theodoric, Ishmael and several of Thomas's men were holding the other end through a small opening in the main stone wall. Quickly he grabbed the end and guided it until it rested flat upon the platform.

ꙮ

It took just minutes for Paul to tie a rope around Taqi and then guide him across the plank as Ishmael and Thomas's men pulled him across slowly, Paul fearful the plank would snap at any moment as it creaked, the wind trying to prise them off like some evil force refusing to let them go. As soon as Taqi was through the hole, Theodoric reached out and grabbed Paul and pulled him in firmly, Paul falling onto the stone walkway that ran inside the wall.

"How did you know there was a hidden access way here?" Paul asked, out of breath, as Ishmael lifted Taqi up, still unconscious. Paul started to shake uncontrollably.

"Believe me, I know every tunnel, every passage way and escape hole. Next time, don't be so bloody fast to throw away your life…or mine with a heart failure."

Reynald appeared through the turret's door some feet away fuming, his face red with rage and still dressed in only his long nightshirt. He saw Taqi still bundled upon the floor with Paul now stood over him. Quickly Reynald lifted his sword and unsheathed it throwing down the scabbard. Gerard closely followed him as well as Stewart, Nicholas, Upside and several other Templars, the flaming torches casting flickering shadows only adding to the look of rage upon Reynald's face.

"Stand aside, Paul, whilst I run that sneaking bastard through!" Reynald bellowed as he approached. Theodoric immediately went to block Reynald's way but he pushed him aside hard and raised his sword in both hands, the blade pointing down. Paul stepped fully over Taqi as he started to come round and raised his arm to block any move Reynald was going to make. Reynald glared at Paul angrily, spit foaming at the sides of his mouth. "This assassin just tried to kill me…now move aside or so help me God I will strike you down too," he fumed.

"I cannot do that…for if this man had wanted you dead, you would already be dead," Paul replied as Theodoric tried to stand between them.

"Theo, get out of my way for by Christ no matter the friendship between us, I will have you arrested."

"My Lord…'tis true what Paul says. And, even if it is not, then think onward…this man is a valuable asset with which to bargain…perhaps even exchange for gold…let alone the intelligence we can get from him," Theodoric explained as Stewart stepped closer to Paul.

"I think you will find that this man came to warn you, not kill you," Paul started to explain as Taqi rolled on the floor half unconscious.

"'Tis the son of Firgany is it not…Alisha's brother no less," Gerard stated as he looked down at him.

"What!" Reynald bellowed even louder at Paul in a long drawn out manner. "So you brought this man and his accomplice into my castle to kill two of my men and have me run through in my sleep?"

"If that was so, then why did Paul just risk his life trying to stop him from escaping and who do you think killed the other assassin?" Theodoric said and deliberately stood back in front of Reynald's sword. "I would check whatever message has been left for you before you run anyone through this night."

Reynald stared at Theodoric hard and his entire body shook with rage. Theodoric raised his eyebrow and tilted his head slightly as if to ask him a question.

"He could be right you know...about exchanging him for gold," Gerard commented and rubbed his chin and then patted Reynald on the shoulder. "I think best you retire and check on your good wife...I will have this one in chains and in the morning we can find out exactly his intentions. What do you say?"

Slowly Reynald lowered his sword, his gaze falling to Paul's hand firmly placed upon his own sword ready to draw.

"I will decide what to do with that man in the morning...," Reynald said loudly and flounced around still full of anger and pushed past Nicholas and Upside.

"'Tis one less I owe you," Gerard said quietly to Paul. "But whatever happens with this one, I strongly suggest you take your family and your men and leave for I know Reynald, and he will snap soon of that I am certain."

"Thank you," Paul replied.

"Thank him...he mentioned the only word Reynald probably heard this night...gold," Gerard said nodding toward Theodoric and then looked down at Taqi. "Take him to the dungeon...and make sure you keep him well observed and bound."

Stewart and Nicholas immediately helped lift Taqi up with Ishmael taking his legs. Paul took a deep breath of relief and as he breathed out, the pain in his shoulder suddenly tore through him as it registered. He grimaced, momentarily going dizzy, Theodoric just managing to support him in time.

"Come, we must have that seen too...and Alisha is going to kill you for sure this time," he said as they began to follow Taqi being carried.

"How do we explain this?" Paul asked in pain.

"Exactly as it happened...and somehow we need to keep Taqi alive and get him out before we leave. If not, he will never leave this castle alive."

"Paul!" Alisha called out from behind as she rapidly walked toward him closely followed by Tenno carrying Ailia. She flung her arms around him when she reached then looked at him, his nightgown covered in blood. "Were they after us?...are you hurt?"

"I could not stop her coming down here," Tenno stated.

Paul looked at Theodoric briefly before taking both of Alisha's hands.

"No...they were trying to leave a warning message for Reynald," Paul answered and hesitated as Alisha looked at him intently. "It is Taqi."

"Oh my Lord...," she gasped pulling her hands away from Paul and covering her mouth in shock. "Is...is?"

"Taqi is still alive. He has been taken to the cells beneath the west wing."

"I must see him at once," Alisha replied, anxious, and spun to rush away. Paul reached out and grabbed her hand, stopping her. She turned and looked at him, puzzled. "What...why do you restrain me so?"

"You will not be allowed to see him. Not yet anyway," Paul answered as Theodoric nodded in agreement. "We shall not leave as planned until we have secured his release with Reynald."

"And you think that animal will agree to let him leave?" Alisha asked angrily.

"We will get word to Al Rashid...we can negotiate this...trust me," Theodoric interrupted. "I know Reynald well enough. But I advise you all still leave as planned."

"No...I will not leave until I know he is safe," Alisha shot back.

"You need to consider other factors in this matter," Theodoric remarked and nodded toward Ailia half asleep in Tenno's arms.

"Ali...we will find a way, you have to believe us on this," Paul said and clasped his hands around hers reassuringly and smiled. "We will."

"Why does the Lord test us so?" Alisha asked quietly, her voice emotional. "Will it ever end?" she sighed and rested her head against Paul as he wrapped his arms around her. He grimaced again in pain.

ꙮ

Paul followed the guard, one of Reynald's own men, down the wide stone stairs toward the iron gated entrance to the cells. He passed Paul a burning torch whilst he unlocked the thin iron door, and then pulled two heavy bolts to release the door mechanism. There were no windows and only one single oil lanthorn to illuminate the main foyer area. It smelt damp coupled with a sickly sweet odour of previous occupants. The air was still and frigid, the cold sharp.

"He is easy enough to find...he is the only prisoner we have here," the guard remarked and gestured toward the far end of the vaulted dungeon that housed eight open iron bar cells. "Keep the light."

Paul knew that Reynald rarely if ever kept prisoners. Too time consuming and costly to keep and feed, preferring to kill them upon capture unless they were a high value individual. As he waved the torch at the end cell, he saw Taqi sat cross legged on the stone bench stark naked, his elbows placed upon his knees, his eyes shut.

"Taqi...it is I, Paul."

"No need to whisper, my friend," Taqi replied and opened his eyes.

"I was assured you would not be ill treated."

"So far I have not...they will simply not feed me, clothe me nor let me sleep. They come in every few minutes and throw water at me. Could be worse...for with water I can endure this for as long as it takes," Taqi explained and stood up slowly and walked over to the iron bars and looked at Paul. "Fear not for truly my training was worse than this," he laughed. Paul let out a little laugh but more from concern masking his fears. "Thank you for the headache by the way."

"I am sorry for that, but I could not let you die needlessly. Alisha has suffered too many deaths these past years," Paul replied and paused as images of Arri ran through his mind. "And clearly I am responsible for this mess, having suggested it in the first place...and your friend...'twas I...I who killed him," Paul sighed. "'Twas also I who helped Reynald escape after his sea escapades...why do I keep making so many errors of judgement?"

"Paul...because you are a good man living in a whole world of evil. If you had not saved Reynald, then I believe your brother would not still be with us no?"

"And what of your friend?...I thought he was one of Turansha's men"

"Much like you, he was my best friend yes...we joined together, trained together and have worked all these past years together, but it was Allah's will he died. 'Tis not a stain upon you for he knew the risks...and I am sure wherever he is now, he will be glad he did not win the fight for he knew of what you really are and what you must do. He must have made a mistake to have been discovered. If he had not made that mistake, we would not now be in this position would we, so you cannot and must not blame yourself, my friend."

"Taqi, you both cannot possibly know of what I am supposed to do..."

"Paul...you think me blind? We were both there when Arri was buried. I saw what you saw and heard what you heard...but did not let on. And let us face it...you have never been what we could call normal have you?" Taqi half laughed and held onto the iron bars and stared at Paul, their faces lit up by the flickering flame of the torch. "And Ali and Ailia...they are at least well yes?"

"For now...but we were to leave this day."

"Then you must still leave if you can. Al Rashid will never agree to a ransom. It is against all we stand for. And Reynald will not allow me to leave alive."

"I shall not leave you here to rot and die."

"Reynald knows that...and once he realises there will be no gold for my release, he will use that as a means to get you to intervene and give him the excuse he has always sought to have you removed. Do you think we do not hear of the many rumours about you, and the scheming that some plan against you and Alisha for fear that you have a divine legitimacy to rule these lands as a king and rightful queen? You put fear into the hearts of men like Reynald, for the Haute Cour knows of your real bloodlines."

"Taqi...how can you know these things?"

"Do you think we do not have spies everywhere...or our own seers like I said before? And Attar...do you not think he speaks to us too?" Taqi explained and reached out and grabbed Paul's arm tightly. "You cannot remain here...you must leave me for Alisha and Ailia's sake."

"The weather turns worse daily...'tis the only reason we are still here and now you are here, then we can delay longer as needs must."

"No, Paul...you cannot delay. Reynald will never change his ways...and I should have slit his throat while I had the chance, but my master forbade it. Reynald will bring a darkness upon this land that will haunt us all throughout the centuries that follow. 'Tis why you must form the new Order and, if possible, the Knights of Saladin."

"How...how do you know of such matters?"

"Like I said, do you think we do not have Sufi seers? If Reynald does not cease his actions, my Order will join with Saladin against him. 'Tis why you cannot delay. You must get Alisha away from these lands. Swear to me you will leave this day."

"No I cannot swear it."

"Then Alisha and Ailia are already dead," Taqi stated bluntly and stepped away from the bars and turned his back to Paul.

"Taqi…you cannot ask this of me. We are lifelong friends," Paul protested.

"Then you should respect the bond we once had. Honour me by saving Alisha and Ailia. Now go for I will not speak with you again in this life if you refuse to hear what I am saying."

"Taqi…look at me."

"Your judgement has not exactly served any of us well so far has it, Paul…so for once in your life, listen to someone else's advice."

"My loyalty to you has and always will be guaranteed and I will not leave you to rot here and die," Paul snapped angrily.

"Loyalty…then show it to Alisha and Ailia and get them out of this place. Then and only then, come back for me. I can hold out…trust me," Taqi said, turning his head very slightly but still with his back to him.

"Very touching," Gerard suddenly interrupted as he stepped down into view slowly clapping his hands. "Loyalty you speak of eh…'tis but a false ideal proffered as some great noble attribute."

Paul moved the flaming torch toward Gerard to see him better as he approached.

"That simply demonstrates your own cynical view of people," Paul replied.

"Really and you demonstrate yet again your naivety to people for let me tell you something about loyalty…most people who profess loyalty to you are not at all. They are loyal to their own need of you and what you can do or offer them. They are only loyal to their need of you…and once their needs change, so will their loyalty," Gerard explained and smiled broadly, placing his hands upon his waist.

"That may be your experience of the people you mix with, but that is not mine. You only perceive that which you see by your own making. I have true and loyal friends and I shall not let my friend die here," Paul retorted.

Gerard laughed and stepped closer to look at Paul closely. He looked at him for several moments in silence before smiling broadly again. Taqi looked over his shoulder at both of them.

"You cannot even keep the loyalty of your own wife, who beds a man you called a friend."

Taqi turned around fully hearing this and looked at Paul, puzzled. Paul looked at him quickly as Gerard folded his arms and waited for Paul to respond.

"Paul…deny this," Taqi demanded and grabbed the iron railings, staring at Gerard fiercely.

"Ha see! He cannot for I speak the truth," Gerard explained.

"No…she would never do such a thing," Taqi exclaimed. He looked at Paul hard, waiting for him to refute Gerard's claim but he did not. "WHO?" he suddenly shouted angrily.

"Oh you know…the blonde handsome one who has always had an eye on her…Nicholas," Gerard smirked, seeing the obvious frustration and anger in Taqi. Paul just shook his head at Gerard, disappointed. "Like I said, you need to harden up and fast. You will then see we are not so different."

1 - 9

"I shall never be like you," Paul replied quietly, Taqi still shaking his head in anger. "And should people abuse my loyalty, that is their error and a matter they will have to answer for to the Lord themselves."

"You still honestly believe all that horse shit? Do you really think the good Lord listens to yours or any of us…our prayers? If he does, he must be deaf or cannot understand, or just twisted," Gerard replied and laughed again, shrugging his shoulders. "Do you think I have never prayed?"

"Depends what you prayed for?" Paul replied.

Gerard let out a loud laugh and took several minutes to calm himself down and wiping a tear of laughter from his cheek.

"I respect and admire you more than you realise, Paul. You have physical strength, more personal courage than most I have ever met…yet your naivety fails you. I am sure even Taqi here would have to agree with me on that?" Paul looked at Taqi. He shook his head slightly no. "You will learn… or die."

"I cannot believe Alisha did what he says," Taqi said with a heavy sadness in his voice and looked down at the floor.

"'Twas a mistake, Taqi…"

"And you forgive her?" Taqi asked, still looking down.

"Yes…totally and utterly and my loyalty remains the same as ever before…if not stronger," Paul answered.

"Never make a beautiful woman your wife my father once told me," Gerard said and smirked.

"You had a father?" Taqi retorted and looked up at him in defiance.

"Hmm…a subtle but effective way of inferring I am a bastard. Good point, for I have been called far worse," Gerard replied, his tone mocking. "But mark my words…you, Taqi…will be safe here as long as Reynald's patience is served well. You are an asset he can bargain with for he knows the high regard Rashid has for you despite what rules your Order may aspire to keep. The guards are under orders not to harm you…simply keep you awake so you are too tired and will become…more compliant. He now knows you could have sliced his throat from ear to ear and he has read the note from Al Rashid you so kindly delivered to his bed post…," Gerard explained and stepped closer. "I am not your enemy…never have been," he then said quietly. "The guards outside are set to watch you do not kill yourself." Paul looked at Gerard, bemused, questioning in his mind if he was being genuine or if it was some clever ruse. "You helped save our lives once…'tis not forgotten by me…and secretly I have to confess that Reynald's actions of late are getting worse. But please try to remember me as not all bad and a complete bastard, for I do try and rein him in."

Two guards stepped down into the cell area carrying a flaming torch and large pitcher of water.

"Seriously?" Taqi asked and shook his head, holding the iron bars.

"Yes I am afraid so," Gerard replied. "But I shall ask they warm the water slightly," he whispered jokingly then pulled Paul aside as the guard threw the water all over Taqi, some splashing back on Paul.

Taqi blinked as the water ran down his face and licked his lips briefly. Steam rose from the water as it hit the cold stone floor.

"'Tis already warmed…for 'tis piss," Taqi remarked and looked at Gerard and raised an eyebrow, refusing to give the guards any satisfaction. "And by the taste of it, the person who did it has a sexual disease."

The guard holding the bucket looked at his colleague, then into the bucket then quickly left the cell area, scratching at his crotch.

"Ah 'tis a pity we do not have you both in my Order…a pity," Gerard smiled trying not to laugh at the guard hurriedly walking up the stairs. "Come Paul, I believe Reynald demands an audience with you. Apparently you saw the Princess naked."

Paul looked at Taqi as he winked at him. It was freezing in the dungeon and he feared for how he would cope with the cold. Taqi nodded he should leave.

"Now give Ali and Ailia my love and they must not worry."

"Yes, before anyone else does," Gerard mocked and ushered Paul up the stairs first turning back to look at Taqi. Taqi scowled at him hard, Paul just shaking his head trying to disregard his deliberate crass remark.

ꙮ

Alisha, biting her thumb nail in apprehension, sat in the tall chair nearest the fire just staring at the flames waiting for Paul to return with news of Taqi. Sister Lucy lay on the bed with Ailia in the small side room chamber both asleep as Princess Stephanie used the garderobe behind the curtained off small corridor that led to it.

"Move aside you freak," Reynald said loudly outside the door drawing Alisha's immediate attention.

The door suddenly swung open as Abi stood blocking the way in, Reynald half hanging off the door release. Tenno stepped up to Reynald as he squared up to Abi.

"This man…demands he speaks with you," Abi said still barring Reynald's way as his face turned red with a growing rage.

"No…let him in," Alisha replied and rushed over to Abi and put her hand upon her arm. "Please…'tis after all his castle."

"Too bloody right it is…now let me pass. How dare you bar me!" he shouted close to Abi's face. She simply looked back at him and shook her head disapprovingly.

"Abi, Tenno. Please…just let him enter. I will be fine."

"Any trouble…," Abi said and frowned at Reynald, intimating to her sword with a quick glance and placing her hand over the pommel. "We are just here."

Reynald flounced past her into the room and stood fuming whilst Abi slowly closed the door. When it was almost shut, she quickly opened it again, scowled at Reynald then closed the door.

"I have summoned your husband for I need answers this night or by Heaven heads will roll," Reynald blurted out angrily.

Alisha moved to the inner door, looked in on Ailia, who was still asleep,

Sister Lucy looking up. She nodded at her silently. Slowly and quietly Alisha pulled the door shut.

"What questions?" she asked standing up straight and facing Reynald. She felt for her dagger and checked it was secure before placing her hands across her tummy.

"Your husband…he vanishes for nearly a month to stay with whom we have no idea save his version of events. Immediately upon my return I am assaulted in my own chambers…my own fucking chambers!" Reynald spat angrily and paced rapidly up and down the end of the room. "And the assailant is none other than your very own brother…so you tell me, what am I to think?"

"Sire…from what I have heard, they came to warn you and offer their services to ensure peace…for all."

"Fucking horse shit. Absolute shit! An envoy or embassy could have done that. No…there is more to this. 'Tis your husband…a right royal bloody thorn in my arse."

"Sire. We are due to leave this very day, weather permitting. If my husband had anything to do with it, he would have waited to do such a thing until after we had left. You know he is a very smart man," Alisha replied, softly spoken.

"Too damn smart for my liking," Reynald replied and walked over to the large window and looked out as the sun started to rise over the battlements. "Your weather seems to favour you this day…but I cannot allow you to leave until I am satisfied you or your husband had no part in this," he explained, turned and looked at her, his eyes falling upon her chest, then down her slender figure to her hips. He licked his lips and pulled his beard in his hand several times as he stepped closer to her. Alisha took a deep breath and stood up straight refusing to be intimidated knowing Abi and Tenno were just outside. "Unless of course we can negotiate something," he sneered as he walked around her eying her up and down. "Yes…compensation I think. Maybe even let your brother leave."

"Leave…but will he be alive when he leaves? For you are renowned for your clever trips and clauses," Alisha shot back defiantly.

"Ha, so you would consider the negotiation?"

"You have not stated what you wish in return?"

"'Tis pretty obvious is it not?" he asked and leaned close to her and sniffed her hair, closing his eyes as he did. "Hmmm. You smell like a real woman should. And full of fire, passion and desire. Just how I like them."

Alisha remained perfectly still trying to mask the anger mixed with fear running through her. Her eye caught movement at the curtain to the garderobe corridor as Princess Stephanie's foot briefly flashed into view before she silently stepped back.

"You would allow my brother his freedom for sleeping with me?"

"As I thought…a sensible worldly aware woman. You are so much more suited to this world than your husband. And you know men and the power you solicit over them," Reynald spoke quietly as he walked around her looking with lustful eyes. He put his hands up to touch and cup her breasts but she quickly stepped back. "I love that fire in your eyes. Always have since the first day I saw you in Tortosa. I told you even back then the day would come when I would have you."

Alisha looked at him hard with utter contempt in her eyes as he looked down at her thighs. He stank of sweat and iron from the blood still left in his unwashed hair. She involuntarily shuddered thinking how Princess Stephanie must feel when he takes her at his whim.

"Hell will freeze over first before you could even touch my rotten corpse for I would rather kill myself than let you lay a single finger upon me…you disgusting immoral godless man," she said, her eyes widening.

"Then you just signed your brother's death warrant for I would rather see you watch him burn for your insolence and I will still have you at my choosing," Reynald snarled back.

Behind the curtain, Princess Stephanie stood with her hands across her mouth trying not cry, her entire body shaking with emotions of both fear and betrayal. Tears streamed down her face and she was nearly sick. She stepped back a pace and took a sharp intake of breath. Both Alisha and Reynald heard something behind the curtain but just as Reynald took a single step toward it, Paul opened the door and rushed in, his hand already covering his sword handle. Reynald froze and looked at Paul as Alisha stood perfectly still.

"What manner of intrusion is this?" Paul demanded.

"'Tis no intrusion for she invited me in. Ask your freak friends outside," Reynald replied. "We were just discussing negotiation terms for her brother…your friend."

"He was trying to do you a favour and a great service…if you were not so blind to see it."

"You two sorely test my patience…in my castle…and with a constant demonstration of a total lack of respect for me," Reynald bellowed.

"'Tis out of respect that I check my reasoning and temper with you for all I see is an angry embittered man capable of so much more but for his own arrogance and stupidity," Paul replied.

Princess Stephanie took another step backwards in alarm.

"I owe you…," Reynald sneered as he approached Paul and put his hand upon his arming dagger.

"Pull that knife from beneath your gown, and it will be the last thing you ever do," Paul stated and stared at him hard.

"You dare to threaten me in my own castle surrounded by all of my own men and knights?"

"This is but stone…and your men…how certain of your men's loyalty are you? For like you I too have men within these walls, far better trained than even your Templars…most of which I suspect would not side with you should you test my resolve," Paul replied confidently and with a total self assurance that caught Reynald off guard.

"You mean your freaks?"

"Do you wish to tell them that…and Thomas and his men to their faces?" Paul replied and stepped closer to Reynald. Alisha could hardly breathe as she stood bolt upright listening to every word and watching them both. She clutched her dagger tightly, prepared to use it on Reynald if she had to.

The door suddenly swung open and Gerard stepped in looking at them all in turn.

"Shut that fucking door!" Reynald snarled. Gerard looked at Alisha and Paul and quickly closed the door as he stepped down into the chamber. "With you on the other side."

"Reynald…My Lord…and friend," Gerard said softly and approached Reynald. "We can all hear what is being spoken outside. Thomas and his men are all there, as well as half of my knights," Gerard explained. "This will not end well for any of us if you insist on pushing the matter."

"'Tis treasonous…I will have them all burned at the stake as an example."

"Reynald…that will not happen," Gerard stated. "We are low on men and knights as it is…and all we will be left with is a bloodbath for both sides. 'Tis her they follow…all of them."

All three men looked at Alisha as she gulped and stepped backwards, her hand to her chest, alarmed.

"Then we just execute her and be done with this madness." Reynald remarked and looked at Alisha, his eyes wide and menacing.

"I defy you to try it...for your head will be on the tallest post of this castle by midday I swear," Paul said, his voice low and threatening.

"Lord...we cannot afford nor win this fight. You risk losing everything...and for what? And we owe this man our very lives."

"So what exactly do you suggest?" Reynald demanded as his eyes flashed from Alisha to Paul and back again.

"Let me ransom Taqi back to Al Rashid, for I know he favours him like his own son...and let these people go with all their followers...and this conversation here today shall forever remain between us four. We need never see them again. If not...I can promise you one thing, it will end badly for us I am certain of that."

"I will not leave without my brother and I demand he leaves with us," Alisha stated.

"You do not make demands of me!" Reynald shouted and moved toward Alisha. Before he got anywhere near, Paul was already beside her, his sword drawn and pointing just inches from Reynald's chest.

"I know you think you rule these lands...but in truth you are ruler and master of nothing...and if you think you can knock my blade away in time...just try me," Paul said slowly and deliberately calmly.

"Gerard...are you just going to stand there and do nothing?" Reynald asked, his eyes fixed on Paul's.

"No, My Lord, I am going to do something," Gerard replied and opened the door so Abi and Tenno could see in. He quickly raised his hand for them to stay still. "My Lord...'tis time you rested fully. You have not slept this night and you are sorely tired. Later, later when everyone is again calm, we can discuss the matter of Taqi."

"You what?" Reynald sneered angrily at Gerard.

"My Lord...have I ever let you down yet or given you wrong advice? These people will be gone by the end of this day one way or another," Gerard explained and beckoned him over. "Come on. It has been a long night."

Tenno stepped into the room and put his hands upon his hips and stared at Reynald.

"You and all your men are banned from ever entering my castle or any of my lands again. I will give you just two days to be gone from my borders or I will have you hunted down. And I am only giving you two days by way of payment for your deed in saving us...but the debt is paid...is that understood?" Reynald said through gritted teeth, flounced around and walked away from Paul, pushing past Gerard hard. As he stormed out of the room, Gerard looked at Alisha and Paul as she quickly held him.

"I seriously do advise you all pack up and leave, preferably before he awakes," Gerard said and half smiled at Paul. "I can have some of my knights escort you some of the way if it helps?"

"Thank you...we shall leave this day," Paul replied as Alisha looked up at him, alarmed.

"Not without my brother," she exclaimed.

"Sssh Ali...we shall do what is necessary," Paul replied quietly then looked at Gerard. "Thank you...and I hope this will not affect my brother's position?"

"It shall not. He is a good knight and I can ill afford to lose any. For what it is worth...I do see a change in Reynald of late. 'Tis why I stay close to him for he claims he has visions too...of himself wearing fists of iron and crushing Saladin," Gerard explained quietly as Tenno stared at him hard. "We have very few knights of the land we can call upon...so no, if Brother Stewart wishes to stay, he is welcome. Godspeed your journey is a safe one."

Tenno held the door open wider and Abi stood back allowing Gerard to step through. He nodded back at Alisha then Paul and without further words left. Abi stepped back inside the room and closed the door behind her. As the door latch was secured, Princess Stephanie pulled the garderobe curtain aside covering her face with her hands silently crying. She had heard all that Reynald had said. Alisha immediately put her arm around her and sat her down upon the tall chair. She sobbed openly. Alisha looked at Paul for some guidance but all he could do was shake his head with sadness. Sister Lucy entered the room and knelt before Princess Stephanie and gently pulled her hands down.

"Look at me, child," she said softly. Princess Stephanie sniffed and tried to stop crying as Alisha rubbed her back. "We must all leave...but in time, if you still wish it, we will come back for you."

Princess Stephanie sniffed again and wiped her cheek. She looked at Paul then to Alisha to seek confirmation from them. Alisha smiled and nodded yes. Princess Stephanie lowered her head and sobbed again.

"I shall make arrangements now for our departure...and, Paul, we must speak with Theodoric about Taqi. But our priority now is to get the women as far away from here as possible before this day is done," Tenno stated. "Agreed?"

Paul nodded yes as Abi nodded likewise in agreement. Paul moved to the window and looked down in time to see Gerard walk across the inner courtyard toward the Templar guard room. He stopped and looked up directly at Paul and raised his right hand. 'Fists of iron and Godspeed' Paul thought to himself as Gerard's words echoed through his mind. He raised his hand back in acknowledgment then turned to look at Alisha as she comforted Princess Stephanie. He shuddered momentarily as he thought on the words that the men all follow her…she had the power. She looked over at him and feigned a brave but tired smile.

"Paul," Abi said and walked over toward him. When she reached him, she checked the wound in his shoulder. "You must get this seen to now. 'Tis a small star but sometimes they tip them with poison."

"What?" Alisha asked, alarmed.

"Probably not as they came to warn Reynald, not kill him. Poisons do not linger long on the spikes. But it still needs to be removed and cleaned. Come with me," Abi stated and led Paul toward the main door. "We shall be back shortly."

Tenno opened the door for them to leave.

"Please be quick," Alisha asked, Princess Stephanie looking up at Paul.

Paul nodded and followed Abi out of the room. As soon as Tenno closed the door, Abi grabbed Paul by the shoulders and leant down to look him directly in the eyes.

"I have brought you out so I may clean and seal this wound…but also for Theodoric to show us a way to remove Taqi this day from the dungeon. If we cannot do so today, then we must stall leaving until we can. If not, despite his boasts, he will die."

"You mean break him out?" Paul asked, surprised.

"We have the men and the means so yes if we must…unless you can think of a better way?"

"I cannot risk confrontation with Alisha and Ailia present. You must get them out of Kerak first and only then will I get Taqi out. You know Reynald believes he wields fists of iron and in his own destiny…he will not allow Taqi to be taken quietly…whatever the outcome or number of men that would be killed."

Abi looked at Paul in silence for a moment. She knew he was right.

"Fine…then this is what we shall do."

Chapter 70
Crossing Destiny!

Port of La Rochelle, France, Melissae Inn, spring 1191

"But Reynald is mad almost...he will never let Taqi leave alive so am I correct in assuming Abi and Paul forced his escape?" Gabirol asked.

"You could say that," the old man answered and looked around the table at each of them, silently impressed that despite the late hour they were still listening intently. "Theodoric knew of the castle's design very well, but he knew not of any secret passages that would aid them in getting Taqi out."

2 - 22

"So what did they do?" Sarah asked quickly.

"Paul immediately went back to his chamber and packed as much of their belongings as possible, which was not much, then put Alisha and Ailia onto Adrastos, and along with Tenno and Percival they left the castle along with several of Thomas's men and Sister Lucy also upon a horse to make good speed. Tenno protested they should all leave together and come back later for Taqi, but Paul was insistent. Whilst Reynald slept, they would get Alisha and Ailia as far away as possible from Kerak. Theodoric briefed Stewart, Upside and Nicholas that they were leaving."

"For where?" Simon interrupted.

"'Twas far too dangerous to head west with many patrols of Saladin's forces operating in that area and had effectively sealed it off. They could not risk being intercepted by men who did not know of Paul or without a signed warrant from Saladin or Husam. Lord Montferrat and his port of Tyre was virtually surrounded and the other ports of Jaffa and Acre were too far to reach in one journey, so it was agreed they would head for Jerusalem direct and from there on to Tortosa where ships were still available," the old man explained.

"Did Nicholas and Stewart go with them?" the Templar asked.

"No, despite protesting they should. Princess Stephanie was heartbroken that

they were leaving without her. There were quite a few tears when they had said their farewells quickly and quietly, Princess Stephanie remaining in their chamber as they departed hastily. She knew if she left with them, Reynald would without doubt chase them once he awoke and realised. Alisha at first refused to leave saying she could not bear to be separated again under any circumstances, but Ailia...she simply smiled and told her all would be well. 'Twas a simple remark but one that Alisha knew to be the right decision. She gave Paul a long hug and kissed him, checked she had her dagger and departed. And so it was that Abi and Paul waved them off and then watched them from the watchtower, only then planning how best to get Taqi out. But it was not a straightforward operation..."

"How so?" Peter asked.

"Because Kerak Castle was purpose built as a defensive castle of war...the best of its kind and despite Theodoric knowing every aspect of it, he was the first to point out that getting Taqi out of the dungeons was impossible," the old man explained and paused briefly. "The only option being to get Reynald to sign his release...which meant for some diplomatic negotiations between them...and gold of course."

"And did they succeed?" the Hospitaller asked.

"Firstly Stewart and Nicholas took the day's gate log and altered it so it did not show Alisha's party having left the castle so as far as Reynald was aware, when he did finally crawl out of his drunken slumber, everyone was still in the castle. Princess Stephanie asked Reynald if he would meet with Paul to discuss terms on Taqi and tried to persuade him to see sense in getting Al Rashid on their side."

"What was his response to that then?" Gabirol asked.

"He agreed Paul and his entourage could stay a short while longer than his initial demand they all leave immediately...but this was mainly because Theodoric went and saw him, detailing how they could get Al Rashid on side...to get him and his men to do the killing, including assassinating Saladin himself. This part Reynald liked."

"And meanwhile Alisha and her group headed for Jerusalem?" Ayleth asked. "I hope they made it."

"By staying on at the castle, Paul was able to fool Reynald long enough into believing Alisha and Ailia were still in the castle, helped by the fact that Princess Stephanie pretended to visit her. Alisha supposedly refusing to leave her chamber after Reynald's visit and feeling unwell, plus women's problems. Reynald did not even notice Tenno and Percival's absence...at first."

"That sounds ominous," the Templar remarked.

The old man looked at him and nodded his head yes.

Crac de Moab, Oultrajordain, Kingdom of Jerusalem, January 12th 1187

Paul sat opposite Theodoric beside the small wooden chess table set up near the second smaller window of the chamber. Thomas poured some wine into three tankards set up on the main table near the fireplace. The large intricately patterned and expensive curtains were all drawn and the two lanthorns cast long shadows across the room. Princess Stephanie sat in a large chair watching Paul and Theodoric in silence, her chief maid sat on a small stool beside her repairing Reynald's linen socks.

"'Tis late Paul, perhaps we should leave this game. I am sure Reynald will be wondering where you are too," Theodoric said quietly looking across to Princess Stephanie.

"He is in the hall…drinking. Can you not hear him?" she replied sadly and sighed as she sat up straight. "Do you think Alisha will be in Jerusalem by now?"

"If Tenno rode the horses hard, yes. If not, then certainly by tomorrow," Theodoric answered and moved a chess piece. "Check!"

Paul looked at where he had moved and shook his head. After a few moments studying the board, he moved his queen.

"I believe that is checkmate!" Paul replied and stood up. He looked at Princess Stephanie. "I pray Ali and Ailia are safe wherever they are this eve. At least they will be too far away for Reynald to intercept or stop now."

"And Taqi?" Princess Stephanie asked softly, her hair looking almost gold in the light from the fireplace.

"We are forbidden to enter there…though Nicholas has assured us he is bearing up well considering the cold," Paul replied.

"Aye he is one tough little bastard, excuse my language," Thomas remarked and handed Theodoric a tankard and offered the other to Paul. "But I am telling you now…he grows weak."

Suddenly the door burst open banging loudly against the stone door jamb. Princess Stephanie jumped with fright as Reynald stood in the doorway clearly drunk, Gerard behind him trying to pull him back and help steady him to stand upright.

"So this is cosy….," he bellowed and entered the room, Gerard shrugging his shoulders. "You all ignore me and shun my hospitality to join me in the hall…why the insult?"

"My Lord," Princess Stephanie said and stood to greet him.

"And where is your wife for I have seen little of her these past two days? Does my personage offend her that much?"

Abi opened the small adjoining room door and stepped into view hearing the commotion. She looked at Reynald hard.

"Reynald…come, let me take you to our chamber and calm you…you know," Princess Stephanie said trying to distract him and started to gently pull him toward the door. "My Lord?"

Reynald flounced his arm hard against her knocking her sideways. Quickly Paul moved to go to her aid.

"Stand exactly where you are…she is my property not yours to do with as I wish as befitting a husband," Reynald yelled angrily and wiped his hand across his face, wine still visible in his beard. "What say you?"

"I say you are drunk…and your behaviour is not befitting of a husband…certainly not a Lord's behaviour," Paul replied, staring at Reynald as Gerard raised his eyebrows.

"Ha! You clearly do not know many lords then." Reynald laughed out loud in response and nudged Gerard and pointed to Paul. "You…'tis your naivety and soft heart that will be your downfall…now where is your wife? For I owe her an apology."

Princess Stephanie looked at him then to Paul, the fear in her eyes showing as they widened. Gerard noticed this and looked at Paul with suspicion.

"She has not been well…she rests," Abi interjected and proffered with her hand to look inside the small room.

"And you prefer this company to mine?" Reynald snapped and grabbed Princess Stephanie by the arm tightly. "And this…," Reynald said half spitting as he pulled out the note Taqi had pinned to his bedpost. "Do you believe we can trust what is written upon this?" he asked and waved it close to her face, forcing her to close her eyes as it smacked against her.

"If they had wanted you dead…you would not be standing here this night…and Gerard…you know Al Rashid. You know he is a man of his word. Turn him against Saladin and you will have victory in these lands. Turn him against you…you will be dead before the year is out," Paul explained as Reynald stood shaking from rage and drink.

Princess Stephanie yanked her arm away hard and moved backward toward Paul rubbing her arm in pain. Reynald glared at her. Ishmael stepped into view from his almost hidden position against the far wall and moved toward her. His stare said all Reynald needed to know.

"Gentlemen…we all have much to consider. I suggest we sleep upon matters and resume this conversation in the morning with clear heads… agreed?" Gerard interrupted and stood beside Reynald and helped steady him as he swayed drunkenly.

"We do not side with assassins," Reynald blurted out, pushed Gerard aside, looked at Princess Stephanie and shook his head disapprovingly. "Make sure you are in my bed by the time I return," he ordered then stormed out of the room, Gerard watching him as he left, shaking his head.

"Paul," Gerard said quietly and turned to face him. "I did warn you there is a change in him…history I am sure will not remember me kindly, but I do what I must in these trying times. I look to men like you, and you," he said as he looked over at Thomas, "to stand by us. If not, I fear the divisions between us will be the death of us all. You are not the boy I once slapped down in Rochfort…and contrary to what Reynald just said, it is men with a mind like yours that we sadly lack in these lands."

Paul looked at Gerard, partly stunned by his words. Gerard winked, smiled and gestured for Princess Stephanie to follow him out. Putting on a brave face, she nodded silently at Abi, Theodoric, Thomas and then Paul, both fearful and embarrassed. Her maid quickly gathered up their things and followed her out of the chamber. Gerard nodded at Paul and pulled the door shut.

"Well that's it then. We are all in balls deep this time," Theodoric said and clapped his hands together then raised an eyebrow as he looked at Abi, who raised an eyebrow back at him. "Okay…maybe not all of us," he smiled.

"I do not believe he will see the benefits of taking heed of Al Rashid's warning. His ego is too big to accept it…and he is still fuming that his very chambers were breached," Paul remarked, beginning to pace up and down as he thought.

"There is a poison in his mind for he was never this irrational before," Theodoric commented as Abi nodded in agreement with him.

"Then we must be ready to leave immediately. I will speak with Reynald in the morning…but I fear it will make no difference," Paul said and rubbed his chin.

"What does your heart whisper?" Abi asked.

"Like Theo said…we are in balls deep…there will be trouble," Paul answered and smiled at Theodoric.

"Don't pick up too many of my bad comments," Theodoric laughed back.

"I shall have horses and supplies readied for I think the only way we are leaving here with Taqi…is if we take him…by force," Thomas explained and raised his eyebrows. Abi nodded in agreement with his comments.

"Damn…I knew I should have lost some weight," Theodoric joked trying to make light of the seriousness and tension and rubbed his hands over his stomach. Thomas grinned. "Not fat before you say it!"

"I suggest you all sleep. I shall keep watch," Abi said as Paul looked toward the door.

"I will only rest once our horses are ready as I said," Thomas replied.

Paul's mind wondered how Alisha and Ailia were doing. He took comfort knowing they were protected by Tenno and Percival and far enough away from Kerak and Reynald.

ꕥ

Paul awoke with a jolt. Still fully dressed, he had lain down to rest and despite his mind being unsettled he had eventually fallen asleep. He moved to sit up but he felt heavy, his limbs aching. He pulled his sword aside so he could sit up. His chest burned inside and he went to cough but could not. He felt short of breath and light headed. His shoulder fired wave after wave of excruciating pain down his entire left side. Theodoric lay beside him also fully dressed but sound asleep. Thomas was obviously sleeping with the horses for he was nowhere to be seen. He could see Abi's legs as she lay upon the single bed in the adjoining room, the door ajar. Ishmael was asleep sat upright in the main chair, one of his two swords resting across his lap. Paul tried to clear his dry throat and rubbed his neck but he did not wish to wake everyone. The early morning sun was just beginning to break on the castle walls.

"Cough as loudly as you wish for they cannot hear you," Firgany said behind Paul.

Quickly he turned around in shock and surprise. There was no one else except Theodoric snoring beside him. Puzzled, Paul ran his hand through his hair. He sighed and closed his eyes and sat in silence for a few moments. He felt the side of the bed next to him sink as someone sat down, a hand touching his left shoulder with an instant burning pain shooting through him with an intensity that caused him to screw up his eyes in pain.

"Theo, what are you doing?" he asked and opened his eyes. His jaw visibly dropped as he saw Firgany sat beside him, his hand placed firmly upon Paul's injured shoulder. He blinked not believing his eyes or the physical sensation of his presence. Firgany was wearing the same robe he had worn to his and Alisha's wedding. He smiled reassuringly and looked at Paul with a pride he could sense.

"Do not worry, they cannot hear us," Firgany spoke softly, his eyes glistening with a look of approval and contentment Paul had never seen in a person's eyes before.

"How is this possible?"

"You are not exactly well at this moment. Did you not realise the fever that burns within you?" Firgany asked and smiled. Paul shook his head no. "'Tis from the wound and the foul water thrown upon Taqi. Some entered the open cut."

"Have I died?" Paul asked, alarmed, and looked at Theodoric and went to push him, Firgany just grabbing his forearm in time.

"No...but you are in that state that allows me to see and speak with you."

"Why only now?"

"Because now is the time when you and my son need me. Reynald this very minute beats him in his frustration and anger. If you do not intercede, Taqi shall surely be joining me yet his allotted time is breaking," Firgany explained and smiled, which confused Paul. "Say hello to Alisha for me when next you see her."

∞

Paul gasped for air and sat up fast, opening his eyes wide. Theodoric opened his eyes and looked up at him concerned seeing the sweat beading down his forehead. Paul looked at his hands and the fact that he was still lying upon the bed not sitting. He looked around the room for Firgany.

"Paul...what is it?" Theodoric asked as Ishmael stood up raising his sword, looking around the room too.

Quickly Paul stood up, pulled his clothing down to straighten it out. Grasped his sword and unsheathed it. Abi entered the room tightening her sword belt.

"'Tis Taqi...he is being beaten...quickly, we must go to his aid," Paul explained and rushed for the door.

"Paul…you must wait," Abi called out but he was already out of the door. She looked at Theodoric as he rolled off the bed and pulled out a small arming dagger. "You will need a greater weapon than that for what is about to unfold."

"Here," Ishmael said as he threw his second sword, Theodoric just catching it.

Ishmael and Theodoric quickly followed Abi out into the corridor just as Princess Stephanie opened her door opposite, looking alarmed. She tied off the strap of her night gown around her waist and hurried after them as they all ran off down the corridor toward the main stairs.

Paul could hear Reynald grunting with exhaustion and the sound of his fists lumping into flesh as he assaulted Taqi. Two of his own personal guards stood up to bar Paul's route as he ran down the wide stairs toward the iron gated entrance to the dungeons. Light streamed in through the only single window to his right ending in a burst of light upon a single wooden table. The two guards stood together and smirked at Paul as he approached, their hands tucked into their sword belts. Both wore their helmets, which made Paul realise Reynald must have warned them of possible trouble.

"Out of my way or so help me Lord I shall part your heads from your shoulders this very hour!" Paul demanded pointing his sword at them held with both hands. The two guards looked at each other and laughed as another blow upon Taqi echoed out. "NOW!" Paul shouted, swung his sword up and crashed it down upon the table shattering it. As splinters flew, the table fell in half with a loud thud. The two guards looked on in horror and amazement. Paul swung the blade back toward them. Instantly they moved aside, one pushing the other hard to get out of the way. As they shuffled nervously past Paul, his eyes staring into theirs, Abi ran into view. Quickly Paul turned to see Reynald throw another punch on Taqi, who was tied up by the hands, hanging lifeless from the vaulted ceiling. Paul swung the iron gate open with a loud bang and ran toward the end cell. "Reynald!"

Reynald looked up, staggered backwards and went to stand up straight. He was covered in blood…Taqi's blood! He laughed when he saw Paul run into the cell. Without hesitation Paul swung his sword against the iron chain holding Taqi up. It sparked with a brilliant flash as the sword cut through it like a knife through soft bread. Reynald blinked in surprise momentarily but rushed to grab Paul as Taqi fell upon the filthy stone floor. Instinctively Paul thrust his right elbow into Reynald's face hard knocking him backwards onto his backside. Paul put his left arm around Taqi and helped to move him against the cell railings. Taqi's hands and feet were still tied as he coughed up blood in pain. Paul pointed his sword back toward Reynald as he jumped to his feet. Abi rushed in looking at the scene.

"Unfasten him!" Paul yelled and threw his arming dagger at Abi. She just caught it and knelt down beside Taqi. "We are leaving this hour with Taqi."

Reynald stepped forward with both his hands raised and smirked at Paul.

"You have just given me the perfect excuse to mount your head upon a spike over the main gates," he grinned.

"Not before your head is thrown to the birds," Paul replied and held his sword with both hands pointing it at Reynald. "Move a step closer and I swear by all that is holy I shall end your life this very minute."

Abi quickly cut though the ropes holding Taqi's feet together but she could not loosen the iron cuffs around his wrists. She lifted him to his feet. He looked at her through his bloodshot and swollen eyes. He feigned a brave smile, his teeth all covered in blood, rolled his eyes and passed out. As he went limp, Abi threw him over her shoulder, held him in place and drew her sword just as Ishmael and Theodoric appeared at the entrance. Theodoric yanked the set of keys that hung from the guard's belt as he stood perfectly still. As soon as Theodoric lifted the keys into view, the two guards ran up the stairs.

"You will never exit this castle alive," Reynald boasted and wiped his sweating face.

"Follow me...and I will kill you," Paul stated as he backed out of the cell following Abi carrying Taqi.

"Oh I shall follow you," Reynald said loudly and smirked again as he started to follow Paul as he began to back up the stairs, Ishmael leading the way. "You had better run me through right here and now for I am following you," Reynald goaded.

Paul did not know if Reynald had finally gone mad or had a death wish as he confidently followed him step for step. Ishmael held the heavy wooden door open so Abi could walk through into the wide corridor that led along the western wall toward the inner bailey keep courtyard. Abi ran along it with Taqi on her shoulder as if he weighed nothing. Ishmael beckoned Theodoric to follow her as Paul kept Reynald at a sword's distance. Paul then stood still and stared at Reynald hard and positioned himself ready to strike him. Reynald froze, his eyes blazing and wide. He laughed out loud and put his hands upon his waist. He suddenly threw himself at Paul using his left arm to knock the sword aside. Paul let himself fall backwards and used Reynald's own weight to throw him over. As he passed over, Paul used his left hand to grab Reynald's belt, causing him to land heavily, winding himself, Paul then rolling onto his side still firmly holding Reynald's belt. He flung his sword around in his hand and pointed it down directly above Reynald's throat. Reynald just looked up at him and laughed again. He could end it all right here and now, Paul thought to himself. Do not hesitate, do not hold back. Think of the many lives you will save. He gripped his sword handle tightly, his knuckles turning white, Reynald seeing the decision had been made in Paul's eyes. Reynald did not struggle…he just let out a resigned sigh as if wanting death.

"NO!" Princess Stephanie suddenly screamed from the far end of the corridor as she appeared, out of breath looking shocked, her hands to her face.

Both Paul and Reynald turned their heads together to look at her. She shook her head no. Paul was not sure what she was implying. He looked back down at Reynald as he started to laugh at him. Paul pushed him down hard and stood up. Quickly he moved away toward Ishmael holding the end door open. As Reynald rolled over on the floor, Princess Stephanie rushed to his side but he simply pushed her away aggressively and started to walk toward the door, Ishmael slamming it shut with a loud echo. Princess Stephanie immediately followed Reynald.

As the loud bang of the door echoed out, Paul caught up with Abi and Theodoric on the far side of the large vaulted anti-room. It was whitewashed and the morning sun shining through the arched windows made them squint their eyes as Theodoric started to open the exit door. Suddenly the door burst inwards as one of Reynald's guards pushed his way into the room followed by several more. Theodoric backed up to stand beside Abi shielding Taqi. Paul ran to stand in front of them as Ishmael guarded their rear. Brother Upside ran in behind Reynald's guards, sword drawn closely, followed by Nicholas. As they all moved to positions where they could all see each other, the alarm bell outside started ringing to alert the rest of Reynald's knights and men. The other door swung open with a loud bang almost falling off its hinges as Reynald kicked the door and stepped into the room. He paused as he took a deep breath and wiped his hand across his face. He stared hard at Paul and smirked. Gerard ran into the room behind Nicholas followed by Stewart. In alarm Stewart immediately moved toward Paul but Gerard grabbed him by the arm and held him back. Confused, Stewart looked at Paul for an answer as Reynald started to move toward them, Princess Stephanie entering the room.

"Too soft...I said it would be your downfall. You should have killed me whilst you could," Reynald stated through gritted teeth.

"Just hold on a moment, My Lord," Gerard said and raised his hand for him to stop.

"Not this time, Gerard. This time this man has gone too far," Reynald snarled back.

Abi gently placed Taqi upon the stone floor. Stewart and Nicholas both seeing the bloodied state of him looked at each other. Upside shook his head disapprovingly at Reynald.

"Let us pass or many of you will die," Abi stated matter of factly and raised her sword and swung it about her head several times making a loud whooshing sound as the blade cut through the air before finally stopping and pointing it at the main bulk of Reynald's men whilst half crouching over Taqi protectively. "The odds are not in your favour."

"The fucking arrogance!" Reynald bellowed. "'Tis all false bravado for you are outnumbered."

Paul looked at Reynald briefly then at Gerard.

"You know this is madness...you also know your Order does not surrender unless outnumbered three to one or more yes?" Paul asked and quickly looked back at Reynald. "Well, we do not surrender ever," Paul stated. Stewart pushed past Gerard. "No, Stewart...this is our fight and our decision...I am sure Gerard would allow you to retire from this fight?"

"He stays exactly where he is or we will consider him on your side," Reynald yelled.

All stood in silence for several moments as both sides weighed up their options. Paul could sense that Gerard was not party to Reynald's ranting.

1 - 9

"Your great Lord Reynald will bring ruin and death upon all of you, if not today, then certainly within weeks…months at best," Abi stated.

Theodoric raised his sword and stood closer to Paul and looked at Reynald.

"Reynald…you were once in this very same position stood beside me… what has happened to you?" he asked, looking at Reynald.

"You dare to ask me such questions when you stand with those traitorous bastards trying to help an enemy assassin escape," Reynald shouted and pointed to Taqi.

"He was not your enemy!" Paul retorted as Gerard held back several more of his knights at the doorway. "You have broken your promise, again!"

"You, you have always been a Muslim lover…and…and I bet you schemed and planned all manner against us whilst you were away supposedly in the desert for nearly a month. You plot against us," Reynald shouted and shrugged his shoulders. Princess Stephanie slowly moved herself around the side of the wall so she could watch both groups. "Kill them now…go on kill them. I order it or by Heaven I will have you all in chains before the day is done!"

Gerard looked at Reynald, bemused. Stewart looked at Paul and in that instant made a decision as time was running out. He moved to stand beside Gerard, paused and looked at him.

"You know I cannot stand with you on this order. Please explain to Lord Reynald the finer points of our Order's rule and how we can challenge an order…I am now challenging any order you may now be forced to make if you follow his instruction," Stewart explained, his heart beating so hard and his stomach tied in knots. Gerard simply nodded at him in silence and looked over at Reynald as Stewart walked to Paul and stood beside him, nodded an acknowledgment and immediately drew his sword. Paul shook his head no he must not. "This is one decision, my brother, I should have made a long time ago."

"Oh how fucking sweet and lovely. Okay Gonfanier…you can join them all in hell," Reynald shouted and waved his hand at Stewart.

Nicholas and Upside moved to stand on either side of Gerard, blocking the doorway. Paul started to usher Ishmael to follow him closely as Theodoric knelt to lift Taqi up. Abi quickly slung him over her shoulder again as Paul made it clear he was heading for the doorway. Princess

Stephanie could hardly breathe as she watched helplessly as Reynald's knights formed up behind Nicholas, Gerard and Upside. Nicholas gulped hard whilst Gerard rapidly weighed up the unfolding scene before him. Reynald started to laugh. Paul looked at Nicholas.

"Nicholas…Upside…this is a crime committed here upon Taqi…a crime pure and simple. No man is above the law of our God. When exposing a crime is treated as a crime, then we know we are being ruled by criminals…," he stated and quickly looked back at Reynald, who just laughed out loud again at his words. Gerard raised his eyebrows and shook his head. "Look at how this so-called lord uses you and your Order for his insane bloodlust…what changed in him?"

All in the room looked at Reynald as he stood alone.

"Do not preach in my castle to me, boy!" he shouted angrily. "And who cares what you think. When you have lost the respect of all your peers and people you looked up to, then you no longer care…I lost all of that a very long time ago…didn't I, Theo?"

"'Tis never too late, My Lord, to step back onto your true path of destiny," Theodoric answered.

"Horseshit!" Reynald shouted and raised his arms, exasperated and animated. "Absolute fucking horseshit," he shouted again and louder, his face turning red. "If I am like this, 'tis your doing with all that so-called sacred and esoteric rubbish you fed me in Aleppo…do you remember, about so-called fucking destiny and my bloodline. If I had never listened to you we would not now be in this position…and you…you," he shouted pointing his finger at Paul. "I bet he has filled your head with the same horseshit… go on! Tell me I am wrong."

"Yes, go on tell us he is wrong for I too have seen your parchments with Elohim written beside your name," Gerard interjected and folded his arms.

"What?" Paul asked, surprised. Then he recalled how his father had written Elohim upon his parchments back in La Rochelle to explain the makeup and meaning of the words, not that he was implying he was Elohim himself. "How wrong can you be? 'Twas just my father's writing to explain its meaning…I am no Elohim."

"Then explain the sword," Gerard remarked.

"You know all about this sword as do you, Reynald…," Paul replied and looked at Reynald, who was now pacing up and down rubbing his fingers across his forehead.

"Oh I know all about that damned sword and all it brings with it…crossing destiny does not work in your favour believe you me, boy."

"We are leaving," Paul stated and started to move toward the door. Nicholas took a deep breath and stood before him and looked at him hard but confused too. Gerard simply raised his eyebrows waiting to see what he would do. Paul raised his sword as Stewart readied his. "You are either on my side, by my side…or in my fucking way…now choose wisely," Paul stated, his voice becoming deep as the energy from the sword surged through his body.

Princess Stephanie started to cry seeing that a fight was now unstoppable. She looked at Reynald as he roared with laughter. Nicholas looked behind him at all the other Templars now formed up and Reynald's knights. Slowly he turned to face Upside, their eyes locking. Upside feigned a smile and slight nod. Both drew their swords as Gerard stepped back a pace. Paul braced himself ready for the onslaught disappointed in Nicholas as he pointed his sword at Paul and their eyes met. Reynald laughed even louder.

"Paul," Nicholas said, his sword shaking, his eyes widening. "See this sword…" He paused and looked at Gerard. "'Tis yours for as long as I draw breath," he stated clearly and loudly, immediately stepping forward and took up position beside Paul. "Always have and always will be by your side."

Upside raised his eyebrows and rolled his eyes in an exaggerated fashion and quickly moved to stand the other side of Paul, shaking his head at Nicholas. Paul gulped hard with emotion, took a deep breath and looked at Gerard.

"You always get me in balls deep every time," Upside muttered at Nicholas then winked at Paul.

Reynald stopped laughing immediately and looked at Gerard and outstretched his hands toward him, shaking his head.

"Gerard!" Reynald snapped. "Do something!"

Gerard raised his hand to his mouth, more to hide his smile from Reynald. He then rubbed his chin several times as he looked at Paul intently. He had a grudging respect for him and even admired him. Yes he knew he had superior numbers still, but in the confines of the ante-room, he also knew any fighting would be costly in men and, even then, there was no guarantee who would come out victorious.

"My Lord…it would seem we have a dilemma on our hands."

"There is no dilemma here," Princess Stephanie interrupted and started to walk across the room toward Paul's group. When she stopped, she looked first at Gerard, then Paul and finally to Reynald. "You all forget one simple fact here," she stated and took a deep breath clearly shaking with fear and emotion. "This is my castle…my lands and my men!"

"Pah!" Reynald rasped and clapped his hands by his sides mockingly.

Gerard rested back slightly and looked on intrigued but saying nothing.

"What happened to you?" Princess Stephanie asked and slowly walked toward Reynald staring him in the eyes. "Where is that courageous, honourable, charismatic and noble man I fell in love with all those years ago?… For look at you now," she asked so all could hear.

"I am a noble lord and pray you never forget that or your place, woman," Reynald snarled back. Gerard shook his head and placed his hands upon his hips. "You would side with these traitors…these Muslim loving devious conniving and scheming peasants!"

"Peasants you say," Princess Stephanie repeated and looked back at Paul, his eyes searching hers and seeing the fear in them. "That man there, the very same man who saved your life twice….TWICE!" she shouted, "has more nobility in his little finger than you now possess."

"What!" Reynald fumed and pulled out his arming dagger, grabbed Princess Stephanie by her throat and half bent her backwards placing the dagger's blade against her chest.

Paul immediately moved to help her but Abi grabbed the back of his robe, stopping him.

"Reynald…enough of this," Gerard said calmly and began to walk toward him.

"Stop where you are for I see you are all against me," Reynald snarled as spit ran from his mouth, his teeth gritted in anger, his eyes darting from one man to the next. Taqi started to open his eyes and tried to move as he came round. "Him…I want his head on a pole now! Do you hear me…do it," he commanded.

Several of his own knights moved to step forward nervously when Gerard raised his hand for them to stop, his Templar knights moving to block them.

"Stay where you are!" Princess Stephanie called out despite the dagger being pushed up against her chest nicking her skin and forming a rivulet of blood. Pain was running through her back as Reynald forced her backward. "I repeat, Reynald…this is my castle and my men. Check our wedding contract...and let us see what the Haute Cour has to say of this matter shall we."

"You cheap whore!" Reynald yelled and pushed her to the floor aggressively. She went to crawl on her side but Reynald kicked her hard in the ribs. She let out a moan but held her pain refusing to show how bad she was hurting. She looked up at him defiantly, her eyes blazing with anger and pain.

"Too far my friend, too far," Gerard said and shook his head disapprovingly.

Paul tried to move but Abi pulled him back again.

"My castle...my men," Princess Stephanie said and stood herself up slowly. She pulled her dress straight and looked at the men before her. "You are under my roof, in my castle and you follow my orders. I am ordering you to let these people leave without harm or malice upon them."

"Oh no you don't," Reynald yelled and pulled her hair, forcing her to fall backward upon her shoulders hard. "You stay down, woman, or by Heaven I swear I shall put you down like an unwanted dog for good!" Reynald snarled, pointing his dagger at her.

Princess Stephanie rolled onto her side, jumped to her feet and in one swift move punched Reynald as hard as she could using the palm of her hand up into his nose as she had seen Tenno teach Alisha, the crack of his nose breaking echoing in the room. He staggered backwards stunned, his eyes wide until he hit the whitewashed walls, his legs striking a wooden bench that ran the length of the wall. He raised the dagger toward her but before he could stand up properly again, she kicked him squarely in the groin and several men groaned and winced in sympathy as she did so. He recoiled in pain but looked up at her, his face full of rage.

"I heard every word you spoke to Alisha in her chambers when you tried to bargain a night with her in exchange for Taqi," Princess Stephanie stated calmly, pointing her finger at him as Reynald tried to catch his breath whilst covering his groin with both hands. "I was in the very same room and I heard all you said...about your whoring and killing...you will never ever lay a finger upon me again that I do swear, you animal...and may I remind you that you only have position here because of me and I have barons who will stand by my side, not yours, so do not test my resolve."

"Whore!" Reynald screamed and grabbed her by her long hair again and pulled her close to him. Panting and trying to catch her breath she stared into his glaring eyes as he put the dagger up against her throat. "So I have nothing left to lose by opening your pretty little neck now do I?"

Princess Stephanie gulped hard, her eyes wide with terror but she was not going to change her mind now.

"Go ahead then...do it! The man I loved is no longer anywhere within you. You are but a shell of the man I once knew...when he died inside, I too died...bit by little bit daily. Not any more...so go ahead...finish what you have started and put me out of this living hell I endure with you," she said, a tear running down her face. "All the killing you have done...it has only served to all but kill you inside instead. Have you forgotten the words you once boasted to me, when first we met...that Eastern teaching?" she asked, trying to reach the man she once knew. He shook his head no, his pupils beginning to shrink. "A man who conquers himself is greater than one who conquers a thousand men in battle...do you remember?"

All looked on hesitantly, Abi checking out the number of men in the doorway still. She bent down and picked up Taqi under her left arm, Theodoric grabbing his other side in support.

Reynald looked down at Princess Stephanie as she just stared back at him, her arms hanging limp and submissively down. Her eyes glistened beautifully but filled with terror. He looked down her soft white skinned neck as she breathed in short sharp intakes, his blade across her throat. He looked closer at the blade as the sun reflected off of it and he saw his own filthy reflection. He blinked, shocked at the sight of himself. As if seeing through a clearing mist he looked into her eyes, his rage fading from his features. He looked up in time to see his young daughter Alix push past the men and into the room. Her eyes widened in alarm when she saw her mother bent backwards, her father holding a knife to her throat.

"Papa!" she called out and immediately ran toward them.

Reynald lowered Princess Stephanie to the floor, pulled the dagger away and fell down upon the bench shaking his head bewildered at his own actions. He dropped the dagger just as Alix flung her arms around Princess Stephanie and looked at Reynald, confused.

"Let them go...all of them...just let them go," he said quietly and waved his hand.

Gerard immediately nodded at the men for the door to be cleared. Abi and Theodoric quickly dragged Taqi out of the room as Ishmael and Paul covered them. Princess Stephanie sobbed, her eyes closed as she hugged

Alix, both now sat on the floor. After a minute, she coughed, wiped her eyes and quickly stood up. She held Alix's hand tightly and faced Reynald.

"We shall be leaving with them. You value this castle so much…then I hereby freely pass it to you with glee. I shall travel to Jerusalem with Alix and arrange for the appropriate papers to be drawn up."

"Are you divorcing or annulling out marriage?" Reynald asked, his voice almost broken. "But I love you," he said shaking his head and a tear welled in his eyes.

For an instant Princess Stephanie recognised the man she had once fallen in love with. There was just a spark of him still inside, she told herself, but she quickly shook her head no.

"I will not seek a divorce or annulment. But for my sanity and the safety of our daughter, we shall remain in Jerusalem until the man I once knew finds a way back to us," she said emotionally. "Kiss your father goodbye, Alix."

Alix nervously stepped toward him, when he grabbed her and pulled her close to his chest and wrapped both his arms around her. For a minute Princess Stephanie feared he would try and harm her and gasped hardly able to breathe.

"I…I love you both…I do," he said quietly, closed his eyes and kissed Alix on the cheek and held her. "'Tis a madness the Lord has cursed me with," he whispered and kissed her again.

"Come, Alix…we must go." Alix pushed herself away from Reynald and clasped Princess Stephanie's hand. She turned and walked toward the door not looking back once as Reynald just sat bewildered. She looked at Gerard as they walked past him. "Try and get back the man he once was… for all our sakes."

"What do you think I have been trying to do these past months?" Gerard shot back and grabbed her arm. "Perhaps you should have done this a long time ago," he continued in a whisper. She stared at him for a moment shocked by his remark. "He swears he does all of what he does to protect those he loves."

Princess Stephanie looked back at Reynald sat on the bench, his head lowered. She rubbed her hand across the cut upon her chest.

"The only thing he loves is killing and power," she sighed and looked back at Gerard. "And you know that is the truth for he has forgotten who and what he was."

Gerard went to speak but hesitated. He let go of her arm.

"I am sorry, My Lady...and if you are also now travelling to Jerusalem, you will need more of an escort than Paul and his few men...so please take some of my men...as several of them are already going," he half joked, looking at Nicholas and Upside.

"'Tis a kind gesture, Master Gerard. One that will not go unrecognised," she replied. "You have changed also...for the better I might add."

"We have all changed," he answered and clicked his fingers at one of his sergeants. "Fetch me my scribe set. I have orders to write, and make it quick," Gerard said and looked back at Reynald, who was sitting forwards resting his elbows on his knees, his head in his hands shaking from side to side. Gerard sighed heavily at the state of his friend.

Paul walked toward the stables, checking behind him in case Reynald changed his mind. Thomas was stood by the main entrance and looked on surprised to see an injured Taqi being carried by Abi and Theodoric protected by Stewart, Nicholas and Upside. He ran toward them.

"No Thomas, back quickly for we needs must leave now," Paul called out.

"What have I missed?" he asked.

"Everything...and Reynald seeing sense...but I am not sure for how long so we must leave now," Paul answered just as Princess Stephanie rushed toward then with Alix running by her side to keep up.

"Paul...we are coming with you," she called out. Paul frowned. "Just try stopping us."

Within minutes Thomas had all the horses brought out already saddled and ready to go along with the rest of his men. Stewart, Nicholas and Upside were changing their Templar robes when Gerard walked across the courtyard accompanied by the rest of his Templars.

"Stand by!" Abi said aloud drawing their attention, Ishmael wielding both his swords.

Theodoric led two horses pulling Princess Stephanie's caravan into view. He stood still as Gerard walked directly for him. Gerard stopped just feet away, his men all forming up behind him.

"Fear not we are not here to stop you. You will need more men to escort the Princess Stephanie...and I would be remiss in my duties if I did not furnish you with appropriate forces and support," he explained and proffered a sealed warrant for Paul to take. "Take it, man…'tis my sealed orders giving you temporary investiture of our Order and authority over my Templars, whom I charge to your command…here are the volunteers," he explained as twelve of the Templars behind him stepped forward. "'Tis long overdue for you naturally command men…I told you one day you would be part of our Order," Gerard smiled as Paul took the sealed warrant, more than a little surprised. "And you three," he called out looking over toward Stewart, Nicholas and Upside. "You are all in breach of marching fighting order protocol. You are incorrectly dressed…now put your mantels back on… unless of course you have all resigned?"

Nicholas looked at Upside, puzzled, then to Stewart.

"But Master…we directly disobeyed you," Stewart remarked.

"I do not recall any such thing. I do recall someone questioning the reasoning and validity of an order made in error as per our Order's rule… correct me if I am wrong?" Gerard explained. Nicholas smiled as Upside raised his eyebrows again and started to put his mantle back on. "'Tis a great honour to be chosen as the Order's Gonfanier and I know not of any better candidate capable of that responsibility…so please do not make me have to go through all the process of choosing another."

Paul did not know how to take Gerard's gesture but he was in no position to question why. He could see the pride in Stewart. He looked back at the caravan as Thomas nodded indicating Taqi was safely inside along with Princess Stephanie and Alix.

"Never thought I would be saying thank you to you…but thank you," Paul said to Gerard and offered his hand.

"I have much to do here. I grow old and war fighting is a young man's business. I shall do what I can to steer Reynald back into line…and should you see your friends, and maybe even Saladin, let him know some of us seek a peaceful existence…some more than others. And when you hand over your friend, put in a good word to Al Rashid from us here."

"I shall," Paul answered as Gerard shook his hand. "But I am a little surprised at this," he said lifting the warrant up.

"'Tis a pragmatic response from me…There is a very large shit storm coming our way and I need all the men I can get. That will also afford you some safety and security should you need it to get to Tortosa and home," he explained and paused briefly. "Plus 'tis an expedient manner of getting you out of my hair once and for all," Gerard said seriously…then smiled.

Gerard looked into his eyes for a few moments. Paul could sense he wished to say more but he didn't speak. He broke the handshake, bowed his head slightly at him and then Stewart before turning away. As he walked through the men he just raised his hand farewell. Paul looked down at the warrant again. Is this why his parchment had always shown him as a knight? he wondered And what had Reynald meant when he said crossing destiny does you no favours?

Port of La Rochelle, France, Melissae Inn, spring 1191

"And just like that Reynald let them go?" Peter asked bluntly, almost disbelievingly.

"Yes...'twas partly the shock of seeing Princess Stephanie so defiant and asking for death at his hand. Then having his daughter see them like that...it momentarily shook him to his senses," the old man replied.

"Momentarily you say?" Gabirol asked.

"Yes...'twas indeed a curse that was afflicting his very mind."

"Like that Bull's Head Bandit?" Simon asked.

"Almost identical indeed for Reynald had alas lost all recognition of moral boundaries. There was still a greater fury that burned within him for he had become blinded by his own invincibility and position too...but also his own sense of destiny!" the old man explained. "'Twas the thirteenth of January when Paul looked back at Kerak Castle for what he hoped was the last time. He did not feel like a leader of men but as they all rode off he looked ahead at Stewart carrying the Templar standard, Nicholas and Upside either side of him. Theodoric drove Princess Stephanie's caravan whilst Abi attended to Taqi's wounds and when Paul looked back at the rear guard of Templars, he knew and realised that everyone was there because of him, his actions and decisions...and willingly so."

4 - 29

"I still do not understand what you mean about 'crossing destiny'," Ayleth commented.

"Reynald was told a long time ago, in a similar fashion to some of Paul's experiences, that he had a destiny, one whereby he would not be allowed to eradicate the faith of Islam as he had vowed spurred on by the death of his first and only true love, Constance," the old man started to explain and moved upon his chair looking

uncomfortable for a moment. "But he believed nothing was foreordained and that he could set his own destiny...'tis why he constantly and deliberately orchestrated conflict between him and Saladin. That was his destiny he believed...for he had seen great battles to come whereby the souls of many thousands on all sides were slain in a sea of blood."

"So his original intentions were good and inspired?" the wealthy tailor asked.

"Yes I suppose you could say in his mind they were."

"So are our destiny's foreordained?" Sarah asked.

"It is my understanding that life is like a large storehouse. We enter one door and the exit is set on the other side at a predetermined location and distance. As we walk through that storehouse, we encounter many obstacles, hurdles, trials and tribulations, as well as many good times. Well, most of us do. Also there are many boxes we can open, look in and learn from. We can also take out from those boxes, but we must also put something in them otherwise they become empty for those who follow in our footsteps, especially our own children...and like a heart with no heartbeat, they become useless. Reynald constantly took out and instead of listening to his heart, for the heart is the only teacher any of us ever really need, he simply smashed his way from one box to another...and as Princess Stephanie said, in so doing killed his own heart."

"I have seen too many men turn that way," the Hospitaller interrupted and coughed. "I too almost turned that way..."

The Templar leaned over and rubbed his brother's shoulder reassuringly.

"Did they all reach Jerusalem safely and join up with Alisha then?" Simon asked.

"Can someone like Paul just be charged with a commission of warrant directly into the Order?" Gabirol asked.

"In special circumstances yes. How do you think Gerard started off? Can you ever imagine him following orders starting as just a knight?" the old man answered, the Templar nodding in agreement. "Paul had more than proved himself as a natural leader and intelligent. He certainly fell within all the strict criteria for admittance to the Order...but perhaps Gerard meant what he said."

"About ridding himself of Paul once and for all?" Gabirol commented.

"Yes, though a bond had grown between them and as I said, Gerard had developed a begrudging admiration and respect for him."

"I always knew that Gerard was not all bad," Sarah said and smiled at Ayleth and nudged her elbow.

"I still cannot fathom why we two have been given a warrant and commission to do whatever is contained here. Before we continue, can you not at least give us

both a clue how so and why?" the Templar asked, his brother nodding in agreement with him.

"I suppose now is as good a time as any to reveal parts of your true past also," the old man replied and looked at them both in silence for a moment. "You know of Hugues de Payens as we have already discussed?"

"Of course, as do all Templars...being one of the founding knights of the Order... in fact the first Grand Master even," the Templar replied immediately.

"Then know that within your warrants are copies of your family trees...you will see Hugues de Payens writ upon it for he was your great grandfather on your mother's side but also your great grandmother was in fact his wife, Catherine St Clair... which is another pronunciation of your own surname no less."

Sarah gasped loudly in surprise as the Templar looked stunned, the Hospitaller just lowering his head and laughing silently. He shook his head several times before looking up at the old man.

"Hang on," Gabirol said and quickly flicked through his notes. "Here...you said earlier that Hugues de Payens visited Alba and met with King David the First of Scotia. The king subsequently granting him and the Knights Templar the Chapelrie and Manor of Balantrodach...where these two must first go from here yes?"

The old man simply smiled and nodded yes.

"And you swear you speak the truth?" the Templar asked emotionally.

"I swear it. If you need confirmation, you can find it with the Marshal here in La Rochelle. He will happily decipher the code upon them to authenticate and validate all that will be given to you."

"Given to us?" the Templar asked, bemused.

"Yes...for there are deeds and titles as well as financial matters that legally belong to you both," the old man explained.

"But...but if we had not accepted these, then, then...," the Templar started to say but stopped.

"But I knew you would," the old man smiled.

The room fell silent as the Templar and Hospitaller looked at each other utterly confused and overwhelmed.

"Well if you need some new clothing," the wealthy tailor joked.

"I bet Alisha was relieved to see both Paul and Taqi arrive safely in Jerusalem then," the farrier stated after several more minutes of total silence in the room.

"She was that indeed," the old man smiled.

"You are not going to cry again are you?" Simon asked the Hospitaller bluntly as he stared at his sealed warrant held in both hands. He simply shook his head no.

"My brother and I have never been given anything, ever," the Templar stated.
"Next you will be telling us they are related to Paul or Alisha?" Peter remarked.

City of Jerusalem, Kingdom of Jerusalem, January 17th 1187

Stewart halted his horse at the edge of the tree lined road where the road opened out from the fertile hillside to the flat plateau before them. He pulled up the Templar standard that had been rolled up and attached along the side of his saddle. Quickly he unfurled it and pulled the banner taut. The midday sun blazed fiercely upon Paul's back and shoulders as he drew up alongside Stewart and Nicholas. Paul had been given a Templar mantle to wear as part of accepting Gerard's warrant. Though he knew it would only be temporary and he nevertheless had mixed feelings about wearing it. Half of him felt like a fraud but the other half felt proud. Thomas and his men had likewise been offered one each for the duration of the journey but refused, though it was Thomas who persuaded Paul he should wear one for ease of travel and passage through the various watchtowers and road outposts. Jerusalem shimmered and looked like it was surrounded by water. He recalled the first time he had seen the city. Theodoric applied the main brake on the caravan and wiped his brow. He was soaked in sweat. Paul was not sure if his injured shoulder was burning from the heat of the sun or if the wound was smarting. Soon he would see Alisha and Ailia again and he smiled.

"Brother...you must lead us in," Stewart remarked and gestured for Paul to move forward. He frowned at him. "'Tis our Order's tradition...," he smiled.

Paul looked to the rear of their small column.

"Thomas!" he called out just as Princess Stephanie opened the small sliding cover to the door of the caravan. She smiled at Paul as Thomas rode past. "Thomas...please will you join me at the front as we enter?"

"Would be an honour...I just pray the rest of my men have not fallen back into old ways and are presently otherwise engaged in the whore house," he laughed.

"Then let us find out," Paul replied and pulled his horse about and started to move off toward Jerusalem. He felt cold and shivered despite the heat and wondered if he was suffering from the heat or was indeed ill with a fever as Firgany had apparently told him. How would he explain that and what had happened to Alisha? he pondered.

ᘓᘐ

Paul stood alone waiting patiently inside the entrance area of the Templar Headquarters. He was covered in dust and sweat seeped through his chain mail and mantle. He removed the small spurs upon his boots and laughed to himself knowing Adrastos would have thrown him if he had worn them whilst riding him. Theodoric and Abi were already in the Hospitaller's main hospice getting Taqi administered to by Roger des Moulins himself. It would be good to see him again, Paul thought, and rubbed his face where he had stitched his wound back in La Rochelle. He smiled again thinking how things had changed for the better between him and Stewart since that event. Despite Reynald's severe beating Taqi's injuries were mercifully minor save several broken ribs and a dislocated shoulder. As he waited, his eyes fell upon the large strange mural he had studied in utter bemusement so many years previously. He shrugged his shoulders with a light laugh as he now looked upon it fully understanding all its meanings and symbolism. He took in a deep breath of the cool air inside the building and the silence all around him. In the distance a door closed and he listened as footsteps echoed from an approaching person. Paul looked at the dark star on the mural and the image of the crucifixion with the small tree shoot growing from it. Another door shut and echoed out directly into the long vaulted arch corridor as Count Henry appeared wearing his familiar cloak. He smiled broadly when saw that it was actually Paul stood before him. Quickly he approached and clasped Paul's forearm as Paul did the same with his.

"I hardly recognised you…what with the beard and, well…wearing all that get up too," Count Henry said, smiling. "My Lord, you have certainly grown. Please explain how this is so," he asked and stood back a pace to look at Paul.

"My Lord, 'tis a long story…but I must request of you that you pass on a message to Al Rashid most urgently. We have Taqi with us, now being attended as we speak for injuries sustained from Reynald."

"What…how? Was Reynald attacked?"

"No…Taqi was sent to warn Reynald but also proffer negotiations of working together. I am afraid I interceded and somewhat ruined the whole mechanism…from which Taqi was subsequently captured and personally beaten by Reynald."

"And you wish me to send word to Al Rashid but what exactly?"

"Gerard wishes to open negotiations on behalf of Reynald…but also that Taqi is with us and will be returned to his Order if they will accept him back."

"Paul!" Alisha called out as she stepped into view, the sun shining beams of light all around her as she moved, Ailia holding her hand tightly and Tenno stood behind them. Quickly they approached. "Paul, my love, you are here," she said and put her arm around his neck, kissed him on the lips softly, her eyes wide and excited to see him. "And Taqi?" she asked with alarm in her eyes.

"He is with us…he sits with Abi and Theo in the hospice," Paul replied just as Sister Lucy entered the corridor, heard what he said then quickly turned around gathered up her skirt and ran off toward the Hospitaller's hospice. "'Tis so good to see you both," Paul continued and rubbed his hand through Ailia's hair, knelt down and pulled her close and took her up in his arms. Tenno stood his usual bolt upright and nodded slightly. "And you are a sight for sore eyes, my friend. Thank you for watching over my family."

"'Tis my honour as always," Tenno replied in his clipped fashion and bowed his head slightly again.

"Papa…you stink," Ailia giggled and held her nose as he held her. Alisha laughed with relief and kissed him again, clearly happy and relieved to see him.

"I do not care," she remarked and smiled, her eyes not moving from his. "And he brought my brother with him." She then kissed him again softly and slowly.

"I…I shall speak with you later when you are refreshed for I see you have more pressing matters," Count Henry remarked, smiling, and placed his hand upon Paul's injured shoulder, blood instantly seeping through the chain mail and material of the mantle. "Ah…I see you too are injured. You must have that seen to…and that is an order. See, I can do that now you wear that," he joked referring to his mantle.

It was only then that Alisha realised Paul was wearing a filthy dust covered Templar mantle. Paul saw the look of alarm register in her eyes.

"'Twas just a temporary measure. I shall explain," Paul said reassuringly.

"Then do so as Roger sorts out that wound once and for all," she replied and started to pull him toward the main exit. Count Henry smiled and simply nodded at him and Tenno.

"I told Mama you would be here today," Ailia said and put her little arms around his neck, resting her head upon his uninjured shoulder.

"She did," Alisha remarked as she led them out into the courtyard.

Brother Teric appeared from the direction of the stables. He stood still as soon as he saw Paul with Alisha and Ailia.

"'Tis not possible," he laughed. "I have just spoken with your brother and Nicholas but I never thought I would see the day when you would be wearing our mantle…or have you answered King Guy's aria ban and call to arms?"

"Not for long," Alisha interjected and held him closer.

"No not at all…but follow me and I shall explain, my friend," Paul replied and smiled.

"Destiny crosses our paths again does it not?" Brother Teric asked and walked with them as Paul put his left arm around Alisha. "'Tis a good day."

Tenno nodded yes to himself as he followed closely behind them.

"And Percival…he is okay?" Paul asked.

"He trains with Thomas's men as he does all day and every day," Brother Teric answered.

As they walked across the courtyard Paul caught sight of Princess Stephanie and Alix being led away by the Patriarch Heracles and several of his entourage. He would catch up with her later, he thought to himself, relieved she was away from Reynald.

Chapter 71
The Tears of War

Hospitallers' quarter, Jerusalem, Kingdom of Jerusalem, January 17th 1187

Alisha entered the long cool corridor of the Hospitallers' great hospice and infirmary. She wore her long green dress she had not worn in years, Paul having found it at the bottom of their travelling trunk. It was the first dress he had ever seen her wear and the same day she stole his heart completely and effortlessly. Paul held Ailia in his arms, Tenno following closely as always now. Brother Teric spoke some pleasantries to two Hospitallers dressed only in their single full length working order white and blue robes. Brother Teric faced Alisha and beckoned her to follow. After a short walk along the corridor, they turned off into a side passage that had eight doors, four on either side. Incense burned away filling the air with a pleasant fragrance, the marbled floor gleaming with a clean shine. Brother Teric checked the small chit he had been handed and knocked upon the far end door to room 5.

"Enter," Master Roger called out.

Brother Teric smiled and winked at Alisha as she eagerly approached the door. As he held the door open for her, she rushed inside and froze as she looked in shock at Taqi sat up in bed but his eyes hidden beneath a wrap of bandages. She gasped, which immediately drew Taqi's attention. Master Roger stepped closer to her and smiled seeing the concern upon her face.

"He looks worse than he is. The bandages are to help remove infection he has within his eyes," he explained reassuringly in his usual calm and soft voice.

Alisha moved quickly to sit in the chair beside Taqi's bed, clasping her hand over his and kissed the side of his face.

"Allah be praised you are safe," Taqi remarked and smiled, placing his left hand over her face to check it was really her. "'Tis wondrous indeed to know you are here and safe."

Alisha smiled but tears welled in her eyes seeing how bruised and swollen his face was. A single white sheet covered him up to his waist but she could clearly see the almost black bruises up his side and the distended areas where his ribs had been broken. She kissed his hand and held it tightly as Paul and Tenno stepped into view. Paul silently pointed to his own eyes whilst looking at Master Roger. He simply shrugged his shoulders and indicated with a slight nod then shake of his head he was not sure if he would go blind or not. A light knock at the door drew all of their attention as Attar appeared. He smiled and bowed his head in greeting and stepped inside.

"Paul, please come and see me in my quarters when you can, please. I have cleaned out his wounds, checked his lungs are not damaged and rinsed his eyes with rose water and applied some honey based ointments. Attar, 'tis good timing. Perhaps you would avail yourself to help me with Taqi's eye infection?" Master Roger said as Attar moved closer to Taqi. He simply nodded in silence and sat in the chair opposite to Alisha.

Ailia looked on puzzled at everyone and pulled her small comfort blanket close. Paul hugged her as Tenno looked at Taqi, concerned. Master Roger indicated with a slight nod of his head for Paul to follow him outside. Tenno took Ailia from him as he followed Master Roger into the hallway and walked to the main corridor. The whitewashed walls made the interior look far bigger than it actually was.

"Just tell me straight. With the swelling and infection, will he lose his sight?" Paul asked quietly.

"I cannot answer for certain. The infection is severe. I have seen men with lesser lose the eye. Perhaps you can get Theodoric to make up some of his famed threefold water?" Master Roger explained and asked.

"Blind…he would rather be dead!"

"'Tis early days yet. I am afraid Reynald knew exactly what he was doing. Just enough damage to incapacitate him and enough muck thrown at him to infect him so he remains alive but not well enough to be of any trouble. He was fortunately incredibly fit and otherwise in good health," Master Roger said and paused as he looked at Paul, who was shaking very slightly, his face pale and despite the heat, not sweating. "You, my friend, I also note are unwell."

"'Tis just a mild fever."

"I think not. I must finish some paperwork...new statutes and rules on dress code to get rid of the impracticable closed cape in favour of a new open version. Silly details but it makes a massive difference in the field. But come and see me nonetheless when you are ready and I can give you something for your fever."

"Thank you. I shall. But how long do you think it will take before we know about his eyes?" Paul asked and looked back toward Taqi's room, concerned.

"Hard to say. But he will not be going anywhere soon that is certain."

Paul pondered Master Roger's words. They could not leave until Taqi was fit enough to travel again. No way would he leave him alone especially if Reynald was due to come as King Guy had decreed. Time was not on their side. He would see if Theodoric could make up some threefold water but also if there was a way he could get Taqi back to Al Rashid sooner rather than later. His thoughts were interrupted as Percival, Thomas and Abi entered the corridor, approaching fast, their footsteps echoing out.

"Thank you...and I shall visit you later," Paul said and bowed his head slightly to Master Roger. "Thank you."

"'Tis good to see you arrived here safely," Percival called out and pulled Paul close, hugging him briefly. Abi smiled just as Thomas nodded at him. "But promise me no subterranean adventures whilst we are here."

Paul stood back a pace and looked at Percival.

"I promise no visits...and thank you for bringing Alisha and Ailia here safely," Paul replied.

"That was easy enough," Percival remarked. "The next part of getting to Tortosa will not be as easy."

Port of La Rochelle, France, Melissae Inn, spring 1191

"How come Taqi, as a Muslim, was allowed to be treated by the Hospitallers or was it simply because he was a friend?" the farrier asked.

The old man looked across at the Hospitaller to answer.

"In our hospices we are free to treat all and any person of any race, creed, gender or religion. Our Order is clearly divided into our military brothers, like myself, and those who work with the sick...and they treat all who come to them," the Hospitaller answered.

"I hear your Order is equal to the Templars'. Is this so?" the farrier asked further.

"I think we could agree upon that," the Hospitaller replied as his brother nodded in agreement.

1 - 6

"The Hospitallers', like the Templars', is still a religious Order that has privileges granted by the Papacy," the old man explained. "Like the Templars they too are exempt from all authority save that of the Pope, and it pays no tithes and is allowed its own religious buildings. Most of the more substantial Christian fortifications in the Holy Land are built by the Templars and the Hospitallers, who alone hold seven great forts and 140 other estates in the area. The two largest of these, their bases of power in the Kingdom and in the Principality of Antioch, are Crac de l'Ospital and Margat. The property of the Order is divided into priories, subdivided into bailiwicks, which in turn are divided into Commanderies. Frederick Barbarossa, the Holy Roman Emperor, pledged his protection to the Knights of St John in a charter of privileges granted in 1185 which initially stirred some rivalry with the Templars but thankfully by Master Roger's diplomatic hand, a closer working relationship now exists between them as I mentioned previously. But back to your question. Taqi was treated like any other. The hospital in Jerusalem is large enough for two thousand patients and the wards are staffed by a Brother-in-Charge and twelve assistants, though Taqi was afforded a room alone for obvious reasons. There are even separate wards for women staffed by female servants. There are four physicians and four surgeons and as Alisha and Paul saw, the wards are kept clean and well ventilated. There were about three hundred Brothers altogether resident in Outremer that year. Food was always lavish to say the least because the Order knew the basic connection between recovery and eating good food. They learnt this from the many Arab influences in terms of the practice of medicine."

"Why do they do all that?" Ayleth asked, puzzled, and faced the Hospitaller.

"Because helping to heal the sick is understood as an act of Christian love," the Hospitaller replied. "Every poor man and woman should not just have good treatment, but the best and most luxurious treatment possible."

"And Taqi received that?" the farrier asked.

"Yes and in person from Master Roger mainly until Paul could organise their departure for Tortosa," the old man answered.

"I wish to know why would it not be so easy to travel to Tortosa, as you said earlier?" Ayleth asked.

"Because Saladin had many raiding parties out upon the land. King Guy had decreed all men fit enough for warfare must muster in Jerusalem...they must not engage in hostilities and avoid them at all cost until he could determine how many knights and men he actually had at his disposal. This meant many of the pilgrims and trade routes were left unguarded and unescorted parties would be liable to attack from either Saladin's forces or bandits who were seizing upon the approaching instability in the region," the old man explained.

"I take it Taqi would be staying in Jerusalem then?" Gabirol asked.

"Attar had been sent by Al Rashid upon hearing of his position, courtesy of a carrier pigeon no less, which just proved yet again how effective his own network was at passing on intelligence fast...," the old man started to explain.

"Did he lose his sight then?" Sarah asked bluntly.

The old man looked at her and shook his head no.

"Luckily for Taqi he received the best treatment from Master Roger when he required it the most. Plus some infusions made up by Attar."

"Such as...and why did Roger need to speak with Paul alone?" Peter asked.

"Attar brought a special bean that when roasted and crushed then mixed with other herbs helped Taqi's body fight the infection within his eyes. 'Tis called caffe or coffee, from the Arabic word qahwa, which changed to qahwi then to qahfi to caffè. The Arab world has given birth to many thinkers and many inventions, among them the three-course meal, alcohol and this coffee. Muslim mystics treasure it," the old man started to explain.

"Where does this caffe drink come from?" Sarah asked. "Perhaps we can sell it here."

"It comes from the highland areas of the countries at the southern end of the Red Sea, Yemen. 'Twas the Yemenis who gave it the Arabic name qahwa, which originally meant wine, and Sufi mystics used it as an aid to concentration and even spiritual intoxication when they chanted the name of God," the old man continued to explain then paused for a moment. "But I digress from your question why Master Roger requested Paul to meet with him...it was so he could introduce him to one of his best knights...a tall and rather odd character at best," the old man explained and chuckled to himself. "He was once a Templar, but by the request of Master Roger he joined the Hospitallers instead."

"How was he odd?" Simon asked curiously.

"Odd is perhaps the wrong word," the old man answered. "The knight I speak of was an orphan found abandoned within Cashtal yn Ard, or the Castle of the Heights...'tis a well preserved chambered tomb situated on raised land overlooking

the parish of Maughold on the Isle of Man. The monument where he was found was originally a megalithic chambered cairn of a conical heap of stones built as a landmark. Some say it was used as a communal burial place for ancient chieftains and their families but now most of the stone cairn has been stripped away. The large firmly set stones create a dramatic burial site and it was providential that a very young boy, Theodoric, just happened to be visiting when he found the baby wrapped in swaddling. Even as a child he had the whitest of hair and the most piercing blue eyes."

"Isle of Man you say...the place you mentioned previously?" Gabirol asked.

"Yes...and Theodoric took the baby to the small church of Saint Mary of the Isle Douglas where the young Theodoric had been working as an apprentice upon its construction. Remember how I explained that the Isle of Man and Anglesey were and are populated by Irish Aryans and were sacred spots where the Arch Druids based themselves...the Arch Druids being the highest ranking members of Britain's priestly class who inherited their knowledge from the Babylonian Brotherhood via the Phoenicians?"

"I recall and I made notes because you stated it was connected to the mystical Isle of Avalon," Gabirol stated.

"Good...but this knight...incredibly brave and both physically and mentally strong, was different in that he openly opposed any belief in what we call God as we are taught...," the old man explained. "He believed in an eternal soul and a form of a collective conscience...which is why he got into so much trouble within the Templar Order...but Master Roger liked him and saw something in him."

"You mean he was what I think our local Father at church terms an 'atheist'...is that the correct term?" the wealthy tailor said.

The old man nodded yes in agreement.

"What was this knight's name?" the Hospitaller asked.

"Master Douglas!"

"My Lord," the Hospitaller exclaimed, visibly surprised. "You mean Lone Master Douglas?"

"Yes...that is another name he was afforded. Lone, for he was acknowledged as a Master of the Order but commanded no men."

"How is that possible?" Gabirol asked, perplexed.

"Master Douglas, despite his claims of being an atheist, was incredibly knowledgeable and entrusted with the highest initiate secrets of both the Templars and Hospitallers...as well as those of the Sufi!" the old man explained and looked at the Hospitaller.

"We knew of him well enough...but," the Hospitaller started to explain until the old man placed his finger upon his lips requesting his silence.
"So why would Master Roger want Paul to meet him?" Simon asked.

Hospitaller's quarter, Jerusalem, Kingdom of Jerusalem, January 17th 1187

A single Knight Hospitaller sergeant stood watch at the junction of the corridor leading to Master Roger's chambers. Several small ceramic oil lamps flickered away set within several equally spaced alcoves. The late evening was quiet save for the distant moaning of a patient somewhere off in the distance. The sergeant nodded acknowledgment to Paul and knocked upon the door gently.

"Enter," Master Roger called out. The sergeant opened the door for Paul. He bowed his head slightly as he stepped through the low doorway to see Master Roger sat behind his large wooden table, a Hospitaller flag draped in front of it hanging down to the floor. A lanthorn illuminated the room, Master Roger smiling broadly as the door closed behind Paul but he immediately jumped to his right grasping his sword handle as he caught sight of a tall man to his left who had been hidden by the open door. The tall man raised his left eyebrow, then smiled as he looked across at Master Roger. "Paul…here is Master Douglas, whom I wish you to meet. You have much in common."

"We do?" Paul asked puzzled as Master Douglas offered his hand. "Honoured to meet you," he said and went to shake his hand. Master Douglas grasped Paul's forearm as Paul gripped his in return. Even in the semi darkness of the corner of the room Paul could see his blue eyes. They immediately reminded him of Kratos. His grip was firm and Paul could easily feel the solidness of his forearm muscles through the long sleeve chainmail as it fitted him tightly. He held his stare. "Do I know you already?" Paul heard himself ask aloud.

"Not from this life time," Master Douglas replied in a strong confident but well spoken manner. "But I shall make it my business to know you in this one."

"I hear you do not believe in God," Paul remarked as they broke their grip and stood apart as Master Roger stood up.

"Not the pathetic jealous and vengeful God your Bible speaks of…no I do not." Master Douglas answered and studied Paul's face carefully, looking for his reaction. "Do not get me wrong for I will stand up and defend any man or woman's choice to believe in whatever they wish...and that includes the boy lovers of the den...but I will not be told how I must see things nor be told how I must understand matters."

"I like a person who is not afraid to speak his mind. But why do you not believe in what Christians believe?" Paul asked.

"I like a man who wastes no time in getting to the point," Master Douglas smiled and stepped closer to Paul to look at him better. "If you speak to an unknown and unseen person by yourself alone, you are considered mad. Do it in a crowd and it is accepted as talking to a higher deity, a God, and you have religion. So you tell me why sending thought messages to a Jewish ghost, Holy Spirit whatever, telling him you will accept his jealous and vengeful love under the conditions of his laws as your absolute master, removing your own free will and judgement, only to then ask him to remove a curse that was passed down to you because an old woman that was made from the rib of a man ate a magical apple because she was told to do so after talking with a speaking snake...so ask me again why I do not believe as Christians do."

Paul looked at Master Roger quickly but he just shrugged his shoulders and smiled back. When Paul looked back at Master Douglas, he was tall and imposing, yet the look he gave Paul when he raised both his eyebrows made him laugh. He could not contain his laughter despite covering his mouth with his hand. Master Roger started to laugh. When Master Douglas raised his eyebrows even further, Paul laughed even more.

"I...I am so sorry...for laughing," Paul exclaimed, waving his arms as he tried to contain himself.

Master Douglas looked at Master Roger, puzzled, but then started to laugh himself. As Master Douglas placed his fingers from both hands around his sword belt he started to roar with laughter. As the three looked at each other laughing, Paul eventually managed to calm himself down. Whether it had been a mixture of the release of tension or tiredness, he was not sure, but it was the first time since Arri had died that he had laughed. The enormity of that simple fact was not lost on him as he wiped his eyes. He sighed and laughed lightly at the same time. Images of Arri laughing flashed through his mind. For a few moments Paul stood still, Masters Roger and Douglas looking at him closely as they stopped laughing.

"I had forgotten what it was like to laugh," Paul said quietly. "Forgive my impoliteness."

"'Tis no impoliteness I assure you. We are indeed alike as Master Roger has informed me. 'Tis an honour to make your acquaintance. I have heard much of you and I know your father well," Master Douglas said and nodded at Paul.

"The honour is mine I am sure," Paul replied and stood up straight. "But my father has never mentioned you."

"No, not surprising for we differed on many things...especially my affection for your mother."

"You knew my mother too?" Paul asked, bemused.

"Oh yes. I make no apology when I tell you I prayed to our so-called Lord in Heaven to have her love me...as well as other times in my life but the 'Almighty' is either deaf, powerless or simply chose to ignore me. 'Tis why I questioned his existence for I was once an initiate of the mysteries you know of and others to come," Master Douglas explained and moved to sit upon a bench that ran along the width of the room. "When I heard you were here I requested a meeting...for my own selfish reasons of interest."

"I do not understand," Paul replied and looked over at Master Roger.

"Master Douglas does indeed know many things. 'Tis why he is afforded the rank he holds but refuses to lead others," he explained and proffered Paul a single chair opposite the table.

"I refuse to lead men for I was responsible for the death of my entire squadron...I do not ever wish to have that responsibility again," Master Douglas explained plainly.

Master Roger shook his head no at him.

"'Tis a debate we have oft argued over...but Master Douglas here served with your father a long time ago but left to serve alongside Brother Elek," Master Roger explained as he sat himself down.

"But you knew my mother too?" Paul asked looking back at Master Douglas.

"Yes. She captured the heart of many a man, including mine. Do not take offence or insult for I loved your mother dearly. I always have and always shall...and Brother Elek, you do understand and realise he knowingly came to your aid that day?"

"None taken," Paul replied and sat down. His mind raced with a hundred questions why his father had never mentioned him before. It almost infuriated him that yet again he was learning something new about his father's past. Perhaps the fault was his own? he wondered thinking back upon the many times his father had asked him to join in discussions about his past but he had refused preferring to be outside playing or making boats. Then the words started to sink in about Brother Elek. Slowly he looked up at Master Douglas.

"What do you mean he came knowingly?"

"He knew his time would end if he came to warn you about that arse Turansha…but he swore to us your mother had visited him in a dream and asked him to intervene…which I am pleased to see he did and consequently you stand before me alive and well. It validated what Elek believed," Master Douglas explained.

Paul immediately thought back upon when he believed he had seen and spoken with his mother and Elek in a dream state. A lump swelled in his throat as he recalled both that meeting and when Elek was killed beside him. Knowing that he had deliberately come to his aid knowing he would be killed filled Paul with a sense of guilt but deep appreciation at the same time.

"So despite all you have seen and learnt, you do not believe in a God?" Paul asked as his mind fought to make sense of what he was hearing from this tall and enigmatic man sat before him.

"I did not say I do not believe in a God. 'Tis the only one single factor I consider in all matters…what I do not believe in is religion. There is a massive difference. I understand how religion is used to convey codes and meanings…but I believe there is a better way. 'Tis a matter I have discussed many times with Master Roger here and previously with your very own father. 'Tis that contention between us that separates us," Master Douglas said and gave a reassuring smile that solicited trust as he leaned forward and clasped his hands together. "Your father taught me one valuable lesson that has always stayed with me…one he claims he was told by a wise man who could grow no beard, make of that what you will, in a great land across the western sea."

"I am intrigued. What did he teach you?" Paul asked.

"Your father told me the last time I ever saw him that we all have two sides to our natures, our very souls. He likened them to two hungry wolves of which only one can win dominance," Master Douglas said and smiled as he rubbed his large hands together. Paul looked at him intently, trying to work out roughly how old he was. At least in his middle fifties he thought despite still having a full head of white hair that grew downward to a point in the middle of his forehead. "One wolf is evil. It is anger, jealousy, greed, resentment, inferiority, lies and ego. The other is good, full of joy, peace, love, hope, humility, kindness, empathy and truth."

"And which wolf wins?" Paul asked.

"Whichever one you feed the most," Master Douglas replied and sat back up straight and looked at Paul in silence for a few minutes. "Now hear me, young Paul…you do not need religion to have morals…if you cannot determine what is right and wrong from what is within you, then you lack empathy. Morality is always doing what is right no matter what you are told or what your religion is. Unquestioning blind faith religion is doing what you are told no matter what is right. And the principal enemy of progress against advancement to lay fair and just laws, reduce the reasons for war, is religion. What of a God that tells me how to raise my own family, to exercise patience and tolerance yet hypercritically loses both and proceeds to then drown out his own creation and then again destroys them by fire and brimstone. 'Tis not so much God I have a problem with…'tis his followers in whatever form they kill and destroy in his name. We are all born as an unwritten book, our pages empty and naturally atheist at heart. Then religion steps in and fills the pages to the point we can longer read our own lives. And faith…'tis just a blind excuse to opt out of any personal responsibility for one's actions and to evade the hard work of thinking and evaluating what everything in life is about. Religion is sadly too oft used by men in power to oppress the populace to the point whereby it becomes a self perpetuating lie that leads to many oppressing themselves willingly. Life has taught me that as long as men are willing to kill and maim in the name of their religion or god, then we shall all never know a world of true peace and without war! That much I do know of this world."

"You see why I wished for you two to meet," Master Roger laughed. "Most people find Master Douglas intimidating and offensive in his views yet you laughed."

Paul nodded yes then looked at Master Douglas as he smiled broadly.

"'Tis refreshing to see…and so like your father, though you do have your mother's eyes," Master Douglas replied.

"I suspect you do not make your views known to many?" Paul remarked.

"Oh he does and without reservation," Master Roger answered. "He is lucky not to have been tried for heresy on many an occasion. Master Douglas here, like your father and Firgany, has tried to bring forward an attitude of openness and learning not restricted by dogma and fear…but all it did was put their lives in jeopardy. 'Tis a hard lesson to learn that most people simply do not wish to question too much that which they are told, especially by a God they have been told since birth is infallible."

"Those who are able to see beyond the shadows and lies of their culture will never be understood, let alone believed by the masses," Master Douglas said quietly and shrugged his shoulders.

"That is very profound. I must remember that," Paul remarked.

"They are not my words but those of the Greek named Plato. You can learn much if you read his works," Master Douglas replied and winked.

"Ah, I have his works my father left to me but I confess I have not read much," Paul explained. He thought for a moment upon Master Douglas's previous comments. "But your statement earlier that you do not believe in a God per se…how do you balance that with everyday life?"

"'Tis simple for as I said, I do not believe in a hypercritical God who sits upon a white cloud and looks down upon us daily ruling us by fear…that rule and that fear is made by men who interpret the ancient scriptures then twist them to suit their own desires and cravings for control and power. That at least your father and I always agreed upon. But I do believe in the divine love of a greater consciousness…that our souls are indeed spiritual. I only ever ask people if they believe in a higher purpose…and to help others without expecting reward," Master Douglas said and leaned forward looking at Paul intently as if studying every reaction in his eyes and face.

"Then what was it that you did not agree upon?" Paul asked, not moving his gaze from him.

"Your father believed, probably still does, that all of us are made up of good and evil equally, very similar to what I say about the two wolves within us…but I believe that some people…they are just pure evil through and through. That they have a soul that has never developed beyond service to self with no understanding or empathy. They are the type you cannot reason with no matter what ideology or logic you use…"

"Ah…as my father once told me, morals are wasted on the immoral?" Paul remarked.

"Oh…so perhaps your father has changed since last we met for that is a statement he would have never used before."

"I know that some people do bad things due to their own physical ailments…nothing to do with their soul," Paul said as he recalled the Bull's Head man he had killed years previously.

"Perhaps…but a person like Turansha…his soul is truly dark," Master Douglas said and stood up. He smiled broadly and offered his hand for Paul to shake. "It has been a genuine pleasure to meet you. I hope we shall become better acquainted whilst you stay here."

Paul stood up and shook his hand.

"A strong firm grip just like your father. But now I must bid you all goodnight," Master Douglas said and nodded at Master Roger. He nodded back in acknowledgment.

"I look forward to further discussions with you. You bring a refreshing new attitude to things that interest me," Paul replied as Brother Douglas broke his handshake and opened the door.

"You have not heard anything yet…trust me," he smiled as he winked at Master Roger.

Paul turned to face Master Roger as Master Douglas left the room and closed the door quietly behind him.

"An interesting and formidable character I think you will agree?" Master Roger said and offered Paul to sit down. "Now I understand we need plan to get you and your family out and away from the madness that is rapidly engulfing these lands. So please, sit and I will see how best we can do this with what few men I have left at my disposal."

"You need not have to. I have Thomas and his men, plus Abi, Tenno, Ishmael and Percival. But why do you have so few men?"

"Because King Guy has ordered all knights and Orders to muster here. We as an Order are under obligation to oblige his said arriere ban. But you and your family, you need to be away from here…and you know full well why so I need not spell it out do I?" Master Roger explained and looked up at him. Paul was not sure if he was referring to his friendship with him and his father or the claimed fact that he and Alisha were of a certain bloodline. Either way, if he could help secure a safer passage for him and his family, he was more than willing and happy to accept it whatever the reasoning. Master Roger could see Paul was thinking and taking his time to respond. "Crimson Thread!" he stated and raised his eyebrows then smiled.

ꙮ

It was early morning when Paul found his way to where Alisha and Ailia had been put up. Brother Teric led him to their room on the third floor of the Templars' headquarters. Princess Stephanie, who refused to stay in the royal suit within the other quarter, had been given the room beside theirs and Tenno and Abi a smaller room opposite so he could be near. Ishmael, Percival, Thomas and his men had all been bunked in a separate empty billet. As Paul had followed Brother Teric it felt strange to be back within the headquarters again. He felt heartened that Master Roger would be assisting him to get his family back to France. His stomach rumbled and he realised he had not eaten anything since his arrival.

"Thank you for escorting me. I had hoped to see Taqi again but I understand he sleeps well at the moment," Paul said quietly as Brother Teric indicated which room to enter. The door opposite opened slightly and Tenno peered out from the darkness. He recognised them and nodded very slightly before closing the door again quietly.

"Does that man ever sleep?" Brother Teric whispered and smiled. Paul smiled back and shook his head no. "'Tis a pity you cannot stay with us, my friend, for we are in sore need of men of your calibre. I would be honoured to serve beside you."

Paul looked at him, surprised and touched by his sincere remark.

"If I did not have family here with a mad man out there somewhere who wishes us all dead, then I would stay...and the honour would be mine I assure you," Paul replied then looked down at his Templar mantle. "This I am afraid I must return to your Master for I shall have no further need of it."

4 - 38

"No...keep it. As a memento of your brief time within our Order. I am sure your father would approve. Something to tell your grandchildren one day eh?" Brother Teric said quietly and put his hand upon Paul's shoulder. "You embody everything a true Templar aspires to be. You have even taught me things I never even considered. So thank you."

Paul did not know what to say and was unaware that Alisha saw and heard all that was spoken between them as she looked through the door peep hole having heard them arrive unable to sleep wondering where he was. She looked at Paul dressed in his Templar mantle and armour. She had always thought how handsome and brave Nicholas had looked in his uniform, but now as she looked at Paul, her heart burst with pride and sorrow at the same time. He stood tall and upright. The light cast from the few small oil lamps set within the tiny alcoves along the corridor made him look older and tired, she thought. She would never forgive herself for what she had done with Nicholas but she would try to regain Paul's trust no matter how long it may take, she swore to herself. Paul looked her way sensing her presence. He saw the small peep hole was open but as the room inside was dark he could not see her face. She stepped back a pace but then closed the small slide cover and quietly opened the door. Wearing a long dark blue night robe, she hid herself behind the door so they could only see her face as she looked at them. She smiled as they both acknowledged her.

"Go, my friend, and rest," Brother Teric whispered and ushered him toward the door just as Princess Stephanie opened her door. She bowed her head at them.

"I heard talking. Sorry if I have interrupted," she explained quietly as she fastened the bow around her waist tightly, the cream night gown hanging close to her figure.

"'Tis only us, My Lady. Apologies for disturbing you this late hour," Brother Teric said and looked at her. To him she was all and everything in a woman he had ever dreamt of. He held his gaze until she lowered her eyes, embarrassed. "My Lady…I am so sorry for I stare," he quickly said and started to back away. He smiled at Paul and raised his hand. "I shall see you in the morrow," he said and turned his back, walked a few paces then stopped. Quickly he turned around and walked back. "My Lady, I am so sorry I have lost all manners this eve. Forgive me."

"Brother Teric…do not be so silly. I disturbed you. Goodnight…all of you," Princess Stephanie replied and stepped back into her chambers. Her eyes met Paul's briefly. Alisha stretched out her hand and grabbed Paul's hand. "Goodnight."

Brother Teric stood and stared at the door as she shut it. He turned to face Paul and laughed quietly embarrassed as Paul shook his head and smiled. Quickly Brother Teric turned and walked away down the corridor briskly shaking his head to himself.

"That man is so in love with her," Alisha whispered and pulled Paul into the room. "Just as this woman loves this man," she said, leaned up and softly kissed him upon the lips. The room was dark save the early morning light just making its presence felt through the spaces between the wooden shutters. Ailia was asleep in the small bed set in the far corner of the room.

"Taqi…how is he?" Paul whispered as soon as she broke the kiss and looked up at him, her arms wrapped around him.

"He is fine and Attar remains by his side. But how are you for we have not had any time alone since your arrival?"

"I am fine…especially knowing you and Ailia are safe."

"For now," Alisha stated and pulled Paul closer, resting her head upon his chest. "I cannot ever express or show you how much I love you, Paul," she said softly, her voice emotional. Paul smelt her hair as he always did savouring the familiar scent. He kissed the side of her head and put his arms around her and closed his eyes and they stood holding each other.

"You know I have learnt that grief is the price we pay for loving…my love for Arri was so strong, the grief I feel inside will never fade," Paul whispered as tiredness started to overwhelm him as he held Alisha. Just her physical presence beside him gave him a sense of calmness he could never feel anywhere else. She squeezed him tightly. "I love you and Ailia so much too that God forbid anything happens to you, the grief alone by equal measure to that love would kill me."

"Please, Paul…do not say such things. I need you to always live…no matter what happens to us. When we get home," Alisha said softly and paused, laughing to herself at the realisation she had called La Rochelle home. "When…we get home we shall set up a light upon the point to remember our Arri."

Port of La Rochelle, France, Melissae Inn, spring 1191

"Ah I really feel for Brother Teric. Unrequited love eh?" Sarah interrupted the old man.

"And unrequited love for Count Henry remember," Simon stated, recalling what the old man had explained much earlier in his tale.

"You have a remarkable memory, Simon," the old man smiled. "But yes, unrequited love for him too with his love for Isabella, the sister of Queen Sibylla."

"What purpose did Master Roger have in introducing Paul to Master Douglas save the obvious fact he once knew his father?" Gabirol asked.

"Paul's father was not infallible shall we say…and Master Douglas knowing of

Paul's presence requested the meeting. It was Master Douglas who had argued with Paul's father that there must be a better way to carry the secrets and codes other than the purely military arm of the higher initiates of the Templars. His fear being what if they were all killed in service?...but also because it restricted other men who perhaps were better minded and suited to carry the information. At the time Philip was more than a little over protective in the codes being held purely by men of military prowess and might. 'Twas the main contentious issue between them," the old man explained.

"But is that not the very same thing Paul now advocates and spoke of with his father, who seemed to agree with him?" Peter asked.

"That is so...for Philip had changed much himself. 'Tis why he agreed the time had come to form a new order of architects, builders and Masons who would be entrusted with the secrets...'twas Master Douglas who inscribed upon a stone tablet at Balantrodach...'and the nine shall remain hidden until the time awakens them. Then will man know of their great deeds'."

"What does that mean?" Ayleth quizzed.

"It refers to those same nine original founding Knights Templar buried there... but who must be moved," the old man explained and looked at the Templar and Hospitaller.

"So Paul's idea was identical to Master Douglas's?" the Templar asked.

"Indeed...and they would have cause to discuss much on the means and ways how to achieve this matter as well as start the process to form a Muslim contingent of Templars."

"That surely will never happen?" the Templar shot back instantly.

"Never say never for it will surely come to pass...," the old man replied and paused for a moment. "For the new Order Paul and Master Douglas spoke of would be open to all men and women with the only condition being that they believed in the eternal nature of our soul and a higher divinity whether they were from Hindu, Jewish, Christian or Muslim backgrounds...it matters not."

"To discuss all this and organise, it must have taken more than just one meeting surely. And did Paul really set aside his Templar commission?" the Hospitaller asked.

"Yes he set aside his Templar commission but kept the mantle as advised. Master Roger offered him a position within his Order to train as a physician under his direct tutelage but he declined for it would have meant staying in Jerusalem. And yes Paul and Master Douglas spent many more hours in each other's company for Alisha and Paul had no option but to stay longer than they wished or planned for."

"Why?" Simon asked bluntly.

"Because there were far too many roaming forces of Saladin's army and King

Guy's insistence that all knights and men at arms muster in Jerusalem. Even Queen Tamar, who was due to travel to the city, was barred from travelling and had to wait in Antioch. She had promised her people she would visit Jerusalem and return with holy relics claimed by the peoples of Georgia. What forces King Guy did have spare were dedicated to keeping the main land bridge of supplies open from Acre to Jerusalem for without it the city would soon run out of supplies. Saladin knew this fact only too well."

"So what did they do?" Ayleth asked.

"Paul spent as much time as he dared learning from Master Roger but also teaching Alisha and Ailia all about Jerusalem, the Dome of the Rock and other matters. Whatever illness Paul originally had when he arrived in Jerusalem did not seem to affect him. Perhaps it was the infusion Attar had made him but the fever despite lasting a couple of weeks eventually passed...or at least appeared to. He even managed to get in some drawing. Even Princess Stephanie sat for him," the old man answered.

"Do you have that drawing too?" the wealthy tailor asked.

The old man nodded toward the large leather folder.

"You will find it in there. 'Tis numbered I believe as sheet 9," the old man smiled.

Quickly Gabirol opened the folder and leafed through several vellum and parchment sheets until he saw one with a tiny number 9 in the corner. He removed it slowly and laid it out flat for all to see.

Fig. 67: Princess Stephanie.

"My Lord," the farrier said as he studied the picture of her. "I think I must surely have to travel to Outremer for these women are beyond beautiful."

"Hmmm. She looks a little hard to me," Sarah remarked. Stephan laughed at her comment.

"I think you would look hard too if you had to deal with the likes of Reynald as a husband," Ayleth joked. "I would say she looks confident and assured...not hard."

"Perhaps," Sarah shrugged and sat down.

"I can see why Paul would be tempted," the Hospitaller remarked and pulled the drawing around so he could see. "We only ever saw her fleetingly and at a distance usually on the very few occasions we saw her."

"So this is her?" Simon asked.

"Without a doubt," the Hospitaller answered. "Notice the head band she wears. 'Twas one of her known recognisable items of jewellery, of Druid origin so rumour had it."

"Celtic design," the old man confirmed and smiled. "'Twas given to her by Philip himself many years previous."

"Hey you, I want one," Sarah remarked and nudged Stephan in the side.

"I wish to know if and when they ever left the city?" Peter interrupted.

"Well let me explain. Brother Teric moved Alisha and Paul to other, more homely, premises a short distance from the Templar quarters. Abi, Theodoric, Sister Lucy, Tenno, Percival and Ishmael went with them whilst Thomas and his men remained within the Order's enclave. It was decided the best time to travel to Tortosa would be when Queen Tamar could meet them half way...but also give Taqi enough time for his eyes to hopefully heal."

"Hey, they must have made it back as that lanthorn is lit every night as Alisha said would be done upon their return," Simon interjected loudly and smiled broadly.

City of Jerusalem, Kingdom of Jerusalem, January 1187

Paul walked with Brother Teric across the main courtyard toward the stables where Thomas and his men were cleaning their equipment in the shade beneath a wooden lean to. The sun was already fierce despite the early hour.

"Princess Stephanie requests your attendance to go for a ride but I have advised strongly against doing any such thing for now. She grows bored and restless and seeks stimulation," Brother Teric said as they approached Thomas, who was stood sharpening his sword. "I would sorely love to stimulate her," he muttered quietly then looked at Paul alarmed. "I…I just said that out loud didn't I?"

"You did," Paul laughed. "Fear not I shall not repeat it."

"Forgive my crass vulgarity…alas she has that effect upon me."

"I have noticed."

"Have you?" Brother Teric asked and stopped and held Paul's arm to stop him. "Is it that obvious?"

"To me it is. I see the way you have always looked at her."

"Oh my Lord…I pray she does not see it."

"Perhaps it would be a good thing if she did. She may look at you the same way."

"I am neither blind nor stupid. 'Tis too much to hope for…besides, I have seen the way she looks at you, often times." Paul looked away briefly knowing what he said was true. "Worry yourself not, my friend, for I see much and say nothing. I am just glad to be near her and to service her…I mean serve her, oh Lord. I shall cease my tongue now," he laughed.

"Look up," Paul exclaimed and nodded toward the main entrance of the headquarters as King Guy rode in followed by a column of his own knights, their bright banners, horse coats and mantles a brilliant explosion of colour against the white and sand walls enclosing them.

"I had hoped we had missed him…he will be taking Princess Stephanie out this day. I note he still makes his knights fit horse blankets…in this heat. Does the man never learn?" Brother Teric asked shaking his head dismissively.

Just as King Guy pulled up, Master Douglas walked across his path heading toward Paul and Brother Teric. He was eating a piece of unleavened bread. King Guy steadied his horse and looked down at him, bemused, and outstretched his hand as if to demand an explanation. Master Douglas stopped, looked up at the king, squinted as he was silhouetted but then just raised his hand up, bit another piece of bread and continued to walk toward Paul and Master Teric, who chuckled to himself.

"Master Douglas is certainly a law unto himself is he not?" Paul commented and smiled seeing the look of disapproval upon King Guy's face.

"That is true. You know that man followed your father literally to the ends of the earth for many years."

"Yes I do…yet my father never told me anything about him. In fact many people," Paul sighed.

"I am sure he had his reasons. You can ask him when next you see him once we have gotten you home," Brother Teric stated then nudged Paul. "Any chance you could run me off a similar image of that drawing you did of Stephanie?"

Paul looked at him and smiled. He nodded yes just as Master Douglas stopped in front of them still eating.

"Hello, boys," he said smiling broadly. "I see the Peacock is back."

As soon as Master Douglas said Peacock, Paul's mind returned to the time when Tara was killed when he first journeyed to Outremer, the same day he first met King Guy. He laughed to himself as he recalled Theodoric's words on what you call a peacock with no feathers. Just a cock!

"The king has come to inspect how many knights he has at his disposal. He plans for war, my friends," Brother Teric explained as Master Douglas just stared back at the king, a look of utter contempt upon his face.

"Indecisive, weak and easily influenced I am afraid. The sooner we get you on your way the better," Master Douglas said and faced Paul. "So come with me. We have some serious planning to do whilst our great king there takes the princess on a jolly. If your friend Taqi is fit enough to travel soon, then we need have him returned to his master before the real shit starts to land upon our heads. It may mean sending him one way with his own escort whilst we head a different way for we cannot risk going via Al Rashid's fortress route."

"If we can join with Count Raymond, he would give us secure passage to Tortosa for he still has a treaty in place with Saladin…we could travel unmolested surely?" Paul asked.

"'Tis why King Guy is holding most of his knights and men here, lest any be tempted to join with Raymond. If things get any worse between them, there will be war between them let alone with Saladin," Brother Teric explained as Princess Stephanie walked into view, her head covered in a white veil tied back with her favourite head band set in place with her golden hair plaited to the sides. She saw Paul and smiled at him. "Just nod back, do not wave." Paul looked at Brother Teric, surprised. "Trust me, Paul, for I know of orders from Reynald requesting the king seeks evidence to use as just reason to divorce her whilst seeking the favour of the barons here. Your name was mentioned as being the reason of her waning affections for Reynald."

"What?…but I am not going to do anything," Paul protested.

"It matters not," Master Douglas stated. "You are just convenient to have her removed, stripped of her titles and divorced with all her wealth going to Reynald."

"The scheming bastard," Paul muttered through gritted teeth as Princess Stephanie walked around toward a horse being readied for her. She looked over at him surprised he did not acknowledge her. "More reason we leave here soonest."

"At last you are beginning to understand the politic of this land," Brother Teric said and patted Paul's shoulder.

"I fear I shall never understand the politic of this land," Paul replied as Princess Stephanie was helped up into her saddle. She sat like a man with her legs either side as she refused always to sit side saddle. She took the reins and steadied the horse then looked again toward Paul. She shook her head, bemused, then pulled the horse around. "You know she will seek me out later and ask what is wrong."

"Then make damn sure you do where there are plenty of people and not alone," Master Douglas said. "But for Balian I fear we would already see conflict between the king and Raymond."

"Why?" Paul asked and watched as Princess Stephanie rode out of the main entrance briefly glancing back at him again.

"Because Raymond refuses to recognise Guy as the rightful king and why he keeps all of his knights in Tiberias. The treaty he has with Saladin only fuels the fires of dissention, especially when both Gerard and Reynald call him a traitor openly," Brother Teric explained.

"'Tis true," Master Douglas confirmed. "Things are tense here because of the factional rivalries between Raymond, who as you probably know was previously regent for the kingdom. 'Tis why he refuses to accept Guy of Lusignan as king, following the death of the child king, Baldwin the Fifth, Guy's stepson, last year. King Guy has summoned Gerard to accompany Master Roger, as well as Balian and Joscius, Archbishop of Tyre and Reginald Grenier, Lord of Sidon, to go to Tiberias and negotiate with Raymond and try to bring him back into the Christian fold."

"So Gerard is soon to be here?" Paul asked.

"Aye...and if you are still here he will expect you to serve your commission. He knew what he was doing when he issued it. So come for time is not on our side," Master Douglas said and ushered Paul to follow him. "Let us check upon your assassin friend."

Paul and Master Douglas walked along the main corridor of the Hospitaller infirmary. It was cooler inside. Master Roger appeared from the adjoining corridor with Percival and Abi.

"Ah Paul...perhaps you will speak with your wife," Master Roger said as he approached, Abi raising her eyebrows. Paul looked at them, puzzled, and Percival indicated with his thumb over his shoulder. "She is in the Knights of Lazarus wing helping with the sick. We could not talk her out of it."

"And Ailia...where is she?" Paul asked.

"With Sister Lucy and Theo," Abi answered. "Taqi is well. Attar sits with him and is playing some Sufi flute music...but Ali I am afraid refuses to listen to us, insisting she help with the sick."

"Knights of Lazarus...are they not the ones with leprosy?" Paul asked, alarmed. Abi simply nodded and indicated over her shoulder toward their sectioned off ward at the far end of the large arched corridor. "I must stop her immediately."

"Good luck with that," Percival said and stood aside gesturing for him to pass. "We have tried this past hour but she insists it is something she must do as penance."

"Penance!" Paul said and quickly headed down the corridor.

A sergeant of the Order of Lazarus sat upon a small wooden stool in front of the door and looked up at him, his eyes heavy and bloodshot. He simply leaned over and pulled a heavy green dividing curtain back upon its rails to reveal the eight beds inside occupied by members of the Order in various states clearly in their last hours. The dormitory was white washed and cool, the beds all made up with clean white cotton sheets. Paul went to enter when the sergeant put his arm across blocking his way. He shook his head no silently. Paul stood still and watched in silence as Alisha sat beside one of the lepers and gently bathed his forehead with a water soaked cloth. She smiled beautifully and spoke with the man. Paul could not hear what she was speaking but the sick leper laughed lightly and placed his heavily bandaged hand upon her forearm. Quickly and with concern he retracted his hand, but she gently took his hand back and held it with both of hers. The man's face was mainly covered in blood marked bandages but his eyes were clear and looked normal. She stroked his hand softly and smiled at him as he just stared into her eyes. A lump of unspeakable pride welled up in Paul's throat as he quietly observed her interaction with the sick man. She laughed again at something he said. It was pure delight to see her laugh again and he realised in that instant how much he had missed seeing her laugh. Abi stood beside him and looked on. She sighed and just shook her head. Paul could not help but smile at her. Music from Attar's flute drifted on the air like a distant almost heavenly tune off in the distance.

"Now that is the mark of a true queen," Percival whispered from Paul's shoulder.

Alisha must have heard him for she looked up, saw them all standing at the door and smiled, her eyes meeting Paul's. Paul sensed she was in no danger and knew what she was doing. He smiled back at her and nodded his head and mouthed 'I love you'. She smiled and then continued to talk with the sick Knight of Lazarus.

"Please sire…let her stay awhile. She has an uplifting and godly presence," the sergeant sat near him asked, his eyes almost pleading as he stared up at Paul.

Paul looked at Abi as she simply shrugged her shoulders and reluctantly nodded in agreement.

"We must make sure we clean her thoroughly afterwards," she whispered close to Paul's ear. "But she will be fine I am sure."

"Where is Tenno?" Paul asked quietly.

Tenno's hand suddenly appeared from the other side of the door as he sat around the corner just out of sight having been there all along keeping an eye upon her. Paul laughed lightly.

ഇ ര

By the time Alisha had seen to all the patients, Sister Lucy had already put Ailia to bed with the promise that both her mother and father would check in on her later. Theodoric retold her, for perhaps the twentieth time, a story about a young princess who was saved by hiding inside a cave of water. He changed it slightly every time and she delighted in always picking him up on the difference. As advised by Master Roger, Alisha wished to strip off and bathe completely with all of her clothes to be washed too. The evening was cool and mild for the time of year and Paul escorted Alisha to the lower floor of the building to use the baths that were situated below. The water was always fresh and running through a system Master Roger had himself designed. They both knew Sister Lucy and Theodoric would not mind their lateness. Tenno and Abi left in order to eat whilst Percival went to check on Adrastos and the other horses before retiring for the night. Stewart and the other Templars were all at last vespers so they had the bathing chamber to themselves. When Paul opened the door that led down to the sunken baths, Alisha stood still and listened as the sound of male voices singing drifted upon the air in a beautiful harmonic wave that seemed to echo louder as it filled the stone and marble bath chamber. Alisha gently clasped Paul's hand.

"I know not what that song is but it tells me you must now join me in bathing," she said softly and smiled at him looking intently into his eyes. "Master Roger would insist would he not?"

"Ali…why did you tell Abi you felt you had to administer to those men today for penance?" Paul asked and held her hand to his chest.

She frowned at him, her eyes looking at him as if to ask why he need ask such a question for was it not obvious? She sighed and shook her head side to side and looked down.

"'Tis so obvious is it not?" she said sadly. "I wronged you and I do not know how I can make amends and put right that which I have broken."

"Ali…look at me…we have been over this so many times," Paul said softly and raised her chin with his right hand to look up at him. Her eyes were filled with emotion but looked beautiful. "We can never undo what was done…but my trust for you is stronger than ever before. We have started to make a new plate remember." Alisha closed her eyes, a single tear running down her cheek. "It was something that had to happen," Paul explained. Alisha opened her eyes wide with surprise at his remark. "Kratos taught and showed me many things whilst I was with him. If you had stayed with me out of guilt, that would have been wrong. If you had to choose between us, I would have told you to choose him," Paul started to explain and paused seeing the look of panic register upon her face. "To choose him for if you stayed with me and things did not work, you would always regret the choice and resent me. But you came back to me with no doubt left in your heart as there had been before…this I know and feel and that is far more important to me than the physical act that occurred. I will not lie, it hurt and at times it still does, but I need only look in your eyes, your cheeks as you smile, the way your hair hangs over your shoulders…and that you are the mother of two miracles granted unto me," Paul explained and cupped her face in his hands. She blinked as another tear fell. "You need never apologise again or do penance for I know the pain and regret you torture yourself daily with. 'Tis not what I wish…for I wish to see you laugh again…as you did today."

"And Arri…what of him?"

"Arri is a scar cut deep within our souls…it will never fully heal and nor should it for we shall never forget him."

"Never!" Alisha replied emotionally and bit her bottom lip.

"I learnt that true open and honest pure love is not just about forgiving, but understanding and dedicating a commitment to protecting that person's heart with the same passion you use to guard your own. That is how I feel for you. And Arri…not a day passes when I do not think of him. A thousand reminders a day touch my soul and he would not wish to see you suffer that much I do know. Grief as I said never ends…but it does change, its sharp edges softening with time. It is a passage and path we must all walk but it is not a place to stay or dwell within. Grief is certainly not a weakness when it eats away at your very heart and crushes your soul, and nor is it a lack of faith for it is simply and truly the price we pay for loving so much."

"They are beautiful and touching words…but how do you know about Arri?"

"I just do. I know he watches us."

Alisha gulped emotionally as both eyes dropped a tear.

"The intensity of my love for him was such that I face an equal intensity of pain and sorrow so deep…that I do not know how to even breathe at times," she replied sadly. "I love you and I want and need you now more than ever," she said softy and kissed him, her lips gently pressing against his, the intensity of her embrace surging though his body reminding him of their first embrace. She pulled away and opened her eyes searching his. "If you will have me again, I wish to be with you joined as one."

Port of La Rochelle, France, Melissae Inn, spring 1191

The old man stopped talking and sat in silence for a few minutes that seemed to take an age to pass. Simon looked at Gabirol, who shrugged his shoulders. Ayleth held her hands to her mouth anxiously.

"Are you all right?" Miriam asked softly and leaned over toward him placing her hand upon his left hand.

"Oh forgive me. 'Tis the late hour and I tire," the old man answered and looked at her. He placed his right hand over hers and immediately she felt a sense of great calmness overcome her. She let out a gasp and laughed lightly at the emotion that swept over her. "I am sorry...," he smiled and released her hand.

"How did you do that?" Miriam asked, perplexed, and rubbed her hand, smiling.

"I have no idea," the old man replied and smiled broadly.

"So did he lay with her?" the Genoese sailor interrupted, Sarah giving him one of her looks and frowned hard. "Just curious."

The old man nodded his head yes and then took a small sip of drink from his rose hip water filled glass.

"'Twas like the first time all over again...the intensity of the act but also with the added deep and true love of two people that have shared much...and lost much together. 'Twas neither awkward nor filled with thoughts of Nicholas as one may have expected. Paul slowly undressed her, then she him. They bathed together and afterwards, by the light of a single candle in the bathing chamber, they lay down upon the deer pelts and furs set up upon the raised lounging area. As they joined and became as one, outside in the distance Thomas and his men sang a song, their harmonies filling the evening air with a beautiful sound that made people stop where they were to listen."

"Didn't anyone disturb them?" Ayleth asked, embarrassed.

"Nearly...for Sister Lucy came looking for them and having been informed by Master Roger they had gone to the bathing chamber, she sought them out. She almost disturbed them, but saw them in time and slowly, as well as very quietly, backed out and stood guard almost at the doorway. Princess Stephanie appeared and asked after them and went to enter but Sister Lucy barred her from entering with one of her looks and slight shake of her head. Princess Stephanie realising what was obviously taking place sighed very visibly. Sister Lucy sat her down upon one of the stone benches set inside the entrance and comforted her. She understood herself only too well that deep empty and utterly hopeless sense of unrequited love that she clearly recognised in Princess Stephanie's eyes for Paul."

"I think it is beautiful," Sarah remarked staring off in a world of her own as she spun her hair around her finger. Stephan smiled at her seeing her deep expression.

"It was indeed for both felt they had truly and openly joined as one soul. 'Tis an experience few of us are privileged to have. If such a thing as the Hieros Gamos does exist, that true sacred marriage, then they both partook of that mystery that night.

'Twas such an experience that Paul wrote Alisha another poem the following day which he presented to her as they both sat with Ailia and admired the bright blue colours of the Dome of the Rock. Recalling what the female had told him previously beneath the pyramids, he did indeed write her stating he would always return to her no matter the length of time he was ever gone, to always wait."

"I would love to have read that," Ayleth remarked.

"You can for it is within the pages of Paul's folder," the old man replied and pointed to the leather journal. "I know she would not mind if you read his words. They shared an experience that bound the chains of love between their hearts that would never again come undone. 'Twas far more than a physical act for it was a spiritual act."

"You mentioned that Thomas and his men sang a song they could all hear. What was that?" Peter asked.

"'Twas a song they always sang having been taught it by their forefathers and theirs before them. It recounts a prophecy when the lion walks with the lamb and the dark sun has passed and Aquarius sits in the heavens' place, when the goddess of love is joined with Jupiter at the feet of the Virgin, then shall all the world be as one...never to be undone. 'Tis a song that has to be heard to appreciate how the sounds and harmonies touch the soul...and even if you do not understand the words, for they were spoken in the language of the forest, they echo within the soul... some to the point of moving them to tears," the old man explained.

"This is burnt around the edges?" Gabirol remarked as he removed a small parchment note that had been in a fire.

"Yes it is, but the words are still visible," the old man replied.

"'Tis in French this time," Gabirol remarked and flattened the scorched note. "Shall I?" he asked, looking up briefly at the old man. He simply nodded yes. Ayleth nodded yes too immediately eager to hear Paul's words and so he started to read it. "Now that you are again back with me here, I have nothing to fear. With you is where I belong, and together we are eternally strong. There are no words to describe how beautiful and special you are or that can express my love for you. To put them into words would be to define them, to quantify them, which limits them, imposing a beginning and an end, for there is no definition fitting enough. I love the taste of your sweet tender kiss, never I pray to again miss. The way you hold me so tight, everything is forgiven now and so truly right. So know always, no matter how far or out of sight I may be, I shall always return to thee...my wife and her eternal loving embrace, the one whom I honour with total love, devotion and grace."

"Simple but beautiful," Ayleth commented and sighed.

"Words when written from the heart need not make sense or read particularly well to others, so long as it is felt and understood by the recipient, that is all that matters," the old man said looking at her.

"Oh for such words to be spoken just once to me," she said out loud then immediately blushed, realising her words.

"Your time will surely come...it will," the old man smiled reassuringly.

"How did the note become burnt?" Simon asked.

The old man, his smile vanishing, looked at him.

"Alisha and Paul managed to stay in Jerusalem until the end of February, by which time Taqi's bandages were due to be removed, but also word arrived of Reynald's imminent arrival.

Hospitallers' quarter, Jerusalem, Kingdom of Jerusalem, February 22nd 1187

Alisha, escorted by Tenno, stood in the cold early morning air with Ailia watching as Stewart dressed in his full Templar fighting order tightened the saddle straps around his horse then pulled down the black and white blanket with the Templar markings on. He smiled when he turned and saw Alisha with Ailia stood by her side, though she was shivering with the cold. Tenno simply nodded slightly. Several Templars stood readying their horses and equipment alongside a contingent of Hospitaller knights showing their opened cape modifications Master Roger was implementing.

"What brings you here this early hour?" Stewart asked and approached them.

"I heard you were leaving on a joint patrol today with the Hospitallers… and Paul, he does not sleep well these past nights…I fear he still harbours a fever he has not had time to recover from. Attar gives him that drink, cuafi, but that does not seem to help," Alisha explained just as Brother Upside and Nicholas appeared leading their horses to join the men. Upside elbowed Nicholas hard, Alisha feigning a look of disapproval to him. "Brother Upside…there is no need of that upon Brother Nicholas."

"Yes there is. There is always reason to knock this one about," Brother Upside joked in reply.

"Good morning to you," Nicholas said politely and part bowed his head. "We have Thomas and his men attending today too. 'Tis a pity Paul does not join us for his company would be most welcome," he continued and looked at Ailia and smiled.

"My papa is not too well, Mr Templar," Ailia replied and half hid herself behind Alisha's dress.

"Is he not?" Stewart asked, concerned.

"He has a slight fever still that is all or I am sure he would have joined you. I came to bid you all a safe patrol and to return speedily for we have need of leaving soon for Tortosa."

"Then please pray tell us when you plan to leave for I am sure Brother Teric can clear it with Master Jakelin for us to escort you," Nicholas said, Tenno nodding in agreement.

"I am sure we can do that," Stewart agreed then stepped closer. "Ali…I know you well enough so please, why have you really come to see us this early hour?"

Alisha blushed and laughed nervously as she held Ailia's hand tightly. Nicholas and Brother Upside listened intently their curiosity roused.

"Paul speaks in his sleep…or has done several times these past few nights," she began to explain quietly. "He calls out that girl Tara who was killed and also Elek…but," she hesitated as she looked down at Ailia and rubbed her hand through her hair before looking back at Stewart. "But he also calls out for your mother. 'Tis something he has never done before. Then when he wakes he speaks of having to serve as a knight…Both Orders want him and he is torn and says that perhaps he owes a debt of duty for all that everyone has done…yet I for all my selfish sins do not wish this of him."

"We can break his legs so he can never join either," Brother Upside interrupted, looking serious, causing Ailia to frown at him. "I was joking."

"Then best we get you all away from here and back home to where you truly belong," Stewart replied and placed his hand upon her shoulder reassuringly.

"'Twas after he wore the mantle and took Gerard's brief commission…it somehow affected him," Alisha explained as Tenno nodded in agreement.

"Then we must dissuade him of any such ideas," Nicholas said and knelt down to look at Ailia. She smiled at him. "You have your mother's eyes, young lady, and I bet your father's heart. What do you say about your father staying here as a knight…with us?"

Alisha looked at him and frowned hard but Nicholas just winked up at her then looked back at Ailia. Briefly she looked at Alisha then back at Nicholas.

"My papa has done enough," Ailia said quietly and shook her head no then quickly looked up at Alisha.

0 - 0

"There is your answer. She misses nothing despite her young age," Nicholas said and stood up. "Advise Paul to have your brother ready to leave when we return. None of us can afford to delay any longer...agreed?"

"And if Master Jakelin does not approve?" Alisha asked and held Ailia close to her side.

"You know he will...if not, he loses a knight," Nicholas replied and bowed his head slightly.

"And I was just getting used to this again," Brother Upside remarked and pulled a face as he tugged at his mantle, making Ailia laugh lightly.

Alisha looked at Stewart as he nodded in agreement the same.

"Thank you...all of you. Please be safe," Alisha said, her voice full of emotion. "Thank you."

Alisha opened the bed chamber door slowly to see Paul kneeling beside their only single travelling trunk. He was still dressed in only his white night gown. Sister Lucy gestured for Ailia to keep quiet and to follow her as Tenno held the door ajar. Alisha mouthed a thank you to him as she entered the room quietly. The door shut with a slight clank of the handle but it did not disturb Paul, who was clearly deep in thought as he folded his Templar mantle. She stood in silence and watched him for several minutes as he ran his finger over the Templar cross. He opened the trunk and saw the silk scarf Firgany had given Alisha years previously on their sea voyage together. He recalled the words he thought Firgany had said warning him of Taqi being assaulted by Reynald.

"I forget...I am sorry. I shall remind her to wear it," Paul spoke out to himself still unaware Alisha was in the room. He pulled the scarf to his face and smelt it, her perfume upon it. "I love her with all my heart and all my soul, Firgany...and I miss your wise counsel."

"And I love you too," Alisha said softly and stepped towards him.

He opened his eyes, surprised but pleased to see her as she quickly knelt down beside him. She cupped her hands around his face and kissed him on his lips. When she finished she stared at him whilst still holding her hands to his face. She smiled, her eyes filled with emotion as she looked into his seeing a sadness she had never seen before. She shook her head to question him but he feigned a brave smile and sat up straight.

"I am sorry if I kept you awake again…'tis the dreams this place causes me to have," he explained then lifted up her scarf. "And this, I forgot to ask you to wear it again as your father asked me too."

"What…how do you mean? I mean when?" Alisha asked, looking puzzled.

"The night we took Taqi from Reynald. 'Twas Firgany that appeared to me…in a dream too. He told me that Reynald was beating him and also asked me to remind you to wear your scarf to remember him by."

Alisha sat back upon her legs and rested her arms down. She sighed but smiled at the same time. Gently she took the scarf, Paul's yellow and black with crimson thread headband falling from it. He laughed to himself seeing it fall to the floor.

"I do not need any scarf to remember him by…and you can tell him that next time he appears," Alisha replied and pulled Paul closer, wrapping her arms around his neck tightly. "But what else troubles you in your dreams?" she whispered.

"Tears…so many tears of war. 'Tis all I see. I saw a pigeon bring a message from Al Rashid in a dream about Taqi. Then it really happened a few days later when Attar recovered it. Now I am torn for this sense of guilt that keeps hitting me that I too should stand and fight alongside my friends and brother either as Templar or Hospitaller…yet my own selfish needs always call me back to you. Am I so wrong to think such selfish acts?"

Alisha shook her head no as tears welled in her eyes.

"You know, I have so stopped trying not to cry these days for it is all I seem to do. But you…no it is not selfish to wish it so for I too feel it and wish it too. So let us cry the tears of war that it may wash away the pain, blood and sorrow and go home…a home we should never have left… please."

"I thought I was taking us to a better life," Paul replied sadly.

"You did. We must never forget the unbelievable sights we have seen.

The true friends we have made along the way…and those we have lost. And when we return, then together you and your father can do what is required of you so the whole world may one day learn the truths of this world…that is your destiny…so let the tears of war fall where they may for it is not a fight you have started."

"No it is not…but I fear it is one I should finish…and I know Abi thinks the same."

"Then finish it where and in the best way possible…by educating people to that which they have all lost sight of and forgotten. Awaken the true spirit within people, then and only then will the tears of war finally stop falling, and that as we both know is not a naive or foolish hope for we have seen what is possible," Alisha stated, her tone almost pleading with him as she grasped his hands tightly. "This place, whatever forces are at work here, they debilitate and exhaust you and for that reason alone we shall leave upon the return of Stewart's patrol," she explained as Paul stared into her eyes. "Until then, you must rest…and I shall lie with you." She rested her head against his chest and held him as he gently placed his arms around her and simply held her.

Chapter 72
End to All That Was

Paul opened his eyes whilst trying to sit up. His vision was blurred as he reached out for Alisha lying beside him. When his hand touched her she stirred and turned to face him. All around her shone a bright light blocking out everything else. She frowned puzzled seeing the same light around him. She sat up quickly and clasped his hands tightly. In amazement they looked around themselves but could only see white.

"My dear sister…it appears you forget that I was once your brother," Kratos spoke but was nowhere to be seen.

Alarmed, Alisha looked at Paul as he tried to focus his eyes.

"Do not worry, Ali…this is what this place does to me," Paul said reassuringly and turned to look behind him. "I am sure Kratos is here somewhere…just wait."

"You are learning how this all works," Kratos spoke again and started to step through the light beside them as if passing through a downpour of water. He smiled and rested upon his staff and nodded at them. "'Tis but a brief visit from me for I have Abi's child I must watch over."

"I have not forgotten what you told me…I have just been otherwise engaged in matters of living and trying to get by. But what brings you now?" Alisha asked, puzzled, and shook her head, wondering if she was actually dreaming.

"Ali, this is no dream," Kratos explained and winked. "But I am here to warn you that you must leave now if you can. Lord Toron, whom you know as Humphrey, Princess Stephanie's son, will arrive soon. He has promised Reynald he will prove her love for you, Paul, so he may be granted his divorce and gain her titles and castle," Kratos explained simply. Alisha looked at Paul, concerned and fearful he had feelings for Princess Stephanie too. "Do not worry, Alisha, for it is all but a cunning ploy to serve Reynald's greedy aims for he knows he has lost Stephanie."

Alisha sat up closer to Paul and held him tightly.

"Then we shall be away first thing this day," Paul replied.

"Taqi will be ready. And Alisha...Theodoric needs must tell you who your real father was for he has still not revealed it. Ask of it when next you see him...for you must," Kratos remarked then looked over to his right. "Now look yonder distance. Tell me what you see."

Alisha and Paul looked up but all they could see was whiteness. As they both strained to look harder, the white seemed to open revealing the image of what appeared to be the Dome of the Rock, but it was night time yet, surrounded by many strange lights that stretched off all around it like a thousand small fires, but they were not made of fire. As far as the eye could see were many buildings of strange construction where Paul knew only hills presently stood.

"'Tis the future you show us. Why?" he asked as he held Alisha close while she looked on in fascination. Kratos simply nodded as they continued to watch.

A very bright ball of light suddenly descended and hovered directly above the Dome, illuminating its brilliant gold covered exterior. After a few moments it shot back upwards. It instantly reminded Alisha of the bright light that had come down and hovered over her upon the ship many years previously. It reminded Paul of the light that came down at Arri's grave. He gulped hard as he recalled that sad day.

"'Tis indeed the future and you are being shown this so you can make notes and speak of such matters for there will come a time, as this fourth age of man passes over into the fifth, flight of the Phoenix as you already know and understand, when men will need to be reminded that despite all they see and hear, with much fear no less, that a promise was made not to abandon them. In the transition stage many will be scared and terrified by wars and rumours of wars, of great and worsening upheavals of natural disasters...when the seals and prophecies of the old books appear to be all coming true...that is when they must be reminded all hope is not lost. These lights will again reappear to start that process. But they must be made aware of the fact beforehand...and that is where you come in for you must find a way to carry the warnings forward so they never forget," Kratos explained and paused. "Men must remain positive for it directly affects the very world you exist upon."

"I have tried to do so, but I simply do not know how to," Paul replied as images of an old derelict cathedral started to appear.

"Remember this?" Kratos asked and smiled. "This is how the world as a whole now stands. It will decay further...but as you have seen previously in your shared vision, this cathedral will be rebuilt...the old Church will pass and a new one will be born from its ashes...just like the Phoenix again... and in that time, the last of the line of popes will know it to be so for he will be the one who acknowledges the third secret of Fatima and where and when it will come to pass," Kratos explained as the image shifted to another ball of light as it lowered slowly over the grave of Arri, Paul himself visible in the image exactly as he had experienced it. He shuddered as Alisha shook her head with sadness. "You must forgive me...both of you for showing you this painful scene again. 'Tis not my desire to hurt you. But I must tell you, Arri is no longer there."

Alisha looked at him in shock, then expectant joy.

"Is he alive...has he risen?" she asked excitedly, but then sighed and lowered her head. "What am I saying?"

"He has been removed for when the day comes, in the future, you would not want his physical remains to be abused or desecrated. I hope you will forgive me but I had them removed to a far more secure location..."

"Where?" Alisha demanded.

"Be angry with me if you must...but I cannot tell you that yet...but I shall all in good time," Kratos replied softly and looked at her. "Please trust me for I have never let you down yet have I?" he asked.

Alisha shook her head no, confused.

"Then trust me when I tell you that you must insist upon Thomas and his men escorting you away from here. Paul can take Taqi to Al Rashid, but as Raja told you when last you saw her in a similar vision, 'tis the Vikings who would protect you. Their swords are the finest ever made by normal means. Do you remember?"

Alisha thought back upon that time and nodded yes silently and rested against Paul.

"What does that mean?" Paul interrupted and pointed at a new image of Jerusalem as he knew it. It was being bombarded by flaming shots fired from large trebuchets but a large candle could be seen in front of the scene burning down fast. It had a large X with a smaller x attached to it etched into its side.

"That, my dear friends, symbolises that the candle for Jerusalem burns down fast. Time is running out and is why you must leave. You know what the X means...like it or not that is you three, Ailia being the small x."

"No…for I know what the meanings are behind the X and small x…we are neither a royal family nor a holy family," Alisha protested.

"Then what are you?" Kratos asked softly and raised his eyebrows questioningly.

"Paul…tell him. We are just ordinary people. I do not want it," Alisha protested again as emotion welled up, expressed in her face. "I demand to know where you have taken him."

Kratos looked at Paul, but he carried on looking at the image of Jerusalem being bombarded, a sickening knot tightening in his stomach, but also the realisation that what Kratos was saying made perfect logical sense. After all they had been through and seen, it was almost impossible to deny what he claimed. A realisation was beginning to register within him that indeed there was something quite clearly different about them, or at least how others perceived them. He knew in his heart Alisha was certainly different. Kratos finally looked at her. He tilted his head slightly and smiled, his eyes looking deeply into hers. He did not need to say any words for she knew his answer. He would not be telling her whatever she demanded or however long she pleaded. But as he looked at her intently, she was also overcome with a sense of calmness and knowing that he had done the right thing. As he stared into her eyes, she became very sleepy and closed her eyes.

Alisha woke up with a jolt and grasped at her chest, breathless. She sat up and started to nudge Paul to wake him. Slowly he started to come round and opened his eyes wearily.

"Kratos!" she exclaimed.

"Yes…'twas him," Paul replied and sat up slowly, his head feeling dizzy. He pulled himself up against the bedstead and looked at Alisha. "Ali…we must leave this very day," he said with a dry voice, his throat feeling sore.

"Yes," she said and jumped up upon her knees in front of him, her eyes falling to the windows as rain fell against them hard. "Oh Lord…look at the weather," she exclaimed sadly at the severe heavy rain outside and rolling dark clouds.

A slight rap upon the chamber door drew both their attention.

"Come in," Paul called out.

Theodoric opened the door and stepped inside.

"Sorry to trouble you both...hope I haven't interrupted anything," he said and clasped his hands together, which Paul immediately knew meant he had something to tell them as he always did so. Alisha and Paul both shook their heads no. "Good good. Hmm...you can see the weather no doubt...bit freakish to say the least. 'Tis like someone does not wish us to leave yet doesn't it," he explained and paused. He was clearly thinking things over in his mind. "Princess Stephanie's son Humphrey will be here in two days. Stewart and his contingent will be meeting him to escort him in...but...but in the mean time all non-essential travel for all has been banned by order of the king."

"What...but we must leave today...we must for we have been warned," Paul stated and swung his legs off the bed to stand.

"Who has warned you?" Theodoric asked, puzzled.

"'Twas just a dream he had, that is all," Alisha answered as Paul stood up but immediately fell backwards upon the bed, unsteady on his feet.

"I do not think you are in any fit state to travel anywhere this day," Theodoric remarked and stepped closer. "But on a good point," he started to say as Paul looked up at him. "Taqi...his bandages have been removed and he can see. The ulcers upon his eyes have gone. He is very lucky indeed."

"That is wonderful news. I must go and see him," Alisha said and jumped off the bed and hurried to open their travel trunk.

Theodoric looked at Paul.

"Dream you say?" Theodoric asked quietly and raised his eyebrows suspiciously.

"Yes...you know the type," Paul replied as he watched Alisha pull out her heavy dark blue dress. "Just a dream," Paul sighed.

Port of La Rochelle, France, Melissae Inn, spring 1191

"Forgive me for I simply cannot get my mind around this concept that this Kratos can appear to them both in a dream," Peter remarked, waving his hand.

"'Tis a lot to accept on face value I grant you. But if you have ever studied the ancient Vedic and Buddhist philosophies, which remember can be traced back thousands of years before Christ, they all teach of the power of the spirit to be able to travel and to learn of things on different plains of existence...and also to see others and communicate with them. Some claim to be able to also transport their physical

bodies great distances," the old man replied politely despite Peter's apparent agitation as he scratched his head. "Are you okay, Peter?"

"Yes...I am just tired and all that you tell us...'tis so much to accept and take on board," Peter replied.

"As I said before, I am not here to change you but to explain and show you things. How you interpret them is ultimately down to your own perceptions and what you are comfortable with."

"I do recall that year for we sheltered inside the castle at Tiberias unable to send out patrols for the weather was foul to an extreme for nearly two weeks...probably longer," the Templar explained confirming what the old man had said.

"Yes it almost seemed like God himself was stopping Alisha and Paul from leaving Jerusalem," the old man sighed and shook his head. "If only the weather had not been so horrendous I feel so much would be different".

"One thing you have never answered, and that is who was Alisha's true blood father?" Gabirol asked.

The old man looked at him for several long minutes in silence.

"Don't tell me it will turn out to be Reynald himself," the farrier laughed.

All in the room looked at him, Simon laughing at first until he saw the serious look upon Sarah's face as she looked at the old man. All then looked at him in anticipation.

"If I said to you he was a prince of the House of Edessa would that make sense to any of you?" the old man asked.

"I know you said at Edessa there is a mound identical to the one in England, Silbury isn't it, and that Jesus was somehow related to the kings of Edessa...they wore a crown of thorns or something...," Simon stated, struggling to recall the information. "And they carried a small purse?"

"Simon, one day you will awaken to your own abilities, for yes they did indeed carry a form of purse, as is depicted on many ancient deities, pharaohs and kings... but I have never mentioned thus far," the old man smiled. "Her father was a knight from Edessa but his father before him married into the line of Charlemagne...but his own bloodline, as I have said before, came from the Desposini...of true royal blood lineage."

"You are guarded on what you tell us about her father. Why?" Ayleth asked softly.

"I hope you will trust me when I say that her father was far more than just a knight and prince of Edessa...but it has no relevance any more save to say that his line was pure...and he too could wield the sword Paul carried. That is all I am able

to tell you I am afraid," the old man explained solemnly. "He also carried an identical sword to that used by Charlemagne himself."

"I guess you will not be telling us more on him?" Gabirol asked, disappointed.

"Perhaps I may. But it is for another time for the continued safety of others," the old man explained.

"So with all the foul weather I take it Alisha and Paul did not leave when they had hoped?" the wealthy tailor asked.

"No," the old man simply replied.

City of Jerusalem, Kingdom of Jerusalem, February 25th 1187

Alisha and Paul looked down into the open stone slab covered yard through their main window. Sheets of water ran down the wooden slats of the window shutters from the heavy downpour. Ailia sat opposite Taqi at the main table as he watched her fascinated whilst she drew pictures with charcoal sticks. Abi and Tenno stood up when the sound of horses started to echo from outside.

0 - 0

"Here they come," Paul said and pointed toward the main walled entrance as a Templar banner and the banner of Lord Humphrey of Toron fluttered just above the height of the outer wall. "Princess Stephanie will be relieved to see her son arrive safely."

Alisha leaned closer and opened the slats wider in time to see Stewart turn his horse into the main courtyard alongside Lord Humphrey. They were closely followed by the rest of the Templar contingent. Stewart led them all toward the main Templar headquarters gate. It was difficult to make out the other Templars and Hospitallers due to the heavy downpour. Ailia jumped down from her chair and rushed over to see the passing column in time to see Princess Stephanie walk into view accompanied by Brother Teric holding a weather shield above her to stop her getting soaked. Quickly they hurried after the mounted column.

"Eager to hear word of Kerak and her son," Tenno stated as he looked down at them.

"Well his banner is there. Thankfully Reynald and Gerard are not with them," Paul remarked as Abi nodded in agreement. "We better get ourselves over there."

"Does this mean we can leave now Uncle Stewart is back?" Ailia asked, looking up at Paul and smiling.

"I hope so," Paul answered and looked over at Taqi. "I hope so."

꧁꧂

Paul and Abi walked along the main corridor of the Templar headquarters toward the main assembly room. Two Templar guards stood outside on either side of the doors as several other Templars, some looking very young, Paul thought, hurried back and forth, whilst several sergeants and turcopoles busied themselves carrying wet coveralls and mantles to the drying rooms, others bringing refreshments and food. Abi frowned hard at a very youthful looking Templar who was staring at her. A flash lit up the interior as lightning thundered outside with a loud clap, several horses outside neighing in fright. Paul would check on Adrastos afterwards, he told himself.

"Sorry, sire, you cannot enter here," one of the Templar guards said and blocked Paul's way at the door.

"Can he not?" Abi replied and stepped forwards looking down at the guard. "I suggest you check again."

"They can enter," Stewart called out as he appeared from a side passage wearing just a long white robe and drying his wet hair. "I have been soaking wet for four straight days," he explained and smiled as he approached.

"'Tis good to see you back safe and well," Paul remarked.

"'Twas an interesting trip. We have also picked up several new knights… you can tell can't you?" Stewart commented and looked down the main corridor at several bemused looking knights. "And Humphrey brings more worrying news…so come in for I think you will need to hear it."

The guard acknowledged Stewart's words and opened the right hand door of the two. Stewart motioned with his head to follow him inside. Abi looked down at the guard as he stared up at her.

"Ah…Paul. Just the man I need to speak with," Humphrey said from across the room, seeing Paul enter. Princess Stephanie was standing by his side holding his hand. She looked over at Paul. "I am just waiting for Count Henry and Master Jakelin to arrive and then we can begin."

"Begin what?" Paul asked.

"Preparations to deal with Count Raymond and Saladin," Humphrey replied.

Paul looked at him, surprised at his new found confidence. Steam rose from his soaked surcoat and mantle as heat from the nearby fire warmed him. All looked back at the main door as Master Jakelin entered accompanied by Count Henry.

"Ah good, I have not missed anything yet then?" Count Henry asked and closed the door behind them. "Master Roger will be along soon."

"No...but please, make yourselves comfortable whilst I quickly change into drier clothes. I have much to explain," Humphrey said and smiled at his mother. She looked at him pleased to see he was safe, but there was sadness in her eyes as she feigned a brave smile.

"What do you mean make preparations against Raymond?" Paul asked curiously.

"I will explain all when King Guy himself is present. Has he been notified of our arrival?" Humphrey asked Brother Teric.

"Aye, sire, he has," Brother Teric replied.

"I must hurry and change then," Humphrey said and walked toward the eastern wall of the room, waved at his mother briefly and left through a small side door closely followed by two maids and a young squire.

Paul could see concern etched across Princess Stephanie's face. She looked at him and smiled gracefully.

"I think we shall be waiting a while for the king is presently otherwise engaged," she explained softly and clasped her hands behind her back. "You promised me you would make another image of me...do we have time now?"

"I have not brought my items to do so. Perhaps later," Paul replied.

"You will be gone before we have time again I fear," she shot back and looked away unable to hide her obvious sadness. She looked down in silence for an awkwardly long time before Brother Teric coughed on purpose to get her attention. She shook her head and looked up directly at Paul and gulped, clearly emotional. "I am sorry. Forgive my churlish behaviour. I should be pleased my son has arrived safe and well...but it is tinged with sadness for I know it means you shall all now be leaving soon."

"But you are coming with us are you not?" Paul asked, surprised.

With her hands still clasped behind her back she simply shook her head no, emotion etched deeply in her face. She looked as though she was about to burst into tears but she controlled herself just as she always did.

"I have received word that Reynald intends to take my daughter back to Kerak with him but also, if I leave, to have Humphrey stripped of his position and titles," she answered and took a deep breath. Brother Teric shook his head in disgust. "And yet my dear son still sides with Reynald even then and so begs I stay. He says he needs me and my counsel."

"Then have Humphrey and Alix come with us," Brother Teric interrupted. All in the room looked at him, surprised at his comment. "Do you honestly think I wish to stay here when all hell is about to be let loose and we end up fighting our own brothers…against Raymond? For that is what is being planned."

"It will not come to that," Stewart remarked and put his towel down across one of the large chairs. If it does, then this city, this whole kingdom will fall."

"So he blackmails you?" Paul asked, shaking his head, and walked over to her. When he reached her she stepped back a pace and put her hands across her front.

"Please…do not pity me…for like you we have both lost a child and like you, I shall do all and whatever is required of me to protect my remaining children," she explained emotionally and struggled to stop herself from crying. "No!" she said, her tone clipped as Paul reached out to take her hands. "Please…just no." She knew if she touched Paul she would break and collapse into tears. She wished he would just hold her but knew it could not be so.

Paul moved closer to her but she backed away further. The main door opened and Master Roger entered accompanied by his scribe and two sergeants.

"King Guy will attack Lord Raymond if he continues to refuse to recognise him," Brother Teric explained and looked at them each in turn. "You all know full well Reynald likes to be known as the Red Wolf of Kerak but also the chief enemy of Islam and he will do all and anything to get his war with Saladin…and men like Lord Raymond stand in his way, so by influencing the king, even if it means war with Raymond first, Reynald is looking to the next stage already."

Paul turned and faced Master Roger and Count Henry and looked at them, seeking their opinion. Count Henry walked over to him.

"What Brother Teric speaks is true I am afraid," he explained. "King Guy will indeed attack Raymond. Gerard has actually tried to warn him against it but he does not listen for as we stand this hour, Saladin masses his forces to attack Kerak."

"Good then I hope he seizes it for I hate that place now…and put a stop to Reynald's madness," Princess Stephanie remarked.

"My Lady, I urge caution in what you speak," Brother Teric said quietly.

"To add to all of that, our sources tell us that both Reynald and Turansha's men seek out Saladin's sister Sitt al-Sham Zumurrud. She is somewhere en route from Damascus but they wish to seize her and hold her for ransom," Master Roger explained and sat himself down. "And Alisha's sister, Queen Tamar of Georgia, heads to meet her caravan."

"Why does Turansha wish her caught?" Paul asked, puzzled.

"Because he has fallen foul of Saladin once too often now and he and his men have all been outlawed," Count Henry answered.

"How long until Reynald arrives here?" Princess Stephanie asked.

"Two weeks, maybe three depending upon how successful Saladin's assault upon Kerak proves to be…but I suspect it is a deliberate minor assault to draw us out or give Raymond more time to secure his position. I believe Saladin hopes King Guy will split his forces and try to relieve Reynald at Kerak whilst also attacking Raymond and leaving Jerusalem exposed," Master Roger detailed as Count Henry shook his head.

"So what does King Guy intend do?" Paul asked.

"We have already advised him he cannot divide his forces nor let Jerusalem be so exposed…so Reynald will need to fend for himself on this one," Count Henry replied and looked at Princess Stephanie.

"Good…he needs to be brought down somewhat," she stated and sighed heavily. Slowly she turned away from them and walked to the end of the room and looked out of the tall arched widow out across the city as more dark thunder clouds rolled in. She clenched her hands together and closed her eyes.

"My Lady," Brother Teric said and went to approach her but Master Roger stopped him.

"How soon can we leave?" Paul asked Stewart quietly.

"If Master Jakelin allows it, we can leave as soon as this storm passes," Stewart answered.

Princess Stephanie heard his reply, quickly turned around and hurried for the main door covering her face trying to hide her distress. She pulled the door handle but the door did not move. Angrily she grabbed the handle with both hands but still it would not open.

"Open this fucking door!" she yelled and kicked the door. Brother Teric rushed over to the door and simply turned the handle as she stood staring, her hands clenched tightly into fists. Brother Teric opened the door. She looked at him briefly then quickly stepped through into the corridor and walked away fast.

"She is torn…utterly torn," Brother Teric remarked as he held the door open and watched her walk away.

ꕥ

Paul left to follow Princess Stephanie but Brother Teric rushed after him and reminded him of what he had been warned. Through the pouring rain he watched her walk across the main courtyard and out of sight. To his right he heard laughter coming from the main stable entrance. He looked over and was just able to see Thomas standing with Percival and Master Douglas and several Templars sheltering out of the rain. He needed to check on Adrastos so decided now was as good a time as any.

"Please go and check on Princess Stephanie," Paul asked Brother Teric.

"Don't need telling twice," he replied and immediately ran off after her.

Paul laughed to himself seeing him run so fast. He looked back at Thomas and the others. He pulled up his hood and ran across the open area to them. Half way across a loud crack echoed out as lightning struck just beyond the wall in a brilliant flash. Thomas waved Paul to hurry up then grabbed his arm to stop him as he ran into the shelter.

"Out in a storm with a sword…not a good idea, my friend," Thomas laughed as Paul lowered his hood.

"The gods sense the pile of shit heading this way," Master Douglas remarked with a large grin upon his face. "I have just been acquainting myself with these fine men…well, men at least," he joked.

"He has a sharp wit this one," Thomas remarked, smiling.

"Tell me, Paul…did you name this bunch of reprobates with their gospel names?" Master Douglas asked.

"No…why?" Paul answered bemused.

"He does not believe they already had these names…too convenient and like the disciples in the Bible," Percival explained and raised his hand to greet him.

"He thinks surely you must have given us our names…changed them just like Jesus did," Thomas explained.

"Do not be absurd," Paul laughed and looked at Master Douglas then Thomas, who shrugged his shoulders in an exaggerated fashion.

"Absurd you say…think on," Master Douglas laughed. "Even Jesus… just how and where in the fuck did he just happen upon such names like Mathew, John, Luke, Philip, Thomas…in this Jewish and Arabic named fucking land?"

Paul looked at him and went to respond, but then thought on his words, realising what he was implying. Percival raised his eyebrows.

"I think you tease, Master Douglas," Paul finally said.

"Aye that I do…but still a good fucking question no less," he laughed back.

"So why are you all here for surely not to discuss that?" Paul asked.

"Keeping an eye on our horses in the storm for they hate thunder," Thomas replied. "The Destrier warhorses are fine but the palfrey and sumpter pack horses scare all too easy."

"We were also speaking on how we can argue our case to leave…now that Taqi is well enough to travel. Master Douglas says we should just go… for arguing with King Guy is useless and he will not permit it under the present circumstances," Percival explained as he stepped forward, Thomas nodding in agreement.

"'Tis true," Master Douglas remarked. "I have said I am more than happy to add to your number for safety. But as I have explained to these…men," he said and laughed briefly, "that arguing with King Guy is like playing chess with a pigeon. No matter how good you are the bird is still going to shit on the board and strut around like it won anyway."

Paul laughed upon hearing his analogy as did Thomas seeing his reaction.

"Then argue we shall not…and leave regardless and I am sure we would all be most agreeable to accepting your generous offer," Paul answered.

"'Tis a deal," Master Douglas smiled and proffered his hand for Paul to shake in agreement.

"Okay, men…we are truly screwed now," Thomas joked.

"Aye that you are," Master Douglas replied and winked with a large grin.

"Ah my protégée no less. I told you long ago you would serve alongside an army of kings did I not?" Theodoric said as he appeared from the farrier's tack area eating some fresh bread.

"Theo...a sight for sore eyes...and yes you did, but I see no kings," Master Douglas shot back joking, then held both of Theodoric's arms and laughed. "I heard you were hiding out somewhere in this city."

"'Tis good to see you again too, my dear friend, very good indeed," Theodoric replied.

Port of La Rochelle, France, Melissae Inn, spring 1191

"So when did Alisha and Paul finally get away?" Ayleth asked.

"The weather unfortunately only got worse so it meant a lot of time was wasted for them. Paul spent many an hour alone with his thoughts, mainly pondering the comment Husam had stated back in Cairo," the old man said quietly.

"What comment?" Sarah asked.

"When Husam revealed that he knew Paul had helped Reynald and Gerard escape after the naval engagement. War was coming and Paul could not shake off the deep sense of dread and guilt that it was, as Husam stated, ultimately down to his actions."

"He cannot take that upon his shoulders," the Templar remarked shaking his head no.

"We know that but it did not stop Paul from feeling it. Perhaps it was the place affecting him as he told Alisha, but either way, it played heavily upon his conscience," the old man sighed. "'Twas the comment that Husam made that any blood Reynald and Gerard may spill would be down to his decision. But what made matters worse was that he overheard Upside talking with Theodoric and Master Douglas about Nicholas and Alisha. Upside said he had seen the look in Theodoric's eyes and how he looked at Kratos and Sister Lucy as if they knew in advance what would happen between them. Paul felt embarrassed for Alisha and that they were discussing the matter with Master Douglas but a sense of dread also filled him. If Theodoric sensed or knew what was to come, then why had he not informed him before it happened? He felt betrayed almost by his lack of action but also very concerned for what else did he possibly know and was not telling him? That is why Paul kept himself alone for much of the time those last couple of weeks in Jerusalem."

"So they did leave?" Ayleth asked again.

"Yes...yes, my dear, they did," the old man replied and took a deep breath and sat himself up straight. "Though Paul was able to confide in Tenno and voice his concerns over what Theodoric had done...more correctly not done, Paul nevertheless even began to doubt Theodoric's real intentions, but that was fatigue of the mind. Tenno gave him a good word of advice about people in general."

"Which was?" Gabirol asked after the old man had sat in silence for a while.

"I am sorry...Tenno informed him that all people show three faces to the world and you can never second guess or truly know someone, except when you loved someone totally like Alisha and Paul did...with total openness and honesty, the bad aspects of themselves and good."

"Three faces? I've heard of being two faced," Simon grimaced.

"Yes...and it is quite true in most cases," the old man replied. "In Tenno's homeland they say you have three faces. The first face, you show to the world. The second face, you show to your close friends and your family. The third face, you never show anyone. It is the truest reflection of who you are."

"I have to agree with that," the Hospitaller remarked.

"He also said that you don't know how strong you are until being strong is the only choice you have, which Paul liked and made a note of as Tenno said he should always remember that," the old man explained and looked up at Ayleth. "Then the day was upon them when the weather finally cleared. 'Twas still unseasonably cold but Paul made sure everyone was up early and ready to leave. Alisha was not happy that she would have to travel in a different direction to Paul, who would be escorting Taqi back to Al Rashid to a rendezvous point. It meant being apart for a day at most, but Alisha did not want Paul out of her sight for even a small moment," he detailed and sighed heavily. "It was by now March the thirteenth and the start of the Muslim year 583, in Arabic history date terms...and word had already reached King Guy that Saladin had taken his troops to the water hole area of Ras al Mai and sent letters out to neighbouring countries asking for volunteers for the forthcoming Jihad. His brother Al Adil, governor of Egypt, was preparing to lead his forces out of Cairo towards Syria within the week... and Husam al Din Lu'lu, Paul's good friend of course, was already taking fifteen galleys down the Nile toward Alexandria, and in the far north, Taqi al Din with many troops had already reached Aleppo and was watching the frontier with Antioch. It was the month of Muharram when large numbers of Muslim pilgrims were travelling home from Mecca. Later Saladin left his troops at Ras al Mai under his nephew Taqi al Din and took his own guards to protect pilgrims. In doing so he had called off his attack on Kerak as it had served its purpose of being a purely delaying ploy...and as soon as Saladin was away, Reynald and Gerard wasted no time in travelling to Jerusalem."

City of Jerusalem, Kingdom of Jerusalem, March 13th 1187

Paul walked along the line of horses and men formed up in twos accompanied by Master Jakelin. All of Thomas's men nodded at him as he passed them. Several of Master Roger's Hospitallers were with them. The sky was blue for the first time in weeks but the air was still cold. Stewart rode into view accompanied by Nicholas, Upside, Brother Teric and eight other Templars.

"Where is your friend Taqi and family?" Master Jakelin asked, looking around as Stewart pulled his horse into position near the front of the column.

"He will be here shortly with Alisha and Ailia. Abi and Tenno are sorting them a cart in which to travel with Sister Lucy and Theodoric," Paul replied just as Thomas and Master Douglas rode onto view from the direction of the main stables.

"Paul, we have received word by heliograph Reynald has travelled through the night to avoid ambush. He is but moments away," Master Douglas explained and leaned lower. "So we need to leave now."

"We are coming," Theodoric called out as he held open the main heavy wooden door to their accommodation. Alisha stepped out holding Ailia's hand closely followed by Sister Lucy carrying two bags and Ishmael holding their large travelling trunk. Taqi stepped down onto view wrapped in a dark Hospitaller cape. He still looked tired and squinted in the bright daylight.

They were half way across when Tenno steered a large four wheeled caravan into view and drew up just short of them, Abi riding her horse and guiding Tenno's horse as well as Adrastos. One of Thomas's men, Philip, steered their water wagon into the middle of the column behind Thomas. Paul immediately realised then that they did not have a horse for Taqi.

"I pray this weather holds…and we have no horse for Taqi," Paul remarked and looked up, a few clouds rolling over gently. "I shall have to resolve that now."

"We do not have time," Master Douglas remarked. "He can ride with me for my steed can take us both or on the water cart or ride with you."

Within minutes Ishmael had loaded all their belongings into the rear of the large cart whilst Theodoric and Sister Lucy sat up front waiting patiently. Taqi hugged Alisha tightly.

"Fear not, dear sister, for I shall see you again. Besides we still have tonight together...and Paul is not the only one who sees things," Taqi said reassuringly and stood back a pace from her. "I am proud to be your brother and I shall miss you more than ever...and you young Ailia," he said and rubbed his hand through Ailia's hair.

"Stay safe...and please no more sneaking into Reynald's chambers," Alisha replied and bit her bottom lip, determined not to cry. "Please get him to Al Rashid safely and hurry back to us," she said turning to look at Paul.

"It is all arranged and Al Rashid knows where to meet us. We shall not linger and come straight after you. Your sister's, Queen Tamar's, caravan is neutral and her treaty with Saladin still remains so you will be safe with them until we arrive for she cannot move presently in either direction," Paul explained and took her hands and kissed them. "We leave here as one but once at the northeastern road, we shall have to leave you...but it is only for one night and a single day."

Ailia tugged at Paul's cape. He reached down and picked her up and looked into her eyes.

"You promise you will come for us?" she asked, trying her hardest to look serious, which made Alisha laugh.

"I promise. I will always come back for my little princess...always...and my queen," Paul answered and pulled Alisha close and kissed her on the lips, Ailia pulling a face of mock disgust. "Now come, we must leave."

Paul lifted Ailia up to the rear of the caravan and kissed the side of her face as she wrapped her arms around his neck. She refused to let go until Alisha gently pulled her little hands away from Paul. Reluctantly she stood up in the doorway and frowned, which made Paul laugh.

"Where is Princess Stephanie?" Abi asked as she drew up near them.

"She is not coming to see us off. She said her tearful farewell last evening. She said she could not endure this day," Alisha answered.

Tenno took the reins of his horse from Abi and quickly mounted.

"So we all know who is going with whom yes?" he asked.

"Yes. Master Douglas, Percival, Ishmael, Stewart, Brother Teric, Nicholas and Upside are coming with me to meet Al Rashid and deliver Taqi. The rest of you will head to meet up with Queen Tamar's caravan, where we shall meet you tomorrow eve latest," Paul explained and noticed Count Henry walking towards them fast. Just as he reached them he sighed and shook his head as the sound of many horses started to echo out from the main entrance approach.

"Ah damn…'tis too late," Count Henry stated and slapped his thigh in annoyance.

All looked toward the main arched entrance as Reynald and Gerard rode into full view, their banners flying behind them and a full squadron of Templars at the vanguard. Amid a loud cacophony of noise and horses' hooves echoing out, they all entered the main courtyard just yards away. Reynald pulled his horse up hard, directed himself toward Paul immediately upon seeing him stood with Count Henry.

"'Tis a fine fresh morning is it not?" Reynald bellowed and sniffed the air in an exaggerated fashion and pushed his targe shield higher up on his back. "You can smell the blood of war already," he boasted and grinned.

"Lord Reynald…'tis good to see you have arrived safe and well," Count Henry replied courteously.

"Good my arse…I am the last person you wish to see," Reynald replied and wiped his hand across his face as Gerard pulled up beside him. Both looked down the line of Thomas's men and other knights formed up. "And this is for what?" Reynald demanded.

"We are leaving," Paul replied instantly. "So we need not take any of your time."

"Not so fast," Gerard said and dismounted. "Where are you going?"

"Home…back to France," Paul answered.

"Not with my men," Gerard shot back.

"Master Gerard…they are only doing their duty in escorting them away as per standing orders for the protection of pilgrims," Master Jakelin interrupted.

"Horseshit for I see no pilgrims," Reynald laughed. "Running away more like cowards."

"Do we really have to do this right here and now?" Paul asked and looked up at Reynald shaking his head disapprovingly. "With or without your permission…or knights, I and my family are leaving."

"I thought the king banned all travel?" Reynald replied and grinned as he looked down at Alisha.

"Not all…besides you have just travelled," Paul remarked.

"With a full complement of knights and sergeants," Reynald shot back and gestured with his hand. "If you go out and travel through hostile lands, as we know Saladin has many raiding parties and troops out there, you will put the lives of these good men at risk for nothing."

0 - 0

"'Tis a risk we are prepared to make," Thomas interjected loudly as he pulled his horse around to face Reynald.

"But one I am not prepared to let my knights take when you can easily wait here until things become safer," Gerard explained looking at Alisha then Paul.

"Things will only get worse here and you know it," Paul replied.

"Well you cannot leave for you took up Gerard's commission did you not?" Reynald laughed as Master Jakelin looked at him with disdain. "Oh he did not tell you...ha! You should have read the commission closer...for by accepting it, no matter how short a time, you are committed to serve for at least four months," Reynald explained and laughed again as Paul looked at Gerard hard. "By my reckoning that still leaves at least another month and half to serve." Alisha held onto Paul's arm tightly. "Oh, and you cannot resign until after those first initial four months."

Stewart quickly dismounted and walked over fast upon hearing Reynald's claim.

"Fine, if that is indeed true, then as a Templar he can escort his family away from here and serve his term out in Tortosa can he not?" Stewart asked.

"Brother Stewart, be careful how you address Lord Reynald," Gerard said and frowned at him.

"And I thought you had changed...if only a little for the better," Alisha snapped, looking at Gerard, shaking her head with disgust.

"Hey, I need men...and good men especially with what is coming," Gerard answered and raised his hands. "And with your skill and that sword of yours...well."

"This sword will never serve you," Paul shot back, angered at Gerard's coldness.

"Then we shall escort them," Nicholas called out and turned his horse around and moved closer. Upside raised his eyebrows but followed suit. "We can resign right here and now if needs must, Master," he stated and looked down at Gerard.

"What is it with you?" Gerard asked and shook his head. "Your love for this family is obsessive."

"'Tis even more than that, Master," Nicholas replied and dismounted. "The Order has been my family for many years...but this family...'tis the very family that our Order is all about is it not?"

"Hah what utter horseshit!" Reynald laughed out loudly.

Alisha turned her head slowly and looked up at him, her eyes narrowing. He scowled back but as he stared at her, the intensity of her look unnerved him momentarily then his horse bucked as if startled. Quickly Reynald had to pull hard on the reins and calm his horse. Taqi smiled unable to hide his amusement. All went eerily quiet as all looked at Reynald, including Gerard.

"I order that you let Paul escort his own family away," Count Henry spoke up, breaking the silence. "If as you claim the commission you gave him is legal, then knowing Paul, he will honour it...but only after his family is away from here. He can even wear his Templar uniform." Alisha looked at him alarmed. "Fear not, Alisha, for as a Templar Reynald cannot touch him for he falls under my command, not his," he said and winked as he turned slightly away from Reynald. "And, Master Gerard, might I remind you to whom exactly you answer."

"You cannot remain here as a knight," Alisha whispered to Paul closely.

"I suspect you really go to join with Count Raymond," Reynald snapped dismissively.

"If King Guy does not make peace with Raymond, you will lose this city that I do know," Paul replied, looking at him directly. "There are far more smart men out there allied against you this day."

"Perhaps it is Saladin you choose to join," Reynald remarked and smirked.

"I had hoped after our last meeting you would have seen sense...but I see not," Paul replied and shook his head.

"Well we shall just have to see what the king has to say all about this won't we," Reynald smirked.

"The king already knows about this and Paul has his blessings to go," Princess Stephanie said, stepping into view from behind the large caravan. "You forget his queen is my friend," she remarked as she walked closer. "You Lord Reynald will let these people be on their way without delay and there will be no accusations levelled at any person's behaviour or insinuations for I know only full well your plans."

"She has gone truly mad," Reynald laughed loudly and looked back at his own column of men.

"If I have it is only because of you. But you will let them leave this hour. If you do not, you shall never see your daughter or I ever again."

"Do not threaten me, woman," Reynald snapped angrily, his long hair swinging around his face as he turned fast to glare at her.

"You let them leave…and I will gladly have all my titles, deeds and lands signed over to you without delay, nor settlement for me…and a divorce without all the unnecessary theatre you wish to incite," Princess Stephanie explained calmly and placed her hands across her stomach and smiled at him disarmingly. Reynald looked at her, puzzled.

"No you cannot do that for us," Alisha said and grasped Princess Stephanie's arm.

"'Tis not for you I do it trust me," she whispered back and smiled again at Reynald. "Well, Lord Reynald?"

"And you…," Reynald said waving his finger at Paul. "You will leave… and never come back for you are a constant thorn in my arse."

"I leave here today and I swear it when I say I hope I never come back or see you again…but I will deliver Taqi back to his master first. I can even speak with Count Raymond…for you must all see sense and join together to deter Saladin," Paul explained and paused as he realised everyone was listening. "If you cannot, your new found titles and land will not remain yours for long."

"Oh, let me guess, you and your mad seer have seen it all in a vision," Reynald mocked.

"You of all people should know better," Theodoric said aloud, looking at Reynald. He shook his head, disappointed at him.

"Do you agree to my terms or not?" Princess Stephanie interrupted.

"'Tis some scheming trick," Reynald replied.

"As they leave those gates, I shall by almighty God follow you to see the king and the whole damn court and swear under oath all that is mine to be yours…and you are welcome to it…except Alix."

Reynald rubbed his beard and looked at Gerard, who nodded yes very slightly. As Gerard looked at Paul, he winked.

"'Tis a deal I think…oh but Paul…do not bother seeking counsel with Raymond for I think we are past that," Reynald said calmly with a broad smile upon his face, the smile vanishing as Attar walked past him slowly staring at him. "And take him with you."

Princess Stephanie pulled Alisha close and hugged her.

"I know what I am doing...now go and be safe," she whispered then kissed the side of Alisha's face. "Please...and be happy."

Alisha could see and sense the anguish in her eyes as Princess Stephanie bravely fought to contain her emotions and forced a smile.

Gerard stepped closer to Paul and put his arm around his shoulder and started to walk with him away from Reynald.

"'Tis indeed a fine line I tread these days. I said what had to be said in front of Reynald...but what I said of the commission was alas all true and valid," Gerard explained quietly. "But I know what you speak of is sadly all too true...Reynald fails to see that at the moment...but he will if you leave him to me." Paul stood still and back a pace to look at Gerard, confused at his remarks and behaviour. "Wear the Templar mantle again...it may just save your arse. I will make sure it is noted on record that you served out your term by the time you arrive in Tortosa. Who knows, perhaps when I visit La Rochelle in the future you will avail me of your presence and hospitality."

Paul was not sure what to make of Gerard's comments but he sensed he was a man with divided loyalties and a growing conscience.

"Okay you bunch of fucking ladies, are we leaving today or here for happy chats?" Master Douglas yelled out loudly. Reynald sat up on his horse straight, surprised to see him. "Yes, 'tis me again, Lord Reynald... and I am so glad you resolved this matter all by yourself."

Master Jakelin laughed as did Nicholas at his comments. Reynald just pointed at Master Douglas as he moved himself to the front of the column ready to lead it out. Attar quickly fetched his small horse and mounted it whilst Princess Stephanie and Alisha hugged each other once more. Alisha then placed Ailia into the large caravan and climbed up inside. Taqi mounted Adrastos and slowly rode past Reynald, staring at him hard. As everyone took their positions, Princess Stephanie stood proud and looked on ignoring Reynald, who was looking at her intently curious and puzzled. Count Henry moved to stand by her side. Brother Teric bowed to her as he rode past her.

"I hope your daughter did not hear Master Douglas," Gerard remarked as Taqi pulled up beside Paul.

"I think she has heard far worse of late," Paul replied and proffered his hand to shake. "Do not take this the wrong way, but I hope it is a very long time before we meet again."

Gerard took Paul's hand and shook it firmly.

"Likewise…you are an extremely bad influence on my best men."

"Perhaps if they are your best men, you should listen to what they say."

"I do, believe me I do," Gerard replied, let go of Paul's hand and stood back. "You and I have come a long way since our first encounter in Rochefort-sur-Terre have we not?" he asked and smiled, Paul not really sure what to make of his question. "Now leave before Reynald changes his mind."

"How did you resolve the assault by Saladin at Kerak so quickly?" Paul asked.

"'Twas just a ruse and no assault came…for he was not there himself…but I suspect he will return with greater numbers next time. Now hurry, go."

Taqi reached down and helped Paul mount Adrastos to sit in front of him. Paul looked back to check Alisha and Ailia were in the caravan and saw Theodoric raising his hand confirming they were ready. Reynald sat looking on bemused not quite sure of himself and concerned why Princess Stephanie seemed so calm and collected. Paul looked at her and as their eyes met, she gulped hard as her throat tightened with emotion. She felt lost and alone and all she wanted to do was run and jump into the caravan with Alisha and Ailia, but she knew she had to remain calm in order for her friends to leave. Master Douglas called out an order and the column started to move, Stewart looking back briefly as he hauled up the Templar standard to check Paul was following. Gerard moved back towards his own column of men still formed up. Paul bowed his head at Princess Stephanie before turning away, Reynald looking at him then back at her suspiciously as her eyes followed Paul and Taqi as the column slowly filed out through the gates, Alisha waving from the rear of the caravan. When the last rear guard horse had vanished from view, Princess Stephanie stood perfectly still whilst Gerard's men started to dismount. Eventually she turned her back on Reynald and walked away.

Port of La Rochelle, France, Melissae Inn, spring 1191

"So they got away," Ayleth sighed with relief.

"They left Jerusalem for sure, its streets now filled with pilgrims forced to stay longer than planned, and knights from all kingdoms. They made good time to the northwestern highway and the weather held," the old man replied but lowered his head.

"And Alisha was to head for her sister's, Queen Tamar's, caravan whilst Paul took Taqi northeast to meet Al Rashid yes?" Gabirol asked.

"Yes...that was the plan and intention," the old man answered and looked up again. "They had only been travelling an hour when Count Henry caught up with them in order to meet up with Al Rashid himself. He wished to convince him to either stay neutral or join with his Order and not Saladin."

"We had heard such rumours at the time that Count Henry was dealing with the Ashashin direct," the Templar remarked as his brother nodded in agreement.

"He also wished to move on to see Raymond in person afterwards...for word was already reaching Saladin's ears about the dissention between King Guy and Raymond. Saladin had no intention either of renewing the previous truce with the king but he did with Raymond," the old man explained as Gabirol wrote down what he was saying.

"Why could Queen Tamar not move her caravan?" Simon asked.

"Because Saladin had asked her to remain where she was until he could secure the region. Too many bandits were taking the opportunity of the turmoil to exploit and raid caravans whilst the pilgrim escorts all remained within Jerusalem by order of the king. She had a sizable escort of her own but even so, Saladin had requested she wait and that his sister would be allowed to join her, so she did."

"I was in Tiberias at that time and we knew that Raymond had allowed Saladin's reconnaissance troops to pass through his lands unmolested. In fact we even joined them on two occasions when it was known Turansha was massing all of his men in the region," the Templar explained. "We were waiting for orders from Gerard on what we must do should King Guy engage against Count Raymond, but it was Count Henry who turned up briefly ordering us to ignore any orders coming from Gerard until further notice. 'Twas a tense and confusing time for sure."

"'Twas indeed...," the old man sighed.

"So you are saying that Count Henry had authority over Gerard despite him being the Grand Master of the whole Order?" Peter asked.

"Yes he did for it was the Prior de Sion who had authority over the Order," the old man answered. "Not that Gerard would agree with that rule, which is more the pity."

"Why?" Ayleth asked quietly.

"For if he had respected Count Henry's orders and words of wisdom, all would have been so different...for all that was, would forever be changed as a consequence."

"Did Paul leave Alisha and Ailia then to take Taqi to Al Rashid?" Sarah asked hesitantly, sensing the sadness in the old man's tone.

"Yes, yes he did. 'Twas early the following morning that Alisha hugged Paul tighter than she had ever hugged him before. Paul had pulled the fur collar around her face to protect her from the cold wind that blew in from the north. He did not wish to let her out of his sight for a second but he knew he had to take Taqi to his rendezvous. The night before Paul had time to do a quick drawing of Ailia...," the old man sighed and shook his head as he took a deep breath.

"Here is this the drawing for I saw it earlier," Gabirol asked and pushed into the middle of the table a small charcoal drawing of a young girl, its edges burnt.

Fig. 68: Ailia.

"Oh my Lord," Ayleth gasped and put her hands to her mouth in alarm and then looked up at the old man.

"'Tis burnt...like Paul's poem," Sarah remarked and pulled the picture close. "This is not a good sign."

"'Twas the beginning of the end...an end to all that was before!" the old man sighed heavily, unable to hide his sadness. "Paul kissed Ailia and promised her he would come back to her. Taqi bade Alisha an emotional farewell and swore he would be there for her and Ailia should the time ever come. Theodoric tried to cheer everyone up as he usually did and before the sun had fully broken over the mountains to the east Paul found himself sat upon Adrastos watching Thomas lead the

caravan column away down the northern highway toward the ancient Roman town of Beit She'an, 'tis near enough to Tiberias should they need to travel there. Saladin's sister often used it as a staging post when she travelled to and from Damascus. Paul saw Alisha and Ailia waving from the rear as Tenno glanced back and waved briefly before they vanished over the lip of the dip in the land and out of sight."

"So who exactly went with Paul and Taqi again?" the wealthy tailor asked.

"Abi, Ishmael, Stewart, Percival, Master Douglas, Brother Teric and Count Henry and of course Attar but also Brothers Upside and Nicholas and four other Templars," the old man replied.

"Not that many then should they get ambushed," the farrier remarked.

"No...not many at all, but still enough," the old man sighed. "And they made good ground to the rendezvous point without incident."

"Where was their rendezvous point then?" Ayleth asked.

"Their meeting point was on the hill Jebel Sabarta overlooking the old ruins of Pella set in the valley below. It afforded Al Rashid plenty of cover from the mountains to approach from the east, not the open and exposed north and west," the old man explained and shook his head. "Thomas would rest briefly at the Pella ruins to refill their water wagon...you may recall they always travelled with one...before moving on to Beit She'an."

Rendezvous point, Jebel Sabarta, Principality of Galilee, March 14th 1187

The midday sun burned directly overhead but the cold wind from the north cut into all of them as Paul's group pulled up at the small marker stone set within a small alcove of open area. The hillside was dotted with brush and trees, the ground awash with vegetation after the weeks of rainfall. Abi looked across at Paul with Taqi sat behind him. It reminded her of the Templars' actual seal of two riders upon a single horse. She could see the tension in his face and worry as he looked west toward the lowlands stretched out beneath them knowing Alisha and Ailia were just miles away from them.

"Paul, they are well protected. They have enough experienced knights and Tenno will certainly see to it. Thomas and his men will not let them down," Abi said reassuringly but a knot pulled taut in his stomach.

"They will be with Queen Tamar before nightfall," Count Henry commented as Taqi dismounted from Adrastos nearly pulling Paul off with him. "But after I have spoken with Al Rashid I must leave and get word to Count Raymond, for the king does not even know I am here."

"Does he not?" Brother Teric asked. Count Henry shook his head no in silence and smiled. "It would be madness to return alone."

"At least if Tenno runs into any problems at Beit She'an, they do not have far to seek safety with Raymond in Tiberias," Percival remarked and looked towards the small shining strip on the horizon that was the Sea of Galilee.

Paul looked east at the mountains, the snow capped tip of Mount Hebron on his far left visible. He wondered how long they would have to wait for Al Rashid to show, impatient to get away and after Alisha and Ailia.

"Will we have to wait long?" Percival asked as he dismounted, as if reading Paul's mind.

Taqi looked around the small clearing and up the track that snaked off up the side of the mountain and out of sight around a corner flanked by huge boulders. He looked down at the dust covered sand and gravel path then looked back toward Percival.

"No…not long at all for they are already here," Taqi smiled. He raised both his arms up high. "Isme Taqi!" he called out.

No sooner had he spoken than all around the group, the brush and tall grasses seemed to move and rise upwards. Nicholas and Upside immediately drew their swords as men appeared when they pushed back cloaks covered in the grasses and brush that had perfectly camouflaged them. Taqi smiled as the nearest man approached tying off the camouflaged cape around his waist revealing his pitch black cloak and weapons. Only his eyes were visible through the thin strip of his black head cover. He grasped Taqi's forearms to greet him but said nothing.

Master Douglas looked on ever watchful as Abi protected their backs. Several horses suddenly appeared from behind the large boulders and trotted down toward them. Paul noted all the men on the ground were armed with high power crossbows all held ready in the aim but pointed downward slightly. The rider in the middle of the approaching horsemen pulled up and dismounted. Paul knew immediately it was Al Rashid just from his sheer physical presence. He unwound his head cover as he walked up to Taqi and smiled.

"I am afraid we do not have time for our usual pleasantries for Turansha and his men are in this very region…and he has a lot of men with him," Al Rashid explained looking at Taqi and Paul in turn. He looked up at Master Douglas. "Master Douglas…we meet yet again. If I did not know better I would swear you are trying to join us."

"Not in this life time, my friend," Master Douglas replied, smiled and bowed his head. "'Tis good to see you again also."

Abi moved her horse into position beside Paul.

"Ah the great Abi Shadana no less. I had heard you were dead many times over already," Al Rashid said looking up at her.

"As you can see I am still very much alive…but it concerns me this news of Turansha," she replied.

"The man is an outlaw to all sides now…and sadly his numbers grow as more fanatics throng to his call for an all out Holy Jihad…even to the point of vowing to destroy Mecca itself and the Kabba! His brutal and savage methods know no bounds at all," Al Rashid explained. He looked at Taqi as he moved beside him. "And you, my friend, are fortunate we need every trained Ashashin we have otherwise you know you would not be accepted back into the brotherhood," he continued and smiled, patting Taqi on the shoulder. "But you are one of my best so we can bend some rules." Taqi looked over at the rider on the horse next to Al Rashid's. He smiled and bowed at the rider, which puzzled Paul. Al Rashid noticed this. "Ah…so it was not me you were eager to be reunited with," he laughed and beckoned the rider to come closer. "Come…show yourself."

Abi looked at Paul, bemused, as Taqi appeared to blush.

"As you wish, My Lord," a female voice replied as the rider removed her headdress, flung her head back and shook her long hair aside out of the way of her face.

Percival looked up at her, his mouth dropping open in surprise, shocked by how much like Nyla she looked. She looked down at Taqi intently and smiled.

"A female?" Master Douglas remarked and shook his head.

"Female yes…deadly…more so," Al Rashid remarked proudly. "They make great assassins and get into places many of my men cannot."

0 - 0

"I bet," Percival said as he stepped closer to look at her.

"'Tis rude to stare," Taqi stated almost laughing at the way Percival was staring open mouthed at the woman. She looked down at him and narrowed her eyes in disapproval. "You do not want to mess with her believe me."

"I am sorry. I believe you," Percival replied and stepped back as Al Rashid laughed.

"Well done, Attar, for organising this...and you, sire," Al Rashid said looking at Count Henry. "It is my honour to be in your presence again despite the circumstances. You must know that Saladin has put a bounty upon Turansha's head now he has finally woken up to the man's evil intent."

"The honour is all mine I assure you," Count Henry replied and bowed his head slightly. "I also know Saladin wishes you to join forces with him."

"As does Count Raymond. But you should know we join with no sides," Al Rashid replied.

"That I do, but these are changing times and you may have to," Count Henry said and looked toward Paul and Abi. "Reynald wants war on everyone. And I do mean everyone."

"What of Grand Master Gerard's intent?"

"He will follow and join whatever side appears to be winning despite my warnings to cut the elm if he disobeys my orders," Count Henry explained as Paul looked at him puzzled. "I shall have to explain that to you another time."

"Taqi al Din, Saladin's nephew, as we speak, plans to move his troops to the fortress of Harenc (Haram) on the frontier of Antioch. He will be there in force by mid April at the latest. Count Raymond raises much suspicion he is pro Muslim and too friendly with Saladin for he has made it known he will allow Saladin's reconnaissance troops to pass through his lands. I think it is purely a strategic move by Raymond in his refusal to recognise King Guy. Raymond has already allowed a Muslim garrison to occupy his fief in Tiberias, probably hoping that Saladin will help him overthrow Guy," Al Rashid explained.

"But I thought Saladin was preoccupied in his northern territories?" Count Henry asked, looking concerned.

"Not any more, my friend, for Saladin has pacified his Mesopotamian territories, and is now eager to attack the Crusader kingdom to remove Reynald, no one else just him; he does not intend to renew the present truce when it expires shortly for he has a lot of internal pressures from within his own camp to deal with Reynald once and for all...sooner rather than later," Al Rashid explained and raised his eyebrows.

"We know the truce is about to expire and is why we have commissioned Balian to seek terms with Raymond to recognise the king and have Reynald banished," Count Henry explained.

"'Tis too late for that for we know Reynald has already convinced King Guy that Saladin is massing his troops, and Reynald's men are already attacking Muslim pilgrims and caravans in an attempt to disrupt this. 'Tis all part of Reynald's great stratagem as you call it," Al Rashid said and looked at Paul as he finished.

"'Tis a bloody dangerous strategy to play then," Master Douglas remarked.

"Very," Al Rashid simply stated then looked toward the western horizon as several large plumes of black smoke gently climbed skyward from the area near Pella.

Paul, seeing Al Rashid's face change to one of concern, spun around to see the plumes rising faster and ever higher and in an instant his stomach knotted and pulled so intensely it hurt. His heart exploded with fear.

"Ali…oh my Lord," Paul gasped and ran back to Adrastos and jumped up into the saddle, took the reins and without even looking back immediately sped off down the track toward the columns of smoke with an absolute knowing it was connected to Alisha.

"Paul…no!" Abi called out and immediately set off after him.

"Is he always this impetuous?" Al Rashid asked.

"My Lord, my sister's caravan is travelling in that very area," Taqi replied, concerned.

Al Rashid took one look toward Paul and Abi riding off, clicked his fingers for his horse to be brought to him. Quickly he mounted his horse as Brother Teric, Nicholas and Upside sped off in pursuit, Nicholas almost throwing up fearing for Alisha.

"You better fetch a horse from our main party and follow fast," Al Rashid said and slapped Taqi on the shoulder, then quickly set off after Paul and Abi immediately followed by all of his own mounted Ashashin. Master Douglas did not hesitate and set off after them while Count Henry, Stewart and Ishmael helped hurry Taqi along. As soon as Taqi mounted a horse, he sped off closely followed by the female Ashashin. Stewart threw the Order's standard at one of the accompanying Templars and raced off to follow as fast as his horse would carry him. Death was in the air.

Bibliographic References – Book 3

81: After - 'Some Administrative, Military, and Socio-Political Aspects of Early Muslim Egypt'. http://www.wikiwand.com/en/Egypt_in_the_Middle_Ages. Athamina, Khalil (1997). In Lev, Yaacov. War and Society in the Eastern Mediterranean: 7th–15th Centuries. Leiden: BRILL. pp. 101–114. ISBN 90-04-10032-6. Bianquis, Thierry (1998). 'Autonomous Egypt from Ibn Ṭūlūn to Kāfūr, 868–969'. In Petry, Carl F. Cambridge History of Egypt, Volume One: Islamic Egypt, 640–1517. Cambridge: Cambridge University Press. ISBN 0-521-47137-0. Bonner, Michael (2010). 'The waning of empire, 861–945'. In Robinson, Charles F. The New Cambridge History of Islam, Volume I: The Formation of the Islamic World, Sixth to Eleventh Centuries. Cambridge: Cambridge University Press. ISBN 978-0-521-83823-8. Brett, Michael (2001). The Rise of the Fatimids: The World of the Mediterranean and the Middle East in the Fourth Century of the Hijra, Tenth Century CE. The Medieval Mediterranean. Leiden: BRILL. ISBN 90-04-11741-5. Brett, Michael (2011). 'Egypt'. In Robinson, Chase F. The New Cambridge History of Islam, Vol. 1: The Formation of the Islamic World, Sixth to Eleventh Centuries. Cambridge and New York: Cambridge University Press. ISBN 978-0-521-83823-8. Halm, Heinz (1996). The Empire of the Mahdi: The Rise of the Fatimids. Handbook of Oriental Studies. 26. transl. by Michael Bonner. Leiden: BRILL. ISBN 90-04-10056-3. Kennedy, Hugh (1998). 'Egypt as a province in the Islamic caliphate, 641–868'. In Petry, Carl F. Cambridge History of Egypt, Volume One: Islamic Egypt, 640–1517. Cambridge: Cambridge University Press. ISBN 0-521-47137-0. Kennedy, Hugh N. (2004). The Prophet and the Age of the Caliphates: The Islamic Near East from the 6th to the 11th Century (2nd ed.). Harlow, UK: Pearson Education Ltd. ISBN 0-582-40525-4.

82: Yarnall, Judith (Jan 1, 1994). Transformations of Circe: The History of an Enchantress. University of Illinois Press. ISBN 0252063562. Braund, David (1994). Georgia in Antiquity: A History of Colchis and Transcaucasian Iberia, 550 BC–AD 562. Clarendon Press. ISBN 0198144733. Lordkipanidze, Otar (1968). 'Colchis in Antiquity'. Archaeologia. Boardman, John; Edwards, I. E. S. (1991). The Cambridge Ancient History. Volume 3. Part 2. Cambridge University Press. ISBN 0521227178. Ivanchik A.I. 'Cimmerians and Scythians', 2001 Terenozhkin A.I., Cimmerians, Kiev, 1983 Cimmerian. (2006). In Encyclopædia Britannica. Collection of Slavonic and Foreign Language Manuscripts – St Cyril and Methodius – Bulgarian National Library.

83: After – 'A Historical Research of the Ten Tribes Scattered Into the Nations' Part 1 by Prof (Dr) WA Liebenberg. Academic Proofread by: Ed Garner BTh. MSc. 'Maximinus Thrax' by Wasson, Donald L. 'Historia Augusta, Life of Maximinus.' Ancient History Encyclopedia Limited.

84: After - Kadri, Sadakat (2012). Heaven on Earth: A Journey Through Shari'a Law from the Deserts of Ancient Arabia. Macmillan. ISBN 9780099523277. Massignon, Louis (1982). The Passion of al-Hallaj, Mystic and Martyr of Islam. Translated by Herbert Mason. Princeton, NJ: Princeton University Press. https://en.wikipedia.org/wiki/Mansur_Al-Hallaj.

85: Bahā' al-Dīn Ibn Shaddād (2002). The Rare and Excellent History of Saladin. Ashgate. ISBN 978-0-7546-3381-5. Imad ad-Din al-Isfahani (1888). C. Landberg, ed. Conquête de la Syrie et de la Palestine par Salâh ed-dîn (in French). Brill. Nicolle, David (2011). Saladin: The Background, Strategies, Tactics and Battlefield Experiences of the Greatest Commanders of History. Osprey Publishing. ISBN 1849083177. Extracts from -

https://wikivisually.com/wiki/Salah-al-Din_Yusuf_ibn-Ayyub.

86: https://en.wikipedia.org/wiki/Saladin Bahā' al-Dīn Ibn Shaddād (2002). The Rare and Excellent History of Saladin. Ashgate. ISBN 978-0-7546-3381-5. Imad ad-Din al-Isfahani (1888). C. Landberg, ed. Conquête de la Syrie et de la Palestine par Salâh ed-dîn (in French). Brill.

87: After http://www.cogandgalley.com &

https://weaponsandwarfare.com/2009/03/26/islamic-ships-and-shipbuilding - full sources listed.

88: After - http://www.theinfolist.com/php/SummaryGet.php?FindGo=byzantine_navy – full sources listed.

89: After - Gibb, H. A. R. (1973). The Life of Saladin: From the Works of Imad ad-Din and Baha ad-Din. Clarendon Press. ISBN 978-0-86356-928-9. OCLC 674160. Husain, Shahnaz (1998). Muslim heroes of the crusades: Salahuddin and Nuruddin. London: Ta-Ha. ISBN 978-1-897940-71-6. OCLC 40928075. https://en.wikipedia.org/wiki/Saladin

90: The Jewish Religion: A Companion, published by Oxford University Press.

91: After - Theosophy, Vol. 59, No. 5, March, 1971 (Pages 145-150). The Path – December 1892. Reincarnation in the Bible — William Brehon. Theosophical University Press.

92: After - Encyclopedia Mythica Folkways: 'Reclaiming the Magic & Wisdom' by Patricia Telesco. 'A Dictionary of Symbols' by J.E. Cirlot. A Dictionary of Angels by Gustav Davidson. 'The Origin of Consciousness in the Breakdown of the Bicameral Mind' by Julian Jaynes. 'Genesis Revisited' by Zecharia Sitchin. From 'The Ashes of Angels - The Forbidden Legacy of a Fallen Race' by Andrew Collins. 'Book of Enoch the Prophet' by R. Laurence. 'The Legends of the Garden of Eden and the Angels' by Alfred Hamori.

https://www.bibliotecapleyades.net

93: 'The City Of Ten Thousand Swords' by Rendall 2002 after - ancient Indian poem.

94: After – al-Khiḍr, The Green Man- http://khidr.org/ Article on the Green Man. http://www.ancient-origins.net/myths-legends/unraveling-nature-and-identity-green-man-002620

95: After – 'At the Gates of Dawn: A Collection of Writings' by Ella Young. Also – 'The coming of Lugh : a Celtic wonder-tale' by Ella Young. Published by Biblio Bazaar (2009) ISBN 10: 1110936435 ISBN 13: 9781110936434

96: Three writings by Dr. Don: Reflections. http://www.donhuntington.com

97: After article - http://www.ancient-origins.net/myths-legends/lost-cycle-time-part-1 by Walter Cruttenden.

98: After - lleneverthopman.com/female-druids/ & from www.themagicalbuffet.com

by Ellen Evert Hopman.

99: After – 'The Character and Legacy of Henry II' by Dr Mike Ibeji. 'Eleanor of Aquitaine' By John Simkin - spartacus-educational.com.

100: After – 'The Lost Gospel. Decoding the Ancient Text that Reveals Jesus' Marriage to Mary the Magdalene' by Simcha Jacobovici & Barrie Wilson. Was the cave of Abraham in Shechem or Hebron. https://christianity.stackexchange.com

101: After - article - commanderysaintmichael.wordpress.com. Philip Coppens at http://philipcoppens.com

102: After – Article by Armando Mei - http://www.ancient-origins.net/ancient-places-africa/36400-bc-historical-time-zep-tepi-theory.

103: After – 'The Jesus Papers' by Michael Baigent. 'The Book of Enoch' Chapter 20. R.H. Charles, Oxford: The Clarendon Press. Prof. Arysio Nunes dos Santos

Universidade Federal de Minas Gerais - http://www.rickrichards.com/

104: After – 'Heliopolis: Egypt's radiance' by Philip Coppens.

http://philipcoppens.com/heliopolis.html

105: http://knightstemplarvault.com/king-melchiors-diadem/

106: 'Sarasvati - Vedic river and Hindu civilization' by Dr. S. Kalyanaraman (October 2008)

Sarasvati Research and Education Trust. 'Saraswati – the ancient river lost in the desert' by

A. V. Sankaran - http://www.iisc.ernet.in/

107: 'Thomas Becket' by Ben Johnson - http://www.historic-uk.com. Fulcher of Chartres, A History of the Expedition to Jerusalem, 1095–1127, trans. Frances Rita Ryan. University of Tennessee Press, 1969. William of Tyre, A History of Deeds Done

Beyond the Sea, trans. E.A. Babcock and A.C. Krey. Columbia University Press, 1943. Philip K. Hitti, trans., An Arab-Syrian Gentleman and Warrior in the Period of the Crusades; Memoirs of Usamah ibn-Munqidh (Kitab al i'tibar). New York, 1929.

108: After – 'Gilgal Rephaim, Circle Of Og King Of Bashan' by: C K Quarterman. 'Did Biblical giants build the circle of the Refaim?' by Barry Chamish - netmedia.net.il

109: What Is the Strongest? The Contest Between King Darius' Three Bodyguards by Andy Naselli - http://andynaselli.com.

110: Gods Warriors –

111: after – James Webb: article - New Dawn No. 48 (July-August 1998)

http://www.newdawnmagazine.com

112: After - Excerpt from: The Nine unknown men – 'The Dawn of Magic' by Louis Pauwels & Jacques Bergier. From Bharata to India: Volume 1: Chrysee the Golden by M. K. Agarwal. www.decodinghinduism.com Quoted text taken from the ancient Hindu text the Mahabharata. 'Decoding God Puzzle' by Andy.

www.ingramcontent.com/pod-product-compliance
Lightning Source LLC
Chambersburg PA
CBHW022016050726
47499CB00004BA/948
9781912562473